Songs of
Earth and Power

OTHER BOOKS BY GREG BEAR

Songs of
EARTH & POWER

The
Infinity Concerto

AND

The Serpent Mage

GREG BEAR

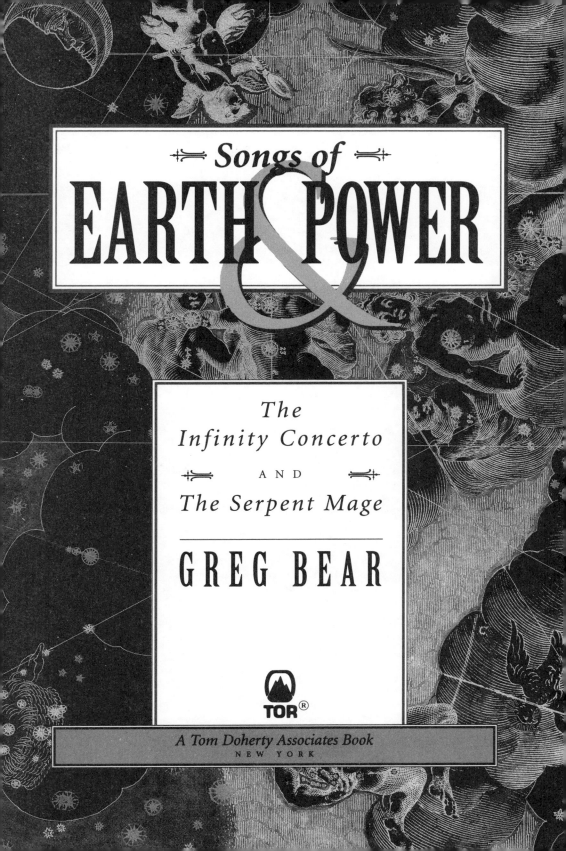

TOR ®

A Tom Doherty Associates Book
NEW YORK

SONGS OF EARTH AND POWER: THE INFINITY CONCERTO AND THE SERPENT MAGE

Copyright © 1994 by Greg Bear

This volume comprises the novels of *The Infinity Concerto* (1984) and *The Serpent Mage* (1986), substantially rewritten for this edition.

This book is printed on acid-free paper.

A Tor Book
Published by Tom Doherty Associates, Inc.
175 Fifth Avenue
New York, N.Y. 10010

Tor® is a registered trademark of Tom Doherty Associates, Inc.

Design by Patrice Fodero

Background art: Barbara Wiggins Designs

ISBN: 0–312–85669–5

First Tor edition: December 1994

Printed in the United States of America

0 9 8 7 6 5 4 3 2 1

Book One

THE

INFINITY

CONCERTO

If a man could pass through Paradise in a dream, and have a flower presented to him as a pledge that his soul had really been there, and if he found that flower in his hand when he awoke—Ay!—and what then?

—SAMUEL TAYLOR COLERIDGE

What song did the sirens sing?

—ANCIENT RIDDLE

1

re you ready?

"Huh?" Michael Perrin twitched in his sleep. An uncertain number of tall white forms stood around his bed, merging with the walls, the dresser, the bookcases and easels.

He's not very impressive.

Michael rolled over and rubbed his nose. His short sandy hair tousled up against his pillow. His thick feathery red eyebrows pulled together as if in minor irritation, but his eyes stayed shut.

Look deeper. Several of the forms bent over him.

He's only a man-child.

Yet he has the hallmark.

What's that? Throwing his talents in all directions instead of concentrating? Never quite able to make up his mind what he is going to be? A ghostly arm waved at the easels and bookcases, at the desk swamped with ragged-edged notebooks, chewed pencils, and scraps of paper.

Indeed. That is the hallmark, or one of—

The alarm clock went off with a hideous buzz. Michael jerked upright in bed and slapped his hand over the cut-off switch, hoping his parents hadn't heard. He sleepily regarded the glowing green numbers: twelve-thirty in the morning. He picked up his watch to check. "Damn." The clock was eight minutes late. He only had twenty-two minutes.

He rolled out of bed, kicking a book of Yeats' poems across the floor with one bare foot. He swore under his breath and felt for his pants. The only light he dared use was the Tensor lamp on his desk. He pushed aside the portable typewriter to let the concentrated glow spread farther and spilled a stack of paperbacks on the floor. Bending over to pick them up, he smacked his head on the edge of the desk.

Teeth clenched, Michael grabbed his pants from the back of the chair and slipped them on. One leg on and the other stuck halfway, he lost balance and steadied himself by pushing against the wall.

His fingers brushed a framed print hung slightly off balance against the lines and flowers of the wallpaper. He squinted at the print—a Bonestell rendition of Saturn seen from one of its closer moons. His head throbbed.

A tall, slender figure was walking across the print's cratered moonscape. He blinked. The figure turned and regarded him as if from a considerable distance, then motioned for him to follow. He scrunched his eyes shut, and when he opened them again the figure had vanished. "Christ," he said softly. "I'm not even awake yet."

He buckled his belt and donned his favorite shirt, a short-sleeved brown pullover with a V-neck. Socks, gray Hush Puppies and tan nylon windbreaker completed the ensemble. But he was forgetting something.

He stood in the middle of the room, trying to remember, when his eyes lit on a small book bound in glossy black leather. He picked it up and stuffed it in his jacket pocket, zipping the pocket shut. He dug in his pants pocket for the note, found it folded neatly next to the keyholder, and glanced at his watch again. Twelve forty-five.

He had fifteen minutes.

He trod softly down the wall-edge of the stairs, avoiding most of the squeaks, and half-ran to the front door. The living room was black except for the digital display on the video recorder. Twelve forty-seven, it said.

He opened and closed the door swiftly and ran across the lawn. The neighborhood streetlights had been converted to sodium-vapor bulbs that cast a sour orange glow over the grass and sidewalk. Michael's shadow marched ahead, growing huge before it vanished in the glare of the next light. The orange emphasized the midnight-blue of the sky, dulling the stars.

Four blocks south, the orange lights ended and traditional streetlamps on concrete posts took over. His father said those lights went back to the 1920s and were priceless. They had been installed when the neighborhood houses had first been built; back then, they had stood on a fancy country road, where movie stars and railroad magnates had come to get away from it all.

The houses were imposing at night. Spanish-style white plaster and stucco dominated, some two stories tall with enclosures over the side driveways. Others were woodsy, shake shingles on walls and roofs, with narrow frame windows staring darkly out of dormers.

All the houses were dark. It was easy to imagine the street was a movie set, with nothing behind the walls but hollowness and crickets.

Twelve fifty-eight. He crossed the last intersection and turned to face his destination. Four houses down and on the opposite side of the street was the white plaster single-story home of David Clarkham. It had been deserted for over forty years, yet its lawns were immaculately groomed, hedges trimmed, stucco walls spotless, and Spanish wood beams unfaded. Drawn curtains in the tall arched windows hid only emptiness—or so it was reasonable to assume. Being reasonable hadn't brought him here, however.

For all he knew, the house could be crammed with all manner of things . . . incredible, unpleasant things.

He stood beneath the moon-colored streetlight, half in the shadow of a tall, brown-leafed maple, folding and unfolding the paper in his pants pocket with one sweaty hand.

One o'clock in the morning. He wasn't dressed for adventure. He had the instructions, the book and the leather keyholder with its one old brass key; what he lacked was conviction.

It was a silly decision to have to make. The world was sane; such opportunities didn't present themselves. He withdrew the paper and read it for the hundredth time:

"Use the key to enter the front door. Do not linger. Pass through the house, through the back door and through the side gate to the front door of the neighboring house on the left, as you face the houses. The door to that house will be open. Enter. *Do not stop to look at anything.* Surely, quickly, make your way to the back of the house, through the back door again, and across the rear yard to the wrought-iron gate. Go through the gate and turn to your left. The alley behind the house will take you past many gates on both sides. Enter the sixth gate on your left."

He folded the note and replaced it. What would his parents think, seeing him here, contemplating breaking and entering—or, at the very least, entering without breaking?

"There comes a time," Arno Waltiri had said, "when one must disregard the thoughts of one's parents, or the warnings of old men; when caution must be put temporarily aside and instincts followed. In short, when one must rely on one's own judgment . . ."

Michael's parents gave parties renowned throughout the city. Michael had met the elderly composer Waltiri and his wife, Golda, at one such party in June. The party celebrated the Equinox. ("Late," his mother explained, "because nothing we do is prompt.") Michael's father was a carpenter with a reputation for making fine furniture; he had a wide clientele among the rich and glamorous folk of Los Angeles, and Waltiri had commissioned him to make a new bench for his fifty-year-old piano.

Michael had stayed downstairs for the first hour of the party, wandering through the crowd and sipping a bottle of beer. He listened in while the heavily bearded, gray-haired captain of an ocean liner told a young stage actress of his perilous adventures during World War II, "on convoy in the Western Ocean." Michael's attention was evenly divided between them; his breath seemed to shorten, the woman was so beautiful, and he'd always been interested in ships and the sea. When the captain put an arm around the actress and stopped talking of things nautical, Michael moved on. He sat in a folding chair near a noisy group of newspaper people.

Journalists irritated Michael. They came in large numbers to his parents' parties. They were brash and drank a lot and postured and talked more about politics than writing. When their conversation turned to literature (which was seldom), it seemed all they had ever read was Raymond Chandler or Ernest

Hemingway or F. Scott Fitzgerald. Michael tried to interject a few words about poetry, but the conversation stopped dead and he moved on again.

The rest of the party was taken up by a councilman and his entourage, a few businessmen, and the neighbors, so Michael selected a reserve supply of hors d'oeuvres and carried the plate upstairs to his room.

He closed the door and switched on the TV, then sat at his small desk—which he was rapidly outgrowing—and pulled a sheaf of poems from the upper drawer.

Music pounded faintly through the floor. They were dancing.

He found the poem he had written that morning and read it over, frowning. Yet another in a long line of bad Yeats imitations. He was trying to compress the experiences of a senior in high school into romantic verse, and it wasn't working.

Disgusted, he returned the poems to the drawer and poked through the TV channels until he found an old Humphrey Bogart movie. He'd seen it before; Bogart was having woman trouble with Barbara Stanwyck.

Michael's troubles with women had been limited to stuffing love poems into a girl's locker. She had caught him doing it and laughed at him.

There was a soft tap on his door. "Michael?" It was his father.

"Yeah?"

"You receiving visitors?"

"Sure." He opened the door. His father came in first, slightly drunk, and motioned for an old, white-haired man to follow.

"Mike, this is Arno Waltiri, composer. Arno, my son, the poet."

Waltiri shook Michael's hand solemnly. His nose was straight and thin and his lips were full and young-looking. His grip was strong but not painful. "We are not intruding, I hope?" His accent was indefinite middle-European, faded from years in California.

"Not at all," Michael said. He felt a little awkward. His grandparents had died before he was born. He wasn't used to old people.

Waltiri examined the prints and posters arranged on the walls. He paused before the print of Saturn, glanced at Michael, and nodded. He turned to a framed magazine cover showing insect-like creatures dancing on a beach near wave-washed rocks, and smiled. "Max Ernst," he said. His voice was a soft rumble. "You like to visit strange places."

Michael muttered something about never having been anywhere strange.

"He wants to be a poet," his father said, pointing to the bookcases lining the walls. "A packrat. Keeps everything he's read."

Waltiri regarded the television with a critical eye. Bogart painstakingly explained a delicate matter to Stanwyck. "I wrote the score for that one," he said, lips pursed.

Michael brightened immediately. He didn't have much money for records—he spent most of his allowance and summer earnings on books—but he did have a Bee Gees album, a Rickie Lee Jones concert double, and the soundtrack albums for the original *King Kong*, *Star Wars* and *Citizen Kane*. "You did? When was that?"

"Nineteen-forty," Waltiri said. "So long ago, now, but seems much closer. I scored over two hundred films before I retired." Waltiri sighed and turned to Michael's father. "Your son is very diverse in his interests."

Waltiri's hands were strong and broad-fingered, Michael noticed, and his clothing was well-tailored and simple. His slate-gray eyes seemed young. The most unusual thing about him was his teeth, like gray ivory.

"Ruth would like for him to study law," his father said, grinning. "I hear poets don't make much of a living. Still, it beats wanting to be a rock star."

Waltiri shrugged. "Rock star isn't so bad." He put a hand on Michael's shoulder. Usually Michael resented such familiarities, but not this time. "I like impractical people, people who are willing to rely only on themselves. It was very impractical for me to want to become a composer." He sat on Michael's desk chair, hands on his knees, elbows pointed out, staring at the TV. "So very difficult to get anything performed at all, not to mention by a good orchestra. So I followed my friend Steiner to California—"

"You knew *Max Steiner?*"

He nodded, smiling. "Sometime you must come over to our house, visit Golda and me, perhaps listen to the old scores." At that moment, Waltiri's wife entered the room, a slender, golden-haired woman a few years younger than he. She bore a distinct resemblance to Gloria Swanson, Michael thought, but without the wild look Swanson had had in *Sunset Boulevard*. He liked Golda immediately.

So it had all begun with music. When his father delivered the piano bench, Michael tagged along. Golda met them at the door, and ten minutes later Arno was guiding them around the ground floor of the two-story bungalow. "Arno loves to talk," Golda told Michael as they approached the music room at the rear of the house. "If you love to listen, you'll get along just fine."

Waltiri opened the door with a key and let them enter first.

"I don't go in here very often now," he said. "Golda keeps it dusted. I read nowadays, play the piano in the front room now and then, but I don't need to listen." He tapped his head. "It's all up here, every note."

The walls on three sides were covered with shelves of records. Waltiri pulled down big lacquered masters from a few of his early films, then pointed out the progression to smaller disks, scores released by record companies on seventy-eights, and finally the long-play vinyl records and CDs Michael was familiar with. For scores composed in the 1950s and 60s, he had tapes neatly labeled and shelved in black-and-white and plaid boxes. "This was my last score," he said, pulling down a bigger tape box. "Half-inch stereo eight-track master. For William Wyler, you know. In 1963 he asked me to score *Call It Sleep*. Not my finest score, but certainly my favorite film."

Michael ran his finger along the tape box labels. "Look! Mr. Waltiri—"

"Arno, please. Only producers call me Mr. Waltiri."

"You did the music for Bogart in *The Man Who Would Be King!*"

"Certainly. For John Huston, actually. Good score, that one."

"That's my favorite movie," Michael said, awed.

Waltiri's eyes sparkled. For the next two months, Michael spent most of his free time in the Waltiri house, listening to him recite selections on the piano or carefully play the fragile masters of the scores. It had been a wonderful two months, almost a justification for being bookish, something of a loner, buried in his mind instead of hanging out with friends . . .

Now Michael stood on the porch of Clarkham's house. He tried the handle on the heavy wooden door: locked, as expected. He removed the key from his pants pocket. It was late for the old neighborhood. There was no street traffic, not even the sound of distant airplanes. Everything seemed to have been muffled in a blanket.

Two months before, on a hot, airless August day, Waltiri had taken Michael up to the attic to look through papers and memorabilia. Michael had exulted over letters from Clark Gable, correspondence with Max Steiner and Erich Wolfgang Korngold, a manuscript copy of a Stravinsky oratorio.

"Up here, it feels like it's the forties again," Michael said. Waltiri stared down at lines of light thrown by a wall vent across a stack of boxes and said, "Perhaps it is." He looked up at Michael. "Let's go downstairs and get some iced tea. And on the way, instead of my talking about myself, I would like you to tell me why you want to be a poet."

Sitting on the porch, Michael sipped from his glass and shook his head. "I don't know. Mom says it's because I want to be different. She laughs, but I think she means it." He made a wry face. "As if my folks should worry. They're not your normal middle-class couple." He squinted at Waltiri, who leaned forward, head inclined like a watchful bird. "She might be right. But it's something else, too. When I write poetry, I'm more in touch with being alive. I like living here. I have some friends. But . . . it seems so limited. I try hard to find the flavor, the richness, but I can't. There has to be something more." He rubbed his cheek and looked at the fallen magnolia blossoms on the lawn. "Some of my friends just go to the movies. That's their idea of magic, of getting away. I like movies, but I can't live in them."

The composer nodded, his slate-gray eyes focused above the hedges bordering the yard. "You think there's something higher than what we see—or lower—and you want to find it."

"That's it." Michael nodded.

"Are you a good poet?"

"Not very," Michael said automatically.

"No false modesty now." Waltiri wiped condensation from his glass on the knee of his pants.

Michael thought for a moment. "I'm going to be."

"Going to be what?"

"I'm going to be a good poet."

"That's a fine thing to say. Now that you've said it, you know I'll be watching you. You must become a good poet."

Michael grinned ruefully. "Thanks a lot!"

"Think nothing of it. We all need someone to watch over us. For me, it was Gustav Mahler. I met him when I was eleven years old, and he asked me much the same thing. I was a young piano player—how do they say—a prodigy. 'How good will you be?' he asked after he heard me perform. I tried to dodge the question by acting like a young boy, but he turned his very intense dark eyes on me, cornered me, and said again, 'How *good?*' I puffed up and said, 'I'll be *very* good.' And he smiled at me! What a benediction that was. Ah, what a moment! Do you know Mahler?"

He meant Mahler's music, and Michael didn't.

"He was my god. The sad German. I worshipped him. He died a few months after we met, but somehow I felt he still watched me and he would be disappointed if I didn't make something of myself."

By early September, Waltiri had taken Michael even further into his confidence. "When I began to write music for movies, I was a little ashamed," he said one evening when Michael came over for dinner. "Even though my first score was for a good movie, Trevor Howard in *Ashenden.* Now I have no regrets, but at the time I asked myself, what would my heroes say about writing for silly films?" He shrugged in resignation. "It was next to impossible to work otherwise. I married Golda in 1930. We had to live. Times were hard then.

"But always before me was the shining splendor of perhaps doing serious music, concert-hall material. I wrote some on the side—piano pieces, cantatas, exactly the opposite of the big orchestral scores for the studios. A little has even been recorded recently, because I am so well-known as a film composer. I wanted to do an opera—how I loved the libretti of Hofmannsthal, and how I envied Richard Strauss that he lived in a time when such things were easier! 'Dream and reality are one, together, you and I alone, always together . . . to all eternity . . . *Geht all's sonst wie ein Traum dahin vor meinem Sinn . . .* ' " He laughed and shook his head. "But I am wandering.

"I had one last fling with serious music. And . . . " Waltiri paused in the dim, candlelit dining room, his eyes again focused on the distance, this time piercing a framed landscape over the china cupboard. "A very serious fling it was. A man my own age then, perhaps a little older, by the name of David Clarkham, approached me at Warner Brothers one day. I remember it was raining, but he didn't wear a raincoat . . . just a gray wool suit, without any drips on it. Not wet, you understand?"

Michael nodded.

"We had some mutual acquaintances. At first, I thought maybe he was another studio vulture. You know the kind, maybe. They hang around, bask in other peoples' fame and fortune, live off parties. 'Lounge lizards,' somebody called them. But it turned out he was knowledgeable about music. A charming fellow. We got along well . . . for a time.

"He had some theories about music that were highly unusual, to say the least." Waltiri went to a glassed-in oak bookcase, lifted a door, and withdrew a small thick volume in a worn wrapper. He held it out for Michael's inspection: *Devil's Music,* by someone named Charles Fort.

"We worked together, Clarkham and I. He suggested orchestrations and arrangements; I composed." Waltiri's expression became grim. His next words were clipped and ironic. " 'Arno,' he tells me—we are good friends by this time— 'Arno, there shall be no other music like this. Not for millions of years have such sounds been heard on Earth.' I kidded him about dinosaurs breaking wind. He looked at me very seriously and said, 'Someday you will know exactly what I

mean.' I accepted he was a little eccentric, but also brilliant. He appealed directly
to my wish to be another Stravinsky. So . . . I was a sucker. I applied his theories
to our composition, using what he called 'psychotropic tone structure.'

" 'This,' he tells me, 'will do exactly what Scriabin tried to do, and failed.' "
Michael didn't know who Scriabin was, but Waltiri continued as if with a long-
rehearsed speech.

"The piece we wrote, it was my forty-fifth opus, a concerto for piano and
orchestra called *Infinity.*" He took the book from Michael's hand and opened it
to a marked passage, then handed it back. "So we get infamous. Read, please."

Michael read.

"Or of strange things musical.

"A song of enchantment.

"Judge as you will, here is the data:

"That on November 23rd, 1939, a musician created a work of undeniable
genius, a work which changed the lives of famous men, fellow musicians.
This man was Arno Waltiri, and with his new concerto, Opus 45, he created
a suitable atmosphere for musical CATASTROPHE.

"Picture it: a cold night, Los Angeles, the Pandall Theater on Sunset
Boulevard. Crowds in black silk hats, white tie and tails, long sheer gowns,
pouring in to hear a premiere performance. Listen to it: the orchestra tuning,
cacophonic. Then Waltiri raising his baton, bringing it down . . .

"We are told the music was strange, as no music heard before. Sounds
grew in that auditorium like apparitions. We are told that a famous composer
walked out in disgust. And then, a week later, filed suit against Waltiri! 'I am
unable to hear or compose music in a sensible fashion!' he said in the court
deposition. And what did he blame? Waltiri's music!

"Consider it.

"What would prompt a well-known and respected composer to sue a
fellow composer for an impossible—so doctors tell us—injury? The case was
dropped before it ever reached court. But . . . what did that concerto sound
like?

"I submit to you, perhaps Waltiri knew the answer to an age-old question, namely, 'What song did the sirens sing?' "

Michael closed the book. "It's not all nonsense," Waltiri said, returning the
tattered volume to the shelf. "That is roughly what happened. And then, months
later, twenty people disappear. The only thing they have in common is, they were
in the audience for our music." He looked at Michael and lifted his eyebrows.
"Most of us live in the real world, my young friend . . . but David Clarkham . . . I
am not so sure. The first time I saw him, coming out of the wet with his suit so
dry, I thought to myself, 'The man must walk between raindrops.' The last time
I saw him, in July of 1944, it was also raining. Two years before, he had bought
a house a few blocks from here. We didn't see each other often. But this wet
summer day he comes to stand on our porch and gives me a key. 'I'm going on
a trip,' he says. 'You should have this, in case you ever wish to follow me. The

house will be taken care of.' Very mysterious. With the key there is a piece of paper."

Waltiri took a small teak box from the top of the bookshelf and held it before Michael, pulling up the lid. Inside was a yellowed, folded paper, and wrapped partly within, a tarnished brass house key. "I never followed him. I was curious, but I never had the courage. And besides, there was Golda. How could I leave her? But you . . . you are a young man."

"Where did Clarkham go?" Michael asked.

"I don't know. The last words he said to me, he says, 'Arno, should you ever wish to come after me, do everything on the paper. Go to my house between midnight and two in the morning. I will meet you." He removed the note and key from the box and gave them to Michael. "I won't live forever. I will never follow. Perhaps you."

Michael grinned. "It all sounds pretty weird to me."

"It is very weird, and silly. That house—he told me he did a great deal of musical experimentation there. I heard very little of it. As I said, we weren't close after the premiere of the concerto. But once he told me, 'The music gets into the walls in time, you know. It haunts the place'

"He was a brilliant man, Michael, but he—how do you say it?—he screwed me over. I took the blame for the concerto. He left for two years. I settled the lawsuits. Nothing was ever decided in court. I was nearly broke.

"He had made me write music that affects the way a person thinks, as drugs affect the brain. I have written nothing like it since."

"What will happen if I go?"

"I don't know," Waltiri said, staring at him intently. "Perhaps you will find what lives above or below the things we know."

"I mean, if something happened to me, what would my parents think?"

"There comes a time when one must disregard the thoughts of one's parents, or the warnings of old men, when caution must be temporarily put aside and instincts followed. In short, when one must rely on one's own judgment." He opened another door in the bookcase. "Now, my young friend, before we become sententious, I've been thinking there is one other thing I'd like to give to you. A book. One of my favorites." He pulled out a pocket-sized book bound in plain, shiny black leather and held it out for Michael.

"It's very pretty," Michael said. "It looks old."

"Not so very old," Waltiri said. "My father bought it for me when I left for California. It's the finest poetry, in English, all my favorites. A poet should have it. There is a large selection of Coleridge. You've read him, I'm sure."

Michael nodded.

"Then, for me, read him again."

Two weeks later, Michael was swimming in the backyard pool when his mother stepped out on the patio with a delicate walk and a peculiar expression. She nervously brushed back a strand of her red hair and shielded her eyes against the sun. Michael stared at her from poolside, his arm flesh goose-bumping. He almost knew.

"That was Golda on the phone," she said. "Arno's dead."

There was no funeral. Waltiri's ashes were placed in a columbarium at Forest Lawn. There were features on his death in the newspaper and on television.

That had been six weeks before. Michael had last spoken with Golda two days ago. She had sat on the piano bench in her front room, straight-backed and dignified, wearing a cream-colored suit, her golden hair immaculately coifed. Her accent was more pronounced than her husband's.

"He was sitting right here, at the piano," she said, "and he looked at me and said, 'Golda, what have I done, I've given that boy Clarkham's key. Call his parents now.' And his arm stiffened . . . He said he was in great pain. Then he was on the floor." She looked at Michael earnestly. "But I did not tell your parents. He trusted you. You will make the right decision."

She sat quietly for a time, then continued. "Two days later, a tiny brown sparrow flew into Arno's study, where the library is now. It sat on the piano and plucked at pieces of sheet music. Arno had once made a joke about a bird being a spirit inside an animal body. I tried to shoo it out the window, but it wouldn't go. It perched on the music stand and stayed there for an hour, twisting its head to stare at me. Then it flew away." She began to cry. "I would dearly love for Arno to visit me now and then, even as a sparrow. He is such a fine man." She wiped her eyes and hugged Michael tightly, then let him go and straightened his jacket.

"He trusted you," she had repeated, tugging gently at his lapel. "You will know what is best."

Now he stood on the porch of Clarkham's house, feeling resigned if not calm. Night birds sang in the trees lining the street, a sound that had always intrigued him for the way it carried a bit of daylight into the still darkness.

He couldn't say precisely why he was there. Perhaps it was tribute to a good friend he had known for so short a time. Had Waltiri actually wanted him to follow the instructions? It was all so ambiguous.

He inserted the key in the lock.

To discover what is above or below.

He turned the key.

Music haunts the place now.

The door opened quietly.

Michael entered and shut the door tight behind him. The brass workings clicked.

Walking straight in the darkness was difficult. He brushed against a wall with his shoulder. The touch set off an unexpected *bong,* as if he were inside a giant bell. He didn't know if he had crossed a room or made his way down a hall, but he bumped against another door, fumbled for the knob, and found it. The door opened easily and silently. To Michael's left in the room beyond was another doorway leading into a smaller room. Moonlight spilled through French doors like milk on the bare wood floor. All the rooms were empty of furniture.

The French doors opened onto a bare brick patio and a desolate yard, with a brick wall beyond. The door handles felt like ice in his hands.

He exited from the rear of Clarkham's house. A flagstone path curved around the outside to the side gate. When he had entered the front door there had been no moon, but now a sullen green orb rose over the silhouettes of the houses on the opposite side of the street. It didn't cast much light. (And yet, the moonlight through the French doors had been bright . . .) The streetlights were also strangely dim, and yellowish-green in color.

There were fewer trees than he remembered, and those leafless and skeletal. The air smelled antiseptic, electric and mildewy at once, as if it had been preserved and then had spoiled for lack of use. The sky closed in, pitch black and starless. Through the windows of the houses across the street came fitful brown glimmers, not at all like electric lights or television. More like dull reflections from dried blood.

He walked gingerly across the dried, patchy grass to the front door of the house on the left. As predicted in the instructions, the door had been left open a crack. Warm, welcoming light poured in a narrow shaft from within. He pushed the door open with a damp palm.

Entering, Michael saw a small table perched alertly on delicately curved legs on the polished wood floor of the hallway. A brass bowl on the table presented fruit: oranges, apples, something blue and shiny. Down the hall about eight feet and to the left opened a rounded archway to the living room.

He closed the front door. It made a muffled, pillowy sound.

A faint mildewy smell issued from the walls and floor and hung in transparent wisps through the hall. Michael approached the archway, nose wrinkled. The house was lighted as if somebody lived there, but the only sound he heard was that of his own footsteps.

In the living room, a lone, high-backed, velvet-upholstered rocking chair occupied the middle of a broad circular throw rug before the dark fireplace. The throw rug resembled a target of concentric circles of tan and black. The chair faced away from Michael and rocked slowly back and forth. He couldn't see who, if anybody, sat in it. He had just realized he was not following the instructions when the chair stopped rocking. It held steady for an unbearably long time. Then it began to swivel counter-clockwise.

Suddenly, Michael didn't want to see what sat in the chair. He ran down the hall, around a short bend and into an empty room.

"Do not stop to look at anything," the note had said. He had hesitated, he told himself, not stopped; still, he felt the need to be more cautious. He made sure no one followed, then departed the house through the rear door and found himself on yet another brick patio. To his left rose a white trellis arch overgrown with wisteria. Fireflies danced in oleander bushes to each side. Beyond the patio, glowing paper lanterns hung motionless over a stretch of empty flower beds.

Michael was startled to see someone sitting behind a glass-topped wrought-iron table under the wisteria trellis. Except for the wan flicker of the paper lanterns, there was little illumination, but he could make out that the person at the table wore a long dress, pale and flounced, and a broad hat half-obscured by inky shadow.

Michael stared hard at the seated figure, fascinated. Was someone supposed to meet him, take him farther? The note had said nothing about a woman waiting. He tried to discern the face beneath the hat.

The figure rose slowly from the chair. The jerky quality of its movement, a loose awkwardness, made his flesh crawl. He backed up, stumbled down the porch steps into the garden, and twisted around to fall on his face. For a second or two he lay stunned and breathless. Then he looked over his shoulder.

The figure had left the table. It stood at the top of the steps. Even hidden by the dress, every limb bent in the wrong places. He still couldn't see the face beneath the hat.

The figure took the first step down from the patio, and Michael jumped to his feet. The second, and he ran across the garden to the black wrought-iron gate at the rear. The latch opened easily and he swung from the gatepost, halting in the alley to get his bearings. "To the left," he said, his breath ragged. He heard footsteps behind, the sound of the latch. Was it the fifth or sixth gate to the left? The alley was too dark to allow him to re-read the note, but he could make out gates in the obscurity—gates in the walls on both sides. Trees loomed thick and black above the opposite wall, leaves hushed, dead still.

He counted as he ran . . . two, three, four, five gates. He stopped again, then passed to the sixth.

A lock blocked the iron latch. He knew instinctively he couldn't just climb over—if he did, he would find nothing but darkness on the other side. He fumbled frantically for the key in his pocket, the only key he had been given.

The figure in the flounced dress had closed the distance between them to six or seven yards. It lurched slowly and deliberately toward him as if it had all the time in the world.

The key fit the lock, but just barely. He had to jerk it several times. A sigh behind him, long and dry, and he felt cold pressure on his shoulder, the rasp of something light and brittle brushing his jacket sleeve—

Michael flinched, crouched, pushed the gate open with his forearm, and fell through. He crawled and scrambled across broken dirt and withered stubble, fell again, gravel digging into the flesh of his cheek. No use fleeing. He closed his eyes and clutched the crumbling clods and twigs, waiting.

The gate clanged shut and the latch fell into place with a *snick*.

Several seconds passed before he even allowed himself to think he hadn't been followed. The quality of the air had changed. He rolled over and looked at the stone wall. The figure should have been visible above the wall, or through the openwork of the gate, but it wasn't.

He let his breath out all at once. He felt safe now—safe for the moment, at least.

"It worked," he said, standing and brushing off his clothes. "It really worked!" Somehow, he wasn't all that elated. A strange thing had just happened, and he had been badly frightened.

It couldn't have taken Michael more than fifteen minutes to do everything in the instructions, yet dawn was a hazy orange in the east.

He had crossed over. But to where?

2

Perversely, his next thought was how to get back home. He walked cautiously to the gate and peered over. There was no alley, only a broad bank descending to a slow-moving gray river about a hundred yards from shore to shore. In the hazy dawn light, the river ambled through a hilly landscape devoid of trees, banks bristling with rank weeds.

He turned and surveyed the field before him. It had once been a vineyard but was now overgrown with dry scrub. The vines had died, leaving thick gray stumps tethered to stakes tilting crazily in dirt crusted with crisp, sere dead leaves. The weeds themselves weren't faring too well.

As the smoky dawn brightened, the rear of a blocky rectangular mansion emerged from mist and shadows. Michael walked through the dead vineyard, squinting to make out details within the mansion's dark outline.

It wasn't in very good repair. One whole wing had been ravaged by fire, leaving only masonry and charred timbers. Michael was no expert on architecture, but the design seemed old and European, like a chateau in France. There was no sign of life.

He came upon a narrow path through the weeds and dead vines and approached the building, feeling as if he were an intruder. He hadn't the slightest idea where he was. His arms prickled with goosebumps in the clammy, chill air, and his stomach growled for breakfast.

The house was even larger than Michael had thought: three stories tall, the bottom story recessed five or six feet. Five broad corbeled stone arches supported the overhang. As he approached, he observed that a yard-wide chunk of stone and plaster had fallen from the middle arch.

The path led up to the central arch, where Michael stopped. The air of desertion and decay didn't encourage him. A dark oak door set into the wall beneath had been decorated with two carved mirror-image whorls occupying the top and bottom frames, surrounded by intertwining serpents. Two bronze lanterns jutted from the stone beside the door, their glasswork broken and jagged.

Michael made a fist and knocked on the door. Even after several episodes of heavy pounding, there came no answer from behind the rough, cracked wood.

He backed away and looked to his left and right. To each side of the door were bricked-up windows, and beyond them more alcoves in the stone wall. He stumbled through old dead bushes to the next alcove on his right and found another door, again without an exterior handle. He tried prying it open with his fingers but it wouldn't budge. The last door on the right had been plastered over. He returned to the second door and tentatively pushed at it with one hand, feeling the smooth rolls of the serpents beneath his fingers. It swung inward with a whining creak.

Michael looked over his shoulder anxiously: still alone, unobserved, though he couldn't help wondering what might be hiding in the ruined vineyard.

With a stronger shove, the door swung open all the way, rebounding with a heavy thud from an inner wall. Indirect morning light allowed him to see a couple of yards into the gloom of a dark hallway. Simple brickwork walls, stone floor: empty. He advanced slowly. About fifteen feet in, the hall turned a corner. A bar of light slanted across the floor from that direction.

Michael peered around the corner. Beyond lay a large and long-abandoned kitchen. He stepped forward gingerly, his feet kicking up great black wafts of felt-like dust. Yard-wide iron pots and brick-based stoves and ovens filled a chamber at least seventy feet long and sixty wide. Everything smelled of old spilled wine and dusty decay. Light shafted down through a long, narrow horizontal window about twelve feet above the floor on the opposite wall. Apparently the kitchen was in a kind of basement; from the front it lay below ground level.

The hall through which he had entered flanked a brick enclosure which might have been a storage locker or refrigerator. A white-enameled metal door hung ajar on corroded hinges, revealing only darkness within.

On the south side of the kitchen a stairwell rose into deep shadow. He crossed the cluttered floor between the iron-grilled stove and the enclosure, feet striking mounds of broken crockery and heavy, smaller pots beneath smooth rivers of dust. He climbed the stair.

Swinging doors waited at the top, one knocked from its hinges and propped against the wall, the other kicked and splintered askew. He pushed the leaning door aside and stepped into a dining hall.

Three long dark wood tables filled about half the space, chairs upended neatly on the table edges. Carpet gave way to wooden parquet flooring beyond the tables. The room could have held a respectable-size ball, and stretched to the front of the house, where tall arched windows afforded a view of the rising sun. Morning light smeared silvery-gray across the table tops.

The room smelled of dust and a rather bitter tang of flowers. He looked to both sides and decided to try the broad door on the right.

That took him into an equally decrepit and impressive foyer. Here, modern-looking overstuffed couches had been spaced along the walls beneath more tall arched windows. A demolished grand piano cluttered a small stage like a crushed beetle. At the opposite end of the foyer was an immense staircase, transplanted from a castle or luxury liner, with gold banisters mounted on turned pillars of ebony. He looked up. A balustrade ran from the staircase across the length of an upper landing.

"*Ne there! Hoy ac!*"

The largest woman he had ever seen leaned over the stone and metal railing of the balustrade, directly above him. She pulled back. He traced her elephantine steps by the agonized creaking of the floor as she approached the stairs. Through the rails her shapeless body appeared to bulk at least a thousand pounds; she stood six and a half feet tall; her arms, thick as hams and like in shape, were covered by the long sleeves of a black caftan.

"Hello," he said, voice cracking.

She paused at the top of the staircase and thumped her palm on the railing. Her face was little more than eyes and mouth poked deep into white dough, topped with well-kept long black hair. "Hel-lo," she repeated, her tiny eyes growing almost imperceptibly larger. He couldn't decide whether to stand his ground or run. "*Antros.* You're human. Where in hell did you come from?"

He pointed to the rear of the house. "Outside. The vineyard gate."

"You couldn't have come that way," the woman said, her voice deepening. "It's locked."

He took the keyholder from his pants pocket and held it up. "I used this."

She made her way down the stairs slowly, taking each step with great care, as well she should have. If she fell, she was heavy enough to kill herself and bring the staircase down with her. "A key!" She peered at it hungrily. "Who gave it to you?"

Michael didn't answer.

"*Who gave that to you?*"

"Mr. Waltiri," he said in a small voice.

"Waltiri, Waltiri." She reached the bottom and waddled slowly toward him, her arms describing arcs with each step to avoid the span of her hips. "Nobody comes here," she said, vibrating to a slow stop a few feet from Michael. "You speak Cascar or Nerb?"

He shook his head, not understanding.

"Only English?"

"I speak a little French," he said. "Took two years in high school. And some Spanish."

She tittered, then abruptly broke into a loud, high, sad cackle. "French, Spanish. You're new. Definitely new."

He couldn't argue with that. "Where am I?"

"When did you get here?" she countered.

"About half an hour ago, I think."

"What time was it when you left?"

"Left where?"

"Your home, boy," she said, some of the gravel tone returning.

"About one in the morning."

"You don't know where you are, or who I am?"

He shook his head. A slow anger grew alongside his fear.

"My name," the huge, corpulent woman said, "is Lamia. Yours?" She lifted one arm and pointed a surprisingly delicate finger at him.

"Michael," he said.

"What did you bring with you?"

He held out his arms. "My clothes, I guess. The key."

"What's that in your coat pocket?"

"A book."

She nodded as best she could, her head almost immobile on the thick column of her neck. The effort buried her chin in flesh. "Mr. Waltiri sent you. Where is he?"

"He's dead."

She cackled again as if that were ridiculous. "And so am I. Dead as this house, dead as a million dreams!" Her laughter scattered from the walls and ceilings like a flight of desperate birds. "Can you go back?"

"I don't know," he said. Then, plaintively, "I want to."

"You *want* to. You come here, and you *want* to go back. Don't you know *how?*"

He shook his head.

"Then you're stuck here. You're dead, too. Well, at least you have company." If her unbaked features could convey any emotion, she might have appeared wistful. That turned to sudden, almost childish concern. "But you must leave this house! Nobody stays here come night!"

By this time Michael was trembling, and angry at himself for being afraid. The way the woman stared at him, saying nothing, made it all worse.

"Well," she said finally. "You'll learn soon enough. You'll return to this house tomorrow morning."

"It's only morning now," Michael said.

"You'll need the rest of the day to straighten out your situation. Come with me."

She walked around the staircase and opened a large door at the front of the house. He followed her shimmying form down a long flight of stone steps to a rocky field, then across a narrow path to a dirt road which wound its way through more low, treeless hills.

Lamia pointed a delicate finger at the end of an immense arm. "There's a town—a human town—about three miles up this road, beyond the field and over a bridge. Go there quickly. Don't loiter. There are those who have no great love for humans. There's a seedy hotel in town, bed and board; you'll have to work for your keep. They stick together in the town. They have to. Go there, tell them Lamia wants you put up. Tell them you'll work." She stared at the book bulging his jacket pocket. "Are you a student?" she asked.

"I guess so," he said.

"Hide the book. Full morning tomorrow, come back and we'll talk."

She turned without waiting for any reaction and labored up the steps to the door, shutting it behind her. Michael looked this way and that, trying to squeeze meaning out of the barren hills, ruined old house, and rocky front yard.

He wasn't dreaming. It was all quite real.

3

Michael had not reckoned with feeling scared, being hungry, or facing the acid realization that he had no idea what to do. He had nothing to fall back on, no reasonable guide; he had only Lamia's words. Lamia herself, whatever she had to say, was hardly reassuring. Her brusqueness and her almost certain insanity made Michael all the more desperate to find a way home. He decided to try the gate again, to climb over it if need be; perhaps the river and the countryside beyond the gate were illusory. Perhaps he could just jump and find himself back in the alley . . .

Back with the figure in the flounced dress and broad hat.

That thought stopped him halfway across the field, behind the ruined mansion. Fists clenched, he turned and trudged back over the rocks and clods between the dead vines.

He was on the dirt road again, following Lamia's directions, when he heard pounding hooves. A group of five horses and riders galloped along about half a mile behind him, raising a small plume of dust. He hid behind a boulder and watched.

The riders approached the narrow path leading to the house and slowed to confer with each other. Michael had never seen horses or men like them. Uniform mottled gray—all but one, a dazzling golden palomino—the horses were large and lean, hide clinging so closely to jutting muscles they appeared to have been flayed. The men were tall and thin, with a spectral quality most strikingly evident in their faces. All of them had reddish-blond hair, long narrow jaws without beards, and square large eyes beneath formidable brows. Their clothing was pearly gray, differing from the horses' coloration only in the way it diffracted the early morning sunlight.

Done conferring, the riders took the path to the house and dismounted near the steps. The horses kicked at clods of dirt as their masters entered the house without knocking.

Michael squinted from his awkward vantage. He decided it would be best for him to leave the area and get to the village as quickly as possible.

The walk took about forty-five minutes. All the way, he kept glancing over his shoulder to make sure the riders weren't coming up behind him.

His wristwatch had stopped working, he noticed; the sweep second hand was motionless. The dial read one-oh-seven. But he could judge time by his growing hunger.

The village first appeared as an irregular line of brown blocks set against the horizon. The closer he approached, the less impressed he was. Small mud-brick houses leaned on each other, defining the outskirts of the village, their thick thatch roofs rising to conical peaks. Tiny twists of greasy smoke slid from the peaks of most of the houses. In the still air, the smoke gradually settled into a ground-hugging haze. Beyond the mud-brick houses, larger two-story buildings connected by stone walls presented a unified dreary green-brown exterior.

A low unguarded gate led through the walls into the village proper. He walked between the gateposts, kicking up wisps of smoke and ground fog. A sign neatly painted on the gate arch, facing toward the village rather than out, proclaimed:

EUTERPE
Glorious Capital of the Pact Lands

A few people were about in the mid-morning, women carrying baskets and men standing and talking. They all stared at Michael as he passed. He stuck his hands firmly into his pants pockets andreturned their stares with furtive glances. The women wore pants or brown, sack-like dresses. The men wore dust-colored pants and dirty tan shirts. Some walked from house to house carrying bundles of dried reeds.

To Michael's discomfort, he was attracting a lot of attention, though nobody advanced to speak to him. The place had a prison atmosphere, quiet and too orderly, with an undercurrent of tension.

He looked for a sign to show him where the hotel was. There were no signs. Finally he gathered up courage and approached a pale round-faced man with thinning black hair, who stood by a wicker crate to one side of the narrow stone-paved street.

"Excuse me," Michael said. The man regarded him with listless curiosity. "Can you tell me where the hotel is?"

The man smiled and nodded, then began speaking swiftly in a language Michael couldn't understand. Michael shook his head and the man made a few motions in the proper direction, lifting his eyebrows.

"Thanks," Michael said. Luckily, the hotel was nearby and rather obvious; it was the only place that smelled good. There was no sign in front, but the building was slightly more elegant than its neighbors, with a pretense of mud bas-relief ornament over the door and windows. The odor of baking bread poured from the first floor windows in billows. Michael paused, salivating, then walked up the front steps and entered the small lobby

A short, bulky man wearing a gray kepi and coveralls sat behind the counter. All the furniture was made of woven wicker or—like the counter—of narrow, close-fitted bricks. The carpets in the lobby and hall were thin and worn, and the coarse cloth upholstery on a wicker couch placed near the door was tattered, barbed with feathers and fibers.

"Lamia told me to come here," Michael said.

"Did she, now?" the man asked, his gaze fixed on Michael's chest. He seemed unwilling to acknowledge that anyone could be taller than he.

"You speak English," Michael said. The man agreed with a curt nod. "She said I should work for some food and be put up this evening. I should return to see her tomorrow."

"Did she, now?" he repeated.

"She wants me to work."

"Ah." The man turned to look at the rack of keys mounted behind the counter—baked clay keys, bulky and silly-looking. "Lamia." He didn't sound pleased. He wrapped his fingers around a key but didn't remove it from the hook. He stared again at Michael's chest. Michael leaned over until the man could look into his face, and the man beamed a broad smile. "What kind of work?"

"I . . . anything, I guess."

"Lamia." He removed the key and looked at it longingly. "She never sent anyone here before. You a friend?"

"I don't know," Michael said.

"Then why's she looking after you?" the man went on, as if Michael had answered in the negative.

"I don't know much of anything," Michael said.

"You're new." He stated it nonchalantly, then frowned and peered at Michael's face more closely. "By God, you're *new!* How'd you meet Lamia if you're new? But—" His whole aspect changed abruptly. He came alive, lifting his hand and shaking his head vigorously. "No questions. You *are* under her charge, or you wouldn't say so, believe me. Let it stand at that. Yes! Stand at that." He considered something profoundly puzzling, solved it, and brightened. "Since you're new, you'll go in with the teacher." He came around the counter with a jaunty swing of his long arms. "Double up. It's a small room and my wife'll work the skin off your fingers and the kink out of your arms. You'll eat plain like the rest of us." He chuckled ruefully, winking. "There isn't anything fancy, believe me, but this place is quiet at night. You'll sleep on cottongrass, and when the alarm rings—"

At that instant, a bell clanged loudly. The sound seemed to come from all directions. "My name," the stout, long-armed man said, "is Brecker, and we'll be going downstairs now. That's the alarm. Risky!"

Michael assumed Brecker was assessing the situation, but the innkeeper called out, "Risky!" again and a thin worried-looking woman about the same age leaped down the stairs, bandy legs taking them three at a time.

"I *heard,*" she said in irritation. Michael looked through the lobby's smoky windows and saw people hurrying about in the streets. "It's Wickmaster Alyons and his coursers again. They must have been at the Isomage's house, and now they're here."

Michael followed them down stone steps into a dirt-walled cellar. They squatted by the wall closest to the steps, among large bottles of brown liquid and straw baskets filled with potatoes. Brecker patted the floor beside him and Michael sat.

"Why the alarm?" he asked.

Risky tossed her lank hair and spat into a corner. "The riding of the noble Sidhe against the race of man," she said, her voice thick with sarcasm. She appraised Michael with a cool eye. "You're new," she said. "Where's Savarin?"

"Probably watching them from upstairs," Brecker said. "As usual."

Even with the cellar door shut, Michael heard the sharp clatter of hooves. There came a high-pitched keening, and then a voice resonant and hypnotic.

"*Hoy ac!* Meat-eaters, followers of the Serpent! Praise Adonna or we unleash your babes and return the Pact Lands to dust and desert!"

Brecker shuddered, opening and closing his hands in spasms, and Risky's lips became thin and white. The hooves clattered off. Moments later, bells rang again through the town.

"Welcome to Euterpe," Risky said to Michael as she threw open the cellar door and scrambled up the steps. Brecker followed, motioning for Michael to return with them to the first floor.

"Tomorrow," Brecker told Risky, "our new lodger goes back to the Isomage's house, to Lamia. He's new, you know."

"He's much too young to be anything else," Risky said. "And he's not like the rest of us. Not if *she* wants him." That said, she seemed to make an effort to put everything from her mind. "Show him the double."

"My thought, too. With Savarin."

"Might as well. There's a lot for him to learn."

The double on the second floor waited at the end of an ill-lit corridor. The room was small, its dark walls paneled in thin strips of gray pasteboard. The floor was tiled with mica that flaked under his shoes. Two beds had been stacked bunk-style in the narrow space, and a washbasin on a flimsy stand made of sticks and wicker occupied a corner. At least there were no insects visible.

As he stood in the doorway, wondering who Savarin was, Risky came up behind him and argued with Brecker over what work Michael was to do. Brecker gave him a nervous glance and took Risky down the corridor, where they whispered.

Michael caught most of the conversation despite their precautions.

"If he's under Lamia's protection, should we work him at all?" Brecker asked.

"Did she forbid it? I say, work him. We can always use hands."

"Yes, but he's different from the rest of us—"

"Only because he came from the Isomage's house."

"And shouldn't that mean something?"

"Lamia doesn't scare me," Risky said. "Now, if Alyons brought the boy in under his arm and said, 'Show him a good time,' maybe then we'd spare him some labor."

That seemed to settle it. Risky showed him the washroom—"Modern, one upstairs and one down," she said, but no running water and no plumbing. She gave him a crust of bread and a glass of thin milk, then set him to work wringing fresh-washed linens through a stone mangle in a laundry room behind the kitchen. As he turned the handle and fed in sheets and pillow casings, he munched on the bread.

"No crumbs on the sheets," Risky warned. She peered at him critically. "You look hungry."

"Starved," Michael said.

"Well, don't eat too much. We'll just take it out in more work."

Carrying dried sheets upstairs, Michael noticed that only two rooms were occupied out of the twelve in the building; the double he shared with the unknown Savarin, and the largest, a suite. "We don't go in the suite but once a week," Risky explained.

"Who's in it?"

"Hungry and curious. Hungry and curious. Takes new ones a while to learn how the land lies, doesn't it?" She shook her head. "You'll meet him this evening. Brecker's already planning a gathering."

In the hotel's service court, he was put to chopping sticks—or rather making the attempt. He raised blisters quickly on both hands and felt miserable. He had never enjoyed hard physical labor. As he swung and missed, swung and missed, swung and splintered, swung and finally split a bundle of sticks cleanly, he wanted more than anything to be home again, in bed with a book on his lap and a ginger ale on his nightstand.

By dusk—which came somewhat early, he thought—he had cut thirteen bundles of sticks into sizes that would fit in the hotel stove. Brecker inspected the small pile and shook his head. He stared at Michael's chest as he said, "No doubt you'll do better later. If you get to stay here. But never mind. There's the meeting tonight." His face took on a contented expression and he winked. "Word gets around. You're good for business, tonight at least."

They allowed Michael a half-hour to clean up for dinner. Having eaten only the bread and drunk two glasses of the translucent bluish milk, he was ravenous again. He went to his assigned room and lay on the lower of the two bunks for a moment, eyes closed, too tired to really want to eat and too hungry to nap. He washed his blistered hands in the basin of water and picked at a splinter beneath his fingernail. A pungent herbal smell came from the basin. Michael sniffed the soap—a fatty, grainy bar with no odor at all—and wiped his hands on a rag. The odor departed rapidly.

He removed his shirt and wiped himself from the waist up with a damp cloth, then used the primitive facilities in the lavatory at the end of the hall. He suspected he would carry the slops bucket downstairs the next day, unless . . .

What? Unless his talk with Lamia went well? What would she do besides talk to him, and what was her connection with the riders, the Shee as Risky called them?

He was too exhausted to be terribly curious. Night had fallen swiftly. He descended the stairs to dinner with drooping eyelids and sat at the smooth-worn, stone-topped table next to Brecker.

Dozens of wax candles lit the table, inserted in clay holders before each seat. There were twelve seats, all filled. The table's occupants—five women and seven men—regarded Michael with intense interest whenever his head was turned.

Michael sat as straight as he could, trying to be dignified and not fall asleep. As Risky carried out a bowl of vegetable soup, Brecker stood and raised a cup of watered brown ale. "Patrons and matrons," he began. "We have among us this evening a newcomer. His name is Michael, and he's young, as you see; the youngest I've ever met in the Realm. Let us welcome him."

Men and women raised their cups and shouted in a bewildering array of tongues, "Cheers!" "Skaal!" "Slainte!" "Zum Wohl!" "Here's to Michael!", more than he could separate out. He lifted his cup to them. "Thank you," he murmured.

"Now eat," Risky said. After the soup had been noisily consumed, she removed the bowl to the kitchen and brought in a pot filled with cabbage and carrots and large brown beans, as well as plates of a sliced raw vegetable Michael had never seen before, resembling a brown-skinned cucumber with a triangular cross-section. There was no meat.

His eyelids drooped and he caught himself just in time to hear, " . . . so you see, lad, we're not in the best situation here." This from the tall, strong-looking fellow with the full salt-and-pepper beard sitting across and one chair to the left of him.

"Huh? I mean, sorry?" Michael said, blinking.

"I say, the town is not in the best of circumstances. Ever since the Isomage lost his war, we've been confined to the Pact Lands in the middle of the Blasted Plain. No children, of course—"

The plump auburn-haired woman beside the strong man shushed him and rolled her eyes. "Except," he continued, giving her a harsh look. "And you'll pardon the indiscretion, but the lad must know his circumstances—"

At this several people called out, "And where's Savarin?"

"He should be the one tutoring the lad," the auburn-haired woman said.

"The lad," the man pushed on, "must know that there are children of a sort, to remind us of our peril. They reside in the Yard at the center of Euterpe." The auburn-haired woman crossed herself and bowed her head, moving her lips. "And there's not an instrument in the entire land to play."

"Play?" Michael asked. The group looked at each other around the table.

"Music, you know," Brecker said.

"Music," Michael repeated, still puzzled.

"Lad," the strong fellow said, standing, "you mean to say you don't play an instrument?"

"I don't."

"You don't know music?"

"I like to listen," Michael said, feeling fresh alarm at their amazement. More glances were exchanged around the table. Brecker looked uncomfortable.

"Boy, are you telling us it wasn't music brought you here?"

"I don't think it was," Michael said.

The auburn-haired woman gave a shuddering moan and backed her chair away from the table. Several others did the same. "Then how did you come here?" she asked, no longer looking at him directly.

"He's not a *Child,* is he?" a stout woman at the end of the table wailed. Her male companion took hold of her arm and urged her back into the seat. "Obviously not," he said. "We know the Children. His face is good."

"How did you get here, then?"

Michael, haltingly and with some backtracking, gave an account of Waltiri, the note, Clarkham's house and the crossing over. For some reason—perhaps his weariness—he didn't mention the figure in the flounced dress. The gathering nodded in unison when he was done.

"That," said the strong man, "is a most unusual path. I've never heard of it."

"No doubt Lamia could tell us more," someone said, Michael couldn't see whom.

"I know," said a deep, gruff voice. The crowd fell silent. Brecker nudged Michael and pointed out a man seated across from them and to the right. "The occupant of the suite," he murmured.

Older than the others, none of whom seemed more than forty or forty-five, this man carried a thin curly cap of white hair, and his pale pink face, shadowed with tones of weary gray, wore an expression of bitter indifference. His pale blue eyes searched from face to astonished face. "He never says *anything,*" Brecker whispered to Michael, eyes wide.

"Boy," the man said, standing, "my name is Frederick Wolfer. Do you know of me?"

Michael shook his head. The man was dressed in a yellowed and frayed tuxedo and a formal black suit shiny and ragged with age. The elbows of the jacket had been patched over with gray cloth, and in the patches, new holes had been worn. "Did Arno Waltiri mention me?"

"No," Michael said.

"He sent me here," Wolfer said, his jaw working. He raised an unsteady hand. "He sent a man already old into a land that doesn't tolerate the old. Fortunately, I have fallen in with good people." A murmur went around the table. "Fortunately, I have withstood the rigors of war, of Clarkham's attempt to build an empire, and the internment of all of us here in the Pact Lands. All of that . . ." He paused and gazed at the ceiling, as if he might find the proper words floating up there. "Because on a summer night, who knows how many decades ago, I went to a concert and listened to a piece of music, music written by Arno Waltiri. I know the name, yes indeed. I am the only one left alive of those who were transported by his music. The only one. Boy, you must understand our circumstances. All of us here, with the exception of you, all the humans in the Realm, or Sidhedark, or Faerie Shadow, or whatever you wish to call this *accursed place—* we are here because music transported us."

"Enchanted," said the auburn-haired woman

"Crossed us over," said a plump, black-haired man.

"Me, when I played trumpet," said the strong fellow.

"And I, piano," said another.

Wolfer held up his hand to stop the voices. "I was not a musician. I was a music critic. I believe that Waltiri took his vengeance on me . . . by setting me among musicians, forever and ever."

"We loved music," Brecker said. "We added something to human music which it does not ordinarily have—"

"Except for Waltiri's concerto," Wolfer interjected.

"We took from ourselves, and made music as the Sidhe have played it for thousands of years. Made it whole. And crossed over." Brecker chewed on a stray bit of food, swallowed, and added, "All of us love music."

"And here," Risky said, "there is none."

"The Sidhe say their Realm is music," the strong man said, "but not for us."

"Ask Lamia why you're here," Risky suggested

"And be careful of that woman, boy," Wolfer said, seating himself with painful slowness. "Be very careful indeed."

4

Michael barely remembered lurching up to the room after dinner, and he had no memory at all of falling asleep. But he awoke at an unknown hour, in complete darkness, to hear the room door open, footsteps, and the clump of something heavy on the mica flooring.

My roommate, he thought. *Savarin.* He dozed off again with a vague wonder as to what sort of Queequeg the Realm could conjure.

At dawn, his eyes flew open and he stared up at the bulges between the slats on the bunk above. He rolled over beneath the scratchy covers and stared at a trunk over against one wall, beside the washstand. The trunk had been fashioned of the ubiquitous wicker, equipped with heavy cloth straps.

He hadn't dreamed at all during the night. Sleep had excavated a pit in his life, a time when he might as well have been dead. Nevertheless, he felt rested. He was contemplating getting out of bed when someone knocked on the door. Simultaneously, a bushy-haired head peered over the edge of the top bunk.

"Light's up," Risky said behind the door. He heard her go down the hall.

"Good morning," said Michael's roommate. He was about forty, with a pronounced nose, graying brown hair, and large bright eyes. His withdrawn chin sat on a thin neck with almost no Adam's apple.

"Good morning," Michael said.

"Ah, American?" the man asked.

Michael nodded.

"My name is Henrik Savarin. You're in my bunk."

"Michael Perrin. I'm sorry."

"From?"

"Los Angeles."

Savarin nimbly stepped down the bunk ladder and landed on the floor with a soft plop. He had slept in his brown pants and loose-fitting shirt, and had wrapped his feet in felt tied with lengths of rope.

"Short blanket on top," he explained. He untied the knots in the ropes and pulled off the felt, then slipped his feet into canvas shoes without socks. "Musician?"

Michael shook his head. "Student, I suppose."

"A scholar!" Savarin grinned and slid his palms down his pants legs in a useless attempt to remove wrinkles. "In a land full of those crazy about music, a scholar like myself." He held out his hand. "Pleased to acquaint with you."

Michael shook Savarin's hand. "I'm not really a scholar," he said.

"They pry, you know." Savarin pointed his nose at the closed door. "Myself, I regard it as most impolite to pry. So no questions for now. But . . ." He raised his hand and smiled again. "I'll tell you. I study the people here, I study the Sidhe and their languages, and I sometimes teach. In my day I taught music, but played a piano only poorly. Still, music caught me. I crossed, as they say."

Michael dressed quickly and followed Savarin downstairs into the dining room. The morning sun revealed that the brick walls were covered with faded hand-painted flowers, arranged in decorative rows in imitation of wallpaper. The dinner of the night before had been cleared without a trace. Only Savarin, Michael and the old man Wolfer were in the dining room. Wolfer ignored them. He sat at his own small table near a window and slowly ate his porridge, contemplating the indirect morning light with raised eyebrows.

Savarin held his spoon on the table upright in one fist as Risky dropped a starchy sphere of porridge into his bowl, then poured thin milk over it from a clay pitcher. She did the same for Michael. The porridge smelled faintly of horse corral, but it didn't taste bad.

"Lamia wants you this morning," she reminded Michael before returning to the kitchen. Her tone was aloof, as if he were no longer a curiosity or an asset to the inn, and therefore no longer counted for much. Savarin grinned at Michael and cocked his head to one side. "You have an acquaintance with the large woman at the Isomage's house?"

"That's the way I came here," he said. Savarin stopped eating.

"I'd heard the rumor," he said, frowning. "Most unusual. From the house, you mean?"

"From the gate in the back."

"Most unusual indeed." Savarin said nothing more until Risky came to take the empty bowls. She removed the half-full bowl from under Wolfer's spoon and carried it away, whistling tunelessly.

"Did you know," Savarin said, his voice loud for Risky's benefit, "that the Sidhe feel little affection for humans, one of their many reasons, because we often whistle, as our hostess does this moment?"

Michael shook his head. "Who are the Shee?"

"Alyons and his coursers, among many others. The masters of the Realm. Very sensitive. Whistling irritates them greatly. Any human music. I believe if you had whistled your way across a Faerie path when they lived on Earth, they would just as soon have flattened you with barrow stones as said good night. Angry about the despoiling of their art, you see."

Michael nodded. "Who is Lamia?"

Savarin shrugged. "You know more than I. A large woman who lives in the Isomage's house."

"Who is the Isomage?"

"A sorcerer. He angered the Sidhe far more than someone who simply whistles." Savarin smiled. Risky returned with a pitcher of water, which she poured into clay mugs, setting one before Wolfer, one before Savarin, and one before Michael. Savarin tsked her and shook a finger. "The tune," he said. "Bad luck."

Risky agreed with a nod. "Bad habit," she said.

"The Shee sound like they—" Michael began, but Savarin interrupted.

"Pronounce it correctly. It's spelled S-I-D-H-E, from the ancient Gaelic—or rather, the ancients Gaels heard the Faer calling themselves by that name. They pronounce it somewhere between 'Shee' and 'Sthee.'"

"Yes," Michael said.

"Try it."

He tried it. "The Shthee—"

"Close. Try again."

"The Sidhe—"

"That's it."

"—sound like they're pretty cruel."

"And difficult. But we do, after all, intrude, and I've been told they came to the Realm to escape humanity. There's been enmity between us for a long time."

"But no one in Euterpe wanted to come here."

"All the worse, no? Do you speak German?"

"No."

Savarin smiled valiantly, but it was obvious he was disappointed. "So odd," he said. "Only one or two German-speakers in the Realm, and yet Germany was so advanced, musically." He leaned across the table. "So you don't know much about Lamia?"

Michael shook his head.

"Learn as much as you can. Carefully. I hear she has a temper. And when— if—you come back, tell me."

"If?"

Savarin waved the word away. "You'll return. I have a feeling about you . . . you're most unusual."

Michael left the hotel a few minutes later. Brecker followed him into the street and handed him a frayed cloth bag with a piece of bread in it. "I hear Lamia's larder is empty . . . usually," he said. "Good luck."

Michael went back down the road he had taken the day before, his heart pounding and his hands cold. A small crowd gathered at the village outskirts to watch him leave.

He neither saw nor met any Sidhe riders. He saw nothing moving, in fact; neither animals on the ground nor birds in the air. The sky gleamed pale enameled blue above, and the muddy horizon was relieved by patches of orange, similar to a layer of smog. The sun was warm but not hot, not very bright in fact—he could look at it almost indefinitely without hurting his eyes.

Yard by yard he returned to the house, feeling as if he were enclosed in a transparent bowl that prevented the Realm from reaching in and making itself real to him, and likewise prevented his thoughts from reaching out to encompass what he saw.

Near the path leading to the house, his vision narrowed. He focused on the front door, which hung half-open as if he were expected. He walked down the path.

Pausing on the porch, he took a deep breath and felt his chest hitch. The oppressive gleam of the sky-bowl seemed to keep even the air from his lungs. He swallowed at the air again, with little better result.

His room. His books. Saturday afternoon movies on TV. Mother and Father. Golda Waltiri with a tear running down her cheek and more swelling up in her eyes. Michael felt hollow, full of echoes.

He heard horses coming. He turned to look; the door jerked wide and a thick arm reached out to grab him, pulling him inside before he could even yelp. Lamia's grip was painfully strong. She let him go, then took hold of his coat collar and lifted him level with her head, peering at him intensely through her tiny dough-wrapped eyes. "Into the closet!" she whispered harshly. She half-dragged, half-carried him across the floor and opened a narrow closet door behind the grand staircase, thrusting him inside. He fell back against soft dusty things and tried to hold back tears, shaking so hard his teeth chattered.

Through the closet door, he heard footsteps. The front door shut with a click, as if just enough energy had been expended to bring it completely closed, and no more.

He heard Sidhe voices again, commanding and melodic, speaking in a haunting, half-familiar language. Lamia, her tone softened, subservient, replied in English. "I've felt nothing." Another voice continued at some length, fluid and high-pitched but distinctively masculine.

"No one's been here, no one's passed through," Lamia said. "I tell you, I felt nothing. I don't care what's happening in town. They're all fools, you know that better than I."

Michael reached out in the darkness to get leverage to stand. His hand touched rough fabric, then something soft and smooth which he couldn't identify, like leather but thinner and supple as silk.

The Sidhe voices took on a snake-like threatening tone.

"I remain at my station, I watch," Lamia said. "You force me to stay here, you keep my sister at the gates; we are your slaves. How can we defy you?"

Michael picked out one word in a rider's response: Clarkham.

"He has not come here," Lamia said. That ended the conversation. The front door swung open and a sound resembling wind announced the rider's exit. Michael felt for a doorknob on the inside of the closet door. There was none.

Lamia opened the closet. "Come out," she said. He blinked and took a step forward, tripping over something soft and tough. Before he could look back in the closet and see what it contained, she whirled him around and slammed the door shut. "They'll raid the town tonight, looking for somebody. They won't raid Halftown; they never do. So I'm sending you there. First, though, listen to me and answer some questions."

Michael shrugged out from under her hand and backed away. "I have questions, too," he said.

"By what right? You've come here, you should know as much as there is to know."

"But I *don't!*" His voice ended in a high wail of frustration. The tears came freely now. "I don't know anything, not even where I am!"

"In Sidhedark," Lamia said, turning from him. "In the Faerie Shadow. The Realm," she continued, more gently. "You are no longer on Earth."

"I've been told that. But what is this place?"

"Not Earth," Lamia murmured. She walked ahead, her bulk rippling. "Follow me."

"Can I go home?" he shouted after her, hanging back.

"Not this way. Perhaps not at all."

Suddenly deflated, Michael followed her down a broad hallway, into the burnt-out wing of the house.

5

Years ago, there was a war here," Lamia said. "The entire plain was scourged. The river turned to steam, the trees became serpents and crawled away, the land cracked like open wounds, revealing all of Adonna's past indiscretions, its abortions. And in the middle of it all . . ." She paused, swinging her thick arms to take in the ruined wing. "In the middle, this house stood alone. The Isomage lost everything, almost. But he escaped, and he still had enough power to threaten them with great harm if they didn't make a pact with him. For their part, the Sidhe were to create a livable territory within the Blasted Plain, and gather all humans here, all those who had crossed over and were being persecuted. The Sidhe were not to harm them, but would tend them. For his part, the Isomage would go far away and work no more magic in this part of the Realm." She turned her tiny eyes on him and Michael saw a gleam of defiance and strength that seemed out of place in the massive, paste-white face. She closed her half-buried eyes and hardly seemed human. "I was young then." She took a deep, quivering breath and let it out through her small, narrow nose with a low whistle.

They stopped by a long charred table with fragments of chairs scattered around it. In the rubble which covered the table, Michael could see glints of tarnished silver plates, bent and melted forks and knives, slumped metal cups and shattered glassware, all dusted with fine gray powder and chunks of wood and plaster. The smell of smoke still hung thick in the air.

"Years ago. Ages," Lamia mused softly. Moving one columnar leg at a time, slow and ponderous as an elephant, she swung around to face him and pointed with her quivering left hand in his general vicinity. "You crossed over with something powerful. I know you did. Are you aware of it?"

Michael shook his head.

"You'll know what it is, soon. This is a strange place; take nothing for granted. And above all, *obey.*" She growled the last word and advanced on him, stopping a yard away when he began to back up. "You still have a book. I told you to hide it. The Sidhe don't like human words, any more than they like human song. Why didn't you obey me?"

"I don't have anyplace safe to hide it."

"You doubt whether I can protect you, whether I will be obeyed?" Her voice sounded no more menacing than usual, but Michael felt a tremor ladder up his back nonetheless. He said nothing.

"I am the second guardian. Did you meet the first?"

"I don't know."

"You would know, my boy. Believe me, you would know."

He thought of the figure in the flounced dress. "I think maybe I did."

"Were you afraid of her?"

He nodded.

"You're less afraid of me, that's obvious. And yet . . ." She smiled, the curve of her lips barely shifting the great flaps of her cheeks and jowls. "I am the one who controls the other. Is that clear?"

"If nobody ever comes this way, why are you here?" Michael asked. Lamia tittered, holding one hand over her mouth and pretending coyness in a way that made his stomach uneasy.

"Now," she said. "There are a number of things you must do. You're new; you can't know half what it takes to simply stay alive. And believe me, you don't want to *die* here. To keep alive, you'll have to be trained."

"I don't want to stay. I want to go back." He clenched his hands. He still couldn't believe the situation was irreversible.

"To go home, you must move ahead," Lamia said. "There's only one person with the power to send you back. He's a great distance from here, and to reach him you'll make an arduous journey. That's why you must be trained. Do you understand me now?" She leaned over and peered at him. "Or are you stupid as well as young?"

"I'm not stupid," Michael said.

"Parts of the Realm are quite beautiful, though few humans cross the Blasted Plain to see them. The Sidhe appreciate beauty. They leave the ruins for humans."

"Are you human?" Michael asked.

Lamia's white skin purpled slightly. "Not now."

"Are you a Sidhe?"

"No." Her laugh was a deep grumble in her massive torso. "Now you've had your questions. Any more and—"

"If I don't ask questions, how will I learn?"

Her arm struck out like a scorpion's tail and her hand slammed into the side of his face. He spun across the charred floor and fell into a mound of ashes, raising a choking cloud. She pushed through the cloud and grabbed him with both hands by the shoulders, lifting him clear and dangling him over the floor. Gentle, almost sweet, her voice reached him through the haze of ash and pain as if she were miles away.

"You'll go to Halftown. You'll take instruction from the Crane Women. Got that?"

"The hotel—"

She shook him once, making his bones pop. "You don't deserve the luxury. The Crane Women are called Nare, Spart and Coom. Tell me their names."

He couldn't remember.

"Again, then. Nare, Spart, and Coom."

"Nare, Spart . . ."

"Coom."

"Coom."

"They're expecting you. They'll teach you how to survive. Maybe they'll teach you how to see and hear and judge situations better. Think that's possible?" She held him with one hand and brushed him down with the other. Her touch was feverishly warm. She set him down near the table and looked up longingly at the burnt-out rafters.

"It was the middle of a banquet," she said. "They took us by surprise. We used to have parties every night. It was beautiful."

Terrified and furious, Michael tried to control his trembling but couldn't. He wanted to kill her.

"Go," she said. "Tell the innkeeper and his wife that Lamia no longer needs their services. Take yourself over to Halftown. The Crane Women. What are their names?"

"Nare, Spart, and Coom."

She grunted. "Go, before the Sidhe return."

He fled from the ruined wing, through the hall and across the entry to the front door. Book bouncing against his hip, he ran down the road to Euterpe until his lungs ached, ready to burst. Tears of rage streaked his face.

He stooped by a cracked, glazed boulder and pounded on it until his hand bled. "God damn you, god *damn* you!"

"Better be quiet," the wind whispered. He jumped and whirled around. Nobody.

"Remember where you are."

He screamed. Something luffed his hair and he looked up. There, translucent as a spider's web, gaped a narrow and colorless face. It rotated and vanished.

Cupping his hands over his mouth, smearing blood on his chin, Michael stumbled and ran the rest of the way to Euterpe with little concern for his lungs or his legs.

RISKY ACCEPTED HIS explanation with seeming indifference. Brecker nodded and accompanied him upstairs to the room. "You didn't come here with anything, so there's no luggage for you to pick up," he said. "But you can help me clean it." They swept the floor in silence. Michael was confused by the token labor.

"It's not my dirt," he said. "I've only been here one night."

"We all do our bit," Brecker said. "It's what keeps us going."

"Even when there's nothing to do?"

Brecker leaned on his straw broom. "Where'd you get that bruise?"

"Lamia hit me."

"Why?"

"I don't know," Michael lied.

"For asking dumb questions, likely." Brecker resumed his sweeping. "It's a hard land, boy. Wherever you came from, it seems you led an easy life among reasonable people. Not here. Mistakes cost." He held a pan down for Michael to sweep dust and mica flakes into. "Mistakes cost dear."

Savarin was climbing the stairs as they descended. Michael passed him with a shrug. "Moving already?" Savarin asked, staring after them.

"To Halftown," Michael said.

"Might I accompany you?" Savarin asked.

Michael shrugged again.

"This could be most useful."

The road to Halftown stretched to the east of Euterpe for two miles.

"We call it east, anyway," Savarin explained, walking beside Michael. Michael kept his hands in his coat pockets, one wrapped around the book of poems. "Where the sun rises, you know."

Michael said nothing, staring at the ground as they walked.

"Where did you get the bruise?"

"Lamia hit me for asking questions."

Savarin pursed his lips. "Tough customer, Lamia, I hear. Never met her myself. What sort of questions?"

Michael looked suspiciously at Savarin. "What do you know?"

"You might have gathered by now that when new people show up, I am their tutor. I know as much as any human here, I suspect—with the exception of the Isomage; but he's been gone for decades now."

"Where the hell is this place?"

"Some people claim this place *is* hell, but it is not. I would venture a guess that it is the legendary land of Faerie, which some consider the place of the dead; but none of us trapped here died on Earth, so your guess is probably as good as mine. Ask Adonna. Adonna made it."

"Who's Adonna?"

"The *genius loci,* the god of the Realm. Most of the Sidhe pay obeisance to it. From what I gather, it's not in the same league as whatever made our universe. Much cruder." Savarin winked. "But be careful to whom you speak when you make such critiques."

"So we're in a different dimension?"

Savarin held up his hands and shook his head. "Not to be quoted. Scholar that I am, and as hard as I've researched, I'm still remarkably ignorant. Facts are hard to obtain. Frankly, I was hoping you could provide a few."

"Who are the Sidhe?"

"The mortal enemies of humankind," Savarin said, his face suddenly grim. "There are all kinds of Sidhe, not just the ones who bear a passing resemblance to us. There are the Sidhe of the air, called Meteorals by some—"

"What do they look like?"

"Translucent, drifting creatures, resembling spirits. There are the Sidhe of the forests, called Arborals; they are green as grass. Umbrals will always be found in shadow, and at night can be very powerful. Pelagals are reputed to be ocean-going, but we only have rumors of a distant ocean here. Riverines live in streams and rivers. Amorphals can be a different shape each time you see them. Most of the Sidhe, however, belong to the kind called Faer—like Alyons and his coursers.

The Faer resemble you and me and we can even interbreed, but they're a very different race, ages older than the current stock of humanity."

"And what is Halftown?"

"Where the Breeds live. Born of female Sidhe, sired by human males, most often."

"They won't live with humans?"

"They're a sad lot," Savarin said. "They're reputed to live forever, like the Sidhe, and like the Sidhe they have no souls. But like humans, they change— their peculiar way of aging. Humans don't accept them. Sidhe isolate them, but find them useful now and then. Many know Sidhe magic." They walked on in silence for a few minutes. "Who's to watch over you in Halftown?"

"The Crane Women," Michael said.

Savarin was impressed. "Very powerful. Ugly as sin, and they wouldn't mind my saying so. They're the oldest Breeds I've heard of. Was it Lamia who sent you to them?"

Michael nodded. "I don't go anywhere on my own. I mean, I don't have any choice."

"Maybe that's something to be thankful for. Less mistakes made that way."

"Is Lamia a Breed?"

"I don't think so. There are many stories about her, but nobody really knows what she is. I suspect she was a normal human once, but did something the Sidhe didn't like. She was at the Isomage's house when I came here."

Beyond a rise, the road bisected the Breed settlement, which was laid out in an irregular circle. Halftown covered about ten acres, brown and dun and weathered gray buildings arranged along concentric half-circle streets, the ends of each street letting out on the main road. The land around Halftown was hummocky, as if ploughed by a giant and careless farmer, and the ground was poorly drained. Standing pools of brackish water lay in the hollows and exuded a marshy green smell. A branch of the river flowed past the other side of the village, little more than a sluggish green creek.

"Observe the houses," Savarin said, stopping to tie a string on his cloth shoes. "What would you say of them?"

Michael examined the flimsy structures and then, to make sure he had missed nothing, examined them again. "They're shacks," he said. "They look like the houses in Euterpe." Savarin straightened. "You're still not observing. See what you already know." He pointed to the barren landscape: grassy shrub, hammocks and puddles, low bushes and scattered boulders.

"Jesus," Michael said under his breath. "They're shacks. Made of wood."

"*Wood,*" Savarin emphasized. "Do you see any trees?"

"No."

"That's how you tell Halftown from Euterpe. Breeds have Sidhe relatives, and that means connections with Arborals. Arborals control all the wood in the Realm. Humans are only allowed sticks and wicker and grass."

Michael felt dizzy. He still hadn't accepted that the Realm was real—yet every moment it became more and more complex.

"There aren't any trees at all?"

"Away from the Blasted Plain, there are forests everywhere. But no wood for you and me. Very few humans leave the Pact Lands. Sidhe traders bring in goods every fortnight, in accord with the Isomage's pact, but even they face danger on the Blasted Plain."

Michael saw his first Breed, a male, as they came within a hundred feet of the outer circle of huts. The Breed was slightly taller than Michael, with long, lank red-brown hair and a powerful build. He stood in the middle of the road, a staff in one hand and a bored expression on his face. He held out his staff to stop them.

"I recognize you, Teacher. I know this boy human, too. Lamia warned us about him—but she said nothing about you."

"I come here often," Savarin said defensively.

"The coursers came last night," the Breed said. "No more humans allowed in Halftown. Except, of course . . ." He pointed his finger at Michael.

"I think you'd better go," Michael told Savarin. "Thanks for helping me."

Savarin frowned at the Breed. "Yes. I'm sure discretion is best. But I've never been barred from Halftown. I hope it's not permanent. This is where I get most of my information." He sighed, cast a sunny smile on Michael and turned around. "Learn quickly, friend. And come tell me what you've learned, if you can."

Michael accepted his outstretched hand. Savarin returned the way they had come, leaving him alone with the Breed guard.

A cool breeze rippled their hair and clothes. "So where am I supposed to go?"

"To the Crane Women. Come."

Michael followed him down the road. Through Halftown, the thoroughfare was paved with brown brick and cobbles. The huts seemed cleaner, though flimsier than those in Euterpe. Small plots around each house were filled with rows of healthy green plants; he couldn't see any flowers.

Other Breeds stared at him through windows and open doors. The men were almost as tall as the Sidhe Michael had glimpsed at the Isomage's house. The women were slender, handsome enough, even noble-looking, though few were what Michael would have called pretty. Their faces were hard and sculptured, too much like the men's.

His escort led him out the other side of the village and away from the road, toward the creek. Across the water, perched atop a broad low mound, sat a larger hut shaped like a half-deflated soccer ball, covered with sticks, dirt and thatch. Except for two round glass-paned windows and a stone chimney poking through the top, it could have been a yurt—one of the portable dwellings used by central Asian nomads. The yard around the hut was strewn with small boulders and piles of debris, sorted and categorized—a pile of pebbles here, sticks to one side, bones and animal skulls there, other mounds he couldn't identify. The smell was of ancient garbage, richer and more suggestive than dust, but not overtly offensive. Stakes marked the perimeter of the mound and scraps of fabric fluttered from them like sad, decrepit banners.

"How do I get across?" Michael asked as they stopped at the water's edge. The Breed pointed out flat stones just beneath the slow-moving surface.

"They await you," he said, and began his walk back to Halftown. Michael swallowed the tightness in his throat and stepped out onto the first stone. The water swirled around his shoes. He thought about falling into the water to force himself to wake up, stop dreaming, but if he hadn't been shocked out of sleep by the things that had already happened, the murky creek was unlikely to do the trick. Besides, he had no idea what lurked in the depths.

He was sick of being afraid. He clutched his book tightly and stepped onto the second stone. He concentrated so hard on not falling that he failed to notice a figure standing on the opposite bank until he had crossed. He looked up with a start.

"Hello," he said quickly. Beyond any doubt, this was one of the Crane Women.

The figure was female, in a bizarre sort of way. She stood an inch or two shorter than Michael, slightly stooped. She still possessed a roundness in her elongated, leather-skinned limbs which demonstrated femininity, but her arms hung almost to her knees. Her face was oblate, wider than tall, with narrow long eyes beneath thin flat brows. Her legs, clothed in ragged pants, stretched very long in comparison with her torso. She lifted one hand and wriggled spider-like fingers in front of her flat chest. The fingers were long and dark and tapered to thin black nails.

"Hello," he repeated.

She looked him over slowly, nodding with a steady rhythm as if feeble. Her short-cut hair had the color and texture of goose down.

"*Jan Antros,*" she said. "Just man-child." Her voice was a gnarly squeak with undertones of heavy wind.

Michael shook his wet feet and reached with one hand to empty his left shoe, then his right. He never took his eyes off her. The shoes squelched when he put them on again. "I'm Michael," he said, trying to be agreeable.

"You're a delicate, incredibly fragile, very frail indeed, piece of tissue," came a melodious voice from the hut. Another woman with similar features leaned from one window. Her face was a puzzle of wrinkles and red and purple tattoos. "You don't look important."

Behind Michael, where she couldn't possibly have snuck up on him, a third woman stood on one spindly leg with the other tucked close to her chest. More than any of the others, this one scared Michael. She had long dusty-red hair tied in a single braid that reached to her knees. "The Flesh Egg sends us a weak man-child. She expects us to process, train?"

"Are you Nare, Spart and . . . Coom?" Michael asked, trying to keep his teeth from chattering.

"I'm Nare," said the Crane woman standing on one leg.

"Spart," said the one at the window, and

"Coom," said the downy-haired figure who had first addressed him. "Want us teach?"

"I don't know what I want," Michael said, "except to go home."

The Crane women chuckled together, sounding like leaves skittering over rock.

"Won't hurt you," Coom said, backing off a foot. "Much." Her hair seemed alive in the breeze.

"We don't mind man-childs," said Nare at his side, circling.

"But there's one thing you must want," said Spart in her beautiful voice from the window. She spat into a nearby pile of debris.

"To survive," Nare said.

"Live in Sidhedark."

"Fight to live."

"Fight to stay human."

"Understood?"

Michael could do nothing but nod. In the moment he turned away from the hut, Spart left the window and stood between Nare and Coom. She was the tallest of the three and had the longest, most Sidhe-like face. Tattoos formed an intricate tangle of leaves and branches and whorls wherever her skin was bare.

"You'll build a house on this mound, away from ours thirty paces," she said. "Wood will be brought to you this evening. Until you've built your own house, you don't exist."

"What'll I do now?" he asked. He had focused on Spart; he suddenly realized the other two were gone.

"Be patient." Spart's voice had much of the hypnotic quality he'd experienced while listening to Alyons and the coursers. "You can do that, can't you?"

"Yes."

"Go and sit where you want your house. Wood will come."

The Crane Woman returned to their hut, leaving him on the stretch of hard-packed dirt by the creek bank. He shifted from one foot to the other, then looked over the water to Halftown. He shaded his eyes and stared at the sky.

Not a cloud was visible. Enameled sparkling blueness stretched overhead, blending with orange and green along the horizon. About thirty yards away from the hut, and an equal distance from the creek bank, two boulders nestled against each other, forming a natural seat about a yard wide and two and a half feet tall. Michael crossed to the boulders and sat on them, looking at the sky again. Sometimes it seemed to be made of cross-hatches of colors, hundreds of colors all adding up to blue. Yet it wasn't like a painting. It was very alive, disturbing in the way it seemed to shift, to bulge *down* and retreat up.

He felt drugged. Until now, alone, with no instruction but to wait, it was as if he had not seen anything clearly. Now the clarity flooded down on him from the sky. The sky, by its very unreality, seemed to show how real everything was.

But this reality wasn't the same brand he had experienced on Earth. This was more vivid, more apparent and simpler.

He knelt beside the boulders and plucked a blade of grass, peeling it along its fibers, rubbing the ragged edges, smearing the beads of juice on his fingertips. He felt a tickle on his arm. A tiny, translucent ant crawled among the light, silky hairs, rainbow-hued like an opal. Until now, Michael hadn't thought to wonder if there were insects in Sidhedark. Not many, apparently.

What about birds, cats, dogs, cows? He'd seen horses, but . . . where did the milk come from?

He was tired. He leaned back on the rocks and closed his eyes. The darkness behind his lids soothed, still and restful. Wind sighed over him.

He had slept. He sat up and rubbed elbows stiff from pressing against the rock. The sun was setting. No clouds yet, but unmoving bands of color hung above the horizon, pale pinks and greens at the highest, and just above the sun's limb a particularly vivid stripe of orange. Michael had never seen a sunset like it.

He looked to the east. The sky there was an electric blue-green.

Stars shone already in the east, as sharp and bright as white-hot needle points. Instead of twinkling, they made little circling motions, like distant tethered fireflies. Michael had sometimes used *Whitney's Star Finder* on summer nights to pick out the few constellations visible through Los Angeles' thick air. He couldn't recognize any now.

The air had cooled considerably. Orange light flickered in the windows of the Crane Women's hut. He had a notion to peer in and see what they were up to, but he rubbed the bruise on his cheek and thought better of it.

Only then did he notice that his wristwatch was gone. He grabbed for the key in his pants pocket, but it was missing as well. He still had the book.

He felt almost naked without the key. He resented the thievery; he resented everything about the way he was being treated, but there wasn't a thing he could do.

The last of the sun slipped behind distant hills, burning muddy orange through the smoky haze which he surmised lay over the Blasted Plain, beyond the boundary of the Pact Lands. Where the sun had been, a sharply defined ribbon of darkness ascended from the horizon and blended with the zenith; and then another to one side, and yet another on the opposite side, resembling the shadows of cloth streamers in a celestial wind.

Michael listened. The land all around was silent, but from the sky came a low humming, like wind stroking telephone wires. When the darkness was complete, the humming went away.

Then, starting in the east and progressing westward across the sky, the stars steadied, as if precipitating out of solution and pasting themselves against the bowl of the heavens.

There were stars in the dirt, as well. He pulled his feet up on the boulders and looked down. Things sparkled and glinted between the few blades of grass. Soon these glows faded and the land settled into night with a breezy sigh, as if all the Realm were a woman lying back on a pillow.

No, indeed, Michael thought; *this is not Earth.*

He sat on the rocks for some time before he heard the voices. They came from the creek, but he couldn't see who spoke; there was no light but the stars and the now-faint orange glow from the hut's windows. Concentrating on the source, forcing his pupils to their maximum dilation, he discerned a low-slung boat-shadow gliding down the creek, and then a few figures standing on the prow. The boat nudged the bank and he heard footsteps coming toward him.

He stood up on the rocks like a housewife afraid of a mouse. "Who's that?" he called.

The hut door swung open. Spart stood silhouetted against swirling, furnace-orange light. The approaching shadows passed through a shaft of light from the door and were outlined briefly. There were four, three male, one female, murky green in color, all naked. They were obviously Sidhe, with the same elongated features and spectral grace, and each carried a broad, stubby log.

They surrounded Michael. At a signal, the four simultaneously dropped the logs from their shoulders onto the dirt with resonant thumps.

"*Dura,*" said the female. The beauty of her voice made Michael shudder.

"Your wood, boy," the Crane Woman called from the hut door.

He turned and croaked, "What do I do with it?"

But the hut door closed and the naked Sidhe walked away. The female glanced back at him with some sympathy, he thought, but she said nothing more. The night's blackness absorbed them.

He remained standing on the boulder awhile, then sat. The four logs rested on their ends, each about a foot and a half wide and a yard tall. He was no carpenter like his father; he couldn't calculate how many board-feet there were in the logs, or how much of a house he could build with them.

Not a very large one.

He leaned back and closed his eyes again.

"*Whose boy are you?*"

He thought he was dreaming. He wiped his nose reflexively.

"*Hoy ac!* Whose house?"

Michael spun around on the boulders and looked in the voice's direction. There was only a log.

"*Rup antros, jarl wiros,*" said the voice, like that of the Sidhe woman but with a fuzzy quality. "*Quos maza.*"

"Where are you?" Michael asked softly. The night air was quite chilly now.

"All around, antros. It's true. Your words are Anglo-Saxon and Norman and mixes from the misty north and the warm south. Ah, I knew those tongues once, at their very roots . . . affrighted many a Goth and Frank and Jute . . ."

"Who are you? Who?"

There was silence for a moment, then the voice, much weaker, said, "*Maza sed more kay rup antros.* It's strange to be broken for a human's house. Why so privileged? Still, all wood is passing; the imprint must fade . . ."

The voice did indeed fade. Though the night was still and quiet thereafter, Michael got no sleep.

6

He was almost as cold as the rocks he sat on when the dew settled around him in the early dawn. The sky turned from black to gray and mist slid over the mound and creek in glutinous layers. Narrow vapor trails four or five feet in length shot through the mist with quiet hissing sounds. Michael was too chilled to care.

He twisted his stiff neck around and noticed the logs no longer stood around the boulders. Sometime during the night, they had fallen into jumbles of neatly cut beams and boards. The bark of each log lay scrolled next to its partitioned innards.

Michael wasn't encouraged. Like a lizard, he waited for the sun to come up and warm his blood. He hadn't resolved anything during the night—the hours had been spent in a cold stupor—but his conviction of inadequacy had solidified.

The sun appeared in the east, a distant red arc topping a hill beyond the main branch of the river. Without thinking, Michael uncurled his arms and legs and stood on the rock to catch the first rays of warmth. His bones cracked and his legs almost collapsed under him, but he staggered and kept his balance. Dew had soaked his clothes.

The hut was quiet and dark, likewise the village. In a few minutes, however, just when he thought he might be catching some warmth from the new day, he heard activity from the Halftown houses. Curls of smoke began to rise from their stone and mud-brick chimneys.

He heard a woman singing. At first, he was too intent on just getting warm to pay much attention, but as the voice grew near, he angled his head and saw a young Breed female fording the stream on the flat rocks, barefoot. She wore cloth pants hemmed at the knees and a vest laced shut with string. Her hair was raven black—uncharacteristic, he thought—but her face bore the unmistakable mark of the Sidhe, long with prominent cheeks and a narrow, straight nose. She carried four buckets covered with cloth caps, two in each hand. She glanced at Michael on her way to the Crane Women's hut.

"*Hoy,*" she greeted.

"Hello," Michael returned. She stopped before the door, which opened a crack. A long-fingered hand stretched out and took two buckets, withdrew, then emerged to take two more. The door closed and the woman reversed her course. She paused, cocked her head at Michael, then started toward him.

"Oh, God," he said under his breath. He was just warm enough to shiver and he badly needed to piss. He didn't want to talk to anyone, much less a Breed woman.

"You're human," she said, stopping about six paces from the boulders. "Yet they gave you wood."

He nodded, arms still unfolded to catch the warmth.

"You're an English speaker," she continued. "And you come from the Iso-mage's house. That's all they say about you in Halftown."

He nodded again, glanced away, swallowed. Beneath all the cold and misery churned a steady current of shyness. The Breed woman's voice was disarmingly beautiful. He would have to get used to Sidhe and Breed voices.

"It will be warm soon," she said, walking toward the stream. "If you have time today, come to the village and I'll give you a card for milk and cheese. Everybody needs to eat. Just ask for Eleuth."

"I will," he said, his voice cracking. When she had crossed the creek, he clambered down from the rock, walked some distance away, and hunkered to hide while he urinated. He felt like some animal, barely domesticated. A pet of the Breeds.

The door to the Crane Women's hut opened and Spart emerged carrying a roll of cloth. She stared at him balefully, unfurled the cloth and flapped it. An exaltation of tiny birds flew from its folds and circled the house, then headed north. Without explanation, Spart returned to the house and closed the door behind.

Massaging blood back into his legs, Michael looked doubtfully at the piles of lumber. He picked up the sheets of bark and discovered that they could be peeled into light, strong strips with a ropy toughness. He thought about how to put a hut together and shook his head. He'd need tools—nails, certainly, and a knife and saw.

Even as he speculated halfheartedly, he asked himself what the hell good it was, building a house where he didn't belong. He had reached the point during the cold night of knowing beyond doubt this was no nightmare; he felt sober and scared and severely chastened. Never again would he go looking for adventure. Adventure was misery and degradation and terror; it wasn't worth the weird beauty.

"You have a long way to go."

Nare stood behind him. Her large eyes stared at him critically, large, like an owl's but darting from point to point on his body. She had undone her long red-gray hair and it fanned over her shoulders and down her back in an unbraided radiance, spreading to its widest point behind her knees. "Now that you have the grace of wood, what are you going to do with it?"

"I need tools."

"I don't think so. Are you aware what the grace of wood means?"

He thought for a moment. "Humans don't get much."

"Humans get scrap. Not even Breeds can get wood all the time. The finest wood is reserved for the Sidhe. Like as not they have ancestors in it."

"I don't understand," Michael said.

"The Sidhe are immortal, but if they die in battle or through some other faulting, the Arborals press them into trees. They dwell there a while, then request oblivion. Arborals do their work, and we have wood."

"I heard a voice last night."

Nare nodded. Bending over, she picked up a plank and held it out to Michael. One long forefinger pressed against the edge and a notch fell out. "Feel and press. Riddle how it all goes together. Wood was shaped into a house by the Sidhe that dwelled within. Just puzzle it. *Maza.*"

"Today?" Michael asked.

"Today is all the time you have." Nare headed for the creek and dove in like an otter. He didn't see her come up.

For the next few hours, trying to ignore his hunger, Michael took each board and beam and pressed, poked and rubbed the surfaces until he found the removable pieces. At first he took the small pieces and tossed them aside, but thought better of it and gathered them into a small pile.

It became obvious that he could fit some of the pieces into holes in the planks, and use them to slide into notches in the beams. It reminded him of a wooden puzzle he had at home, only much more complex. When the sun was high, he had managed to assemble two planks and one beam, with no idea where to go from there. He didn't even know what shape the house would be.

Spart, the Crane Woman with tattoos all over and the melodious voice, came to him from the hut and offered a wooden bowl filled with cold gruel, a piece of fruit and a puddle of thin milk. He ate it without complaint. She watched, one long arm twitching, and removed the bowl from his hands when he was done.

"When you have finished the house, you will go into the village and announce yourself at the market. They will allow for your food. Also, while you're here, you can carry messages for us, and otherwise make yourself useful." She glanced at the pile of wood. "If you haven't puzzled it by dawn tomorrow, it's not your wood any more."

He stared at her tattoos. She didn't seem to mind, but she bent down and tapped the wood meaningfully. He set to work again and she walked back toward the house.

"Is it safe to drink the water?" he called after her.

"I wouldn't know," she said.

By evening, with all his ingenuity he had succeeded in figuring out that the house would be square, about two yards on each side, without a roof or floor. He would apparently have to gather grass or something for the roof, and that discouraged him. He was ravenous, but no more food was brought out.

Maybe they'll feed me when I'm done, he thought. *If . . .*

He discovered the bark could be used for lashings. As the sun and sky went through the same twilight phenomena of the day before, Michael kicked a beam with one foot and held his hand out in front of him. "It's impossible."

But . . .

He knelt and picked out a square, thick beam whose use he hadn't discovered. He pressed along the grain and it fell apart in neat, almost paper-thin shingles. Then the plan seemed to come together in his mind. He assembled planks and beams, slipped tenon into mortise, lashed the wood with strips of bark, and took five long, thin curved pieces to make the framework of the roof. When darkness was complete, he had almost finished putting on the shingles. He had one string of bark and two pieces of pressed-out wood left, yet the house seemed complete.

Spart stood outside when he emerged through the low door. She looked at the string in his hand and shook her head in pity. *"Fera antros,"* she said. "If you had built it right, you wouldn't have any pieces left over."

For a moment, he was afraid she might have him dismantle the hut and start all over again, but she pulled a bowl from behind her back and passed it to him. His meal this time: vegetable paste and a thick, doughy slice of dark bread. Spart squatted beside him as he sat on a rock and ate.

"There are many languages among the Sidhe," Spart said. "Some are very ancient, some more recent. Nearly all the Sidhe speak Cascar. It would be an advantage to learn as much Cascar as you can—and you need all the advantages you can get."

"Some speak English," Michael said.

"Most speak it because it is in your mind. In-speaking. And English was spoken in the last lands many of us inhabited on Earth, English and other tongues—Irish, Welsh, French, German. We also speak Earth languages you wouldn't be familiar with, all old, most dead. Languages come easy to the Sidhe. But no human tongue can replace Cascar."

Not being hungry made Michael bolder. "How old are you?"

"There are no years here," Spart said. "Seasons come and go at the whim of Adonna. How old are you?"

"Sixteen," Michael said.

She stood and took his empty bowl. "Tonight, in the dark, one of us will test you. You will not be able to fend us off, but how you react will shape the way we teach you. Sleep or not, as you will."

7

Inside, the house was drafty and small and the floor was no comfort, but it was better than nothing. He sat in a corner, trying not to sleep, awaiting the promised test.

There wasn't much he could do to prepare. He wondered if they would hurt him. He had never been much of a fighter; it had always taken him too long to get angry. Consequently, he had little experience with his fists.

Not having slept the night before, he couldn't keep his eyes from closing. He groaned as he realized he was falling asleep. His head bumped his knees—

And jerked up at the sound of hooves. He heard a horse nicker and sneeze. Still dark. A large splash in the river.

He was so tired. Being tired and alert at once gave the experience a surreal edge, as if things weren't bizarre enough already. He had to decide whether to stay in the house—and perhaps have it knocked down around his ears—or go outside.

All his life he had been slow to act, thoughtful, predictable. Perhaps being unpredictable would give him an advantage . . . He stood. The roof hung a bare half-inch above the top of his head. Hunkering down, he bunched his leg muscles to spring through the doorway. If he could run fast enough, perhaps he could get away.

Michael leaped through the door, keeping his head down, jaw clenched, hands crooked in fists before him—and butted headlong into something tall and solid. He rebounded and fell back, clapping his hands to the top of his head.

A Sidhe stood over him, wearing bright silver chain mail and sporting a long, wickedly pointed pike. Michael's vision swam; he barely saw the Sidhe lower the pike and prod his sternum.

"*Vera ais. Sepha jan antros pek,*" said the Sidhe in a low voice. Michael regained his breath and looked around frantically. A few yards away, a Sidhe horse stood relaxed, pale gray blankets wrapped around its neck and withers, with a silvery saddle and no stirrups or reins. "*Vas lenga spu?*" Michael's fear melted any anger he felt, but sharpened his perceptions. Even in the dark he could now see the Sidhe in detail: a spectral face and long, reddish hair; huge eyes with reverse epicanthic folds; long-fingered hands gripping his pike, fingernails trimmed to metallic points; boots made from the same silvery-gray material as the saddle; pearl-gray cape hanging loose around his shoulders to his calves.

The pike pressed harder, breaking skin, drawing blood. Michael squirmed and cried out.

"*Vas lenga?*"

"Leave me alone!" Michael shouted. He grabbed the pike and let it go immediately; it seemed to have sharp edges all around and cut his fingers.

"You don't belong here," the Sidhe growled. "Do you know who I am?"

"No!"

"I am Alyons, Wickmaster of the Blasted Plain and Pact Lands. Some call me *Scarbita Antros*—Scourge of Men. How did you get here? Why are you living in a house of wood?"

"I was sent here," Michael said.

"*Quos fera antros, to suma antros.*"

"The boy is in our charge."

Michael recognized Nare's acid voice. She stood to one side, between them and the Crane Women's hut, and Spart stood on the other side. Michael couldn't see Coom. Alyons made no move, but his hands applied an ounce more pressure to the pike. Michael felt it scraping bone and cried out, but tried not to squirm again. "What is he doing here?" Alyons asked, eyes still on Michael, like a hunter unwilling to release his prey.

"I have told you," Nare repeated. "He is in our charge."

"He's human. You don't train humans."

There was a rapid exchange in Sidhe between Spart and the Wickmaster. Alyons' face filled with deep-set lines of hate, turning his smooth chiseled features into a mummy mask. He lifted the pike a hair's breadth. "If I kill the boy, I remove a burden, no?"

"Probably," Spart said. "But what would we do to you, in turn?"

"You're *t'al antros*," Alyons said contemptuously. Coom stepped from the shadows behind him.

"We are very, very old," Spart said, "and the Sidhe of the Irall come to us to ask questions. Would you like your name mentioned when we respond—horse thief?"

The lines of Alyons' face deepened, if that were possible. "It wouldn't upset me," he said. He lifted the pike a hair.

"And when Adonna's priest comes for *temelos?*" Spart asked.

Coom dropped a hand on Alyons' shoulder and pulled him roughly away, dragging his face down to her level. "Ours!"

"Then take him," Alyons said with great calmness. He shrugged her off and walked to his horse, seeming to glide on rather than jump. "But I will go to the Arborals and question the grace of wood."

"They brought it," Nare said.

"You are a crude and foolish *fricht*," Spart said.

"Ours," Coom repeated.

Alyons leaned forward. The horse seemed to turn to smoke, every curve blurring and smoothing. Then, in silence, they were gone. Michael lay on the dirt, his chest bleeding sluggishly, his hands bloody from contact with the pike. The Crane Women were gone, as well.

He got to his feet and made for the shelter of the house. Inside, he tried to keep his lungs from heaving and held his mouth with his bloody hands to stifle sobs. He wasn't sure what had just happened—whether the Crane Women had tested him, or he had actually been visited by Alyons. The Sidhe's voice still haunted his ears, rich and deadly as venom.

Within minutes, however, Michael could hardly stay awake. There sounded a vibrant chirping nearby, repeated several times—birds?—and that was the last thing he remembered until his arm was grabbed. "Get out of my house," he demanded groggily.

"*Jan antros.*" Coom leaned over him, the light of dawn through the door outlining the side of her head. "Not eyes-full! We promise test . . ."

"Go away," he said, "please." And he was alone in the hut.

Morning came and went, and the day, and it was near evening again when he awoke, stiff and still exhausted. He felt his chest. The blood had clotted and the wound had been smeared with white paste. It was tender but didn't ache. The cuts on his hands had scabbed over.

A bowl of mush and fruit waited by the door. He ate slowly with his fingers, head full of fog, past all thought. The temptation to give up, throw it all in, grew with the pain in his body and the tiredness clamped to every muscle.

When he finished eating, he rolled over and looked at the dirt floor. Idly, he drew a line in the dirt with his finger, then wrote a line of words, and another, half-purposefully, until he had scrawled a poem.

> The scraping on the roof at night—
> Chitin or nail or stiff, hot hair—
> In dark of August, summer's heat
> Constructs a limb of dust and air.

> If you step out to watch the clouds,
> Silent lightning will prance and grin.
> While on the roof the summer waits
> And if you try to go back in . . .

> Why, Hello! The season is a spider.

Half the time, when he wrote a poem, he had no idea what it meant. The back of his head seemed disconnected from all present circumstance, as though facts and images seeped in slowly and were jumbled along the way.

But in these lines the menace was obvious. He was scared clear through, and he had no way to fight his fear. Not yet, perhaps not ever.

He stood by the door of his house and watched the sun go down, hands in his pants pockets. Nare came out of the hut and strode toward him. When they were face to face, she took his hands in hers and peered at the palms, then pulled apart his blood-stained shirt and examined his chest.

"How did I do?" Michael asked with an edge of bitterness.

"You are no good to us asleep. You were to go to the market today, get yourself a card."

"I mean, how did I do last night?"

"Terribly," she said. "He would have killed you. And later . . . You are a terrible warrior."

"I never *wanted* to be a *warrior*," he said incredulously.

She held out her twiggish fingers and shrugged elegantly. "The choice is to be a warrior, or die," she said. "Your choice."

Coom and Spart crossed the stream and entered the hut.

AS NARE STOOD motionless beside him and Michael waited nervously, the stars twirled into view. Coom and Spart emerged with eight long torches and began staking them in a circle between the house and the stream. They lighted the torches by cupping their hands behind the wick and blowing on them. Sparks and flame shot up into the night and an orange circle of light shimmered within the perimeter.

"Time is difficult to measure in the Realm," Spart said, approaching Michael and taking him by the hand. The sensation of her long, strong fingers around his own quelled any protest. She led him into the circle and motioned for Coom to join them. "You will learn our functions now," Spart said. "Coom is an expert in what the Sidhe call *isray*, physical combat. Nare is versed in *stray*, preparation of the mind. And I will teach *vickay*, the avoidance of battle as a means to victory. Tonight, since it is the simplest and easiest of the three, you will learn from Coom the beginnings of how to survive a fight with human or Sidhe."

Coom walked around Michael slowly, with high, almost prancing steps. Nare and Spart watched from outside the circle of torches. Michael regarded Coom warily, hands at his sides, head inclined slightly. He jumped as she reached down and grabbed a leg to reposition it. "Don't fall over," she said. "Like stool. One leg to be like two." She continued her circling. "Morning, you run to Halftown, run back. Tonight, you just stand up." She shot out one arm and pushed him. He promptly fell on his butt and scrambled to his feet again. She reached out and shoved once more. He stumbled but stayed upright. She circled and shoved from another angle. He toppled forward on his face. "Like stool," she repeated. She shoved again, and again, but he remained standing.

His face flushed and his jaw hurt from clenching his teeth, but he was surprised at how calm he felt. The methodic circling, shoving, went on for an hour until he kept his balance no matter what angle Coom attacked from.

The torches guttered. "Ears," Coom said. Nare and Spart extinguished the feeble flames. Clouds obscured the stars now; except for the feverish orange glow from the hut windows, there was no illumination. He couldn't see any of the Crane Women. He listened to the sound of their feet moving, trying to guess how many circled him. A hand pushed hard on his back and he went to one knee, then got up quickly.

"Ears," Coom said again. He sensed a footfall nearby and braced himself instinctively in the opposite direction. The blow came, but he kept his balance.

Another hour passed. He was groggy and his legs ached abominably. His shoulders were sore and swollen. For a time he rotated in the darkness, until he realized he couldn't hear their footfalls any more. He was alone. The Crane Women had returned to their hut.

He felt his way to his house and collapsed in a corner. He couldn't sleep. He rubbed his arms and shoulders and contemplated past gym classes, where he had never performed enthusiastically. It wasn't a matter of being weak or clumsy; he could run well enough, his coordination was good, his frame sound. Michael had just never cared that much, and the gym teachers had seldom inspired confidence in those who didn't profess to be jocks.

Inspiration wasn't the issue here. Whatever he thought, however miserable he was, tomorrow he would run until he dropped—which he was sure he would. No protests, no complaints.

After the incident with Alyons, Michael fully appreciated his position.

Obviously, things could get much worse.

8

T he Sidhe do not use swords," Spart told Michael. They squatted on the ground outside his house, facing each other with legs crossed.

"But Alyons has a pike—"

"That is his wick. He uses it only against humans."

Michael nodded and looked away, resigned to the ambiguities. Spart sighed and leaned toward him.

"You are supposed to wonder what Alyons does with his wick."

"Act wicked?" Michael said, trying for a smile. Spart leaned back and narrowed her eyes to even tighter slits. "Okay," he gave in. "What does he do with it?"

"The wick is his symbol of rank. It confers his power of office, of labor. It signifies that he has the strength to guard the Blasted Plain and the Pact Lands, and to uphold the pact made between the Sidhe and the Isomage."

"So why did he stab me with it?"

"Like many Sidhe, he hates humans."

"Do you hate humans?"

"*T'al antros,*" she said, tapping her chest with her finger. "I am half-human."

"Why don't Sidhe use swords?"

"They have no need. A Sidhe warrior is frightening enough without. And there is honor involved. Death is final for a Sidhe. There is nothing beyond except being pressed into a tree by the Arborals. That is not even half a life, and it does not last. So it has been established that the Sidhe may combat each other only by means dependent on their own skill and power, by which we mean magic and strength of will."

"I'm going to learn magic?"

Spart shook her head. "No humans ever conquer Sidhe magic. You'll have to learn how to flee, how to be inconspicuous. You cannot hope to best a Sidhe in grand combat. Your only chance is that a Sidhe will consider combat with a human shameful, worth only small effort. Take advantage of that. In the rare instances where you might be called into grand combat—" She slapped her hand against the dirt. "You will simply die. Dying in the Realm is as permanent for humans as death anywhere for a Sidhe. So do not provoke a warrior."

"I don't understand—"

"You will, in time. Now you will go to Halftown and do our errands. After, you will run. There is an order of grains to be delivered here, and you will—"

"I know. Ask for food for myself."

Spart regarded him with infinite patience, blinked slowly, and turned away.

Halftown was quiet, matching the somber, overcast morning. Michael tried being cordial to the Breeds, but they returned no greetings; curiosity about him seemed to have lapsed. They were like ghosts intent on some irrevocable task; only a few of the women had any obvious hint of life and joy in them.

Michael followed the curving market street that branched from the main road near the center of Halftown. The lone market consisted of a house (in Cascar, a *caersidh,* pronounced roughly "ker-shi"), round like most of the others, and a covered courtyard twice the area of the house itself. The courtyard was filled with tables and shelves stacked with provisions—foods in one corner, housewares, liquors (in bottles which looked suspiciously like the ones in Brecker's cellar in Euterpe) in another, and the simple types of clothing in a third. The middle of the courtyard was the counter, and there the market manager held sway.

Spart had said the manager's name was Lirg. He had a daughter, Eleuth; she delivered milk to the Crane Women's hut. Lirg never took cash—the Sidhe abhorred money, which seemed a bit strange to Michael, considering the legends of pots of gold and such—but kept careful track of Halftown's balances.

Michael gathered the economy was loosely based on fulfillment of assigned tasks and dispersal of goods according to need, not unlike the simpler forms of communism he had learned about in Mr. Wagner's class at school. Allotments of supplies were brought across the Blasted Plain. As Michael skirted the courtyard, three large, big-wheeled wagons, each drawn by two Sidhe horses, lumbered in from the opposite end of the market street.

The wagons were filled with food and supplies. A Sidhe driver sat on the lead wagon, tall and aloof, dressed in iridescent browns, the cut of his clothes not substantially different from that of Alyons, except he wore no armor and carried no wick. The horses were lathered as if they had been driven hard, and a peculiar golden glow lifted from the backs of the wagons like sunlit dust. The glow dissipated, leaving a sweet-bitter scent in the air. Lirg stepped down from his counter and directed the unloading of the supplies. The Sidhe driver took down his tailgates and several passersby pitched in to help. Few words were exchanged. The supplies were either carried into a covered shed in the fourth corner of the courtyard, or placed directly in the market stalls. There was no rush to inspect the goods; they differed not in the slightest from those already available, and assured only continuity, not variety.

Michael watched until the wagons had been unloaded and pulled aside, then entered the courtyard, reluctant to make himself obvious. The driver shut the tailgates and smoothed the wood with his hands, leaving trails of golden glitter on the boards. He then walked around the horses and patted each on the haunch with more precision than affection. Everything he touched was left with a sparkle.

Lirg was back at his counter when Michael approached. The Breed fastened him with a steady gaze, one eye dark and the other half-shut by a scar. Lirg's hair was more brown than red, and his skin tan instead of pale. "Your needs?" he asked, leaning forward on thickly muscled arms.

"I'm here to pick up grain for the Crane Women. And to be put on your list."

"What list?" He examined Michael intensely, then nodded. "The card. I see. Food only . . . that is all we can spare, even for pets of the Crane Women."

"I'm not a pet," Michael said between gritted teeth. "I'm a student, and I'm doing what they tell me to do." Lirg grinned at that, and Michael blushed.

"I see. Daughter!"

Eleuth emerged from the house with four sacks of grain. She put two of them by Michael's feet and hefted the other two onto her shoulders.

"I can carry them all," Michael said.

"I've told my daughter to help you," Lirg said. That seemed to settle it. Eleuth gave Michael a look suggesting he not argue. Michael picked up his two sacks.

"Am I on your list . . . on the card?"

"You are," Lirg said. He turned to a Breed customer and Michael left the courtyard, Eleuth following a few steps behind.

"What are they teaching you?" Eleuth asked as they approached the creek.

"They're trying to make me stronger," Michael said.

"Why don't you just stay in Euterpe? They have their own allotment. You could do well there."

"That's not the way things worked out," he said. "I suppose I'm being trained so I can go home again. I hope that's the reason, anyway. I have to find the man who can do it."

"A Sidhe magician could send you home," Eleuth said. Her voice was extraordinary; he didn't want to look at her for fear of being unable to look away again. "I think one could, anyway. That's what Lirg says, that the priests of the Irall could send humans home again if they really wanted to. There's something mysterious about that, I can't help thinking. Because, you see, the humans are still here."

Michael considered her words for a moment, then started to cross the stream. "Anyway, I have to learn how to live here."

Eleuth nodded. "If you're new, there's a lot to learn, I guess."

They set the sacks down outside the door of the Crane Women's hut.

"Where's your mother?" Michael asked. Humans didn't live in Halftown; he knew that much.

"I don't know," Eleuth said. Her face was simple and composed. "Most of us have Sidhe mothers, and our fathers are missing—or in Euterpe. We never know who they are. So I suppose I'm unusual, second-generation Breed . . . my father a Breed, my mother human."

He knocked on the door and Spart opened it. She peered at Eleuth, Michael and then the sacks and said, "Fine." She closed the door again.

"Does that mean you're free today?"

He shook his head. "I have to run to Euterpe and back." He walked to his house.

"You built that yourself?" Eleuth asked, following.

"Sort of."

"Like a Sidhe warrior. Must build his own dwelling . . . but very clever, really, for a human."

Michael glanced at her; Eleuth's expression was still composed and simple. She wasn't ragging him. "Thanks for the help," he said. He felt very awkward.

She looked around the mound with an expression of awe mixed with distaste, then smiled at him and said good-bye. As she forded the creek, Michael watched the way her legs moved. They were long, graceful. His face flushed. She was pretty in a way; no, not just pretty (perhaps not pretty at all) but beautiful. But then, how did he know what passed for beauty in the Realm?

An attraction to a Breed, he was sure, could be perverse and would only complicate his life more.

"Man-child!" Nare came toward him, carrying two thick sticks about seven feet long. "Run to Euterpe. Hold this over your head going and in front of you returning." She gave him a stick. He hefted it and groaned inwardly.

"Then what?"

"When you are strong enough, you learn how to use the stick." With the other stick, she lightly tapped his own just outside one hand's grip. "Or I break all your fingers. Now go."

Michael began to run. He crossed the stream without slipping and congratulated himself on his newfound coordination. Leaving wet shoe prints, he took the first hundred yards in stride, though the stick made his arms ache. Within a half mile he was still going strong. It was in the third quarter of the first mile that he was sure the stick would drag him down, and that once on the ground, he would die.

He tried to remember how to breathe when running: steadily, without letting his legs pound the air from his lungs.

His mouth was dry and his lungs began to feel as though they'd been sprayed with acid. His arms were twin upright pillars of pain, and his knees wobbled; still, he was determined to keep going. He'd show them he was good for something. He had had enough humiliation—

His toe caught a rock and he sprawled headlong in the dirt. The stick bounced end-to-end and rolled ahead of him. He picked dirt from between his teeth and felt his bruised lips and nose, trying to control his agonized gulping for air.

A half-hour later, he stood with his hands on his knees before the outskirts of Euterpe, his face beet red and his legs liquid. He dropped the stick on the ground beside him. He wasn't sure he would ever be able to lift it again. "Christ," he said. "I'm nothing but a wimp. He might as well have killed me."

It took him a couple of minutes to become aware of the small crowd standing nearby, just outside one of Euterpe's small pedestrian gates. They watched him curiously, saying nothing at first. He tried to stand upright and winced. The auburn-haired woman he had last seen at the hotel dinner stepped forward. "Why did you come back?" she asked, voice thick with anger. "Breeds not good enough for you?"

He regarded her from under his brows, breath ragged.

"They're getting me in shape," he said. He didn't want anybody to be angry— why should humans be mad at him?

"Why do you need to be in better shape?" a man asked from the back of the group.

"I don't know," Michael said. He picked up the stick, his fingers barely agreeing to close on it, and turned around to start back.

"Michael!"

Savarin came through the gate. Michael leaned on his stick, grateful for a friendly voice and an excuse to rest a bit longer. His chest now felt as if it were filled with water. He coughed and wiped his forehead.

"You're in training?" Savarin asked.

Michael nodded and swallowed.

"Well, that can't hurt."

"Oh, yeah?"

"They are teaching you . . . how to fight, perhaps, how to fight Sidhe?"

He shook his head. "They're teaching me how to run away from Sidhe."

Savarin scowled. "When can you return? There are people I'd like you to meet."

"I don't know. They're going to make me run more errands for them. Maybe later."

"If you can, come to the schoolhouse—it's on the other side of the street from the Yard. In the middle of town. I teach languages, other subjects. Come see me."

Michael agreed and pointed with the stick. "I have to go back now."

"Look at that!" a high-pitched masculine voice shouted from the crowd. "They give the bastard a fortune in wood!"

"Be quiet!" Savarin cried, waving his arms and advancing on the crowd. "Go home!" The crowd broke up with resentful glares at both of them.

Michael tried to pick up his pace again. Halfway, the agony subsided and the run became easier. He had heard of second wind but had never experienced it before. His body seemed to resign itself to the situation and make the best of things.

It was late morning when he came to the creek and crossed it, then clumped to where Spart stood on the mound. She took his stick and called to the other Crane Women with a sharp whistle.

Coom emerged from the hut to inspect him. She palped his legs and arms and shook her head violently, tossing her dust-gray hair. "*Usgal! Nalk,*" she said, pointing to the stream. "You stink."

"That's not fair," he said, frowning resentfully.

"Things won't be fair again until you've bathed," Spart said. "Then follow Coom away from here and keep on working."

"But I'm exhausted."

"You didn't run without stopping," she said. In the hut, Nare cackled and withdrew her face from the window.

Michael dragged his feet to the stream and removed his clothes. He was down to his underpants before any notion of modesty occurred to him. He glanced back at Spart. She sat on her haunches plaiting reeds into a mat. She paid him no attention. He kept his underpants on and dipped a foot gingerly into the water.

Of course, it was freezing. He closed his eyes. They would think him an idiot or a coward if he always hesitated. He stepped back and then ran forward, plunging in feet first. The shock was considerable; when he surfaced, he could hardly breathe and his teeth chattered furiously. Still, it was better to bear the hardship than put up with more ridicule.

As he rubbed the silty, mica-flecked water over his skin, he again noticed the pungent herbal smell. Apparently that was the nature of water in the Realm. He crawled out of the creek—which was about four feet deep in the middle—and shook his arms and legs, scattering ribbons of water across the bank. Still damp, he put on his clothes, but held the jacket by its yoke and carried it to where Spart plaited her reeds.

She turned her attention away from her work to look him up and down and shook her head pityingly. "Only a fool would dive into water so cold."

Michael nodded without argument. That was their game; he could go along with them. "Thanks," he said.

And so it went for the first five days.

9

The Crane Women ran Michael around the level grasslands, with the stick and without it, sometimes one or two of them pacing him and giving directions. They seemed tireless. When he was near collapse from exertion, they wouldn't even be breathing hard. After a while, Michael suspected Sidhe and Breeds just didn't get tired. He asked about that once, and Nare simply smiled.

He learned the Pact Lands within the vicinity of Euterpe and Halftown quickly. There wasn't all that much to learn—grasslands, the curve of the river, one fork and an oxbow beyond the fork.

He asked about the Blasted Plain. Spart told him that part of his education would come later. He could see the haze beyond the perimeter of the Pact Lands, and occasionally make out black spires rising through orange-brown clouds, but his radius was never more than six miles from Halftown, and the Pact Lands, he surmised, extended at least ten miles on all sides.

Sometimes, his exercises seemed ridiculous, designed to humiliate him.

"Five times you have missed the mark," Nare said, standing over him. Her shadow bisected four concentric circles drawn in the dirt ten feet from where he squatted. He had been set to tossing pebbles, trying for the central circle. After an hour he had only hit the center three times.

"I've missed more often than that," he said.

"You miss my words, too," Nare said. "You fail to understand anything we've been showing you. Five tests." Michael tried to remember the times he had been tested in any meaningful way. "Not a good sign," she went on. "Don't you see the truth behind the tests? Must we explain in words? Words are so beloved to you!"

"They're clear, at least," Michael said. "What do you want me to learn? I've done everything I can to cooperate—"

"Except use your head properly!" Nare grabbed his arm and hauled him to a standing position. "This is not a bull's-eye. These are not pebbles. You are not training, and this is no series of useless games."

"Funny," Michael said. He regretted saying it immediately; he had vowed that whatever the pressure, he would not behave like a smartass.

"You're a crack-voiced child, and worse, *jan wiros.* What have you learned?"

"I think . . . I think you're trying to teach me how to survive by thinking a certain way. But I'm not a magician."

"You are not required to be one. How would we have you think?"

"With confidence."

"Not that alone. What else?"

"I don't know!"

"If we tried to turn you into a magician, we'd be even more doltish than you. You're not special. But Sidhedark is not like Earth. You must learn how the *Realm is* special, how it supports and nurtures us. You cannot be told. Words spoil the knowledge. So we must torment you, boy, to make you see. The Sidhe returned language to humans thousands of years ago, but they never explained how language can destroy. That was deliberate."

"I'm trying to cooperate," Michael said sullenly.

"You cooperate so you can show us you aren't a fool." She smiled, a hideous and revealing expression which didn't reassure him at all, and probably wasn't meant to. Her teeth were cat-sharp and her gums black as tar.

"IN *BETLIM,* LITTLE combat, warriors not kill. Best," Coom said. They circled each other with the sticks held before them in broad-spaced hands. "*Lober,* not hurt. Win. Strategy."

Michael nodded.

"One thing very bad," Coom said. "*Rilu.* Anger. Never let mad control! Mad is poison in *betlim.* In great combat, *rilu* is *mord.* Hear?"

HE NODDED AGAIN. Coom touched his stick with her own. "Disarm you now."

He gripped his stick tighter, but that only made his hands hurt more when, with a whirl and a flourish, she whacked his stick straight up in the air, parallel to the ground. He caught it as it fell, wincing at the pain in his wrists.

"Good," Coom said. "Now you hear why you learn. Hear that stick is wick; you are Sidhe given power of *pais* where you stand. I take wick and take land from you. Stop me—maybe stop me. Hear how I move. Take control of air. Of Realm."

Then she did an amazing thing. She leaped up, braced her feet against nothingness, and sprung at him with her stick. He retreated, but not before receiving another bone-rattling blow. She hung before him a moment and landed on her feet. "Good," she said. "Stronger."

She disarmed him again, this time whacking the stick out of his reach before it came down. He walked over to pick it up and turned to see Coom standing where he had been.

"Gave up ground," she accused, disgusted.

"You took away my stick."

"Didn't take away most important weapon." She threw down her stick and backed up a pace. "Come at with *kima.*"

He didn't hesitate. She reached around with one spider hand as his stick came down on the spot where she had stood, grabbed hold and slammed it to the ground.

He could feel the bones in his back pop before he let go.

"Little defeats teach potential," Coom said. "Not to waste my time, you will train with this." Spart came from the hut carrying a headless mannequin with bush-branch arms. It held a smaller stick, tied to leafy "hands" with twine. Michael groaned inside, then resigned himself to the indignity.

"Take this off thirty paces and hammer it into the ground. Then fight with it," Spart said.

He did as he was told, clutching the cloth, straw and wood mannequin and using his stick to pound it in like a stake. He assumed a stance before the mannequin, imitating Coom and feeling foolish—

And it promptly swung up its stick and knocked his to the ground. The mannequin vibrated gleefully, twisted on its stake and became limp again.

When the hair on his neck had settled, Michael retrieved his stick and resumed his stance, a little farther back. They sparred for a bit, the mannequin having at least the two disadvantages of being staked to the ground and using a shorter, flimsier stick. Michael wasn't encouraged.

He had no illusions that the fight was fair. He got his lumps.

10

As the predawn light filtered through the plaited reed door cover Spart had given him, Michael scrawled another poem in the dirt floor.

Night's a friendly sort
Oh yes likes to throw a
Fright now and then—when
The wind hums—but after
You're dead will gladly
Share a glass of moon.

Nothing more than exercise, he thought—not worth recording even if he had the means, which he did not—no pencils or writing implements of any sort but the stick, no paper but what was in his black book. And he hardly considered his work worthy of the book.

The Crane Women usually arose fifteen minutes before sunrise, which gave Michael a short time of being alone and at leisure—time more important than sleep. He used the time to read from the book or write in the dirt, or just to savor not having anything in particular to do.

He heard the door to their hut creak open. He took the book, zippered it into his jacket pocket and wrapped it in the folds before hiding it in the rafters overhead.

"Man-child! *Jan viros!*"

Michael came out of the house and saw Coom approach, Nare two paces behind. They looked like hunters unsure of their prey—and he was their prey. The Crane Women were masters at unnerving him. He could never predict their moods or attitudes. He should have been a nervous wreck, but he found himself adapting.

"More run," Coom said. "To Euterpe and back. With *kima.*"

He grabbed the stick without hesitation and ran. Behind, Nare called out, "This evening is *Kaeli.*" She said it as if some special treat were involved. Michael hefted the stick before him and crossed the creek. He did not see the watery hand which rose up, grasped at his ankle and missed.

He could make it to the town without collapsing now. He took some pride in his improvement. For the first time in his life he felt the exultation of the body in sheer activity, the meshing of breath and legs, the matched, almost pleasant ache in all his muscles.

At first, he stayed away from the outskirts housing, not wanting to bring on another confrontation. But he was curious what Savarin was up to, what the teacher had meant the last time, that there were people he wanted Michael to meet. He decided to enter Euterpe and go to the schoolhouse—and the populace be damned. He had his stick and he felt a little cocky.

He was up to the main gate when he almost bumped into the teacher. They laughed and Michael put down his stick, breathing deeply and wiping sweat from his face with his shirt sleeve.

"I thought I might catch you during your morning constitutional," Savarin said. "And warn you. Best stay out of the town for the next couple of days. Alyons has been harassing us since your arrival. The townspeople are upset. They're liable to strike out at you without being aware of what they're doing."

"I haven't hurt them," Michael said.

"No, but you've brought trouble. Things here are marginal, at best. Alyons threatens to reduce our allotment if anything else happens to upset him."

"Is that why they shouted at me the last time?"

"Yes. I still want you to meet some people, but later. And I also want to tell you . . . something's planned for tonight—the Halftown *Kaeli*. Have they invited you?"

"Nare mentioned it before I left. I don't even know what it is."

"It's very important. *Kaeli* is when the Sidhe get together to tell stories, usually about the early times. I'd like you to listen closely and tell me what you hear. I've only heard one—and that from a distance. I was hiding in tall grass. Now, with the Breed guards so tense, I don't dare. Nobody is allowed near Halftown now . . . That's what makes me think something is afoot."

"What?"

"Best not to ask for trouble yet. But a *grazza*, perhaps. A raid by Riverines and Umbrals. Keep an eye out, and be careful."

"You want me to come back and tell you about the *Kaeli?*"

"Of course," Savarin said, his eyes brightening. "But a couple of days from now, when things are more settled." He looked around nervously. A few faces peered from nearby windows, and two men loitering by the gate cast glances at them. "Until then," the teacher said, gripping Michael's hand and releasing it with a wave as he made for a different gate. Michael picked up the stick, held it over his head, and began the return leg of his run.

His body took over almost immediately and he forgot Savarin, forgot the *Kaeli*, forgot almost everything but the sensation of distance covered.

THE BREEDS OF Halftown marched in double file over the grassland, dressed in dark brown and gray cloaks, conversing casually in Cascar and calling to those farther forward or back in the lines. The air was still and cool; the sun touched distant hills and ribbons of evening cascaded slowly to the hazy horizon, revealing the stars with their tiny circling motions.

Behind the lines marched the Crane Women. Michael walked abreast of Spart, wearing his jacket. (The book rested in its nook in the tiny house, as secure as he could make it.) He had washed his clothes in the creek earlier, as a concession to formality; they were still slightly damp even after drying near a fire Nare had kindled. Holes revealed his knees, and the shoulder of the jacket had separated at the seam.

The Crane Women wore short black coats that emphasized the length of their legs and the shortness of their torsos. They walked with arms folded, jutting elbows making them look more then ever like birds. They seemed to carry more of an ancient reserve with regard to *Kaeli* than the other Breeds, and didn't talk.

Those assigned to choose the site had gone on ahead during the late afternoon. Now a bonfire blazed a few hundred feet down the path, squares of peat and dried brush-wood providing the fuel. Circling the bonfire was a perimeter of poles, each topped by a leafy green branch. When the Breeds had gathered within the circle, Lirg came forward and paced around the fire. Michael sat beside the Crane Women, crossing his legs on the grass stubble and dirt.

Lirg spoke in Cascar for a few minutes. Michael understood little of what was said; he had difficulty even picking out the meanings of individual words in the long discourse. There seemed to be many words in Cascar with the same or subtly shaded meanings, and the syntax varied as well.

Spart leaned forward and tapped Michael on the shoulder. "You haven't learned the tongue, have you?" she asked.

"I've only been here a couple of weeks," Michael said defensively. Nare blew out her breath. The Crane Women looked at each other, then Spart sidled forward and placed both her hands around Michael's head.

"Tonight only," she said, "You have a boon. It won't last." She removed her hands and Michael shook a buzzing out of his ears. When the dizziness passed, he listened to Lirg. The Breed was still speaking Cascar but the words became limpid; Michael could understand all of them.

"Tonight," Lirg said, "we invoke the sadness of the time when we were grand, when the Sidhe marched between the stars as easily as I circle this fire." He passed around to the other side, his words piercing the crackle of the flames. "Each will share the tale, the part of his ancestor, and as conclusion, I will tell of Queen Elme and her choice."

First to pick up the thread was a tall brown-haired Breed who announced himself as Manann of the line of Till. As Manann spoke, Michael was enchanted by the way the language adapted to poetry—half-singing, half-speaking, until he could no longer tell the difference.

The Earth, home to us all, has spun
A thousand polar dances since
The war called Westering, won
First by men, who decreed that none

Of the race called Sidhe should possess
Souls beyond the border of Death.
Unwitting, the Mage who made us less,
Who imposed this inward emptiness,

Gave to the Sidhe life without end.
And then time came for the wheel to turn
Again. The Sidhe thus damned did send
To defeat the vain and gloating men

Who had in cruel and thoughtless rage
Robbed us of life beyond matter.
The Sidhe bid the responsible Mage
To work their own vengeance and engage

His power to transform men to beasts.
Triumphant Sidhe in sweet passioned
Irony watched mankind decreased.
Yet in the shape of the small, the least

Of claw-foot, scruff-fur animals,
None who had once been men could tell
How to once more open the portals
Of shadowy death; how immortals

Could reclaim the boon of a soul.

Holder of the Wick of Battle,
Ysra Faer of the line of Till
Confined men-beasts and all allies—
Also made beast, and beast-form still—
On Earth, walled-in like cattle.

"How many races were there?" Michael whispered to Spart, uncertain whether he spoke in Cascar or English. She turned her dark eyes on him and answered, "More than four . . . we do not know for sure, now. Much has been forgotten. Many of the animals of Earth were once kin of the Sidhe and humans of old."

Manann sat and another stood, a young woman with beefy arms and a face squatter than usual. "I am Esther of the line of Dravi. I take the challenge of the end-rhymed song, but I *correct* Manann of Till . . ." Laughter rang through the circle. "He forgets my line's honored form, and I follow *that* now."

All tribes, brothers and sisters hand in hand,
In glory Sidhe set out to march the stars.
Through this spacing, histories multiplied
As numberless as the shore's sea-ground sand.
Yet in swifting time, all progress died.

All glorious rise swings back to fall, sure
As the new-born Sidhe on time's cruel road
Came to their doom by chance or anger's blade.
Exaltation turned to slow decay, the pure
And good demeaned, ideals not lived but played.

Lacking worthy goals or adversary,
Star-marcher Faer in easeful ways declined.
None took on the hard discipline of the Sidhe.
Mere sibling strifes trained the warrior wary;
Tribes found bitter freedom in their jealousy.

From the line of Dravi, Wickmaster Sum
Foresaw the impending doom; in darkness
Deeper than ever known, against the races
Of the Great Distance he warred, to come
To glory, to draw in battle traces

Of pride and courage lost since war with Man.
The Great Distance breeds minds unlike our own,
With unfamiliar thoughts of foreign
Shape. Of this war called Quandary none can
Recall the tale, only the outcome, when, worn

From victory more costly than defeat,
Destroying what sloth, misrule and ease
Had not already, the wasted Sidhe
Swung Earthward the ravaged Faerie fleet.
Among their dead: Wickmaster Sum, of Dravi.

Having long since beaten humanity,
The last drops from the river of Sidhe
Thought Earth to be their choicest
Harbor, refuge for a well-earned rest.

Esther of the line of Dravi took her seat, and Fared of the line of Wis continued.

By way of right succession, Krake
Of the line of noble Wis did take
The Wick. As Wickmaster of Sidhe,
Krake brought us home from the endless sea

Of dark-storied, sinister space.
Yet on Earth, no peace, for the race
Of resourceful, unquenchable Man
Had crawled, across an age's span

Up from beast by nature's road
Of Change and Pain, with Death's sharp goad.
While Sidhe declined in sibling strife,
Man struggled back to conscious life.

Though new-born Man was then quite young
Krake knew on human history hung
The fate of his weary, worn Sidhe,
Too weak for one more victory.

Nizandsa, of Serket's family,
Now extinct, made this plea:
"We must find the one called Mage,
Imprisoned as serpent this long age.

"He has the knowledge to restore our
Souls, whose lack has caused a dour
Decline. Perhaps a trade of liberty
Can return to us the essence of Sidhe!"

But Krake, we are told, did not agree.
"In Man old or new I cannot see
Any answer for our many troubles.
With human help, a problem doubles!

"Power to men, releasing the Mage,
Can only resurrect the rage
Felt in their dread animal fall.
No power to Man! That would end us all."

Nizandsa's faithful lost this debate.
Krake, unhappy still, filled with hate,

Ordered his coursers to halt all
Dissent. In Great Combat, the pall

Of disgrace again gloomed over us.
Nizandsa's murder ended all trust
Between the branches of the Sidhe,
The third curse of a trinity.

Lirg stood now and walked around the fire again. "The new breed of men,"
he began, voice low and almost devoid of song, "had regained their former shape,
but not their past glory. They could not keep what had made the men of old the
grand enemies of the Sidhe. And the Sidhe, themselves, had long since lost what
made them great." He came to the side of the fire where Michael sat between the
Crane Women, and looked over their heads at the Pact Lands beyond. "I tell the
story now of the family to which we all belong, the line of the Mage Tonn's
breath-daughter, Elme.

Assuming the wick from father Tonn,
Queen Elme defied the scorners of
Man, brought Sidhe to new-found
Harmony, and against the will of
God-like sire, loved and married—

A distant keening sound carried over the plain, interrupting Lirg and causing
the Breeds to stir for the first time in half an hour. Nare, Spart and Coom leaped
to their feet and out of the circle before Michael could blink twice.

Clouds moved quickly across the sky. The keening faded, grew louder, and
faded again as if carried on uncertain breezes. From farther away still came the
sound of horns unlike any Michael had ever heard; horns that seemed to laugh
and cry at once.

As one, the crowd scooped up dirt and extinguished the bonfire. Michael
stood aside, not knowing where he fit in, deciding it was best to keep out of the
way.

With the bonfire reduced to embers and smoke, seeing was difficult. A drop
of rain struck his forehead, then another. Wind tugged at his jacket—or he
thought it was the wind. A green veil of luminosity flashed behind the hills.

"Man-child! This way!" Spart grabbed his arm and pulled him after. "*Kaeli*
is over for tonight. Adonna sends its hosts!"

The first burst of rain soaked Michael instantly. He followed the indistinct
form of a Crane Woman across the fresh mud and bent, beaten grass. Puddles
were forming everywhere. The wind gusted and pushed him this way and that.

"Where are we going?" Michael asked. The figure didn't answer, but kept
running ahead, gesturing. He fell into a hole up to his knees in water, tried to
balance and slid up to his thighs. Wiping his eyes, blowing muddy water from
his nose, he splashed out of the hole and yelled, "Hey! Wait up!"

The figure paused for him. It gestured again as he clambered after. Running was difficult; the rain fell so thick he had to clasp his hand to his mouth to keep from breathing water. Still, the figure forged ahead, relentless.

Sheet-lightning flared again, throwing the landscape into gray brilliance. Michael stopped. He heard something roaring very close—the river, he thought, yet the figure ahead gestured again: Follow. "Where are we?" Michael cried out. No answer came. He stepped forward tentatively, lost his footing, and yelled in surprise. His mouth instantly filled with rain. Choking, he slid on scrambling feet and butt down a muddy bank, over an edge—

And into rain-filled space.

It took him a moment to realize he had fallen into rushing water. He kicked and thrashed about, trying to find the shore, but currents like strong fingers wrapped around his feet and pulled him under. Pressed between powerful walls of water, he opened his eyes and felt the darkness of the night pass into blacker insensibility.

His lungs were about to burst when he was flung from the water like a salmon clawed by a bear. He hit the mud face-down and turned his head just enough to take a breath, inhaling both air and mud tossed up by the weakening rain.

He rubbed his eyes clear. The lightning flashed silent and green. In the strobing glare he saw the foaming, racing water a few feet away. Reaching from the water, trying to grasp his legs and retrieve him, were four transparent hands. He jackknifed his legs and dug his fingers into the mud to pull himself farther up the bank.

One shoulder and an arm struck a cold, solid mass—a boulder, Michael thought. He wrapped his arms around it . . . and the boulder shifted. Looking up, blinking at the remaining drops of rain, he saw a man-shaped piece of night tower over him. Steely, bone-chilling hands lifted him from the bank. He tried to scream for help but a hard, cold palm clamped over his mouth, numbing his lips and jamming his tongue against his teeth.

His head was immediately wrapped in a thick cloak.

Then, after probing his ribs and legs roughly through the icy fabric, the shape hesitated. It pulled Michael's head into the open and he stared into a face as black as the bottom of the sea, with two starry points for eyes. Harsh breath like a freezer's charge of air prickled his nose.

"*Antros! Viros antros!*"

With a cry of rage, the frigid shadow flung him aside. He rolled through space, rotating in a world of lightning and darkness, rain on his lips and mud in his eyes. The impact seemed to come after the mud, but everything was confused.

Michael lay on his back, certain that every bone in his body was broken.

Far away, and growing fainter, the keening wavered with the wind until both faded, and silence covered the wet, tormented land.

11

Caught in a beam of sunlight, a drop of water hung from the tip of a blade of grass, more beautiful than any diamond. Round, filled with shimmering life, the drop grew until its freedom was assured. It fell in a quivering sphere and broke over his forehead, cool and gently insistent.

Michael saw a glowing mist, golden above and blue to either side, surrounding a new droplet on the grass blade. He blinked and the mist resolved into sun half-hidden by clouds. Tall green grass rose on all sides. For a moment, he felt no need to do anything but stare. Indeed, it seemed that all his life he had been nothing but a pair of eyes.

But soon he remembered his hands and they twitched. There was some reason he was reluctant to remember his body, and when he moved his legs the reason became clear: pain. His torso, as he lifted his head and looked down on it, was surprisingly clean. Rain had rinsed the mud from his jacket. He tried to sit up, then gritted his teeth and fell back.

Limb by limb, he took inventory until he was sure nothing was broken. Pulling back his jacket and shirt, he found a mass of welts on his side. His arms were heavily bruised, especially under his armpits, where he had been hoisted by the shadow. His teeth felt as if they were on fire. He vaguely remembered being slapped from the river, the hands rising from the water to pull him back . . . and the shadow with eyes like stars.

He stood, legs wobbly and vision spinning. The river lay about fifty yards beyond an embankment. He must have walked the distance; there was no sign in the unbent grass that the water had flowed so high as to carry him here. Or— the shadow had flung him clear.

Had he encountered another kind of Sidhe—an Umbral?

Shading his eyes against the cloudy glare, Michael looked from his elevated vantage across the plain. He stood on an island of grass in the yellow-green sea of mire. For as far as he could see there was nothing but the storm-soaked plain and the distant hills. No sign of Euterpe or Halftown; no sign of anyone.

It seemed he was the only living thing besides the grass.

Black curls of flood water still snaked from the low hills to the river. The river itself had returned to its channel, once more slow and sluggish.

Michael sat. River-borne, he must have come from upstream, and that was where he would return when he was strong enough.

His back prickled. He turned stiffly to look in the opposite direction. Less than a hundred yards beyond the grassy knoll, the Pact Lands came to an end. He had almost been washed onto the Blasted Plain.

The air beyond the border hung like smoke in a thick gray-orange haze. The river waters roiled muddy gray-blue right up to the demarcation, then flowed turgid yellow-green and sickly purple, like pus from a long-infected wound.

The Blasted Plain itself spread in an expanse of black, gray and brown boulders across glistening, powdery umber sand. Through the murky air, Michael could see tall curly twists of rock like broken strands of glue. The Blasted Plain was more than the sum of its parts, more living than dead, but nothing alive was visible: malevolent, made of things long buried, hard emotions long suppressed, mistakes covered over.

Death, despair, foulness and horror.

Michael shuddered. The shudder grew into tremors of delayed shock. He descended the knoll as quickly as his unstable legs allowed and began his march over the grassland, upriver to Euterpe and Halftown—or so he hoped—and away from the desolation of a war he could hardly imagine.

After a few minutes, he began to draw on reserves he had built up during the past weeks of training. He walked for the hour or so remaining until dark, then slept fitfully under the open night sky, and resumed at dawn.

He would not die. He would not starve.

He had survived; and in that simple fact, Michael found a dismaying, pleasurable pride.

THICK SWATHS OF fog shouldered in over the plain, driven before the sun's warmth. Michael followed the sandy river bank, crossed the shallow ox-bow where the river rippled and glittered over rocks and pebbles, and climbed another hill to get his bearings.

The roofs of Halftown clustered about two miles away like broken nut shells on a brown and gray cloth. He broke into a run along a trail of hard, clayey sand.

In Halftown, things seemed to be carrying on as usual. Several buildings had suffered rain and wind damage, and Lirg's market courtyard had nearly been flattened, but the Breeds went about their business as if the commotion of the night before had been commonplace.

The hut of the Crane Women was unscathed. Nare squatted between two piles of animal bones, holding a long split stem of grass in her teeth and weaving reeds into a thick mat for sitting. Coom was nowhere to be seen. Spart, he discovered, had silently stolen close and walked behind him as he approached the mound.

Michael grinned at her over his shoulder. "Worried about me?" he asked. Spart's eyes widened and she bared her black gums.

"It wasn't you they were after, nor any human," she said.

"I got that impression," Michael said. He stopped before his house and lifted one foot to scrape mud from his shoe. "What happened?"

"There was a raid on the Breeds," Spart said. She walked toward the door of the hut, her jaw working as if chewing cud. She did not seem glad to see him.

"I took care of myself," he said defiantly, squaring his shoulders.

"You escaped Umbrals and Riverines." She turned on the hard-packed dirt before the doorway. "They're branches of the Sidhe who worship Adonna most fervently. Adonna needs Sidhe blood to do its work, but it cannot touch the pure Sidhe. So it comes for us. We're adequate for its needs, and few care if a Breed is lost. You were lucky, man-child, not skilled."

Michael looked between the two Crane Women, his face reddening. "I survived," he said. "God damn it, I survived! I'm not just some piece of garbage everybody kicks around! I have my rights and I . . . I—" He was speechless. Spart shrugged and entered the hut. Nare cocked a glance at him, smiling around the stem in her teeth. She removed the stem and spat into the dirt.

"You survived, boy," she said. "But you did not help anybody else. Three Breeds were taken last night, including Lirg of the line of Wis."

Michael thought of the black face with freezing breath and eyes like stars. He shuddered violently, then straightened again and stuck out his jaw. "What will happen to them?"

"Adonna has its uses for them. We said that, boy. You don't listen."

Michael suddenly felt deathly exhausted and despondent. He had never lived in a place so cruel and unpredictable. The thought of continuing to struggle seemed to pull wool around his brain. He dropped loosely into a crouch before his hut and held his chin in his hands. "What about Eleuth?" he asked a few moments later.

"She was not taken," Nare said. "She is only one-quarter Sidhe. Her uses would be limited."

"Do they always attack on a night of *Kaeli?*"

"Not always. Often enough."

"So why so you hold them out in the open?"

"We are still of the Sidhe," Nare said. "We must keep the customs, even when it is dangerous."

Michael pondered that for a time, and decided it didn't really make sense. But he didn't want to pursue that line of questioning. "I'm going to run now," he said. Nare didn't react. He wanted to get into Euterpe and talk with Savarin, find out what happened to the humans. At least with Savarin, he could ask questions and not be ridiculed.

He started off at a gentle lope, hoping to ease the exhaustion and funk from his body. As he approached Halftown again, he slowed. Glancing behind to see if he was watched, he took the path leading through the village.

Eleuth swept debris from the courtyard as Michael approached. She glanced at him without slowing her broom.

"I heard," Michael said. "I'm sorry."

"He serves the god now," Eleuth said. Sad, her voice sounded even more beautiful.

"Are you going to work the market alone?"

"I'll try."

He opened his mouth, but decided he really had nothing to say. He bent down to pick up a piece of shingle.

"Throw it in the pile," she said, poking the broom end at a neat stack of splintered boards.

"If I can help . . ."

She regarded him with a placid expression, though her cheeks were wet. He had never seen a Sidhe or a Breed cry before. Perhaps she could cry because she was three-quarters human.

"I mean, if there's anything I can do . . . ?" he said awkwardly.

She shook her head and continued sweeping. As he turned to walk away, she said, "Michael."

"Yes?"

"I will take my rest later this day. May we visit then? I'll be better."

"Sure. I'll be back by my place at—"

"No. Away from the Crane Women."

That suited him. "I'll meet you here."

Though every muscle ached, it was the sort of pain he felt might be driven away by exercise. Once outside Halftown and on the road, he picked up his jogging pace as ache gave way to exertion.

Twice now his life had been threatened. Such things seemed to be expected in the Realm. The Crane Women, each time, had treated his horrible experiences as just another minor hurdle. Michael couldn't accept that.

He wasn't sure he could trust the Crane Women to help him to his goal; he knew he couldn't trust Lamia. Even the humans had little altruistic interest in his fate; Savarin probably cared for Michael only so long as he gathered information. Only Eleuth accepted him for what he was, and desired his company.

He ran even faster.

Whatever else he thought about them, one thing was obvious: the Crane Women's training was doing him no harm. He felt better, stronger; on Earth, he might have been laid up for a week after being roughed up and nearly drowning.

Euterpe had come through the storm with little damage. Some of the walls were water-stained, and one or two had been shored up after the dissolution of a few bricks, but little more. Obviously, what Nare had said was true: the Umbrals and Riverines had sought Breeds, not men.

Michael made his way through the streets, walking quickly to avoid curious onlookers. Even so, a gaggle of women dressed in muddy brown skirts and shawls, sitting on benches near the inn, tittered at him. He hunched his shoulders, shook his head to clear his thoughts and crossed a narrow, cheerless triangle adjacent to a large, low one-story ochre brick building.

No signs announced the fact, but Michael supposed this was the dreaded Yard. He circled the building and saw Savarin's school on the opposite side, a square, low-roofed structure with a clumsy steeple rising over one corner. As he climbed the brick steps, he heard a high-pitched warbling wail from the depths of the Yard and the muffled slam of a heavy door.

Savarin stood near a wicker lectern in the empty single classroom, leafing through a small pile of gray papers. The teacher looked up, his eyes widening at the bruises on Michael's face and the state of the boy's clothing: muddy, grass-stained, shirt and jacket torn. "You look more like a savage every day," Savarin said. "Was I right about last night—more than a storm?"

"A—what did you call it?—a raid."

Savarin nodded, standing, circling Michael and touching his jacket solicitously. "*Grazza,* similar to the Arabic *grazzu,* you know. My God. I knew Halftown was hit—"

"Right in the middle of *Kaeli,*" Michael said. "They took three Breeds, including the market manager. How often do these raids happen?"

"Often enough to make me suspect Alyons cares little for the Breeds, and that the Pact does not fully apply to them. Yet they follow Sidhe customs—"

"He doesn't give a damn for them," Michael said, surprised by his anger. "I'd like to kill that son of a bitch."

Savarin regarded Michael solemnly for a moment. "I hope your memory of the events was not affected."

"I remember well enough," Michael said. "The Crane Women even let me understand Cascar for a while."

Savarin's face betrayed almost comic envy. "Then tell," he said. "Do tell all."

For an hour and a half, Michael reconstructed the *Kaeli* and the events after. Savarin grabbed his sheaf of gray papers and scribbled notes frantically with a sharp stick of hardened charcoal. "Marvelous," he said several times throughout. "Names I've never heard before, connections made! Marvelous!"

When Michael finished, Savarin said, "I suspect Adonna would have done with us all, Breed and human. But it acts very slowly. A god's time must be different from ours. In its moment of hesitation, we might fit our entire history in the Realm . . ."

"What happens to the Breeds they took?"

"I've heard the Umbrals and Riverines share them in their temples. Work magic with them. I know little beyond that. Perhaps some are taken to the Irall."

"What's the Irall?"

"Adonna's greatest temple, ruled by the Faer but accessible to all Sidhe. How many did you say were taken?"

"Three."

"Then it might not be an even split. Perhaps the raiders had a tiff of their own, dividing the captives."

Michael didn't like the word, *divide.* It sounded entirely too accurate.

"As for *Kaeli* songs, I've heard some outlines before, but never so many details. A shame Lirg didn't have time to tell more about Elme. I suspect some very important history is connected with her." He put his notes on the lectern and sat beside Michael on the classroom's front bench. "Questions are going around town. Why are you here, and why are you with the Crane Women and not your own kind? The townspeople resent you because they fear Alyons' displeasure. Our position is precarious, and you introduce an element of uncertainty."

"Is there anything I can do?" Michael asked.

"Perhaps." Savarin smiled, then frowned as he inspected Michael's bruises. "You should be resting, not up and about."

"I'm fine. Tell me more about the Crane Women." *Come on, teacher,* he thought. *Teach.* "Why are they so old . . . and how old are they?"

"I'm not positive," Savarin said, "but I believe they date back to the time of Queen Elme herself. I've heard they're Elme's daughters, but that hasn't been confirmed, and of course they'll never tell. Sometimes the Sidhe send their priest initiates, or their most promising young warriors, across the Blasted Plain to the Crane Women for training."

"Well, I'm no warrior and certainly no Sidhe. The Crane Women make me feel stupid. If the Sidhe hate humans and Breeds so much, why is Alyons supposed to be protecting us? Does he protect *anybody,* really?"

"Yes," Savarin said, scratching his nose between two fingers. "Somewhat. Things here would be much worse without him, much as I hate saying it. But he loathes us. He makes sure we stay put, and between whatever protecting he does, he makes our lives miserable."

"He wanted to kill me."

"I'm sure you go contrary to everything he holds dear," Savarin said, chuckling. "You are being treated in a most unusual way—like a Sidhe in many respects."

Michael looked down at the hard-packed dirt floor. "I have a million questions, and nobody knows the answers, or will tell me if they do."

"If the Crane Women haven't told you by now," Savarin said, "perhaps being ignorant is part of your training. Ignorance loves company." He smiled. "I've someone I want you to meet . . . if you're free, that is."

"I'm free," Michael said with a touch too much defiance.

12

The last person to arrive in the Realm before you was—is—a young woman."
Savarin led Michael down a narrow alley. Their feet squelched in the still-
damp mud. "She's been here two years, counting by days—which is more
reliable than counting by seasons. I've told her about you, and she wishes to meet
you. She is from your country, the United States."

"Where in the United States?"

"New York."

"Savarin, how long have you been here?"

"Perhaps thirty, thirty-one years."

"You don't look old enough," Michael said, astonished.

"Here, we get old to a point, then no older. Our souls are aware there is no
place for them to go, and so they take better care of our bodies. Aging stops,
even for old Wolfer."

Michael was silent for a moment, letting that sink in. "What's your friend's
name?"

"Helena." Savarin turned left and waved for him to follow. At the end of an
even narrower, T-shaped alley, a door was set into a mud-brick wall. The T's
extensions branched to the right and left, ending in blind walls. Within the doorway a flight of steps led up into shadow. The feeble glow of a candle in a sconce
at the top of the stairs lit their way as they climbed.

Savarin straightened Michael's coat collar and tugged his shirt collar out
around it, shook his head at the hopeless task of making him presentable, then
turned to a fabric-covered wicker door and lightly rapped it with his knuckles.

"Yes? Who is it?"

"I've brought a visitor," Savarin said, winking at Michael.

The door opened with a dry scrape and a woman not much older than
Michael stood in the frame. She smiled nervously and glanced at Savarin,
smoothed the lower half of her blouse with her hands, and glanced at Michael.
She wore a short skirt made of the same dun-colored cloth most of the humans
and Breeds had to make do with. Her blouse, however, was white and cottony,

cut short around her shoulders. Her face was broad, with generous black eyes and wide full lips. Her hair was dark brown with hints of red. She was well formed, slightly plump, but as tall as Michael and able to carry her figure well.

"Helena Davies, this is Michael Perrin." Savarin waved his hand between them.

"Hello," Michael said, offering his hand. Helena took it—her fingers were warm and dry, slightly callused—and stepped back.

"Please come in. Savarin's told me about you."

The apartment was separated into two rooms by a plastered brick wall, the door between hung with curtains made of pieces of hollow twig strung on twine. Two chairs of woven cane stood in opposite corners, covered with tiny gray pillows. In another corner, a wash basin sat on a stand made of sticks, much like the one in the inn room Michael had first shared with Savarin.

"I'm brewing herb tea," Helena said, showing them to the seats. She pulled out a bedroll and went behind the curtain to retrieve a white ceramic pot and three mugs. She set them down on a second wicker stand and pulled the bedroll close to Michael's chair, then sat on it, serving the tea and handing them their mugs. She stood abruptly, her hands going this way and that as she searched for something with her eyes. She said, "Ah!" and walked briskly to a box on the window ledge, from which she withdrew honeycomb wrapped in waxed cloth. "Honey for your tea?"

"Please," Michael said. She broke off a bit of comb and handed it to him. He dropped it into his mug. Realizing his mistake, he started to fish out the melting bits of wax, then gave it up. Helena laughed, but not unkindly, and sat down again.

"I'm so *nervous*," Helena said. "Henrik tells me you didn't come here the way the rest of us did."

Michael didn't want to repeat what was becoming, to him, a tiresome story. "How did *you* get here?" he asked.

"Helena was a budding concert pianist," Savarin said. She shrugged modestly and held her mug to her lips, looking at Michael over the rim.

"Prokofiev," she said.

"Pardon?"

"I was playing Prokofiev. I'd been practicing the Piano Concerto No. 3 for a month, preparing for a recital. I was very tired. Up in the morning with Bach, and around all afternoon with Prokofiev."

Michael waited for her to continue. She returned his gaze intently, then laughed and went on. "My fingers and wrists felt numb, so I decided to take a walk. The music was in my head. I could feel it. In my body, too, especially my chest and arms." She touched a spot above her right breast. Her breasts swung enticingly free beneath the blouse. "Like I was having a musical heart attack, you know?"

Michael shook his head.

"Anyway, I was dizzy. I stood at the top of a flight of stairs in my apartment building, and at the bottom was nothing but a pool of mercury—you know, quicksilver—and I stumbled. Put my foot in it. Woke up here." She set her cup down and wiped her lips delicately with a forefinger. "I still don't like stairs, even living on an upper floor."

"That was two years ago?" Michael asked.

"Give or take. How did you get here? I mean, Henrik explained, but I'd like to hear it from you."

All of Michael's confidence, built up (he had thought) during the weeks of training, dissolved in her presence. She was fresh, lively, young and completely human. He stumbled over his words, then bore down and performed a passable re-telling of his experiences. When he had finished, Helena looked out the small curtained window, the subdued light from the alley soft on her face.

"We don't understand anything about life, do we?" she said. "I thought this was like purgatory for those who spent too much time with music and too little time in church. At first, I mean. I was that naive."

"Many people feel a religious confusion when they first arrive," Savarin said. "I'm studying it."

"You study *everything*," Helena said, reaching out with a slender hand to touch Savarin's arm. "Isn't he too much?"

Michael focused on the contact with a twinge of envy. "You're from New York?"

"Brooklyn. And you?"

"Los Angeles."

"Oh my *gawd*," she said, shaking her head. "A crazy Californian. I've never heard of Arno Walt . . . what's his name. Did he ever write serious music?"

"For movies," Michael said.

"Nothing else?"

"Well, the concerto . . ."

"I've never heard of that, either."

"I think it was suppressed or something. It got him into a lot of trouble."

"Well, music's a big world. And I do suppose composers have a hard time, even harder than pianists. What are you doing now that you're here?"

"I'm training," Michael said before he had a chance to think.

"Training for what?"

"I don't know." He grinned sheepishly. Helena regarded him with apparent shocked surprise.

"You must know what you're training for," she said.

"To get my strength up, I suppose."

"You don't look particularly sick to me."

"Weak," he said. "I mean, I just never did much physical exercise."

"A bookworm like Henrik, I suppose," Helena said. "Well, then it's good for you there are so few books here."

"Michael brought one with him."

"Oh, did you? Can I see it?"

"I don't have it with me." He was surprised how touchy the subject was to him; he recalled Lamia's expression when he told her he had a book. "It's just a volume of poetry."

"More's the pity it's not a book of music. I'm terribly out of practice." She held up her hands and spread her fingers, crooking the pinkies slightly. "I'll bet you think musicians are terribly vain," she said, sighing. "Talk too much."

"No, not at all."

"Most of the people here are older than me. Some have been here for a hundred years or more. Isn't that amazing? Yet most don't look any older than Henrik, and those who do, were older when they came here. I think it's all very profound."

"It is," Michael agreed, though he might have chosen a different word. He could hardly keep his eyes off of her. To his embarrassment, he was getting an erection. He held his hands in his lap and tried concentrating on other things— Alyons and his coursers, the Umbral.

"I wonder if we'll ever figure it out," Helena continued. She seemed aware of Michael's shyness—even of his predicament, and appeared to enjoy it. "Will you be staying with the Crane Women for long? I mean, will they let you live in town?"

"I don't know. I don't really know much of anything. I'm so ignorant, but . . ." He wanted to just blurt everything out to her, bury his head in her— He raised his eyes from the blouse. "I have to go," he said. The thought of Alyons had made him presentable again. "They might need me for something."

"Oh, I'm sorry," Helena said, standing. He wondered what Savarin was to her—just a friend? "Can you come back? I'd like to talk some more—remember old times."

He glanced down at her hips and thighs, then at her breasts and face, her eyes. No doubt about it. She was beautiful. "I'll try," Michael said. "When would . . . uh . . . be convenient?"

"I work early mornings doing laundry." She displayed her hands. "Ugly, aren't they?" she said, holding them up before his face again. "No labor-saving devices in the Realm. You can come in the afternoon. I'm usually here otherwise. Do call." She smiled radiantly.

"I have to go," Michael said to Savarin.

"Certainly," Savarin said. He accompanied Michael.

"Good-bye, until later," Helena said.

"Bye," Michael said, waving awkwardly. At the end of the alley, Savarin chuckled.

"She likes you, my boy."

Michael merely nodded.

"And I suppose you won't be seeing me as much, or telling me so many interesting things?"

"I'll tell you whatever I learn," Michael said.

"After you tell Helena." Savarin cut off Michael's weak protest with a smile. "No, I understand. Everybody's priorities are for the immediate. I am cursed with an interest in the long-term."

They parted at the outskirts of Euterpe and Michael returned to Halftown, his thoughts crowded and confused.

13

For the first time, life in the Realm had some purpose besides survival and the now-distant goal of returning home. Michael wandered down Halftown's curving market street, thinking of Helena's face, of her lips and the way they moved when she talked to him.

He found the flattened courtyard and picked through the rubble to the front door of Lirg's—now Eleuth's—house. He knocked on the door frame. There was no answer for a moment, then Eleuth swung the door wide open and stared at him, blinking wide-eyed.

"Hello," she said. Her face seemed older, worn.

"You wanted to talk with me?" Michael asked. He compared Eleuth's strange beauty with Helena's brisk familiarity and felt slightly repelled.

"I need company," Eleuth said. "But if you have something to do . . ."

"No," Michael said. Queerly, his repulsion was turning to a distanced kind of attraction, something he could handle. Eleuth motioned for him to come in and closed the door softly behind.

The house was decorated very differently from the human dwellings he had seen: solid-looking, clean wooden furniture draped with rugs and fabrics, lamps burning sweet-scented wax in corners away from the windows, a ceramic brick firepit in the center of the house with a chimney poking through the roof. Thick, intricately patterned rugs hung from iron rods between wall and chimney, dividing the interior into four rooms. He sat on a bench and Eleuth sat across from him on the edge of the firepit, which was dark and covered with a brass mesh screen.

"It's not as if Lirg's dead," she said after a few awkward minutes of silence.

"What will they do with him?" Michael asked.

Eleuth lowered her gaze and reached down to adjust a boot. "He will serve Adonna."

"Whatever that means," Michael said.

"It means he will add his magic to the rituals. That will weaken him. Breeds are not like Sidhe full-bloods. Magic tires us. The more human blood we have, the less power to spare."

"And after that?"

"These are cruel thoughts," Eleuth said, face twisting suddenly. "I'll never see him again, either way. He was a good father."

Her words came slow and sweet. The brief expression of grief smoothed into sadness. The sadder she became, the more Michael was attracted to her. It took very little effort to sit beside her and reach for her hand. For the first time, he felt in control. She looked up at him with tears in her eyes. "What is death like on Earth?"

That took Michael aback. Except for Waltiri, he had never experienced the death of a loved one on Earth. Friends, parents, grandparents were all still living, as far as he knew. Death was an intellectual exercise, something to be imagined and not deeply felt. "Final," he said. "Everybody keeps saying humans have souls and Sidhe don't, but I know a lot of humans who would disagree."

"It makes no difference here," Eleuth said. "So I'm told. Young people must rely a lot on what they're told, no?"

Michael lifted his shoulders. "I suppose."

"Breeds are less constrained then Sidhe. We are already among the lowest. We don't have much farther to fall."

"Humans aren't exactly respected here, either," Michael reminded her.

"But the Sidhe leave them alone. The Umbrals don't come to snatch them away."

"That's because we're useless. We have no magic. Have you done magic?"

Eleuth nodded slowly. "A little. I'm learning, but not quickly."

Michael patted her arm and stood. "I should get back to the Crane Women." He didn't particularly want to go, but he had no idea what more he could do here—or didn't want to consider the possibilities, suddenly.

Eleuth stood, eyes still lowered, and reached to touch the back of his hand with one finger. "When we are alone, we are most vulnerable," she said. She looked up at him. "Both of us need strength."

"I guess that's true," Michael said. There was an awkward moment as he tried to figure out how to say good-bye. Finally, he just smiled and sidled out the door. She looked after him, eyes as wide as when he had entered. Just before the door closed, he saw her turn away with a slow elegance that sent shivers down his arms.

His confusion multiplied as he crossed the stream and walked across the mound to the huts. Grateful none of the Crane Women were outside, he entered his small dwelling and stood with head brushing the ceiling rafters. His face was marked by lines of reddened sunlight gliding down the opposite wall.

Michael wasn't disturbed that night, except by a distant, deep hum that filled the land for a second or two. When that passed, he lay on the plaited reeds and stared up into darkness. For a dizzying moment, it seemed that it wasn't the world that had changed, but himself; that somehow he had twisted around to present a new face. He didn't feel sixteen years old.

He felt full, expectant . . . waiting.

14

Spart roused Michael early the next morning, taking him by the hand and
dragging him from his hut, all the while making strange half-humming, half-
whistling noises. She seemed to be trying for a tune and not quite finding it,
but the closer he listened, the more he realized the sound went beyond tunes.
Before he was awake enough to think clearly, she stopped and strutted around
him, her critical eye sweeping him from head to foot. "Ready?" she asked, halting
before him with hands on hips.

"I suppose I must be," he said.

"We are going on a trip. We will cross the Blasted Plain. You will come
with."

"Okay," he said, swallowing. "Breakfast first?"

Coom emerged from the hut and tossed him a gray-green lime the size of an
orange. Nare offered a crust of bread from the window. He knew better than to
protest; besides, Sidhe food seemed to satisfy more. At least, he was seldom
ravenous.

They walked along the banks of the river in the early morning sun, through
waist-high reeds and feathery-fronded water plants he couldn't identify. Creepers
like green rubber hoses slithered down to the water. Ahead, to the northeast, a
patch of intense blue glittered above the faded orange ribbon that seemed to
drape across the Blasted Plain.

The Crane Women plunged along ahead and behind him. He remembered
some of the landscape from his unexpected journey during the *Kaeli*. After two
hours of steady hiking, they reached grassland that had been hit hard by the
storm. The grass lay bent and disheveled like matted hair.

Four hours later, he recognized the mound where he had awakened, with its
topknot of greener grass, and he saw the border. But the Crane Women veered
northwest, pushing and climbing out of the reeds and following a winding trail.

Three hours later, always coming within view of the border only to veer away,
Michael was tired enough to halt and utter a weak protest. The Crane Women
had been bounding along like children on an outing, acting much younger than

they looked (if he could apply any human age at all to them). "Please!" Michael called out after them. "What are we doing, where are we going?"

Spart waved him along. Michael sighed. He'd given up trying to find motives for what they did. At the very least, the Crane Women were elusive.

And now they eluded him. He had paused and kneeled for a second to untangle his foot from a root, and when he looked up, they were gone. But he was not exactly alone. At the top of a low hill about half a mile away stood a horse—a Sidhe horse, its rider nowhere in sight.

Michael searched the hill nervously with his eyes, then walked toward the animal. An unaccompanied Sidhe horse was unusual in the Pact Lands. He had never seen one, at any rate. As he climbed the gentle slope, the horse lifted its head and whinnied. It trained its ears in his direction and turned on pumping legs to face him. Michael stopped; he felt no need to approach any closer. It might be a trap. A Sidhe could be lying on the other side of the hill, waiting for someone curious.

"Right you are to be cautious," Spart said, rising as if out of the ground a few yards behind him. "Do you know what that is? Do they still have them on Earth?"

"Of course," Michael said. "But not exactly . . . it's a horse."

"The Cascar word is *epon*," Spart said, "a word so old it predates the earliest horses. There were other steeds in those times, stronger, even more noble. They did not last the wars. Shall we have a closer look?"

"If you say so."

"Yes," Spart said. "It is part of what you must learn."

The horse pawed at the dirt and bent to nip blades of grass. As they drew closer, it reared up briefly, then trotted straight for Spart. She held out her broad hand and it buried its nose in her palm, closing its eyes and nuzzling.

The horse's coat, up close, was velvety-shiny, the muscles packed tight beneath. Its legs were long and its head narrow and lean, almost bony. The mane hung low on the neck but was well kept; the horse had been curried recently.

"Where's it from?" he asked.

"It crossed the Blasted Plain just a short while ago," Spart said. She gently slapped a cloud of golden dust from its withers. "Its masters await us beyond the borders. It will guide us across, and if we stay close, the *sani* will protect us." She held her palm out; flecks glittered on it like bright chips of mica. "Would you like to ride?"

Michael shook his head. "I've never ridden a horse."

"You'll have to learn. Should it be now?" She wasn't asking Michael; she was addressing Coom and Nare, who walked casually up the other side of the hill, Nare with a blade of grass between her lips. They nodded noncommittally.

Spart squinted at Michael and shrugged. "His choice," she said. "The horse is borrowed, after all." She walked around the animal, feelings its flanks and withers, caressing its hindquarters.

Nare chuckled throatily and squatted a few yards away pulling the grass from her lips and inspecting it. "When you plan to ride a horse," she said, "you walk up to it, look it in the eye, say, 'You are my soul, I am your master!' Believe it. Then . . . you mount."

"Is that all?" Michael asked. Coom laughed, a sound like dragging slate between clenched teeth.

"Yes," Spart said. "But to believe it, you must be able to ride like the Sidhe. No human can ride like the Sidhe. They already have souls. There is little room for a horse."

"I might be able to learn," Michael said defiantly. "Maybe I'll ride just as well."

"Then try." Spart cupped her hands to provide a stirrup. "Left foot up, right foot over."

"No saddle?"

"Unless you brought it with you."

He put his left foot in her hands, grabbed hold of the lower neck and swung up and over. For a moment he hung in empty air, and then he landed on his hands and knees, the wind knocked out of him. The horse stood a few paces away, shaking its head and snorting.

"If you can't ride a horse," Nare said, watching from where she sat, "act like one."

Michael got to his feet. "It's fast," he said.

"Some other time," Spart said. Once again, he felt his worth drop to zero. To regain some of his pride, he approached the horse a second time and patted its flank. It turned its pearly gray head toward him, large silver eyes blinking enigmatically. "Ho," he said. "Hi ho. Something like that. Are we going to be friends?"

The Sidhe horse flicked its tail at an imaginary fly and lifted one foreleg. "Listen," Michael whispered in its ear, after pulling the head down gently to his level with one hand on its nose. "I'm in bad enough shape without your dragging me any lower. They think I'm a klutz," he nodded at the Crane Women, "and I agree. If you won't be my soul, how about just being my buddy?"

The horse raised its head, butting his hand away, then cocked its ears in his direction and gently bumped its nose into his chest.

"Is it possible you have a way with horses?" Spart asked.

"I wouldn't know."

"Try again," Spart suggested. "If you succeed, maybe you won't have to cross the Blasted Plain on foot." She held her hands out to form a stirrup again. He stepped up and swung over onto the horse's back. The horse wriggled its back muscles and shook its head but stood steady. Michael wrapped his legs tighter and asked, with a small quaver, "Do I ride it now?"

Spart's eyes turned west, where a cluster of three Sidhe horsemen moved slowly across the grassland about a mile away.

"Who's that?" Michael asked.

"The Wickmaster," Spart said, blinking slowly and reaching to take the horse by the chin.

"Why is he here?"

"Wants to meet the ones who wait for us," Nare said, standing. "Come. Let's cross now."

The Crane Women walked down the opposite side of the hill. The horse followed. Michael had no idea how to give it directions, and now did not seem the best time to ask. Alyons and two coursers paced their animals about a hundred yards away, both groups heading toward the edge of the Pact Lands and the haze beyond.

The Crane Women paused at the border. The green grass stopped along a geometrically perfect line, to be replaced by the glistening black and umber sand of the Blasted Plain. Nare bent to scoop up some of the sand; it trickled between her fingers as light and lifeless as the dust in a vacuum cleaner bag. She brushed her hand on her pants, face creased with distaste.

"We'll walk close to you, to the horse," Spart said. Coom inspected the horse's flanks closely.

"Is it the dust that protects us? I mean, the *sani*."

"Part," Coom said. She, too, kept an eye on Alyons and the coursers, who had stopped at the border about sixty yards to the north. Alyons eyed them coldly, caressing his golden horse's shoulder with sure, smooth strokes. Michael wondered why the Wickmaster wasn't acting more boldly.

Nare crossed first. The horse followed reluctantly, carrying Michael, its flanks rippling. "Forty miles," Spart said, pointing east. "Desolation. Ruin of war. Good training ground. But you should be careful. Adonna buries its mistakes; dig deep enough beneath the Realm and you'll find them again."

The tortured spires of once-molten rock rose on all sides, some bending back to form loops and arches. The ground opened up in cracks and chasms, farting sulfurous wisps and acrid mists. Scattered over the terrain were pools of churning yellow-orange liquid like pus-filled wounds. Michael's eyes smarted sharply until Spart told him to bend down and administered a dark viscous cream high on each cheek. There was nothing she could do for his sense of smell, however. The dust billowed thick and irritating around them. Michael took a strip of cloth from Coom and tied it over his nose and mouth; the others did the same. His nose ran constantly. Whatever dignity he gained by being on horseback, he lost by snuffling beneath the cloth.

He worried that they weren't carrying food and water. If they stayed for any length of time, the oversight would be unfortunate; they would find no sustenance on the Blasted Plain.

By dusk, they had made it to a flat pan of rock topped by smaller, sharp-edged boulders. Michael dismounted to help them clear a space about four yards across, lifting and tossing the boulders carefully to avoid slicing his hands. Then Coom took a small wood wand from her pouch and drew a circle in the dirt around the clearing. "Rest here," she said.

"Will the circle keep things out?" Michael asked, thinking of pentagrams.

"No," Coom said. She didn't elaborate on its purpose. Twenty yards behind them, Alyons and his coursers halted but did not bother to dismount.

The orange light oppressed. Michael was anxious to move on but Nare shook her head firmly. The Crane Women sat within the circle and Michael stood near the center. The horse stood beside him, head lowered, eyes half-closed. It looked very tired. "Are we resting for the horse's sake?" he asked, voice muffled by the scarf. The Crane Women, like the horse, had also lowered their heads. None of them answered. "I get it," he said. "Something saps the horse's strength when it's here, but it protects us . . ." They neither affirmed nor denied his theory.

A heavy brown cloud flowed above their heads, riding a pseudopod of gray-orange mist. Each liquid particle in the mist was as large as a drop of rain but did not fall. The mist swung around the circle but did not enter.

Alyons and his coursers were outside the periphery of the cloud. They stared intently at the Crane Women and Michael, who fancied he could feel Alyons' hatred even at this distance.

An hour later, Spart and Coom stood up abruptly. Michael shook his head; to his surprise, he had fallen asleep standing up.

He offered the horse to Nare, who mounted without comment. Spart broke the drawn circle with her foot and they continued east. The Sidhe followed not far behind.

Darkness was coming, and the Crane Women hastened to leave the Blasted Plain before nightfall. Michael's feet kept getting stuck in the dust, much worse than sand at a beach; he was soon exhausted and regretted giving up the horse.

With sunset—transformed by the orange haze into a sinister ritual of darkening brown sky and ribbons of ascending tan and ochre—they neared another sharply defined border. What lay beyond wasn't clear; the air thickened at that point, revealing only shadowy presences that could have been tall boulders or the tops of trees.

The horse picked up its pace and they had to run to keep up. Michael did his best, but was the last across the border. For a second, he had a terrifying notion that if the Crane Women left him behind, he might not be able to cross by himself; but there no force tried to prevent him.

"Welcome to the Realm proper," Spart said.

Trees! Huge, spreading leafy canopies rose before them, muting the last of the daylight into green murkiness. The air smelled clean and sweet and felt moist and cool. The dust that had accumulated on their skin and clothing sloughed off, leaving them hot and sweaty, but not besmirched.

The horse cantered to a grassy glade to crop an emerald-green dinner. Nare hopped from her mount and sauntered up to a tree, which she patted with her long-fingered hands, grinning broadly. Michael stretched out his arms and inhaled, soaking up the coolness and greenness and peace.

For as far as he could see in the dusk, the trunks of trees rose in well-spaced disorder. Between them grew shrubs thick with red and purple berries, tall lilies with white flowers delicately fringed blood-red, patches of blue flowers abutting the glades.

The forest seemed surreal in its perfection. After a few minutes, Michael became uneasy again. He looked back to the border, with its abrupt barrier of orange haze, to see where Alyons and the coursers were. They were not visible.

Spart approached him with both hands behind her back. Her grin was more subtle than Nare's. Coom sat on the lowest limb of a tree, watching him like a bird.

Withdrawing her left hand, Spart revealed a flower. It didn't belong to any of the flowering plants he had spotted—it was translucent, as if made from a soft glass. It could have been plastic except for the delicate tracery on its petals. She seemed to be offering it to him, so he reached out to accept. She snatched it back and hid it behind long, fanned fingers.

"What color is it?" she asked.

"Yellow," he said.

She pulled away her hand. The flower was bright blue.

"Okay, blue, but it looked like—"

"The Realm is not like Earth. On Earth, all things sit on a base of chaos, as here, but the foundations are much finer. The foundations of the Realm are coarse. Everything is open to suggestion. On Earth, the chaos is hooked into stability by a law which says you can never win . . . you understand?"

Michael shook his head.

Spart sighed and held the flower closer. "Earth is a more accomplished creation. In the Realm, everything is fluid. Look. What color is the flower?"

"Still blue," he said, but as he said it, he realized the flower had been yellow all along. "I'm . . . I'm sorry. It's yellow."

"Since you cannot win even *betlim,* a small combat," Spart said, "you must be like the flower. Suggest! Take advantage of the fluidity, the seams of the Realm. Magic may be beyond your reach, but not suggestion." She held the yellow flower out to him. This time she let him hold it, but as her fingers released it, Spart herself vanished. Nare and Coom and the horse as well were gone. Michael fumbled the flower and it fell to the long green grass, landing on three dew-flecked stalks.

The flower was pink.

Michael sat, then lay back on the grass, puzzled by what Spart had just told him. Nearby, the flower wavered on its tripod of grass stalks in a lazy, rich breeze. He smelled the mingled scent of tea roses and jasmine. Night was falling rapidly and the sky turned deep blue, with subtle highlights of magenta. The woods loomed black. Wind soughed between the trees, waving the shadow limbs back and forth hypnotically. Michael felt his eyelids closing . . .

"We have company."

He jerked awake. Nare squatted beside him with another stalk of grass held in her lips. She pointed to a second group gathered around a small, bright fire about forty feet away.

"They're Sidhe!" Michael whispered. But they weren't Alyons and his coursers, who were still not to be seen. Five males with long hair and beards, dressed in gorgeous metallic reds and greens and blues, circled the fire, glancing into the darkness in the direction of Nare and Michael. A sixth appeared, younger than the others, his suit white with black checks. Whether their clothing was armor or thick garments, Michael couldn't tell, but the portions limned by the fire dazzled his eyes.

He turned and saw Coom to one side of the group, conferring with a white-haired, white-faced Sidhe wearing velvety black robes. As the Sidhe moved, Michael saw rich gray patterns in his robes—or rather, suspended just above the fabric, for they seemed to float, and changed with every motion.

"Who are they?" Michael asked.

"They are from the Irall," Nare said. "They've chosen an initiate. They bring him to us for training."

"Why to you?"

"Because we're older than most Sidhe. We know the old ways, the old disciplines." Her expression spoke volumes to Michael: at last, the Crane Women had someone interesting to train, someone worth the bother.

The younger Sidhe detached himself from the fire and walked to the perimeter of the encampment. He braced against the smooth massive trunk of a tree and let himself slide down on his haunches. He peeled a piece of fruit, seemingly unaware that Nare and Michael were just a few yards away

"What is he being initiated into?" Michael asked.

"The young one is entering *temelos,* the circuit around priesthood. He is in for rough times, very rough indeed. The priesthood is not easily arrived at, nor easily kept."

"What's his name?"

"Biridashwa," she said. "We will call him Biri."

Michael looked back toward the border and the brown darkness of the Blasted Plain. He could make out distant red glows like lava fissures creeping up the spires of rock; flitting green balls; and high above the plain, a small lone sphere of lightning, silently flashing.

Then he spotted another fire glowing deep in the woods. Its light was broken by three shapes: Alyons and his coursers.

"What do they want?" Michael asked, gesturing. "They keep following us."

Nare shook her head. "The Wickmaster wishes to speak to the Sidhe of the Irall. He won't get a chance."

"Why?"

Nare smiled a crooked smile like the one she often used to express her opinion of Michael's abilities. "Why do you think Alyons is Wickmaster of the Pact Lands, and not of his own circuit in the Realm proper?"

"I don't know," Michael said. "Why?"

"Too many questions," Nare said, and kept silent for the rest of the night.

15

og drifted through the trees and over the camps, dropping a glistening layer of dew on the grass, flowers and Michael. He came awake to the sound of heavy bootsteps nearby, and rolled onto his back, alarmed. The young Sidhe stood two strides away, white and black against the gray, face pale in the early morning.

"I am requested to see you are awake," Biri said. He looked tense, unhappy. The forefingers and thumbs on both his hands rubbed together.

"I'm awake," Michael said, getting to his knees. He was in awe of the young Sidhe. His companions seemed so different from Alyons and his coursers. Michael tried to penetrate the fog and find the Wickmaster, but saw only bright silver and great tree shadows. He brushed the dew from his face and arms and shivered.

"They haven't taught you *hyloka?*" Biri asked.

Michael shook his head. "Whatever that is."

"I'm told we will train together. Perhaps we can help each other."

"You're going to be a priest."

Biri looked at the ground "My guardians will leave soon. I'll cross the Blasted Plain with you. Where are the *Geen Krona?*"

"The what?"

"The Crane Women."

"Not far, I'm sure." But he was never sure about the Crane Women.

Three tall figures stepped from the mist and strode toward the camp. Michael stood quickly. He immediately recognized Alyons' slender, powerful shape. They passed within five or six paces of Michael and Biri, ignoring them, and halted just beyond the Sidhe camp. Biri backed up and whispered to Michael. "They followed you here?"

Michael nodded. "Alyons doesn't like me."

The Wickmaster spoke in Cascar with the guardian dressed in black. The coursers stood motionless to one side, in casually defensive poses, while the guardians looked upon them with unconcealed distaste.

"He's asking for a new audience with the *Darud,*" Biri said.

"Who's that?"

"The chief of the *Maln*, the Black order. That's Tarax—the one in the black *sepla*. Alyons used to be a member, but he committed some crime. He was punished by being sent to the Pact Lands to oversee humans and Breeds."

"What are they saying now?"

Tarax had half-turned from Alyons and approached one of the coursers. A few words were exchanged and the courser backed away, bowing slightly.

"Tarax has told Alyons to be thankful for what he has. I think Tarax berates the courser for some error in ritual before a member of the *Maln.*"

Michael watched Tarax closely, fascinated by the movements of the white-haired Sidhe. "Is he older than the others?"

"A human might think so. Age doesn't matter much to the Sidhe. Especially here."

"Well, *is* he?" Michael persisted.

"I don't know," Biri said. As if suddenly aware he was speaking to a mere human, Biri stiffened and took a step back.

Alyons bowed to Tarax and turned, gesturing for his Sidhe to follow him away from the camp. His eye caught Michael's and held; the Wickmaster's face showed no expression, but Michael felt his hatred nonetheless.

"He's very angry now," Biri said. "I think the Crane Women have been talking with Tarax. Alyons was hoping for leniency. Tarax told him there is no such thing among the Sidhe."

"Great," Michael said. "Now he'll really have it in for us."

"I don't think so," Biri said. "Not as long as I'm here. The Crane Women have an honored status, especially when they train a novice. They are no longer just old Breeds. Alyons doesn't dare displease them."

"And when you're gone?"

Coom descended the trunk of a nearby tree and jumped to the ground with a light thump. She brushed bits of bark from her clothing and squinted at Alyons and his coursers as they vanished into the fog. Nare walked up behind Michael and Biri, carrying fruit in a newly-woven grass mat.

"Breakfast," she said, laying it between them. "Eat well. We cross the border this evening. It's best to be nourished, but not sated, when we cross. This is our last meal today."

"Why cross this evening?" Michael asked. "Isn't it more dangerous?"

Coom snorted. Nare tossed him a blue fruit similar to the one he had seen in the between-house. He caught the fruit and turned it in his hands. Half of it was furry and soft like a peach, sky-blue; the other half dark blue, apple-hard and shiny. At no point on its surface did it show a stem or other blemish.

Spart stood a few yards away, near a sapling. "Eat," she said.

AT MID-DAY, THE Sidhe brought their horses forward and mounted. Tarax approached Spart and handed her a packet of *sani*; there would be no horse to protect them on the return trip. Instead, they would have to rely on Biri's pure Sidhe magic, undeveloped as it was.

Tarax held out his hands and Biri clasped them. The look that passed between them was one of long acquaintance, even dedication, but no apparent affection.

Tarax broke the clasp first. Before departing, he turned to Michael and surveyed him coldly. "So this is the Flesh Egg's favored, is it?" he said, his voice deep and level. "To be trained with my Biri, by the oldest of the Breeds."

Having delivered these few obvious words, Tarax returned to his group and they mounted. The shadows around the trees seemed to double and shift—and horses and Sidhe were gone.

Biri sighed. "You are the first human he has spoken to in centuries. The last one . . . best not to describe what happened to *him.*"

When the shadows of the trees fell long and the sky changed hue, the Crane Women led Biri and Michael from the forest, moving south to cross the border at another point. Michael paced steadily behind Spart as they traversed a brief, emerald-azure savanna. Beyond the high, moist grassland stood an orderly row of waxy brown rocks, shining in the sunset like polished wood. The highest was about thirty feet, the lowest barely a stepping stone. Where the rocks straddled the border, they became blackened and cracked, tumbled to one side. Nare took the giant slabs one by one, climbing to the highest and jumping from rock to rock, the others following until they stood on the border, which plainly divided one boulder about ten feet tall.

Beyond the border, dust piled high around the rocks. Biri crossed first, staying upright as he slid and ran down an incline of dust. Coom and Nare followed. Spart tapped Michael on the shoulder, urging him ahead. He tried to imitate Biri's grace but ended up sliding down the incline on his butt. They quickly ran ahead to avoid the acrid clouds they had raised.

"Now we move as a group," Spart said. "Close together." Biri brought out the bag of *sani* and sprinkled a little on each of them, muttering something in Cascar as he did so. They walked due west until the dusk settled into darkness, and then halted. Michael looked around at the orange band of fading light on the horizon, at the dust now inky black, at the gluey arches and spires to the north, and shivered.

"Why are we stopping?"

"Because we won't be able to see much longer," Spart said. This time it was Biri who removed a wand from his white-and-black checked coat and drew a circle around them. Where the lines joined, he sprinkled more *sani,* then stepped back.

"Now watch," Spart said as they gathered and sat in the middle of the circle. "See what even a young Sidhe can do in the Realm."

Biri reached out with his long, muscle-knotted arms and touched a spot directly before him with his index finger. The muscles in his face tightened and his lips moved silently. The rock began to glow, and presently the cold was dispelled by a steady pulse of heat. The glowing spot mesmerized Michael. "Will I ever be able to do that?" he asked Spart in a whisper.

She shook her head, not in denial, but as if the question irritated her. Michael leaned back, frowning. *Well, will I?* he asked himself. He held his hands out to the warmth. He was thirsty—he had swallowed some dust and it tasted like the bitter part of a bad apple—and hungry, but he knew better than to ask about food.

Presently his legs cramped and he unfolded them and lay back. The others remained sitting, staring at the glow. He leaned on his elbow, stretching his legs behind Spart. His eyelids began to droop.

He awoke, his whole body jerking and trembling. His eyes opened and he became aware that he was standing, the toes of his shoes on the edge of the circle Biri had drawn. He faced away from the heat into darkness. Something urged him to cross over the line, but he couldn't.

In the fixed starglow, Michael made out a purple shape beyond the circle. Each time he blinked, it changed form and appeared closer. The battle between the urge to step over the line and the strong desire to stay inside the circle jerked him harder now; his legs and arms twitched like marionette limbs in the hands of an inept puppeteer.

The purplish shape was close enough now to stand face to face with him, but it had no face. The shape consisted of smooth rings of varying sizes stacked atop each other, with several more rings gliding up and down the thing's exterior. Michael blinked and the shape became an assemblage of irregular rounded blobs.

He blinked again, and the shape was his mother, smiling and beckoning with her arms.

Again, and it was Helena, waving for him to follow her as she stepped back.

"It's a little *obvious*, isn't it?" Biri said, standing beside him. "You haven't met one of these before?"

Michael shook his head. "What is it?"

"An abortion. A creation too inconsistent to match up with the Realm."

"One of Adonna's mistakes?"

"Gods don't make mistakes," Biri said solemnly, with no touch of irony. "What are you going to do?"

Michael laughed hysterically. "What should I do?"

"Do you wish to see it as it really is?"

"Should I? I mean no, no."

"I've seen them many times," Biri said. "They are mostly harmless to a Sidhe, even to capable Breeds. Only humans are susceptible. It was the power of the Isomage that liberated them from their deep tombs. The Blasted Plain has much worse to offer."

"Can it hurt me?"

"It can do worse than kill you. Whenever a human child is born, one of these is liberated. The child has no reservoir of waiting souls from which to draw, so its search allows certain patterns within one of these to enter the Pact Lands. The child is branded. The same could happen to you if you slept here outside a circle."

"You mean, I'd be possessed?"

"These are not intelligences. They are abortions. You would be more *eaten* than possessed. Your soul is a rare thing here, heavily armored within your body. What happens to it when they crack that armor is not explainable in your languages."

Michael tried to retreat from the edge of the circle, but couldn't. "I'm stuck."

"It cannot hurt you in here. You can play with it, in a sense; it can no more leave you than you can back away. You can learn from it."

"I don't want to. I want it to go away and leave me alone."

"A Sidhe uses the abortions to prove his interior—"

"I don't care!" Michael shouted. "I'm not a Sidhe! Make it go away."

"I can't," Biri said. "Only you can release it." The novice walked away, smiling gently, and squatted near the glowing rock.

"Spart," Michael said, "help me!"

No reply. He couldn't turn his head to see the Crane Women. The shape now resembled Eleuth. She looked very sad, as if she had lost something vital and he was responsible. She looked down. She became a cylindrical *something*, lines of light crawling up its surface like worms, leaving trails of fire.

He tried to find a clue within himself. They wouldn't leave him in this fix (he hoped) if they didn't believe he had some way of getting out of it. He had to think it through . . .

No, in an emergency, thought would be too slow. What if humans had something to make up for their lack of magic, something instinctive? He searched, waited, but the necessary remedy wouldn't come forth.

The cylinder split like a pared cucumber, revealing an interior compounded of offal and tiny, unidentifiable skeletons. The bones of the skeletons linked and spun, churning the fleshy parts into liquid, which streamed through the lengthening slits and spattered on the dark ground. The segments became slithering smooth snakes without discernible head or tail. They rolled into spirals and the spirals lifted to vertical positions, then met at their edges.

They flowed into the shape of Arno Waltiri. He sat upright in a coffin, sallow-fleshed, eyes open but dead and sunken. His jaw fell abruptly and music came out, sharp and painful. Michael's skin seemed to blister as the music surrounded him. The corpse flopped forward, draped over the lower half of the coffin lid, and revealed another body behind it: his own.

"Wait," Michael protested. It was stealing all these images from inside him. If he could stop the flow . . .

"Wait," the ragged Michael in the coffin mimicked, shaking its head from side to side.

"Stop," Michael said. He shut his eyes and concentrated on doors closing, dams cutting off water at their sluice gates, capping toothpaste tubes, corking bottles. He tightened his mind down until his entire brain seemed to shrink and harden. *You can't steal anything more. I've put a lock on it. Loose minds must not entwine, must not combine—*

Michael opened his eyes and saw nothing but darkness beyond the circle. He relaxed; he was in control again. He backed away and lay down again by the glowing rock, glancing at Biri, who lay on his back, head turned in Michael's direction.

The Sidhe nodded and closed his eyes.

THEY SPENT TWO days and three nights in the desolation, Spart engaging Michael in endless and repetitive drill with sticks, running him over the sharp boulders until his feet burned in agony and his shins and hands were scraped raw. The dust in his wounds stung like acid and left tiny black lines slow to fade.

When he wasn't training, Michael watched Nare and Coom preparing Biri. The young Sidhe endured everything stoically and performed his exercises flawlessly. The most spectacular thing he did was to reduce a boulder nine or ten feet across to rubble by running around it and chanting. When the dust had cleared, Biri stood atop the heap, brushing his clothes down. Nare and Coom walked around him, features blank.

Michael knew they were much more pleased with Biri than they were with him, and it was obvious why.

Despite Biri's apparent ease, Michael was seldom able to engage the Sidhe in any meaningful conversation beyond amenities and Biri's occasional advice, which galled Michael even more than silence.

"Why do you even bother with me?" Michael asked Spart. "You could train the Sidhe to do whatever you want."

Spart agreed and shook her head in despair. "We do indeed seem to enjoy wasting time," she admitted wryly. "It's fortunate we are immortal and can afford to be foolish."

Only on the last night on the Blasted Plain, as they prepared to cross the border into the Pact Lands, did Biri open up a bit. "When I am done here, I have a good thought, and a bad," he told Michael.

"What?" he asked, his tone hardly concealing his resentment. If Biri had not answered, Michael would not have much cared, but the Sidhe pointed across the Plain and said softly, "It is good to go back to the Sidhe territories, but it is less good to fulfill my purpose there."

"What *will* you do with the Breeds you've captured?" Michael blurted. "When you're a priest, I mean."

For the first time, Michael saw Biri become visibly angry. He advanced on Michael and stood over him. "The Faer do not worship Adonna *that way*," he said, his voice cold and crisp.

"Some of the Sidhe do," Michael said. Spart looked between them curiously, as if anticipating some kind of fight and perhaps welcoming it.

"*Not* the Faer," Biri reiterated, backing away. He glanced at Michael from under his brows and returned to his preparations. Michael sucked in a deep breath.

"Hold it," Spart commanded, continuing to stare at him curiously. Michael held his breath, inwardly fuming at the indignity. "Not your breath, your mind. Hold it in again."

Michael let his breath out with a whoosh. "I don't understand," he said.

"Just now, Biri probed you to learn your intentions. It was a very young thing for him to do, and he didn't succeed."

"He tried to read my mind?"

Spart shrugged and took Michael's hand. "You are indeed a man-child," she said. No further explanation was offered.

Night had fallen when Nare ordered them to follow behind her. Michael walked ahead of Spart, who was at the end of the line. He stumbled less often. "I'm getting more agile," he said to no one in particular, enjoying this small accomplishment. And he had to try extra hard for the next few minutes to keep from making himself a liar.

Coom carried a stick which she had caused to glow at one end. The dim yellow luminosity was all they had to travel by. Michael didn't ask why they couldn't wait until morning. He felt some trepidation about what they might encounter, with no circle to protect them, but it seemed part of the plan, the test.

They marched down into a gully and then followed the long depression. The plain was silent except for the sound of their footsteps. Michael lost himself in the rhythm of putting one foot ahead of the other, keeping up with the circle of light from the glowing stick.

"Ssst," Nare hissed. Michael looked up and followed the direction of the eyes of those ahead. On the edge of the gully, outlined against the stars, sat a giant inverted skull, its blunt jaw poking at the sky.

The group stopped and Coom raised the stick higher. The object rose at least thirty feet above them. As Michael peered closer, he saw it wasn't a skull, but a huge shell. The occupant—or occupants—of the shell curled over the rim of the gully, long blue-black slug-like things protruding from the skull's "eyes." They joined just beyond the two holes, forming an elongated body which split again into three stalks, each sporting a mouth like a pair of toothed dinner plates hinged with filamented flesh. The stalks waved above the group, mouths opening and closing with faint clacking sounds.

Where the skull's nose would have been, an arm with a triangular cross-section slithered, its end covered with tentacles, each tentacle tipped with a blob of flesh that glowed in the dark. The creature or creatures waved this arm like a watchman's lantern.

Michael stood his ground only because the others did so. His instinct was to either run or have a heart attack. The breath in his lungs rasped like a file cutting steel. His pumping blood sounded loud enough to shake the rocks loose. Indeed, a few pebbles clattered down into the gully as the thing slithered on, and it turned its stalks as if to peer after them.

Biri's face expressed unabashed awe, his expression intensely watchful, fascinated.

The monstrosity either didn't see them or ignored them, passing with cruel slowness. More rocks clattered, the stalks swiveled again, and the skull-snail dragged its shell away from the gully with the sound of huge fingernails on acres of sandpaper. Michael shuddered uncontrollably and sat down. Biri looked back at him and made as if to wipe his own brow, a gesture which endeared him to Michael enormously. Spart poked Michael in the ribs to get him moving again.

ONLY A FEW minutes later, they crossed over into the grassy prairie of the Pact Lands, not far from the river. The group made it to the mound by early morning, and Michael went to his hut and collapsed.

He shook from exhaustion and emotion. Not until his body had shivered itself free did he fall over on his side and sleep.

Outside the hut, Biri stood to face the newly risen sun, holding his small wand high in the air. He then sat on his chosen spot and his head slumped forward. He, too, slept.

16

ichael sat up and rubbed his eyes; he had felt, rather than heard, Biri's presence outside his hut. "Yes? What is it?"

"My wood was delivered last night," Biri whispered. "I've built my quarters."

Michael pushed through the door cover. A new hut, little different from his own, sat on the mound about twenty feet away. He was not fully awake and felt awkward in the Sidhe's presence. "Good."

"Before I met you, I'd never spoken to a human being. I'd never even heard of the Pact Lands until my journey began."

Michael's bowl of porridge waited to one side of his door. He bent to pick it up and began scooping the warm goop into his mouth with two fingers. "Where are you from?" he asked. "I mean, not that it would do me any good to know . . . I'm pretty ignorant about everything outside the Pact Lands."

"Shall we trade stories?" Biri asked. "The Geen Krona believe if we train together, we should behave honorably, and not fight or argue. I am very interested in where you came from, and how you traveled here."

Michael told Biri about his circuitous route to the Realm. Biri nodded at the key points, but frowned when Michael mentioned the figure in the flounced dress. Michael put aside his empty bowl and said, "Now, you."

"To the north, across broad savannas and beyond *Nebchat Len*—that's a lake, almost a sea, very deep—there is a forest called *Konhem*. That's where I was born." He paused, glancing at Michael from the corners of his deep-set eyes. "Do you know much about the Sidhe?"

Michael shook his head.

"We are seldom told who our parents are, especially when we've been chosen before birth, sometimes before conception, for the priesthood. By tradition, our fathers are ashamed of showing weakness by loving a female and getting her with child. That is why young Sidhe are so rare." He turned his gaze toward Halftown. "I think there are more Breeds born than Sidhe. At any rate, I've never met another Sidhe younger than myself. And our mothers return to their clan after giving birth, leaving the children to be cared for by the Ban Sidhe. They are the

Mafoc Mar, the Bag Mothers, clanless females who serve the members of the Maln, the Black Order." He stopped and sketched a design in the dirt with his wand. When he lifted his wand, the design rubbed itself out. "Do you understand?"

"I think so," Michael said. "I don't speak much Cascar, but I've heard of the Ban Sidhe. On Earth, they're supposed to come and claim the dead."

Biri cocked his ears forward slightly, something Michael had never seen a Breed do. "The clanless Bans not in charge of raising young take Sidhe dead to the Arborals, or to their tombs, whichever is willed."

"Where is this forest, and the savanna? We met in a forest . . ."

"That was a small forest, just a patch. The savanna—the *Plata*—stretches around and beyond this patch, to Konhem, the deepest, darkest forest in the Realm. I lived in Konhem for a time. Then I was taken into the mountains called *Chebal Malen,* the Black Mountains. I was given up to Tarax . . ."

Biri leaned forward and stared into Michael's eyes. An extraordinary thing happened. Michael's view of the mound and the Crane Women's hut faded and he seemed to stand before the white-haired, black-robed Sidhe, peering up from a low angle. Tarax stooped and gently grasped a small, slender hand—not Michael's, but Biri's. That faded—Michael could vaguely see the huts again—and was replaced by the vista of an enormous flat-topped mountain with jagged slopes dusted by swirling drifts of snow. Then he stood on a perfectly flat plain, surfaced with cyclopean blocks of stone stretching for miles on all sides, cloud shadows flowing over the stonework. Ribbons of cloud flew straight up from the slopes on the opposite side. "The Stone Field is not on the highest mountain in the Chebal Malen, but it is very cold and harsh there. Tarax built a four-room caersidh out of stone and I lived there for many seasons while he tutored me. Finally, I was considered worthy and he took me to the Sklassa, the fortress of the Black Order. Until now, I have never known anything else." He smiled at Michael. "The trip across the forest and savanna was wonderful. I have never seen so much change."

"What does a priest do?" Michael asked.

Biri drew back and sighed. "That I cannot tell you."

"I mean, do you attend Adonna, take care of sacrifices, that sort of thing? I'm just curious what—

"I cannot tell!" Biri said, standing swiftly. "No human must ever know what happens in the Irall. I've spoken too freely already." He stalked off to his hut, leaving Michael to ponder Sidhe moods and Sidhe secrets.

If anything, he thought, it was the Black Order, the Maln, that sounded like it should be kept secret. Was training novices the only thing the Black Order did? Even among the Sidhe, Tarax had been impressive—if only for overshadowing and cowing Alyons.

The Crane Women walked up the side of the mound opposite Halftown, pushing their knobby knees with their hands as if going up some long, exhausting grade. They cackled softly among themselves and shook their heads. Nare saw Michael sitting on his boulder and straightened sharply, regarding him with large, accusing eyes.

Their faces are so strange, he thought. *So human, but the way their eyes curve up, the way they blink almost from three-quarters to one side...*

Spart called across the mound, "Boy! You'll come with us today." He sighed, climbed down from the rock, and reached into the hut for his shoes.

They walked several miles away from Halftown, due east. He wondered why Biri wasn't going with them and Coom seemed to hear him think. "Sidhe trains different," she said. "Share some, not today." She cackled softly again and Michael felt his neck hair rise.

"He already knows what you'll need to learn today," Spart said. She walked ahead of the rest, holding out her wand and pointing it here and there at the horizon. Soon a mist began to rise, swooping across the river and enveloping them. Spart rejoined the group, and they squatted to rest—all for Michael's sake, he imagined, since the Crane Women never seemed to tire.

"Do you remember the color of the flower, boy?" Spart asked, shuffling nearer and peering intently at his face. She grimaced, wrinkles distorting the snakes and vines tattooed in red and purple across her face.

"I remember it changing," he said.

"What advantage does the Realm give you?" she asked.

"There are ways to change it."

"What is magic, boy?"

"I ... I don't know. Yet."

"Will you ever know?"

He didn't answer. Coom stalked closer, goose down hair frizzing in the mist. Nare stood behind him; he could hear her steady, patient breathing.

"Some think the Crane Women will live forever, training and teaching," Spart said. "Do you believe that?"

Michael shrugged, then nodded. "I don't see why not."

Spart chuckled in the back of her throat and pushed her wand into the dirt. "Biri is a curious novice. He made you *see* today. What do you think of the Sidhe now?"

"Strange," Michael said, squinting in a stray shaft of sunlight.

"Will you ever understand Sidhe, or Breeds?"

"Probably not," Michael said.

"Because you're human?" Nare offered.

"No, because you're Breeds ... and he's Sidhe," Michael countered, uncertain what he meant.

"At this stage, your mind is all confusion," Spart said, tying in to his uncertainty. "You don't think clearly. You are slack. You can't feel what we teach. Your spirit is like a limp sail on Nebchat Len."

"You have sailboats?" Michael asked.

Spart sighed. "You see? Every breeze pushes you this way and that. Now listen close. We have less time to teach you now. Other tasks await us." She looked at her companions. "Less time than you'll think. You must learn quickly. Remember the flower. Remember, the Realm works for you. And *you* ..." She stood. "You have less time." She pulled a flower from her pouch and dropped it to the ground before him. "What color?"

"Blue," he said. He looked up from the flower. The Crane Women were gone. He turned quickly, trying to catch some glimpse of them in the mist. They had deserted him.

The flower was yellow.

A deep, bass humming ascended and swept over the grass like the passage of a helicopter, the mist blew away in translucent spirals. The grass spread out in green and yellow fans and wind scoured his face.

Michael stumbled a few steps backward and came up against a square-cut stone marker about as tall as he was. A few yards away, a shadow in the mist, stood another marker. Both had been carved with circled swastikas that faced each other over a stretch of fresh-cropped grass.

The more the mist cleared, the more obvious it became that a kind of path was aligned between the markers; not a path traveled by horses, people or even carts, however. The grass had not been trampled—only neatly cut short.

Again came the humming and the sensation of motion overhead. The hair on his arms bristled and his whole body tingled.

Something white wavered at the boundary of the mist, a few dozen feet down the path. It detached itself and swept along, a human-like figure from the waist up, a trailing blur from the waist down. As if Michael didn't exist, the figure passed by and vanished in the opposite haze.

The Sidhe of the air, Michael thought—a Meteoral, like the one he had seen on the road from Lamia's house. He picked up his stick and scurried to the edge of the path, where he squatted in the taller grass, shivering, trying to be inconspicuous.

Several more flew by, the air swirling in their wake. They weren't immaterial but he could almost see through them. They cast only the vaguest of shadows in the muted sunlight. The tops of their heads floated a good eight feet above the ground, and they seemed in proportion to that height. At first he could not tell whether they had male or female features, but he soon realized they were all female, with slender, hard-edged faces and somber expressions. Soon, a steady stream of Meteorals flowed down the path, growing more and more distinct as the sun burned away the mist.

At first, none of them paid him any attention. He tried to hide in the deeper grass, however, and stepped on a dry stick. It snapped loudly. His heart clenched like a fist.

The stream of Meteorals scattered in all directions. Michael heard whispers overhead, then all around, as if they had regrouped and were lowering themselves in an enveloping canopy.

Directly in front of him, the air glimmered and crackled.

His skin tingled painfully as a rush of white filled his view. He caught a glimpse of a hideous, angry long face drawn into a scream, fingers shaped into claws. His cheek stung and he grabbed it with his hand. His fingers came away bloody.

"Sed ac, par na antros sed via?" The voices came from all directions, from a hissing multitude, exhaled like a chill wind.

"You are on a trod," came a softer, no less menacing single voice right next to his ear. He turned slowly to face a Meteoral stooping in the grass. The grass seemed to pass right through her. He could feel her breath on him sweet as ether. "You are the human from the house of the Isomage, no?"

Michael nodded. His legs froze and pins and needles traveled up his thighs.

"You should not be here."

"The Crane Women—"

"Have no *power* over us." The face shimmered and stretched, becoming even more hideous. The eyes were the most substantial things in the face, large, completely white and without pupils. A hand swung up one side of his head and the fingers stretched and clenched. Blood from Michael's cheek dripped onto his jacket.

"They brought me here. Talk to them—"

"We despise Breeds as much as we despise you."

The face vanished. Michael's legs were too numb to support him. He fell back into the grass and cried out through clenched teeth at the pain as the circulation returned to his legs. He looked down at the spots of blood on his shoulder and the front of his jacket, and saw that his clothing had been neatly sliced to ribbons. The leather of his shoes flopped in shreds, as well.

"Help me," he murmured, crawling away from the trod. He left drips of blood and scraps of cloth behind. "Please *help me*. God, please take me back . . ."

A long ribbon of pearly white formed over his head. He looked up, cringing, and saw a chain of Meteorals swoop low above him, each face conveying some new expression of curiosity, anger, irritation, even humor. And with each passage, his clothes twitched, snagged, lifted, becoming more and more ragged. The Meteorals' trailing arms drifted over him like smoke, silently slashing, flaying.

Michael closed his eyes and buried his face in his arms, lowering himself to the ground, certain he was going to die. He just didn't want to see it happen. Where were the Crane Women? Had they done all their work, the weeks of training, just to let him be sectioned like bologna in a deli? He felt a rush of cold air on his naked back. His jacket and shirt had completely fallen away. The first stab of pain hit him, slow, excruciating, as something moved along his back. *No.* He felt a burst of anger. *God damn them all. Why does everyone have to be so cruel, so full of hate? I don't hate them.*

Suddenly, he seemed to be sitting somewhere else, watching but not seeing in the midst of incredible stillness and calm. He had had the same feeling when poetry flowed from his pencil so fast he could not tell from where it came.

A kind of *looseness*, in his hands as much as his head. He watched himself stand, sweep at the air with his stick, grimace. He—that distant Michael, braver and stronger than he could have imagined—seemed to be grinning back at the Sidhe hovering around him.

The stick was little use. He'd have to take advantage of the chaos. Blue flower, yellow, but really pink.

Grass, actually, and air, right here.

He ran, holding the stick before him, knees parting the hip-high grass smoothly. Part of himself had been left behind like a squid's decoy cloud of ink.

Not magic, but interesting; the Meteorals didn't seem to notice where he really was.

Naked, he ran through the sunlight and warm gentle breezes, legs pumping on their own, lungs drawing in and growing, heart leonine. He imagined his heart growling, surrounded by a wind-tossed mane. He imagined himself a glass gazelle, a Sidhe horse turning into a quicksilver blur. The grassland fled beneath him, *afraid* of his feet; he held the center and the Realm passed under, not the other way around.

Meteorals flanked him. He dodged. Blue flower, pink.

Here, he thought in a place below thought, *you can reach down and use your mind to accomplish things impossible on Earth. Because Adonna is not a mature god, and the Realm isn't polished.*

Was that what the Crane Women wanted him to learn?

He dodged, leaving more shadows. The Meteorals swirled around the shadows like snow-devils.

Long after he knew he had escaped, Michael continued to run. No body carried him; he was nothing more than eyes. He could not feel his muscles, only the stick he held before him. He *was* the stick, his body the comet's tail of its flight.

Michael Perrin fell and rolled, stuffing grass and dirt into his mouth. The stick bruised his ribs. He sprang up with legs and arms splayed. His head fell forward and his arms went out from under him.

The whole world suddenly filled with pain. His body demanded to curl up like ash, his muscles burned so badly. His vision clouded, red and uncertain.

He felt his fear again. His heart was a small, tight snake, not a lion. *"God,"* he gasped. "God, please."

"Quiet." Spart stood over him, hands on hips, arms elbowed out like bird wings. She bent and felt his arms and back with a worried frown. He heard Nare and Coom conversing in Cascar to one side.

"You did well," Spart said. "Much too well, actually."

The agony and fear faded. *Is it night?*

No.

17

Did they want him dead? Why did they leave him between the markers—to put him out of the way, so they could concentrate on Biri? Or was there something else—a conspiracy, perhaps—of which Michael knew nothing?

When he opened his eyes and stared at the roof of his hut, it all seemed like a dream. In the Realm, however, there was no dreaming... perhaps because one cannot dream within a dream. In the mind, anything can happen. Anything can be accomplished, given control of the milieu, knowledge of the very convenient underlying rules. Was that what the Crane Women were trying to tell him?

Spart leaned over and peered into his face, making him jump. He hadn't been aware she was in the hut.

"I was good, huh?" he asked, expecting no more encouragement than usual.

"Survived again," Spart said laconically. "When you can do what you did at will, you will be acceptable."

"What did I do?"

"Out-seeing. In Cascar, *evisa*. You threw a shadow. Do you remember what it felt like?"

He tried to recall the sensation, like picking out the muscles that made one's ears wiggle. He had never been able to make his ears wiggle, however, or his nose. On Earth, he had often dreamed of flying. It had been so simple to fly: just by discovering and flexing a certain muscle in his neck and head, he could lift himself from the ground a yard, two yards, higher with more strain. Upon waking, he could never locate the muscle—nor could he now.

"I'm awake," he said. Spart pulled her hand away from his chest. "Maybe I'll just do it when I really need to." He sat up on his elbows.

"What if you do not know you need to until it is too late? You are just beginning. Don't get your hopes up."

"What hopes? I haven't had any *hope* since I came to this place."

"Ah!" Spart pulled her lips back from her black gums and long teeth. "You hope for those *geen*."

"Who?"

He suddenly felt weak and fell back. The weakness throbbed. As he twisted his head, he saw Nare on one side of him, Coom on the other.

"*Ba* (click) *dan*," Coom said. "Okay?"

Nare bent closer to examine his limbs.

Michael fought dizziness and tried to sit up. "Other than being a little banged up, I'm fine," he said, words slurred.

"Something," Coom said. "Did something."

"What?"

"Up. Outside."

He stood awkwardly, joints aching, and realized he was naked. Spart pushed him with unusual gentleness through the doorway and they pulled him forward by his arms until he stood in the middle of the mound. The air seemed bright and thick. "Do you feel anything?" Spart asked as they circled him. Coom made soft clucking sounds. "Anything odd?"

"No. Nothing. Well . . . I feel a little sick. Why?"

"Be certain!" Nare snapped. "Where is it?"

"On one of his limbs, probably," Spart said. "Hiding."

"*Daggu*," Coom said, barking the word like a curse. He was filthy, stained with grass juice and blood, but he didn't feel badly injured. Still, the way the Crane Women regarded him, with tight narrow expressions, worried him. Coom glanced down at his calf and bent over. She held out her left hand, wriggling her fingers slowly, and suddenly snapped it down to his ankle, plucking something up and holding it at arm's length.

"Do you see it?" Spart asked.

"What?" He tried to make out what Coom held.

"In the sun," Nare said. Coom brought her hand up closer to his face. Something about two inches long glinted in her long fingers. He squinted and traced its silhouette. It resembled a slender crab, translucent, almost invisible. In all the dirt and mess, he wouldn't have noticed it at all; he certainly hadn't felt it.

"What is it?" he asked, shivering. He could feel his strength returning already.

"This night, while you sleep," Nare said, "it would kill you. It's a gift from the Meteorals. When they give one of these to another Sidhe, the bite produces mystic dreams. Humans and mostly-humans can't dream here, so it kills them."

"Jesus," Michael said.

"Remember," Spart said, her eyes fixed on his. "You *can't* dream here. There are no dreams."

Coom carried the tiny creature into their hut.

"It will entertain us tonight . . . and then, we'll add it to our collection," Spart said.

Biri had watched all this from the door of his hut. The young Sidhe drew his reed curtain closed and Michael stood alone and naked, as hollow as a dead tree.

Inside his hut, stashed in a corner, a change of clothing awaited him. The pants, shirt and cloth shoes resembled what the Crane Women wore but were even more ragged. Still, they were clean. He put them on. The fit was tolerable.

Michael felt the by now very familiar sensation of apprehension and help-lessness. He had survived. He had done something strange, son thing he wasn't sure he would ever be able to repeat; yet in the face of the Realm's mystery, he had not learned much.

What he had learned was that the Crane Women cared little for his safety—or they were crazy enough to put him into situations where he could get killed.

He came out of the hut again to see that the sky was brightening. He had slept all day after his ordeal. After eating the fruit and porridge Nare had left for him, he went to the stream to bathe. He scrubbed off all the dry grass and dirt stains, then poured water over himself. When he had shivered dry, he went to a relatively calm pool and peered at his reflection.

His cheek was swollen and the scratches were pink and puffy, but they didn't seem infected. His forehead was bruised, as were his ribs and feet.

Biri came up to him as he finished dressing. "What do you want?" Michael asked, looking off to one side.

"They played games with you. Not the Crane Women—the Meteorals."

"Everybody plays games with me."

"If they had meant to kill you, you wouldn't have escaped."

"Maybe they did try to kill me, and I'm just better than anybody thinks."

Biri shook his head.

"Dammit, nobody believes I'm worth a crap! Why can't I just do something right and be recognized for it?"

"Do you know what you did?"

"Yeah. I survived. We've been through all that."

"The Crane Women were—"

"I don't give a damn what they were doing. I'm not wanted around here. Tell them," he nodded at the hut, "tell them I'm going to spend the night with my own people. Not with Breeds." He hesitated. "Not with Sidhe."

"I'll tell them. And after tonight?"

"I'll worry about that later."

"What will Lamia do?" Biri asked.

"What do you know about her, or care? I don't want to be here, that's all."

Biri watched as Michael crossed the river and walked west. He carried his book in one frayed pocket; it slapped against his hip with every step.

In Euterpe, Michael located the alley where Savarin had led him, turned left into it and at the end walked up the flight of steps to Helena's doorway. He knocked on the frame but received no answer. Standing for a moment, convinced his luck wasn't going to improve for some time, he descended the stairs and nearly walked into her.

"Michael! What happened to you?" She reached up and touched her fingers solicitously to his face.

"I'm leaving the Crane Women," he said. "I want to live in town. I thought you'd help me find a place."

She blinked at him. "Maybe Savarin can help you."

"I thought . . ." He was too numb for finesse. "I thought maybe I could stay here."

"Oh, I don't think so," Helena said, smiling broadly. She patted him on the shoulder. "Come on. Let's find Savarin."

At the hotel, Risky told them the scholar was teaching classes. "Why did you to leave the Crane Women?" Helena asked as they walked through the streets.

"Sick of them," he said. "I just want to find a way to go home."

"So do we all," Helena said ruefully. "But most of us have learned to accept that there's no going back."

"Someone could send us back."

"That hasn't happened yet." She peered at him and squinted sympathetically. "What did they do to your face?"

"They took me out on a hike and left me on a trod. I was almost killed. That's part of the training."

Helena shook her head.

THE SCHOOL WAS in worse repair than most of the buildings in town. There were no windows in the brick frames and the door hung askew, allowing Savarin's dulcet tones to escape across the clear sunny morning.

They waited for Savarin's lecture—conducted mostly in French—to end. The five townsfolk sitting on the brick pews got up and shuffled out, their expressions resigned. Savarin lifted his arms in greeting. "My flock," he said, pointing to the backs of the departing five. "Enthusiasm incarnate."

"Michael needs a place to stay," Helena said.

"Why? You have your place outside Halftown."

"I don't want to be there," Michael said. "I'm leaving the Crane Women."

Savarin frowned. "That's not good," he said. "I'm afraid there's no place in town for you. You don't have a job, and jobs are important. Outsiders are few and the accommodations are slim even for those living here."

"I'll work at something."

"You don't understand." Savarin sat on the end of a pew and spread his hands. "Lamia ordered you to the Crane Women. The townsfolk are in awe of Lamia, no matter how irreverent they may seem. If you displease her, you have no place here. Go back."

Michael shook his head.

"Savarin is right," Helena said. "I mean, I've only been here for a short time, and I have to accept things as they are. Getting along, doing things the accepted way."

"Can't I share your room?" Michael asked, glancing from one to the other. Helena's sympathetic smile was weaker this time.

"You're young," Savarin said. Michael turned away, unable to bear the thought of another lecture.

"Look," he said, "I know I'm young, I'm stupid, I'm clumsy. So what? I need a place to stay. I need *freedom.*"

Savarin laughed bitterly. "Freedom? Show me a human in the Realm who has freedom. Why should you be different?"

"I didn't want to come here! Music didn't bring me here."

"No?" Savarin said. "You walked here, on your own volition. You knew you were going someplace. You tried harder to get here than we did. So you are a little less free. There's no place for you here in town." He tried to soften his words by adding, "Not that we wouldn't put you up if we could. But things are balanced very delicately now."

"We can't afford to rock the boat," Helena restated.

"I might manage to get you some food," Savarin said.

"Me, too," Helena said. "And maybe some better clothes. Where did you get those?"

Michael looked at Helena imploringly, and realized his few hopes had been exploded. Without a word, he turned and left the school.

"Michael—"

He ran. Letting the familiar pleasures and pains of exertion fill him, blanking out his worries, he covered most of the distance to Halftown before forcing himself to slow to a walk.

He didn't even know who he was any more. At one time he had been the young, bright son of well-to-do, talented parents, living in a prosperous neighborhood in a famous city, hoping—trying—to be a poet. Now he was ragged, bruised . . . yet stronger and swifter; and he had been forced to do something quite wonderful . . . or die. He didn't know who his friends were. He was angry at Savarin and Helena, but he didn't actually blame them . . .

The Realm was a tough place to live.

He entered the market courtyard in Halftown. The Breeds paid little attention to him; he was none of their concern. But Eleuth saw him from the workshed, where she was wrapping cloth goods for a customer, and her face lit up with a smile. When she saw his bruises, the smile changed to a frown of concern. She finished tying the package and handed it to the tall Breed woman, who glanced at Michael sternly in passing.

"Hello," Michael said.

"They've been testing you again," Eleuth said, perching on a stool in front of him. Standing, she was a couple of inches taller. On the stool, her face was level with his.

"How'd you guess?" He smirked, holding out his scratched arms.

"And they won't let you stay in Euterpe."

"Did you see me going there?"

She shook her head. "I'm learning. Very slow, very difficult, but by just looking at you I can see a little of what happened. Why did you leave the Crane Women?"

"I don't want to die," Michael said. "And I don't think they much care if I do."

"You could be wrong," Eleuth said. "But stay here. I have to work for a while."

"I don't have anyplace else to go," Michael said.

Eleuth smiled. "I mean, stay here with me. You can help. As long as they let you."

Michael watched her return to her customers. Suddenly, a different kind of panic assailed him. What was he going to do, sleeping with a Breed woman under the same roof?

What did she expect him to do?

18

I'm closing now," Eleuth told Michael as dusk settled. "Today seemed shorter than usual, didn't it? Adonna's whim, I suppose."

She showed him how to pick up the baskets of merchandise from the tables and where to put them in the shed, away from the elements. He helped her draw a tarp over the displays of heavier merchandise. "Nobody steals anything here?"

"Certainly, they might," Eleuth said. "But even Breeds can afford a few safeguards." She didn't explain, simply grinned at him as she closed the gate to the market courtyard. "Now. How long has it been since you ate?"

"About a day and a half," he said. He hadn't noticed, but the reminder awoke his hunger.

"I have some broth cooking, some Faer dishes . . . I hope it will be enough. I mean good enough for you."

The house next to the market square was soon lit with oil lanterns and candles. Eleuth kindled a fire in the pit, placed bread on the bricks to toast, and stirred a pot suspended over the flames. She offered Michael a cup of water from a cloth bag, cooled by evaporation, and asked him to sit on one of the two wooden chairs.

"How old are you?" Michael asked as she finished gathering utensils and set a wicker table for them.

"Oh, that's not a definite thing here," she said.

"Can you guess?"

"Not much older than you, by the looks."

"But I'm sixteen, and you're . . . bigger."

"That's natural for those with Sidhe blood. We grow up very fast here."

"Your father was half Sidhe?"

Eleuth nodded. "My mother was human. She died long ago. I don't remember her very well. Now if I were full Sidhe, I'd either remember everything, or nothing. Depending on what I choose."

Their eyes met and he looked away, face flushing. "I feel so stupid," he said quietly. Eleuth handed him a ceramic bowl filled with vegetable broth. It smelled spicy and was; his tongue burned pleasantly after a few swallows.

"Bread?" she offered. He took a piece of the durable, brown-crusted bread. "We all learn here, all the time," she continued, sitting across from him. Her legs were so long, so graceful. "Isn't that true on Earth? I mean, mortals have finite lives; they must spend all their short years thinking themselves to be very ignorant."

"I guess." A few more swallows and the soup's warmth passed up his neck and into his head. His scalp broke into a sweat.

"As for me, I'm not terribly bright, even for a Breed. By Sidhe standards, I'm very slow. Lirg was a fine father, but I think I was a disappointment to him."

"He'd rather have had a son?"

"Oh, no!" Eleuth laughed. "Sidhe always prefer daughters. Magic is more powerful in a family with daughters. But in my case, I inherited very little."

"What can you do with magic?" Michael asked "I've seen some things, but . . ." He trailed off.

"We probably shouldn't talk about it," Eleuth said. She took his empty bowl and filled it again. "You're not a Breed. I'm not sure why you're here or why they tolerate you. Do you know?"

Michael shook his head. "I wish I did. I mean, I think I wish I knew. Maybe I don't want to know."

"You must know eventually," Eleuth said. They ate in silence for a while. Then she picked up their empty bowls and stuck them in a pot of sand. She spun the pot on its pedestal and plucked the bowls out, clean.

"You can sleep next to the hearth," she said. She took a rug down from its bar and laid it on the floor, then produced two blankets and a robe. "This was Lirg's," she said, handing the robe to him. "I'll sleep now. In the morning, you can pick out some other clothes. Good night."

He lay on the rug and pulled the blankets over him. Eleuth banked the fire in the pit and pulled the screen over it, then slipped behind another hanging into her room.

He lay in the ember-lit dark for a few minutes, his mind turbulent but blank. His eyes shut.

Sleep without dreams occupied no time at ail. He came awake to the sound of weeping. It was Eleuth. Groggy, uncertain what to do, he sat up on the floor and listened for a minute, chin on his knees. Finally he stood, the old clothes binding him where he had twisted in his sleep. He approached the hanging.

"Eleuth?"

The sobbing became softer. "Eleuth, what's wrong'?"

"I'll be quiet," she said, her voice muffled.

"No, what's wrong?"

He pulled aside the hanging and saw her lying on a wooden pallet, blankets pulled up around her neck. Her face was streaked with tears which glinted in the light of the room's single candle.

"I can't remember all the transactions," she said. "No matter how hard I try, I can't keep the accounts in my head."

Michael leaned sleepily against the wall. "Then use paper."

"Oh, *no!*" Eleuth said, shuddering as she wept. "We do not write anything down. That is . . . wrong. Lirg would be very disappointed in me." She wiped her face with her hands.

"So you're different. Everybody's different."

"I'll be all right," she said. "Go back to sleep now." She lay on her back and stared at the ceiling. He let the hanging slip back.

"Michael?"

He stopped at the edge of the bedclothes. "What?"

"Are you afraid of Breeds? I mean, do you hate us?"

"No," he said. "They're no worse than humans. Better than Sidhe, as near as I can tell."

He heard her bare feet on the floor. She pulled back the hanging and stared out at him. Nothing was said for a time, then she motioned for him to come join her.

"I'm mostly human." she said as she held back the blankets. He started to climb in with his clothes still on, but she made a face and pushed him gently back. "Not with those," she said, undoing the strings which belted his pants. "Take off that shirt. You deserve much better."

He felt strange, excited but sleepy, afraid but calm. She smiled at his underclothes as he untied the fabric and let it hang in front of him. She took his hand and pulled him down beside her, then kissed his forehead.

"You're tired," Eleuth said. "Tonight we sleep."

"I don't want to sleep just yet," he said. He put his arms around her, bunching the coarse but pliant fabric of her gown in one fist. He nuzzled her neck and she lifted her chin, closing her eyes. Then he kissed her. She tasted slightly electric, as if he were licking a dime. With one hand he undid the ties on the upper portion of her gown, revealing her breasts. They were dotted with pearly-gray freckles and her sternum rippled in the hollow between. He touched her skin gently with one finger, then rubbed his cheek against her breasts, feeling her warmth. She held his head and squeezed him closer, kissing his hair.

"Sweet," she said. "*Sona, dosa, sona.*"

"What do I do now?" he asked, looking up at her, eyes half closed.

"Sleep, Michael," she crooned, stroking his brow. She nestled down beside him and he felt the bare stretch of her leg against his. He moved instinctively, but she restrained him. "Sleep," she repeated, but he didn't hear her finish the word.

THE MORNING BEGAN as a patch of gray light shining on the floor. Michael opened his eyes and looked at the light from where his head lolled over the side of the bed. He rolled on his back and saw Eleuth leaning on her elbow next to him, hair concealing her hand. She smiled and bent to kiss him. "You kept me very warm," she said. She ran her hand down his arm, tickling the hairs.

They made love. It was the most wonderful thing, and the most silly thing. It had nothing of lust in it, only necessity. They lay holding each other and he secretly surveyed her breasts and stomach, and she secretly enjoyed him looking at her.

Eleuth got out of bed, climbing over him with her hand cupped between her legs. She dipped a white cloth in a ceramic jar full of water and cleaned him off, then slipped on her pants and shirt. "No market this day," she said. "But I have a few things to do."

He lay on the cot, half-covered with blankets, watching as the gray light became yellow.

It was one of the most—no, the single most wonderful thing that had happened to him. He was pretty convinced of that. He couldn't remember anything finer, and yet . . .

It had its drawbacks. In all the time he had spent here, there had always been some hope that it was all a dream, some long-play fantasy. But throughout his few pubescent years, he had never been able to have a fantasy so real or vivid as what had happened this morning.

Ergo, he was not fantasizing. He had more than suspected as much. The drawback was that it was now proven.

And yet . . .

A certain hollowness remained. He was relaxed, as if a knot had been untied between his legs that he had hardly realized was there until now. He had acquitted himself well; Eleuth had enjoyed him, and he sensed the knot flex and tighten as he remembered her enjoyment. His pleasure had been real but unspectacular, sure to get better with practice. Hers had been real and prolonged.

So what about the hollowness? He couldn't put his finger on it. Like everything else in Sidhedark, the accomplishment (and that seemed a truthful but ridiculous word to use) came with a little hard gnarl of unease, of impending disaster.

Michael realized that even if he made it back to Earth, he would still have that gnarl buried inside of him.

Maybe that was part of growing up. Oddly enough, making love didn't make him feel any more adult. It was perhaps the most childish part of being grown-up.

He was dozing when Eleuth entered, carrying three pieces of fruit. She handed him two of them and he smiled at her.

"There's a legend on Earth, saying that if I eat this, I have to stay here forever."

"I wouldn't object," Eleuth said, sitting on the bed beside him. "You've already eaten fruit here, haven't you?"

He nodded. "Can you teach me to speak Sidhe?"

She shook her head slowly. "It's more difficult than a human language. Lirg tried teaching my mother. Only the Sidhe have a real knack. Sometimes, it's not even a language in your sense."

"But I've been able to make out words."

"Yes. Sometimes we use different words to mean the same things . . . And when we communicate, we in-speak. You allow me to speak your language. I in-speak . . . look into your mind, and find the words. I wish Lirg were here to explain it to you." Her eyes moistened again. Michael reached out to touch her shoulder. She lay down beside him. "What will you do today?"

"Go to Savarin, I think," Michael said. "He didn't help me yesterday, but there are still things I need to know."

"I'll teach you what I know," Eleuth said.

"I'm grateful for that, but he's a teacher. He may be able to explain things more clearly."

"Oh."

They ate their fruit.

"Can you help me here?" she asked, glancing at him with eyes narrowed, as if puzzled.

"Sure," Michael said. "Why don't you tell me what you need done before I go to Euterpe?"

Together they counted rolls of fabric and pots. Eleuth brought out pants and shirts for him to try on, and he found some that fit reasonably well. Shoes were more difficult. Sidhe and Breed feet were longer and narrower than human feet. Michael found a pair made out of canvas-like material that didn't actually pinch his toes, and Eleuth watched him with her vague puzzled expression as he stamped about, trying to get them to fit. "They'll never believe it back on Earth," he said. "Faeries wear tennis shoes." Then he laughed at the thought of trying to explain things at home. It was the first time he remembered laughing in the Realm. Eleuth smiled.

She sewed a pocket into his shirt to hold the book and as she cut the thread with her teeth and tied it off, she said, "I'm expecting a shipment this afternoon. Could you come back to help?"

"Sure. I thought everything just appeared out of nowhere," he teased. He pointed at the covered racks of merchandise in the storage room.

"Oh, no," Eleuth said, her long face betraying mock distress. "I'm not nearly that skilled."

He left when the sun was just below zenith and walked the distance to the human town at a leisurely pace. Something had loosened in him; he could observe things without the nervous tightness that had prevailed before. It seemed he now had the time to put everything in perspective.

He also confronted the fact that he would soon have to tell Eleuth he couldn't stay forever, that he didn't love her. He wasn't sure what he felt for her; gratitude, affection.

But there was one image he couldn't erase from his mind: that of the Crane Women—immortal, but because of their human blood, changing with age. How long would it take for Eleuth to change?

A few Breeds—a male and two females, all of that cast of features that indicated they were older than Eleuth, but how how much older he couldn't tell—directed a horse cart along the road. They passed Michael without acknowledging his presence, holding their long heads high, their dull brown clothes rippling like fur to an unwanted touch. He turned to watch the cart, noting the wood-spoke wheels, the well-fitted but unornamented frame, the simplicity of the harness.

At the inn, Brecker greeted him civilly while sweeping out the small lobby and told him Savarin was indeed back in his room. Michael climbed the stairs. Behind the wicker door, he heard Savarin humming to himself. Michael knocked on the wicker. "It's me."

Savarin swung the door wide and smiled half-expectantly, half-sadly. "You've forgiven us, I hope?"

"Yeah," Michael said. "I found a place in Halftown."

Savarin invited him in and leaned through the door, peering down the hall to see if anyone followed. "We want you to understand, it's not you we're afraid of."

"I know," Michael said. He didn't want to discuss it, but he knew Savarin would air the issue for a while. He sat on the edge of the washstand, lightly so as not to crush it.

"It's just that we have to be careful. We stand between Lamia and the Sidhe, between rules that change from day to day. Have you had any trouble from the Crane Women?"

Michael shook his head. "I haven't seen them. I came here—"

"You still have to be careful. Where are you staying in Halftown?"

"That isn't important." Michael said. "I want you to tell me what you know about Sidhe language. I can't get anywhere if I can't understand what they're saying."

Savarin cocked his head to one side and lifted his eyebrows. "Tall order. You have to be largely Sidhe to pick up on all of the tongues. I'd say the resemblances between Sidhe and human languages are strong, but the syntax and methods of understanding are quite different. For example, the Sidhe use a meta-language . . . a language of contexts. And Cascar is like a hundred languages thrown together. They never run out of words that mean the same thing, or very nearly. I can't speak it well. I can sometimes make myself understood, but . . ."

"I understood it for a time," Michael said. "During the *Kaeli*. One of the Crane Women touched my head, and I understood everything they said."

"And what was that like?"

Michael thought back. "Like listening to music. Each word seemed to be the equivalent of a note. Notes are always the same in music, but place them next to each other and they sound different . . . or lengthen the notes, shorten them. Use the same word in a different context, and it means something else . . . sounds different."

"Perhaps you should be educating *me*," Savarin said.

"But it didn't last. I don't remember anything from that night, except what they said . . . and even that's fuzzy. They were singing, but not singing. I need to know so—" He stopped himself. "I just need to know."

"Because you still plan on leaving the Realm," Savarin said.

Michael turned his eyes away and pointed his index fingers together.

"I don't recommend that. First of all, Alyons will hunt you. No human can escape his coursers. Second, Lamia will resent even the attempt—and, as I've said before, I don't want to cross her. I don't know what the Crane Women will do."

"I haven't thought much about that," Michael said. "I'm just struggling. I don't want to be anyone's responsibility."

"Just thank the stars you are," Savarin said. "I've known people, when they came here, Alyons took them—and we never saw them again—despite the Pact! We dare not object. What happens to them, where does he take them? Nobody knows. But you! You seem to be protected. He has not taken you ... even though he's tried." He put his hand on Michael's knee and stared at him earnestly. "Go back. Keep up the training. It's for a purpose, I'm sure."

"I don't see it that way," Michael said.

Savarin shrugged and seemed to give in.

"Then we'll discuss Cascar and Nerb. Do you know the difference?"

"No."

Savarin explained that Cascar was a younger, less formal language. He believed it had arisen after the Sidhe returned to Earth, and that it was the proto-language out of which had arisen several of the major human language groups, the most familiar of them, for Savarin, belonging to the Indo-European branch. "Certainly the words sound familiar," he said. "Their word for us—a word which never changes, you notice?—is *antros*. Sometimes they call us males—*viros*, as in virile, no?—or female, *geen*, and the latter they apply to their females as well—but as a kind, we are always *antros*. A *spit-word*, so to speak.

"As for Nerb, not many Breeds speak it, and none of the Sidhe I've encountered."

"I haven't heard much about it, if anything. So say something to me in Cascar."

"Pir na? Sed antros lingas ta rup ta pistr."

"What's that mean?"

" 'Why? Humans talk as if they have stone tongues.' It's something a Breed once told me. *Lingas* means both language and speaking and tongue. Context is important, and pitch, as in Chinese. There are other Cascar words for language, meaning eating with the tongue, spitting with the tongue, magic with the tongue. Calling birds with the tongue. All different."

"How do they learn it?"

"They're Sidhe," Savarin said laconically. "It comes naturally to them. Nearly every Sidhe and Breed I've met knows how to speak the human languages I'm familiar with. Do they suck the knowledge out of my mind? I don't know. But they only speak Cascar around humans when they don't want us to understand, or when they wish to be belligerent." He paused, looking almost sad. "There's another language I've heard hinted at. I know almost nothing about it but that it exists. One of its many names is Kesh. An unspoken language, used during the star-marches. Not, as you might suspect, a kind of telepathy, but something different.

"And to make things even more confusing, I'm tracking down evidence that the Sidhe picked up words from humans—words from tinker's cant, Celtic languages, etc.; picked them up during their last centuries on Earth. There is a section in *Hudibras* by Samuel Butler—if I can remember ..." He screwed up his face in concentration and peered at the ceiling. *"But when he pleased to shew't, his speech/ In loftiness of sound was rich;*

A Babylonish dialect
Which learned pedants much affect;
It was a party coloured dress
Of patch'd and py-ball'd languages;
'Twas (Irish) cut on Greek and Latin
Like fustian heretofore on sattin.
It had an odd promiscuous tone,
As if h' had talk'd three parts in one;
Which made some think, when he did gabble,
Th' had heard three labourers of Babel;
Or Cerberus himself pronounce
A leash of languages at once.' "

"We're like little babies here," Michael said, sighing.

Savarin nodded. "Now perhaps you can tell me why they simply haven't slaughtered us all?"

"Do they hate us that much?"

Savarin's expression brightened. "Can you tell me anything about the Council of Eleu? Does that sound familiar?"

Michael couldn't remember hearing anything about it.

"Then listen closely. You're going to be associating with Breed and Sidhe more and more, whatever your personal wishes may be. Just listen for it. 'Council of Eleu.' And if you find out anything, tell me immediately! To answer your question, no, not all of them hate us. And the Council of Eleu has something to do with those who tolerate us."

Something flashed into Michael's head and he struggled to keep it, to clarify it. A group of tall, pale figures talking about him. Something about his bedroom in the house on Earth . . . but it was gone before he could grasp it. "I'll let you know if I hear anything," he said. "How's Helena?"

"Well," Savarin said. "She worries we gave you the wrong impression, that you hate us, hate her."

"I don't hate anybody," Michael said. "I'd like to talk to her some more."

"Certainly. She's working now, I'm sure, but we could walk over later."

"No. I'll go myself."

"Certainly," Savarin said. His lips normally carried a slight sardonic smile; now the expression took on sharp significance. "I believe there is something you must know, very soon."

"What?"

He grimaced. "Human sex is dangerous here."

"Why?"

"Such things are closely regulated. We do not want children. The Sidhe and Breeds can have young—we cannot."

Michael just looked at him.

"The people who have been here longest, and the Breeds, say it is because there are no seedling souls in the Realm. A human child is born empty. A Sidhe or Breed child is expected to be that way, and already has an internal . . . how would we say . . . compensation. But human children are vessels waiting to be filled. They are filled by creatures from the Blasted Plain—Adonna's own aborted children, some say." He set his lips and waved off any further inquiry. "Talk about it is considered obscene. No more."

"There's just one other thing," Michael said. "I'm a young fellow and naive— everyone keeps saying that—but I still don't understand. Why do humans put up with all this crap?"

"What else can we do?" Savarin scrutinized him intensely, as if looking for something hidden. Then the perpetual half-smile returned and the scholar leaned back, folding his hands and cracking his knuckles. "You'll learn soon enough," he said in a low voice, eyes languid. "Why not go and talk with Helena now? She should be done with her work."

Michael didn't expect to be dismissed, but Savarin was obviously thinking about other things. Michael stood and held out his hand. Savarin grasped it and shook it loosely, then fluttered his fingers in the direction of the doorway. "Go," he said. "And thank you for coming back. We thought we'd lost you when you ran away."

He nodded and shut the wicker door behind him. Savarin resumed humming, keeping it low enough so it couldn't be heard more than a few feet outside.

Michael snapped his fingers while he walked, caught himself, and stuffed his thumb into the fabric tie of his pants. It was early afternoon and the town was slowing down: shops closing, people strolling in pairs down the narrow streets, some heading for the ramshackle school, others just walking, talking. Michael saw an Oriental man and woman speaking what sounded like Chinese.

His last question—and Savarin's subsequent expression—kept echoing in his mind. Resistance seemed only natural when somebody oppressed you. Michael's father had often talked about his student days at UCLA—talk which had bored Michael slightly, but came back to him now as a model of how Americans, at least, behaved when they thought something was wrong. Michael wondered if the humans in the Realm could organize a protest, maybe set up a blockade. Keep Sidhe out of Euterpe at least . . . passive resistance.

He grinned at how silly it sounded. Alyons could handle a blockade in short order. Some people would probably get killed. Maybe he'd be the first.

He still found it hard to believe that he could die in the Realm. Death had been a difficult enough concept on Earth, but here, with everything topsy-turvy and so many fantastic phenomena, how could anyone actually *die*? So what if it wasn't a dream, he told himself. It wasn't exactly reality either.

His reverie carried him to the steps below Helena's doorway.

He walked up slowly, apprehensive. He rubbed his chin to check the length of peach-fuzz. A few of the real whiskers he had started were getting quite long now; he hadn't thought about them until this moment, but he wished he had a mirror and a pair of scissors to snip them off.

He had a panicky moment just before knocking, when he told himself it would be best just to run away, head out across the—

Helena opened the door.

"Hi," he said, dropping his hand from his chin.

"Hi yourself. I heard your footsteps."

"Yeah," Michael said. "I wanted to apologize for running away like that."

"No apology needed," Helena said. She opened the door wider and invited him in, then left the door open and blocked it with a brick. She seemed subdued. "It must be rough on you. Confusing."

"I guess. Anyway, that's no excuse to act like a little kid. To be rude, I mean."

"I'm glad you came back," she said, standing a few feet away. "Would you like to sit?" They sat and Helena bit on a thumbnail, watching him but not really seeing him.

"Is something wrong?" he asked.

She seemed to reach a decision and leaned forward, staring at him earnestly. "Michael, will you swear something for me? Double swear? Because I'm taking a big risk."

"What risk?"

"Will you swear?"

"Swear to what, Helena?"

She stood nervously and paced in front of him, waving her arms as she spoke. "You're a sweet fellow, but you didn't understand what we meant yesterday. You know how strange you are, being taken care of by Breeds and so on."

"I guess," Michael said.

"Don't guess. Do you know?"

"It's strange to me, that's for sure."

"Well, it's even stranger for us. Nobody from here—I mean humans—has ever been given that treatment before. So it makes us wonder, are you a double agent or what? A Sidhe who just looks human?"

"I'm not a Sidhe," Michael said, laughing.

"No, I don't think you are. You sweat when you're nervous." She giggled and placed her hand reassuringly on his shoulder, letting the fingers linger, gripping him. "So you have to swear to me, you're not a double agent, you're not a plant or whatever put here to catch us."

"I swear," Michael said.

"Your eyes look so human," Helena said. "Such a nice green color. What's happened to you since yesterday?"

Michael blinked at the change in subject. "I found a place to live in Half-town."

"Oh, where?"

"You wanted me to swear. I did. So what next?"

Helena kneeled before him, curled up her legs, threw her head back and looked at him intently. "You know Savarin. He's a scholar. There are other people you haven't met, except one of them came to see you that night they gave the dinner. When you came to town. A short, heavy fellow with black hair."

Michael didn't remember him.

"Well, anyway, he saw you, and thought sometime we'd have to decide whether to contact you."

A bell rang in the town plaza. Michael went to the window to listen.

"So you're contacting me," he said softly.

Helena stood and leaned on the sill beside him. "That's the warning bell," she said, voice quavering. "Alyons is here, or some of his riders. So I'll tell you quickly. We found a cache of Sidhe metal. Never mind where. Some people here are keeping it, making it into . . . things. A piano, for one. What I wouldn't give to hear a piano again! But they won't let us play it, of course, until after—" She stopped abruptly, her face paling. Hoofsteps sounded in the narrow alleyway. "Michael!"

"What?"

"Are they after you, or did you bring them here?"

"I'm *not* one of them," Michael said. She grasped his arm.

"They're outside!"

Alyons and two of his coursers paced at leisure on horseback toward the door at the end of the alleyway. Alyons glanced up and spotted Michael in the window. Michael pulled back.

"*Antros!* Your presence is demanded!"

"They *do* want you," Helena said, terrified.

"It looks that way."

"Oh, don't tell them anything. I'm so frightened. Where will they take you?"

"I don't know," Michael said. He stepped into the hall and looked the opposite way. If he could only get back into that mindset again . . . He turned to Helena and took her hand clumsily in his. He had a crazy urge to laugh. "A piano, eh?"

"Shh!"

"That's not what I had in mind," Michael said, "but I guess that's pretty subversive."

"Man-child!" Alyons called.

He kissed her hand and felt a flush of pride mix with his fear. A Sidhe appeared in the door at the bottom of the stairs. Michael unceremoniously pushed Helena back into her room and shut the door. He stood at the top of the steps, looking down on the courser with what he hoped passed for imperious disdain. "What do you want?"

The courser began climbing, giving no answer. Michael looked to either side of the Sidhe, wondering if he could play the uncertain flower down the stairs. There was only one way to find out. With all his speed and concentration, he dashed down the steps, trying to send a shadow to one side and swerve himself to the other. The courser grabbed him without hesitation and placed him under one arm as easily as he would a trussed piglet, then turned and marched out the door, presenting him to the Wickmaster.

They exchanged a few words in Cascar and Michael looked directly at Alyons.

"So you're learning from the Crane Women," the Wickmaster said. "But not too well."

The courser spoke again and they laughed. "Never make a shadow when there are only two ways to send it," Alyons advised. He hefted his wick and motioned for Michael to be tied and led behind his horse. They skillfully reversed the horses in the narrow alley and left with Michael in tow. He looked over his shoulder and saw Helena at the window, her face pale. His hands were roped together; he could not wave, only lift and shake them as if he were a prizefighter celebrating victory. For a moment, he had feared the Sidhe would take her, as well.

They pulled him out of town, walking their horses just fast enough to keep him half-running. They joined another group of four, making a total of seven Sidhe, and jerked Michael down the road to the Isomage's mansion.

19

The troop led Michael up the path to the Isomage's house, jerking sharply on his rope as he fell back. Alyons dismounted and strode inside while the others waited, silent and aloof.

After some minutes, Alyons emerged and grabbed the end of Michael's rope. He reeled it in, coiling the coarse brown jute with quick jerks around his arm until he stood just two feet from Michael, towering over him. "She wants to speak with you, man-child." His expression stony, Alyons' eyes seemed fixed in their sockets as he turned away, pulling Michael by his tied and outstretched hands. The Wickmaster seemed to be in a state of controlled rage, which perversely made Michael more optimistic; if the circumstances weren't to Alyons' liking, perhaps Michael wasn't in as much trouble as he'd thought.

The interior of the house was as he remembered, only darker and cooler. The sun lay languid and orange on the horizon. The day had been particularly short.

The staircase led up into brighter light from the narrow windows along the entryway. Lamia stood on the balcony, her tiny, finely molded hands gripping the railing.

"Is he down there?" she asked.

"As you requested," Alyons said, his tone dripping contempt.

"Send him up to me."

The Wickmaster took his time undoing the rope, his long corded fingers cool against Michael's arms. "Go," he said. He pointed up the stairs and gave Michael a hard push. Michael ascended, rubbing his reddened wrists and watching the daylight grow dull. He didn't fancy staying in the house after dark, but even less did he fancy traveling with the coursers at night, or walking back to the town alone.

He met Lamia on the landing. A change had come over her. He could see it even in the fading light. Her skin was waxen, her face tighter, as if she wore a restraining mask. Around her eyes, scaly patches had started to flake away and her hands were crisscrossed with tiny thin wrinkles like cracks in bread dough.

He stopped five paces from her. Lamia made no move toward him, instead regarding him with a wavering gaze. She seemed half-dead with exhaustion.

"You grieve me, boy," she said softly. "I set you a task and you run from it."

"I don't enjoy being a slave," he said.

"You're . . . no . . . slave." Her voice carried bitter humor. "You're freer than I am, freer than Alyons down there." She gestured with a trembling hand and immediately returned it to the railing to support herself. Michael stared down into the lower floor's gloom. Alyons stood by the foot of the stairs, head bowed, twisting and coiling the rope with his fingers.

"They keep trying to kill me," Michael said.

"Who, the Crane Women?" Lamia tittered, a dead dry sound of rolling pebbles. She motioned for him to come closer. He hesitated and she made as if to reach out with one hand and strangle him. "Closer!" she growled.

He advanced one stride. She edged a few inches along the railing. The dry wood creaked beneath her weight. Her arms bounced in slow, oily waves beneath the fabric of her gown. "They are teaching you how to stay alive."

"I can stay alive on my own, in Euterpe with all the others."

"You will not stay in the town. The town is for fools, cowards too afraid to make their own way."

"I'm not too afraid."

"You're too stupid to succeed, then." She lowered her voice and pushed back from the railing, tottering for one awful moment. Michael retreated two steps in case she fell; he saw her as a poorly balanced sack of venomous fluids, about to topple and burst. But Lamia kept her balance. "You require tempering," she said. "Come with me. We have to talk alone."

She wobbled and thumped through a doorway leading to a second floor hallway. This part of the house seemed in better condition than the ground floor; as far as he could tell in the twilight, the walls were intact, and the thickly carpeted floor muffled her ponderous steps.

She reached out with her left hand and pushed wide a door, motioning for Michael to enter first. He sidled past her and stood in a broad empty room. Candles burned in sconces set high on all four walls. The room's floor was dark polished hardwood. A second Lamia labored upside down in the depths of the wood as she followed him. She closed the door and leaned against it, breathing heavily.

"Are you sick?" he asked.

She shook her head. Her small eyes, enclosed in scaly flesh, saddened as she looked beyond him at the empty room.

"You have a duty, boy," she said distantly. "Have you learned more about this house, about the Realm?"

"A little," Michael said. "Not nearly enough."

"You know that the Isomage lived here?"

He nodded. "I don't know who he was . . . Was he David Clarkham?"

"Is, boy. He *is*." Her lips formed an upward-tilting curve suggesting a smile.

To each side, the skin of her cheeks separated in more fine cracks. "You know that he wishes to save us?"

Michael shook his head. "Why isn't he here, then?"

"His enemies drove him away. I told you. The battle that destroyed this entire plain. They forced all the humans in their control to live here in desolation and pain. I've never been to the town; I cannot leave this house. But from this house I have a . . . small influence. In my cursed condition, I can help. Do you understand?"

"No." There was pleasant defiance in his ignorance. It warmed him.

She rolled her hips and dragged her legs to the middle of the room. He caught a whiff of her odor, unpleasant and dead sweet, like decaying flowers. "You must not defy his plan," she said. "The Sidhe opposed to us simply wait for their chance . . ." She shook her head. The skin of her neck crackled.

"Then why do they give you any power at all?" Michael asked.

"They cannot hurt me more than they already have. There is a treaty over this land, over the plain. We suffer our punishment, but if they make any further moves against us, the treaty crumbles . . . and a power buried deep in the land is unleashed against the transgressors. There is a stalemate. To the Sidhe, it seems we are defeated. Perhaps we are . . . and perhaps not. But should humans break the treaty . . ." Her voice trailed off again.

"Why am I important?"

"Important?" She spat on the floor, then walked to the spot where her spittle beaded on the polished surface and with infinite pains, bent to wipe it with the hem of her gown. Her skin crackled like crumpled paper as she pushed herself back to her upright posture, cheeks pinking, jaw tight with the effort. "Important," she murmured, as if chewing the word. "You are not *crucial*. You are simply a messenger. But to help at all, you must survive. You must continue to train with the Crane Women."

"Do I have any choice?"

Lamia turned her back on him. "I have some influence over the Wickmaster; but only some. If you do not return to the Crane Women, he will take charge of you. What he'll do with you, I don't know."

"I have no choice, then."

She swiveled slowly, arms out, in grotesque parody of a pirouette. Michael looked at the far wall and saw a long, horizontal wooden bar mounted beneath the candles—a practice bar for dancers. "May you never know how cruel life is," she said. "Or what can be lost . . . and yet remain alive. Go back to the Crane Women. Resume your training."

Michael stood silent in the candlelight, then turned and left the room. He descended the stairs and stopped before Alyons, who let the rope fall free from one hand.

"*Jakap?*" the Wickmaster asked. The rope unwound like a struggling snake.

"Lamia orders me to go back to the Crane Women."

"She orders nothing," Alyons said. "I am Wickmaster."

"You can't hurt me," Michael said.

The Sidhe leaned over, bringing his face level with Michael's. "You are right, man-child. I can't hurt you if you do as she wishes. But step out of line, just once . . ."

"Wickmaster!" Lamia stood by the balustrade, limned by the faint glow from the dancing room. "Obey the Pact."

Michael dodged the Sidhe's grasping hand and walked out the door. "I'll ride back," he said, trying to conceal the tremble of anger and fear in his voice

"On which horse?" Alyons asked, closing the front door with a solid thump. "Which is yours?"

"Your horse," Michael said.

Behind him, Alyons barked a short laugh. "My horse. Such a beautiful and golden horse, such a temptation, my horse . . . even for humans. Mount then, *antros,* show us your skill."

Michael touched the golden Sidhe horse delicately, then mounted as he had been instructed. He wondered idly if it were possible to steal the horse, and decided that would be very unwise. But his feet kicked out of their own volition, heels sharply prodding the animal in the flanks.

The landscape, locked in long, gray twilight, suddenly blurred around him. The horse's flesh flowed like hot steel under the saddle and between his calves, and Michael felt an incredible pulse of power as they streaked along the road. His body seemed to melt and he grasped the horse with his arms and legs in sheer terror, shouting for it to stop. His words drowned in the wind.

Michael had an impression the coursers were right behind him, but when he tried to turn and look, the landscape made such bizarre gyrations that he closed his eyes.

Suddenly, everything settled. He clung to the back of the horse to keep from sliding off. They stood on the mound, the horse's breathing shallow and steady. It jerked its head and shivered. He slid from the saddle and barely managed to land on his feet.

Alyons' mount rejoined the coursers standing around the Crane Women's hut. The horses' skins gleamed in the furnace glow from the window; the Wickmaster's cape reflected the myriad tiny glimmers in the dirt of the mound as he dismounted from a borrowed animal. The horseless courser ran gracefully and swiftly over the road and across the creek, stopping at the edge of the mound.

Banners of dark glided up from the horizon, announcing night.

Spart emerged from the hut, glanced at Michael without comment, and turned to Alyons. They spoke in Cascar for several minutes. Michael shivered in the river of cool air flowing from the south. The coursers murmured among themselves.

Nare called to him from the window. He walked unsteadily to the hut. The Crane Woman's luxuriant hair was animated by a current of warm air flowing through the window and caught the inner glow, forming a golden nimbus around her face.

"To Lamia?" she asked. Michael nodded. "Is she different?"

"She's sick, I think. Her skin's all patchy." He was relieved. Apparently he was not going to be chided for running away. "I didn't want to come back," he said, the words tumbling out all at once.

"Of course," she said. She closed the window.

Alyons glided aboard his horse and the coursers moved off slowly into the dark. For a moment, Michael stood by the hut, then returned to his own shelter. Biri was nowhere to be seen.

He thought of Eleuth and Helena. He hoped Helena wasn't worried—and then hoped she was. He pondered his own neutral feelings. All emotion seemed to have drained out of him.

"Wait and see," he murmured, curling up in his hut, pulling his jacket higher around his neck. He squeezed his eyes shut.

That night, before sleep, the darkness behind his eyelids roiled with thoughts of home, the Isomage's mansion, the crinkled, flaking lids of Lamia's eyes.

MICHAEL AWOKE BEFORE dawn and listened to the humming sky. As the humming faded, he peered out his door to see a pale band of gray on the horizon. Clouds had moved in during the night, and though the air wasn't exceptionally cold, flakes of snow fell, melting as soon as they touched the dirt.

Eleuth came from Halftown an hour later, wrapped in a light shawl and wearing knee-high boots. She carried four buckets of milk, as on the day Michael had first seen her. He stood in front of his hut but she barely looked at him as she walked past. Biri watched both of them from his door. When the buckets had been deposited outside the Crane Women's hut, she began her return trip.

"Eleuth," Michael said. She stopped, still not looking at him. "I couldn't come yesterday."

"So I heard."

"I want to thank you." Those words sounded particularly callous, as if his need to say them belied their meaning.

"Are you all right?" she asked. "I heard Alyons took you from the human town."

"I'm fine. I'll try to see you today."

Eleuth finally faced him and nodded. Biri regarded her with seeming disinterest. She glanced at the young Sidhe. To Michael's surprise, a flash of hatred crossed her face. She ran across the stream.

Spart stood beside Michael. She offered him a cup of milk.

"Where does the milk come from?" he asked, sipping.

"Always questions."

"Always."

"From herds of horses beyond the Blasted Plain. It is brought into Halftown and Euterpe twice each month. It keeps well, and it nourishes." She sighed. "But I remember the fine milk of Earth, rich and full of the taste of the plants cows and goats ate." She smacked her lips and took the empty cup. "You kept the Breed woman company?"

Michael nodded. He wasn't embarrassed; he saw no reason to worry about appearances in front of the Crane Women. Spart blinked and stared off into the distance.

"Do you feel anything, having done this?" she asked.

"Grateful," Michael said.

Spart lifted the corners of her lips and cocked her head. "Human male, grateful?"

"I'm not a monster," he said defensively.

"Do you think she gives, not takes?"

"She's sad," he said. "She's alone now."

"So you take."

Michael did not like the course of the conversation. "The Sidhe never eat meat?" he asked. The question had waited for weeks. Spart jerked and turned slowly to look at Biri's hut. The door cover was drawn and all was silent within. "No," she said. "Even in-speaking the thought is painful. Never eat flesh. Only humans eat meat. It is the sign of their defeat."

"All Sidhe are vegetarians?"

Spart looked him firmly in the eye. "Always and ever. That is why we have magic and you do not."

"Never?" Michael pursued, sensing something unsaid.

Spart moved away, shaking her head. "The subject is not fit for discussion."

"What do they sacrifice to Adonna?" He thought of Lirg.

Spart turned on him and advanced until her nose nearly pressed against his chin, looking at him as if he were some oddity, an out-of-place curiosity. "Always forbidden, on occasion mandatory," she said. "Do you know that law?"

"I don't think so."

Spart glanced at Biri's hut once more, then walked back to her own.

"Can't we even hold a discussion longer than four sentences?" Michael called out after her. She did not answer. He kicked at the dirt, angry with himself, unable to find the center of his emotions, angry with Spart for implying his ignorance. "Jesus."

Out of habit, he began his warm-up exercises. Tiring soon of that, wondering when his training would continue, he entered his hut and lay on the reed mats, clearing a space to reveal bare dirt. He picked up one of the pieces of wood he hadn't fitted properly into the framework and drew a line in the dust. "I'm a poet," he said to himself, quiet but firm. "I'm not a soldier. I'm not a goddamn jock. I'm a poet." He closed his eyes and tried to think of something. Surely he could write about what was happening to him. About Helena, Eleuth. About what Biri had told him.

But it was all a tangle. Their faces came and went, bringing no words with them. Instead, he began to recall things about Earth. The sadness almost overwhelmed him. He missed his father and mother, the school—he even missed the ridicule and being a dreamy kid in a world of jocks and New Wave robots. He felt like crying. He was being asked—no, forced—to think and behave like an adult, to make life-and-death decisions, to *choose,* and he was not at all sure he was ready to give up his youth.

Michael had always been mature, in the sense of being able to think for himself. Given time enough, and equanimity, he could puzzle through most problems and reach a conclusion others might regard as advanced for his age. But confronted with love, violence, sex—miscegenation—what could he conclude?

Only that home was better. Safer. How could one ask for more than warmth, food, peace and quiet, a chance to learn and work?

" 'There's no place like home,' " he murmured, and snickered. He tapped his heels together. Oz was a national park compared with Sidhedark. The Realm was more like a history lesson rather than a fairy tale—something out of World War II. Internment camps—the Pact Lands. The Blasted Plain, like some bizarre crater from an even more bizarre bomb, filled with mutated monsters. The Crane Women—drill sergeants.

Surely he could write about *that.*

The stick began to move. He applied it to the dirt and was pleased with the old, familiar feeling of tapping Death's Radio, the source of poetry. In *Orphé,* a film he had first seen at age thirteen, Death had come for the modern beat poet Orpheus as a woman in a large black limousine. The limousine's radio played provocative nonsense phrases that impressed Orpheus with their purity and poetic essence. When the poetry came pure and clean, Michael sometimes felt he was tuned to Death's Radio.

Here she comes
Bottle in hand
To the mike
Swaying now
Gravel voice
Filmy gown
She will die
Her singing
Will kill her
We will all
Listen, her
Blood and boozy breath
On our savage ears.

The stick came to a halt and he tapped it on the tiny hole in the dirt that concluded the poem. He had written a similar poem a year ago, after seeing Rickie Lee Jones in concert. But that poem had been flowery and melancholy-sweet, like bad Wordsworth, and this version was lean, essential—almost too spare for his tastes. No masterpiece, but a tugger. He frowned.

Sometimes he had the impression that he wasn't really the author of a poem, that Death's Radio allocated poems by queue number and not personality. But this was a particularly strong sensation. He hadn't written this poem. Somebody, somewhere, had heard his in-speaking and transformed it for him.

His hand reached out and scrawled *Just ask* beneath the poem.

Ask what?
Gnomisms. Puzzlements.

Names are but the robes of fools,
And words the death of thought.
Your realm lies not in matter's tools
But in what song has wrought.

He dropped the stick. The letters had gathered all the dirt's sparkles into their tiny valleys and banks. They blazed in the hut's gloom. He hadn't written them; it was more as if he had been speaking with someone, and the markings in the dirt had appeared as they talked.

"Man-child!"

He left the burning words in the dirt and backed out through the reed doorcover. Spart stood before his hut.

"Yes?"

"You will not train today," she said.

He stood with a chill draft circulating around him. "So?"

"You are not a prisoner. Just don't attract Lamia's attention again, and don't say you plan to run away. The Wickmaster has enough chores." Her face briefly pruned into a broad grin. "When you are not training, you are free to leave the mound. Without our company." She paused and looked around meaningfully. "After all, where will you go? Not far. Not far."

"I could cross the Blasted Plain, like when we went to meet Biri," he said.

She laughed. "I think you are too smart to try that. Not yet."

That was true enough. "What will you do with Biri today?"

Spart shook her head and held her finger to her lips. "Not for humans to know." She walked off and he dropped the door cover, then looked back at the words in the dirt, now dark. He reached out with his foot to erase them, but thought better of it and pulled the book from its hiding place under the rafters. It opened in his hands to Keats's long poem, "Lamia," which he had first read a few years before and forgotten. It did not illuminate his situation, nor did it shed much light on Lamia; it did, however, raise his curiosity as to why she was called that. No part of her was serpentine.

Except that she was shedding her skin.

He closed the book and put it in his new-sewn pocket. Outside, the mound seemed deserted. For a second he had a crazy notion to search for the Crane Women and Biri, observe them secretly—but that was as unlikely as escaping across the Blasted Plain alone.

He set out for Halftown.

As he approached the market square he heard a commotion. Three tall Breed males—including the guard who had first met Savarin and Michael on the outskirts of Halftown—stood at the gates to the market, glaring at a small crowd gathered around. The discussion was in Cascar and it sounded heated.

Eleuth stood to one side, head bowed. Michael walked up to her. "What's going on?"

"The market is no longer mine to manage," she said. She tried to smile but her lips wouldn't cooperate. "Since Lirg was taken away, I haven't been running it at all well. So the Breed Council claims."

Michael looked at the guards and the crowds and felt his face redden. "What will you do now?"

"They'll assign me a new house and find a new manager. I'll move."

"Can't you fight it?"

She shook her head as if shocked by the idea. "No! The council's decisions are final."

"Who's in charge of the council?"

"Haldan. But he takes direction from Alyons, who oversees everything in the Pact Lands, especially in Halftown."

"Is there anything I can do?"

She touched his cheek appreciatively. "No. I will be assigned another job, one better suited to my abilities."

He felt a surge of guilt as she stroked his cheek.

"I'm learning more quickly," she said, her voice distant. "Soon I'll be able to do things a young Sidhe can do."

"Magic, you mean."

"Yes. Michael, we could go away today . . ." The look of misery in her face, and desperation, was almost more than he could stand. "To the river. It looks like it will be warmer . . . perhaps we could swim."

Michael grimaced and shook his head. "I'm not sure I'll ever swim again."

"Oh, the Riverines are seldom a problem in the daytime. Besides, I can see them long before they reach us."

That hardly reassured him. Why not spend a day with her, though? It wasn't an unpleasant prospect. But his distance from her had grown now that it was obvious she needed someone, needed to lean on him. "I can't help anybody now," he said. She looked down at the ground.

Finally the guilt—and a basic desire which made him feel worse—drove him to agree. "What about the market?" he asked as they left.

"It is taken care of now. Come."

The sun had reappeared, driving away most of the clouds. The afternoon was pleasantly warm. The river flowed broad and slow and was also warm—which would have surprised Michael, had they been on Earth. The water was clear enough to see long silver fish gliding in the depths, just above ghostly reeds. Eleuth lay naked on the bank and Michael lay on his side, facing away from her, his head supported in one hand. "How is the novice Sidhe doing?" Eleuth asked.

He couldn't read her tone, so he turned away from the river to look at her. "Fine, I guess. I don't know what it takes to be a priest here—a priest of Adonna."

"It takes compromises, my father said once. He once tried to worship Adonna like a Sidhe, but it wasn't productive. All the Sidhe have compromised. They worship Adonna, Adonna lets them live here."

"How can worship be coerced?"

"Some Sidhe are very dedicated to Adonna. They feel a kinship."

"What kind of kinship?"

"Adonna is like the Sidhe, Lirg said once. 'We deserve each other, we and our god; we are both incomplete and lost.' What is the god of Earth like?"

"I'm an atheist," Michael said. "I don't believe there's a god on Earth."

"Do you believe Adonna exists?"

That took him aback. He hadn't really questioned the idea. This was a fantasy world, however grim, so of course gods *could* exist here. Earth was real, practical; no gods there. "I've never met him," Michael said.

"It," Eleuth corrected. "Adonna boasts of no gender. And be glad that you haven't met it. Lirg says—said—" She suddenly fell quiet. "Does it bother you when I talk too much about Lirg?" she asked.

"No. Why should it?"

"Humans might wish the talk to center on themselves. Not on others. That's what I've heard."

"I'm not an egotist," Michael said firmly. He looked at her long limbs, so lovely and pale and silky, and reached out to touch her thigh. She moved toward him, but the movement was too automatic, too acquiescing. He flashed on an image of Spart; what Eleuth would someday become.

"I'm confused," he said, removing his hand and rolling on his back. Eleuth gently laid her chin on his chest, staring up at him with large eyes golden in the low-angled sunlight.

"Why confused?"

"Don't know what I should do."

"Then you are free, perhaps."

"I don't think so. Not free. Just stupid. I don't know what's right."

"I am right when I love," Eleuth said. "I must be. There is no other way."

"But why love me?"

"Did I say I love you?" she asked. Again he was taken aback. He paused another minute before saying, "Whether you do or not," which was certainly witless enough.

"Yes," Eleuth said. "I love you." She sat up, the muscles on her back sleek like a seal's, her spine a chain of rounded bumps. The sun almost touched the horizon, orange in the haze of the Blasted Plain. Her skin looked like molten silver mixed with gold, warm and yellow-white. "On Earth, do humans choose the ones they love?"

"Sometimes," Michael said, but he thought not. He never had. His crushes had always been involuntary and fierce.

"A pure Sidhe male does not love," Eleuth said. "He attaches, but it is not the same as love. Male Sidhe are not passionate; neither are most Breeds. Liaisons between Breed males and females are usually short. Lirg was different. He was passionate and devoted to my mother." She sounded regretful. "Sidhe women are passionate, desiring, far more often. They are seldom fulfilled." She turned to face him. "That is why there are Breeds in the first place. Sidhe females and human males—almost never the reverse. So why are you confused?"

"I told you," he said.

"Not really. You don't love me? That confuses you?"

He pressed his lips together and finally nodded. "I like you. I'm grateful . . ."

Eleuth smiled. "Does it matter, your not loving me?"

"It doesn't feel right, making love and not feeling everything."

"Yet for all time, Sidhe males have not loved their *geen*. And we have survived. It is the way."

Her resignation didn't help. It twisted the perverse knot a little tighter, however, and the only way he could see to forestall the discussion was to kiss her. Soon they were making love and his confusion intensified everything, made everything worse . . . and better.

As dusk settled, they walked back to Halftown, Michael trailing his shirt in one hand. Eleuth held on to his arm, smiling as if at some inner joke.

20

The market courtyard was empty when they returned. Eleuth entered the house and began to stack her belongings in one corner. When she came to a brown rug, rolled and tied with twine, she paused and smiled, then undid the twine. "Do you have to go back right away?" she asked.

"No," Michael said.

"Then perhaps I can show you some of what I've learned." She unrolled the brown rug on the floor, smoothing the wrinkles, going from corner to corner on her hands and knees. "They'll leave me here for tonight, but tomorrow I must be gone. Lirg would be pleased with how far I've come; if I practice one more night here, it's almost like having him present." She kneeled on the rug and motioned for him to sit at one corner. "Lirg says the reason Breeds have a harder time with magic is because they're more like humans. They have more than one person inside them . . . but no soul."

Michael opened his mouth to express doubts about that, but decided he wasn't the one to judge.

"I'm not sure what he means . . . meant by that. But I feel the truth in it. Whenever I do magic, and I'm one person, it works. Sometimes my thoughts just split up, and many people talk in my head, and the magic fades. For a Sidhe, there is only one voice in the head, one discipline. So it's easier for a Sidhe to concentrate."

"Maybe that's what he meant—just concentration."

"No, it's deeper than that," Lirg said. She sighed and sat up on her knees. "Anyway, when you bring it all down to one person willing one thing, magic just flows. The next hardest thing is controlling it. Little magic is easy to control. For a split second you tie up the Realm with your head and there it is, what you want done is done. The Realm flows for you. It's almost automatic, like walking. But big magic . . . that's very complicated. Shall I explain more?"

Michael nodded. His mouth felt dry. Eleuth lay on the rug, staring at him steadily with her large dark eyes, her straight hair falling around her shoulders and curling over one breast.

"The Sidhe part of a Breed knows instinctively that any world is just a song of addings and takings away. To do grand magic, you must be completely in tune with the world—adding when the world adds, taking away when the world takes away. Then it becomes possible to turn the song around, and make the world be in tune with you, for a few moments, at least. A world is just one long, difficult song. The difference between the Realm and your home, that's just the difference between one song and another." She closed her eyes and chanted. *"Toh kelih ondulya, med nat ondulya trasn spaan nat kod."*

"What does that mean?"

"It means something like, 'All is waves, with nothing waving across no distance at all.' "

Michael gave a low whistle and shook his head. "And you feel all that?"

"When it works," she said. "Now sit farther back, on the edge of the blanket. I won't be able to talk to you for a while, because I can't listen to you in-speak. Understand?"

"Yes." *Maybe.*

She stood in the middle of the blanket and held out her arms, then swung them to point at opposite corners, as if doing slow exercises. Michael looked at the corner on his left and saw a curl of darkness, as tiny as a thumbnail, seem to screw the rug to the floor. The rug tensed under his knees as if alive.

She held her arms down at her side and closed her eyes, lifting her chin. Her fingers straightened.

For the merest instant, four glowing pillars rose from each corner and passed through the roof into a greater darkness high above. She held out her hand, fingers clenched into a fist, and spun once. Her eyes flashed just as he blinked and in the moment his lids were closed, the room seemed bright enough to be seen clearly through the skin.

She knelt in front of him, extended her fist, and uncurled it. A beetle lay in the middle of her palm, like a scarab but deep metallic green, with velvety green wing cases. It moved slowly, turning as if confused.

"That's very nice," Michael said, not sure whether to be impressed or not.

"It was a cold night, with clouds and the sky filled with light," she said. "It was a kind of road, hard and black, with white lines and golden dots and grass imprisoned in rock on each side, and trees in the grass." She pointed to the beetle. "This was . . . there. So I brought it back."

Michael blinked. "I—"

"I brought it for you from your home," Eleuth said. "You live in a very strange place."

The beetle crawled a half inch across her palm, then stopped and rolled over. Its legs kicked feebly and it was still. Eleuth looked down on it with concern and touched it gently with one finger. Drops of water glistened on the finger, as if it had searched through wet grass.

"Is it dead?" Michael asked.

Tears brimmed in Eleuth's eyes. "I think so. I have so much to learn."

IT WAS DARK and very cold when he returned to the mound. The windows of the Crane Women's hut glowed brightly. Spart waited for him between the huts, standing on one leg. She crooked a finger at him, lowered her leg, and strode to his hut. He followed. She gestured for him to pull back the cover and he complied. She snapped her fingers and the letters of the poem in the dirt glowed. "Where did that come from?

"I'm a poet," he said, resenting her intrusion. "I write poetry. There's no paper here, so I write it in the dirt."

"Yes, but where does it come from?"

"How should I know? It's poetry."

"Do you know how old this poem is?" she asked, pointing to the last few lines. "In its Cascar version?"

Michael shook his head. "I just wrote it."

"It is dangerous to write such things. Your play with the Breed girl is making you a very interesting student." She walked away on her long limbs like a two-legged spider.

"It's *my* poem," he called after her. He heard a scratching noise behind him and saw Nare peering around the door into the hut's inner darkness. She mouthed a few words, her eyes focused on the glowing scrawls. "Tonn's *Kaeli*," she said, grinning at Michael. She straightened and followed Spart.

The air smelled of dust and electricity, though the night sky was cloudless. He lay on the grass reeds, shivering, and thought briefly of Eleuth and what she had done, then more lingeringly of Helena. He wondered what Helena was doing, and when he would get to see her again . . . and he wondered if she could ever be as affectionate as Eleuth.

(What Eleuth had done . . .)

But that seemed too much to hope for.

21

The few times Michael saw the Crane Women training Biri, they spoke Cascar and he couldn't understand precisely what was happening. They continued to work with Michael, and as the days passed and the weather grew colder, Nare finally devoted a day to teaching him how to harness *hyloka,* or drawing-of-heat-from-the-center. He was just beginning to get the hang of the discipline when she abandoned him. For a week, they concentrated on Biri from dawn to dusk.

On a bitterly cold morning, Michael emerged from his hut and saw Biri in the middle of the mound with the Crane Women. They surrounded him with linked hands, their eyes closed and faces upturned to the cool blue sky. Snow fell around them in lazy, swaying flakes. Michael sat cross-legged on the dirt before his door.

For hours, the group simply stood, doing nothing.

Michael wrote poems in the hardening dirt and scratched them out, peering up now and then to see if anything had changed. He tried to recapture the sensation of an inner, separate voice, but failed.

Finally, Biri collapsed between the Crane Women and they broke away, backing up, crouched over like birds of prey, their eyes wide and lips tight and grim. They went to their hut and left Biri where he lay. Michael went to him and bent over, reaching out hesitantly to touch his forehead. "Are you all right?"

"Go away," Biri said, eyes tightly shut.

"Just asking," Michael said.

Spart came running from the house, arms swinging. "Go!" she screeched. "Leave him alone! Get out of here!"

"Forever, you mean?" Michael asked resentfully, dancing ahead of her shooing hands.

"Come back at dusk." She looked down on Biri, who hadn't moved.

"Is he all right?"

"No. Go now."

Michael walked across the stream, then looked over his shoulder at the frozen tableau of Spart and the prostrate Sidhe. He frowned and kicked at small rocks on the road to Euterpe.

The snow fell more heavily, forming speckled caps on the bushes and grass clumps by the roadside. He practiced *hyloka* as he walked, and felt a gradual spreading of warmth from the pit of his stomach.

How many days had he been in the Realm? His concentration was broken by the question and he cooled rapidly in the icy air. He had lost count of the days; perhaps two months, perhaps two and a half or three. Everything had merged into training, running, casting shadows, with highlights of terror, of Eleuth's affection, and thoughts of Helena.

He frowned and bore down on *hyloka* again, feeling new heat rise in his chest and spread down his arms. He smiled and swung his arms experimentally. The chill was dispelled. When Euterpe was in sight, he quickened his pace. His face was flushed and his fingers tingled.

He thought of Biri lying on the ground in apparent agony and was very glad he wasn't a Sidhe. He felt almost giddy with relief that he was Michael Perrin. He was even glad to be in the Realm, because otherwise he wouldn't be so warm, standing in the snow; so warm and comfortable. He kicked his legs and didn't notice the thin trickle of smoke.

Michael was prancing exuberantly by the time he reached the outskirts of Euterpe. He jigged past the outer houses, grinning and humming. He wondered vaguely why he was so happy, and turned up the street to Helena's alley.

A thin coat of ice crusted the cobbles in the central gutter. As he danced, his feet didn't so much crack the ice as melt it. He left steaming tracks as he leaped and ran around the corner of the alley, hollered as he passed between the blank stone walls. In his ecstasy, Michael seemed to find the inner voice again, and was about to chant a snatch of poetry when he came to the bottom of the stairs. He stopped and smoothed his hands on his pants legs. He didn't want to be less than dignified around Helena.

Michael's feet hissed on the steps. He stood by Helena's doorway, knocking on the frame. His nose twitched—something burning. He looked around, puzzled, hoping it was only a cooking fire and not the building. The smell grew stronger.

He lifted his hand to rub his nose.

The sleeve of his shirt smoked. He stared at it for a moment, dumbfounded. Heat radiated from his skin. Flames curled from the edge of the fabric, small and dull at first; then the entire sleeve ignited. He clawed and tugged his way out of the shirt, casting it to the floor, where it sent up volumes of gray smoke. He dropped to his knees and pulled the book from its pocket, dropping it as his fingers scorched the binding.

The pants caught next and he kicked out of them, brushing bits of char and smoking fragments from his legs.

The walls of the hallway reflected an orange glow, but the clothing had extinguished itself. His breathing was deep and rapid. His whole body tingled and euphoria mixed with his astonishment and fear. He wanted to dance again, but instead decided it was time to do some hard thinking.

About something left untended . . . let out of control. And that was . . . what?

Hyloka. He hadn't stopped the drawing of heat from the center. He shook his head in comic exasperation and concentrated on the center of warmth, gradually damping it. His hand still glowed ruddy. He damped more. Normal skin color returned.

With the heat vanished the euphoria. Michael suddenly realized he was standing naked in the middle of the hallway, surrounded by the blackened remains of his clothes . . .

In front of Helena's door.

It was worse than any nightmare of embarrassment he had ever had. He had burned his clothes off his back. He bent to pick up the book, and without thinking he pushed on the wicker door. It opened—there were no locks in Euterpe—and he darted inside.

Several seconds passed before he was calm enough to realize she wasn't home. Chilled again, he looked around for something to wear. The closet—a wicker armoire—yielded a long skirt which he tied around his waist. He found a kind of short jacket which barely fit his shoulders and was about to sneak out when the wicker door swung open again.

Helena came in with several scraps of cloth draped over her arm and a sewing kit in one hand.

"Hello," Michael said by way of warning. She turned slowly and regarded him with wide eyes.

"What in hell is wrong with you?" she asked a moment later. He shivered, mortified, but managed a miserable smile. "I burned my clothes," he said.

"Jesus H. Christ." Helena propped the door open with her foot, as if contemplating escape. She glanced down at the blackened rags in the hallway and shook her head, confused. "Why?"

"I was trying to keep warm," Michael said. "It got away from me. I was, you know, drawing heat from the center . . . Spart calls it *hyloka*—"

"You're only making it worse," Helena said, relaxing. She folded the fabric over the back of a chair and laid the sewing kit on the seat. "Start at the beginning."

Michael explained as best he could, and when he was done, Helena nodded dubiously. "So you dress up in my clothes. That's my only skirt, you know."

"I wouldn't fit in your pants," Michael said.

"Indeed you wouldn't. What are you going to do? Wear my only dress around? Do you have other clothes?"

"No. Just those." Michael pointed toward the hall. "I was—"

"Why did you come *here to* burn your clothes?"

His mortification turned to misery. He stammered and felt the start of tears. Then he saw she was enjoying the whole situation, egging him on. "I was coming to visit. It was snowing."

Helena suddenly started laughing. She bent over and fell back on the chair, knocking the kit to the floor. "I'm so-orry," she cackled. "I'm really so-o-o-rry!"

Michael saw the humor, but couldn't bring himself to join her. "I'll go now," he said.

"Not in my dress, you won't. What are we going to do? I don't have any men's clothes here."

"Borrow some, maybe," he suggested hopefully.

She restrained her mirth and picked up the sewing kit. "Actually," she said, walking around him, "you don't look half bad. Maybe I'll let you wear it."

"Helena, please."

"All right. I shouldn't laugh."

"I'm sure it's very funny," Michael said. "I'd be laughing, too, but it's me standing here like an ass, and in your apartment, too. And it's me wearing your clothes—"

"Why did you come back? I've seen so little of you."

"To talk. Until a few days ago, they've kept me busy." He hoped she hadn't heard about Eleuth; he didn't know what kind of gossip network there was in Euterpe. No doubt he would soon find out. "You won't tell anybody, will you?"

"No. Michael, you are the most unusual person I've ever met, and you get weirder every time I see you."

"It's just this place, everything about it."

"Oh. *You're* normal, then."

"Yeah . . . No, I mean, not like everybody else—"

"Enough, enough," Helena said, holding up a hand. "I'll go find Savarin and tell him you need some clothes. He might know where to get them—fabric is scarce around here, you know. You can't just cook it off every chance you get." She giggled. "I'm even bringing home stuff mangled in the tubs at the laundry," she said, pointing to the cloth. "It's part of my job to patch it up."

"Don't tell Savarin. Don't bring him here, *please.*"

"But we'll need an excuse. Some reason why you need new clothes."

"Tell him I wore mine out training."

"Sure. And walked naked through town to my apartment."

"Then make something up! Please."

"I'll be circumspect. I'll tell him it's a secret. You know what he'll think then?" She put on a prim expression. "Well, let him think whatever he wants." She went to the door. "I'll be back shortly. Don't go anywhere."

"You don't need to tell me that," he said.

She gave him one final glance, shook her head, and closed the door. Michael looked down at the blouse that barely fit across his chest, and the dress, and gave a helpless groan. He sat on the chair and rubbed his face with his hands, then lifted his head and looked around the small apartment.

Sitting on the wicker table near the chair was a rounded piece of what appeared to be driftwood. He wondered where it had come from; Helena had it displayed prominently, a treasure. Wood was highly regarded by the humans. The Breeds were forbidden to trade wood, and he doubted Sidhe traders would supply any to humans. He wondered if he could procure some for Helena, perhaps a board from his hut; anything to make up for what he had just done.

Near the window looking down into the alley she had placed a tall, columnar ceramic vase with three leafy sticks giving out one small yellow bud. He walked over and sniffed the flower. It had no odor.

The rest of the room was quite spare. Still, after his hut, Helena's apartment seemed like the height of civilization.

An hour passed before she returned with a cloth bag and held it out to him. "Go into the back room and put these on," she said. "Savarin asked Risky for some leftovers. She had them from a tenant who disappeared years ago. They should fit."

Michael did as he was told and used the opportunity to examine her sleeping quarters. The bed was made of—what else?—wicker, with a mattress stuffed with vegetable fiber, not precisely straw. Over it lay two plain, thin blankets. The area was barely large enough for a single bed. On the walls, someone—probably Helena—had painted red and blue flowers, clumsy but, to him, charming.

Helena examined Michael critically when he returned through the curtain. "Well," she said, finger to cheek, "it's not the tailored look, but it will have to do."

"There's no pocket for my book," he said. He held up the volume, which was starting to look the worse for wear.

"I'll make you a pocket with some scraps," Helena said. "Give me the shirt." He removed the shirt and handed it to her.

"So you won't be needing any warm clothes, hm?" Helena asked as she cut out a patch pocket and began to apply it.

"I don't want to use *hyloka* again until I know how to control it," he said. He sighed. "There are so many really strange things to watch out for."

She looked at his naked chest as she sewed on the pocket. He shifted on his chair and pretended interest in the window. He wasn't scrawny but his skin was pale and he thought he would never pass for a pin-up.

"You're getting heftier," she said. "Must be the training. Too bad baggy clothes hide it."

Snow was falling again. "Does it get real cold here?"

"Looks like winter's getting started, but you can't always count on it. When winter sets in for sure, it gets *very* cold. The laundry shuts down, everything stops. Winter is a good time to hide things. The Wickmaster hardly ever comes through then. He doesn't want to see how miserable everybody is. He has to keep us reasonably well-cared-for, and what he doesn't see, he doesn't have to correct."

She finished the sewing and put the needle away. "There. A pocket." She passed the shirt to him and turned her chair around to watch as he put it on. "A regular ragamuffin. Have you thought much about what I said?"

He buttoned the front and slipped the book into place. "Said?"

"About our group."

"Oh. I've thought about it. I'm wondering what you'll do with a piano."

She stood and peered out the window into the alley, then drew closer to him. "It's not just the piano," she said. "It's bigger than that. The piano's nice, though." A distant look came into her eyes. "I'm *so* out of practice. My fingers are ruined." She wriggled them and made as if to pound a keyboard. "Stiff. Calluses. But like I was saying, we have other plans. Savarin thinks we can trust you. The Wickmaster seems to hate your guts. Of course, maybe that's just a ruse . . . Humans who have gone over to the Sidhe." She looked at him sharply. "You're more mixed-up with the Breeds than with the Sidhe, and the Sidhe and Breeds aren't exactly close. But we have one reservation."

"Yes?"

"Why are the Crane Women so interested in you?"

He felt vaguely guilty and grit his teeth. "I think because of Lamia," he said. "But listen, if you don't trust me, forget it. Don't tell me anything."

"You don't know why you're being trained?"

"I'm probably the most ignorant person in the Realm."

Helena laughed. "Don't be upset. We have to be careful. You know how serious things are. What do you know about the Pact?"

"That the Isomage, or David Clarkham, or whoever he is, fought a battle and won concessions."

"He lost."

"Yeah, but he made the Sidhe agree to set up the Pact Lands. I suppose having Alyons watch over us was part of the agreement."

"Savarin says Alyons was sent here as punishment for breaking a Sidhe law. But what I'm getting at is, if we put up some kind of resistance, or try to change things, the Pact is off. Alyons can do what he wants with us."

"You're not thinking of resisting?" He remembered Biri running around the rock, powdering it, and Biri was just a young, inexperienced Sidhe. What could a Wickmaster do, if all their restrictions were removed?

"Yes!" Helena affirmed, eyes wide with excitement. "Isn't it about time?"

"Is Savarin the leader?"

"Heavens no. Someone you have yet to meet."

"But you and Savarin think I shouldn't know his name."

She hesitated, then shook her head. "Not until we're positive you can be trusted."

"Do *you* trust me?"

"I think so," Helena said. Then, after a moment, "Yes, I trust you." She smiled broadly and rocked gently in her chair, giving him a sly smile. "Nobody could be an undercover agent and burn his clothes off on my doorstep."

Michael felt his chest muscles loosen with relief. "So what are you going to do?"

"We're still planning. Nothing's final. But if this really is winter, maybe we can get on with it. They've been planning ever since I came here, and long before. The central committee is very careful."

"Thanks for the clothes," he said, remembering how Eleuth had clothed him before.

"Nothing to it. Try not to destroy them."

"No guarantees," he said ruefully. "Sometimes the best intentions go way wrong."

"Don't I know it," she said. She fastened her gaze on him and bit her lower lip.

"What's wrong?"

"You're handsome," she said.

"Bull."

"I mean it. You're attractive."

"I think you're beautiful." The words came out before he could think.

Helena's expression didn't change for a moment, but then a slow, warm smile emerged and she touched his knee with her hands.

"I mean it, too," he said.

"You're sweet. What time do you have to be back?" Her tone became businesslike and she went to the window again.

"Dusk," he said.

"That'll probably come early today. You want to learn why we're so sure we can resist, and succeed?"

"I suppose," he said.

"You'll have to be sure, now," she said sternly. "I'll be taking you to someplace pretty unpleasant."

"How can I—? Oh, okay. I'm sure."

"Do you have a strong stomach?"

"I guess."

She frowned at him, then held out her hand. He took it and stood up.

"There are several lessons for you to learn," she said. He felt his heart quicken hopefully, but she put on a shawl and held the apartment door open for him. "I have friends in the Yard. They'll get us in. There's somebody I want you to meet. A Child."

22

The Yard was at Euterpe's center, a broad, flat brick building surrounded by streets uncharacteristically wide for the human town. Helena marched ahead of him with a look half of puzzlement, half of resolve. "Nobody likes to go here," she said. She looked over her shoulder at Michael. Her eyes were a little wild, like a wary deer. "Savarin comes here more often than the rest of us."

The entrance to the yard was narrow, barely two feet wide, blocked by a heavy woven wicker door a foot thick. Helena pulled a knob and glass chimes tinkled faintly within. A peephole slid open in the brick wall beside the door and a yellow, bleary eye peered at them.

"Sherebith, it's me," Helena said. The wicker door opened with a hollow scraping sound.

"Yes, Miss Helena. What can I do for you?" A yellow-faced, plump woman in a long gray gown stood in the half-open entranceway, one arm on the door, the other folded across her chest. The plump woman stared at Michael with neither trust nor liking.

"This is a friend," Helena said. "I'd like him to see the Yard and meet Ishmael. Michael, this is Sherebith."

Michael held out his hand. "Glad to meet you," he said. The woman looked at the hand, grimaced in disbelief and opened the door wider. "Come in," she said in a resigned tone, marching ahead of them. "He's been quiet today. The others are following his example. Thank whomever for small favors."

Sherebith led them down a dark corridor made of close-spaced bricks the color of dried dung. Faint light entered through narrow slits at intervals of six or seven strides; the only other illumination came from wax candles ensconced between the slits. Despite the musty smell, the floors and walls seemed clean and well-tended. Sherebith went first, followed by Helena and then Michael, who had the nagging urge to look over his shoulder.

The interior was silent. At the end of the corridor, another heavy wicker door studded with more glass chimes. "Alarms," Helena said, tinkling one with a finger. Sherebith opened the door and set them all ringing.

The door led to an open court about ten feet square, walls and overarching parapet also of yellow brick and devoid of ornament. In each of the four walls opened another door. Sherebith stepped to the one directly opposite and unlatched it. As it creaked open, a damp odor wafted out, combining the worst traits of musty cellars and the sewer sludge Michael's father used on the family garden.

The candles burned dimmer in the heavy air beyond. There were no slits for lighting, but covered ventilator holes in the ceiling admitted dim barred spots of day.

The room's opposite walls were lost in darkness. Square brick columns supported the low ceiling, each side holding a guttering candle. They walked past pits dug into the floor, each about ten feet on a side and faced with brick and tile. Michael counted seven. "Compound three," Sherebith said. "I call it Leader of the Howl Compound, because of Ishmael. He's the big one. The instigator." She pointed to benches near each pit. "When the compounds were built, people thought perhaps the parents would like to come visit their Children now and then. Nobody has, not since the first few months. Only me and the caretaker. I'm the warden." She smiled, revealing snaggled, yellow teeth. "I'm the only one who cares about them, who's kind to them, except the caretaker."

"What about Savarin?" Helena suggested gently.

"Him? He has reasons to come here. He gets them upset sometimes. No love for Savarin. Does he listen to them when night's down and they hear the calls from the Plain, things you and I can't hear? *No.*" She pointed to her small, curled ears, hidden beneath straight strands of graying hair. "Calls from their real kin. The bodies mean nothing. It's what's in the bottles that counts, not the shapes nor the labels."

She led them to the middle pit. Michael glanced into the other pits as they passed; the walkways were only a yard wide, and it was difficult to stay calm with the unknown on each side. Each pit held a single pale, reclining figure, some child-sized, some larger. He couldn't make out details.

Sherebith leaned over the middle pit. "Ishmael," she called softly. "Ishmael, are you home?" A thin gray figure stirred in the shadows.

"Yes, Mother." The voice was thick, deep and cultured, imbued with an abysmal sadness. Michael felt a tug on some emotion that he could not immediately identify.

"I'm not his real mother," Sherebith confided with a slack-lipped smile. "But I'm the only one he knows."

"Ishmael," Helena said, kneeling on the walkway. The pit was as deep as it was wide, and the walls were faced with slick gray tile. Except for three bowls, receptacles for food, water and waste, all arranged neatly against one wall, Ishmael's pit was bare, and the pale, loose figure within it, naked.

"Yes," the figure said.

Michael's eyes had adjusted well enough that he could make out the details of Ishmael's face: small, round, disproportionate to such a tall body. The large hands hung from arms which sprouted thin from stooped shoulders and widened to grotesque forearms and wrists.

"We have some questions," Helena said.

"I'm not otherwise occupied," Ishmael said with a thin chuckle.

"Has he been here since he was born?" Michael whispered.

"Almost," Helena said. "He was one of the first. He's been here since the War."

"Time passes," Ishmael said. "Questions." He stood, paced, and squatted again, leaning against the tiles and stretching his pale legs out on the floor.

"Who are you?"

"Product of lust. A sideshow for the guilty. Something so evil it must be evilly confined through all its endless life. An abortion walking. Victim."

Helena glanced at Michael to gauge Ishmael's effect on him, then returned her attention to the pit. "Who are you?"

"An abortion!" Ishmael's voice rose. "Born of man and woman."

"You killed your parents."

"I don't remember." Coy.

"You tried to kill others."

"You are so *informed.*"

"Who are you?" Helena persisted. "Your real name."

"Call me—"

"Stop that." Sherebith said quietly. "His true name is Paynim. He's one of Adonna's own."

"Paynim," said the figure, "Ishmael. No matter."

"He took the child's body when it was born. There are no souls here." Sherebith walked around the pit and stared at them owlishly from the shadows, hands limp by her sides. "I am the only one who cares."

"Adonna cares!" Ishmael wailed. "Adonna bred me—"

"Buried you," Sherebith said, pacing behind Helena and Michael, making Michael edge uncomfortably close to the pit.

"Adonna freed me."

"You rose from the Blasted Plain. You still call to your friends there."

"No friends." Sad, deep.

"Then what are you?" Helena asked.

"Out of time, mired in the Realm, given form by Adonna. Ishmael."

"What are you capable of?"

The Child shook his head. Michael could barely make out his grin. The air was stifling. Michael wanted badly to be outside.

"I stare at the Realm. I foresee."

"What do you foresee?"

"Rebellion."

"When?"

"Soon, soon."

"Who will win?"

Michael looked at Helena, then at Sherebith.

"The Pact will be broken. Alyons will lose everything."

Helena's expression was triumphant. "That's the second time he's used those words. He told Savarin the same thing. We'll *win!*"

Michael frowned. The Child had folded his hands in his lap, face composed.

Sherebith kneeled beside the pit and looked up at them. "Nobody cares for them," she said with solemn pride. "I am the only one."

"And the caretaker," Helena reminded her.

"And him," Sherebith agreed with a shrug.

Behind them, a short lean man dressed in brown pants and a knee-length baggy shirt pushed a wicker cart across the narrow walkways. From the sides of the cart hung the paper and wicker bowls used by the inhabitants of the pits. Three covered containers poked from a recess in the top of the cart. Helena and Michael stepped aside and he passed along the narrow walkway, bowls rapping hollowly the sides of the cart. Michael looked at the man's face. He seemed to concentrate on some inner melody, gliding under the bands of light from a ventilator; his eyes were sunken, useless, as blue as a newborn kitten's. "The caretaker," Helena whispered into Michael's ear.

"The only one," Sherebith affirmed, gaze fixed on Ishmael in his pit.

MICHAEL FELT BONE-COLD and weary as they emerged from the Yard. Sherebith closed the door behind them and latched it without a word. For the first time, Michael knew what it felt like to want to die—to get the misery over with.

That was an insight freely given by Ishmael.

Helena took a deep breath and brushed her hair back from her face. "Now you see why we don't go there often."

"They're kept in the pits . . . because they hurt people?"

"They're monsters," Helena said, walking across the road. "Didn't you *hear* him?"

"Yes, but he's been there . . . how long? Decades? That would turn anyone into a monster."

"I've only heard stories," Helena said, staying one stride ahead. "They killed their parents, or they murdered other people. Or they escaped to the Blasted Plain and lived there and made raids on Euterpe until they were caught, or killed. And when they were killed, a . . . foulness came out of them." She shuddered, her shoulders jerking spasmodically. "This isn't Earth, Michael."

"I know that," Michael said, his voice rising. "But the way they're treated! If they're so bad, why not just kill them?"

"We can't kill them," Helena said. "Alyons can. Not us. Alyons hasn't killed any of them for a long time. None have escaped for a long time. They're human . . . sort of. I don't wish to talk about it anymore."

"All right. Then about Ishmael's prophecy. How do you know he—it—is telling the truth?"

"Sherebith will tell you. Once you get past all the crap, Ishmael never lies."

"Maybe he misleads. I read about the sibyls—"

Helena turned on him, jaw thrust out and fists clenched. "Look! We have little enough to go on, nothing to encourage us. We take our reassurances where we can."

"From Ishmael?" Michael said, his face flushing. "From someone you lock up as a monster?"

"A special monster," she said. "Don't try to set us straight about the Realm, or about what we're doing, Michael. We've been here a lot longer than you have."

That seemed to settle it. They were silent the rest of the way back to Helena's apartment. She walked up the stairs ahead of him. "You want to come in?" she asked.

He considered. "I want to know what I can do to help. I don't like Alyons any more than you do. Maybe less."

"Then come in," Helena said.

23

Helena busied herself cleaning up in the back room behind half-drawn curtains. Michael listened to water splashing, toilet articles clinking, Helena humming to herself.

He was disturbed. Something was wrong, but what exactly eluded him. The perverse mood brought on by Ishmael's words was passing; what was wrong, or seemed wrong, was much more mundane.

Helena. When she was away from him, he had doubts she could ever be more than she was at this moment—friendly, but distant. When she was in his sight, the doubts shrunk to mere points, blocked by his infatuation. She was quick, pretty, human. She would never look like the Crane Women. She came from Earth. From home.

Yet he didn't feel at ease around her. He was more comfortable around Eleuth than Helena.

Helena parted the curtains and smiled. "Thank you for waiting. I always have to wash myself after visiting the Yard." She offered him a damp rag. He didn't feel any dirtier than usual, but to please her, he rubbed off his face and wiped his hands.

"There," she said, throwing the rag into a corner and sitting in the second chair before him. She adjusted her seat until it was square with his. "You know how much I feel for you," she said.

He didn't reply for a moment. Her eyes locked his; he had to make an effort to look away and swallow. "I know *that* you feel for me," he said, concentrating on the curtained window. "I don't know how . . . or how much."

"Now *you're* being obscure," she said. "I care for you a great deal. You're a very sweet boy. True, you're caught up in things you don't really understand, but so am I. So are we all. You do the best you can."

He shrugged, his thick red eyebrows drawn together. She smiled. "You're smart, attractive, and anywhere else I would probably be in love with you, right this minute. I'd want you to write poetry for me. I'd play the piano for you." Her smile broadened. "You may hear me play a piano soon, anyway. If we were in Brooklyn—" Her face stiffened and she shook her head, looking away. "But we're not. We have to see that. I can't love you, not like I should. Today you've seen why."

"I have?"

"The Yard. To love you properly, I'd want to give myself to you completely . . . and I can't." She searched his face and reached out to touch his cheek. "Don't you see? They've taken love away from us. We might make a mistake, a slip. I couldn't stand the thought of having a Child."

He was dumbfounded.

"Poor Michael," she repeated.

"I don't see—" he began. But he did see. She was being perfectly reasonable. And yet . . . there was that wrong thing, that still-nagging point of disturbance.

"Friendship is very important here," she said. "We live by it. We all have to work together, or they'll overwhelm us. We all have to resist every way we can. I need you. We need you. As a friend."

He still didn't have any reply. He wanted to show her he knew what she was about to say, but he couldn't.

"We can't be lovers, Michael. Do you understand? I hope you do. I need you to understand, now, before it gets all . . ." She waved her hand and cocked her head to one side. "All crazy."

"I do understand," he said. It was too late. He felt it even more strongly now. Not being able to have her made him love her all the more. He knew it was perverse, but it wasn't a new emotion; it was just that the denial unveiled it completely. He had to be near her any way he could. "Friendship is important to me, too," he said with a weak grin. "I really need friends here."

"Good." She laid her hand on his knee and regarded him earnestly. "We need your help."

"How?"

"If you truly want to be one of us, to resist Alyons and the coursers and to free us all from the Sidhe . . . you have to listen for us. Let us know what you hear."

He laughed. "The Crane Women don't tell me anything," he said. "I feel like a goddamn mushroom with them." He was surprised by the bitterness in his voice.

"Yes. I know the joke," she said. "We all feel that way. But Savarin says you're right in the thick of things. There's a Sidhe living not ten yards from your hut, and the Crane Women are training you. I've told Savarin I bet you're already learning things no other human knows. Like how to burn off your clothes." She smiled. "We still don't know why you're being trained. Probably only Lamia could tell us that. But there *must* be things you can learn, knowledge you can pass on. You could learn about the land beyond the Blasted Plain—"

"I've been there," Michael said.

"See!" Her excitement doubled. "Wonderful! You could tell Savarin what it's like, what we'll find when we break out!"

"It's not wise to even think about crossing the Blasted Plain," Michael said. "Even the Sidhe have to dust themselves with *sani* and use their horses for protection. It's dangerous."

"We know a little about the powder. Can you get some for us?"

"I don't think so," he said. "I don't know where it is, or even if the Crane Women have any . . ."

"But if you could get into their hut, look for it . . . They must have *some.*"

"I wouldn't even want to try," he said.

"Why not? They're half-human."

He chuckled. "The forgotten half. You should see their windows at night. Like they have a blast furnace inside. Orange light, flickering. You'd think it was on fire."

"Can't you even look?" The goad in her voice was not particularly sharp, but surrounded by the silkiness, the hint of doubt, it hurt.

"I'll let you know," he said after a pause.

"We'll need it soon."

"How soon?"

"Within a fortnight. Two weeks. Sorry—I start to talk like the old folks here." She gave him a questioning look, lifting her eyebrows. She was practically begging.

"I'll try," he said.

"Marvelous!"

"I better be going back now." He wanted to be alone, to think things over and subdue the buzz of confusion and disappointment.

"Don't cause any trouble," she said. "Don't try to run away again. Just work with us . . . help us. You heard what Ishmael said."

"I heard." They stood and she kissed him on the cheek, gripping his arms tightly.

FOR THE NEXT week, he hardly had time to think. The Crane Women suddenly integrated him into Biri's training, without explanation—and without reprieve.

The day after he'd spoken with Helena, they took Michael and Biri to a barren mound about two miles south. Coom supervised Biri and Spart kept watch on Michael as they tried higher and higher levels of *hyloka.*

The Crane Women were positively grim. Spart barked out her instructions, her voice growing hoarse as the hours passed. Before the day was done, Nare instructed Michael on how to block his aura of memory—which, among other things, would prevent a Sidhe or Breed adversary from in-speaking. "Occult the knowledge," she told him. "Not just your immediate knowings, but the knowings of your mother and father, your forefathers . . . memories of your kind. No eyes will see, no minds will use what you do not wish them to have."

Snow fell more frequently during that week. The season was indeed going over to winter, in fits and starts, as if the air itself were undecided. But more days were dark and cold than otherwise. Michael's *hyloka* kept him warm under the most frigid conditions.

Spart schooled Michael on how to throw a shadow while asleep, and how to sleep like the dead, his heart barely beating, while at the same time his mind stayed alert. He controlled his breath until he seemed not to breathe at all. He explored his inner thoughts, paring them down to the ones most essential to his exercises.

For a time, he forgot about Helena and Eleuth. What little spare time he had, Michael spent exercising these new abilities, reveling in the potential that was being unlocked without resort to Sidhe magic.

He could not locate the inner voice that had briefly conversed with him in poetry. He did find, however, a good many other unexpected things in his mind. Some edified him, some astonished him, and others made him wilt with shame. When he complained he couldn't stand any more introspection and asked if this was just incidental to the other disciplines, whether it could be foregone, Spart told him that a warrior must know all there was to hate in himself, or his enemy would use it against him.

"Blackmail?" Michael asked.

"Worse. Your own shadows can be thrown against you."

Biri's training seemed similar, but at a higher level. There was no repeat of the torturing circle-formation the Crane Women had exercised against the young Sidhe. Nevertheless, Biri became thinner. He was less talkative and seemed more resentful of Michael's presence. Michael avoided him.

In and around all the other exercises, there was running with and without sticks, physical training from a taciturn and frowning Coom, verbal harangues from Spart when he didn't pay attention.

He hated it, yet the training exhilarated him. He missed Earth even more but he began to feel as if he could survive in the Realm.

There was no training on the eighth day. Biri and the Crane Women left the mound before sunrise. Michael was asleep and had no idea where they went.

He walked around the mound in the early dawn, calling out their names, looking at the fresh footprints heading south, wondering if now was the time to look for the *sani* in the Crane Women's hut. He lingered near the hut, frowning, feeling he was about to betray them. Still, they were not exactly friends—taskmasters, tyrants, not friends.

Then why did he feel beholden to them?

He began to sweat and ran away from the mound, going to Eleuth's new quarters in Halftown. She was cleaning clothes and preparing for more of her own exercises; he half-listened as she described the Sidhe magic she now knew.

"If I brought a beetle back now, it would stay alive," she said proudly, smiling at him.

"No need," he said gloomily.

"You are bothered. Why?"

He walked around the small apartment, one of four units in the single-story wood building. The room was barely fifteen feet on a side, divided in half by a curtain: clean, neatly arranged, but somehow oppressive. Eleuth didn't seem to find it so.

"What are you going to do?" he asked.

"I'll be assigned another task soon," she said, looking down at the floor, eyebrows raised.

"Like what?" he pursued.

"The decision hasn't been made yet."

He was about to say something that might make her feel miserable but he caught himself. He was upset. He couldn't stand her calmness but that was no excuse to pass on his gloom. "The Crane Women are gone today," he said. "I don't want to stay on the mound. Would it bother you if I stayed here?"

She smiled; of course not.

She fixed a simple dinner for them. In perverse exchange, he briefly put up his wall against in-speaking, leaving her fumbling for words, without ready access to his memory of English. She was chastened, but remained outwardly cheerful.

After they cleared the remains of dinner, Michael asked her whether she could transfer someone between the Realm and Earth. He thought the question innocent enough; he just wanted to know how capable she was.

"Why are you angry?" she asked.

"I'm not angry."

"No?"

He shrugged and admitted perhaps he was. "It's not your fault."

"I feel that it is."

"Always so sensitive!"

She backed away and he flung up his arms in irritation and frustration. "I'm sorry," he said. "I don't know what to do or say any more."

"You wish to return to Earth?"

"Of course. I always have."

"You would consider it love if I returned you to Earth?"

The question took him aback. "Can you?"

"Would you consider it love?"

"What do you mean, love? It would be wonderful, yes."

"I'm not sure I can," she said. "I wouldn't want to fail you."

He paced around the room, scowling and mumbling. "Jesus, Eleuth, I'm just confused. Very, very confused. And angry.

"With whom are you angry?"

"Not you. You've never done me anything but good."

She smiled radiantly and took his hand. "I would want everything I do to be good for you, to be love for you."

He felt even more miserable. What if he never did go home, would it matter much? Could he make a life here in the Realm, even in the Pact Lands? Others had lived in worse conditions and been happy, or at least not miserable. Eleuth sensed the drift of his thoughts and gripped his hand all the tighter.

"It could be a good life here," she said. Her hopeful tone stung like a dart in his temple.

"How?" he asked, shaking her hand loose. "I don't belong here! I'm human, and you're—" He pounded his hand against the wall. "And *she's* human, and that's the problem, isn't it?"

"The woman in Euterpe?" Eleuth asked, staring at the back of his head.

"Helena," he said. He imagined it to be the most vicious thing he could say: the name of the woman toward whom he felt as Eleuth deserved to have him feel toward her. As Eleuth wanted him to feel.

"Humans have many more troubles than Breeds, actually," Eleuth said. She didn't sound upset or jealous. He turned toward her. Her face gleamed half in shadow, half brightened by the afternoon light from a high window. Her eyes were large and deep and calm.

"Please," Michael said.

"You could love her, and be with me," Eleuth said.

Tears began to flow down his cheeks. He felt guilty and vicious and furious, every thought part of a turbulent, rising whirl. "Don't say any more. Please, no more."

"No," Eleuth said, standing and reaching for his shoulder. "I'm sorry. I don't understand. I cannot be . . . jealous. Sidhe women are not jealous. Who can be jealous of males who cannot love, cannot attach?"

Michael sat on a bench and rubbed his eyes with his palms. None of the calmness exercises would work now. He couldn't bring down his level of misery, or control its effects on his body, the tension in his neck and arms.

"I could love you while you loved her," Eleuth said. Michael didn't seem to hear. She sat beside him and put her head on his shoulder. "I could do many things for love, and what I cannot do, I will learn." She stroked his back with one hand. "It is all a Sidhe woman ever expects."

Michael dried his cheeks with the back of his hand and hugged her, feeling a sudden fierce affection for her, an urge to protect her.

He stayed with her that night and the next morning returned to the Crane Women's mound. The huts were still empty. He entered his own hut and stashed the book in the rafters, then sat on the mats and tried to think of a poem. Not even an opening line would come. His head was empty of words. Full of turmoil; empty of expression.

BY LATE MORNING, he made his resolution. He would search for the *sani*. He didn't know right from wrong himself; perhaps Helena and Savarin did.

In Biri's empty hut, the plaited mats were neatly folded in one corner. He looked everywhere in the hut and found no sign of the powder.

He crossed to the Crane Women's hut and stood by the door. Peering through the windows, he saw only darkness within. He tried to pry the door open with his fingers, but it seemed latched. He pushed, hoping it would open. It didn't. Then he pushed harder and something wooden clicked within. The door swung outward slowly.

The Crane Women obviously didn't feel the need of locks. So what—if anything, or anyone—did they have guarding the hut? The thought didn't give him much pause; he was beyond practical concerns.

The sunward window cast a shaft across the room, illuminating shelves stacked with bottles. The contents of one of the bottles wriggled pinkly in the beam. His eyes adjusted slowly to the gloomy corners. In the center of the room, a cylindrical brick oven rose almost to the roof, with four mouths opening around its circumference. A ceramic platform surrounded the oven, shiny white and indented with a regular series of mortars. A few pestles lay on the table, and small piles of powder of differing colors and roughness. The fire was out, but the oven still kept its heat; he could feel it on his face and outstretched palm.

Across the room from each other were two sets of shelves, both packed tight with bottles full of teeth and small fragments of bone. Other bottles held roots and vegetable matter. A bottle containing a forked root had been the first to catch his eye; even now, the root spasmed, jiggling the bottle on the shelf.

Yet another shelf was devoted to bottles of dusts. None of the containers were labeled. If they had discernible uses, only the Crane Women knew what they were.

Beyond the closest set of shelves rose a partition made of wooden boards, on which thin sheets of tough, pearly tissue had been stretched between pegs to dry. Below the sheets hung the skeletal forearm of a small clawed animal. The claws appeared to be made of gold.

On the other side of the room, partly hidden behind a drape of gray cloth, a glass box sat on a table. In the box lay pieces of frosty crystal finely carved into abstract shapes. Each crystal had a single clear facet like a peephole. Michael pulled the drape aside with forefinger and thumb and opened the box's lid.

The temptation was too great; he removed a crystal and held it up to his eye. Like a slide viewer, the crystal contained an image. Green rolling hills and a wonderfully vivid sky appeared to Michael. He was about remove it from his eye and pick up another when a woman walked over the hills. With a shock, he recognized her. She was a much younger Coom. Her name, the crystal informed him in no obvious way, was Ecooma. She smiled and swung her arms, her long, shapely legs outlined beneath a wind-blown red dress. Her face resembled Eleuth's, but was even more comely. She passed out of range of the crystal eye, prompting him to turn with it to follow her, but to no result. The crystal maintained one steady point of view.

A second crystal showed a high mountain pass. Swift clouds threw shadows on a snow-covered slope beyond. The naked female standing on a rock, undaunted by the obvious cold, was called Elanare. She stretched her arms out to the wind, long red hair trailing behind her. In her youth, Nare had been even more lovely than Ecooma.

Michael lifted a third crystal. Spart—Esparta—stood among a group of young human women, seated on marble benches in a small stone amphitheater. The women wore short white dresses tied around the waist; Spart wore a long black gown and her hair was tied up in a bun with sparkling gold thread. She was speaking to the women, and they laughed now and then as if surprised and delighted. Though her beauty was more subtle than that of Ecooma or Elanare, to Michael she seemed the most lovely of all.

Gone were their distortions of face and frame, rolled back by time. He gently laid the third crystal in the box and reached for a fourth. The one he picked revealed a man and a Sidhe female from the waist up, arms around each other. The man was ruddy-skinned, with a thick brown-black beard, wry intelligent eyes and a sharp short nose. The Sidhe's facial features were so evocative and familiar that Michael was sure he must have seen her before, however impossible that was.

They were Aske and Elme, the crystal informed him, and there was good reason for their portrait to reside in the glass box. They were the mother and father of the Crane Women, and of seven other Breed children whose pictures resided in other crystals.

He put the crystal down quickly, his arm hairs tingling with premonition. He quickly searched the rest of the hut for *sani* and spotted a pouch resting on a low wooden table near the door. He hastily sprinkled some of the contents into his palm and saw the unmistakable golden flakes he needed. He poured the flakes back into the pouch and retied the knot.

Now that he had found what he needed, Michael felt a sudden tingle of panic. He looked around to see if he had disturbed anything, knowing there was no way to conceal his invasion from the Crane Women. Hopeless. They would catch him, and what would they do?

He fumbled at the door latch, pulled it open sharply to leave—

And jumped back with a yell. There stood Biri, covered with mud and blood, his eyes wild and mouth gaping wide as if in pain. Black blood oozed from the corner of his mouth and dripped from his hands, spotting his *sepla*. He made small whining noises deep in his chest like a hunted animal.

Michael retreated into the hut, horrified, his throat constricting. Biri rolled his eyes back and twisted his head horribly.

"Michael, oh, human *Michael*," he groaned. "What have I done?"

His body contorted and he raised his hands in supplication. Then he straightened and ran. Michael looked after him as he leaped the stream and ran past the limits of Halftown.

Nare, Spart and Coom walked onto the mound from the opposite direction, skirting the piles of rock and bone. They turned as one and stared at Michael in the doorway of their hut. He slipped the pouch into his pocket surreptitiously.

Spart put her arm around his shoulder and walked him to his own hut, then stopped and turned him to face her.

"Was he hurt?" Michael asked, swallowing. "What happened to him?"

"You have witnessed Biri's shame," she said. "You must tell no one. He has survived his test."

"What test? For the priesthood?"

"Yes," Spart said, her expression unusually grim. "Tarax sent Biri's favorite horse across the border. Biri hunted it down and slaughtered it. When he recovers, he will be ready to serve Adonna." She focused her eyes on his and frowned, releasing his shoulders. "What you have, what you know . . . you will use it wisely?"

Michael swallowed hard, twice, almost choking. Then, tears in his eyes, he said, "I will."

The Crane Women entered their hut and shut the door behind them. Michael stared across the grasslands, wondering if he would ever again feel like a whole person.

24

The snow fell thick and heavy, leaving a blank white page on which were lightly sketched the horizon, Halftown, the huts and a few gray gaps in the clouds. The stream flowed dark and shiny gray, a thin shelf of ice projecting from each bank. Little ice-blades sliced the smoothly rushing water.

Michael stood on the bank and watched the stream. The falling snow seemed to calm him. His discipline isolated him from the cold. His mind felt just as isolated from reality, aloof.

The pouch of *sani* rested in his pocket.

Biri sat outside his own hut, head bowed. The Sidhe hadn't spoken once, hadn't eaten. Coom had washed his hands and face and wrapped a reed blanket around him.

There had been some perfunctory training for Michael that morning—a run with the stick across the fields, while Spart paced him and checked his skin temperature with long, black-nailed fingers. He had thrown a shadow for Coom, skillfully enough to delay her catching him by a few seconds. He had blanked his aura of memory well enough to prevent Spart from in-seeing. All this, as the snowflakes careened slowly down like drunken, frozen dandies, oblivious to the dark emotions around them.

"I'm going to Euterpe," he told Coom, who squatted outside the Crane Women's hut, keeping an eye on Biri as she pounded a rock to powder with a harder rock. She nodded.

He left the book in the rafters of his hut. He wasn't expecting trouble, but if any came, the book wouldn't help and he didn't want to lose it or see it damaged.

The road seemed longer, extended by the snow's whiteness. When he came to Euterpe the town was as private and closed-down as a sleeping face. He walked through deserted streets, glancing at brick walls and tile roofs, worn-out wicker baskets piled in a heap, carts carrying buckets of frozen human waste. He saw everything as if for the last time. The sensation of fated closure was strong, emphasized by his numbness.

He took the familiar alley, approached the familiar entrance and stairs and climbed slowly and quietly. He reached for the bag. When he came to the wicker door, now draped with a cloth cover, he held his hand up to knock, then hesitated. He heard voices inside. Helena had a visitor.

He felt, if such a thing was possible, even more deeply isolated and sick at heart. He pushed the door. It became party to his stealth and opened with only a faint scrape. The voices continued. He pulled aside the curtain to the bedroom, knowing it was wrong to invade someone's privacy, but feeling his own grievance was stronger.

Savarin and Helena lay on the narrow cot, covered mercifully by a dun-colored blanket. Helena saw him first. Her eyes widened. He lowered the curtain and backed into the front room, pulling the *sani* from his pocket and laying it on the front table. There came scuffling and creaking from behind the curtain, the rustle and quick breathing of clothing hastily put on. "Stay here," Helena murmured. "Don't come out. I'll talk to him."

She emerged from behind the curtain, combing out her hair with her fingers, looking at him sidewise, her face white. "Michael," she said.

"I brought it," he said, pointing to the wicker table. "What you need. What you wanted."

"I'm sure you don't understand," Helena said, coming closer. "It's—"

"Please," he said. "Enough. I'll go."

"Let me *explain!*" The note of desperation held him. "It's not what any of us wants. Savarin can't have children. Before he left Earth—"

"Please, enough," Michael repeated.

"He's safe, don't you see? You're not. You're not safe. That's the difference. That's the only difference." She came closer, holding out her hands. Finally she stopped, hands circling to form small shields. She struggled for something more to say. "We need your help."

"You've had my help," he said. "You have the powder. I'll go now."

As Helena called his name, louder and more frantically, he ran down the stairs and back to the street and out of Euterpe. His long stride carried him without apparent effort. He seemed suspended within his body, isolated from the exertion, his breath smooth, the machine running even better without his interference. He passed a woman clutching a cloak about her head and shoulders.

As if on an endless cycle, he was going to Halftown. Awareness that it was all drawing to a close, that his adventure in the Realm was about to end, had grown even stronger in him, like a thick flame that gave no light.

25

Halftown lay subdued and quiet in the mid-afternoon snowfall, its half-circle streets covered with shallow drifts. Michael wasn't thinking clearly and it took several extra minutes for him to find Eleuth's quarters. He stood outside the door, his mind almost as blank as the fields of snow between Euterpe and Halftown.

As he knocked, it occurred to him that not for an instant did he suspect betrayal behind this door. (Had Helena betrayed him? Or had she just done something that, in his youth, he couldn't begin to fathom?)

The door opened. Eleuth examined his downcast face and took him by the arm, leading him inside without a word spoken. She sat him on the bunk and took the small stool for her own seat. Several deep, jerking breaths were necessary before Michael could say, "I have to go back now. There's nothing more I can do here."

She nodded, then shook her head, then nodded once more. "Do you need my help?" she asked.

"Of course. I can't do it myself or I'd have done it already."

"Then I'll help," she said. "We have to wait until dark, and we can't do it here. Somebody might see us, or feel what's happening. Until night, you'll stay here, have something to eat?"

"I'm not hungry," he said.

"You'll need all your strength," she said. She served him a bowl of vegetable stew. After he finished eating, she took the bowl and pulled back the covers on the bunk. He sat down. She adjusted the pillow for him and he lay back with his eyes open. Deliberately, with another deep breath, he closed them. His face became as rigid as ice.

Even when Eleuth was sure he was asleep, his face remained stiff. She sat watching him for some time as the snow fell faster outside and the wind rose. Then she went around the room, removing objects from the dresser drawers, from shelves, and from the low table. She assembled the articles in a cloth laid over her lap: white face cream, though it really didn't matter, she thought; a few twigs from a flowering tree beyond the Blasted Plain; some stones from the Plain

itself, dusty to the touch, and the dead green beetle she had summoned from
Michael's neighborhood. When she had pulled in the corners of the cloth and
made a bundle by tying them, she sighed deeply, smoothed back a few loose
strands of hair with both hands, and stared out the window at a white world she
doubted she would experience much longer.

With darkness, the snow stopped and the wind died, leaving the Pact Lands
in muffled silence. Michael awoke and ate more of the stew while Eleuth painted
her face with the white cream. "It reflects the light," she explained.

The inevitable unreality of everything fell on him now in an avalanche. Why
should he be dismayed by betrayal? None of these people existed. They were all
phantoms; to find his way home, all he had to do was enact some formula which
would bring him out of his trance, his waking nightmare.

He forgot all the proofs he had accepted in the past about the Realm's existence. They were dim, feeble things compared with his present pain. Eleuth tied
a blanket-cloak around his neck, in case his discipline slipped in his distraction.
Then she took his hand, lifting the bundle in the crook of her arm, and led him
into the night.

Michael followed her through the snow without speaking. Her grayish outline
advanced into the darkness beyond Halftown and away from the road, the stream,
the mound, taking him in a direction he had never gone before.

The grass was frosted with snow that powdered with the brush of their legs
and fell on their feet, melting into their cloth shoes until they were soaked. Only
hyloka kept their feet from freezing.

When they were far enough away from everything to suit her, she cleared a
patch of snow away for him to sit, laid out the cloth and arranged the articles,
then squatted opposite him. He could barely see her. A few stars, too near, peeped
through rifts in the clouds. The cream on her face glowed and he followed her
movements that way.

"You wish to go home," she said, her tone more stern than he had heard it
before.

"Yes," he said.

"You wish to get there by Sidhe magic."

"I do."

"There is risk. Do you accept that?"

"Yes." He did not much care.

"Do you accept this gift from me, given out of love?"

"I do." He felt a pressure in his chest. "I appreciate this very much, Eleuth."

"How much?" she asked, almost bitter.

He shrugged in the darkness. "I'm not worth much. I don't know why you
feel so strongly toward me."

"You acknowledge that love?"

"Yes."

"Do you return it?"

He leaned toward her dim features. "I love you, too," Michael said. "As a
friend. As the only friend I have here. Wherever we are."

"As a friend, then," Eleuth said, her tone less astringent. She laid the twigs on the cloth in a circle, pointing toward the center. Near one of the twigs she placed the beetle. Next to another she placed one of the pebbles. The rest of the pebbles she piled on one corner of the cloth.

"Is that all you need?" Michael asked.

"That, and my training," Eleuth said. "I'm still not very good." She stood, took his hand, and made him stand in the middle of the circle of twigs. "For you, I wish I were a full-blooded Sidhe," she said, holding out her arms. She assumed the same pose he had seen in the crystal portrait of Nare. "But Lirg's blood is strong and good and I rely on him, too. Wherever he is now." She danced lightly around him, spinning from one toe to the next. He turned his head to follow her. "Face straight ahead," she said.

After a few minutes she stopped, breathing heavily. "Did the Sidhe pass his test?" she asked.

"Yes."

"Did he take his flesh, drink his blood?"

"I think so."

"He left the Crane Women this evening," she said. "He goes to his new home. Perhaps he will see Lirg."

"I don't know."

"Do you know what your friends in Euterpe are doing tonight?" she asked.

"No."

"All the Breeds stay in tonight. We don't know either, but we have our suspicions." She resumed the dance, reaching now and then to brush his shoulders with her fingers. "Michael," she said, breath harsh, twirling around him. "Look straight ahead. It is time for you to go home . . . very soon."

Light sprang up around his feet. He glanced down and saw the twigs burning brightly from the outside in, like so many fuses.

"Out of love," Eleuth said. She formed her arms into a circle. Two circles of light leaped from the arcs of her fingers, rose and fell around him, stopping at waist level. The twigs burned to their ends. He stood in the middle of a radiance of fire that rose around his feet but did not burn.

Eleuth stood rigid in front of him, arms held high, breasts pulled taut against her rib cage, stomach flat, heaving. Her hair fell in disarray and her eyes closed. She twisted her head to one side. "I will guard," she said. "For as long.

As.

I.

Can."

Her eyes opened black, rimmed with blazing red. He fell toward them. His feet lifted from the cloth. The circles tightened around his waist like belts, cinching close. The fire spread to Eleuth, crackling and hissing, searing the darkness until the land around them flared bright as day. When the flames touched her navel, she flinched and screamed.

The fire surrounded her. Arced outward to the snow-covered grass. Melted the snow into steam. Dried the grass and set it ablaze. She twisted in her own fire, mouth open to reveal darkness much deeper than the night. Michael rose toward her and felt the cold electric destruction of the power she had unleashed.

"Please," she said, barely audible over the crackle and roar. "I will guard. Careful! Out of love—"

She became smaller and darker, twisting in the fire until she receded to a black point.

Michael no longer stood on the cloth, on the grassland, but flew high above, looking across the infinite expanse of the Realm, its forests, plains and mountains spread beneath like a topographical relief map. The river snaked far to the northeast through forests, scrub lands, blank desert and swamps. He saw a mountain surrounded by a city with walls like a tangle of silvery roots—

And a black, spiky something beyond.

To the north he saw a broad lake glowing cobalt in the night—Nebchat Len, possibly. Beyond the lake stretched more forest, and beyond that, massive jagged mountains. Looking straight down, he saw the Pact Lands mounted in the middle of the Blasted Plain, a yellow-green circle surrounded by forbidding orange-tinted darkness. This darkness seemed to writhe, rise up to grab him. Then everything writhed—and vanished.

He could have been suspended in nothingness for all eternity. The sensation of time left him. In the void was a flicker of light, somewhere above where his head had been. He became aware of a canopy of leaves, then of something beneath his feet, hard and gray. His circle of vision expanded. His head filled with rushing blood, and the sensation of weight returned.

Michael closed his eyes and rubbed them. The rush of exultation dizzied him. He wanted to jump, to shout.

He glanced at his wrist to see what time it was—what time the trance had come to an end. But his watch was missing. He still wore the clothes Helena had scrounged for him; his feet were still shod in cloth.

A flicker of fire played around his ankles. He stared down at the fire, watching it brighten, fade and brighten again. Suddenly it flashed up around his calves until it obscured the sidewalk. Tendrils rushed to wrap his wrists like shackles and crawl up his chest like serpents.

"No!" he screamed. "NO!"

He doubled up as if kicked in the stomach. Curled, he flew backwards into darkness, winding along a jagged reverse course and surrounded by a comet's tail of fire.

26

Michael lay on his stomach, gravel and dirt pressed to his face. His legs sprawled across dry grass. He opened his eyes to the twilight and saw dark bushes with greasy green-black leaves. Rolling on his back, he encountered a featureless gray-blue sky, low and oppressive. A few muddy stars glistened wetly in the expanse.

Something rustled nearby. The path on which he lay crossed a yard of sickly grass and ended at a red brick porch. Dull orange paper lanterns hung from the trellis arbor arching over the porch.

He got to his knees. The rustling grew louder. He stood, turned, and started back from the touch of dry, cold fingers against his face.

The figure in the flounced dress stood less than a yard from him, arm bent at two crazy angles and pointing toward his head. The shadow of the wide-brim hat still obscured the features, but Michael was more certain than ever that it was a woman, caught between the Realm and the Earth, probably as crazy as Lamia.

He wondered what he had to fear from her.

She advanced, lurching as if one leg was shorter than the other, or improperly jointed. The sleeved arm extended again and Michael smelled dust, mildew, something metallic. He backed away several steps. He had been home—

You are home.

The voice, soft as the still twilight air, reached around his ears and touched the back of his head.

You are home.

He focused on the fingers of the figure's hand. They were thin, colorless; they could have been twigs wrapped in strips of coarse cardboard. They abraded each other with the sound of dead leaves in a breeze.

Beyond the guardian waited the gate to the alley. He looked over his shoulder for the merest instant, trying to see if he could go back through the house— reverse his course—but *she* stood there, barring the way. When he wasn't watching she could move with incredible speed. He faced her and slowly backed toward the gate.

Stay.

Images of incredible luxury, voluptuousness. Gardens filled with flowers and thick vegetables, luscious ripe berries studding intense green bushes. Tomatoes red as arterial blood. The pink and dusky flesh of eager, hungry women.

If he stared at her—she was gaining on him, lurching—she might catch him. Already her hands reached out, fingers rubbing with sandpaper sounds in anticipation. If he turned to break for the gate she might leap quick as darkness and have him anyway.

She played him like a fish on a line. He was trapped, no way out this time. There was only one way for the trance to end—in her garden, caught between the projected paradise and the dry, somber twilight reality.

Reality. As real a doom as any.

Still, he had learned a lot since he had last encountered her. There might be one way to elude her.

He searched for the hidden impulse, found it feeble but present. Between the Realm and Earth it would work only intermittently, and weakly. Still, he had no choice but to try.

He turned his back on her, concentrated, closed his eyes, pressed hard on nothing—and threw a shadow.

The gate seemed an incredible distance away—only a few yards. Behind he heard drapes of fabric rustle frantically, sensed the arms close around something, pass through empty air. The guardian screed like a bat or a far-off falcon.

He ran down the alley. Sixth gate on the left. But he no longer had the key! He couldn't open the lock, couldn't pass through. He felt rather than heard his pursuer leaping after like a wave of foul dead air.

At the locked sixth gate, he did not hesitate. He ran to the seventh, some yards farther, and found it without a lock. He jerked it open, making the rusty hinges and spring scream.

The guardian's hand grasped his shoulder and flung him back as if he were made of paper. He toppled and slid across the pavement, rebounding from the brick wall opposite. The gate slowly closed, its spring softly singing. He knew he would never have time to open it again if it latched.

He would never reach it, anyway.

But the guardian held back, rocking on hidden limbs like a nightmare toy, a puppet pulled by idiots.

He pushed against the wall with arms and shoulders, leaping, using all his new prowess to make it through the gate. The gate clanged shut behind him.

Michael stood in a long, narrow lot, bordered on all sides by low red brick walls. Some distance away over the end wall he could see the outline of the rear of Lamia's house, the Isomage's ruined mansion.

Perhaps the sixth gate wasn't the only way.

Bordering the path that led to a gate in the distant second wall were two long trellises, thickly wrapped in dead brown ivy. He hurried between them.

"Not that way!"

He stopped. The voice had come from his left, as much a dry croak of pain as a warning.

"She will have you before you reach the end."

"Hide!"

"Watch for her!"

The voices came from the ivy-covered trellises. Against all his instincts he slowed to a walk, his legs cramping with fear and indecision.

Then he discerned them, caught in the vines, limbs entwined: corpses. Emaciated, skin slumped like dry leather, jaws gaping, arms and legs skeletal, eyes hollow. But their heads turned to follow him and they strained against their bonds, lips pulled back over yellow teeth.

"Don't let her have you! Die first!"

"Watch for her!"

"Not that way. She'll get you!"

In fact, the gate seemed farther away now than when he had begun. The closer he came, the more it receded and the longer the trellises were. And the more writhing mummified bodies he saw in the grasping dead ivy.

"If she has you, you never die . . ."

"If she loves you, you sleep . . ."

"And awaken here."

"Live forever . . ."

"But decay!"

Maniacal laughter all around. The corpses struggled horribly, pieces of skin flaking to the ground. Some reached out imploring claw-hands, others strained their hollow chests against the vines, heaving and thrashing and shaking the trellises until they seemed in danger of falling over.

The guardian stood on the same path now. He hadn't seen her pass through the gate; perhaps she didn't need to. As she walked, the wide hat inclined slowly from left to right. She surveyed her past victims, lurching down the path to certain conquest over another.

She collected them. Had them, used them, placed them here. She savored her collection, her work well done. This was her paradise of vegetables and succulent fruits, the garden of her labors.

Stay.

He half-ran, half-stumbled crabwise, trying to find the center of impulse again. But he had no clear way to throw another shadow. The guardian, dress folding and pressing to outline her distorted frame, had risen a foot above the path and accelerated toward him like a piece of fabric on a spinning clothesline. She pitched head-forward in her flight until the hat pointed directly at him and the dress fanned out, a deadly trailing blossom.

He turned and fled from his doom, screaming.

Ahead of him, Eleuth stood on the path, so close he couldn't avoid running into her.

And passing through. He stumbled and fell on the ground. Glancing back, face contorted, he saw the translucent Breed woman spread her arms before the hurtling guardian.

They merged. There was a drawn-out cry as the fabric and distorted body tangled in mid-air and fell to the ground like a downed bird. Michael ran. The gate at the end of the lot was much closer. He reached it in a few strides, opened it, looked back at the guardian still crumpled and *hissing* on the pathway, and saw Eleuth's final shadow gently spin with the force of their collision. It floated from the path, face empty *(She is dead! She is dead!)* fading, fading, until it vanished completely.

Michael stood on the field behind the Isomage's house. With a hollow clang, the gate latched itself and the wall vanished.

Once again he looked across the Pact Lands, down the slope to the broad river. His breath was ragged, his elbows and knees were scraped and bleeding, and his head hurt abominably.

The trance was far from over.

27

Late afternoon in the Realm. From miles away, Michael could smell smoke. A thick column of black rose over Euterpe. Hardly able to walk, he stumbled across the field to the front door of the Isomage's house. In the distance he heard thunder and indistinct shouts and screams. The wind shifted and all fell quiet.

The parlor, ballroom and dining room of the house waited empty and silent except for a whisper like sand or dust falling. He climbed the stairs to confer with Lamia, ask what had gone wrong with his journey and what was happening in Euterpe.

He didn't particularly wish to know.

The room of candles was deserted and dark. He crossed the wooden floor, footsteps echoing sharply even though he still wore his cloth shoes. The echoes struck like returning knives—breath, heartbeat, the rub of Michael's fingers against his bristly chin.

He noted with a start that he had the beginnings of a beard.

Michael walked farther down the hall, away from the open landing. Shadows ruled the house; all the candles sat dark in their sconces or lay shattered on the floor. "Lamia?" he called, quietly at first, then louder. His throat still hurt from screaming in the Between. He ventured into the darkest recesses of the hall, dragging one hand lightly against the wall. The wall vibrated like a bell at his touch; the entire house seemed alive, fearful, shrinking back.

He touched a doorjamb and turned into the doorway. From a half-drawn curtain, twilight sneaked into a small sitting room. Lamia sat in a chair facing the window.

"Please," Michael said. "I need help."

She didn't answer, didn't move. He approached the chair cautiously, fearful of her bulk, her quiet, her fierce concentrated expression as she faced the waning light.

For a moment, the dim lighting and the folds of her skin concealed the fact that she wore no clothes. She sat naked and still in the large chair. Michael was convinced she waited for him to come close enough to reach out and grab. But nothing moved. She didn't even breathe. Was she dead?

He reached out to touch her shoulder. His finger curled back involuntarily into his palm and he forced it to straighten.

The skin gave way, first an inch, then two. Repelled, unable to stop, he continued pressing. She hissed faintly and her head folded in like a collapsing soufflé. Her arm and chest collapsed and she fell into a pile of white translucent folds, sliding from the chair to the floor.

Not Lamia, but her skin—shed completely. He stooped, gaping in horrified fascination, and rubbed the leavings between his fingers. Such a familiar texture. He had felt it before—in the closet downstairs, when she had hidden him from Alyons.

She kept a closet full of her own shed skins.

But then, where was she? Hiding someplace, vulnerable, like a soft-shell crab or snake still damp and tender?

"*Boy.*"

He swiveled on his heels and saw her in the room's opposite corner. She wore a dark gray robe and blended into the shadows. She was half again as tall and fat as she had been. Her voice was deeper, more appropriate to the mountain she was becoming. Everything about her vibrated as she stepped forward, from her cheeks to the flesh of her hands.

"You tried to go back, didn't you?"

His mouth was dry. He nodded. She came within two yards of him and stopped, momentum swinging all her flesh toward him like a cresting wave . . . and resilience drawing it all back until the motions damped themselves. He couldn't see her eyes in the fleshy folds of her face. The nose—tiny and surrounded by the immense cheeks—was her last identifiable feature but for her hair, glossier and more luxuriant than before.

"The Breed girl. I heard about her. Lirg's daughter."

"How did you hear?"

"Hear many things," Lamia said. "Even when I'm . . . not up to my usual. Why didn't you cross?"

"Eleuth didn't get me all the way across. I mean, she did, but only for a moment. I was drawn back."

"The Guardian? Meet her?"

He nodded.

"Escaped."

Nodded again, only once, to signify just barely.

"Your little Breed girl sacrificed herself for you."

"What?" Though he knew.

"She wasn't even half Sidhe, boy. She couldn't do all that and survive the consequences. Even so, her life wasn't enough. You're still with us." This seemed to amuse her, and a little tremor passed through her, accompanied by a deep muffled chuckle. "Do you know what happened while you were gone?"

"How long was I gone?"

"Days, I suspect. Do you know?"

He shook his head. Her smell folded around him: dust and roses and acrid, sweating flesh.

"Your little rebel friends decided to defy Alyons. The Wickmaster has never been even-tempered." Again the deep-buried humor. "There's nothing I can do. Not now. They could have picked a better time. They've given Alyons what he's always wanted—a chance at the humans. To level them, make them pay for intruding."

"What's he doing?" Michael asked, his throat almost closing off the question.

Lamia peered down at her shed skin. "The Guardian. She's my sister, boy. We were Clarkham's wives. Lovers, actually. He brought us here. There were fine times then. Dances, all the people rallying around the new mage. The Isomage, he called himself—equal to the Serpent Mage. Come to bring everybody out of the shadow of the Realm, into the light of his rule. Oh, he didn't hate the Sidhe. He didn't hurt them, not really. He could work magic with music, with what the Sidhe taught us long ago. He was very proud. Soon, he claimed he was the mage reincarnate—born again to avenge what the Sidhe had done to the original human race. His arrogance became too great for the Sidhe to bear. The Black Order sent their armies against us. That was the war . . . the war that made the Blasted Plain." For a long moment she was silent, the cheeks and chin working like dough under invisible hands. "He was not the mage. He could do magic, but he couldn't win. He could only lose a little and call it a draw. He fled. He gave us up, my sister and me. The Sidhe made their Pact with him, but he gave us up. He claimed he had buried powerful magic here, fatal to any Sidhe who transgressed the Pact. He'd fought well enough that the Sidhe had to believe him. So he bargained. He set aside the Pact Lands and put all his people—he thought of them as his own—right here. The Sidhe shrunk the boundaries by half, to let the Blasted Plain act as a barrier. Keep their females from human temptations. Keep themselves pure."

"Are they fighting in Euterpe?" Michael asked.

"What would you do if they are? Go save them all? They're fools. They get what they deserve. Though I'd fight the Sidhe myself if I could. In a week, I'd be able to. If your rebels had waited a week for their foolishness . . . But now I'm in my curse. I eat nothing and grow huge. I shed my skin like a snake and my flesh is fragile as unbaked clay. You, you could grab my arm and tear it off, if you wanted. Here's your chance." She held out her arm. Michael backed away. "But I'll toughen, as I always have before; and the power he left me, that'll come back. Then Alyons will pay, if he hasn't already."

"Please. What are they doing?"

"They made my sister into the guardian, to keep humans from using the Isomage's pathway. She still has a touch of humanity, maybe? She doesn't catch all who would cross. Not you . . . maybe she held back a bit, seeing what you are."

"Tell me!" he demanded, neck muscles cording, lower lip contorted.

"Scourging," she said. "*Scarbita*. Alyons is the *Scarbita Antros*, and there's nothing you can do."

Michael ran from the room, down the hall and stairs. The sky was on a thread's edge of night as he ran down the road, trying not to focus on the wavering smudge of orange light against the gloom.

He was hardly breathing hard when he came within sight of Euterpe. Invoking *hyloka* had restored energy to his tissues and given his senses hallucinatory precision. The brick houses lay in heaps around a central bonfire. He saw mounted Sidhe driving people in lines and clusters ahead of them. Wicks flashed in the firelight. Overhead, the stars seemed to have turned away in fear. The ground glittered with excited pinprick lights.

He left the road and crossed a hill. Most of Euterpe lay in ruins, some of the shattered buildings glowing as if electrified. For a long minute he stared at what seemed the ghost of the hotel, limned in bright outline against the fountains of fire, everything else translucent.

As he watched, the outline evaporated and the hotel was gone.

Piano music drifted from across town. The coursers' mounts reared back and they broke away from their captives to ride back through the flames. Not all of the resistance was broken.

Michael ran around the outskirts, stopping to listen for the music. It came from the last remaining stand of buildings—from the school. Sidhe on horseback darted up and over the flames as if maddened by the music.

The Wickmaster stood on a mound about a hundred yards outside the town, lost in thought. His golden horse waited patiently behind him. Michael tried to keep well back from the firelight, but the Sidhe turned and saw him. For a long moment their eyes held; then Alyons smiled, baring ghost-white teeth, and glided onto his horse.

Michael reversed his run and fled from Euterpe. He wasn't afraid; if fear was a chemical, it had long since been used up in his body. He acted purely as he had been trained. Now it was obvious that his education had been accompanied by a good many subliminal instructions. The Crane Women had tinkered with his aura of memory. He could visualize tactics, methods of escape he never would have thought of on his own.

There was one instruction that he couldn't quite bring to the fore; nevertheless, he acted on it. The Wickmaster's golden horse glided up behind Michael at a leisurely pace, its master exulting. Here was his chance to even the score with the troublesome *antros*, and no one to hold him back.

Ahead, Michael saw the outline of giant teeth—a ring of stones, slightly darker than the night. He ran in that direction—into the jaws and to one side, backing up against a smooth round stone carved with spiral grooves. Alyons slowed just outside the ring. *"Hoy ac!"* he cried.

"Hello yourself, you cruel son of a bitch," Michael whispered.

"Antros! You need the Wickmaster's mercy. Come out and join your own kind. They aren't mistreated, only punished."

"Come in," Michael invited loudly enough for Alyons to hear if he strained; no louder. Alyons lifted his wick to the sky. The tip glowed dull red. His horse paced between the stones, weaving in and out. The Wickmaster chanted softly in Cascar.

He's worried, Michael thought.

"He enters the circle, but he must come closer," said a voice behind Michael. He recognized Spart but couldn't see her.

"Wickmaster!" he cried out. "How did you disgrace yourself? Did you make your masters angry? Were you the lowest thing in the *Maln,* a traitor, or just something they could do without?"

"The *Maln*," Alyons replied coldly, "still accepts me. I do my duty in the Pact Lands. I keep the human filth bottled up."

"They won't take you back," Michael taunted. "How did you insult Tarax?"

"Shy of the mark," Alyons said. Michael could feel his aura of memory being feather-touched. He blocked the probe.

"*Antros!*" Alyons' horse crossed into the inner circle, but the Wickmaster was not astride. Michael pushed up hard against the cold stone.

The point of the wick rose before his face and glowed bright. Alyons flowed into visibility in front of him and lowered the point to Michael's chest. The Sidhe's armor flashed and rippled like living skin. The maple-leaf insignia on his chest seemed to stand apart from the armor, floating with a vitality of its own and changing from moment to moment to oak, then laurel, then back to maple. Alyons pulled the wick back, ready to send it through Michael and pin him to the stone. The Sidhe sang in that weird way Michael had heard the Crane Women sing, as if searching for a tune and not finding it, only the tune was present all along . . .

The dried grass behind the Sidhe flew straight up, swirling into the night. Around the inner circle of the stones, a spiral of dirt fountained upward, the wind of its passage lifting Alyons' hair. For an instant, the Sidhe poised with his wick and Michael again felt the nearness of death.

Out of the ground, with the roar of a dozen freight trains, rose a monstrous steel snake. It had been coiled beneath the grass, and like a spring it lashed out and gripped the Wickmaster in gleaming steel teeth. Clods of dirt struck Michael all over.

The snake lifted the Sidhe high into the air. Then, with the sound of strained metal snapping, it broke apart. The sinuosities straightened and plunged into the dirt like stakes, forming a tripod. The snake's head shuddered at the top of the tripod, in the exact center of the circle of stones.

Alyons, gripped like a mouse, reached down to Michael with a trembling arm. Michael walked slowly around the tripod until he could see the Wickmaster clearly, then let up his memory block.

"The wood, *the wood!*" Alyons whispered. "Quickly! Call the Arborals . . ." His body twisted violently, jamming the snake's steel teeth even deeper through his flesh. His bones ground against the metal loudly enough for Michael to hear, and the tripod swayed.

Alyons died.

Michael had never seen anything like it. Muscles twitching, he looked up at the corpse, fascinated and sick at the pit of his stomach. Alyons had been trapped and executed and he had been part of it. He turned away from the tripod and the limp, bloody Wickmaster.

Spart faced him. Her hair blew back in the night breeze. "The coursers haven't finished," she said. "We must go."

"Who made this?" Michael asked, pointing to the trap.

"Clarkham, who calls himself Isomage."

"Why?"

"I do not know," Spart said. Her voice rasped. Something—the wind, or fear, or just revulsion at the Wickmaster's end—made her shiver. "Perhaps it was his revenge for the imposition of the Pact."

"Did Alyons know it was here?"

"Obviously not," Spart said. She closed her eyes halfway. "No more questions." He followed her as she plodded through the grass. Euterpe's flames were dying. Snow fell again, and he noticed with curiosity that when it alighted on Spart, it did not melt, as if she no longer maintained her *hyloka*.

"I saw Lamia."

"So?" She continued walking without looking back.

"She can't do anything. She shed her skin."

Spart suddenly craned her neck. "Quiet," she said. Overhead came a rushing, wind-whining sound—one Michael had heard before. He looked up but saw nothing in the smoke-palled sky. Snow fell through the smoke as if conjured out of nothing.

Michael had no trouble keeping up with Spart this time; her pace was deliberate, less than brisk. "Use your training now," she told him. "The coursers are still out."

"Don't they know about Alyons?"

Spart did not answer. He frowned at her back and shook his head.

They dodged between the smoldering ruins and piles of bricks and within minutes approached the Yard. It, too, had been demolished. Michael peered over the remains of a thick wall. The pits were open to the night air.

In the least damaged section of town, they passed humans running, or standing in a daze; townsfolk with shackles around their ankles, staked to the ground; men and women huddled in corners, the smoke and diminishing flames adding to the glazed light of panic in their eyes. He didn't see anybody dead, or even seriously injured. Perhaps the Isomage's threat had restrained the Sidhe enough to spare the town from general massacre.

Spart clambered down stairs leading to a basement beneath a relatively intact two-story warehouse. She walked ahead of Michael in the dark, and he followed her by the sound of her footfalls, using his hands to guide him along one wall.

At the end of the corridor was a room lit by glass-chimneyed oil lamps. Smashed wicker boxes and furniture littered the floor. The brick walls seemed to have been sprayed with silvery glitter that sparkled in a way painful to the eyes.

In the middle of the room, shoulders slumped, Savarin sat amidst the debris. He barely glanced up as he heard them enter. His clothes and face were covered with sparkling dust. He looked down at the floor, then, as if reminded of something, looked up again and fastened his dull gaze on Michael. "Traitor," he said, his voice flat and lifeless. "You told them."

"I didn't tell anybody," Michael said but Savarin was obviously beyond argument. The teacher smiled in a sickly way, shook his head and resumed his examination of the floor. Spart pointed to the far corner of the basement room. Seated away from the glow of the oil lamps, Helena, her skin and clothes aglimmer, had drawn her knees up on a makeshift wicker piano bench.

Before her, in the corner, sprawled the smashed and gutted case of an upright piano. Its painstakingly assembled inner works lay warped and twisted a few yards away.

Michael walked to her and reached out to touch her shoulder, but she pulled away on the bench. "I know you didn't tell," she said hoarsely, turning her face away. She tightened her arms around her knees and pressed her chin against her wrists, rocking gently. "We didn't use the dust. They were here a little while ago. I was playing. It was my only chance to play. We used the piano, we played it. But we didn't use the . . . what you brought. Here it is." She handed him the bag. It was empty but for a few grains, the tie loose.

Spart grabbed the bag and pinched it angrily. She took Helena's hair in one hand and shook loose malevolent glitter. "They turned it, they wasted it." She chuffed in disgust and pulled him away from Helena. "They are not worth your time," she said.

Michael looked back at Helena, uncertain what he felt—sadness, perverse satisfaction at his betrayers laid low, horror and anger that people he cared for could be treated thus.

"Isn't there any more dust?" he asked.

"Not for us, not for them. The *sani* is turned. If they try to cross now, it will attract every monster on the plain." She shook the dust from her hand and wiped it vigorously with a scrap of cloth, threw the cloth away, and pulled him up the stairs out of the basement. When he protested that he had to stay and help, her look asked, plain as words, *What can you do?*

Nothing. He followed her.

On the streets, they ran for a short distance, then hid behind the intact corner of a collapsed building as coursers thundered by. "Where are we going?" Michael whispered.

"You are leaving," Spart said. "With or without the powder. It is your time. You go back with me to the mound, then you go on alone."

Only now did he remember the book left in the rafters of the hut. He had forgotten it in his haste to leave the Realm.

"Come!" Spart ran ahead. Instinctively, as the pounding of horses grew louder, he threw shadows. Spart became a crowd of people. The horses halted and reared behind them, screaming with excitement. Michael barely heard the curses of the riders.

They ran along the deserted and snow-covered road to Halftown. Mottled starlight fell between broken clouds. The smell of smoke subsided. Spart ran as fast as ever and he had difficulty keeping up.

Halftown lay empty and quiet before them. Spart slowed and walked him through the town, glancing at the empty buildings, then at Michael, as if to emphasize the solitude.

"Where are they?" Michael asked.

"They will serve Adonna, those who haven't escaped." That was the whining-wind sound he had heard—Meteorals sweeping in. The Crane Women's pact with the Meteorals had been abrogated. Now was certainly not the time to leave, not if he wished to retain any of his self-respect.

"I can't leave," he said. "I have to find Eleuth. I have to help."

"If you stay," Spart said, "the coursers will take you and imprison you with the others. You will be unable to do anything for them. If you escape, perhaps you can help . . . from outside." She was not telling the whole truth—though a few weeks before, he wouldn't have been able to detect her evasion. And it was Spart who had trained him to be sensitive. "Besides, you cannot find Eleuth. She is dead."

The double confirmation—this time from an unimpeachable source—hit him hard.

"She did her best," Spart said philosophically. "She did well, considering."

Michael wept silently as they approached the mound, contrition and loss tangled with an anger turned inward, and also, in flashes, focused on everything he saw around him—the power, the cruelty.

The Crane Women's hut was intact, but his own had been knocked over. Biri's had been removed entirely. Michael searched in the rubble for the book and found it pinned between a shingle and a beam, undamaged. He pocketed it.

Nare and Coom stood behind him. He looked between them, nothing to say, virtually nothing to think. All emotion had fled. He could not go on living and feeling so intensely.

"Soon, you are empty," Nare said.

"*Ananna*," Coom reiterated. "Ready. Now, never."

Spart nodded sympathetically. "One more thing, and then you go across the plain, find the Isomage. In time, you must leave your hated parts behind."

"What?" he asked softly.

"If there is a part of yourself you don't like, you can be rid of it. You still have too many people inside of you. But that can be an advantage for a while. Sacrifice them. When you are in great danger, make one of the selves you don't like into a shadow. Send it forth. It will be real, solid. It will die for you."

"That is something you can do, we cannot," Nare said. Coom nodded agreement.

Michael blinked and shook his head. "Where do I go after I cross the plain?"

"So positive," Nare said, lifting her eyes.

"Follow the river to the sea. No matter how far you stray, always the river," Spart said.

"And what will happen to you three?"

Nare and Coom were gone already. He seemed to remember their leaving, but not clearly. Spart held her hand in front of his eyes. "In-speaking," she said. "Out-seeing. When you are ready, they are yours. The only outright gifts, man-child. Be grateful. We are *never* generous."

Then she was gone, too. He turned to see if they were running from the mound, but there was no sign of them in any direction. The mound was now empty.

Only dust and old sticks, a few stones, a broken mortar and some pieces of glass showed that their hut had ever existed.

Michael was on his own.

28

The border between the Pact Lands and the Blasted Plain was less well-defined now. Michael suspected the circle of corruption was closing, and that soon the Pact Lands would not exist.

He stood on a ridge not far from the river, looking down at the indistinct smudge of red and gray and brown creeping over the frosted grass. Where the border crossed the half-frozen river, whirlpools of mud and bloody-looking water left pinkish foam on the ice and shore.

With no *sani,* with no weapon but his stick, he was indeed empty—empty-souled and empty-handed. For a moment, after leaving the Crane Women's mound, he had hated himself, but even that was gone now. He was a pair of eyes suspended over a vast mental desolation, swept clear of youthful obstructions—but swept clear of youthful ideals as well; of all things beautiful and inhibiting.

He slid down the ridge and across the ambiguous border.

What impressed him most, the deeper into the Blasted Plain he walked, was the silence. He heard only the gentle thump of his feet in the dust, raising little puffs. The dust fell back into place, undrifted by the slightest breeze.

Winter had not touched here. The morning light glowed patchy and orange and shuddered every few minutes as if all the air were a plucked string.

Michael walked quickly at first, then broke into a run. He passed brown pools and smoking crevices, skirted a lava pillar and picked up his pace. The pillar crawled with tiny elongated shadows.

After an hour, a chasm blocked his way, ninety yards across, the rim separated like book pages into razor-thin slices of translucent rock. Sand lay flat across the bottom. At regular intervals, conical depressions blemished the sand like the marks of giant boot spikes.

He walked along the edge for a while, hoping to find a way across. There was a drop of twenty-five feet to the bottom and he didn't fancy a trek across the sand, but finally impatience and the chasm's seemingly endless length changed his mind. He experimentally kicked at the rock slices. With moderate impact, they crumpled into shards, and he was able to dig and kick an angled descent to the bottom.

The sand felt gritty and hard-packed. He walked quickly and carefully, avoiding the conical depressions.

Thus far, he had seen none of the Blasted Plain's inhabitants—unless the worm-shadows of the lava pillar qualified. He was hoping his passage might be easy when a hole directly in front of him suddenly yawned wide. He had to scramble to keep from slipping over the edge and down the loose sandy slope.

A bulbous protrusion rose in the center of the pit. Michael backed away, but not far enough to avoid being sprayed with sand as the protrusion burst like a bubble. He wiped his eyes and heard a deep pleasant voice say, "You don't know what a *relief* it is to be free of Euterpe."

Ishmael, the Child who had prophesied in the Yard, climbed out of the pit. He stood before Michael, lank and naked. His long, pale, dour face was free of wrinkles but still seemed ancient. He lifted one hand on its thickened wrist. "I've been away from my friends much too long." His thick-jointed finger flicked, and from depressions all around leaped more figures, most even less pleasantly shaped than Ishmael. "How may we help you, human?"

"Let me pass," Michael said. His inner emptiness helped steady his voice.

"All pass who will. Would you like guides? These areas can be hazardous, you know."

"No, thank you."

Ishmael sucked in his breath and coughed up a laugh, his eyes jerking wide. "We're the only kin you have here. Don't take all that propaganda they fed you seriously. We're not nearly as bad as our parents make us out to be."

"Perhaps not," Michael said. "But I'll manage on my own." He glanced at the others. There were seven or eight, all with some resemblance to humans, but for at least three the resemblance was passing at best. Their hairless arms hung to the ground or grew into their thighs; their faces were bad parodies. Ishmael approached Michael slowly, arms held out as if to show his good intentions.

"After all that time, we're in the mood to help," he said. His tone became more like a radio announcer's—slick, cultured, less and less believable.

Which self don't you like? Make ready.

"For so long, our talents have gone unappreciated," Ishmael said, full of self-pity. "Our emotions have been neglected."

"Stay back," Michael said.

"Back, back it is," Ishmael said, stopping. He knelt down and peered up at Michael from large yellow-green eyes. "Brother. Born of man and woman. Just like us."

"Quiet," Michael said.

Ishmael took a deep breath. "Where is your powder, traveler? Only a fool would cross the Blasted Plain without powder or a horse."

I believe, Michael thought, *that I would willingly cast off most of what I once was. Like my foolishness, my selfishness and blindness. Can I cast off those things?*

No answer. It was his own decision, his own risk.

Or my reckless defiance. If I had looked at things more closely, and opened my mind to how they might turn out, perhaps Eleuth would still be alive, and Helena—

No, there had been little or no fault in his behavior toward Helena. He couldn't make a shadow from unpleasant memories.

I wish to cast a shadow of the self that took advantage of Eleuth.

For a moment, two Michael Perrins stood in the same spot on the Blasted Plain. Ishmael opened and closed his long fingers. His mouth opened wider and wider until it seemed he had no jaw; his lips peeled back across flexible but very sharp teeth. His face became all mouth, all teeth, the eyes receding and the tongue darting out thin and silvery like a knife blade.

The skin of the Child's shoulders split and blood poured down his chest and arms. Rank brown nettles and thorny vines crawled from the split skin and twined around the mouth, then slid down the rest of the body, the thorns piercing and grabbing hold.

"Time to become real," Ishmael said, his tongue clacking.

The other Children went through their own transformations. Both Michaels remained calm.

What I did was not all that bad, said the Michael about to be sacrificed.

But you cannot be all of me, ever again, said the Michael about to escape. *You are past.*

He stepped aside. The Children moved with astonishing speed toward the shadow Michael, wrapping thorns, teeth, arms, claws and unnamed organs of destruction around him. The shadow screamed and Michael felt a sudden weakness as he ran across the chasm.

Ishmael lifted his mouth from the consuming and wailed, lumbering to his feet to follow, but Michael was already kicking aside the sheets of rock and climbing the opposite cliff. He sliced his hands and laid one shin open from knee to ankle, but made it over the top and stumbled on. The pain didn't slow him much, once he was back on the powdery flatness. The dust flew up into his wounds and his blood fell back into the dust, beading like tiny rubies.

He clutched the book in his pocket. The book meant sanity, words from home, arranged by those who had never been where he was now, who had lived in relative normality and worked in quiet to craft their poems. His fingers rubbed the leather spine through the cloth, and he thought of who and what he had just left behind to perish.

Atonement. Survival.

Yet strangely, the emptiness was less profound now. He had lost; he had gained.

He could see the far border of the Blasted Plain, and beyond, the mist and the tall, snow-dusted tips of trees. The lava pillars had become smaller and stouter, like stacks of slag doughnuts.

At the border the mist swirled opaque as a spill of milk in water. From where he stood it looked tangible, more spider's web than fog. He was less than a hundred yards from the border, yet he slowed, then stopped.

Something long and sinuous stretched above the mist and peered down at him. It was the skull-snail, heads and blood-red eyes searching, body dragging the macabre shell behind. Michael tried to judge how slowly it moved and how much chance it had of catching him if he ran across the final stretch.

It emerged from the mist with an audible sucking sound, its body rippling peristaltically. The skull-shell lurched behind, dragging a smooth furrow in the dust.

What did it want? It wasn't moving so fast he couldn't outrun it; it didn't seem to be threatening, ugly though it was. Its multitude of stalked red eyes focused on him, outer edges arterial bright, inner circle venous. The body glistened like oil on a dirty puddle. Michael half-crouched and held his ground, back prickling at the thought that the Children might have followed him out of the chasm, or were burrowing beneath to pop up in front of him again.

The skull-snail halted, its momentum pushing it a yard farther in the dust. The shell changed colors, jagged bands of brown, black and red crossing its surface. The arm which issued from the "nose" cavity rose seven or eight feet higher and formed a very human mouth.

"Take me with you," the mouth said. The voice was female, unfamiliar to him. "Take me with you," it repeated more quietly. "I am not what I seem. I do not belong here."

"What are you?" Michael asked, glancing around quickly to see if he was being decoyed.

"I am what Adonna wills."

His memory was being tapped, but he didn't opaque the aura. The skull-snail's voice sounded like a Sidhe's and he was curious to know why.

"Who are you?"

"Tonn's wife," the skull-snail said. Tonn had been the Sidhe mage mentioned at the *Kaeli*. "Abandoned. Betrayed. *Take me with you!*"

Michael walked a wide circle around the creature. It made no further move toward him. "You are a mage. Take me where I might live again. And I will tell you where Kristine is."

"I'm sorry," Michael said. "I'm no mage. And I don't know who Kristine is."

He passed through the bitter-tasting mist and over the border. The skull-snail raised its eyes but fell silent as it watched him go where it could not. He walked two dozen yards into the wintered forest before he began to shudder uncontrollably The creature's plea echoed in his head, the voice so lovely—the shape so grotesque, as if a curse had been laid on by a particularly creative and perverse sorcerer.

He lay on the icy grass in the snow-shadow of a majestic oak and cleansed his hands with ice-rime, then rubbed his face and eyes.

It felt like years had passed since he last slept. He damped his body's pains, tried to ignore his wounds and relaxed in the now-dripping grass until his eyes closed.

IT WAS NIGHT when Michael awoke. A light breeze whispered through the tree leaves overhead, brushing their silhouettes over clear gem-like stars. Flakes of snow wobbled down from the leaves, melting as they struck his clothing and skin. The fresh cold smell of frozen grass sap and crushed leaves filled his nostrils as he rolled over on his side.

He had strayed north of the river when he had crossed the chasm. Now, to wash his wounds and clean off what remained of the dust from his passage, he stood on shaky, prickling legs and tried to find the water again. The cut on his shin hurt the worst and his leg felt swollen. His hands were tender, but he wasn't using them nearly as much. For a moment, Michael felt light-headed, and then his feet splashed in the cold reedy shallows. He kicked and wriggled his way through the ice.

He sluiced his wounds thoroughly, then bound them with the reeds, spreading some of the astringent sap on them as the Crane Women had taught him, it seemed centuries ago. In a few minutes his light-headedness passed and he stood in the shallows and removed his clothes to wash more thoroughly.

As he sat on the bank, allowing the night breezes and his heightened body heat to dry him, he listened to the noises of the woods. He had no idea whether he was past the worst of it or not. He felt at peace, however. After so many months in the barren Pact Lands, and the difficulties of his training, he had time to be truly alone, to search for himself in the middle of all his experiences. What he found—now—didn't displease him, but he knew rough edges remained, entire personalities still to be sacrificed.

And however peaceful it seemed here, he had not left the Realm.

He wished for some light so he could read the book, but the starlight, while bright, was inadequate. He massaged his legs with his wrists and forearms and tried to connect with Death's Radio.

Failing that, he whistled for a few moments before he caught himself—looking around guiltily—and then began to make up a poem, murmuring the words.

How often death is simply love.
Make way, make way for the new!

He couldn't go anywhere with that fragment, nor could he force more lines. Being at peace, it seemed, was not the time to write poetry—at least for the time being.

And what in hell did he mean, anyway? Eleuth had killed herself for love— he had killed a part of himself, a kind of counter-sacrifice . . .

Leaves rubbed like dry hands, tree-boughs swayed with dreaming little creaks and groans, snow fell in spirit drifts, grass hissed in the wind. The river grumbled in its bed, making the frozen reeds snap.

"*Antros* . . ."

Michael leaped instantly to his feet. His *hyloka* vanished and the air sucked up his warmth. A few yards away, standing in the darkness with wick in hand, was the tall, unmistakable shape of Alyons.

29

Michael tried not to show his terror. He tried to restore his warmth and control the beating of his heart, which threatened to explode in his chest.

He had seen Alyons crucified by the steel snake. He had watched the life and blood drain from the Sidhe, had heard him call for the Arborals . . .

And now Alyons stood before him, grinning as if nothing had happened. Michael knew the Sidhe were even less likely to return from the dead than humans, yet here was solid-looking evidence to the contrary.

Alyons advanced slowly and stared at a point over Michael's shoulder. "Why so frightened, human?"

There wasn't a thing Michael could say that wouldn't seem ridiculous.

"You thought you could be rid of me so easily? That you could save your people from their own stupidity?"

Michael kept still. His *hyloka* flickered back, but he shivered from fear anyway and the returning heat didn't seem to help. "I didn't—"

"Yes, man-child? Stupid, weak man-child."

"I didn't kill you," Michael said.

"No matter."

"I didn't . . . enjoy seeing you die."

The Sidhe shrugged. They faced each other in silence for a long minute. The Wickmaster's coat flapped in the gentle night breeze; his red hair looked black in the starlight. His eyes were distantly reflective, like mirrors seen from miles away.

Finally, Michael backed off. Alyons didn't move.

"You *are* dead, aren't you?" Michael asked. He could feel nothing inside Alyons; there was no aura. Or . . . he hadn't yet learned how to use the boon.

"I am dead," Alyons confirmed. "Beyond hope even of the trees. And if you didn't kill me, then you lured me to the circle. It's all the same."

"I didn't know."

"If you had known, I wouldn't have been trapped," Alyons said. "I would have read your knowing."

"Sidhe don't leave ghosts," Michael said. Evidence to the contrary . . .

"True."

"Then what are you?"

"I am grief, *Antros*. Your grief, my grief. I am emptiness, not even one left. My horse wanders and does not take a rider now. You have wronged me twice, man-child."

"I don't understand."

"You drew me to my death, yet you did not claim your prize. You disdained."

Michael prepared to turn and flee.

Alyons gestured to the woods. A horse emerged from between the trees. It was wounded on its withers and rump, and its eyes burned wild with recent danger.

"Kill a Sidhe, claim his horse. Disdain the horse, double the insult. You are very stupid, man-child."

"What do I do?"

Alyons pointed to the horse. "Do not waste all that I was. Take my *epon*. Surely, a Sidhe horse will be valuable to you . . ."

Indeed, it would, but Michael no more wanted Alyons' horse than he desired the Wickmaster's company. "I can't," he said. "I don't even know—"

"Tell it, 'I am your master, you are my soul.' It will know you."

"Why do you want me to have it?"

"I have no wishes, no wants. It is the way things are done. Only a human would not know instinctively . . . it is the way."

"You're a shadow," Michael said, revelation dawning.

"With no wishes, no wants . . . and no time limit, if the horse is wasted." He folded his arms as if prepared to patiently wait forever.

"You'll go away if I take the horse?"

Alyons nodded once. "I am not here now. It is only your ignorance that shapes me from darkness. I am nothing but grief and violation."

"Then I take the horse," Michael said. The shadow pointed his wick at Michael and the horse stepped over to him, head down, turning behind Michael to face the image of its former master.

"Grief remains," the shadow said, growing darker. "But the violation is ended . . ." Then, with a harsh, braying laugh, the image became as black as the distant trees and smudged into nothingness.

Michael convulsed violently, throwing aside his fear in a single paroxysm. The horse regarded him with large, puzzled gray eyes. He reached out tentatively to touch its muzzle.

"Gift horse," he said. "You must have crossed the Blasted Plain alone . . . or perhaps he, it, led you." Michael peered into the night where Alyons had stood, as if the shadow might still be there, awaiting its chance. A hundred thoughts plagued him. What if a Sidhe could impress his essence in an animal after death—what if the horse still obeyed the Wickmaster? It could throw him, kill him . . .

Yet as Michael probed, there wasn't the slightest taint of the Wickmaster in the animal. And he could certainly use a horse in his journey.

He lay back in the snowless lee of the oak and regarded his undesired mount for an hour before going to sleep again.

The day was well along before he awakened. The horse kicked frost from the grass and ate breakfast. Michael was ravenous; *hyloka* had to get its energy from somewhere, and he suspected he wouldn't stay warm for long without substantial food.

"Where do we find something to eat, hm?" he asked the horse. It shook its mane and kept an eye on him as it ate. Michael stroked its flank softly, then approached its head and whispered slowly, carefully into its ear. "I don't know if you understand English, but I am your master. And I hope I have room . . . now . . . for you to be my soul." The horse nuzzled his palm and jerked its head back.

"Ready to go, eh?" Michael said. No sense trying to mount as the Sidhe did. He climbed on as best he could, gripped the mane and nudged the animal.

The horse tensed its muscles uncertainly and tossed its head. Then it broke into a trot. Michael laid himself low against its neck to keep tree branches from swiping at his face.

There was very little food in the wintered Realm. He survived off a scant supply of red berries gleaned from bushes and was glad for them, and for the crazy character of the Realm's seasons, that bushes should bear fruit in winter. With so little food, his *hyloka* became undependable, and he quickly learned how to concentrate what warmth was left and light fires with his index finger. It wasn't as neat a trick as the ones Biri had performed, but it made him suspect that his abilities strayed at least a short distance into the domain of magic. He warmed himself by the fires and melted snow for drinking. The horse survived well enough on frozen grass, but gladly drank some of the snow melt, and stayed close at night when the fire burned and smoked.

After some days of that kind of fire-lighting, Michael noticed that the finger was losing its nail. He was soon able to peel back the skin and remove the nail completely. He thoughtfully tossed it in the middle of his most recent blaze and watched it blacken and shrivel. The consequences of certain kinds of discipline began to worry him.

Within a week, he traveled about two hundred miles—there was no way he could be sure of the distance, if distances were ever reliable in the Realm—staying near the icy river. He was hungry all the time and growing thinner. He longed for the porridge the Crane Women had fed him, so bland and so wonderfully filling . . .

On the eighth night, huddled close to his fire with woods all around (and this was a small forest!), the horse standing nearby with its head lowered and eyes hooded, Michael thought about killing the animal and eating it. Part of him remembered Biri immediately after his ritual horse-eating; another part fondly remembered the taste of solid food. He tried the grass, but it was bitter and clearly not fit for humans. He tried bark, or rather chewed on it while searching for grubs, but the bark tasted like quinine mixed with lemon rind and grubs didn't exist in the Realm. He did manage to make a fair tea from the bark, using a queer scooped-out rock as a pot in the middle of the fire, and rolling a cup from the unstewed bark. He thought some of the trees might be laurel, because the leaves were shaped and smelled like the bay leaves his mother had used in cooking; others were obviously oaks, but lacked acorns (and he wasn't sure he could have prepared acorns for eating, anyway—did one do more than just steep them in hot water after crushing?).

By far the majority of the trees were now huge conifers with needles thick as ice plant leaves.

He saw no other animals.

On the ninth day, the pines gave way to more oaks and laurels, the air grew warmer, the snow became patchy.

Within ten miles—about an hour on horseback—the seasons began to change. The trees had never lost their leaves and the grass had never browned off; when the Realm's erratic and premature spring appeared Michael found his first food and wept for joy.

Fruit trees stood in wild orchards, bursting with fruit untouched by any but himself. Apples, pears, peach-like fruit with brown-striped skin, large cherry-like clusters that clearly tasted alcoholic. A pulpy, salty fruit grew on the laurel-like trees and satisfied his craving for meat.

He was relieved of his troublesome thoughts about Alyons' golden horse.

Michael stayed in the wild orchard for two days, even taking the risk of getting mildly drunk on the wine-tasting cherry-fruit. The horse cropped grass contentedly nearby. As Michael lay with his back against a tree trunk, he thought of the *Kaeli* and wondered what the animals had been like that had carried the Sidhe between the stars. He closed his eyes and tried to imagine such a journey, made without fire-ball launchings or spaceships; simply riding on the backs of the original *epon*, stretched out across space like quicksilver or molten gold . . .

He read a few poems from the book, savoring them, his mind warmed by the fruit, his stomach full. He was content despite the past horror and his own shame. He ruefully thought of himself as a comet head at the source of a long tail of experiences, flowing behind him, growing longer and richer. Gradually his reverie muddied and he slipped into a doze. The book tumbled from his fingers and lay in the grass, the wind turning the pages deftly, sighing when it found what it wanted.

An Arboral female stood at Michael's feet, watching him with unblinking green eyes. She walked over to the horse and patted it affectionately, though Arborals had no use for *epon*. Then she looked up at the Meteoral who had luffed the pages in the book, and a face between the tree branches winked at her. She knelt and applied a blue-green paste to Michael's forehead. The paste sizzled, releasing vapors which poured down the sides of his nose and into his mouth.

Both of the Sidhe melted into the woods.

Michael saw a palace of silk and gold, as airy and light as a vast tent, rising above a mountain of ice and granite. A huge cataract of melt-water poured from the caverns in the mountain's side. He was led by a shadowy guide from enclosure to enclosure through the palace, and found within a great king—an Oriental *Khan*—bemoaning the fate of his lost fleet, destroyed by a demon wind far to the east. The Khan had dreams also; dreams of great plains of grass and high snow-capped mountains and trackless desert and wild horses stalked by sturdy bow-legged men with hard, flat determined faces and lank black hair . . . all of that in the Khan's past. Now he ruled the greatest empire of all time, stretching from the Eastern sea across the mountains and plains, south to the mountains of the snow devils, north to the tent-pole of the world.

The Khan's face changed, becoming that of a pale, gray-haired Caucasian, looking younger than his years, sitting on the Khan's throne. He was not of the royal line. The plains of grass faded, the empire vanished into far history, and the pale usurper regarded his palace with an expression of suppressed rage and boredom, of impatient waiting . . .

Waiting for Michael.

The paste evaporated. The visions swirled and Michael opened his eyes slowly. He had never dreamed in the Realm, and he didn't believe what he had seen was actually a dream. It had a certain quality, a stamp, which indicated he had once again had a message from Death's Radio . . . this time, without the use of words.

AFTER TYING UP a supply of fruit in his shirt, Michael reluctantly left the orchard and followed the tree-lined river, which now turned east, sometimes doubling back in a lazy loop or wrapping around mist-shrouded islands. As the horse walked patiently on, Michael stared across the river at the largest of the islands and fancied he saw battlements in rocky crags. He always stayed on the left bank; he could just as easily imagine Riverines lurking in the water, ready to deliver him up to Adonna's forces if he were so indiscreet as to try to ford.

He ate sparingly of his fruit, which stayed at the peak of ripeness. Like all Sidhe food, a little was sufficient.

In the dusk of his fourth day away from the orchard, the horse took an opportune gap in a wall of shrubs and followed a very old, almost overgrown trail up a gently sloping mountain. They spent the night near the crest, Michael sleeping in an open spot near a weathered cairn, the horse nearby, blinking sleeplessly in the dying firelight.

Michael awoke and saw a silvery band crossing the pre-dawn sky. He rubbed his eyes and looked up again. A mother-of-pearl ribbon of light stretched from horizon to horizon at an angle of about thirty degrees. It had moon-like mottlings, and in fact could have been a severely elongated moon, though three or four times broader. As dawn came, the ribbon dissociated into blurred disks which broke down further into an indistinct contrail and vanished.

After breakfast—a chunk of meaty fruit—he walked the horse up to the crest to get his bearings. They looked down the opposite side of the mountain into a long, broad valley. The horse snorted with eager recognition; the atmosphere above the valley was as golden as its skin, and the trees—thick as lumpy moss, from this vantage—seemed suspended in another season entirely, not spring but autumn. They made up a patchwork of browns, oranges and golds. Despite the warmth of the colors, the morning air filling the valley like liquid in a bowl was quite chill.

Michael looked for some time before finding a structure hidden far to one side of the valley. It resembled a tall Oriental pagoda: dark, angular and ornate. He couldn't make out much beyond its general shape.

"Can you think of any reason we should go down there?" he asked the horse. The horse couldn't. "Still, that's where we're going."

Caution had kept him on one side of the river, but he discarded caution now. The compulsion to visit the pagoda in the valley was strong—and had nothing to do with Death's Radio.

30

The slope into the valley was that of a bowl—steep at first, then flattening. On the mountainside, the green trees of the local springtime gave way to autumnal colors until few traces of green remained. The flowers beneath the horse's hooves transformed from blues, pinks and reds to a uniform golden yellow.

The deeper into the valley they traveled, the darker the sky became, until they bathed in rich shadowy gold, like twilight in a smoky old oil painting.

Michael's eye caught a last gleam of blue in a patch of flowers a few yards off the trail. He stopped the horse and dismounted to inspect them.

Four tiny blue flowers, luminous and enchanting, defied the auric suffusion. He could hardly take his eyes off them. He bent down on one knee and cupped them in his hands, then leaned over to smell them. They had little scent, but their color alone was enough to entrance. He picked one and removed the book from his pocket. Opening at random, he pressed the blue flower between two pages, arranging its petals carefully.

With a sigh—half drowsy and half nostalgic for the colors left behind—he remounted and continued toward the pagoda near the opposite slopes.

A wider, winding trail became visible between the trees. Michael guided the horse onto this path and they followed it to a clearing. In the middle of the clearing stood the tall building, black and shiny as obsidian. It sat on a foundation of glazed dark bricks which absorbed the gentle rolls of the clearing. Surrounding the foundation, bushes glistened with waxy yellow-green leaves and large yellow flowers. Around the bushes stretched a lawn of smooth straw-grass, somewhere in color between ripened wheat and bleached bone.

Michael lifted his eyes to the tower. The first impression of a pagoda-like structure was misleading, he saw now. The tower had seven levels and was taller than it was wide. It seemed to have been carved out of foamy black lava. The exposed pockets in the rock serrated every edge evenly, reminding Michael of lace doilies and wickedly sharp obsidian daggers.

Wisdom clearly demanded a rapid retreat. Yet the house or palace was the most striking piece of architecture Michael had seen in the Realm. He wondered whether the Sidhe had built it. They seemed so little interested in the material arts.

He dismounted and took the horse by the muzzle as he had seen Spart do, leading it toward a dark polished granite gate set in a high courtyard wall. The horse's hooves clopped over ochre-swirled tiles of yellow stone. The top of the courtyard wall was protected by sharp upright crystals of golden quartz. Michael looked around, listening, hoping for a faint breeze to relieve the moribund silence and stillness.

The gate had no knocker, but mounted in the wall to one side was a polished wooden dowel tied to a gold chain. The chain passed through two circular eyes screwed into the stone and vanished into a hole.

The horse whickered and nudged Michael's back. He patted its forehead. "Nervous?" he asked. Strangely, Michael wasn't, and that made him wonder if the place was enchanted. "You be nervous for me," he told the horse.

He felt more drowsy. The valley swam in the color of half-remembered dreams. Part of him felt right at home, protected by the half-light, captured in a pleasant reverie . . .

He gripped the dowel and gave it a firm tug, then called out, "Hello? Anybody live here?"

A mirror mounted on a wooden frame swung out from the gatepost, swayed briefly and ratcheted downward until it jerked to a stop about three feet above Michael's head. It angled slightly toward him. He looked into it and was startled to see a tiny face peering right back. All he could clearly make out was an unruly tuft of black hair, two glistening eyes with tawny pupils and a physiognomy not precisely human, yet certainly not Sidhe.

The mirror was apparently angled to reflect images and convey them, through a series of other mirrors, into the building—and vice versa. In a tinny distant voice, the reflected face said something he couldn't make out.

"Pardon?"

"*Hoy ac,*" the face shouted, barely audible.

"*Hoy,*" Michael said. "I need a place to stay the night." *Oh, do you now?* part of him asked.

"*Antros?*" the face asked, astonished.

"Yes," Michael said. "I'm human. May I come in?"

The gate creaked, swayed and swung wide, scraping over an accumulation of pebbles and dust in the courtyard. It apparently hadn't been opened in years. Michael stepped inside and drew the reluctant horse after him.

A deserted courtyard lay beyond the gate. Black stone walls surrounded a well carved from onyx. A black marble crow perched on the rim, water pouring from a slit in its throat. The crow's beak lifted to the dark swirling brown sky and its stone eye regarded Michael with calm curiosity. At the opposite end of the courtyard stood another gate, already open.

A small man waited patiently in the gate. He wore a silky golden robe that pooled in liquid folds around his feet. Michael automatically sought the man's aura of memory. It was unfamiliar and difficult to read, neither human nor Sidhe.

"Hello," Michael said.

The small man nodded. A wispy black beard hung to his chest, and his features were at least in part Oriental. His sallow skin glowed like fine leather. He hid his arms in the sleeves of the golden robe.

"Sorry to bother you," Michael said.

"No bother," the man replied in perfect English, and without probing Michael's aura. "Not many visitors come to my valley, certainly no humans. Introduce yourself."

"I'm Michael. Michael Perrin."

The small man nodded. "I am Lin Piao Tai. What may I do for you?"

"Your valley . . ." Michael gestured beyond the gate, which swung slowly shut, groaning and vibrating. He guided the horse around the fountain, approaching the sallow-faced man. "It's very unusual. It seems to have its own season."

"Only one. A perpetual season," said Lin Piao Tai. "You're traveling. You need a place to rest. You're human and you travel alone—with a Sidhe *epon*. I daresay you haven't been bothered by any of the Sidhe. They scorn these forests. All but the Arborals and Meteorals keep hundreds of *li* away, and even they haven't shown themselves for ages."

"No," Michael agreed. "I haven't seen anybody . . . until now."

"Just as well. Come in. Leave the *epon*—the horse—here. My servants will see to it." Michael patted the horse and followed Lin Piao Tai through the second gate, into the house.

The gate swung shut behind Michael without any visible help. Just inside, a second fountain bubbled softly in a nook. The walls of the nook and the smooth, slightly feminine cup of the fountain were made of pure jet, while the interior of the cup and the floor of the surrounding pool were formed of smooth gray porcelain. The pool itself was illuminated by pale golden candles set in glass cylinders around the rim. Goldfish gleamed in the rippling water, their scales reflecting radiantly in the walls when they swam close.

Lin Piao Tai walked down a black corridor, motioning for Michael to follow. They came to the end of the corridor.

The small man opened a thin paneled door. He lifted his hand and waggled it with studied nonchalance. "Welcome to my home, Michael—if I may call you that."

Michael entered and looked around the large room. The ceiling was at least twenty feet high, made of a warm yellow wood intricately carved with designs of birds and fish. The walls were covered with panels of black and rich brown framing gracefully rendered screens of mountains, forests, and flowing rivers; floor to ceiling, the panels served as fronts of drawers, closets and recesses.

"You must be hungry." Lin Piao Tai pulled the train of his robe aside and with a bare brown foot, drew back a straw mat from the floor, revealing a pit with several pillows spread around the outside and a low table in the center. "My servants will bring food—human food for you, I assume, though no meats—and tea. Be seated, please." Michael descended into the pit and found welcome warmth under the table. A ceramic pot filled with coals kept the entire pit warm.

Lin Piao joined him, arranging his robes to make a kind of sack in which he squatted, legs crossed, like a pupa. "Have you traveled far?"

Michael saw no reason to hold anything back. "From the Blasted Plain," he said.

Lin Piao shook his head, face wrinkling. "I am not familiar with . . . ah! Yes! I remember. Your people are imprisoned there now. They used to wander at will, you know."

Michael's attention was distracted by strange robotic figures entering the room. They wore black robes and stood no more than four feet high, slender, with neutral stylized polished gold faces suggesting neither male nor female. Their hands gestured gracefully, fingers jointed and supple.

Whether they were robots or something else, Michael couldn't decide, and he felt it would be impolite to ask, or to probe Lin Piao's aura.

The servants brought in trays with food and pots of hot tea and set them without sound on the table, bowing and retreating. Michael reached for a jellied cake and savored the rich sweetness. "Delicious," he said. Lin Piao poured him tea. "They've closed down the Pact Lands, I'm afraid," Michael said, surprised to find himself isolated from the memory. He felt so calm—had felt very much at ease since entering the valley—and what, after all, was wrong with that? Everything was so elegant and peaceful.

"I knew that would happen eventually. You humans—if you pardon my opinion—are troublesome. I've had many dealings with humans in the past. On the other hand, I've had dealings with the Sidhe, as well, and I must say I prefer humans." He smiled at Michael. "You don't know what I am. You know I am not Sidhe . . . yet not human, either. My kind is most rare now, all credit to the Sidhe. Rare in my form, at least. Doubtless you've seen my kin on Earth. How is Earth, by the way?"

Michael tried to think of one word that summed it all up, and couldn't, so he boiled it down to three. "Desperate. Cruel. Beautiful."

Lin Piao beamed as if with nostalgic pleasure. "Some things never change," he said. "I am a Spryggla. My kind is as ancient as the Sidhe or the first race of humans, but we allied with neither during the wars. You know about the wars?"

"A little," Michael said.

"How fortunate you could drop by," Lin Piao said, passing covered bowls to him. "We have a thousand things to talk about. I just know it." He turned away, lips working as if silently cursing. "A thousand things."

Michael ate from bowls of steaming noodles in savory broth, and spiced vegetables in eggshell-thin porcelain cups. As he ate he told Lin Piao what had happened to him in the Realm. Whenever he excised something from the narrative, he found himself slipping it back in a few minutes later. He was wary enough, however, not to mention the book still in his pocket.

"Fascinating," the Spryggla said, shaking his head after Michael had finished. "Now you wish to know more about me."

"Certainly," Michael said. That seemed polite, and he *was* curious.

Lin Piao's voice changed timbre, increasing in pitch and becoming more sing-song in delivery. The overall effect was fascinating—and more than a little narcotic.

"Of the thirty races," he began, "the Spryggla were naturally suited to mold dirt, grind stones, make the bricks and plaster and erect the buildings. We loved places in which to live, and we loved them at a time when Sidhe and humans were content to wander under the broad and roofless sky. We built the first walls, and made the lands within them our own. We erected the first houses and the first granaries, and then the first fortresses. At first, we were not appreciated. The others thought we were possessive and greedy, but that wasn't so. We were just preparing ourselves for the finest of our accomplishments, the cities.

"Soon others saw the worth of our cities, and accepted our labors. They lived under our roofs and within our walls. It was our choice whether to go out in the rain or not. The wind became less vexing. There were no animals on Earth at the time; they were created much later, some by the humans, who were excellent in the vital arts, others by the Urges . . . but I stray.

"We built magnificent cities, all dust now I'm afraid, buried beneath the oceans or crushed in the mouths of the hungry Earth. We were essential. Ah, those times were *para daizo*—paradise, that is, within walls . . . but troubled. Soon each kind of glowing light, each intelligence, grew intolerant of its fellows. Tempers shortened, and in those times tempers could be formidable, because our powers were formidable. Factions developed in each race, fomenting dissent and urging separation. There was excitement and intrigue, and no one really suspected where it would all lead. We were powerful but innocent. Knowledgeable but naive."

Michael had eaten his fill and sat back against a cushion to listen. He felt a thrill of expectation. Here at last was the story, simply told, and who cared if it was biased or not, true or distorted?

"Gradually, individuals gathered others around them and became leaders. They called themselves mages. There were four principal mages, called Tonn, Daedal, Manus and Aum, and their power grew at the expense of all the others. They were too strong to really desire war with each other but the lesser mages brought on the conflict through their own ambitions. The war lasted for ages.

"It was not entirely a bad thing, that war. Nobody died . . . not forever. We were like young gods then and injuries of combat, while distressing, could be repaired. But gradually we learned the desperate arts of tact, and lying, and deceit, of gamesmanship and honor. Then we learned distrust and our magic grew stronger. The war became earnest. Enemies found it necessary to attempt to destroy each other." Lin Piao shook his head sadly. "No middle ground. All the perverse pleasures of combat became ingrained—the pleasures of triumph over another, of defeat at the hands of a stronger, of tragedy and loss, contest and victory. These are strong discoveries, and run deep in our blood even now."

Michael nodded, his eyes half-closed. He was awake, but he didn't need to see Lin Piao to appreciate his story. "The other races—what did Tonn turn them into?"

"I am coming to that. Finally, it was discovered how to kill. To kill so that the dead would never return to the Earth. All had immortal souls then, but we were bound to the Earth by such strong desires that death was abhorrent. War became serious indeed. Hate was a thing to be breathed, lived, wallowed in.

"There were winners and there were losers. The losers were treated badly. When the humans under the mage Manus vanquished the Sidhe, they imposed the worst punishment yet—they stripped the Sidhe of their souls. And when the Sidhe regained the upper hand, strengthened by the prospect of complete extinction, the mage Tonn put an end to the war. The Sidhe did not have the means to steal our immortality, but they could put us in more humble packages.

"The Spryggla, followers of Daedal, had always been proud of the work they could do with their hands, so Tonn took their hands away from them and put them in a place where there was no need to build: the sea. They became whales and dolphins. Humans were turned into tiny shrews, to exhibit their true character. Other races were made into other beasts. Some had their souls divided among millions, even billions of smaller forms, like the Urges, who were all transformed into one of their own creations, the cockroach. Aum's people, the Cledar, were music-makers, and their art was stolen by the Sidhe, who called it their own. Then Aum and all his kind were turned into birds."

Michael's eyes closed, but he listened carefully to every word.

"Of all the races, the Sidhe preserved only a few of the Spryggla, that we might build for them. They let us live in comfort, and in time we grew accustomed to our fate. We were given work. They took my ancestors off to the stars with them, and we built great things out there. They returned to the Earth eventually, and I was born."

"How old are you?" Michael asked.

"I don't know," Lin Piao said. "How much time has passed on Earth?"

Michael opened his eyes. "How should I know?"

"Perhaps I will describe something for you, and then you can decide. When I was last on Earth, the greatest human ruler of all time reigned." He spread his hands, his voice thinly hinting sarcasm.

"Who was that?"

"He was a scion of Genghis Khan. His name was Kubla. From shore to shore of the great lands, he demonstrated the new power of the humans, rising again over the sad Sidhe."

Michael tried to remember his history classes. Marco Polo, the opening of China to trade. "That was six or seven hundred years ago, I think," Michael said, peering through slitted eyelids.

"Then I am three thousand and seven hundred years of age, by the time of Earth. And how old are you?"

"Sixteen," Michael said. His eyes flew open and he started to laugh and choke at once. Lin Piao Tai made a gesture of magnanimity. Again, Michael felt his eyelids grow heavy, and languor creep over him.

"And yet here you are, traveling the Realm, free and independent. Marvelous. You seem tired, my friend, and evening is coming. Perhaps you should rest."

"So soon?"

"Time in the Realm still surprises you? My servants will make up a bed-chamber."

"How did you come to the Realm? Why did you leave Earth?"

"Tomorrow," Lin Piao said. Michael followed as the Spryggla went to a wall and pulled back a panel, revealing another dark corridor. In a small, sparsely furnished room, a feather mattress rested on finely woven reed mats, while on a nearby table a tall candle flickered in a glass dish beside a plate of cold tea and crackers—"For the night, should it last longer than expected and you become hungry."

The accommodations were the most luxurious Michael had seen in the Realm. He lay back on the mattress, pulled the blanket around his chin, and fell asleep in seconds.

Beware, beware, his—
Shh! Hiss!
On a dreamless plain, voyagers
Voyage, their eyes shut tight; listen
To the dripping voices.
Children Grow, discard ashes, cinders.
Judas selves linger, ponder;
Judas others ponder, linger;
Rude as strange words in the not-dream.
Ponder, linger, and always scheme . . .

Michael jerked awake, shivering. He felt in deep danger. His body was wet with sweat; the mattress and blanket were soaked. The candle had burned halfway and flickered with his sudden breath, making the close gray walls dance like gelatin.

He turned his head to the other side of the room and saw a gold servant standing a few feet away, its head in shadow. Michael reached out and lifted the candle. The servant's face rearranged itself in blocks like a clockwork puzzle or toy. Suddenly all the pieces slid into place and the face became a smoothly sculpted blank. It bowed to him, but remained where it stood, as if posted to guard.

Michael felt under the covers and found the book, still in his pocket. He lay back and tried to remember what had jerked him awake. Perhaps another brush with Death's Radio. The contacts seemed to come more often now, but he seldom remembered them.

A bell chimed in the hallway outside the room. Lin Piao Tai walked slowly past, carrying a gold and crystal lantern with a leaf-shaped reflector. He winked and smiled at Michael, then motioned for him to follow. "A fine morning," he said as Michael left the bedchamber, buttoning up his shirt. "The finches are singing in the gardens; the lilies are in bloom; breakfast awaits."

They sat under a rose and golden dawn in the middle of an immaculately

groomed garden. Lin Piao had ordered a golden lacquer table set on the slate
flagstones to one side of the meandering pathway, laid with dishes of fruit, cooked
grains and more spiced vegetables. Michael was ravenous and ate an amount that
surprised even himself. Lin Piao Tai picked at his food, watching his guest with
obvious delight.

"There is no finer satisfaction than catering to an appetite, and no greater
compliment than eliminating one," he said. Michael agreed and wiped his mouth
with a raw silk napkin.

"Today, I would enjoy having you tour my grounds. You should see what a
fine place I've made of my prison."

"Prison?"

Lin Piao's expression tilted slightly toward sadness, then brightened again, as
if on cue. "Yes. I have been audacious in my time. Now I pay for it. The Sidhe
do not forgive."

"What did you do to them?"

"I served. Shall we walk?" He led Michael through the gardens, pointing out
tiers and banks of flowers, all of golden and yellow hues. A fine mist blurred the
gardens as they came to a tall black lava wall at the end of the path. "I was a
faithful servant," Lin Piao continued. "In those days, the Sidhe had long since
returned to the Earth. They had dissipated themselves between the stars, you
know—you've heard most of this before? Good. It tires me to relate Sidhe history.
They were not as vigorous as they had once been. They still used Spryggla, and
we still did their bidding, though our numbers had diminished even from the
few of times past."

He pulled his golden robes aside and sat on a smooth onyx bench. "There
was conflict. Two factions of the Sidhe—perhaps more—disputed over how they
should conduct themselves on Earth. The Realm had already been opened to
Sidhe migration, you see, and many Sidhe had come here, rather than remain in
the lands of the new human race. In their squabbles; the factions created various
songs of power, hoping to outdo each other. One faction planned to give the
humans a song of power. I am confused as to the motives behind this—or even
which faction engaged in such foolishness—but I believe it was the Black Order,
and that they wished the humans to be just strong enough to force all Sidhe into
the Realm, where Tarax could control them in the name of Adonna. Praise O
Creator Adonna!" He winked at Michael. "They've done their worst, but it
doesn't hurt to follow the forms.

"I was highly regarded in those days, and so I was given the task of designing
a palace for the Emperor Kubla, who would have it revealed in a dream. When
Kubla Khan built the palace—and it was inevitable he would, given the strength
of the dream and the beauty of my designs—in all its forms and measures it
would embody an architectural song of power, making the Emperor the strongest
human since the wars. I faithfully designed the palace, and others under my
command prepared the dream . . . but a strange thing happened.

"The dream was transmitted improperly. Kubla was tantalized no end by his
vision, but he could not remember it clearly enough to construct it properly.
And when I was placed in his service on Earth, the workers were plagued with

slips of hand and diseases of the eye. The Black Order was foiled. They blamed me. In their court—a most fearsome place, and may you never see it!—they tried me and found me guilty of bungling. For that, I am confined to this valley." He leaned forward, looking up into Michael's face. "Spryggla have magic too, you know. Magic over shapes of matter. We can be very powerful, though not as powerful as the Maln. They took away my magic, all of it except that pertaining to things yellow or golden. They imprisoned me, and I have lived the best I could, with what I have. And lived not too badly, do you think?"

"Not badly at all," Michael said.

"I'm glad to hear it. You're the first company I've had in decades. Now and then, some of the Sidhe call on me, give me commissions, try again to create an architectural song of power on Earth. It was I who conferred with Christopher Wren, and earlier than that, with Leonardo and Michelangelo. But perhaps I shouldn't be telling you these things."

"Why would the Sidhe want you to help them?"

"It all has to do with the factions, the songs of power . . . No, there's certainly no need for you to suffer through all my past exploits, past failures. That's what they were, you know. Never quite as magnificent as first conceived, always interfered with in the final construction. I'm under a kind of curse." He became emphatic. "But not through any fault of my own! I am most unfortunate, caught between warring Sidhe, dragged this way and that . . ."

"Who was your last guest?" Michael asked.

The Spryggla's face darkened. "Someone I'd rather blot from memory. Most unpleasant. Besides, I am honored by a far more welcome guest now, and I must make the most of his company before he leaves!"

They walked back to the black stone house. "My powers are confined to the valley, limited to yellow and gold. I can work moderately well with the neutrals, blacks and whites and combinations thereof. Reds and browns do not interfere with my abilities, but of course I prefer yellows. And I can never leave the valley. As you can see, I lavish my creativity here." He sighed. "I fear I change my surroundings frequently, otherwise I would end in a tangle of baroque embellishment. I would go quite mad."

"May I look at my horse?" Michael asked.

"Of course, of course! How fortunate that I designed quite wonderful stables just before you arrived. Your horse is there now, very comfortable, I trust."

One wing of the house opened to the stables, which were made of gleaming black wood with natural oak stalls. Michael followed Lin Piao along a row of empty stalls, trying to remember something he had forgotten, something important . . .

With an effort, it came to him. Lin Piao swung wide the door to his horse's stall. Michael entered and patted the horse on the rump, checking it over to make sure it was being properly cared for. (Why would he suspect otherwise?)

"I have to leave soon," he said. Lin Piao nodded, his permanent smile somehow out of place. "I have a responsibility."

"Indeed."

"I have to find the Isomage. So I can help my people."

Lin Piao nodded. "An honorable journey."

"I appreciate your hospitality."

"Yours to command as long as you wish."

"Everything seems fine," Michael said, closing the stall door. "Thank you."

Lin Piao bowed. "If I am too zealous of your company, please inform me. I am used to being alone, and perhaps haven't retained all the social graces."

"I don't mind," Michael said. Indeed, he didn't. He was starting to wonder what it would be like to be on his own again in the Realm, without these marvelous surroundings, and this wonderful source of information.

"At any rate, I have work to do," Lin Piao said. "If you will excuse me, make yourself at home. The servants will respond to your needs."

They separated and Michael returned to the garden to sit and appreciate the flowers, the peace. He was becoming used to the limited colors. He had always liked yellow—liked it more and more now—and felt quite at home.

With nightfall, they supped in the main chamber. Lin Piao told him of the vicissitudes of working with the human Kubla, of the Khan's quiet melancholy and towering rages. "He was so nostalgic for his people's beginnings, for the steppes. We had tailored the design of the palace to impress him all the more. It resembled a gigantic Mongol tent, one that might be found in the highest of the seventeen heavens—much finer and more luxurious than the grubby yurts his forebears slept in. All its walls were made of silk. It was a beautiful thing . . . in conception. But when I saw it built on Earth . . . the finished *thing* . . ." He laid a bitter emphasis on *thing*. "I was dismayed. Heartsick. All my work, my conferences with the Sidhe . . . for naught. It was a travesty. It didn't float, it loomed. It was gaudy, encrusted with Mongol ornament. Yet I could not make it otherwise. I was only an advisor, an architect. I could not overrule the Khan. He was desperate to capture what he had seen in the dream. No matter how many advisors and generals and architects I spoke to, none had the courage to go against the Emperor's wishes. Politics, my dear Michael, is a plague found wherever groups of beings gather. I imagine even termites must deal with politics." He smiled. "But you grow sleepy."

Michael's eyes were so heavy he could hardly keep them open. Lin Piao led him to his chamber, and as he pulled the covers over himself, he heard the Spryggla say, "It's very simple, why there are no dreams here. It is to keep the ways clear . . .

"You . . . or I. We are the ones."

Then, oblivion. And in the oblivion, almost immediately, Michael struggled. Death's Radio spoke in him strongly now. He was not dreaming; he was struggling to stay on the ground. There was a great city seen from high in the air; he was almost as high as he had been when Eleuth tried to return him to Earth, but all his seeing focused on the great city, and to one side of the city, black and spiked like the nasty seed-ball of some evil tree, the temple . . . the Irall. Michael recognized it immediately. The temple of Adonna, and he was being drawn toward it . . .

He twisted under the blankets and came awake. He was groggy at first, and almost immediately forgot what had aroused him. There was a noise in the dark room. Michael's eyes seemed glued shut by the secretions of sleep. He took his fingers and pried them open, then rubbed them.

In dim golden candlelight, Lin Piao stood by the sleeping mat, clutching something. There was a look of exulting on his face, and exaltation.

"You have brought it to me," he said. "As it was ordained. To me. Across the worlds. The song. My song."

For a moment Michael didn't realize what the Spryggla held: the black book of poetry Waltiri had given him on Earth.

"That's mine," he said groggily.

"Yes, yes. You have kept it well. I thank you."

"My book," Michael reiterated, struggling to his feet. He reached out for it, but was restrained by two of the golden servants, who stepped from the shadows and held his arms in firm, warm metal grips.

"You don't even know what it is," Lin Piao said contemptuously. The change in his tone was abrupt and it shattered whatever remained of Michael's lethargy. "Didn't I tell you, I worked to transmit the dream? And now I see they've tried again, but this time not in architecture . . . in poetry! And again, somebody interfered. I had heard rumors that your Isomage had part of the song of power. Now I know what he has been waiting for. For you, for this!"

He held up the open book so that Michael could see the page he was referring to. "A human poet is sent the song in a dream. He remembers it, begins to write it down line for line . . . and is interrupted! Practical business, a person from Porlock, sent no doubt by the meddling opposing faction of the Sidhe. And when the poet returns to his paper, the dream is obliterated, only a part of it written down. But Clarkham must have the part never recorded on Earth! And now you have brought the segment not allowed in the Realm, the poem Coleridge recorded, forever a fragment." Lin Piao's eyes flashed as he swung the book up and began to read.

> "In Xanadu did Kubla Khan
> A stately pleasure dome decree
> Where Alph, the sacred river, ran
> Through caverns measureless to man
> Down to a sunless sea."

He turned the page.

> "So twice five miles of fertile ground
> With walls and towers were girdled round—"

The Spryggla suddenly broke off with a choke and batted at the book with one hand as if a wasp had alighted on it. He began to dance, holding the book out at arm's length and squealing like a wounded rabbit. "Traitor!" he cried. *"Human!"*

From between the pages fell the blue flower Michael had plucked at the edge of the golden valley. It landed on the floor, flat and lifeless but startlingly brilliant. Amid all the gold and yellow it stood out like a jewel.

Lin Piao danced away from it, still squealing. He dangled and then dropped the book as if fearing it contained more. One of the servants released Michael's arm and darted for the flower, but at its touch the blossom leaped and seemed to take a breath, expanding and contracting.

"No!" Lin Piao wailed. "Not this, not *now!*"

The servant tried again to pick up the flower, lifting it from the floor and sweeping it as high as it could reach, rushing for the door. But the flower left behind a trail of blue with every motion. The trail dripped color like a swath of paint and then diffused and broadened, pulsing, alive. Lin Piao shrieked as if he were being murdered and followed the servant, staying well away from spreading blueness.

The second servant released Michael's arm and backed away. Its face re-arranged itself in blocks. Michael quickly dressed and picked up the book. The trails of blue had faded. For a moment everything was quiet and seemed perfectly normal.

Then a smile confronted him in the doorway as he tried to leave. Merely a smile, nothing else; bright blue lips with electric blue teeth. It zipped away. Michael peered around the door frame, looking from one end of the corridor to the other. Empty and quiet.

He was on his way to the stables, walking through the main chamber, when he saw brilliant veins of blue creep under the walls, linking to form a cobalt carpet which spread over the floor. Liquid blueness dripped from the closets and drawers and doorways, splashing across the floor, each drop trailing a thread. Michael could not avoid the invasion. It passed under his feet, tingling but pain-less, and crawled up the opposite wall. Faintly, from which direction he couldn't tell, he heard Lin Piao cursing.

Michael's numbness wore off rapidly. He was frightened and pleasantly ex-cited at the same time. The Spryggla's magic was failing. The feeling of power, of overwhelming transformation, was like a tonic. He wanted to dance on the blue floor, slap his hands against the blue walls. "Free!" he shouted. *"Free!"*

But Michael wasn't sure what he was free of. Had Lin Piao actually manip-ulated him, drugged him? He didn't know, but his thoughts were much clearer and his sense of purpose very strong.

He had to get out. He found the door leading to the outer hallway. The black stone seemed unaffected; even the fountain bowl and luminous pool were as they had been when he first entered. Now, however, he saw waves forming in the pool. The ground vibrated underfoot. As the vibration increased in frequency, the waves in the pool took on a pattern, a tessellation of geometric figures. The water rose up in bas-relief, like gelatin formed in a mold.

Michael watched the process, fascinated, until the tessellations suddenly broke down into blue smiles. The smiles lifted from the pool and flashed past him to do their work.

Michael exited to the courtyard and stood there, trying to remember his way to the stables, when Lin Piao came rushing through a side door. His golden robe was singed at the edges and his black hair had turned white. The Spryggla stopped and fixed Michael with a hate-filled stare.

"You did this! You invaded my home, my valley! Monster! Human! I will find a way to destroy you—"

"I meant you no harm," Michael said coldly. "If I can do anything to help—"

A servant came through the door Lin Piao had just used, swaying back and forth as if about to fall over. Its once-golden surface was now the color of tarnished gun-metal. Its charred and tattered robes fell away in shreds. Lin Piao backed off in terror. "It's spreading! Stop it, stop it!"

"How?"

"I admit, you are the one, you are the intended. Now stop it, make it go away! I will stay here forever, I will be content—"

Blue cracks crazed the black stone walls. The cracks joined and the stone shattered as if struck by a hammer. Indeed, the sounds from within the house suggested something pounding to get out.

"I don't know what to do," Michael said. "I'm not a magician."

"But I *am!*" Lin Piao screamed. "How could this happen to me?" His eyes widened and the skin of his face paled almost to white as he saw a great chunk of stone fall from the wall. Above, the pagoda-like tower teetered, crumbling, its serrated edges bathed in blue fire. Bolts of fire spread in fans to all corners of the house and walled grounds and crackled out to the valley.

Michael knew there was no place where he could flee fast enough. Not even throwing a shadow would help. The ground lifted under his feet and the paving stones separated, leaving a bright blue glow. He closed his eyes and opened them just as he was abruptly tossed high into the air. All around, fountains of electric blue rose to the sky, catching the warm dark ochre of night and transforming it into cold, star-specked black.

Michael's stomach lurched. He was without weight or substance, wrapped in eternal cold, eternal ice. Lightning played between his fingers and his hair stood on end. All the wool carpets he had ever scuffed across, all the cats he had ever stroked, came back to haunt him.

He closed his eyes again and lay on the ground, shaken, breathless. The air smelled electric but the ground was still.

A long silence.

He waited for more but the quiet held. Even before he opened his eyes he felt for the book. It rested secure in its pocket.

He looked around. There was little amazement left in him, but all that remained was engaged by what he saw. The house had disappeared, and the gardens with it. In their place spread a field of blue flowers. Blue flowers blossomed all over the valley. The trees of the valley were losing their autumn foliage. The new leaves sprouted rich emerald like the forests outside.

He felt for bruises. For once he had come through an experience in the Realm without cuts, scrapes or contusions.

Michael turned to see the other half of the valley. Right behind him, fist raised as if to strike, stood Lin Piao Tai. Michael drew back, then stopped. The Spryggla was motionless.

He was, in fact, solid blue. He had been transformed into a lapis lazuli statue, complete with his expression of horrified anger.

Twenty yards away, the Sidhe horse whinnied. They walked toward each other, and Michael greeted it with a pat on the nose and an incredulous smile. He had survived, and the horse had survived. They were none the worse for the experience.

But whatever forces had been unleashed to restore the unknown balances of the Realm had not ignored the horse's golden coat.

From tail to nose, Alyons' mount was now a dazzling shade of sky blue.

31

Snow fell on Lin Piao's prison-valley by the time Michael reached the crest of the hill and turned to follow the river. He stopped the horse and looked back through the snow veils. He couldn't make out the spot where the house had stood; the valley was covered with blue velvet, soon to be white. The abrupt reversal of seasons did not surprise Michael; it was Adonna's whim and to question it, he thought with a grin, would not be following the forms.

Several more days were spent crossing through forest. He was still unwilling to give the Sidhe horse full rein, so he never rode it faster than a trot. Again, food became scarce. Michael hardly noticed. His hunger had lessened. What he really needed, as night followed sunset and yet again three times, was an indication he was heading in the right direction, doing the right thing, and not just moving from point to point on a map of foolish incidents.

At night he kindled a fire with his nailless finger and sat by the flames, reading from the book. His interactions with Death's Radio had stopped; his sleep was undisturbed. He read "Kubla Khan" several times, but he had acquired most of it by heart in junior high school. The words seemed at once silly and sublime, pellucid and obscure. Coleridge's preface to the poem was also in the book, reinforcing some of what Lin Piao had said, but Kubla's dream and the building of the palace were not mentioned.

If Lin Piao had been telling the truth, and Michael saw no reason to doubt the broad outlines, he was in possession of part of a song of power. If the Isomage had the second half—the part Coleridge had been prevented from recording—then together, they might be able to break the dominance of the Sidhe and save the humans and Breeds.

Or did he misunderstand the process? How could a song of power be both architectural and poetic? Lin Piao had mentioned encoding; perhaps poem and pleasure dome, as originally broadcast by the Sidhe, could be abstracted into a principle, an aesthetic equivalent . . .

At that point, his mind was lost in vagaries and he closed the book, lying back near the fire.

Proportion, after all, was important in both architecture and poetry.

"Go to sleep," he told himself wearily.

The next morning, at the edge of a broad savanna, with what looked like a mountain (and likely was not) in the hazy distance, Michael found a snare.

It had been tied to a sapling and fitted with a very sensitive rope-and-stake trigger. It hadn't captured anything yet. The horse sidestepped it with a nervous nicker. The snare had obviously been designed to catch a small animal; the sapling couldn't support anything large. The bait was forest roots placed near the trigger in a loop of rope. The roots were still quite fresh.

Michael looked around the bushes and thinning trees. No Sidhe would set a trap for a meat animal; what if it was a magician's snare, set to catch a specimen for some rite? He had seen bones around the Crane Women's mound and hut. But he suspected a human had set the snare. There was something about the snare, a humanness in the casual and elegant way it had been constructed.

He didn't know whether to be hopeful or wary.

He didn't have to wait long. The river broke through the last of the forest and made its half-frozen way across the savanna, straightening and flowing faster in a deeper bed. Michael tried to discern what the towering shape in the distance was, but couldn't. He was positive it wasn't just a mountain.

He was walking the horse on the sandy river bank, skirting patches of river ice and snow, when he felt an imposition. Nothing more than that; simply the awareness of a presence, aware of him.

He stopped and pretended to check the horse's hoof. The imposition grew stronger. He took a deep breath and felt for the aura of memory. He had never needed to probe a purely human aura; now, sensing one—a man—he found it quite easy to search.

He knew how far away the man was, but not the direction. Whoever had set the snare was following him at a distance of about a hundred feet. Yet the frosty grass was barely two feet high.

"Anything I can do for you?" Michael called out on impulse.

More impressions: the man was forty or forty-five Earth-years old. Not a native English-speaker, but able to speak English well enough. "I'm not a Sidhe, you know. I found your trap set in the woods."

Slowly, a heavy-set bearded man with short spiky gray hair rose from a low crouch in the grass, shaking his head and smiling through a broad mustache. "Good trick," he said. "You smell like a Sidhe. I didn't know what you were. *Bozhe moi*, a human, out here!"

The man was a Russian, Michael realized, and a hunter. He didn't come any closer. He stood in the grass, dressed in skins and furs with a cloth bag over his shoulder and a fur cap perched on one side of his head, ear-flaps untied.

"Well," the man said after a pause. "Not like a Sidhe, that is, you don't exactly smell like one. Not sure what you were. I followed you to the Spryggla's valley. You went in, came out . . . Big changes. I followed you here."

"Then you can teach me a few things," Michael said. "I didn't even suspect you were around until I saw the snare."

"Not much of anybody here, you know." The hunter began walking toward him, eyes flashing with caution. "Sidhe don't come here much at all. This whole area, south to the mountains and east to the city, west to . . . the Isomage's hole. Euterpe. You from there?"

Michael nodded. "And you?"

"They never caught me," he said. "I was a dancer." He held out his arms and looked down at his solid frame. "I came here when I was fourteen. *Christos!*" He wiped his eyes with a gloved hand. "Memories. Just seeing you brings them back. Forty years or more. I don't know. Been here . . ." Now he wept openly, standing ten yards away and shaking, wiping his eyes and finally turning away in shame. "Just a boy," he sobbed. "You're not much older than I was, then."

Michael was embarrassed. "They didn't catch you?" he repeated, trying to calm the man.

"Too fast! Much too fast." He wiped his face with his sleeve and faced Michael again, coming a few steps closer. "I haven't talked with a human in . . . I've forgotten how long. I hunt, eat, sleep, go to the city and visit the Sidhe . . . Your horse. That's what made me think you might be a Sidhe. Where did you get it?"

"From the Wickmaster of the Pact Lands."

"Alyons?" The hunter stepped back in awe. "How?"

"He's dead. He thought I was the one who killed him. I wasn't. But he—or rather, one of his shadows—gave me the horse."

"Alyons is dead?"

Michael nodded again. "Killed in a trap set by the Isomage."

"I was there during the Isomage's first battle, long ago," the hunter said, shaking his head. "I watched the pillar of magic, all the colors and monsters you'd ever hope to see. Some of it caught me, changed me, but I escaped. It aged me." He bit his bearded lower lip and looked up at the sky to blink back more tears. "I became the age I am now. I was just watching, but the magic caught me. I fled. Never stopped until I came to the city." He pointed to the hazy mountain-shape. "A Sidhe woman took me in, taught me. I was very slender back then. Handsome. But this is all premature. We need names. I am . . . *Christos!* I've forgotten." He blinked. "I am . . . Nikolai! There."

"I'm Michael."

Nikolai removed his glove and they shook hands. "Your hands are very warm for not being warmly dressed," Nikolai marveled. "The Sidhe have taught you, I suspect?"

"Breeds," Michael said. "The Crane Women."

"Do I pry if I ask where you are going?"

Michael didn't feel ready to answer, so he smiled and shrugged.

"I understand. At any rate, you go to the city. The river passes the city, and you follow the river, correct? Do we continue together?" He stared imploringly at Michael, bushy eyebrows lifted. Michael agreed.

As they walked on, Nikolai revealed the contents of his bag: strips of dried meat, neatly tied in pale white bark. "From something like a rabbit, big eyes," he said. "Stupid for a Sidhe animal." The bag also carried pieces of roots used to bait the snare, and fruit much like the kinds Michael had eaten in the orchard. In a separate pouch Nikolai had nuts, and from his belt hung a small sack of acorn flour. He took a wood-bole pipe from his belt. "To smoke, I have this leaf, dried. Quite tolerable. Never smoke around a Sidhe. They enrage with jealousy. They can't smoke, you know."

"You're tolerated in the city?"

"They welcome me, they do! The females, you'll see. Sidhe males don't live there much now. Very cold. Prigs, I say. The females will welcome you, too. But the horse . . . I don't know about the horse. You tell the truth, that Alyons passed it on?"

"Yes."

Nikolai shook his head dubiously. "We'll see. It's a wonderful place, the city. Built for the Faer by Spryggla, ages ago."

That night they camped on a snow-free stretch of sand on the inner bank of a bend in the river. Nikolai offered his pipe to Michael, who refused it politely. Nikolai took a deep puff and blew the smoke across the still night air, just as the stars settled overhead. "My story," he said, "then yours. Agreed?"

Michael nodded. Nikolai began his story and spun it on at great length, in much more detail than was necessary. Hours stretched on, but the hunter seemed tireless. Finally Michael lay back and rested his head on his arms. Nikolai offered him a small pillow filled with flexible leaves. "Go ahead," he said, "doze. Won't bother me." And indeed, it didn't.

The core of the story was that Nikolai Nikolaievich Kuprin had been brought to the United States from Leningrad to dance in the Denishawn School. He had been dancing since the age of seven—"Really dancing, not just tottering like when I was four"—but not necessarily by choice. Music had always held more attractions for him than dance. Along with the grueling dance practice schedule, he had tried to study piano, and finally had become proficient enough to play accompaniment for the other dancers. "It happened when I was playing Stravinsky," he said, voice softening. "I was at my family's *dacha* in California, in Pasadena, on leave of absence. Nervous exhaustion. They let me play the piano because it relaxed me. I was doing *Rite of Spring* for the next season's presentations . . ." He lifted his shoulders and sighed. "Fourteen, I was. I knew nothing of our world, let alone this! Alyons' coursers almost captured me, but I was naturally canny. They were distracted by the conflict. That was when I came near the battle and saw the finale."

He looked down at Michael, who was nearly asleep.

"A little black-haired boy, watching," he said, eyes welling with tears. "What they did, the monsters they unleashed. The hatred for my people. It's wondrous I can like any of the Sidhe now. Wondrous."

That was the last word Michael heard that night, or heard clearly; Nikolai continued long after he was asleep.

In the morning, Nikolai was still awake by the embers of the fire, staring out across the misty savanna with bright eyes and an alert expression. "One more thing I learned," he told Michael. "Humans do not have to sleep here. Perhaps you can stop sleeping now, too."

The season was changing yet again. Two days later, the enormous city of the Sidhe covered almost the entire northeastern horizon. The sun had warmed, driving out the snow and freeing the river of ice, which crackled and snapped all night as it broke up, and sometimes boomed like cannon. Nikolai suggested they camp on a boulder in case the water rose and flooded the savanna.

Michael offered to let Nikolai ride the horse but he refused. His attitude—half reverence, half fear—worried Michael. There seemed to be something the Russian wasn't telling, perhaps out of politeness, perhaps assuming that Michael already knew.

In the afternoon, less than five miles from the city, they rested beneath a broad laurel-like tree that stood alone on the grassland. "The city is a hundred miles from side to side, roughly guessed," Nikolai said, tugging experimentally on a low-lying branch. The smell of grass and damp soil swirled around them, driven by puffing breezes. "It's surrounded by five walls, with four gates in each wall. Now those towers on the left . . ." He pointed a leaf and sighted along it with his left eye. "That's where the music masters work. Sidhe music. Never heard it, myself. My female acquaintances say it would blast a human brain to blissful ash. Interesting experience, perhaps. And over there, in the golden dome, are Sidhe factories. What they produce I've never been told. Nothing goes in, nothing comes out, but they make, nonetheless."

In the warming sun, the city glistened gold and white and silver, with blue-gray walls and pale gray bridges and roads surrounding a central mountain of Realm granite. Atop the granite a needle-slim spire rose several thousand feet above the savanna, studded with crystals. "We can't see it from here, but on the other side, about ten miles beyond the city wall—"

"The Irall," Michael said. "Adonna's temple."

Nikolai stiffened. "You've been here before?"

"I've seen it . . . from above. In visions."

"What else have you seen?"

"A Sidhe who trained with me showed me the mountains where the Black Order raises initiates for the temple."

"Those mountains lie far to the north," Nikolai said. "Always in snow, wrapped in snow-clouds, black rock with age-old blue ice sheets."

"You sound like you've been there," Michael said.

"Near."

On the western slope of the city's mountain rose a building shaped like a rhombus twisted into a two-turn spiral, about a mile high and three-quarters of a mile across at its base. Around the base, huge tree-trunks supported floors without walls, open to the air. Higher, the trunks branched until they formed a solid thicket around the upper floors. With the trunks and branches providing vertical stability, the Spryggla builders had arranged for transparent panes of many different colors to cover the upper levels, a single color pane to every region separated by a branch. The effect was a miracle of variety and color. Several similar structures, of different size and height, grew up around the mountain.

Closer to them, on the southern slope, sprawled a low flat building consisting of a mesa-like upper surface braced by thousands more tree-trunks. Each trunk was hung with clusters of dwellings arranged in a pleasing haphazard fashion around the building's circumference. Atop the mesa—barely visible as a green fuzz from a distance—grew a thick forest. Yet another building had floors arranged like a stack of cards given a gentle shove. A third had floors tilted to intersect other floors at angles of thirty degrees or more, the whole resembling a crystal lattice.

Between the larger structures, a profusion of street-level houses followed the contours of the foothills, blanketing the lower slopes of the mountain and mottling the heights between ambitious roadways.

Michael regretted he hadn't had more time to talk with Lin Piao. If the Spryggla could build cities like this, they were something very special; he had never seen anything like it and didn't expect he would again.

Nikolai clearly enjoyed Michael's fascination. "The city is always impressive," he said. "Look over there." He pointed with proprietary glee. "That building. They make it like a small mountain, the walls come out in ridges. Caves in the walls. Never been there. What kind of Sidhe lives there, do you think?"

Michael wouldn't hazard a guess. The horse walked along beside them, staring ahead with ears perked, as if looking forward to more familiar company. Impressed as he was, Michael wasn't so enthusiastic. The few experiences he had had with the Sidhe didn't make him relish the prospect of further contact. Nikolai tried to reassure him.

"Listen, in the country, they are bumpkins, rude, unsophisticated. This is the city. Females are very different. Not many males. They welcome me, welcome you. We'll get along fine."

"What about the horse?"

"He's your horse, no? Alyons willed him to you."

"I don't have any proof," Michael said. Nikolai had nothing to say to that.

The walls of the city had been assembled from huge blocks of stone, covered with a bluish ceramic glaze. Nikolai urged him up an incline onto a roadway paved with white stone slabs. The roadway pointed straight as an arrow to a broad, low, mouth-like gate in the shadow of the outermost wall.

"We come in from the rear. This is the face the city turns to the grasslands. Not much traffic, a little-used gate."

The gate resembled the entrance to a huge dark cavern. The wall appeared to be hundreds of feet thick, yet only a hundred feet high; less a wall and more an elevated causeway around the city.

Nikolai stopped at the edge of the roadway and put down his bag. "Here is where I change clothes, stash my food, domesticate myself to the ways of the Sidhe. You are disgusted if your cat brings home a dead animal, no? The Sidhe would dislike my foodstuffs and choice of apparel." He pulled out a simple tunic and pair of pants, stuffed his other clothing into the bag, and hid it in the hollow trunk of a nearby tree.

No guards were visible. Nikolai led Michael a little ways into the darkness, then stopped and sat with his back against the glass-smooth tunnel wall. "We wait a few minutes."

In more like an hour, Nikolai peered into the darkness and nodded. "There," he said. "She comes."

Far off in the gloom, a single figure approached. Michael stood and made himself as presentable as possible while Nikolai looked on. "Who is this contact of yours?" Michael asked.

"An attendant to the Ban of Hours," Nikolai said enigmatically.

The Sidhe woman was taller than Michael by a foot, and Michael was somewhat taller than Nikolai. Her most striking feature was her face, marked with horizontal stripes of orange bordered by lines of charcoal gray. As she walked gracefully toward them, Nikolai gave her an exaggerated theatrical bow. She hardly looked at him, keeping her gaze on Michael. Her eyes were pale gray-blue, like the edges of clouds set one against another. Her lips were narrow, almost severe, in a typically long Sidhe face. She wore a purple-brown cloak edged with a satiny strip of flame red. Beneath the cloak, glimpsed briefly as she walked, was a cream-colored gown with appliquéd floral patterns of pure white.

She wasn't what Michael would have called pretty, but she was extraordinarily exotic.

"Hello," she said. Michael felt his aura being delicately, pleasantly feathered, with nothing of Alyons' bluntness or the Crane Women's forthright probing.

"*Sona rega Ban,*" Nikolai said. "I introduce my friend, Michael Perrin. He wanders, as I—"

Nikolai stopped and cleared his throat behind his hand. The Sidhe ignored both of them, looking at the horse. She smiled and turned back to Michael, then gripped his shoulder in warm, gentle fingers. "I am Ulath," she said. "Of the line of Wis. Your friend is most unusual, Nikolai. The Ban of Hours will enjoy him, don't you think?"

"I certainly hope so," Nikolai said.

"This is your horse?" Ulath asked Michael.

"Yes."

"I've never seen a blue horse, even in the Realm."

"There's a story behind that, *rega Ban,*" Nikolai said. "I'm sure he'll tell it again, when the time is proper."

"Come," Ulath said, "and be welcome to Inyas Trai."

"That," Nikolai said, "is the name of this city, and I advise you not to say it aloud, even when you are alone."

"A superstition, Nikolai," the Sidhe woman said, her voice deepening.

"My lady," Nikolai said, bowing again. "We are but poor—"

"None of your humility. It doesn't belong here."

"No, indeed," Nikolai said, straightening and smiling at Michael. "There is nothing humble about the city of the Sidhe."

The tunnel branched in two in the depths of the wall, one branch leading off into reddish darkness, the other toward a half-circle of daylight. To Michael's relief, they walked toward the daylight.

They emerged onto a narrow, profoundly quiet street that wound between walls of tan and white buildings. Michael felt as if he were at the bottom of a deep river gorge. Crystalline circular mirrors set in the walls reflected daylight all around, throwing luminous patches onto the streets at intervals of a few yards. As the sun passed overhead, new networks of reflection shifted into being, and new patches appeared as the old faded.

Ulath walked a steady two paces ahead of Nikolai and Michael, her robes rustling richly and her thick dark red hair swaying back and forth, a seductive pendulum counterbalancing the roll of her hips.

Nikolai looked around with bright interest, smiling now and then at Michael and silently pointing out one or another feature of Inyas Trai. After a few minutes, having passed only three other Sidhe—all female, and all dressed in some variation of Ulath's garb—they arrived at a broad rugged stone laid into a high-walled, shadowy alcove. Two natural steps provided easy access to the stone's flat surface. Ulath climbed the steps and looked back at them. "Does he know of stepping stones?" she asked. Nikolai shrugged.

"Do you?"

"No," Michael said. Ulath then faced him fully and by the most marvelous kind of out-seeing Michael had experienced, filled his head with the most important particulars of Inyas Trai.

To get from place to place in the huge city, stepping stones simply and directly took one from here, to there. Each stone had seven correlates. A passenger had only to think of the desired correlate, and he was whisked away. Inyas Trai had no vehicular transportation. One either walked, rode a horse (of which there were few in the city) or used the stones.

They stepped. The alcove brightened and faded and they stood in the middle of another stone, at the edge of the roof of a very tall building. Wind whipped Michael's hair. They were nearly level with the peak of the mountain and the air was quite cool. A sweet, spicy odor met them, wafting from slender bamboo-like stalks on one side of the stone. Michael was the last to step down; he was still "seeing" and absorbing the information Ulath had provided.

The city was populated almost entirely by females. Males didn't appreciate urban life; centuries ago, they had retreated to the woods around the Irall, rarely if ever returning. Females ran the city; the Ban of Hours, Ulath's mistress, was the equivalent of a counselor in the city hierarchy.

Michael blinked. He had suddenly become aware that in out-seeing, Ulath had deftly avoided his aura's barriers and plucked out a substantial chunk of personal information. She smiled at him apologetically and walked on, robes and hair swinging.

"Where are we going?" he asked Nikolai in a whisper.

"To the house of the Ban of Hours," Nikolai said. "She keeps the Sidhe records of the city. I will introduce you to Emma, and then I will go on my pilgrimage."

"You didn't mention a pilgrimage."

"You're welcome to come," Nikolai said. "I go to the mountains to witness the Snow Faces. The season approaches."

Michael followed them through an orderly grove of small, thick-trunked trees. They kept to a brick pathway with low railings on each side. "Who is Emma?" he asked.

"You'll see," Nikolai said, his face expressing the tenderest sentiment. He touched his cheek with his fingers and shook his head. "You must promise . . ."

"Promise what?"

Nikolai shook his head violently. "Never mind," he said, whirling and pointing his finger. "Did you see?" Ulath walked on, ignoring them.

"See what?"

"One of the Ban's Arborals. They tend her library."

"The trees?"

Nikolai nodded gravely. "Come. We mustn't lag."

The house of the Ban of Hours was made of wood, magnificently carved and fitted. The roof was high and conical, eight-sided for the first half of its height, then broken into three progressively narrower sections with fewer sides, the highest having three. A brass tower at the apex carried a silver crescent moon. Two wings protruded from beneath the central structure's conical roof at a forty-five degree angle, flanking a triangular courtyard. Flowers grew in disorganized profusion in the courtyard; roses of all colors, including blue, scented the air and also seemed to warm it. Ulath glanced back at Michael.

"The Ban of Hours has lived here for ages," she said. "Since long before the city was built."

"They moved the house here," Nikolai added.

They took a path beside the flowers and entered the Ban's house through a tall, narrow black door at the apex of the triangle. The interior of the rotunda was surrounded by slabs of black marble veined with green. These blocked direct light from windows set in alcoves in the outer wall. Soft, whispering voices issued from behind the slabs. Michael felt dozens of feathery touches on his aura. He gently rebuffed them and the voices stilled. Nikolai stood by Ulath in the center of the room. Both seemed to be waiting.

"The Ban of Hours is very powerful," Nikolai said. "There is confusion in her presence, and time is not the same. Do not be afraid. She will not harm us."

After a few minutes, Ulath shuddered and bowed her head. A tall female dressed in white entered from an adjacent hallway and glided across the smooth stone floor. From high in the tower's interior came a buzzing. Michael turned away from the glare of the Ban's presence and looked up. The lines of the tower spun, filled with golden bees. His thoughts became smooth as he watched the insects.

The Ban took his hand and led him behind a marble slab and up a spiral staircase to the second floor. At the end of a hall lined with brilliantly illuminated windows, they came to a wood-paneled room with a floor cut from the single bole of some huge tree. At the center of the floor's concentric graining stood a wide, low basin of water. Someone or something attended the basin, but Michael could not tell whom or what.

The Ban asked him to wash his hands. As he did so, an incredible perfume filled the room.

"We are in the presence of a poet," she said softly. She clasped his wet hands in hers and led him into an adjacent room.

Here, fine white linen draped the walls and woven reed matting covered the floor. The Ban of Hours spread wide her arms, her hands glowing with warmth and magic. Michael went to her and she folded him to her breasts. "Yes, there has been pain," she said, "and error. It is the way of both our homes. But you know me, do you not?"

He did, and softly, he began to weep.

32

Hours later, fed and left alone in a comfortable sleeping chamber at the end of the southern wing, Michael removed his book from its pocket and hefted it in one hand, frowning.

He had met the Ban of Hours—but he did not remember what she looked like. Ulath he remembered clearly enough, and all the other details prior to the meeting. But he recalled neither the Ban's appearance nor the sound of her voice. He had an impression of a tall Sidhe female dressed in white, but what sort of dress—long, flowing, pale or diaphanous?

No matter how hard he tried to recall, his memory was no more specific than that. Probing Nikolai's aura had proven fruitless; such probes were not very good at eliciting information from recent events, and Nikolai had evidently not been in on much of the meeting to begin with.

Michael's room held a brass bed with a quilted comforter, a bowl of water on a marble stand, and several framed paintings of scenes from Earth. It took him some minutes to realize that the paintings were genuine Corots, with one Turner. So the Ban of Hours was a connoisseur of things Earthly—including, it seemed, himself.

He undressed and washed with water from the basin. Again, the rich, heady scent filled the room—

And like a catalyst, the scent opened his gates of memory sufficiently wide to release one moment:

The Ban raised her eyes and regarded Michael with a warm smile, dimples forming just beneath her prominent cheekbones. Her eyes inclined slightly upward, almond-shaped and deep-set, sapphire blue flecked with silver. "You are determined to go to the Isomage, no matter what the cost?"

Michael nodded.

"No matter that it makes you the pawn of those whose wishes you know nothing about?"

He nodded again, less certain. The Ban sighed and leaned across the inlaid vine patterns of a table top. Between them was a bowl of sliced prepared fruits.

The moment ended. He dried himself with a linen towel and crawled under the soft bedclothes. The sheets felt cool at first, gradually warming against his bare skin.

Tomorrow, he thought. Nikolai would introduce him to Emma—whoever that was—and they would prepare for the trip.

The Ban had approved the trip. That much he also remembered. As for the horse—Ulath had said it was being tended by Sidhe grooms. It was, she had hinted, in sore need of good currying and having its hooves trimmed.

"NO SIDHE WOULD ever have history in a book," Nikolai said at breakfast. "Written words bind. Long memory is best. The past stays alive then; it can change like any living thing."

"So the trees remember?"

Ulath, bringing a bowl of prepared fruits—

The Ban had told him about Emma Livry . . . What about her, though?

—smiled at him and laid the bowl on the table. "The impressed ones remember," she said. "Sidhe such as myself, who have served the Ban. When we have outlived our usefulness in her service, we have ourselves impressed in the wood. It is pleasant, so I'm told, to be released from all the cares of the Realm, and to have only the past to guard, to cherish."

Sun lay bright in the crystal window of the refectory. All around, Sidhe females in a bewildering variety of clothing and skin colors ate decorously while lying on their stomachs, as Michael had heard the Romans once dined. Nikolai lay next to Michael, peeling a blue apple. "I have often wondered what the pure life of the mind would be like," he said. "Halls of memory, corridors of thought."

Ulath lay beside them and rolled on her side to look at Michael directly. Michael felt a flush of embarrassment. He dropped his piece of bread and reached to pick it up. Ulath stopped his hand with her own.

"The Ban is very impressed," she said. "She wonders about you. You come to us, trained like a Sidhe, riding a Sidhe horse. No human has ever done these things in the Realm. The Ban is curious, as are we all." She pointed to the other females in the refectory.

"I'm most jealous," Nikolai said, eating a candied peach.

"You are recently from Earth," Ulath continued. "What is it like there?"

Michael glanced around the room and realized everyone was listening. "Lots of machines now," he said. That hardly seemed enough. "We've been to the Moon."

"I was on the Earth's moon once," Ulath said. "Lovely gardens there."

"Pardon?" Michael wiped juice from his hands on a white linen napkin. The walls of the Ban's room—

Emma Livry, yet another pawn—

"That doesn't sound like our Moon," he said, recovering quickly. "It's dead. No air, no water."

"There are gardens for those who see," Ulath said.

"Ulath has been around," Nikolai confided to Michael. "She knew King Arthur personally."

Ulath regarded Nikolai with mild disapproval, then returned her attention to Michael. "None of us has been able to in-see, to read you," she said.

"Oh?" Michael thought he had been read very thoroughly by Ulath.

"Not where your motivations and plans are concerned. In Inyas Trai, it is polite to be open. Nikolai is very open."

"Nothing to hide," Nikolai said. "Unless some of the males are around." He winked.

"There are no males here now," Ulath said. "We are curious about Michael . . ."

He didn't feel it was wise to open up completely. He told them he had come to the Realm by accident. He mentioned Arno Waltiri's music, skipping a great deal after that—touching only briefly on the Crane Women—and told them about Lin Piao Tai, without mentioning the book of poems. Ulath listened intently, and when Michael was done, stroked his arm. Her touch felt cool and electric, quite different from Eleuth's.

And from the touch of the Ban of Hours. "No matter that it makes you a pawn of those whose wishes you know nothing about?"

Nikolai regarded her attentions to Michael with disapproval. "Come on," he said gruffly, standing and rearranging his city clothes. "Let's find Emma."

Away from the Ban's house, beyond the groves of trees, they came upon a small stone chateau surrounded by poplars and larches. On one side, a mirror-smooth lake diffused the morning sun with a glazed sheen. Swans crossed the lake like small carnival rides, their expanding wakes troubling rafts of water lilies.

The chateau's heavy wooden door was set into an archway carved with foot-high saints. Michael had never gone to church and didn't recognize them. Nikolai crossed himself before one, set at eye level, and murmured, "St. Peter." He took the heavy iron dragon's head knocker in hand and pounded the door twice. "She is quite charming," he said while they waited.

The door opened. A small thin face framed by lank black hair poked out and regarded them with sharp, narrow brown eyes. "Nikolai," the face croaked, and the door opened wide.

"This is Marie," Nikolai said. "Marie, I bring Michael." It was a woman—of sorts. She stood barely four feet tall, thin as a blade of grass, wearing a black shift with long sleeves. White gloves covered her skeletal hands. The corners of her mouth seemed turned down by nature, and her high quizzical eyebrows carried a message: *I'm easily hurt, don't mess with me, I bite instinctively.*

"Is Emma available?" Nikolai asked.

"For you, always," the woman said. "But who's this?" She looked at Michael as if he were some garden slug brought in by the cat.

"An acquaintance," Nikolai said. "From Earth, Marie."

Marie's face softened ever so slightly. "Recently?"

Michael nodded.

"Come with me," she said. "She's upstairs, dancing."

They followed Marie up the stairs to the second floor. Down a short hallway with powder-blue walls, they found a half-open double door. Marie pushed through. "Emma," she sang out harshly, "we have visitors. Nikolai . . . and a friend."

The room was very like Lamia's dance studio on the upper level of the Iso-mage's house; smaller, however, and filled with sun from a broad skylight.

To one side, dressed in a calf-length dancing outfit, stood a girl not much older than Michael, black hair drawn back and tied into a bun, long graceful neck and arms as expressive as the swans in the lake. She descended from her point and rushed to hug Nikolai. "*Mon cher ami!*" she cried. "I am very, *very* glad to see you!"

She pulled back a step and turned him around once, then faced Michael.

"Pay no mind to him, he is a heartbreaker," Nikolai warned. "I know."

"He is human!" Emma said, delighted. She held out her hand and Michael took it. It was flushed, warm, delicate as a flower. Slightly paler than the fingers, however, was the back of the hand, where the skin puckered faintly as if from a long-healed burn.

"From Earth," Marie husked. "Recently."

"Oh! *C'est merveilleux!*" She clapped her hands with childlike delight. "Ni-kolai, you found him and brought him here, so he could speak with us, tell us about home?"

"Partly," Nikolai said. He confided to Michael, "I would do anything to make Emma happy."

Marie brought in a small table and they pulled wooden chairs away from the wall and sat. "Marie," Emma said, "bring wine and some of those delightful cakes the Ban gave us."

She turned to Michael and smiled dazzlingly, then closed her eyes and wrig-gled with delight. "Where are you from?"

"California."

"Do I know . . . California? Yes, I do! In *les Etats Unis*. I have never been there. It is a desert, and very dry, no?"

Marie brought sweet buckwheat cakes, wine, and glasses, and poured and served all around. When Michael had satisfied Emma's curiosity about California, she asked him if he had ever been to France. "No," he said. Her face fell.

"Is it that you can tell me anything about France, how it is? What year is it!"

"1985, when I left," Michael said.

"Left? You left of your own will? Oh . . . I was taken. Not that I am not grateful." For a moment she looked as if she were about to cry, but she brightened immediately and touched his hand. Nikolai looked at the contact with undis-guised jealousy. "So what is Paris like, and France, when you left? So many questions!"

Michael looked to Nikolai for help. "When did . . . uh . . . Emma leave?"

"1863," the hunter replied darkly. "A bad year for her."

"Very bad," Emma said, but not as if she felt it. "So it has been . . . more than a hundred and twenty years. I have hardly known the time. They have been good to me. But sometimes I think I am their toy."

"They love you," Nikolai admonished, then raised his brows and pursed his lips. "As much as they can love, I suppose."

"I dance for them," Emma said. "Their attitude, it is so funny! They tell me Sidhe can dance with far more control, grace, even spontaneity, than can I, yet that is only to be expected. I dance, they say, with a special magic, because I have no magic! It is all physical, no sorcery, no illusion. Ah, but if I had stayed on Earth—"

"If you had stayed on Earth," Marie said, "you would be dead."

"But if *that* had not happened," Emma went on, undaunted, "Nikolai tells me I would have changed the shape of the dance! I mean, the way everyone thinks of dance, ballet."

"You are a legend," Nikolai said. "Michael knows nothing of dance, however. He is a poet. So the Ban tells us."

"Then I will show you dance," Emma said.

"Your practice is over today," Marie said. "You must not overdo."

"Marie is so silly sometimes," Emma said, giggling. "She forgets. Here, I cannot overdo! They protect me. Ulath, the Ban . . . I feel like a . . . how is it? A flower in a conservatory, kept under glass." She shook her head saucily. "I am so delicate, such a fine little toy. Nikolai doesn't think of me that way, though. He knows dancers are tough."

"You are the sister I never had," Nikolai said.

"I am older than he, am I not?" Emma asked, searching the faces around the table. "He is from Earth after I, so I am older. Yet we look so different in time! This place, don't you agree, Michael, it is very strange.

"But no matter. If you wish, you will have me dance for you, perhaps when the Ban requests . . . or anytime."

Nikolai told her they had to leave soon, and she followed them to the door, looking quite distressed until she blew them a kiss, smiled, and ran back up the stairs. Marie stared at them somberly and closed the door.

"How did she get here?" Michael asked. "Like you, like the others?"

"No. The Sidhe brought her here, perhaps the Ban or Ulath or another, even. She is Emma Livry; haven't you guessed?"

"I've heard the name . . . The Ban . . ."

"Emma Livry, one of the finest dancers of her time—but she never had a chance to be as accomplished as her promise. She was just twenty years of age, a beautiful girl. Her dress caught the flame of a gas jet. She was burned," he screwed up his face, "horribly. I am not sure exactly how it was done, but the Sidhe of Inyas Trai came to her, took her. They healed her and kept her here. She delighted them, so young, so beautiful." He inhaled deeply. "Sometimes even the Sidhe do something worthwhile."

Emma Livry. The rest of the meeting with the Ban was suddenly clear as could be, and her words:

"*I venture to guess Nikolai is almost as ignorant of what really happened as you. This dispute over songs of power . . . over the human question . . . it raged in all quarters for centuries.*"

"I know about the pleasure dome," Michael said.

"*Good. Then you are not completely unlearned. That was a minor episode, man-child. There have been episodes far more cruel and senseless. Nikolai will no doubt inform you that Emma was a very promising young dancer who met with an unfortunate accident. It was not an accident.*

"Early in her career, she was approached by David Clarkham. Oh, he had another name at that time—"

"He's that old?"

"Even older. Do you know who or what Clarkham is?"

"Only that he calls himself the Isomage."

She smiled again, conveying an entirely different meaning.

"He approached her with plans for a major ballet in which she would have the starring role. She would dance a quite revolutionary solo. And in that solo, Clarkham would incorporate yet another form of the song of power. Not as architecture, not as poetry, but as dance. He knew that the Maln had gone to great lengths to discourage the transmission of a song of power to the humans, when they realized what humans would be able to do with it—not just drive the remaining Sidhe from Earth, but reunite the Realm and Earth. First the Maln sabotaged their own early schemes by sending a person from Porlock to Coleridge. When Clarkham came along with his plan to bring power to himself by realizing a song, he knew he had to have a great human artist enact the design. Emma Livry was his first choice. The Maln discovered him, however, and before she could dance in his ballet, they stopped her."

"Why didn't they just kill Clarkham?"

"He was much too strong."

"But humans aren't supposed to be capable of working strong magic!"

"Only now do you question Clarkham's character and abilities?"

Michael ignored the gently barbed inquiry. "What did they do to her?"

"She danced in untreated tarlatan. She wished her costume to be pure white, without the dinge of flame retardants. She was waiting backstage. All the Maln had to do was increase the length of a gas jet when she fluffed her dress. She became a pillar of fire, like a butterfly caught in a candle. She ran across the stage, and the flames ate the wind. Poor butterfly . . ." *The Ban lowered her eyes.* "For eight months she lingered in agony. She was so dedicated to the idea of art, such a pure individual, that she invited pantomimes to come look at her writhing, the better to understand the reality of pain."

Michael made a face and shook his head.

"You are disgusted?"

"That's bizarre."

"Perhaps to someone with incomplete understanding. But a Sidhe understands. There is nothing but the song, and all things are the song. Finally, even the Maln relented, and we were allowed to take her away from the pain. We left a changeling in her place, to die for her, and we healed her, on the condition that she never leave Inyas Trai. She never has. We cherish her. Even Tarax has been known to visit, to watch her dance, and Tarax hates your kind with a bitter passion."

The Ban lifted her hands from the table and stood.

"Does that mean I'm in danger?"

She gazed at him, through him, to more important problems beyond. "You are a pawn," *she said.* "In the midst of great forces involved in age-long struggle. You are better equipped than most, but you are still ignorant, and it is not my place to *inform you." She looked at him tenderly. "Though you come to my bosom, and remember me in dreams, and know me for what I have been to your kind in ages past, I have my limitations, too. I cannot protect you beyond the dictates of the* geas *of Adonna."*

Nikolai touched Michael on the shoulder. "No lollypoddling," he said. "You look disturbed. Something wrong?"

Michael shook his head. "No. Not yet."

33

The stepping stone where their pilgrimage would begin lay on the north side of the history grove. No one accompanied Michael and Nikolai as they walked through the grove. Nikolai wore heavy clothes to protect him against the upcoming cold; Michael's clothes were considerably lighter.

Arborals tending the trees stood in the shadows of their charges, male and female both green and naked. They watched but said nothing as the pair passed. "I rather like them," Nikolai said. "They do their work, bother no one, never complain and stay faithful to the Ban. l could live here among them and be quite happy."

"Why don't you just stay in the city?" Michael asked.

"Ah, that's another matter. The city is full of tension. Most of the time the males hide in their woods, or ride in the hills around the Irall. Then there is peace here. But the males return for their *Kaeli*, and then the Ban must be vigilant to keep her humans and Breeds from being hunted and taken away."

"But Tarax watched Emma Livry dance!"

"Tarax, friend, does not know about you and me. Emma he may tolerate, so long as his power is matched by the Ban's—but the Ban can do nothing to protect *me* if I am found."

"So Emma and Marie receive special treatment . . . How did Marie come here?"

"She has always been here, tending Emma. I have never asked." Nikolai looked at Michael sternly. "Perhaps you shouldn't, either."

"Are you upset with me?" Michael asked. The stepping stone was visible through a thin stretch of saplings too young for the history groves.

Nikolai took a deep breath. "No. Envious, perhaps. Worried. You are . . . high profile. They seem to dote on you, as they have never doted on me. I have never spoken with the Ban, not that I recall. You have. Those who attract the attention of the Sidhe face two possible fates. The first is imprisonment, perhaps degradation. Emma is imprisoned, but not degraded, at least not in any way we understand or that she will ever know. She dances; as she says, she is like a flower in a conservatory. I think she enjoys being the flower, being able to concentrate on dance. I would not enjoy that. The female Sidhe tolerate me, enjoy me, but they are not *attracted* to me."

"What's the second possible fate?"

"I don't know," Nikolai said. "Perhaps what happened to Clarkham. "

"Is he human?"

Nikolai lifted an eyebrow. "You seem to know more about him than I do."

"I don't know everything. He's been alive for a long time, and he seems to know a lot about magic."

Nikolai sighed. "Well, for this journey at least, let us travel with light hearts. The Ban has approved, and there is little that will happen on a journey the Ban watches over."

"Nikolai, do you remember what the Ban looks like?"

"No." The stepping stone was deserted, merely a dark flat boulder resting on a white gravel circle. Clouds whisked overhead, shading the sun. Wind carried some of the flower-scent from the gardens around the Ban's house. "Nobody knows what she really looks like, except perhaps Ulath. It is her weapon against Tarax and the Maln."

Nikolai stood on the edge of the stone and reached for Michael's hand. He pulled gently and Michael accompanied him across the stone's surface. Suddenly, they were plunged into intense cold.

A dazzle of white blinded Michael. He covered his eyes with his hands and felt for the opposite edge of the stepping stone. Nikolai took him by the arm and guided him down and into a rock-walled wind-shelter. "Caught me by surprise," Michael said, rubbing his eyes and blinking.

"Much colder than when I was here last season," Nikolai said. The stepping stone perched on the edge of a broad shelf of rock, looking over high jagged peaks. Snow filled the valleys between the peaks, brilliant and white and as smooth as the surface of a pail of milk. Snowflakes swirled violently in the wind that howled around the stepping stone and made the walls of their shelter rattle and vibrate.

"How far do we go from here?" Michael asked, hoping to brace his *hyloka* for the ordeal.

"A mile or so. We wait for the others. Never travel alone, especially with weather like this. Adonna must have a bad toothache today." He grinned and brushed a seat clear for them on a bench-shaped boulder. Drifted snow powdered the dark interior of the shelter. "Will you be warm enough? Ulath seemed to think you wouldn't have any trouble. The Sidhe can come here naked if they wish. Perhaps you could, too?"

Michael's *hyloka* finally took hold. "I'll be fine," he said. He cut back his drawing of heat from within when he felt his pants become warm. This was hardly the place to repeat the incident at Helena's apartment.

Nikolai clasped his gloved hands and stared down at the rugged black stone floor. He sniffed. "What are you most afraid of?" he asked.

Michael shrugged. "All sorts of things. Why?"

Nikolai looked out into the snow and shrugged. "For talk."

"What about you? What are you afraid of?"

"I am afraid of dying here. If I die here, I become nothing. I never go back to Earth. So I am afraid of not being good enough to stay alive. I know I'm afraid, and I live with it. But you . . . do you know what you're afraid of?"

Michael thought of the Ban's comforting, warm arms. "There are lots of things that frighten me, like I said."

"What in particular?"

"I'm thinking. Don't rush me." He looked up at the rock ceiling. "I'm afraid of being normal."

Nikolai grinned broadly. "Thank God. I was worried perhaps you didn't know. Then you would be dangerous. What are you going to do with your fear?"

"Avoid being normal."

"And if you succeed?"

Michael laughed and felt the cold in his stomach dissipate. "Then I'm going to be sorry I have such a hard time getting along with people. With the Sidhe, with women, my friends . . . whomever."

Nikolai stood and peered around the edge of the shelter. "They're coming. Be prepared. Almost anybody can show up here."

"What are the snow faces?"

"A mystery," Nikolai said, sitting again. "In a place where everything is a mystery, we may see something that is mysterious even to the Sidhe. I like that. That's why I come here."

The first pilgrim to join them in the shelter was wraith-like, tall and deathly thin. Michael noticed bright red hair beneath a white hood, and the pale gray eyes of a pure Sidhe. But the look the pilgrim gave Michael and Nikolai had no menace in it, only deep exhaustion—of both body and mind. Michael probed his aura and saw nothing but darkness, as if even memory had guttered out. The Sidhe nodded cordially to Nikolai and sank to his knees on the rock floor.

Five others trooped in one by one: three more Sidhe, one human—heavily wrapped in white—and a Breed. The Breed was a young, strong-looking male, tall and with stiff pale blond hair, dressed much like Michael. At first, Michael couldn't tell if the human was man or woman, old or young. It wore two wooden cups over its eyes, with slits to see through—a precaution against snow-blindness. When Michael probed the human's aura, he pulled back as if burnt.

He had never touched such naked spiritual pain and ugliness. He was left with the impression of foul cancers and leprosy, creeping vermin and monstrous, all-consuming greed.

The five new pilgrims gathered in the lee of the barricade. The trio of Sidhe removed their outer garments and stood naked in the dark nook, hardly glancing at the others. The exhausted-looking one regarded Michael with deep-sunk eyes, then probed his aura gently. To be polite, Michael allowed him access to certain information—language, vague origins.

Nikolai had met them before, apparently, and introduced them to Michael. "This is Harka, Tik and Dour." Harka, the tired-looking one, nodded. Tik and Dour might have just entered maturity; they were younger and more robust and they lacked the calm jaded equanimity of the older Sidhe. "The one bundled up, that's Shahpur—last name I've forgotten—"

"Agajeenian," came a muffled voice through the wrappings. The voice was pleasant, a surprising contrast to what Michael had briefly touched within.

"And I don't believe we've met before," Nikolai said to the Breed.

"Bek," the Breed said, lifting his palm. "My first time. When are we off?"

"When the wind lets up," Shahpur said. His voice seemed more beautiful each time he spoke, very like a Sidhe's. Michael wondered if he had been mistaken in the first probe and tried again. The foulness was indescribable and for a moment he had to struggle to keep from throwing up. The Sidhe stayed away from Shahpur, who said nothing more.

Nikolai tried to keep up conversation. His efforts died. Soon they all stood or sat behind the barricade with only the whistling roar of the wind and the crack and rumble of distant avalanches.

The last light of day faded. The murk within the shelter deepened. Suddenly the wind stopped its bitter assault, leaving only a hollow and fading echo, like the moan of a dying horse. The silence was profound, almost having its own sound as Michael's ears adjusted. Shahpur looked around the edge of the barricade and moved out onto the trail. Bek followed, then Harka, Tik and Dour. Nikolai and Michael left last.

"Sometimes I think this is a shameful thing for them," Nikolai said, nodding at the figures ahead. "I wonder why they even come. Harka grows worse every year. If he was human, I'd say he was dying, but Sidhe don't get physically sick."

"He's blank inside," Michael said. "Maybe they have another way of getting sick. What's wrong with Shahpur?"

"Ah." Nikolai shook his head. "He is cursed. Like me, he wanders the Realm, but the Sidhe caught him once. He escaped, but not before they had their fun with him." The heavily bundled figure turned stiffly around and regarded them for a moment. Nikolai pursed his lips and shut up.

The path followed the contours of a nearly vertical face of granite. Far below, pinnacles of rock spiked through roiling layers of cloud. Their feet crunched the snow gathered in windblown patches along the path and their breath cast almost tangible mists that hung in the air like markers of their passage.

Tik, Dour and Harka were the first to reach a narrowing of the ledge. They turned with their backs to the abyss and sidled along the face, at one point stepping over a yard-wide gap where the ledge had spalled away. Shahpur, Michael and Nikolai had a more difficult time spanning the gap, and Nikolai's foot slipped on the opposite side. Michael grabbed hold of his hand and drew him along to a wider portion, where they lay against the face and took several deep breaths.

"That was not there before," Nikolai said. "The path gets more dangerous every season."

The ledge widened to a broad, rounded lip, giving them at least the illusion of security. Around a blade of rock that had fallen long ago from some higher spalling, they saw the object of their journey. Shahpur followed the leading Sidhe and the Breed, and Nikolai pressed ahead of Michael, panting and cursing.

They all gathered on a broad rock stage before a deep cavelike hollow. "The mountain," Nikolai said. Many miles away, yet as clear as if it stood just yards before them, loomed Heba Mish. "No one knows how tall it is, not even the Sidhe."

Far below the rock stage and cave, clouds poured into a deep chasm, leaving behind wisps which slowly unwound and vanished. At the bottom of the chasm, a deep blue-green slope of ice accepted the falling cloud and scattered it into broad rivers of mist, which slid down worn, rounded grooves. Michael felt dizzy, peering over the rim of the stage. He lifted his gaze and followed a sheer flank of delicately poised snow on the mountain. The white mass reached three-quarters of the way to the peak before being sullied by outcrops of black rock.

"Now we wait," Nikolai said. As if at a signal, the three Sidhe and the Breed moved back into the cave, leaving the humans to listen to the silence.

"What are we waiting for?" Michael asked.

"The Snow Faces," Nikolai replied.

NIGHT CAME AND Michael lay comfortably enough on the chill cave floor. Nikolai slept restlessly beside him. Shahpur sat on his haunches, appearing to be awake. The Sidhe sat with legs crossed, lined up against the opposite wall of the cave.

Michael couldn't sleep. He kept trying to probe Harka. The wraith-like Sidhe's aura was virtually empty of any memory, as if he had been created mere moments before, with no ancestry and no past. Michael wondered if certain Sidhe chose to wipe their lives away. There was a way it could be done with the discipline, boiling memory off with a kind of focused *hyloka* . . .

Nikolai grumbled and opened his eyes. "Waiting is miserable," he said. "Especially here."

"How do you know the right time to come?"

"I have my contacts. Word gets passed along. Arborals whisper, or I listen to Amorphals in their deep cavern homes. Or another wanderer, like Bek or myself or Shahpur, hears about it and the pilgrims begin their journeys. Then we gather. I've always used the stepping stone from Inyas Trai. Others hike and climb. Some never say how they arrive; they just do. Not always, not every season . . . sometimes not for years.

"I've heard the sign first appears in a pool in the Irall. The pool is very deep, with ice at the bottom, and the Sidhe watchers know, when it turns black as night, that the season is coming. They pass the word in secret . . . Adonna might not approve of Sidhe regarding a genuine mystery." He rearranged his legs and closed his eyes again. "In the morning, perhaps, when the wind rises again."

Michael lay in a state between sleep and waking, much like the state he had been in on his second night in the Realm, while perched on the rock waiting for the warmth of dawn.

Orange light slowly filled the cave, accompanied by a low, deep hissing. Michael stood and stretched his cramped legs. Nikolai did likewise, complaining bitterly.

The sun rose beyond Heba Mish, reflecting from the western mountains and casting a dull purple backlight on the snow slope. Clouds in the east became

bathed in flame, green and orange and lavender. Several shafts of light broke
through the clouds and dashed themselves against the unseen side of Heba Mish,
creating an aurora-like edge of yellow around the peak.

High above, the pearly ribbon broke into its separate arcs and faded. Snow
had fallen in the darkness and lay glittering outside the cave.

Nikolai and Michael walked onto the rock stage. The clouds pouring into
the chasm had been depleted. Now there was just a hollow invisible rush of air.
Cracks had formed in the ice and occasional bass rumbles and explosions rose
to their ears as the cracks broadened and the ice calved.

"Here it comes," said Shahpur behind them. Far off, the hiss increased in
volume until it was discernible as a combined wailing and roaring. Icy breezes
slapped at them and rushed through the cave with a ghastly jug-blowing hoot.
The Sidhe and the Breed came out onto the stage, their hair pinned back by the
rising wind. The hooting became continuous.

With sudden violence, the wind drove them back and threatened to blow
them from the stage. Michael felt himself flung down, then lifted until his feet
hovered inches above the rock. He hung suspended for a seeming eternity as
Nikolai and the others clawed for purchase, lying spread-eagled on the stage.
Then the balance of pressures shifted and he fell back. The roar rose to a painful
scream; wind rushed down the gap between the mountains, pouring into the
chasm and leaping over to begin its climb up the white, snow-covered flank of
Heba Mish.

The flank's delicate balance was upset. With barely heard reports, it began
to disintegrate. Mile-wide sheets sloughed off and descended like ragged paper
on a cushion of air. The sheets broke up and the wind snatched at their fragments,
powdering them, grabbing and lofting great billows of snow.

Amoeboid, the billows obscured the side of the mountain, then the rock
outcrops, and finally shot above the peak.

It seemed like hours before the snow reached its zenith. Again the wind
stopped. For breathless minutes the billows hung in a curtain above Heba Mish;
then they descended.

"Now," Nikolai said.

Michael squinted, trying not to lose any detail. The curtain broke up in
residual pockets of unstable air. The pockets sculpted the falling snow, slicing
away this extremity and that, forcing the cloud to push outward here and slide
inward there. A shape slowly emerged from the turmoil.

"Number one," Nikolai said. The features abruptly clarified. It was a man's
face, young-looking, lightly bearded. Michael didn't recognize it. The face spread
over Heba Mish, miles wide, and then decayed. The clouds continued their descent until more features formed. Very indistinct at first, then crystal-sharp, came
the second face—a Spryggla, Michael was certain, because of its resemblance to
Lin Piao Tai. The next face was so familiar he sucked in cold air and almost
disrupted his *hyloka*. Familiar—but who was it? Narrow-nosed, strong and
youthful, sharply chiseled . . .

"Two and three," Nikolai said. "Now it will fall, make one more, and all will
be finished."

Michael stared at the face, trying to recall where he had seen it before. "I *know* him," he muttered. "I know who that is!"

But his memory balked. The fourth face formed, that of a stern and impressive Sidhe, eyes haunted. Michael didn't care. He was so close, and the memory seemed so important he wanted to strike himself, pull his hair—anything to force the answer.

And it came.

The third face was not quite identifiable because of its youth—the man had been old when last they met.

It was Arno Waltiri, now falling into random drifts down the ravaged flank of Heba Mish and into the ice chasm miles below.

34

The Sidhe left first, walking back along the same path but climbing a few yards up to another ledge to avoid the stepping stone. They were not returning to Inyas Trai; they had other destinations which could be reached only by hiking out of the mountains. Shahpur remained on the stone stage, his covered face unreadable, his mind as horribly repellent as before. Only the Breed, Bek, elected to return with Nikolai and Michael to Inyas Trai. "I've never been there before," he said. "And I've run from Sidhe coursers long enough. The city sounds like a haven, for the time being at least."

Nikolai didn't encourage him, but the Breed had made up his mind. Where humans were welcome, surely Breeds would not be despised.

The ledge was even more treacherous after the passage of the winds. Snow had fallen from the sides of their mountain and compacted to slippery ice under their feet. Michael was very tired and glad to see the stepping stone.

He felt as if he had lived a dozen lifetimes, and left something unresolved in each one. He was a many-formed ghost caught between at least two realities, neither of them quite solid and convincing. Who had Arno Waltiri been, that his face should be carved in clouds of snow in the Realm of the Sidhe?

Perhaps Clarkham was not the goal of his travels after all, not the one to return him to Earth or help the humans in the Realm. But Waltiri was dead . . . or rather, Michael had been informed of his death. In the "real" existence of Earth, such a message—such information—was certain. Nobody in Michael's experience had ever been so cruel as to lie about the death of a friend, and he had no reason to suspect Golda.

Perhaps she hadn't known, either. Or perhaps Arno had deceived them all.

Perhaps the composer hadn't even been human.

Michael's thoughts were deeply mired as he stepped up on the stone. Nikolai and Bek followed, Bek with hands trembling, as afraid of the Sidhe as Michael would have been, once.

And should have been, now. In the instant between stones, he heard voices engaged in conversation. Whether the hearing had been arranged as warning, he was never to know. The voices discussed his status in Inyas Trai, his position with the Ban of Hours, the status of humans in the Realm—and mention was made of the Council of Eleu and of the Maln.

He emerged in warm sunlight. Neither Nikolai nor Bek stood beside him on the stone. Ulath and four male Sidhe in pearly gray waited on the gravel surrounding the stone. Ulath's expression was tense, grim. He could feel her aura pulsing angrily, sense her restrained power.

The male Sidhe were coursers from the Irall. He gathered that much before they became aware of his abilities and sealed their memories.

"I remind you," Ulath said, "that he is favored by the Ban of Hours."

The shortest courser stepped forward and held his hand out to help Michael down from the stone. Michael hesitated, then took the hand, realizing he would exhibit his fear otherwise. He didn't know what he would do next. He doubted he could successfully cast a shadow with so little preparation, and so many Sidhe on alert.

"I am Gwinat," said the Sidhe who had offered his hand, "I am your intercept. You are in possession of a horse of the Irall."

"It was given to me," Michael said.

"That is irrelevant. No one, especially a human, can be in possession of a horse from the stables of Adonna's temple."

"It was the horse of Alyons," Ulath said, glancing between Gwinat and Michael. "You are well aware of that."

"And for stealing that horse, Alyons was sent to the Blasted Plain. That was his punishment. We could not reclaim the horse—he put his imprint on it and it would have been of no use to the temple. Sidhe law does not recognize the return of stolen property, anyway—certainly not horses."

Ulath touched Michael on the cheek. "Alyons' shadow took revenge on you," she said. "After Alyons' death, the horse had to be returned to the Irall, or left to die."

"He gave it to me," Michael said hollowly. Then, suddenly crafty, "And I've come to return it."

Gwinat smiled in appreciation, then shook his head. "You were his enemy, and you killed him, no?"

"I didn't want to be his enemy. I didn't kill him."

"Come." The coursers drew up around him, cutting off any hope of escape. Ulath withdrew her hand and backed away. He probed her fleetingly and found regret but no deep sorrow. "The Irall does not approve of the Ban's policy toward humans," Gwinat informed her.

"The Irall has no power over the Ban. She was appointed by Adonna. What does Adonna say?"

Gwinat smiled snakishly and bowed his head. "We will remove this one. That is the law."

Michael.

What? Who is it?

Go with them.

He looked at Ulath but she hadn't sent any messages, and it hadn't felt like the Ban—or Death's Radio. Who, then?

He walked between the coursers, onto the stepping stone which led to the streets below, then through the streets to where their horses—and Alyons'—waited. A small number of Sidhe females watched as the coursers allowed Michael to mount the sky-blue horse, mounted their own, and rode with him through the northern gates of Inyas Trai. Gwinat turned to look back through the gates, still smiling.

"I don't see what even a human would find of value in there," he said softly. "The Spryggla took their revenge on us when they built it, just as Alyons took his revenge on you, eh?"

Michael looked straight ahead, down a wide stone road that passed straight as a shadow through an avenue of black stone pillars, and beyond, to the gates of the temple of Adonna.

They were taking him to the Irall.

35

The Irall loomed, its black central tower smooth and round and featureless, tapering to an anonymous needle point. Around its base irregular clusters of smaller towers poked out from a smooth dome of silky gray rock like crystals, all inclined toward the center.

Gwinat and the coursers led Michael down the dark stone road, between pillars as shiny as polished metal yet as black as night, with gleams buried in their depths like watching eyes that enjoyed his discomfort, his fear.

Nothing the Crane Women had taught him could possibly have prepared him for this.

The entrance was surprisingly small, just wide enough for three horses abreast, and perhaps two heads taller than the coursers riding on either side of Michael. The walls of the tunnel were cupped like the sides of a glacial cave, and what looked like dried flowers littered the floor. The air smelled sweet and dusty, not unpleasant, yet not quite pleasant. Suggestive, haunting, like the smell of *old roses clutched in hands hidden far beneath the sun, petals falling one by one scented, black in always-dark.*

The message came through stronger than he had ever felt it before, just as the light from the tunnel's entrance was cut off by a turn. The coursers pushed on, having no need for the light. Michael, trying to listen for the voice again, heard Gwinat dimly: "We're to take you to the Testament."

As Michael's eyes adjusted, he saw the tunnel had broadened and filled with a faint greenish glow. Ahead, on walkways to either side, two long lines of figures shuffled in single file, eyes staring forward. They were Breeds, and each carried a green ceramic basin filled with black liquid. Michael tried to examine each face as they passed, looking for Lirg, but there were far too many and he wasn't sure he could remember what Lirg looked like anyway.

The tunnel opened onto an immense smoky chamber, its ceiling lost in darkness. The walls on either side were pocked with holes thirty to forty feet in diameter, their lower edges stained by a continuous rusty dripping. The horses splashed in an inches-deep layer of silty liquid rippling across the floor. Alyons' horse—or rather, Adonna's—twitched its ears and withers uneasily.

The next chamber was like the interior of a cartoon beehive, circular horizontal ribs stacked layer upon layer to form a dome. In the middle of the chamber,
a depressed amphitheater with yard-high steps led down to a rusty pool of water.
All Michael could smell now was stale water.

The coursers escorted him around the amphitheater and led him down a side
hallway. They passed a line of marching Sidhe, dressed only in gray kilts.

All of Adonna's attendants were male, apparently; the Irall was a male sanctuary.

"What is the Testament?" Michael asked.

Gwinat turned to him. "The trial chamber of Adonna's judges. The meeting
place of the Maln." He did not need to probe Michael's aura to speak English.

"I thought that was in the mountains," Michael said. Gwinat smiled at the
absurdity of trying to correct human misperceptions.

"I mean, that's where you train priests." Michael remained quiet for a few
minutes, then said, "It's obvious I'm guilty, under your law. Why put me on
trial? Isn't the Maln powerful? Or is my ignorance some excuse?"

"Your guilt is an excuse," Gwinat said.

Michael had to think harder than he had ever thought before. There had to
be some way out of the situation, some supreme *effort* or cleverness the Crane
Women had instilled that he had temporarily forgotten.

Ahead, an electric-blue glow suffused the tunnel like a fog. The horses took
them through wreaths of bluish mist. The mist curled like fingers, curious, cold.

The air cleared and they advanced across a tremendous open space, the interior of the dome itself; all the other chambers had been contained in the walls
of the Irall. Long minutes passed before he sighted a stone table on the otherwise
bare floor, and in tall stone seats surrounding the table, four Sidhe in black robes,
facing inward.

The coursers led Michael in a circle around the table. The four Sidhe in black
watched him closely. The floor crawled with dim patches of blue mist, shot
through with transitory lines of green and black.

"*Tra gahn,*" said one of the four, rising and pushing back the stone chair
with a grating rumble. He looked into Michael's eyes and made a gesture to
Gwinat. Gwinat took Michael's arm and pulled him from the horse, setting him
on the ground with a wrenching pain in his shoulder.

As he turned, he saw that another stone amphitheater now surrounded the
table. On the risers stood a crowd of plumed, dazzle-robed Sidhe males. They
stared at Michael and picked at him with a silent chorus of sharp-edged probes,
seeking a way through his defenses.

"Do you recognize me?" asked the Sidhe standing at the table.

Michael turned, and nodded.

"Who am I?"

"You are Tarax."

"Do you know your crime?"

Michael nodded again. It was useless to argue.

Tarax removed his black robe, revealing a blood-red cloak. He then pulled
back the cloak, unveiling not another layer of clothing, nor his body, but a forest

of leaves, as if his head were supported not by flesh and blood but by a tree. Birds flew from the leaves high into the darkness, their wings beating steadily. The wing beats faded.

Gwinat leaned over him. "Tarax tells us you are guilty," he said, "And that you are the one they want. Even had you been innocent, we would have the authority to take you from the Ban now. Adonna wants you."

36

They led him away from the table. The risers vanished as quickly as they had appeared, and the beautifully dressed Sidhe with them.

"We are going below," Gwinat said. Michael detected a hint of pity in the Sidhe's voice.

The center of the dome of the Irall was occupied by a pit perhaps fifty yards across at its rim. Concentric steps descended to a narrower opening of ten or twelve yards. Gwinat urged his horse down the steps, pushing Michael ahead. The coursers followed. A cold breeze blew up from the center. "Mount," Gwinat said, extending his hand. Michael took hold and was lifted onto Gwinat's horse, sitting before the Sidhe.

Michael's eyes widened as Gwinat booted the animal's flanks. It tossed its head, reared, and kicked off into nothingness. The coursers leaped after.

He closed his eyes momentarily. His stomach twisted and his eyelids fluttered involuntarily, then opened. He blinked against the wind. They plunged down the hole into darkness. Gwinat kept a tight grip with one arm on Michael's waist. To each side, the coursers' beasts stretched out in long, silvery poses of leaping, lips drawn back from gnashing teeth, manes unfurled and gleaming like fire, tails twisting and waving behind. They seemed to nip at the air ahead with their teeth, legs straining for solid ground and finding none.

The darkness was broken only by hanging swatches of luminous green moss on the smooth-bored stone walls. Michael turned to look at Gwinat. The Sidhe had bared his teeth; he seemed to be grinning, grimacing and preparing to scream all at once.

Michael shielded his eyes with his hands. The dry wind stung. The stone walls gave way after several minutes to ice as clear and deep as flawless blue glass.

Far ahead—below—a tiny dot of dim rainbow-colored light appeared, then rushed toward them. Michael flinched, ready for destruction. He felt the horse's muscles relax beneath him. He leaned close to its neck and clasped its mane with what must have been a painful grip, but the animal didn't protest. The walls of the hole vanished; they had fallen for at least a quarter of an hour and now glided over a maelstrom of cloudy, turbid light.

They flew beneath the bottom of the Realm, beyond all solidity, into darkness and terrifying creation. The horses navigated through an upside-down forest of huge icicles with bases hundreds of yards thick. Below, small, brilliant globes of indefinite size flitted over the maelstrom.

Michael silently prayed; not that he would have been heard above the rush of wind which filled the void, pasting his hair to his head and threatening to tear him from Gwinat's grip. "Lord," he mouthed, "I thank you for all I have lived, all I have seen. I am sorry I never acknowledged You, and I hope this is not all for nothing . . . If I die now, I know I have done nothing worthwhile, and have brought pain and death—" He thought of Eleuth's spinning, fading shadow in the Between, and then of the Ban of Hours' accepting, forgiving arms. "I know I am nothing in the face of this, and that this is nothing before You . . ." He was repudiating all his weak attempts at disbelief, and all of his young materialist philosophies. And he was doing it clumsily, with inelegant words and far too many repetitions of "nothing." He was half-crazy with fear, and yet he edited his own prayers . . . In the face of extinction, he worried about style.

Gwinat tightened his hold as Michael began to tremble, then shake. With some surprise, the Sidhe realized the boy was laughing. Tears blew back from the human's face and struck Gwinat's, streaming across his cheeks. For a moment, the Sidhe felt it might be best to simply drop the human into the maelstrom and be done with him. There was something weird and dangerous in this laughter and weeping, something he could not fathom. But he held on and the boy calmed after a time.

The horses pitched downward, away from the ice pillars. Michael was through praying. A wordless, profound silence filled him. Only one thought crossed his mind as they dropped away from the Realm's underside: This must have been the way the Sidhe crossed between the stars, taking their own wind into the emptiness of space, traveling in hordes of millions, so many they would have seemed like a comet's tail, glittering like pearly motes against the stacked razor's-edge blackness.

Ahead, an oval object like an elongated bean drifted over the Maelstrom. The bean-shape clarified into a cylinder about twice as long as it was wide. Spinning slowly on its long axis, pointed down toward the maelstrom, it appeared to have been lathed from a solid piece of brass. Irregular blotches of verdigris marked its surface.

The riders approached the immense, flat top. The expanse loomed like a wall, pierced by an irregular gaping entrance at its center. Michael wasn't able to get an impression of its size until the very last, just as they entered the hole.

The cylinder was perhaps a mile in diameter.

For a moment there was confusion. One of the coursers got ahead of Michael and Gwinat. His animal's hooves twitched a few feet from Michael's face, then swung back and caught Michael on the side of the head. He was knocked from Gwinat's arm and fell away, seeing nothing but warm, mellow red, dimming rapidly to deep brown . . .

Michael's awareness returned in stages. First he smelled dust, acrid and irritating. He sneezed. Then came the pain. His forehead felt on fire. His eyes were open, but he couldn't see until the darkness irised and revealed another, even more profound black.

He was in chains.

His wrists and ankles were shackled to a brass bar with a ring on each end. Chains extended from the rings to another bar a few yards away. Shackled to that bar was a skeleton, clothes and dried skin floating in tatters on its translucent yellow bones.

Michael and his chains floated, weightless. All around was the ineffable presence of something huge, moving. Within a feeble gray illumination he could see nothing but chains, bars and more bodies.

He was floating in a graveyard. He shut his eyes and probed outward to the limit of his range. Only uncertain murmurs came back. The impressions were strong enough to convince him that he was at the center of the brass cylinder, and that the cylinder was an outpost of the Maln—an extension of the Irall.

Michael probed again, and suddenly withdrew cringing as a voice blasted him. He threw up his shields, but they were not strong enough to mask the power and the hate.

"For your crimes, *antros;* for all the creatures that have died that you might eat their flesh; for all that have loved you and been betrayed; for all the so very human things you have done. Together we face a mystery, *antros.*"

It was the voice of Tarax. The Sidhe emerged from darkness and stood on a brass platform.

"Who are you?" Tarax asked, white hair floating in a nimbus around his head.

"I am a poet," Michael said, feeling none of the hesitance or awkwardness he would have once experienced on naming his occupation, his obsession.

"That means nothing to me. Who are you, that you should be protected, that I am prevented from killing you? Now even Adonna requests you. Frankly, I am puzzled. *Who are you?*"

"What does Adonna want?" Michael's throat felt parched and sore from inhaling the acrid dust.

"I do not know. I have served Adonna for a long, long age, and kept his secrets, and admired his creation—"

"His?"

"You are his now. I do not need to be discreet with you. In fact, I have only one function to perform, and since time means nothing to Adonna, I need not be hasty. I know this about you: that you are an evil, and that your worst crime is not the theft of a horse. It is being human . . . and helping the one who calls himself Isomage. You would bring a song of power to him, would you not?"

Michael felt the pressure of the book against his hip. Tarax's platform drew closer and the high priest of the Maln reached out with long fingers to touch the chains binding him to the other bodies. "This is my only task, to release you and send you down the axis to the mist. For all these," he gestured at the hundreds, thousands of corpses, "I have done the honors, and come back a short time later to find them here, returned by Adonna, who took from them what he needed. Most have been Sidhe. Few humans have earned such a demise."

Tarax's robe suddenly came to life. Gray stripes rose from the black fabric, writhing and forming knotwork designs. He touched Michael's chained feet and shoved him slowly, steadily away from the floating graveyard. "Michael Perrin," Tarax announced loudly. "*Antros.*"

An exit opened in the opposite end of the cylinder. Michael looked ahead and saw the rainbow light of the maelstrom. Behind, the graveyard receded into a lattice of brown points, and then was enveloped in obscurity.

He closed his eyes and swallowed hard.

When he opened them again, he saw the flat end of the cylinder, rotating endlessly, brass and verdigris illuminated by the flickering light of what Tarax called the mist. He drifted through the hole, drifted in rushing darkness, and emerged.

Unseen activity below. Something rose from the mist. Darkness sparkled. A pseudopod of night, full of potential, extended and enveloped him. Forms flashed all around, passing in a parade of metamorphosis; faces, bodies, less pleasant shapes. Michael moaned and tried to stop seeing, but couldn't.

There is no magic but what is allowed in our heads.

"No!" He recognized the tone, the intention.

Universes may co-exist in the same wave-train, operating as the harmonics of a complex of frequencies. Analogous to the groove in a phonograph record, which is easily distinguished into horns and strings by the practiced ear—horns one universe, strings another. We may exist in all universes, but "hear" only one because of our limitations, the valve of our desires, our practical, physical needs. All is vibration, with nothing vibrating across no distance whatsoever. All is music. A universe, a world, is just one long difficult song. The difference between worlds is the difference between songs. All Sidhe know this when they do magic.

Michael had been struggling, but now went limp, horrified, waiting. He had not anticipated this. He knew the voice very well—had been searching for it recently, hoping for answers, help.

The book was taken from his pocket, taken away from him, and with it, memory of the poem Lin Piao Tai had sought, the first half of the song of power the Spryggla had thought the Isomage needed. His only secret, his last defense, was now gone.

"You're Death's Radio," Michael said.

I am the Realm. My body is the Realm, and my mind is the Realm.

"Why have you helped me, if you hate me?"

I do not hate. The Creation is flawed. Holding it together has become tiresome. And there is not as much time as once seemed possible . . . not an eternity.

The voice became less hollow. Michael's focus sharpened and he saw the darkness and the clouds of chaos eddy inward, flashing green and yellow and blue, turning rosy, giving off halos of brilliant red.

Before him, on the cut-stone field high in the mountains first revealed to him by Biri, stood an extraordinary figure. He was a Sidhe, certainly, but like no other Sidhe Michael had seen. Despite the lack of wrinkles, the full redness of the hair, the apparent strength of bare arms and legs, the figure looked old and weary. His eyes were black as the void and without whites, and his teeth gleamed stone-gray behind thin lips pulled back in a determined grimace.

He wore a short kilt and a loose tabard tied with a length of golden rope. Around the kilt's hem, branches and leaves twined in gold thread. Michael glanced down but could not see his own body; he had become nothing more than a pair of eyes, at least for now.

"So you recognize me?"

Yes.

The Sidhe came forward. "I went to some trouble to disguise myself. Still, you've been very perceptive. It wasn't my voice you recognized, was it?"

No.

"My delivery. Even a god can't disguise his inmost self, I suppose."

How long have you been . . . a god?

"Not long, actually. Twenty, thirty thousand Earth years. But quite long enough. Do you know what I am?"

A Sidhe.

"Yes, and a very old Sidhe, too. Not of this younger generation. All the Sidhe alive today—with very few exceptions—have forgotten me. All they know is Adonna. They forget Tonn, who led them back to Earth, who opposed his own daughter and the Council of Eleu. I was the leader of the Council of Delf. Do you know who Tonn was, boy?"

The Sidhe mage.

"Good memory. There were four mages, boy, remember them?"

Tonn, Daedal . . .

"Manus and Aum. Others, less powerful, the mages of the lesser kinds. All are animals on your Earth now, not strong enough to re-evolve, or content with their lot. Only humans struggled back, they hated us so much . . . But now so few of your fellows remember why they struggled. Perhaps only one . . . the Serpent Mage. I imagine *he* remembers, oh, yes!"

Michael didn't respond.

"You won't remember this exchange, either. Not for a while. It would not benefit the great majority of the Sidhe to know that Adonna was once one of them. A mage is impressive, but a god must be infinitely more impressive. Aloof. I know my people, how to chastise them and keep them in line. But life in my Realm is just not enough. I've labored long and hard to keep the Realm going, to reconcile all its inconsistencies . . . all the poor judgments of my own creation. And I've sacrificed, too. Whatever personal life I may once have had . . . the respect of my offspring . . . and my own wife."

Michael remembered the skull-snail on the Blasted Plain.

"Yes, yes," Tonn said, coming even closer, until he seemed right next to Michael. "The time has come for a change. Perhaps the Council of Eleu was right. Perhaps Elme was right. It is time for the Sidhe to return to the Earth. Ah, if only poor Tarax could hear me now! He'd lose the very foundation of his life. He'd melt with shame. You, a pitiful human child, must carry the burden—not a powerful and faithful Sidhe. But then, Tarax is remarkably ignorant. All my people are ignorant, except perhaps the Ban of Hours."

Michael conjured back an image of tall figures around his bed on Earth, discussing him. *You?* he asked.

"No, indeed," Tonn said, pulling up a block from the stone field with the palm of his hand and sitting on it. "Not even the Maln, or the Council of Delf. The Council of Eleu chose you. They would be distressed to know I concur. But before any of our plans can be carried out, some obstacles must be cleared away. Some old greeds. We do not precisely agree, but each of us has a use for you."

Then I have no will of my own?

"You have all the will you'll ever need. But you won't need this." He held up the black book. It faded from his hand. "Nor will you need Death's Radio. Time now to forget . . ."

The stone field's blackness intensified and smeared up to take in the sky and clouds, to sweep around Tonn and obscure him.

Once, poets were magicians. Poets were strong, stronger than warriors or kings— stronger than old hapless gods. And they will be strong once again.

The cloud of creation was back in its place. The receding blackness sparkled and churned.

37

M ichael walked and whistled tunelessly, caught himself whistling and stopped abruptly. He looked around warily, his arm hairs tingling. Then he frowned and sat down, wondering why he was still alive.

He had been in the Irall.

He felt his pocket for the book. Gone. He looked around frantically, pushing aside the grass to see if he had dropped it. Everything in his memory was jumbled.

The broad river flowed nearby, noisy as it rushed slick and turbulent over boulders. A few hundred yards beyond the river rose one wall of a canyon, and much closer—overshadowing—the opposite wall, both gray stone streaked with rusty red, jagged and scarred as if the river's gouging had been neither gentle nor discreet. Each wall ascended at least five hundred feet and stretched for as far as Michael could see. Trees clustered in spinneys of fives and tens along the banks, leaves swaying in a cool, persistent breeze—a canyoned river of air to complement the river of water.

"What happened?" he asked, taking a step one way, then back, then another. He remembered meeting Death's Radio, a tall fellow in a kilt and tabard . . . but who had that been? He remembered being told certain things, but he couldn't recall what the things were.

Tarax he remembered quite clearly, and he shivered.

"Michael! Michael!"

Two figures clambered down a rugged trail in the canyon face nearby.

"Nikolai!" he shouted. His difficulties were temporarily driven out by joy. "You didn't make it back to the city!"

"And *you* did?" Nikolai and Bek ran across the river sand, skirting patches of grass. Michael and Nikolai embraced and Michael was surprised and embarrassed at how good Nikolai's warm, strong body felt in his arms. Bek stood to one side, smiling faintly at the reunion.

"I was captured," Michael said.

"We were filtered out, then . . . by the Ban," Nikolai said. They laughed and embraced again. "We were sent here. And so were you. By the Ban? Did she rescue you?"

Michael explained as much as he remembered, which wasn't very helpful. He described the interior of the Irall, the ride below the Realm, and the cylinder above the mist. "After that . . . I think I was dreaming."

"Here? Most unlikely," Nikolai said. "Whatever it was, it must have been real."

"My book was taken away. I've forgotten some things." His face fell. Thinking of the book automatically sent his mind back to "Kubla Khan." He couldn't remember past the first few lines.

"But you survived! No one has ever come out of the Irall alive—no human, anyway."

"And no Breed," Bek said, running his hand through his silky blond hair. "Nikolai told me you were special. Now I believe him! A special *antros.*"

Michael was ready to be offended by the word used so often as a curse, but he probed Bek deftly and found no animosity. Bek returned the probe and met Michael's instant shield. The Breed smiled broadly and shook his head in appreciation and wonder.

By evening, they had gathered dried sticks and grass for a fire. They ate from Nikolai's foraging of the day before—fruit and roots—and rested, saying little. Nikolai cast concerned glances at Michael now and then.

The fire burned to smoke and ashes and a few crackling embers. Bek and Nikolai slept. Michael felt as if he might never sleep again. He sat with his arms wrapped around his knees and stared at the drifting smoke, wondering how he could feel so good when he had lost the final thing of importance to him, when he had no future and no foreseeable prospects. When he was still in the Realm.

He was alive. That was enough. So often he had resigned himself to death—or worse. He thought of the weightless graveyard and the acrid dust.

Even if Clarkham turned out to be useless to him—and vice versa—even if he were a pawn—

He heard a rustling in the grass. What he saw, beyond the sandy oval where Nikolai and Bek slept, made his back go rigid.

Biri stood in the grass, dressed in a black robe with red shoulders and arms. He stared fixedly at Michael and held out his hand, beckoning.

Michael stood and brushed sand from his travel-stained pants. He followed Biri away from the camp until they were out of earshot, their conversation covered by the river's tumult.

"Is this some sort of crossroad?" Michael asked, his voice almost failing him. He cleared his throat.

"No crossroad. I've brought something that may still be of use to you. It is yours, by law. You have survived your punishment, and it has been imprinted." He gestured to a copse of trees. There, visible in the light of the pearly band, stood the blue horse. It nickered and walked forward. Michael reached out to it hesitantly. It nuzzled his palm.

"I've gone through a lot for this horse," Michael said. "This isn't another trick?"

Biri shook his head. "Tarax was furious not to find you back in the cylinder, dead. He released the horse, but not in the same place he was commanded to release you."

"What are you doing here?"

"Fulfilling Adonna's ruling."

"And . . . ?"

Biri looked down at the ground. "Because of Adonna, I have no horse. Because of Tarax, I have no faith in Adonna or the Irall. All my training has been for nothing. My people are dying. We are withering inside. I blame Adonna." The look he gave Michael was almost pleading. "I went to the Ban of Hours. She and her attendants are the only ones who seem to know something has gone wrong in the Realm."

"The Council of Eleu," Michael said.

Biri lifted his head, eyes blazing. "What do you know of them?"

"Not a lot."

"Would you like to know more, as much as I know?"

Michael nodded. If Clarkham was an unreliable savior, then the Council of Eleu might be able to help.

"Ride with me, then . . . or rather, since I have no horse, allow me to ride with you. While your companions sleep."

"Where to?"

"Not so very long ago, I would have thought it an accursed place and shunned it. Now I am less certain. It is not far, if we ride."

Michael looked back at the camp and the sleeping shapes of Nikolai and Bek. He knew Nikolai was asleep, but Bek . . .

"Why shouldn't they go with us?"

"The human has never undergone discipline. He would not survive. The Breed . . ." Biri shrugged. "It would not matter to him. He is without a people, a loner. He does not care that he is a Breed, else it might have some importance to him."

Michael considered briefly. "Lead on."

The blue horse allowed both of them to mount, this time, unlike with Gwinat. Michael rode behind, Biri in front.

"They took me to the Irall," Michael said.

"Yes."

"Did you see me?"

"Yes."

"Why didn't you help?"

"No one interferes with Tarax. Besides, you were going to Adonna. Even initiates know the futility of trying to cross Adonna."

Michael urged the horse forward. Then, fully aware of the consequences, he gave the Sidhe animal a chance to run . . . and to fly. "Tell us where to go," he shouted to Biri as the horse's body blurred and silvered under them.

"South," he said.

38

For a time the horse followed the river and canyon. Michael couldn't tell if they were flying or running, or even precisely where they were. Everything was disarrayed. With a twist of his head the world became a different place, filled with streamers of light and rushing clouds.

"*Abana,*" Biri shouted. "Tell the horse *abana.*"

Michael repeated the word, and what was left of the Realm dissolved. The night became twilight; the streamers and clouds aligned to form a gray-blue heaven. Below, city lights moved across the grassland like water flowing on a wrinkled cloth. "It looks like Earth!" Michael shouted. The wind tasted electric on his tongue.

"It is one of many Earths," Biri said. "The Earths between your world and the Realm. Where the horses go when they *aband.*"

The city lights coalesced into streets and buildings, tilting and swaying far below. Everything appeared cast in a green light, a memorable color indeed— the tint of the Between where Lamia's sister stood guard. "How many Earths are there?"

"Far more than can be counted," Biri said.

"And the horse crosses over?"

"We are only visiting. We are not actually there unless we fall off. The horse grazes the surface, skips along the Earths surrounding the Realm."

The city lights vanished and everything became mixed and indistinct again. Michael reached around Biri and grasped the horse's mane. It felt like cold fire. The horse turned to look back at them, its eye cold and deadly blue, like a ball of ice lit from within. Its lips drew back, revealing teeth as long and sharp as a tiger's. Between the Realm and the Earth—or Earths—it became a very different beast indeed, a true nightmare.

"We're getting near," Biri said.

The horse shivered and the swirl became less intense. He could feel the animal's muscles tighten beneath his legs, preparing to run instead of *aband.*

The Realm returned. The horse hit ground, jolting them painfully, and galloped over a rocky field studded with tiny trees. The night air returned, cold and dry. The sky filled with sharp white stars.

Michael brought the horse to a stop. "How far did we travel?"

"Too far to walk," Biri said, sliding off the horse to the left. "We cannot ride the horse into the protected circle."

Michael dismounted and they walked across the field, stones driving hard into Michael's soft-shod feet. Ahead, vaguely outlined in starglow, crouched a dirt and stone mound, very much like the barrows Michael had seen in history books.

"We have those on Earth," he said.

On one side of the mound stood a stone arch blocked by a circular slab half-buried in the ground. Biri reached to the left of the slab and withdrew a round boulder about six inches across. As if the boulder were clay, he scooped a hollow in it and with one finger planted a fierce white glow in the hollow. "A lantern," he said.

On the right-hand edge of the slab a series of notches had been carved. He placed the fingers of one hand into certain grooves, then touched others in different sequences. The slab sunk into the ground with a grumble.

"Now we enter," Biri said. He led the way.

The stone lantern showed a dank, root-lined tunnel stretching about ten yards into the mound. The floor was cut stone. The chilled air smelled musty.

In the center of the mound opened a chamber about thirty feet in diameter. The chamber's stone walls shone with damp. Silvery-white beard-like fungus hung from the wet surfaces.

Surmounting a stone bier in the middle, two transparent quartz coffins lay within a few inches of each other. In each rested a skeleton. Biri stood on one side of the bier and Michael walked slowly around to the other, peering through the crystal sides.

"Do you know who they are?" Biri asked, his voice soft in the echoing chamber.

"I don't think so," Michael said. The bones in the left-hand coffin, draped in a diaphanous white gown, resembled translucent ivory; in the right-hand coffin, the skeleton was opaque and brown with age and wore nothing but dust and rags. In one hand it clutched a polished wood staff with a bronze head.

Michael completed his circuit and stood beside Biri. "Most of my people reviled her," Biri said, touching the quartz with the tips of his fingers. "When we returned from the stars, we were too weak to destroy your kind. Some Sidhe, including the Mage, revealed themselves to humans as gods and tried to hinder their development. But your kind was not always reverent. Humans grew and matured and found their own skills. They even absorbed and used the lies and dreams the false gods, the Sidhe, revealed, as a flower uses manure.

"*She* thought we should live in peace with you, but at first, her ministers refused to carry out her plans. She was queen; she had guided us home, and she was a powerful sorceress; they couldn't fight her openly. But she began to wander the Earth, trying to find a solution. In time her ministers convinced most of the

Sidhe that the queen was mad, that she had succumbed to the stresses of the journey, that—as often happened then—her powers had broken her mind.

"So she gathered her own followers and formed the Council of Eleu. While other Sidhe tried to control humans, the Council spread knowledge among them. While the Mage, Tonn, spent centuries portraying your gods Yahweh and Baal, and others, the queen opposed him and encouraged humans to develop their own finest qualities. Tonn was stronger.

"Then the queen declared she had fallen in love with a human. She rejected the cold and heartless union with her own males." Biri's face betrayed no irony, no awareness of the implied self-criticism. "Sometimes, even now, her followers believe she truly was mad at that time, but she did indeed love the man, and when he died, as mortals will, she placed his body here. Then, for a thousand years, the Council of Eleu worked with the queen to raise humanity to a level where other Sidhe might be able to accept them as equals. But her enthusiasm ended with her husband's life; in time, the queen herself died, and was laid beside the one she loved, instead of in a tomb of honor, or in a tree where she might pass on her wisdom.

"Tonn founded the Black Order, the Maln, to oppose her wishes, and put Tarax in command. The Maln fought every action of the Council of Eleu. To this day they oppose each other, and the Council of Eleu must work in secret."

"Elme and Aske," Michael said.

Biri nodded. "Adonna is a corrupt god," he continued, "growing more and more senile with time. I cannot serve him. I must serve those who oppose him, and who oppose the Maln."

"You want to help humans?"

"It seems I must, doesn't it?" Biri smiled grimly.

"The Crane Women are Elme's daughters?"

"Elme and Aske had forty children, the first Breeds. Twenty of their offspring married humans, and had children by them . . ."

"How long ago?"

"As far back as nine thousand years on Earth, and as recently as eighty years. Those with less than an eighth Sidhe heritage revert to mortals again, but can still work some magic. Their children spread around the Earth, and many of them lived for thousands of years, surviving many generations of descendants.

"Long, long ago, Elme held court in a beautiful garden, surrounded by high stone walls. She sought the advice of the Serpent Mage, the last of the original humans."

Michael's eyes narrowed.

"Have you heard of the garden?" Biri asked, regarding him curiously.

Michael stared at the skeleton in the radiant gown and did not know how to react. Finally, his eyes welled up, and tears spilled over. He nodded and wiped his cheeks.

All his life he had heard just parts of a wonderful and sad story, and now it had been completed for him.

39

They returned the way they had come, Michael hardly noticed the pyrotechnics; he held on to Biri and the horse and turned his thoughts inward.

He had learned things no history class on Earth could have ever taught him. He suspected there were far more things of which he had heard only partial truths, or no truth at all.

The horse stopped on the ledge overlooking the camp and pawed the ground with its hoof. Its fangs were no longer apparent and its eyes had gentled. Michael swung down from the horse and looked up at Biri.

"I don't trust you," Michael said. Biri returned his gaze with expression unchanged. "Oh, I know you've told me the truth about Aske and Elme, and what you know of Sidhe history. You'd have no reason to lie about that. Perhaps you know I've heard a lot of the story from others. But I don't necessarily believe you've abandoned Adonna."

Biri smiled sharply, eyes cold and fierce. "You'll entertain the thought, however?"

"I'll consider it as a possibility," Michael offered. "But everything is going too smoothly. Everybody wants me to go to the Isomage. Only the Ban of Hours told me I was a pawn, caught between two forces—the Council of Eleu and the Maln. I trust her, I think."

"She is a worthy female," Biri said, nodding his respect.

"I think it's time I acted on my own," Michael said. "I want to return to the Pact Lands."

"They no longer exist," Biri said. "Your people and the Breeds have been moved, put in new communities."

"Camps, you mean," Michael said. "Take me to one of the camps."

"They are closely guarded. Tarax wants no more like you to come to the notice of the Council of Eleu."

"You and I together, we can—"

"I have forsaken Adonna," Biri said, shaking his head firmly, "but I will not fight my own kind."

"Yet you want to serve the Council. You can do that by helping humans."

Biri said nothing.

"I'm not sure that going to the Isomage isn't what the Maln wants me to do. They released me from the Irall, and that makes me suspicious."

"What would the Council have you do?"

"I don't know."

"Who has opposed you most?"

"Human-hating Sidhe."

"The Maln."

"I just don't know . . ." Michael said, confused again.

"It seems obvious," Biri said.

"Then why didn't Tarax kill me when he had the chance? I'm not very strong. Any Sidhe could have killed me. You could, right now, just by raising a finger."

"Perhaps you are not as weak as you think."

"Oh, no?" Michael laughed. "You just hollowed out a boulder and lit a fire in it. It's all I can do to keep myself warm."

Biri dismounted and squatted on the ledge to peer into the canyon. His red-shouldered robe made him look disembodied in the starlight, as if his bust floated on a gray platform over the canyon. "You call yourself a poet," Biri said. "The Sidhe have long regarded poets with respect."

"I am sixteen, maybe seventeen years old by now," Michael said. "In my lifetime, I've written maybe five halfway decent poems, probably less. In the Realm I've hardly had time to write any. And when I've tried, I've heard somebody else's voice in my head giving me suggestions, or just creating things for me. I'm more a pawn than a poet, believe me."

"So what do you intend to do?"

"Maybe sit right here, or travel with Nikolai and Bek. See what I'm really capable of before I make any decisions." He paused, then said under his breath, "From what I've learned, I can't see Clarkham being any help. I'm not even sure he's human, or really cares about humans."

Biri nodded. "If you are a pawn, do you think the forces using you will allow you to remain aloof?"

That stumped Michael. He sat beside the Sidhe and dangled his legs over the canyon. "At least they won't have me behaving like a silly puppet."

"If you *are* being used, either by Tarax or the Council, you face very powerful adversaries should you defy them."

"So what do you suggest I do?"

"Not much, perhaps. Advance in your discipline. Finish your training."

"The Crane Women are gone," Michael said. "I don't expect them to pop up around here anytime soon."

"I can train you," Biri said. He held his hand out in the direction of the camp. "Tonight, while they sleep. Then you can decide." His smile in the dark was radiant, feral. Michael's back prickled.

"And if I decide against the Council?"

"My allegiances haven't solidified," Biri said. "Perhaps you can guide me."

Michael thought for a moment. "Won't Tarax come after you, try to take you back?"

"Why? I am useless to him, useless to Adonna. I am just another disaffected Sidhe. They won't waste their time on vengeance. Only miserable Sidhe like Alyons engage in such silliness."

Michael stepped over to the horse. "So teach me."

"Beginning now," Biri said, getting to his feet.

40

I t might have been the longest night in the history of the Realm. To Michael, it stretched on forever . . . and it was not pleasant. Biri walked with him away from the canyon until they stood in the middle of a broad belt of sand and small boulders.

"First, you must realize you are alone," he began. "For a Sidhe initiate, his aloneness is confirmed by the murder of his horse; there can be no closer relationship and no greater shock than being required to kill his most treasured companion."

"Do I have to kill the horse?" Michael asked, suddenly queasy.

"No. Your feeling toward the animal is shallow, uncertain. You were not raised with it. The *Mafoc Mar* did not pick it out for you from the fields when you were young; you did not grow to youthful maturity with the horse by your side. You must find something else."

"Maybe another shadow-self?"

Biri shook his head in irritation. "That doesn't concern me."

They stood in starlight bright enough to cast shadows.

"No swords, no baubles. Those are all human misunderstandings of magic, human preoccupation with technology. Magic lies purely in the mind. The Sidhe are among the most dishonorable, unreliable creatures on all the faces of Creation, but they have one thing—concentration. What they want, they focus on completely."

Biri sat in the grass and gestured for Michael to do likewise. "You are alone," Biri said. "You are the only thing in existence. You will never truly know there are others. Because humans have souls is no reason to believe they differ from the Sidhe in this, that they are eternally alone."

Michael shook his head. "What about friendship, love?"

"Love does not occur to the Sidhe male," Biri said. "But I can demolish love even so. Did you love the real person, or your image of the person? Did you love an external, or what the person was to you?"

"But there has to be someone, something, to love or to be disappointed with."

"Only yourself. Alone. Life is alone, love is alone."

"Then you don't exist. Nobody else exists."

"Together, we are alone. That is the peculiarity of our being. We never know true community. Not even Sidhe, who can reach inside each other's aura of memory, out-see and in-see; not even Sidhe can avoid being alone. You can never rely on another, not to the core of your being. You can never ultimately trust in another . . . for how is that possible, when you are alone?"

Biri seemed to vanish, leaving Michael on the grass. Alone.

He pulled up a sprig and contemplated it, feeling dead inside. If he was unique, solitary, without any support in all of reality—including his own internal reality—if even his mind was alone, with just one voice, and all else illusory—

The deadness was replaced once again by enormous calm. How often could he have devastating realizations, and then have them smoothed away like a waveless ocean?

How many more revelations would there be, ending in the same assurance of mastery, all illusory?

The blade of grass was alone. Together, they were alone. They were alone together.

The ground of the Realm was alone. The blade of grass was alone with the ground.

Words flowed within him, arguments, changing shape and meaning, having no meaning. He gave them up only after a tremendous, jerking pain swept him.

"I am in love with words," Michael said. "They are my horse. I ride them, use them. But I can never kill them. Even if I cannot use words to get where I am going." The realization of his dependence was enough.

His aloneness suddenly became apparent, without words, truth, meaning or thought.

The only way one can truly be alone is to be at one with everything, everybody . . .

The entire universe, having only one voice.

All the faces of creation, alone.

Michael became aware of what he had been doing when he performed the small tricks the Crane Women had taught him. "To be alone is to be difficult to spot."

He could improve on that. "Aloneness means isolation from needs." He could last indefinitely without food or water.

"I only fight shadows. If I am alone, there is no enemy to fight." And ultimately, no need to fight. "It is crazy to fight when you are alone."

He put down the blade of grass and looked up at the multitude of stars. Biri had helped him build this structure piece by piece, carefully. Now it began to collapse. The whole thing was ridiculous. How could he ever believe such nonsense? Yet as it collapsed, it did not take the calm or sense of mastery with it; they remained.

They had built a boat, crossed a river, and the boat had crumbled just as he stood on the opposite shore.

Biri came up behind him.

"It's all wrong," Michael said. "It doesn't make sense."

"That is the sign over the gate of your acceptance," Biri told him in Cascar. "For a Sidhe, being alone is exaltation, being alone is ridiculous. You must never trust us . . . or our philosophies."

"Then I shouldn't trust you at all?"

"Never trust a teacher."

He didn't seem to be joking. Michael was far from convinced he knew what this final discipline was all about, undeniable though its effects were. And if it was such a discipline that made the Sidhe behave as they did—that segregated males and females, and led to such odd behavior in the males—then he would just as soon be rid of it, effects or no.

But there was nothing he could do now. He felt stronger, better able to cope. They returned to the canyon, Biri following Michael down the path.

The eastern horizon brightened. The long night was finally over. Nikolai and Bek still slept as they approached the camp. The fire had died down to smoking ashes. Biri stayed away from the sleeping figures, staring off down the river.

"What do you plan to do now?" Michael asked him.

Nikolai woke up, rolled over and stared in groggy surprise at the Sidhe. "Who's that?" he asked, scrambling to his feet. Bek sat up on the ground. Biri ignored them.

"I think I will go to the Isomage," Biri said.

"That's where we're heading," Nikolai said, glancing at Michael.

"Not necessarily," Michael said. "Why go there?"

Biri smiled his feral smile.

Nikolai shivered and backed away from the camp. "He wears the cloak of the Maln's initiates!"

"Perhaps because he has some answers," Biri said. "And if you do not go there, someone has to. Besides, he isn't far from here." He gestured downriver. "The river flows into the sea. The Isomage's lands are on the delta." He turned to walk away.

"Where have you been all night?" Nikolai asked, staring at Michael curiously.

"I'm not sure," Michael said. The Sidhe merged with shadows near the canyon wall. As light fell into the canyon, he was nowhere to be seen.

"I've always been interested in the Isomage," Nikolai said. "A tragic, perhaps fearful person." They gathered fruit from the low scrub trees near the river. "Would it be dangerous to go there just to satisfy curiosity?"

"Probably," Bek said.

Nikolai frowned and bit into a tiny pear. "Then we just stay here, or we go back to the Pact Lands—except you say they aren't there any more, and we can't go back. I'm confused."

"At least the Sidhe knows where his answers are to be found," Bek said.

"They may not be the answers I'm looking for," Michael said. "If I'm looking for answers. And I don't know why Biri is going to Clarkham."

"Perhaps Clarkham can tell him about the Council. Or tell us."

"I take it both of you want to go on, to find Clarkham?"

Bek considered a moment, then nodded. Nikolai shrugged. "I'm content wherever I happen to be, so long as none of the Maln are aware of me."

"Then you should go to Clarkham. I'll make up my own mind, in my own time." Michael stalked back toward the camp, pockets filled with the tiny fruit. Nikolai jogged after him.

"Michael, Michael, what is wrong? What did the Sidhe say to you? You have changed . . ."

Indeed, he no longer felt a need for anyone's presence or advice. An ugliness grew inside, replacing the initial calm Biri's discipline had given him.

He stopped, staring beyond a blaze much larger than the one they had left. "Brothers," came a muffled voice from behind the flames. Wrapped in white from head to toe, Shahpur walked around the fire, arms folded at chest-level. "We've been told you need an escort." Harka, Tik and Dour emerged from behind a nearby boulder. Michael looked over his shoulder and saw Bek approaching, his pace measured and confident.

"They're all together," Nikolai told Michael, eyes wide with concern.

"The Isomage welcomes you to the vicinity of Xanadu," Shahpur said. Nikolai groaned.

"Grand, grand!" he cried, swinging his hands out. "Now you do not have any choice. Nor do I."

41

Harka greeted Michael wearily and sat on the sandy riverbank. Tik and Dour stood beside him. The two younger Sidhe seemed nervous; only Bek and Harka remained at ease, Harka perhaps incapable of anything more. Shahpur could not be read.

"We have been watching over you, of course," Harka said. He did not fend off Michael's probe; he was, if anything, even emptier than when Michael had last peered into him. His emptiness was as disturbing as Shahpur's horrible fullness.

"I don't need protection," Michael said.

"The Isomage thinks otherwise. There wasn't much he could do while you traveled between the Pact Lands and here, in Sidhe territories. But he had us meet you in the mountains. He even dared to send Bek into Inyas Trai with you. Now that you approach his domain, we are much freer. We can help when necessary."

"By *help*," Shahpur said, "Harka means we must ensure you come to Xanadu. It is the Isomage's wish."

The Sidhe, however low their status, still retained certain skills. Michael could tell that much just by lightly skimming their auras. He could not escape. He still felt strong, but it was not any sort of strength he could immediately apply; Biri's discipline had somehow confused even his rudimentary skills. If Biri had been with them, the match would have been at least equal; there was nothing he could do to resist now, however.

"It's what I've been planning all along," Michael said. "No coercion necessary."

"Excellent," Harka said. "The Isomage will be pleased. He doesn't have many visitors, as you can imagine."

"What about me?" Nikolai asked.

"All who have helped the man-child are welcome in Xanadu. Shall we begin now, or must you rest after your strenuous night?"

"I'm rested," Michael said. Nikolai squared his shoulders and nodded agreement.

"Fine. It's a pleasant journey. We can be there by late evening. Of course, if we could all ride . . ." He looked enviously at the horse. "But we can't. Bek will tend the *epon*."

For the next ten miles, the walls of the canyon grew higher until they walked through a deep chasm in perpetual shadow. Mosses and ferns crowded the river bank, towering overhead to form a dense canopy that cast everything in verdant gloom. The river became a deep, swift-running torrent no more than thirty feet across.

In its translucent volume, Michael saw Riverines flash like trout, dodging rocks and thick green curtains of reeds in their journey to the sea.

They approached the canyon's end by late afternoon. The walls declined abruptly and the river broadened, pouring onto a wide, forested plain brushed by swift patches of fog; overhead, the sky melted into a color between butter and polished bronze. Trees on the plain took up the bronze color and became pale orange dappled with umbrous green. Golden-edged clouds cast long shadows over all.

The plain sloped gradually to an immense flat sea, placid as a mirror in the last light of day, reflecting the sky with only a darker hint of its own character.

In the red glow of sunset, they hiked through the nearest stand of trees, still following the river. The water sighed and hissed over a broad course covered with small stones. Where the Riverines went when the water was only inches deep, Michael did not know.

Harka urged them on through evening shadows. The forest trail was overgrown and difficult to track even in good light, but the cadaverous Sidhe seemed to feel an added urgency. Bek, Tik and Dour followed some distance behind. Shahpur stayed near Michael, his white form almost silent as he passed through brush and over dry leaves.

Harka puzzled Michael. There was a familiarity about his emptiness . . . but Michael had never encountered a Sidhe with Harka's affliction. If these beings worked for Clarkham, it was possible he had performed some sort of magic on them—subjected them to a *geas*, perhaps. But how could Sidhe be controlled by someone not a Sidhe?

Again and again, Michael concocted plans of escape, and discarded them. His deep-seated anger and confusion fermented. Why had Biri subjected him to such a weird, ridiculous philosophy? Perhaps, Michael thought, to create the stymie he was in now.

Nikolai became more and more apprehensive as they neared the shore of the sea. Finally, the pearly ribbon of light appeared and illuminated their path out of the last stretch of the forest. They walked across sand to the still water's edge.

"It is dangerous to approach Xanadu in the dark, even for the desired visitor," Harka said. "We stay here for the night."

Nikolai followed Michael a few yards up the beach. The others made no move to stop them. Michael bent down and dipped his hands in the sea's glassy surface. The ripple caught the ribbon light and carried it yards away from the beach. The water was neither warm nor cold. Michael brought a wet finger to his lips. It was only faintly salty—more of a mineral tang, actually.

"There's nothing you can do?" Nikolai whispered.

Michael shook his head. "Why try? This is where you wanted to go—and I, too, at first."

"You decided against it."

"If I change my mind, how can I be sure I'm the one changing it? If my mind is changed for me, does an escort make any difference? Perhaps they're merely making us do what we should be doing, anyway."

"I have always felt apprehensive about Harka," Nikolai said. "But to know he works for the Isomage!" The Russian clucked his tongue, then looked at the Breed, Sidhe and cloaked human from the corner of his eye. "Surprises, surprises. What will we do when we see Clarkham?"

"I'm sure he'll let us know what's expected."

The night passed quickly. Michael did not sleep. He sensed a growth of the poison within, a combination of hatred, suspicion and strength that dismayed him. Biri's discipline was blossoming and the flower was ugly.

Dawn disrupted the eastern sky and shattered the arcing ribbon light into fading fragments. The air hummed once again like the beginning chords of a symphony. When the sun had topped the horizon, the hum subsided. The brazen sky brightened to pure butter.

Harka walked past Michael and Nikolai, who lay in the sand, and gestured for them to follow. "We have an appointment and we're already late."

Their path took them at a tangent away from the still sea. Within a mile the sand acquiesced to grass—a perfect rolling lawn spaced here and there with peaceful ginkgo trees, rustled by leisurely warm breezes.

Once the sun reached a certain angle, it blended with the rest of the sky, leaving only an illuminated featureless bowl overhead.

Harka pointed to a green hill that rose with dignified gradualness to a rounded peak about five hundred feet higher than the sea. Surrounding the hill were walled forests and gardens, and atop squatted a pale ivory dome, its size uncertain at their distance. In one side of the hill sank a deep gash bordered by trees; even from miles away, the sound of water plummeting from the gash was audible. The water fell in a torrent down the hillside facing away from the sea and began a sinuous river.

"The Isomage's palace," Harka said solemnly.

They approached a stone wall about fifteen feet high, made of blocks of dark marble. Within the wall waited an open bronze gate, the doors chased with dragons. The gate's only guard was a twelve-foot-tall granite warrior, his fierce Oriental eyes fixed on the lifeless sea, one hand holding a gatepost like a spear. As they passed through the gate, Nikolai regarded the warrior with unabashed wonder.

Within the circumference of the first wall, animals of all description played, browsed and hunted, though the hunts seemed never to succeed. Michael spotted a huge tiger, head hanging as it stalked a herd of translucent deer. The deer, legs like rods of glass, pricked up their ears and bounded away, flushing pheasants from jade-colored brush. The pheasants flapped wings like sections of stained-glass windows as they ascended; then, tiring, they dropped into a nearby ginkgo.

The second wall was constructed of glazed brick and was only eight feet high. Steps mounted up one side and down the other. There was no guard, real or stony.

They now climbed the slope of the hill. At one point they halted and stared out over the river and ocean. Michael estimated they had covered three miles from the outermost wall, which meant the whole circuit was about five miles in radius. The circling walls were broken only by gates at the four compass points and by the meandering river, which emptied into the sunless sea without stirring a ripple.

The third wall was a hedge barely five feet high, but ten thick and studded with long thorns. The gate in this wall was a pedestrian tunnel beneath the hedge. The plaster walls of the tunnel were covered with frescoes of pastoral Chinese life, depicting a long-mustached, round-faced emperor enjoying the peace and fertility of wise rule.

They now passed around the hill, out of sight of the sea. A stone causeway guided them up one side of the fountaining chasm, through a wide strip of cedars. Bridges crossed over verdant rills filled with flowering trees and thick, fragrant bushes. The ground beneath them seemed to breathe, each breath punctuated by a sudden roar of water and a deep, grinding rumble.

Through the gap of one particularly long rill, Michael saw the torrent flush thick chunks of ice, jagged and pale green in the dark waters. The ice bounded from side to side and was finally shattered to milky slush at the base of the hill.

The steps ended in a graceful carved wood pavilion equipped with silk-padded benches. They rested for a few minutes to allow Harka to regain his breath, then crossed the flawless lawn on the hilltop.

Two hundred yards from the dome, a circle of black minarets lanced up from the lawn. They were spaced at intervals of fifty feet; external staircases spiraled to bronze crow's nests at the top. The cages were vacant, but Michael had the strong impression of being watched, if not from the towers, then from the pavilions of glass, stone and wood that decorated the grounds.

The dome itself was constructed of silks held aloft by curving poles. The poles were set in walls of alabaster. Now he could judge the dome's true size: at least three hundred feet high and twice as broad.

They entered the pleasure dome through a spidery arch carved of green soapstone. Harka bade them stop with his uplifted hand and turned to Michael.

"The Isomage meets you as an equal," he said. "That is a great privilege. He is at peace, yet eternally occupied with his work. He invites you as a guest, and as a fellow of Earth. Do you harbor him any ill will?"

"No," Michael said. Clarkham had never done anything to him, had never, in fact, *been* anything to him but a distant goal.

"No," Harka said wearily, "You do not. Nor does your companion." Nikolai regarded the Sidhe with patent mystification. "Enter, then, the fulfillment of the dream and the song."

42

The interior of the silken dome glowed with milky light; the air enveloped Michael in warmth and heady incense. They walked across a black marble floor veined with ice, a layer of chill air flowing over their feet. Nikolai stuck close to Michael, swiveling his head to see everything at once.

The poles supporting the silken tent converged high above, where a gap in the fabric showed the sky. At the center of the enclosure, up a flight of wooden steps carved with dragons and horses, beyond a teakwood fence topped with gold rails, stood a full-sized house: white stucco walls and curtained windows, a sloping red tile roof, all surrounded by perfectly trimmed oleander bushes.

"That's Clarkham's house," Michael said. "That's where I began . . ."

The front door was open but they didn't enter. Instead, Harka led them up the steps and around the yard to the back. The rear of the house appeared quite ordinary, with a brick patio and a well-tended garden of tree roses, outdoor redwood furniture with gaily covered pads, an umbrella-shaded round table on curved metal legs. It was extraordinary only in that it was *here,* a comic discrepancy in an exotic *chinoiserie.*

A dark Sidhe female trimmed the tree roses with bronze pruning shears. At each snip, the roses on the tree she pruned glowed and the air filled with a sweet, sharp fragrance. She glanced up and saw the group gathering beyond the lawn's brick border. She smiled, put her shears down on a folding wooden stand and smoothed her gold-trimmed gray gown.

"Finally!" she exclaimed. "We've been waiting a long time." She walked across the lawn and held out her hand to Michael. He grasped it by the fingers and she beckoned him onto the lawn. The chill of the ice-veined marble was immediately replaced by the warm summer softness of grass. She kissed him decorously on the cheek and led him to the patio. "Please come," she called back to Nikolai. The others bowed and backed away. Nikolai hesitated, confused, then stepped on the grass and followed.

"David has been very patient," she said. Her voice was as sweet as any Sidhe voice Michael had heard yet, like an inviting smile. Her hair swung lustrous, silky black. Her brows angled slightly asymmetrical, one higher than the other, and her lips were more full than the lips of other Sidhe.

They entered the glass doors and passed into the rear room of the house, where Michael had once watched moonlight spill over the bare wood floor. Here, the room was furnished as a study, with an oak roll-top desk in the corner opposite the doors, full bookcases along two walls and an upright piano placed before the gauze curtains of the bay window.

"My name is Mora," the Sidhe said. "We don't have long before he comes down to meet you. Before then . . ." She reached beneath the peplum of her gown and produced a rose from an inner pocket, handing it to Michael. "To decorate your room. You'll be with us for some time, David says."

Michael accepted the rose. "My name is—"

"Oh, we know, we know!" Mora said, laughing. "And this is Nikolai, a friend of Emma Livry."

Nikolai nodded formally and regarded the books and piano with obvious longing.

"Now, I must return to the garden," Mora said. "This is a special season, rare and brief." She laid a finger on the rose in his hands. "This will keep for some time."

She left by way of the French doors, shutting them behind. Michael and Nikolai listened to the tick of a pendulum wall clock mounted over the desk.

Footsteps sounded on the stairs, paused and resumed. The study door opened and a gray-haired man of middle height, appearing perhaps fifty or fifty-five years old, entered. He wore an open-collared shirt and brown slacks and was shod in fawn-colored moccasins. His face was broad and pleasant and his cheeks and chin carried a faint growth of ruddy beard.

"Michael?" he asked, extending his hand. "Michael Perrin?"

Michael nodded and took hold of the hand, shaking it firmly, feeling, as always, awkward over such ritual.

"Very pleased to meet you. I'm David Clarkham. Welcome to Xanadu—or has Mora welcomed you already? Of course. She's a marvel. I'd have a hell of a time running this place without her. I trust you had an interesting journey?"

Michael felt at a loss for words. He nodded again.

Clarkham offered his hand to Nikolai. "Mr. Kuprin. I've admired your daring for years. We met briefly once, though you may not remember. When I visited Emma in Inyas Trai. I was quite heavily disguised."

Nikolai frowned.

"Yes," Clarkham said, smiling. "Successfully disguised. It's getting toward supper, and I've laid out quite a feed to celebrate your arrival. I'm sure you're hungry. Food in the Realm is such a chancy thing. Come with me and I'll show you your rooms, let you wash up. I have another guest here, someone you know, I believe—a Sidhe. He'll be joining us for supper. There's so much to discuss, yes indeed!"

SUPPER WAS MORE of a feast. It was served as the muted sunlight filtering through the silken dome began to wane. A table was arranged on the patio, near Mora's glowing roses, and she brought out bowl after covered bowl of baked vegetables, spiced grains, fresh fruit salads and compotes and green salads. Bread came wrapped in linen in wicker baskets, hot and fresh-baked, served with spiced vegetable butter, the milk of Sidhe horses not being suitable for regular butter.

Michael and Nikolai sat on one side of the table, Clarkham at the head next to Michael. When Mora had finished serving, she sat opposite Nikolai. It was then that Biri strolled onto the patio from the house. He smiled cryptically at Michael and sat beside Mora.

"Fine!" Clarkham said, beaming as he passed the first bowl of food, "We're all here. Mora has done her usual magic"—he winked at Michael—"in the kitchen. What a fine evening this will be."

Michael was less enthusiastic. He ate—he was very hungry—and listened, but said little. Clarkham did most of the talking: domestic pleasantries, the state of the garden, the quality of the weather around Xanadu, what the coming spring might portend for the grounds.

Michael tried not to stare at Biri. Above all else, he wanted to ask two simple questions—why the Sidhe was on such familiar terms with Clarkham, and what Biri's purpose had been in meeting Michael in the canyon.

Biri volunteered nothing, in fact seldom spoke directly to the newly arrived guests. When the meal was done, Clarkham suggested they go inside. Night had fallen and the interior of the pleasure dome had grown somber. Biri stood and passed his hand behind each of a string of paper lanterns hung across the patio just above head level. They began to glow with a guttering yellow light.

The scent of roses was noticeable even inside the house. Michael glanced curiously at the electric lights—the first he had seen in the Realm. The illumination seemed harsher and more grating on his eyes. With that final touch, the house might as well have been on Earth, for all the sensation of normality and comfort—Earth in the 1940s, perhaps, considering the furnishings. Michael was not comforted, however. He had been lulled by appearances too often before.

Clarkham brought out brandy in a crystal decanter and poured snifters for himself, Nikolai and Michael. "The Sidhe love human liquor entirely too much," he explained. "Mora never touches it—says it spoils her heritage. Biri, I suspect, has never tasted a drop in his life. The Maln wouldn't approve, would they?"

Biri shook his head half-sadly. "Alas, no."

"I, however, can drink, and I hope my guests are willing, too." He caught Michael's eye, lifted an eyebrow, pursed his lips, and passed out the glasses. "Master Michael wishes to know what sort of being I am."

"A sensible question," Mora said. They sat in the living room on comfortably overstuffed chairs and a couch, all upholstered in fabric prints of jungle leaves and exotic birds. A fire had been laid and crackled warmly in the fireplace.

"What is he?" Clarkham mimicked. "A question asked often, young man, for the past few hundred years, at least. Much less time has passed here, of course."

"You're not a Sidhe," Michael said, deciding to participate in whatever game was being played. "You're not a Spryggla."

"Heavens, no!" Clarkham exclaimed, laughing.

"Arno Waltiri thought you were human," Michael went on.

"You have that wrong, too, young man. I thought *Waltiri* was human. I doubt very much if Arno was at all deluded by *my* masque."

Michael was taken aback. Clarkham noticed his surprise. "My dear fellow, the game is very complex, and everybody has a stake in it. One can't rectify sixty million years of misery and injustice overnight, or without some turns in the maze."

"Waltiri's dead," Michael ventured without conviction.

"Let's say I have my doubts," Clarkham said. "He is a capable and crafty individual."

Michael couldn't bring himself to ask what Clarkham thought Waltiri was, but Clarkham's tone irritated him. Everything seemed to irritate him now—the light, the company, even Nikolai—as if he were filled with hornets.

"I was born on Earth," Clarkham continued. "In fourteen hundred and ninety-nine. My mother had come over to England some centuries earlier, where she served as *cubicularia* to Queen Maeve herself, before the Queen took to an oak in the Old Forest and her retinue scattered to the islands to escape the charcoal burners. They eventually downed the queen's oak, by the way. Perhaps some of Maeve's venerable smoke resides in the glass windows of a fine English cathedral. But she is no more, and my mother is long dead, too, though she was not mortal. My father *was* mortal, Michael. I am a Breed, if you have not guessed—fifty-fifty. From my mother I learned Sidhe magic, and from my father—well, my father gave me a form which does not unduly reveal my fay ancestry. That is what I am." He waved his hand at Michael. The hornets hummed softly within.

"And you, sir. Question answered one for one."

Michael spoke without hesitation. "I am supposed to be a poet."

"Oh? And are you?"

"Yes."

"Just what I've been waiting for," Clarkham said, exhibiting his satisfaction around the room with a contemplative rub of his chin. "We never have enough poetry."

"To my regret, I have none of my poems with me," Michael said. "And my book was stolen."

"Which book?"

"The book Arno gave me."

"Indeed, indeed," Clarkham mused. "Arno was always quite generous . . . when he needed something done. Did he give any advice with the book?" Clarkham asked.

"He suggested I shouldn't be afraid to take risks."

"To come here, that is."

"I suppose."

Mora broke in. "I'd love to hear some of your poetry."

"I'll have to write some new," Michael said.

"Splendid," Clarkham said. "Biri's been telling us a little about your journey. Quite remarkable. I'm saddened to hear what happened in the Pact Lands. I understand Alyons paid dearly for his excesses."

"Your trap killed him," Michael said. Mora gave a tiny, barely noticeable shudder.

"And he thought you were responsible," Clarkham said. "Poor fool. Never did know which way the wind blew. Not all Sidhe are brilliant, Michael; take that as a lesson."

"I'd thought you might be disappointed to hear I haven't brought the book." Nikolai glanced between them, bewildered and uneasy.

"Heavens no!" Clarkham said. "What use would I have for it?"

"I don't have the first part of the song of power."

"Which one? I've dealt with so many in my time."

"The poem. Coleridge's 'Kubla Khan.' I don't even remember it."

"Then perhaps you'd care to read it again? I have it, right here." He stood and went to a bookshelf, pulling out a book from between two heavy leather-bound volumes. He handed it to Michael with his finger deftly insinuated between the appropriate pages.

Michael glanced at the poem. It was the same text—including the introduction—as in the book Waltiri had given him.

"You thought perhaps the Maln was trying to prevent you from bringing this to me?" Clarkham chuckled. "I've had it for decades. I once told a crazy old Spryggla that I needed it, but only after the fool tried to ensorcel me. For all I know, he spread the word, though his range seemed quite limited."

"He's dead," Michael said. "Or at least, turned to stone."

"And who was responsible for that?"

"Indirectly, I was."

Clarkham took a deep breath. "You are very influential, Michael. You eliminate age-old traditions right and left, break taboos, pioneer new ground. No, it isn't the old material I'm interested in. You have arrived here with potential. The potential is in your poetry. You are in the same position as poor Mr. Coleridge."

Michael turned to Biri. "You've gone over to him, haven't you? You really did want me to come here."

Biri nodded. "Adonna has no influence here. I am free of him."

"Ah, fine old Adonna," Clarkham reflected. "Biri tells me you visited the Irall. I've never been there, myself. I likely would not have survived. I have been a thorn in Tarax's side for many years. Adonna, I suppose, made you forget the meeting. Typical. He's a very old, very weary mage, and he assumes too much responsibility. Valiant in his way, however."

Michael suddenly recovered a memory of Adonna—Tonn—in his kilt and tabard, holding a staff.

"Seeing more clearly now?" Clarkham inquired.

"Seeing what?" Nikolai asked, *sotto voce.*

"I'm remembering some things," Michael explained. Nikolai was obviously not competent to be anything but a spectator in this game. Who else was playing?

"May I ask who, or what, Adonna really is?" Nikolai looked around the circle. Mora took pity on him.

"At one time, he was the Mage of the Sidhe. He made the Realm—a masterpiece, nobody denies that—but he was overly ambitious. He has always opposed the Isomage."

"I never could muster up enough *hubris to* call myself a true mage," Clarkham said. "Others may have, but not I. The mages have earned their positions, their esteem. I simply hope to accomplish what they set out to do, long ago."

"So humble," Nikolai whispered.

Michael leaned forward in his chair. "You brought me here for a reason. Your wife—one of them—cleared the way for me. The other allowed me to escape, when perhaps she could have added me to her collection."

Clarkham kept a perfect poker-face, revealing nothing.

"Please tell me why I am here."

"This evening? I was willing to let you rest . . ."

"Now is as good a time as any."

Clarkham held up his hand and looked at Mora and Biri. "Very well. You are here to finish the final Song of Power. That much must be obvious to you."

It was far from obvious, but Michael nodded.

"I, in turn, will use the song of power to gain control of the Realm, and restore liberty to humans and Breeds."

"You'll use it for nothing else?"

Clarkham tilted his head to the right and tapped his forefinger on the end table, then his middle finger. "You've met Tarax. You know what the Maln is capable of."

"And you've helped me remember Adonna. He doesn't seem such a fiend."

Clarkham's face reddened. "Tonn appears to you as he wishes. Sidhe of his age and accomplishment are very little less than gods, Michael, and enormously devious. I have worked for centuries to simply be able to resist him, and I have succeeded—but I cannot overcome him. It isn't because he is a nice fellow that I wish to conquer him." The muscles of Clarkham's cheek worked visibly and his eyes narrowed. Then, with obvious effort, he brought himself again under control. The ingratiating smile returned. "It isn't an issue I can always be calm about. Tonn is not quite the monster Tarax would have him be, no. But Tonn knows his Sidhe. He designed the Realm for them, and he rules them with a severity which he relaxes only for the Ban of Hours. Can you guess why?"

Michael shook his head.

"Because she was the daughter who stuck by him when Elme defied him. Even though he turned their mother into an abomination, in a fit of . . . I'm not sure what you would call it. Horrid anger. When Elme married a human, it was Tonn who orchestrated her banishment, and devised all her fell tortures. When he couldn't break her to his will, and when the Council of Eleu supported her, then and only then did he put all his power into creating the Realm. He hated humans desperately, Michael."

"Perhaps he's changed his mind."

Clarkham looked surprised, then laughed shortly and sharply. "Obviously he's exercised some influence over you, and without revealing his true nature. For that reason, I suppose I should be a little wary of you."

In the ensuing silence, Nikolai regarded the occupants of the room with growing discomfort. "Michael is for the humans and the Breeds," he spoke up finally. "Michael is a good fellow."

Mora smiled and Biri grinned. Clarkham laughed heartily and without malice. "Of course. He has struggled long and hard to get here, to help his people and mine. We will work together, and all our goals will be achieved. For now, after such a long journey and an excellent dinner, it's best we retire to our rooms and enjoy a comfortable night's sleep. Mora will show you where everything is." He stood and stretched casually. "Good evening, gentlemen."

She led Nikolai and Michael upstairs and showed them the bathroom, their bedrooms and the closet where towels could be procured. She left a scent of roses in her wake. Michael was distracted from his jumbled thoughts by her black, shining hair and teak-colored skin.

There was a fine king-sized bed in his room, the sheets folded back neatly, the white cover pulled down to reveal warm woolen blankets. On the valet near the oak dresser hung a complete change of clothing—slacks, shirt and sweater with new-looking brown shoes made of very supple leather. When he put them on in the morning, he would be better dressed than he had usually been on Earth.

The bedroom walls were decorated with soothing abstract pastel patterns of brown and gray and blue. In one corner sat a tiny rosebush in a brass pot, and beside that, a writing desk with an inlaid leather pad. A gooseneck reading lamp cast a soft glow over the bedstead. Interesting volumes filled a bookshelf near the door—Gerald Manley Hopkins, Yeats, Keats, and Shelley, as well as novels old and new.

Michael shut the door and sat on the bed. With all the comforts of Earth arrayed before him, he should have felt touched despite his caution. But he had no room left for sentiment. He removed his clothes and put on a terrycloth robe. Then he went into the hall, chose a towel from the linen closet, and entered the bathroom.

Hot water, soap, white enamel basin and tub and marble countertop, fern-leafed wallpaper, tiled shower stall. He showered for a long time, until his exhaustion was unavoidable, and dried himself with his eyes closed.

When Michael returned to his room, he found Clarkham standing beside his bed. Clarkham held a box of paper in one hand, thumb clamping down a fine black fountain-pen with gold banding and a clip. "For your convenience," he said, placing the items on the desk. His expression seemed to beseech as he took a step toward Michael. Clearly, he was interested in being friendly, but something came between them, a so-far muted antagonism that might break cover at any instant.

"Sorry," Clarkham said after the moment passed. He walked around Michael and stood in the doorway. "I'm still having difficulty deciding what you are."

Michael shook his head. "I'm not a sorcerer, if that's what you mean."

Clarkham smiled grimly. "Unaware sorcerers are the most formidable, sometimes. But take no heed of my prattle." He made an offhand gesture at the desk. "Exercise your talents whenever you feel the urge. We will all make a receptive audience."

Clarkham left, closing the door behind.

Michael doffed his robe, put on flannel pajamas laid near the bed and crawled under the covers. He reached up to turn off the electric light, fingers wrapping around the hard plastic switch below the glass bulb. Every gesture was so familiar, so strange.

He slept. And this evening, he dreamed.

43

The rose had turned to glass. It lay on the dresser, perfect in every detail, and rang softly when Michael touched it. He picked it up by the stem and inserted it into the lapel of his shirt. It poked from the sweater, still sweetly scented.

As he came down the stairs, three sheets of paper in one hand and the gold-banded fountain pen in the other, he realized that all that had gone before had been trivial.

In bed, he had written five short poems on one sheet. They were more exercises than finished works; tests of his skill. They showed that his ability had not withered. If anything, even while not in constant use, it had grown.

He passed through the French doors onto the patio.

It was an Abyssinian maid,
And on her dulcimer she played,
Singing of Mount Abora.

Mora, however, did not sing of Abora, but of a paradisiacal place called Amhara. Michael probed her lightly and she allowed him into her weave of Cascar words with a smile and a willingness that was quite erotic. Clarkham, seated across the umbrella table from her, did not seem to notice or care. She played her lute-like instrument, occasionally pausing to pluck and tune a string.

Nikolai had already eaten breakfast and sat on a white-painted wrought-iron bench near the low brick wall that separated the patio from the garden of tree roses. Biri was not present.

"I dreamed of you last night," Michael told Mora.

"Yes?" She stopped playing.

"You were singing, just like now, with your lute."

"It is a *pliktera*," she said. "Where was I playing?"

Michael shook his head, smiled, turned to Clarkham and handed him a sheet of penciled poems. "Is this what you're after?"

Clarkham read the poems quickly and laid them on the table. "You know they're not."

"How can I be sure what you need?"

Clarkham stared at Michael steadily. Nikolai shifted uneasily in his seat. Beyond the rose garden, across the black marble and ice floor and near the perimeter of the dome, stood Shahpur, Harka, Bek, Tik and Dour. Far too many for Michael to take on if they combined their power . . .

"I tried to help you last night," Clarkham said.

"You sent me a dream. Not much help." For a brief moment, Michael felt sorry for the Isomage.

Clarkham laughed sharply. "I've dealt with far more songs of power than you, young man."

"I don't need suggestions in my sleep. I've had quite enough from others."

"From Tonn?"

Michael nodded.

"And who else?"

"Whomever. I'm free of them now. I'm on my own." The image came to him clearly; falling free, living up to his purpose. He felt full of strength.

The strength of a bomb.

Arno Waltiri had begun the process. The Crane Women and Lamia—Lamia unwittingly, he assumed—had carried it further; Michael had been forged under their hammers. His journey had annealed him and filled him with the necessary images—images that he would transform beyond all recognition. Clarkham himself had set the timer with the dream sent during the night—awkward as it was, so sublimely ignorant of what was necessary.

"How *pompous*," Clarkham said. "You're only a boy. You've lived what, sixteen, seventeen Earth years? I'm older by many centuries than the city in which you were born."

"Wherever you went, you left disaster and disappointment. Even in the beginning . . . when you worked for the Maln." It was just a guess, but apparently an accurate one.

Clarkham's eyes narrowed and his hands clenched into fists on the table top.

"You were the person from Porlock, weren't you?" Michael continued. "The Maln sent you to interrupt Coleridge. You did your job, but afterward you began to wonder if a Breed could serve Sidhe interests and his own at the same time. And you wondered what Coleridge would have written if you hadn't interrupted . . ."

Clarkham rose to his feet.

"Years later, when you had developed your own magic, you tried to get Emma Livry to dance a song for you. You must have come very close then, because you drove Tarax and the Maln to burn her."

"I loved her," Clarkham said, his voice a menacing purr. Mora looked up quickly but turned from Clarkham's withering glance.

"Who else did you touch?" Michael asked. "And how much better off would they have been if you had simply left them alone? Besides Arno, of course."

"Do you know who Waltiri was—is?" Clarkham asked.

"No," Michael said. He didn't really want to know.

"His people are *birds*, Michael. The Cledar. He was the one who seduced me, not the other way around. I had found a way into the Realm centuries before, but it was his music that opened a gateway through my house that I could not close. He was the one who attracted attention to me in the Realm, and brought the Sidhe down on me to destroy my house and enslave my wives. It was his kind that taught the Sidhe how to use music . . . But he let me believe I was the one controlling things. He was a mage, boy, the last of his people. I'll let you decide how long he has been waiting for this moment, and where he is, now. And how I have turned the tables on him, and on Tonn."

Clarkham stretched his arms, yawning to release his tension. "I suggest we stop this ridiculous talk. Time enough to discuss motivations and peccadilloes when the song is complete. And I know you well enough, boy, to have complete faith in the necessity of your finishing the song. It's inside you already, isn't it? Whether my dream last night helped or not."

"It was a comic opera dream," Michael said. "Do you think that was what Coleridge was trying to say?"

Biri came through the patio doors with a tray of glasses and a clay pitcher dripping condensation. Clarkham frowned and waved the pitcher away. "I have it on authority," Clarkham said. "I have always known the shape of this song, but not its fine details."

"Perhaps the song's secret lies in how its vessels transform it."

"Now you're being obscure," Clarkham said, taking his seat again.

"What was your dream?" Nikolai asked.

"I was in the original pleasure dome. I dreamed of Mora playing, singing. I was a poet—a wild, untamed poet, living in the forests around the palace. Mora was in the emperor's service. She was loved by the court astrologer, a magician— and I loved her, too. We would meet in the cedars. The astrologer became jealous. He advised Kubla to send his fleet to invade Japan, the Eight Islands. And he arranged for press gangs to kidnap the wild poet and send him with the fleet as a galley slave."

Nikolai listened, enthralled. Mora folded her hands on the table top. Biri had set the tray down and was pouring a glass. "And then?" Nikolai asked.

"Then the astrologer planned his marriage to the Abyssinian maid, knowing the fleet would be sent to the bottom of the sea, and his rival with it. A great wind rose and destroyed the emperor's ships, just as the astrologer had foreseen. All aboard drowned. But the young poet's will was so strong he could not be kept away, even in death. He returned to haunt the palace."

"That's what Coleridge was going to write?" Nikolai asked.

"Nobody knows what he was going to write," Michael said. "Why do you need us at all?" he asked Clarkham. "Why not just finish the song yourself?"

"The Isomage is well aware that form is crucial in a song of power," Biri said. "It takes a poet to give it form."

"Indeed," Clarkham said. "Whatever I am, I am not a poet."

"And you think I can equal Coleridge?"

Clarkham considered, then shook his head, no. "You haven't his lyric ability, boy. But you can still give *it form*. You can still finish the song."

"Then I choose not to," Michael said with great difficulty. "You don't deserve the power. You abandoned your wives, and you abandoned Emma Livry. How many others did you hurt? Arno simply gave you what you deserved—some of your own medicine."

"The poor, sad German," Mora said, eyes downcast.

"I was not responsible for Mahler," Clarkham said without looking at her. "Or for his child. That was not my work at all." He smiled at Michael, abruptly calm and friendly. "I've been through a great deal, my boy. I must not be stopped now."

"Then go on without me. You fed me the dream. Give it form. If I can't equal Coleridge, perhaps you can."

"I said I'm not a poet."

"No!" Michael shouted. "You're a parasite. You want power you don't deserve."

"At the very least, I'm a symbiote," Clarkham said, shrugging off Michael's insult. "I interact, inspire. You've been too influenced by Tonn, I suspect, to fully understand my relationship with artists."

"Tonn said poets would rule again someday. I will not allow you to rule."

Clarkham inhaled deeply and let his breath out through his teeth with a faint whistle. "Commendable courage. And stupidity." He pointed to Nikolai. "Look at him."

The corpse in Nikolai's chair was a mass of finely shredded skin and muscle. Blood pooled under the chair. Clarkham raised his finger and Nikolai was restored. "I wouldn't have to be so immature," Clarkham said, "if I were dealing with a worthy opponent. But I'm not. So we'll get our preliminaries out of the way. Produce the final portion of the song, or Nikolai will become what you just saw. But not now. Our emotions have been engaged. There must be time to reflect, to prepare."

"I don't need time," Michael said. He had given Clarkham his last chance, and the Isomage had passed it by with a threat. "I can finish it now."

"I insist," Clarkham said, wetting his lips, eyes fixed on Michael's. "But not right away . . ."

Mora contemplated the tree roses, face impassive. Nikolai simply looked as he had the night before, out of his depth and bewildered. He hadn't felt a thing.

"It's a lovely day. Let Mora give you and your friend a tour. There's much to see here. The pleasure dome was quite a remarkable pattern, and I've gone to a lot of trouble to re-create it. It would be a pity if the object of my efforts were to plunge ahead without full benefit of such artistry." His smile turned almost sweet. "We'll conclude our little dance later. Off with you." He lightly fanned a hand in Mora's direction and left the table.

"You must not underestimate him," Mora said as she led Michael and Nikolai across the marble and ice floor. "The Isomage is a very powerful sorcerer."

"I'm sure he is," Michael said.

She turned and regarded him with a pained expression.

"Then why do you anger him?"

"Because for months now, I thought he was the one who would show me the way home and help the humans in the Realm. Now it's obvious he just wants power. He wants to be another Adonna."

Mora shook her head slowly, almost pityingly, her large eyes steady on Michael's face. "No one comprehends the whole. That is what the Isomage has said, and he must be correct. There is always mystery and surprise."

"He won't harm me until I've given him what he wants. And"—Michael felt the hornets hum louder within—"I don't care anymore. I'm ready to give it to him. So let's tour and get it over with."

Mora cocked her head to one side. "You are saying that a poet from Earth, given a chance to tour Xanadu from end to end, is not even interested?"

This bothered Michael. The opportunity was unparalleled, certainly; but he was not sure he could be enthused by anything now. "I suppose," he said.

"Then come. We'll start at the top . . ."

To one side of the dome, in the middle of a neat circle of cedars, was a black marble staircase leading down into the hill. Mora removed a lantern from a brass plate on the wall and preceded them down the steps. Nikolai followed her closely, and Michael trailed a few steps behind.

"How do you serve Clarkham?" Michael asked her.

"As he wishes me to," she answered softly, barely audible over the whistle of the wind in the shaft.

"And how is that?" Michael pursued, aware he touched sensitive areas.

"When the Isomage came here, there was nothing but ocean. The Maln had ceded it to him in the Pact. David was bitter and exhausted. He had nothing. He had lost everyone he loved; there was only Harka and Shahpur, and they were of little use to him then. He had his power, but no . . ."

She raised her hand and Michael felt her probe him for the right word.

"Inspiration?" he suggested.

"Yes. I also was lost, cast out because I had loved a human. I wandered by the sea, and the Isomage took me in. He was no longer alone, and his strength to imagine returned. That was when he started on the pleasure dome."

"How did the Isomage create all this?" Nikolai asked as they descended into darkness and cold.

"He did not," Mora answered, her voice echoing. "The song already has a variety of forms. He simply took the song as it existed and let it shape the Realm within his territories."

Michael felt the walls with one spread hand; they were mostly ice veined with rock now, and very small veins of rock at that. Ahead sounded an unceasing grumble, a distant roar. The steps vibrated in rhythm with the rise and fall of the grumble.

"The Realm is built on ice," Mora said, "but that ice does not begin for miles yet. This is ice required by the song, cold in the midst of dark. It melts to form the river. And the river—"

They turned a corner and cold blue-green light fell on them. Moisture dripped from smooth slick walls of ice. Rivulets gathered in gutters to each side of the stairway. "The river empties into the sea," Mora said. "It waters the grounds first, so that ice leads to life—cold to warmth. That, too, is part of the song. Some things are not mentioned in any manifestation of the song." She stopped and pointed. Deep in the ice were embedded twisted, elongated fish with the heads of cats and deer. Michael looked closer and saw they were not real, but illusions created by fine cracks; looking again, he saw not fish but frozen reeds capped with eyes. "The song must always be more than its singer can convey."

The steps ended as the floor leveled and they walked directly on ice. Nikolai stumbled in a narrow crack and Michael grabbed his arm. "Not safe for tourists!" the Russian commented wryly.

The ice around them brightened to a pale blue-green, more alive than the dead green of thick glass. Mora led them on to an expansion in the tunnel. "Come," she said, beckoning toward a broad ice bridge.

Above, vaults of ice and marble formed curious traceries, vegetal fans of mineral mixed with the translucent water. Below, the accumulated melt careened from the right and cascaded to the left. The cavern bearing the melt was easily a hundred yards across. The chunks of ice seen from afar now took on more meaningful proportion; they were the size of houses, even mansions. And not all the chunks were ice. As Coleridge had described, pieces of rock were mixed in the tumult. The ice bridge—twisted and doubled-back, obviously natural yet too convenient—took the blows of the rushing bergs and boulders' without a shudder.

They walked along the span, Nikolai reluctantly, afraid of slipping off the rounded surface. The air smelled of cold and mist and was filled with noise: high-pitched grinds and squeals, pounding spray, a deep and momentous impression of motion.

They crossed the bridge and passed into a narrow, low-roofed tunnel, once again as much rock as ice.

Near the exit, rock predominated. They emerged into the dim overgrown light of a deep wedge in the hill—Coleridge's "romantic chasm." Deeper still, a hundred yards below, where they stood on an unfenced ledge, the melt fountained, carrying its ice and rocks in a frothing torrent. Trees formed a canopy over the ledge, glistening with drops of spray. Nikolai shivered.

The ledge took them to the rim of the chasm, overlooking the gardens. The sinuous river flowed like sluggish bronze beneath the warm sky. On the opposite side of the chasm were the steps they had climbed to reach the dome on their arrival. Michael stared down at the base of the falls and the bobbing ice in the deep blue pool there.

"Now we descend to the gardens," Mora said. Michael resisted her hand on his arm.

"We're just wasting time," he said.

"*Please,*" she said.

"Either I do what I was brought here to do, or I leave now," Michael said sternly. Mora backed away and folded her arms across her breasts. Nikolai stood awkwardly to one side, thumbs hooked in his belt.

"Why do you wish to hurry things?" Mora asked in clear sorrow. "There is always time."

Michael looked down the slanting path and saw Harka and Shahpur seated on flanking boulders. There was obviously no chance of escape. He felt the sting of Mora's sadness. "Lead on, then," he said.

The empty Sidhe and the white-wrapped human accompanied them without comment on the rest of the tour. Michael paid little attention to the gorgeous landscaping, the mazes of perfect and ever-blooming flower gardens, the delicate, jewel-like Sidhe animals.

In the early afternoon, Nikolai professed to be tired and hungry, and they made their way up the opposite side of the chasm and returned to the soapstone gate. Harka, Michael and Shahpur hung back a bit before entering the silken tent. At Harka's signal, Michael stopped. Shahpur approached and nodded his shrouded head at the Sidhe.

"We think it wise to warn you," Shahpur said to Michael. "The Isomage will not accept much more defiance."

Harka sighed. "He has been here a long time, with little to do, and not all of his thinking is clear. He still has great bitterness."

"He is powerful," Shahpur said. "He could do you great harm . . ."

"You know that we are different," Harka said. "I have not always served the Isomage in ways that pleased him. He punished me."

"And you still serve him?"

"We have no choice. Now, we warn you only because *he* thinks you could learn from us. We tell you only because *he* wills it. I fled from the Maln with Clarkham; I was his partner. We quarreled, and he gained the upper hand. He poured my self from me like wine from a jug. I have only the hollowness. Shahpur . . ."

"Once, the Isomage was consumed by hatred," Shahpur said. "It bred a disease in his brain like worms in rotten meat. It made him weaker, so he cast a shadow. But the shadow was too strong to simply fade away. He had to cast the shadow *onto* someone. The Isomage chose me. I carry his past foulness."

"He has treated us this way," Harka said, "and yet we have never done him great wrong. If you defy him, refuse him what he most desires, he will consider that a very great wrong indeed. Even empty, I shudder to think what he will do to you, to your companion."

"I won't defy him," Michael said. "I'll give him just what he wants."

"WHAT DID THE humans and the Sidhe lose when they separated?" Clarkham asked after they had finished the early dinner. Bek and Tik cleared away the plates as Mora brought out a tray of brandy snifters. "One lost magic, and the other lost a sense of direction. Bring them together again—that's inevitable—and both will benefit. Ah, but how to bring them together smoothly? Who understands both Sidhe and humans?" Clarkham lifted his snifter and urged Michael to do the same. "Not Tonn. Not an old, decrepit mage losing control of a universe he himself made. Not Waltiri. Not Tarax, a hard and resolute Sidhe with no sympathy for old enemies. Only a Breed."

The brandy was obviously one of Clarkham's evening rituals. Michael sipped
the smooth but potent fluid. "How?" he asked.

"How would I unite them?"

Michael nodded.

"Very carefully. Which do I add first, the water or the acid? An old alchemical
problem—"

"Always add acid to water," Michael said, recalling Mrs. Perry's chemistry
classes.

"Yes. Now I would say the Sidhe are acid, and the humans are water . . .
Adding humans here hasn't done any good. The Sidhe have simply spit them
out, isolated them. But take a few Sidhe and return them to the Earth . . . perhaps
the results will be better."

"We're doing well enough on our own," Michael said, disputing his own
words before they were out. "We don't need Sidhe."

"The Earth is a mess, Michael. No one can see into the minds of others, and
that makes for a nasty and selfish people. What wonders you make are hard and
dangerous. They lack poetry. You fight battles a Sidhe would not even have to
acknowledge—against disease, natural disaster, your own confusion."

"And you want to be in control of the mixing?"

Clarkham nodded. "Can you think of another Breed so qualified, with so
many . . . experiences under his belt?"

Michael shook his head. "You would be the wise one, the benevolent master."

Mora stood behind Clarkham, her hands on his shoulders. Clarkham covered
one hand with his own. "As selfish as any."

Michael's eyes went to Harka, lingering at the edge of the patio.

"It wouldn't be an easy job. Frustrating. Infuriating," Michael suggested.

The early evening light and the glow from the paper lanterns reflected gaily
in the snifters and cast a mellow subdued air across the patio.

Clarkham leaned forward and spread his hands on the cleared table. Between
his hands appeared an image—the Earth, as immediate and real as ever Michael
had seen it, minutely detailed. "All that would be required is to lay a song over
it . . . with the cooperation of humans and Sidhe, guided by the appropriate
leader—myself—and the misery would vanish. The world would return to the
paradise it had once been . . ."

"*Amhara,*" Mora whispered, her face warming to cherrywood brown.

The globe between his hands rushed at Michael. Michael did not flinch. The
image expanded to fill his vision, and he seemed to pass through clouds, over
wine-colored seas, over broad white beaches and jungles and sharp, jagged mountains. He could smell the air, clean and somehow exuberant, filled with pleasure
and challenge. The image vanished like a bubble but the impression lingered.

"Youth," Clarkham said. "A young world again, rid of the guilt, wiped of
the sin and the hatred."

"With you in command," Michael reiterated. At that moment, he launched
his heretofore withheld probe. Clarkham expertly blocked all but the foremost
barb. That portion returned to Michael a brief and horrifying impression of the
inner Clarkham—and a realization.

Use.

Foulness, hatred, almost as repugnant and intense as that within Shahpur. How often had Clarkham shed his darkest shadow? How often had his inner foulness regenerated? He carried a malignancy that could not be eradicated, only reduced, to grow anew.

Shahpur was human; an unprotected soul is flypaper for a cast-off shadow, especially in the Realm.

When Michael had given Clarkham what he wanted, Clarkham would give *him* what the Isomage could no longer comfortably contain. A spiritual *excretion.* How could Michael counter that?

And why should I judge him so harshly? Isn't there a darkness and foulness within me?

Clarkham did not react overtly to the probe. "I will lead. Yes," he said. Only a few seconds had passed. "Who else would you suggest?"

"No one," Michael said.

"Then let us put aside our quarrels. You have the key to help bring paradise to Earth, to help me reunite peoples separated for much too long. Let's cooperate. Our ends are the same." Clarkham gestured for Mora to bring out the pen and paper. She went to the house and returned with a writing tray, setting it before Michael.

"And something special to drink," Clarkham ordered.

Michael reached for the two remaining sheets of paper and began to write. The fountain pen laid its ink in smooth thick lines across the fine linen-grain surface.

The triple circles round him tighten
While from Avernus rise to frighten
The ghosts of voyagers dead while wandering
From edge to edge his shadow Realm . . .

That was just a warm-up. He stared at the white paper, turning his mind from the surroundings. It was like casting a shadow, he thought; the words inside could be drawn out, given shape, sent forth. And they would be deadly.

Again Biri brought out the clay pitcher and thick heavy glasses. He poured a translucent cream-colored fluid and passed the portions around.

Clarkham sipped from the glass Biri gave him and toasted Michael. "The veritable milk of paradise," the Isomage said.

Weave a circle around him thrice . . .

The drink was milky-sweet and biting, with an alcoholic tang. All in all, it was delicious. "Kumis," Biri said. "The drink of Emperor Kubla."

The kumis began to act in Michael almost immediately. He wrote down the last two lines of Coleridge's fragment:

For he on honey-dew hath fed
And drunk the milk of paradise.

And then it was upon him. It flashed and sparkled and came so fast he hardly had time to record it all. He knew he would not have another chance. He tried to catch as much as he could, and he exulted. There was no outside source for this; it came from inside, purely from himself, or rather, that self which connected him with Coleridge, with Yeats, with all the fine poets. That moment when there was nothing but the Word, and it came in perfect waves.

And so the ice, cross ages dripping,
Undermines the silken palace,
Falls beneath the cedars, ripping
As if the years themselves with malice
Seek to still great dreams by gripping
The gardens, walls and golden towers,
Rending from the Khan his powers . . .

Perhaps twenty lines passed so quickly he could not write them down. They were not essential.

As wave to wave, in storm sea floundering,
His galliots beach, unguided at the helm.
Thou Khan, who eats the fruit of Faerie,
Who hastes to leave when bid to tarry,
Listen to the sweet soft critic,
That dusk-wrapped maid on sweet strings playing:
"Palace, towers and gardens," saying,
"Cannot save your soul from pity
Nor build from song a timeless city."
The caverns roar with rising waters . . .

The ground trembled. Clarkham steadied himself against the table.

Drowning to the highest mountains,
Flooding all the Khan's great slaughters
Beneath the whirling, vaulted fountains.

There was more, much more, and it did not simply spin through his head and vanish. The song was created and completed, and Michael knew immediately it was not the song of power Clarkham sought. It never had been. From the very beginning, when they had commissioned Lin Piao Tai to build the palace, the element of destruction had been plain.

Coleridge's poem, and Michael's share in it, were simply decoys, traps meant to snare and destroy those, like Clarkham, who stood in the way of the ultimate combatants. Waltiri, mage of the birds, the Cledar, had sent Michael; the Crane Women and the Ban of Hours had cooperated; Tonn and the Maln had let him pass.

Clarkham grabbed the sheets as soon as Michael stopped writing. He read them, eyes widening, lips working in growing rage. "You are a *traitor*," he said, voice harsh and rasping. "This is not—"

"It's finished. It isn't all there, but I've finished it," Michael said, suddenly exhausted. Clarkham crumpled the pages and threw them on the table. Mora reached for the *pliktera* beside her chair. Clarkham turned to her, but she would not look at him. The ground shook again as Nikolai backed away from the table. From the chasm, the pulse of ice catapulting to the river bed quickened. Clarkham swiveled to face Biri, who stared at him implacably.

"You!" Clarkham said. "You're the traitor. You're still loyal to Tarax!"

"There was no disputing the boy's mission," Biri said. "Tarax and Adonna willed it, as well as the Council of Eleu. All are united against you. Even you willed it. The boy would have turned away, but you brought him here. He would have refused the song, but you forced him to write it. On your own head, Isomage."

Clarkham's face darkened with rage. His hands trembled, waiting to spill their power.

"Better leave," Michael whispered to Nikolai. The Russian didn't need any more encouragement. He leaped over the wall, dodged through the rose garden and vaulted the fence to the icy marble floor. Fine cracks shot across the marble surface behind him, throwing chips of stone into the air as the ground shuddered. Michael reached down to retrieve the pages. He flattened them out and held them behind his back.

"What shall I do with you all?" Clarkham asked. More than ever now, Michael pitied him—and feared him.

Biri took Mora's hand. They walked away from the Isomage, down the brick steps to the lawn. The light through the silken dome reddened and the fabric rippled under the rough touch of a new wind.

Clarkham faced Michael alone on the patio. "Get out!" he cried. The black marble screamed and separated along the ice veins. The lawn rippled and showed gashes of soil. The roses shook. Most of the staked trees had turned to glass; the blossoms shattered and cast their fragments on the dirt.

"GET OUT!"

Michael turned his back on the Isomage, neck hair prickling. He fully expected to have his flesh riven from his bones, but Clarkham concentrated all his power on keeping the palace together.

One of the curved supporting poles snapped with the report of a gunshot. The pole fell and tore out a length of silk. The plaster and brick walls of Clarkham's home split. Chunks slipped away and crumbled on impact. The house's timbers groaned in agony.

As Michael crossed the lawn, barely able to keep his balance, he heard Clarkham shout his name. He looked back and saw the Isomage standing spread-legged on two separated pieces of the patio. The Breed's hair flew out from his head. His hands and arms crackled with energy.

He held up a wickedly glowing finger.

"You may not go!" he shouted over the uproar.

Coils of viscous light oozed from his fingers and expanded above the rose garden and lawn. They sank around Michael, forming a serpentine net of bright green strands.

Michael felt his eyes grow warm, then hot. The shadow he cast was a dark, enveloping thing, alone and indescribably nasty. He sprung away from the shadow, passed through the web and leaped to the broken marble, his own hair charged with power.

And all should cry, beware, beware
His flashing eyes, his floating hair!

The shadow contained all of Biri's Sidhe discipline, all of the poisonous, virulently inhumane nonsense about aloneness and self-mastery through isolation. It was the philosophy of a discouraged, dying race and it had served its purpose—it had filled Michael with the basic will to destroy. Now he had no use for it—except as a defense.

Clarkham leaped to a more stable position and drew in the green web. The shadow struggled, made a sound like crushing rock, and exploded. Darkness scattered the web and dissipated under the fiery dome light.

Clarkham shouted in a language Michael had never heard before, then extruded another web, this one intensely blue.

Michael turned his face away and held up the poem. The lines of ink hissed and crackled. The words shot out in lances of fire over Clarkham's head, setting the house aflame. In seconds, the rear wall and tile roof became a furnace of quicklime, wood and clay. The glass in the French doors exploded and the frames shrank like blackened match sticks. Glowing embers wafted up in the rising heat and ignited the silken tent.

"My work, my work!"

Michael looked down and saw Clarkham run toward the house. The flames beat him back, but he unrolled a sheet of ice from nothing and plunged inside. From the corners of the pavilion, Shahpur and Harka ran to help their master. Shahpur's wrappings puffed trails of smoke.

Strains of music rose from the vibrations of the hill and palace. Michael dodged and ran to escape the falling shreds of burning tent. Only when he was through the soapstone gate did he realize he must be hearing the original Infinity Concerto, as it had sounded decades before.

Mora and Biri waited for him on the lawn beyond the dome's foundation. Nikolai struggled to stand upright a few yards behind them. Biri led the way down the side of the chasm, away from the hill and the fire spreading from the dome to the orchards and cedar forests. In their flight, they passed Bek, Tik and Dour, who seemed to melt into the smoking trees.

They didn't stop until they stood by the granite guard near the gate of the outermost wall. Biri still held Mora's hand. Her face was a mask of grief and remorse.

Nikolai danced from foot to foot, watching the conflagration. "Jesus, Jesus! Look what you've done! I have never seen anything like that! What in hell are you, Michael?"

Michael looked at the papers still clutched in his hands. All the writing had been neatly burned out, line by line, leaving brown-edged shreds held together by margins.

The hill sagged. The conflagration was now a pillar of smoke and fire reaching up to smudge the sky.

"That dream is ended," Biri said, lifting the ruined pages from Michael's hand and scattering them over the grass. "You are free to go now."

"Go where?"

"Home."

"What happens to everybody else? To the humans?"

"That is Adonna's concern. You have served your purpose. You are spent." Biri regarded him with contempt. "You threw off Sidhe discipline. In our eyes, you are nothing now."

Do not reveal yourself. He is merely a wheel, not an engine.

Michael recognized the voice now; it *was* Waltiri. He felt the power still residing in his mind, and smiled at Biri. He did not need to dispute the Sidhe.

The hill now subsided level with the plain. Water flooded from its perimeter in high-vaulting fountains, spreading to form a lake. Ice bobbed lazily in the water. At the center of the lake, a whirlpool formed, its horrible sucking sound audible even at the outer wall. Michael felt a tug in the center of his stomach.

"Clarkham made one mistake," Biri said as they watched the lake vanish. "He trusted a Sidhe." The words struck Mora deeply. She backed away from him and threw down his hand.

"Nikolai," Michael said. "Will you be all right?"

"I am fine," Nikolai said. "Why?"

"Something's happening."

"Your gateway is falling through the Realm," Biri said. "Down to the void. Go home, man-child."

"Michael! Wait!"

Nikolai lunged for him, but a thread pulled tight—the long thread of his existence in the Realm. The grass, scraps of paper, walls, Biri and Mora, Nikolai, all took off around him in a violent spin. He arced high above the Realm and was drawn with incomprehensible speed over the river, grasslands and forests—

Cometing through the Irall, Inyas Trai, across the barren mound of the Crane Women and through the flat, burned village of Euterpe—

Through Lamia's house, where the huge woman lingered in shadow, discarded by all now that her work was done—

Across the ruined field to the softly flickering gateway—

Down the alley, past the slumped figure of the guardian sitting under the trellis—

And into a warm, dark early fall breeze.

Filled with the sound of leaves scattering over pavement, the smells of fresh-mowed grass and eucalyptus, the sensation of complex and ever-changing solidity.

Crickets.

And in the distance, a motorcycle.

44

He stood beneath the moon-colored streetlight, half in the shadow of a tall, brown-leafed maple. Four houses down and on the opposite side of the street was the white plaster home of David Clarkham. It had been deserted for forty years and its lawns were overgrown; its hedges thrust uncontrolled branches in all directions; its walls were cracked and spotted with mud. There were no curtains in the front windows. The FOR SALE sign on the front lawn leaned away from the house, shunning it.

The house was empty.

Michael pulled the hair back from his eyes and felt the growth of silky beard on his cheeks. He looked down at the sweater and shirt and slacks that Clarkham had given him to wear.

In the lapel of the shirt was the glass rose.

He removed it and smelled it. The scent was gone.

45

Michael sat across from his parents in the living room, his discomfort growing with the silence. His mother had stopped weeping momentarily, and his father looked down at the carpet with a face full of pain and relief, the end of grief and the beginning of helpless anger. "Five years is a long time, son," he said. "The least you could have done—"

"There was no way. It was impossible." How could he tell them what had happened? Not even the glass rose would convince them. And five years! It seemed less than five months.

"You've changed," his father said. "You've grown a lot. You can't expect us to just . . . accept. We grieved for you, Michael. We were sure you were dead."

"Father—"

His father held up a hand. "It will take time. Wherever you were, whatever you were doing. It will take time. We . . ." Tears came to his eyes now. "We've kept your room. The furniture, the books."

"I knew if you were alive, you'd come back," his mother said, brushing strands of red hair from her eyes.

"Did you ever talk to Golda?"

"She died a few months after you . . . went away," his mother said. "She sent a letter for you, and there's a letter from some lawyers." She looked down at the carpet. "Such a long time, Michael."

"I know," he said, his own eyes filling now at the thought of their pain. He rose from the chair and sat between them on the couch, putting his arms around them both, and together they hugged and cried and tried to push away the strange time, the long time apart.

After dinner, after hours of catching up on news and telling his folks repeatedly that there was no way he could describe what had happened—not yet, not without more proof—he took the stairs to his room and stood amid the books and prints and the writing table he had now completely outgrown.

He opened the letter from Golda and the papers from the lawyers of Waltiri's estate and lay back on the pillow. Golda's handwriting was elegant, old-world, clear, spread with conservative margins across green-lined airmail paper.

Dear Michael,

    I have not told your parents, because I know so little myself. Arno— mysterious husband! I hardly know how to describe my life with him, won- derful as it has been—Arno requested that our estate be placed in your care, upon my joining him (dare I hope that? Or is something more powerful at work here?), which I believe will be soon, for I have been under great strain. Do not feel bad, Michael, but much of this strain has come from withholding certain facts from your dear parents, who have been so kind to me. But what can we tell them—that you have followed my husband's suggestions—and, despite his last words, perhaps even his wishes? I do not know where you have gone, and I am not even certain you will return, though Arno, appar- ently, was. I am not so old that I may be excused the confusion I feel, but excuse me, dear Michael, for I do feel it. That, and the sadness, the sensation of being in circumstances for which I am totally inadequate either in knowl- edge or mental capacity. Perhaps, on your return, you will know why Arno has made this request, and what you should do with our resources, which are not small. You will also control the rights to Arno's work. There are no other specific requests, and all of these will be detailed in letters from our lawyers. Dear boy. Turn a glass down for us—one glass only, since Arno never drank wine, and told me to drink for him when celebrations were on— when you have safely returned and your loved ones rejoice. As all our people have said for centuries, dear Michael: May there come a time when all shall share their stories, and all will be unveiled, and we may revel in the cleverness and the beauty of the tales thus told. So clumsy, this note, for a young poet to read!

He folded the letter and put it into its envelope, then removed the legal instructions and skimmed them. He would be financially secure; his duties would be to organize the Waltiri papers and provide for their publication, and oversee the publications currently in progress; he could live in the Waltiri home if he so wished.

The letters slid down his chest as he sat up and folded his strong brown arms around his blanketed knees. Of all things now, he wished he could speak with Golda, have her help him with his parents, perhaps put all their minds to rest.

If it would have done Golda any good to know—as much as Michael knew— what Arno Waltiri was, and that he was not dead. Not in any human sense.

And what about the humans in the Realm? Helena, and the others? Adonna— Tonn—had said all would be well, once Clarkham was removed. Michael simply could not believe that, but there was nothing he could do. Not here, not now.

HE WENT TO the bathroom to wash his face. Steam rose from the basin of hot water, curling around his face. He breathed deeply, drawing the steam into his lungs to clear away the sorrow and stress. He looked up through the steam into the mirror.

The position—the angle—wasn't quite right. Familiar, but . . .

Michael presented a three-quarters view. The realization struck like the sound of a cold razor scraping along a blackboard. He stared at the first face of Hebal Mish, the first visage sculpted from clouds of snow. He had changed so much he hadn't even recognized himself.

At first Michael felt afraid. He stood in the hall outside the bathroom, then went to his room and flung open the window to breathe fresh air.

It wasn't over. It would never be over; and he was more involved than ever.

In the depths of the night, a bird began to sing.

Book Two

THE

SERPENT

MAGE

THIS BOOK, FINALLY, IS FOR KRISTINE
—UNBEKNOWNST TO HERSELF,
A KIND OF BEATRICE
1951–1971

1

The pale, translucent forms bent over Michael Perrin once again. Had he been awake he would have recognized three of them, but he was in a deep and dreamless sleep. Sleep was a habit he had reacquired since his return. It took him away, however briefly, from thoughts of what had happened in the Realm.

He is pretending to be normal, one form said without words to her sister, hovering nearby.

Let him rest. His time will come soon enough.

Does he feel it?

He must.

Has he told anybody yet?

Not his parents. Not his closest friends.

He has so few close friends . . .

Michael rolled over onto his back, pulling sheet and blankets aside to reveal his broad, well-muscled shoulders. One of the forms reached down to squeeze an arm with long fingers.

Stop that.

He keeps himself fit.

The fourth figure, shaped like a bird, said nothing. It stood by the door, lost in thought. The others retreated from the bed.

The fourth finally spoke. *No one in the Council knows of this.*

It was a surprise even to us, the tallest of the three said.

Michael's eyelids flickered, then opened. He caught a glimpse of white vapor spread like wings, but it could easily have been the fog of sleep. With a start, he held up his left wrist to look at his new watch. Eight-thirty. He had slept in. There would barely be time for his exercises.

He descended the stairs in a beige sweatsuit, a gift from his parents on his most recent birthday. There had been no candles on his cake, at his request. He did not know how old he was.

His mother, Ruth, was reading the newspaper in the kitchen. "French toast in fifteen minutes," she said, smiling at him. "Your father's in the shop."

Michael returned her smile and picked up a long oak stick from beside the kitchen pantry, carrying it through the door into the back yard.

The morning was grayed by a thin fog that would burn off in just a few hours. Near the upswung door of the converted garage, his father, John, was hand-sanding a maple table top on two paint-spattered sawhorses. He looked up at Michael and forearmed mock-sweat from his brow.

"My son, the jock," Ruth said from the back steps.

"I remember him still carrying stacks of books around," John said. "Don't be too hard on him."

"Breakfast lingers for no man," she said. "Fifteen minutes."

John wiped the smooth pale surface with his fingers and applied himself to a rough spot. Michael stood in the middle of the yard and began exercising with the stick, running in place with it held out before him, hefting it back over his head and bending over to touch first one end, then the other to the grass on both sides. He had barely worked up a sweat when Ruth appeared in the doorway again.

"Time," she said.

She regarded her son delicately over a cup of coffee as he ate his French toast and strips of bacon. He was less enthusiastic about bacon—or any kind of meat—than he had been before . . .

But she did not bring up this observation. The subject of Michael's missing five years was virtually taboo around the house. John had asked once, and Michael had shown signs of volunteering . . . And Ruth's reaction, a stiff kind of panic, voice high-pitched, had shut both of them up immediately. She had made it quite clear she did not want to talk about it.

Just as clearly, there were things she wanted to tell and could not. John had been through this before; Michael had not. The stalemate bothered him.

"Delicious," he said as he carried his plate to the sink. He kissed Ruth on the cheek and ran up the stairs to change into his work clothes.

MICHAEL HAD NOT yet assumed the position of caretaker at the Waltiri house. The time was not right.

After two weeks of job hunting, he had been hired as a waiter in a Nicaraguan restaurant on Pico. For the past three months, he had taken the bus to work each weekday and Saturday morning.

At ten-thirty, Michael met the owners, Bert and Olive Cantor, at the front of the restaurant. Bert pulled out a thick ring of keys and opened the single wood-framed glass door. Olive smiled warmly at Michael, and Bert stared fixedly at nothing in particular until his wife handed him a huge mug of coffee. Shortly after Bert emptied the mug, he began issuing polite orders in the form of requests, and the day officially started.

Jesus, the Nicaraguan chef, who had arrived before six o'clock, entering through the rear, donned his apron and cap and instructed two Mexican assistants on final preparations for the day's specials. Juanita, the eldest waitress, a stout Colombian, bustled about making sure all the set-ups were properly done and the salad bar in order.

Bert and Olive treated Michael like a lost son or at least a well-regarded cousin. They treated all their employees as if they came from various branches of the family. Ben had called the restaurant his "United Nations retirement home" after hiring Michael. "We have a red-headed Irishman, or a look-alike anyway, and half a dozen different types of Latinos, and two crazy Jews in charge."

Michael served on the lunch and early dinner shifts, and he studied the people he served. The restaurant attracted a broad cross-section of Angelenos, from Nicaraguans hungry for a taste of home to students from UCLA. Lunch brought in Anglo and other white-collar types from miles around.

This morning, Bert's mug of coffee did not fix him firmly in the day. He seemed vaguely distraught, and Olive was unusually subdued. Finally, a half-hour before opening, Bert took Michael into the back storeroom behind the kitchen, among the huge cans of peppers and condiments and the packages of dried herbs, and pulled out two chairs from a small table where Olive usually sat to do the books.

Bert was sixty-five, almost bald, his remaining white hair meticulously styled in a wispy swirl. He always wore a blue blazer and brown pants, a golf shirt beneath the blazer. On his right hand he sported a high school class ring with a jutting garnet.

He waved this hand in small circles as he sat and shook his head. "Now don't worry about whether you're in trouble or not. You're a good worker," he said, "and you wait tables like an old pro. You're graceful. You could even work in a snazzy place."

"This *is* a snazzy place," Michael said, smiling.

"Yes, yes." Bert looked dubious. "We're a family. You're part of the family. I'm saying this because you're going to work here as long as you want, and we all like you . . . but you don't belong." He stared intently at Michael. "And I don't mean because you should be in a university. Where are you coming from?"

"I was born here," Michael answered, knowing that was also not what Bert meant.

"So? Why did you come *here,* to this restaurant?"

"I don't know what you're getting at."

"The way you look at customers. Friendly, but . . . spooky. Distant. Like you've come from someplace a hell of a ways from here. They don't notice. I do. So does Juanita. She thinks you're a *brujo,* pardon my Spanish."

Michael had learned enough Spanish as a California boy to puzzle out that *brujo* was the masculine for *bruja,* witch. "That's silly," he said, staring off at the cans on the gray metal shelves.

"I agree with Olive. Maybe even, pardon me, a *dybbuk.* Juanita washes dishes, and I taste the food and maybe yell once a week, but that's both our opinions. Both ends of the rainbow think alike."

"Is Olive worried?" Michael asked softly. Olive reminded him of a slightly plumper Golda Waltiri.

Bert lifted his hands in an expressive shrug. "Olive would like to have half a dozen sons, and the Lord, bless him, did not agree. She adores you. She does not think ill of you even when she sees the way you 'learn' our customers, the way you *see* them."

"I'm sorry I've upset you," Michael said.

"Not at all. People come back. People, who knows why, enjoy being paid attention to the way you do it. You're not in it for the advantage. But you still don't belong here."

Bert put on his look of intense concern, raised brows corrugating his high forehead. "Olive says you have a poet's air about you. She should know. She dated a lot of poets when she was young." He cast a quick, long-suffering look at the ceiling. "So why are you waiting tables?"

"I need to learn some things."

"What can you learn in a trendy little dive on Pico?"

"About people."

"People are everywhere."

"I'm not used to being . . . normal," Michael said. "I mean, being with people who are just . . . people. Good, plain people. I don't know much about them."

Bert pushed out his lips and nodded. "Juanita says that for somebody to become a *brujo*, something has to happen to them. Did something happen to you?" He raised his eyebrows, practically demanding candor. Michael felt oddly willing to comply.

"Yes," he said.

Having struck pay dirt, Bert leaned back and seemed temporarily at a loss for what to ask next. "Are your folks okay?"

"They're fine," Michael said abstractedly.

"Do they know?"

"I haven't told them."

"Why not? They love you."

"Yes. I love them." The dread was fading. Michael did not know why, but he was going to open up to Bert Cantor. "I've tried telling them. It's almost come out once or twice. But Mom gets upset even before I begin. And then, it just stops, and that's it."

"How old are you?"

"I don't know," Michael said. "I could be seventeen, and I could be twenty-two."

"That's odd," Bert said.

"Yes," Michael agreed.

The story spun itself out from there, across several days, each day at eleven Bert drawing up the chairs and sitting across from Michael with his forehead corrugated, listening until the lunchtime crowd arrived and Michael began waiting tables.

On the fourth day, the story essentially told, Bert leaned back in his chair and closed his eyes, nodding. "That," he said, "is a good story. Like Singer or Aleichem. A good story. This part about Jehovah being a fairy, that's tough for me. But it's a good one. I'm not asking to insult you—but, is it all true?"

Michael nodded.

"Everything's different from what the newspapers and history books say?"

"Lots of things are different from what they say, yes."

"I'm asking myself if I believe you. Maybe I do. Sometimes my opinions are funny that way. Are you sure it's better here than going to college?"

He nodded again.

"Smart boy. My son James, from a previous marriage, he's gone to college. The professors there don't know *frijoles* about people. Books they know."

"I love books. I've been reading every day, going to the library. I need to know more about that, too."

"Nothing wrong with books," Bert agreed. "But at least you're trying to put things in perspective."

"I hope."

"Well," Bert said, with a long pause after. "What are you going to do with yourself? What are you getting ready to do, I mean?"

Michael shook his head.

"I feel for you, with a story like that," Bert said. Then he stood. "Time to wait tables."

THE WINTER PASSED through Los Angeles more like an extended autumn, crossing imperceptibly into a wet and clean-aired spring such as the city had not seen in years, a sparkling, green-leafed, sun-in-water-drop spring.

The pearls appeared in Michael's palms six months after his return from the Realm, in the first weeks of that spring. They nestled at the end of his lifeline, insubstantial, glowing in the dark like two fireflies. In two days' time, they faded and disappeared.

The pearls confirmed what he had suspected for some weeks. Events were coming to fruition.

So ended the pretending, his time of normality and anonymity, the last time he could truly call his own.

RAIN FELL FOR several hours after dinner, pattering on the roof above Michael's room and chirruping down the gutters. Moonlit beads of moisture glittered on the leaves of the apricot and avocado trees in the rear yard. Rounded lines of clouds, their bottoms glowing orange-brown in the city lights, moved without haste over the Hollywood hills.

Michael had come upstairs to read, but he put down his book—Evans-Wentz's *The Fairy-Faith in Celtic Countries*—and stood before the open window, feeling the moist air lap against his face.

The night birds sang again, trills sharp and liquid by turns. The trees seemed alive with song. He hadn't heard them sing this late in months; perhaps the rain disturbed them.

Michael closed the window, returned to his bed and leaned back on the pillow. He slept naked, disliking the restriction of pajamas, and he lay in bed as his mind took up signals like an antenna, extending itself and receiving, whether he willed it or not . . .

Tomorrow, Michael would leave the home of his childhood, the house of his parents, to live in the house of Arno and Golda Waltiri. He would assume control of the estate. He had planned the move since telling Bert and Olive he was quitting, but the time had never seemed exactly right.

Now it was right. Even discounting the pearls, unmistakable signs stacked themselves one upon another.

He was having unusual dreams.

He turned off the light. Downstairs, a Mozart piano piece—he didn't know which one—played on his father's stereo. He felt drowsy, and yet some portion of his mind stayed alert, even eager. Moonlight filled his room as the shadow of a cloud passed. Even with eyes closed to slits, he could clearly make out the framed print of Bonestell's painting of Saturn seen from one of its closer moons.

For the merest instant, on the cusp between sleep and waking, he saw a figure cross the print's desolate, snow-dappled lunar landscape. The print was not in focus, but the figure seemed sharp and clear. A young—very young—Arno Waltiri smiled and beckoned . . .

Michael twitched on the bed, eyes closed tightly now, and then relaxed, falling across continent, sky and sea.

He saw—in some sense became—

MRS. WILLIAM HUTCHINGS Cunningham, widowed only a year, had become addicted to long treks in the new forest beyond her Sussex country home. She walked gingerly, her booted feet sinking into the damp carpet of compacted leaves, moss and loam. Early spring drizzle beaded in the fine hairs of her wool coat and cascaded from ferns disturbed by her passage.

The dividing line between the new forest and the old was not well marked, but she knew it and felt the familiar surge of love and respect as she crossed over. The great oaks, their trunks thick with startlingly green moss, tiered with moons of fungus, rose high into the whiteness. Her booted feet sank into the black wet loam and spongy moss and the slick, slippery piles of last autumn's moldering leaves.

Mrs. Cunningham became part of the deep past whenever she crossed into the old forest. There was so little of it left in England now; patches here and there, converted to regular dun brick housing projects with distressing frequency, watched over by (she felt) corrupt or at the very least incompetent and uncaring government ministries. She raised her goose-head walking stick and poked the empty air with it, her face a mask of intense concern.

Then the peace returned to her, and she found the broad flat rock in the middle of the patch of old forest, near an ancient overgrown pathway that arrowed through the trees without a single curve or waver. The trees had adapted themselves to the path, not the other way around, and yet they were centuries old. So how old was the path?

"I love you," she said, with only the trees and the mist and the rock for witnesses. Carefully maneuvering around a black, unmarked slick of mud, she sat on the rock and let her breath out in a whuff.

It was here and not by his grave, in a neatly manicured cemetery miles and miles away, that she came to hold communion with her late husband. "I love you, William," she said, face downturned but dark brown eyes peering up. The mist's minute droplets slipped into the wrinkles of her face and made lines of sheen. She closed her eyes and leaned her head back to feel the droplets land on her eyelids and lips.

"Do you remember," she said, "when we were just married, and there was that marvelous inn, The Green Man, and the innkeeper wanted to see *our* identification, wanted to know how old *we* were?"

For some, such a process, day in and day out, would have signified an unwholesome self-torture. But not for her. She could feel the distance growing between herself and the past, and she could feel the wounds healing. This was how she kept a bandage on her injuries, protecting them with a bit of ritual against the abrasions of hard reality.

"Do you remember, too—" she began, then stopped abruptly, eyes turning slowly to the path.

A tall dark figure, walking on the path miles beyond the trees, yet still visible, approached the rock on which she sat. It seemed she waited for hours, but it was only a minute or two, as the figure grew larger and more distinct, coming at last to the extent of the path that Mrs. Cunningham would have called real.

A tall, pale-skinned woman arrived at the rock and paused, drifting forward as if from ghostly momentum as she turned to look at Mrs. Cunningham. The tall woman had dark red hair and a thin ageless face with deep-set eyes. She wore a gray robe that was really a translucent, nacreous black.

Mrs. Cunningham had not seen her like before. She felt a feather-touch at the back of her thoughts, and the woman spoke. With each word, the uncertain image became more solid, as if speaking finished the act of becoming part of this reality.

"I am on the Earth of old, am I not?" the woman asked.

"I think so," Mrs. Cunningham said, as brightly as she could manage, or dared.

"Do you grieve?"

"No." Mrs. Cunningham's expression turned quizzical, with a touch of pain. "Yes."

"For a loved one?" the woman asked.

"For my husband," she replied, her throat very dry.

"Silly grief, then," the woman said. "You do not know the meaning of grief."

"Perhaps not," Mrs. Cunningham conceded, feeling this was more than impertinence or rudeness, "but it feels to me as if I do."

"You should not sit on that rock much longer."

"Oh?" She tightened her face, resolute.

The woman pointed back up the path. "More of my kind coming," she said.

"Oh." Mrs. Cunningham stared at the path, head nodding slightly, eyes wide.

The tall woman's pale face glowed against the dark trees and misty sky. "I say that your grief is a silly grief, for he is not lost forever, as we are, and you have paid mortality for infinity, and that we cannot."

"Oh," Mrs. Cunningham said again, as if engaged in conversation with a neighbor. The woman's eyes were extraordinary, like holes into a silver-blue arctic landscape, with hints of opalescent fire. Her red hair hung in thick strands around her shoulders, and her black gown seemed alive with moving leaves in lighter shades of gray. A golden tassel dangling from her midriff had a snaky life of its own.

"We are back now," she said to Mrs. Cunningham. "Please do not cross the trod here after."

"I certainly won't," Mrs. Cunningham vowed.

The woman pointed a long-fingered hand at the rock. Mrs. Cunningham removed herself several yards, slipping once on the patch of leaves and mud. The woman drifted down the path, not walking on quite the same level, and was surrounded by trees away from Mrs. Cunningham's view.

She stood, her lips working in prayer, and then returned her attention to the direction from which the woman had come. "The Lord is my shepherd," she murmured. "The Lord is my shepherd. I shall not want—"

There were more, indeed. Three abreast and of all descriptions, from deepest shadows without feature to mere pale wisps like true spirits, some dripping water, some seeming to be made of water, some as green as the leaves in the canopy above, and following them, a number of beautiful and sinewy horses with shining silver coats . . . and all, despite their magnificence, with an air of weary refugee desperation.

Mrs. Cunningham, after a few minutes, decided discretion would be best, and retreated farther from the path—the trod—with her eyes full of tears for the beauty she had seen that day, and for the message of the woman with red hair in the living black gown.

Paying mortality for infinity . . .

Yes, she could understand that.

"William, oh *William,*" she breathed, fairly running through the woods. "You wouldn't *believe* . . . what has . . . just happened . . . here . . ." She came to the boundary and crossed into new forest, and the sensation dulled but did not leave her entirely.

"But whom will I tell?" she asked. "They're back, all—or some—of the Faerie folk, and who will believe me now?"

MICHAEL OPENED HIS eyes slowly and stared at the dawn as it cast dim blue squares on the closed curtains.

Behind the vision of Mrs. Cunningham had been another and darker one. He had seen something long and sinuous swimming with ageless grace through murky night waters, watching him from a quarter of the way around the world. In that watching there was appraisal.

ON THE MORNING of his move, Ruth offered one last time to help him get settled in the Waltiri house. Michael politely refused. "All right, then," she said, dishing up one last homecooked breakfast of fried eggs and toast—consciously leaving out the bacon. "Promise me you won't take things so seriously."

He regarded her solemnly.

"At least try to loosen up. Sometimes you are positively gloomy."

"Don't nag the fellow," John said, holding one thumb high to signal friendly banter and not domestic disagreement.

Michael grinned, and Ruth stared at him with wistfulness and then something like awe. He could almost read her thoughts. This was her son, with the strong features so like his father's and the hair so like her own—but there was something not at all comforting in his face, something lean and . . .

Fierce. *Where had he been for five years?*

Michael walked, suitcases in hand, in the pale rich light of morning. Dew beaded the lawns of the old homes and dripped from the waxy green leaves of camellia and gardenia bushes. The sidewalks steamed in the sun, mottled olive and gray with moisture from last night's rain.

He passed a group of five school girls, twelve or thirteen years old, dressed in white blouses and green and black plaid skirts with black sweaters. They averted their faces as they passed but not their eyes, and Michael sensed one or two turning, walking backward, to continue staring at him.

The possibilities offered by his appearance seldom concerned him; he appreciated the attention of women but took little advantage. He still felt guilty about Eleuth, the Breed who had given her life for him, and thought often of Helena, whom he had treated as Eleuth had deserved to be treated.

For that and other reasons there was a deep uncertainty in him, a feeling that he had somehow twisted his foot at the starting line and entered the race crippled, that he had made bad mistakes that lessened his chances of staying ahead. He was certain about neither his morals nor his competence.

He set the bags down on the front porch of the Waltiri house. Using the keys given to him by the estate's attorneys, he opened the heavy mahogany door. The air within was dry and noncommittal. Plastic sheets had been draped over the furniture. Gritty gray dust lay over everything.

He took the bags into the hall and set them down at the foot of the stairs. "Hello," he said nervously. Waltiri's presence still seemed strong enough that a hale answer wouldn't have surprised him.

The upstairs guest bedroom became his first project. He searched for a storage closet, found it beneath the stairs and pulled out a vacuum cleaner—an old upright Hoover with a red cloth bag. He cleared the hardwood floors of dust upstairs and down, then removed from the same closet and rolled out the old oriental carpets and stair runners, fixing the brass rods to keep them in place. Removing yellow-edged sheets from the linen closet, he made up the brass bed in the guest room, removed the plastic covers from all chairs and tables and sofas and folded them into neat squares.

He then went from room to room in the huge old house, standing in each and acquainting himself with their new reality—devoid of Waltiri or Golda. The house was his responsibility now, his place to live for the time being, if not yet his home.

Michael had spent most of his life in one house. Getting accustomed to a different one, he realized, would take time. There would be new quirks to learn, new layouts to become used to. He would have to re-create the house in his head and cut new templates to determine his day-to-day paths.

In the kitchen, he plugged in the refrigerator, removed a box of baking soda from the interior, and unchocked the double doors to let them swing shut. The pantry—a walk-in affair, shelved floor to ceiling and illuminated by a bare bulb hanging from a thick black cord—had been stocked full of canned and dry goods, all usable except for a bloated can of pineapple that rocked to his touch. He threw it out and made up a list of the few items he would need to buy.

In the triple garage behind the house, a 1939 black Packard sat up on blocks next to a maze of metal shelves stacked high with file boxes. Michael walked around the beauty, fingering a moon of dust from its fender and observing the shine of the chrome. Enchanting, but not practical. Leaded premium gas (called ethyl in the Packard's heyday) was becoming difficult to find; besides, it would draw attention—something he wanted to avoid—and be incredibly expensive to maintain. He peered through the window and then opened the door and sat behind the wheel. The interior smelled new: leather and saddle-soap and that other, citrusy-metallic odor of a new car. The Packard might have been driven out of the showroom the day before. All it needed was air in the tires, and his father would help him remove the blocks, he was sure—just for a chance to touch the fine woodwork.

Michael saw a speck of ivory peeking from between the seat and seatback on the right—a folded piece of paper. He pulled it loose and read the cover.

Première Performance
THE INFINITY CONCERTO
Opus 45
by Arno Waltiri

8:00 P.M. November 23rd
The Pandall Theater
8538 Sunset Boulevard

Within the fold was a listing of all the players in the Greater Los Angeles Symphonia Orchestra. There were no other notes or explanations. After staring at the program for several minutes, Michael laid it back on the seat and took a deep breath.

Parked outside by the east wall of the garage, in a short cinderblock-walled alley, was a late-1970s-model Saab. Michael unlocked the door on the driver's side and sat in the gray velour bucket seat, resting his hands on the steering wheel.

Much more practical.

He had ridden Sidhe horses, *abana* from point to point in the Realm, and touched a myriad of ghostly between-worlds, and yet he still felt pride and pleasure at sitting in a car, knowing it would be his to drive whenever and wherever he pleased. He was still that much a child of his times. After a long search for the latch, he popped open the hood and peered at the unfamiliar engine. The battery cables had been unhooked. He reattached them to the posts. The tires did not need air. It was ready to drive.

Michael knew enough about fuel injection systems not to depress the gas pedal when starting the engine. The engine turned over with a throaty rumble on the first try. He smiled and twisted the wheel this way and that, then backed it carefully out of the alley, reversed it on the broad expanse of concrete before the garage and drove to the supermarket.

That evening, he inspected the living-room fireplace and chimney and brought wood in from where it had been stacked beside the Packard. In a few minutes, a lusty blaze brightened the living room and shone within the black lacquer of the grand piano. Michael sat in Waltiri's armchair and sipped a glass of Golda's Amontillado, his mind almost blank, almost contented.

He was not the same boy he had been when he entered Sidhedark through the house of David Clarkham. He doubted he was a boy at all.

The Crane Women had trained him well; he didn't doubt that. He had survived the worst Sidhedark had to offer—monstrous remnants of Tonn's early creation; the ignorant and frustrated cruelty of the Wickmaster Alyons; Tarax and Clarkham himself. But what had he been trained for? Merely to act as a bomb delivering destruction to the Isomage, as Clarkham had called himself? Or for some other purpose besides?

The flames danced with wicked cheer in the broad fireplace, and the embers glowed like holes opening onto a beautiful and deadly world of pure heat and light.

He drowsed, grateful that no new visions bothered him.

At midnight, the rewound grandfather clock in the foyer chimed and awoke him. The fire had died to fitful coals. He climbed up to the guest room, now his bedroom, and sank into the cool, soft mattress.

Even in deep sleep, part of him seemed aware of everything.

One, the clock announced in its somber voice.

Two. (The house creaking.)

Three. (A light rain began and ended within minutes.)

Four. (Night birds . . .)

Five. (Almost absolute stillness.)

At six, the clock's tone coincided with the sound of a newspaper hitting the front door. Michael's eyes opened slowly. He was not in the least groggy. There had been no dreams.

In his robe, he went downstairs to retrieve the paper, wrapped in plastic against the wet. A man sang softly and randomly in the side yard of the house on the left. Michael smiled, listening to the lyrics.

"Don't cry for me, ArgenTEEEENA . . ." The man walked around the corner and saw Michael. "Good morning!" he called out, shaking his head sheepishly and waving. He was in his early forties, portly, with abundant light-brown hair and a face indelibly stamped with friendliness. "Didn't disturb you, I hope." He wore a navy blue jogging suit with bright red stripes down the sleeves and legs.

"No," Michael said. "Getting the paper."

"Just going to do some running. You knew Arno and Golda?"

"I'm taking care of the house for them," Michael said.

"You sound like maybe they're coming back," the man said, pursing his mouth.

Michael smiled. "Arno appointed me. I'm going to organize the papers . . ."

"Now *that's* a job." The man had walked in Michael's direction, and they now stood a yard apart. He extended his hand, and Michael shook it. "I'm Robert Dopso. Next door. Arno and Golda were fine neighbors. My mother and I miss them terribly. I was married, but . . ." He shrugged. "Divorced, and I moved back here. Momma's boy, I know. But Mom was very lonely. I grew up here; my father bought the house in 1940. Golda and Mom used to talk a lot. My life in a nutshell." He grinned. "Your name?"

Michael told him and mentioned he had just moved in the day before.

"I'm not bad in the fix-it department," Dopso said. "I helped Golda with odds and ends after Arno died. I might know a few tricks about the place . . . If you need any help, don't hesitate to ask. My wife kept me around a year longer because without me, she said, everything stayed broken."

"I'll ask," Michael said.

"Maybe we could walk or run together—whichever. I prefer running, but . . ."

Michael nodded, and Dopso headed down the street. "You were supposed to BEEE IMMORTal . . ."

Michael carried the paper into the kitchen. There, he ate a bowl of hot oatmeal and leafed through the front section. Most of the news—however important and ominous it might seem to his fellows—barely attracted his attention.

Then he came to a small third-page story headlined

CORPSES FOUND IN ABANDONED BUILDING

and his eyes grew wide as he read:

> The unidentified bodies of two females were found by a transient male in the abandoned Tippett Residential Hotel on Sunset Boulevard near La Cienega Sunday afternoon. Cause of death has not been established by the coroner's office. Reporters' questions went largely unanswered during a short press briefing. Early reports indicate that one of the women weighed at least eight hundred pounds and was found nude. The second body was in a mummified condition and was clothed in a party dress of a style long since out of fashion. The Tippett Hotel, abandoned since 1968, once offered a posh Hollywood address for retired and elderly actors, actresses and other film workers.

He read the piece through several times before folding the paper and putting it aside. His oatmeal cooled in its bowl, half-finished.

The bodies might be a coincidence, he thought. As rare as eight-hundred-pound women were . . .

But in conjunction with a mummy, clothed in a party dress?

He called up the paper's city desk and asked to speak to the reporter who had written the piece, which had run without a byline. The reporter was out on assignment, he was told, and the operator referred him to a police phone number. Michael paced the kitchen and adjacent hall for several minutes before deciding against phoning the police. How would he explain?

He had to have a look at that building. Something nagged him about the address. Sunset and La Cienega . . . Barely five miles from Waltiri's house.

He went to the Packard and retrieved the concert program, then checked the glove box in the Saab to find a city map. He took both to Waltiri's first-floor office, dark and musty and lined with shelves of records and tapes, and tried to locate 8538 Sunset Boulevard, the site of the Pandall Theater according to the concert program.

The address was less than half a block from the corner of Sunset and La Cienega.

2

Michael walked briskly up La Cienega's slope as it approached Sunset, breathing steadily and deeply, taking pleasure in the cool night air and the darkness. He could be anonymous, alone without all the handicaps of loneliness; he could be almost anything—a dangerous prowler or a good Samaritan. The night covered all, even motives. To his left, the white wall of a hotel was painted with Mondrian stripes and squares. At the corner, he stood for a moment, looking across the street at the blocky, ugly Hyatt on Sunset, then turned right. His running shoes made almost no sound on the concrete sidewalk.

He passed the entrance of a restaurant built on the site where Errol Flynn's guest house had once stood, then spotted the Tippett building. It would have been hard to miss, anywhere.

It rose more than twelve stories above Sunset, an aging Art Deco concrete edifice with rounded corners. Many of the windows had been knocked out, and black soot ghosted up from several of the gaping frames. A trash tube descended from the roof to a dumpster behind the fence. At ground level, a chain-link fence surrounded the building. The lobby entrance had been blocked by a chain-link and steel-pipe gate.

The building made Michael uneasy. It had once been lovely. It stood out in this section of the Sunset Strip even now, in its present dilapidated condition. Yet it had been abandoned for over twenty years and, judging by the state of renovations, might continue that way for another twenty.

He stood before the gate and squinted to see the obscured address, limned in aluminum figures above the plywood-boarded doors: 8538. The 8 had been knocked askew and hung on its side.

The Tippett building stood on the site of the Pandall Theater. Having confirmed that much, Michael looked around guiltily and glanced over his shoulder at the lighted windows of the Hyatt. Nobody watching.

A hole in the fencing to the left of the gate had been patched with chicken-wire; with very little effort, he could undo the patch and crawl through.

"Odd place, isn't it?"

Michael turned his head quickly. A bearded, sunburned man with thick greasy hair and dirt-green, street-varnished clothes was standing on the sidewalk a dozen yards away.

"Yes," he answered softly.

"It's older than it looks. Seems kind of modern, don't it?"

"I guess," Michael said.

"Used to live there," the man said. "Don't live there now. Want to go in?" The man walked slowly toward him, face conveying intense interest and almost equal caution.

"No," Michael said.

"You know the place?"

"I'm just out hiking."

"Care to know about it?"

Michael didn't answer.

"Care to know about the two women found dead in there?"

"Women?"

"One big, a real whale, one a mummy. In the newspapers. You read the newspapers?"

Michael paused to reflect, then nodded.

"Thought you might have."

"Did you find them?"

"Heavens," the man said, coughing into his fist. "Not me. Someone who didn't know much. An *acquaintance*. Dumb to stay in the *hotel* for a night." He wrinkled his face, expecting skepticism, and added, "It's full."

"Why do you hang around?" Michael asked.

"Because," the man said. He stood about two yards from Michael. Even at that distance he smelled rankly of urine and sedimented sweat. "You know their names?"

"Whose names?" Michael asked.

"The whale and the mummy."

"No," Michael said.

"I do. My *acquaintance* found it on a piece of rock next to them. Gave it to the police, but they didn't care. Didn't mean anything to them. Do you know French?"

"A little."

"Then you'd know what one of the names means. Sadness. In French. And the other . . ."

Michael decided to try for an effect. "Lamia," he said.

The man's face became a mask caught between surprise and laughter. "Gawd," he said. "Gawd, gawd. You're a reporter. I knew it. Odd time of night to be out looking for facts."

Michael shook his head, never taking his eyes off the man. He had not yet tried to read someone's aura on Earth. Now seemed as good a time as any. He found a festival of murmurs, a bright little coal of intelligence, a marketplace full of rotted vegetables. He backed out with only one fact: *Tristesse*. The second name. It suited the guardian of Clarkham's gate. Bringer of sadness.

Lamia and Tristesse. Sisters . . .

Victims of the Sidhe, sacrificed by Clarkham to guard and wait . . . But how could they have found their way to Earth? And who had killed them—or *inactivated* them, since what life they had was dubious at best?

Abruptly and unexpectedly, Michael began to cry. Wiping his eyes, he glanced up at the Tippett building.

"Something wrong? I'm the one should be crying," the man said. "You're not a reporter. Relative, maybe? Jesus, no. None of them would have had relatives."

"What do you care?" Michael asked sharply. "Go away."

"Care?" the man shrilled, backing off a step. "I used to own the place. *Own it*, god damn it! I used to be worth something! I'm not that goddamn old, and I'm not so far gone I don't remember what it was like, having money and being a—" he lifted a hand with pinky extended, raised his eyebrows and waggled his head—"a big goddamn citizen!"

Michael probed the man again and felt the sorrow and anger directly.

"Now everybody comes around here. Goddamn bank never does anything with it, never tears it down, never sells it. Can't sell it. Now there's people died here. Not surprising. I'm going, all right. I've had my fill."

"Wait," Michael said. "When was it built?"

"Nineteen and forty-seven," the man answered, his back to Michael, departing with exaggerated dignity. "Used to be a theater here. A concert hall. Tore it down and put this up."

"Thank you," Michael said.

The man shrugged and waved away the thanks.

Michael put his hands in his coat pockets and leaned his head back to look at the building again. High up near the top, one floor beneath a terrace, a faint red light played over a dusty pane of glass. It burned only for a moment.

Then, on the fourth floor, the red light gleamed briefly again in a broken and soot-stained window. All was still after that and quiet.

Michael shuddered and began the trek back down Sunset to La Cienega.

3

Magic like that worked by the Sidhe was more difficult on Earth; humans could not work Sidhe magic. This much Michael had gleaned from his training in the Realm, Sidhedark. But were these facts or merely suppositions? Breeds—part human and part Sidhe—could work magic; the Crane Women and Eleuth had demonstrated that much. Clarkham, a Breed born on Earth, had nearly bested the Sidhe at their own game.

Michael himself had done things in the Realm that had no other name in his vocabulary but magic. He had channeled the energies of a song of power to destroy Clarkham. And in the year since he had returned to Earth, he had learned that he could still apply Sidhe discipline and invoke *hyloka*, the calling-of-heat from the center of his body, and in-seeing, the probing of another's aura to gain information.

For the time being, he was content not to test the other skills he had learned in the Realm. He had not used *evisa*, or out-seeing, to throw a shadow; there had been no need.

Each morning, he went through his exercises in the spacious back yard. He jogged around the neighborhood holding his *kima*, the running-stick, before him, as the Crane Women had taught him. Several times he jogged with Dopso, who kept up a panting stream of questions and observations. Despite the man's obvious curiosity about Michael, and nonstop talk, Michael liked him. He seemed decent.

Each day, Michael investigated another cache of Waltiri's papers and began to make a catalog of what he found. Within a week, he had worked his way through the garage and knew what lay in each file box—manuscripts, contracts and other legal documents, and correspondence, including an inlaid wooden trunk filled with love letters from Waltiri to Golda, written in German. Even though he had studied German after returning from the Realm, he was hardly fluent, and that handicapped him. He thought about hiring a German-speaking student and acquiring the language more rapidly through in-seeing but decided to put that off for now.

He concentrated on the manuscripts. What little musical training he had acquired before he was thirteen—when he had put his foot down and refused to continue piano lessons—was of little aid in sorting out the Waltiri papers.

Michael recorded the names (if any), opus numbers, and known associations of each musical manuscript. Most were scores for motion pictures; scattered throughout the four and a half decades' worth of work, however, were more personal pieces, even a draft of a ballet based on *The Faerie Queene.*

He spent hours in the garage and then began moving the sorted boxes of manuscripts into the dining room, where he stacked them along a bare wall.

Still no sign of a manuscript for Opus 45, the Infinity Concerto.

At night, Michael fixed himself supper and ate alone. One night a week he joined his parents for dinner, and the visits were enjoyable; occasionally, John would drop by the Waltiri house on one pretext or another, and they would share a beer in the back yard and talk about inconsequential things. Ruth never visited.

Michael did not tell his story to John, even with Ruth away. John seemed to sense that the time was not yet right for Ruth and that they should hear together when the time was right.

All in all, with the exception of the discoveries in the Tippett Hotel, it was still a peaceful time. Michael felt himself growing stronger in more ways than one: stronger inside, less agonized by his mistakes, and stronger in dealing with the ways of the Earth, which were not much like the ways of the Realm.

What impressed him most of all, now that he had gone *outside* and had a basis for comparison, was the Earth's sense of solidity and *thoroughness.* Always in the Realm there had been the sensation of things left not quite finished; Adonna's creation was no doubt masterful, and in places extremely beautiful, but it could not compare with the Earth.

While the Realm had been built to accommodate Sidhe—and keep them in line—and while it contained some monstrous travesties, it had seemed in many ways a gentler place than Earth. What cruelty existed in the Realm was the fault of its occupants. Given Sidhe discipline, Michael had found survival in the Realm proper (as opposed to the Blasted Plain) rather easy. He doubted if survival would be quite so easy in similar situations on Earth.

The Earth seemed not to have been built for anybody's convenience; those who had come to it, or developed on it, made their own way and found and fought for specific niches. The Earth never stopped its pressures . . . nor gave up its treasures easily.

Michael acquired a videocassette recorder out of the stipend paid by the estate and began renting tapes of the movies Waltiri had scored. Watching the old films and listening to the background music, he came to appreciate the old composer's true skill.

Waltiri's music was never obtrusive in a film. Rather than sweeping richly forth with some outstanding melodic line, it played a subservient role, underscoring or heightening the action on the screen.

Again and again one day Michael played John Huston's 1958 film, *The Man Who Would Be King,* reveling the first time in Bogart's Peachey Carnehan and Jack Hawkins's Daniel Dravot, the next in the fine black-and-white photography and the beautifully integrated matte paintings, and finally in Waltiri's subtle score, not in the least period or archaic but somehow just right for the men and their adventure. Michael enjoyed himself hugely; that one day seemed to put everything in perspective and set his mind right. Suddenly he was ready to take on whatever might come, with the same impractical bravado of Carnehan and Dravot. He spent the next day gardening, whistling Carnehan's theme, pulling weeds and trimming back the rose bushes according to the instructions in an old gardening book in Golda's library.

As he trimmed, he thought of Clarkham's Sidhe woman, Mora, and how she had trimmed her roses; and of the rose turned to glass that she had given him, which still lay wrapped in cotton in a cardboard box in the guest bedroom.

His mood darkened the next morning, when again the newspaper proved to be a bearer of disturbing news. An in-depth article began on the left side of the front page and threaded through section A for some two thousand words, describing waves of so-called hauntings in England, Israel and the eastern United States.

The phrase "intrusions into reality" occurred several times in the piece, but overall the tone was light. The reporter concluded that the incidents had more to do with sociology and psychology than metaphysics. He read it through twice, then folded the paper and stared out the kitchen window at the pink roses outside.

The phone rang. Michael glanced at his new watch—it was ten o'clock—and picked up the ancient black receiver. "Waltiri residence. Hello."

"Could I speak to Michael Perrin?" a woman asked, her voice crisp and resonant.

"Speaking," Michael said.

"Hello. My name is Kristine Pendeers. I'm with the music department at UCLA."

"How may I help you, Ms. Pendeers?" Michael said, assuming his best (and unpracticed) professional tone.

"You're organizing the Waltiri estate, aren't you? I've been talking with the lawyers, and they say you're in charge now."

"That's the way it's worked out."

"We have a project here, rediscovering avant-garde music of the thirties and forties. We're interested in locating specific works by Arno Waltiri. Perhaps you've heard of them, or come across them . . . though I gather you haven't been working on the papers very long."

"Which papers?" Michael asked, though he hardly needed to; events were heading in a clearly defined direction: the dreams, the Tippett Hotel, the bodies of Lamia and Tristesse, the hauntings . . . and now this.

"You know, we haven't been able to find a single recording of the piece we're really interested in, and our collection is extensive. And no scores, either. Just these fascinating mentions in memoirs and newspapers, and in this book, *Devil's Music*. That's by Charles Fort. Have you heard of it?"

"You're looking for Opus 45," Michael said.

"Yes! That's the one."

"I haven't found it."

"Is it real? I mean, it exists? We were beginning to think it was some sort of hoax."

"I have a concert program for the premiere," Michael said. "The music existed at one time. Whether it does now or not, I don't know."

"Listen, it's wonderful just having something about it confirmed. Do you know what a coup it would be to find it again?"

"If I find the score, what do you plan to do with it?"

"I hardly know yet," Pendeers said. "I didn't expect to get this far. I'm a connoisseur of film music, particularly from the thirties and forties. I must tell you that doesn't sit well with some of the music faculty here—in Los Angeles, of all places! Can we get together and talk? And if you find anything—you know, the score, a recording, anything—could you let me know . . . first? Unless someone else has priority, of course . . . I hope not."

"No one else has priority," Michael said. "Where shall we meet?"

"I could hardly ask to visit the house. I assume it's not all organized yet."

Michael made a quick decision. "Frankly, I'm over my head," he said. "I could use help. Why don't I meet you near the campus, and we'll talk about having UCLA lend a hand?"

"Wonderful," she said, and they set a time and place for lunch in Westwood the next day.

Over my head, indeed, Michael thought as he hung up.

KRISTINE PENDEERS WAS twenty-two, tall and slender with a dancer's build, and fine fair hair. Her eyes were green and eloquent, slightly hooded, one eyelid riding higher than the other as if in query. Her lower lip was full, her upper delicate; she seemed to be half-smiling most of the time. She wore jeans and a mauve silk blouse.

After less than fifteen minutes in her presence, Michael was already fascinated by her. His infatuations always came fast and died hard—the true sign of an immature romantic, he warned himself silently. But warnings seldom did any good.

They had chosen the Good Earth restaurant. She sat across from him in a double booth. A broad back-lit plastic transparency of a maple tree canopy hovered over them; since they were below street level, the effect was not convincing. Kristine had crossed her arms on the table, as if protecting the cup of coffee between them.

"My major problem is that I don't know much about music," Michael said. "I enjoy it, but I don't play any instruments."

She seemed surprised. "How did you get the position, then?"

"I knew him before he died. We became friends."

"What did he plan to have you do with the estate?" Her half-hooded eyes gave her the appearance of being nonchalant and interested at once.

"To get it organized and take care of things as they came up, I suppose," Michael said. "It's not really spelled out. We had a sort of understanding . . ."

Having said that, he wasn't sure how true it was. But he couldn't say, *I'm being set up for something bigger . . .*

"Did he ever talk to you about Opus 45?"

The waitress interrupted with their lunch, and they leaned back to let her serve it.

"Yes," Michael said. He gave her a brief outline as they ate, explaining about Waltiri's collaboration with Clarkham—to a point—and the circumstances after the performance.

"That's fascinating," she said. "Now I see why the music is legendary. Do you think the score still exists? I mean, would he have . . . burned it, or hidden it away where no one would find it?"

Michael shook his head, chewing on a bite of fish. "I'll keep looking," he said.

"You know, this project I'm working on . . . it really goes beyond what I told you on the phone." She hadn't eaten much of her omelet. She seemed more inclined to talk than lunch. "We're—actually, it's mostly me. I'm trying to put film-score composers back in their proper place in music. Many of them were as talented as anyone writing music today . . . more so, I think. But their so-called limitations, working in a popular medium, for mass audiences . . ." She shook her head slowly. "Music people are snobs. Not musicians—necessarily—but critics. I love movie scores. They don't seem to think—the critics and some of the academics, I mean—they don't seem to understand that music for movies, and not just musicals, shares some of the problems of scoring operas. I mean, it's such an inspired idea, full scoring for a dramatic performance." She grinned. "I'll ride that particular railroad any time you let me."

Michael nodded. "I love movie scores, too," he said.

"Of course you do. Why would Waltiri let you handle his estate if you didn't? You're probably a better choice than most of the people in my department." She held up her hands, exasperated. "Look at this. I'm wasting food again. All talking and no eating."

"All singing, all dancing," Michael said with a smile.

She stared at him intently. "You have a very odd smile. As if you know something. Do you mind if I ask how old you are?"

He glanced down at the table. "That depends."

"I'm intruding."

"No, it's not that," he said. "It's actually complicated . . ."

"Your age is complicated?"

"I'm twenty-two," he said.

"You look younger than that. But older, too."

A silence hung over the table for several seconds.

"Have you gone to school?" Kristine asked.

"Not college, no."

She laughed and reached across the table to tap his hand with her finger. "You're perfect," she said. "Everyone says Waltiri was an iconoclast. You're living proof."

"You've talked to people who knew him?"

"It's part of the project. I know a composer named Edgar Moffat. He orchestrated Waltiri's movie scores and acted as his assistant in the fifties. He's in Burbank now working on the score for a David Lean film. You'll have to meet him. I've interviewed him several times in the last few months. He was the one who told me about the Waltiri estate. He didn't know your name, but he had heard rumors."

"Did he say anything about David Clarkham?" Michael asked.

"That was all before his time, I think. He's only fifty-three."

"Why are you studying music?"

"I'm a composer," she said. "I've been writing music since I was a teenager. And you?"

Michael smiled. "I'm a poet," he said. "I've been writing poetry since . . . for a long time."

Kristine's expression became faintly jaded. "Anything published?"

He shook his head. "I haven't even been writing much lately. Lots of things to think about, lots of work to do."

"Poetry and music," she said thoughtfully. "They're not supposed to be that far apart. Do you think they are?"

How could he answer without making her think he was either pretentious or crazy? What he had learned in the Realm—that all arts were intimately related, that beneath each form lay a foundation that could be directed and shaped to yield a song of power—was not something a student of music at UCLA was likely to understand. "They're very close," he said.

"I've never been word-oriented," Kristine said. "It was a struggle just to get through English classes and learn how to write a clear sentence."

"I don't know much about music," Michael said. "Two sides of a coin." That, he thought, might be a bit presumptuous.

Kristine watched him intently, brow slightly furrowed. "I think the music department has a place for Waltiri's papers," she said. "If the estate agrees, we help you get them organized. Preserve them. Archival folders and boxes, deacidify the papers . . . Maybe that would speed up finding the manuscript."

Such a move could also leave him without a job, or feather-bedding on the estate payroll after he was no longer needed. "I'll consider it," he said. Was that what Waltiri would have wanted?

Kristine pushed her plate away decisively and attracted the waitress's attention with a raised hand, then asked for the check.

"My treat," she said. Michael did not protest.

"When can we talk again?" she asked. "You can meet with Moffat at Paramount . . . Tour the library, the music department. The department head could explain how we take care of collections . . ."

"I make my own schedule," Michael said. "Anytime."

She put down a generous tip and stood with check in hand. He accompanied her to the cash register and then outside. She said, with a hint of regret, that she had to return to the campus. Michael's car was in the opposite direction. For a moment, he contemplated walking with her anyway but decided not to be too demonstrative.

"It was a pleasure having lunch with you," Michael said. She cocked her head to one side and squinted at him.

"You are really very strange, you know," she said. "Something about you . . ." She shrugged. "Never mind. Give me a call if you find anything. Or just want to talk music, poetry, whatever."

She walked off toward the campus, and Michael strolled toward his car. On a hunch, he stopped off in Vogue Records and asked a dark-haired, slender male clerk with a prominent hooked nose if there were any recordings available of music by Arno Waltiri.

"Just the RCA collection," the clerk answered, eyes languid. "You have that already, don't you? Charles Gerhardt conducting?"

Michael said he didn't. The clerk emerged from behind the front counter and took him to the extensive movie soundtracks section and found the compact disk for him. Michael scanned the contents: selections from *Ashenden, The Man Who Would Be King, Warbirds of Mindanao* and *Call It Sleep.*

"Have you ever heard of a recording of the Infinity Concerto?" he asked.

"We can look it up in Schwann, but no, I haven't heard of it."

A search through the thick paperback Schwann catalog revealed that the RCA collection was the only Waltiri album currently available. Michael thanked the clerk and purchased it.

On the way home, he stopped at a stationery store and bought a blank book. He felt it was time to start working on his poetry again, if only to build up his self-confidence and put some conviction in his voice the next time he confessed what he was.

In the car, he removed the plastic wrapping from the book, wrote his name on the flyleaf, and then shuffled through the pages, as he always did when starting a notebook.

In the middle of the book, centered on an otherwise unmarked page, were the carefully typeset words:

Give it up. Finding it won't do anybody any good.

His hairs bristled. Michael felt the message's raised ink with one finger and then slowly closed the book.

4

Michael's father came to the house the next day, a Saturday, ostensibly to finish looking over the woodwork and foundations and make sure everything was in order. He arrived at two in the afternoon. Michael followed him as he made a circuit of the outside of the house, peering into the crawl space vents.

"Your mother's worried about you," John said, using a small ball-peen hammer to sound out the wood immediately within a vent opening. He crawled halfway into the vent, his voice echoing. "She thinks this job might not be all that healthy for you."

"I'm fine," Michael said.

John emerged and pulled cobwebs from his hair. "Seems sound enough on a cursory look. Well, I'm worried about you, too. I haven't the slightest idea where you were those five years, but I'm wondering how much you grew up during that time. What you experienced."

"A fair amount," Michael said. His father regarded him steadily and got to his feet.

"It's funny, the way your mother won't talk. And I suppose I'm funny, not wanting to hear unless she listens, too. She hasn't even hinted that she's curious . . . to you, I mean?"

Michael shook his head.

"Wasn't something like William Burroughs, was it?"

"Nothing to do with dope."

His father's face reddened at Michael's light tone. "Dammit, don't patronize . . . me or anybody."

Michael shook his head. "I don't think you'd believe me."

"I'm not a dullard. I have known lifestyles other than this." He waved his hand around the neighborhood. "Hell, I've even tried dope."

Michael looked down at the grass.

"Something you're ashamed of? Something . . . sexual?"

"Jesus," Michael said, shaking his head and chuckling. "I did *not* run off to

San Francisco and . . . whatever. You can reassure Mom about that." He hated the edge of whine that entered his voice just then.

"We didn't think you had. Believe it or not, we know you pretty well. Not so well you can't surprise us, but well enough to believe you didn't do anything self-destructive. We just think it might not be good for you to stay cooped up in this house all day, going through old papers."

"I've been getting out." He told John about the request from UCLA and pointedly mentioned Kristine. "I also take long walks."

Michael led him through the back porch into the house. John inspected the water heater.

"Looks like the tank's okay, but I'd like to drain it and remove the sediment, see if it's going to rust out soon." John paused and rapped his knuckle on the paneling covering a broad bare space between the heater cabinet and the pantry door.

So what could Michael ultimately tell his father—that he didn't think normal life was going to prevail, that something indefinitely momentous approached this world?

"Any problems elsewhere?"

"I don't think so," Michael said. "I can call in maintenance people if I have to."

"Come on, give your old Dad a chance to feel needed. Is there any better carpenter in Southern California?"

"No," Michael said, grinning.

The door chimes rang. Michael loped to the front door and opened it to find Robert Dopso shifting restlessly from leg to leg on the porch. "Hi," Dopso said, stretching out his hand. "I saw you checking out the foundations. Thought I'd see if you needed some extra kibitzing."

Michael grinned. Three would make the conversation less awkward. "Sure. My father's here. We're looking at the service porch now. Come on in."

"Saturday boredom, you know," Dopso said. "Bachelor's lament."

Michael introduced them. "Robert grew up here," he told his father. "He and his mother knew Arno and Golda well."

"Speaking of Mom, she's invited you over for dinner tonight," Dopso said. "Another reason I came over."

John was still inspecting the wall. "Is there a closet or something on the other side?" he asked. The rap of his knuckles on the paneling made a hollow echo.

"No," Michael said.

"Odd to find an unused space this big." John looked down at the floor and kneeled. His finger followed a thin arc-shaped scrape in the linoleum just beyond the edge of the paneling. "Used to be a door here. I don't think Arno needed to hide skeletons . . . do you?"

Michael frowned and shook his head. Dopso bent down and ran his own finger over the join.

"I don't remember any closet here."

"Still, there was a closet or something, and now it's sealed up." There was a twinkle in John's eye. He winked at Dopso. "Would Arno take it amiss if we investigated someday, when you have time? Probably find nothing but spider webs . . ."

"Probably," Michael said. He didn't want his father or Dopso involved, somehow. The discovery was both exciting and unnerving.

"Come on," John said, walking into the kitchen. "Where's your sense of adventure? An old house, a mysterious space . . . Maybe Arno hid his treasure in there."

"Maybe," Michael said.

"That'd be interesting," Dopso said. "Something to look forward to in a dull neighborhood. Not that it's always been so dull." His glance at Michael seemed to be an attempt to convey some silent message. Michael hadn't the slightest idea what Dopso was hinting at.

After a few more spot checks, they stood in the foyer. John firmly invited him to dinner the next evening. "Let your mother lay out a feast for us. It's in her nature to worry, Michael."

"I know," Michael said, still uneasy. "Dinner tonight at Robert's, and tomorrow night with you and Mom. No lack of hospitality."

"Good. Six o'clock? And let me know when you want to pry loose some paneling."

After Dopso and his father had left, Michael returned to the service porch. He tapped the paneling, idly wondering whether he should feel for secret levers or buttons. It seemed to be nailed tight.

He found a flashlight and went outside to peer into the crawl space again. Prying out the vent his father had replaced, he shined the light under the house and followed the contours of beams, braces, wiring and pipes. The light fell against a dark gray wall of concrete approximately under the service porch.

A basement.

Wiping his hands on his pants legs, Michael went to the garage and searched through a chest of tools. He found a pry bar and a claw hammer and carried them through the back door, setting them on the floor of the service porch.

When had the basement been sealed? He didn't remember any doorway when he had been a frequent visitor to the Waltiri house, almost six years ago, Earth time.

But he hadn't been in the service porch often, either.

Could the door have been sealed during the five years he was away, after Golda's death? Or had Waltiri sealed it himself?

Here was his chance, he thought. He knew there was something unusual in the basement. When a man—or a mage—like Waltiri sealed a doorway off, there had to be good reason. At any rate, Michael could have his father witness the opening, see whatever there was to see, and perhaps then be prepared for the entire story . . .

But if the basement held something dangerous, then Michael did not want his father present. John could not throw a shadow or use any other tricks to escape.

He ran his hand over the panel again, feeling it carefully not for secret latches but to gather some sensation, a clue. He concentrated on what lay behind, closing his eyes and pressing his palm flat against the wood.

Nothing.

But then, the Crane Women had not gifted him with the boon of prescience or second sight. No guiding voices gave him clues, ambiguous or otherwise.

Taking pry bar in hand, he removed the trim from the panel edge, cringing at the squeak of nails pulled from wood. With the strips removed, he inserted the bar in the gap between panel and wall frame and shoved.

The panel held; he succeeded only in bruising his palms. He tried again, with no better result, and moved the bar to another vantage.

After several minutes of fruitless effort, he noticed that the panel wobbled in its seat and that the nails holding it fast had poked their heads a fraction of an inch above the surface. With the claw hammer, he removed one of the upper corner nails and put the bar there, shoving against it with all his might. For this he was rewarded with a groan of wood and a half-inch of give, as well as several more nail heads ready for the claw.

In ten minutes, he had loosened the panel sufficiently to grip it with both hands. He pulled it suddenly free and fell back against the washing machine. Propping the heavy three-quarter-inch plywood panel in the kitchen doorway, he surveyed what was revealed: a door, pristine white, like virtually every other interior door in the house, with a brass knob instead of crystal and a perfectly innocent air.

There was a lock beneath the knob, and in the lock, a key.

Michael reached out and twisted the key and then the knob, and the door opened smoothly inward, revealing darkness. Dry, stale air wafted out, tangy with dust. A sweet, flowery fragrance, somehow familiar, overlaid an odor richer and less easily described. He pocketed the key.

On the right wall he found a black push-button switch. He pushed the top button, and at the base of a steep flight of stairs, a bare, clear bulb cast a dour yellow glow.

Michael walked down the first flight, turned the corner, and peered into the half-lit gloom below. At the end of a second flight of steps, at a right angle to the first, lay a cubicle barely four yards on a side, with a low roof. The cubicle was filled with boxes, some of them covered by a dark fabric tarp. To his right, cramped close to the steps, sat a large black armoire. Michael wondered how such a bulky piece of furniture could have been brought into the basement.

He descended the four final steps, his shadow falling huge across the boxes. The light hung in such a position that he could see almost nothing in front of him; his shadow obscured anything he approached.

He turned toward the armoire and opened one door. The interior, barely visible, was filled with small boxes stuffed with papers. He pulled out a drawer and found more papers: envelopes, packets tied with string, a small wooden cigar box stuffed full with what appeared to be letters. A small wine rack with three dusty bottles had been jammed in the lower corner.

Michael swore under his breath and ascended the stairs to get a flashlight. Returning, he played the beam over the contents of the armoire, seeing that most of the papers were letters, and most of the letters were in German. Curious, he removed a bottle from the rack and read the label, with some difficulty deciphering the *fraktur* lettering:

Doppelsonnenuhr
Feinste Geistenbeerenauslese
1921

The label carried a sundial, the gnomon casting two shadows. Beneath the lettering was a rose and a cluster of red grapes. He replaced the bottle carefully.

On an upper shelf above the drawers, he spotted a black loose-leaf notebook, its spine rippled. The heavy sweet odor . . .

(And he remembered what that fragrance reminded him of—himself, whenever he had touched water in the Realm—the odor of the bearer of a song of power.)

. . . intensified as he opened the notebook. The paper within seemed to squirm under the flashlight beam, shimmering like a film of oil on water, the writing surrounded by warped dimples of oily red, purple and green.

It was a music manuscript. Holding his finger under the title on the first page, he was able to still the play of light enough to read:

> *Das Unendlichkeit Konzert*
> *Opus 45*
> *von Arno Waltiri*

Each turned page exuded a stronger, more clearly defined perfume, until Michael could stand no more. The cubicle seemed to close down around him, oppressing him with the mixed smells of sweet rain, decaying flowers, dust, and endless abandonment. He closed the notebook and shook his head, snorting.

He doubted the notebook and the manuscript within had had these peculiar qualities when the music was first penned. Since that time, something had altered the very paper on which the concerto had been written.

He shuddered and replaced the manuscript, closing the armoire doors.

IN THE CLEAR April afternoon light in the back yard, Michael squatted on the grass and picked at a few blades, face crossed with intense thought.

Everything was laid out before him; he had only to choose what to investigate first. Which gate to take.

He did not have the luxury of not choosing.

5

obert invited Michael in and introduced his mother. Mrs. Dopso was in her mid-sixties, sandy hair frosted with gray, frame small and delicate. "I'm *so* glad we're finally getting a chance to meet!" she enthused, fluttering one hand as if shooing away moths. One of her blue eyes canted upward with perpetual concern, and a blissful smile lighted on her face frequently as she spoke.

They sat down to dinner within minutes of six o'clock. Shadows lay deep in the old house, which was much smaller than the Waltiri home. Robert explained that his mother's favorite hobby was saving electricity. She lighted candles in brass holders on the table, her expression grave as she applied match to wick, then grateful as the flame grew.

"I'd rather let others have the electricity, those who need it more," she said. "Improve our country's productivity, pump it into big factories."

"She's a bit hazy on how the power net operates," Robert explained.

"Perhaps, perhaps," Mrs. Dopso said lightly. "I'm just so pleased to have Michael as a guest. We have so much to talk about."

"Perhaps not all at once," Robert suggested.

"Have you ever heard such a son?" She hurried into the kitchen, hands twisting slowly back and forth at her sides, and returned with a bowl full of steamed vegetables. Next came a cheese and tuna casserole, followed by a plate heaped high with uniformly sliced bread of virginal whiteness. "It's not a feast," she said. "It's just *food,* but the talk is more important than the dinner."

"Mother knows you're the caretaker for the Waltiri estate." Robert scooped vegetables onto his plate. He handed the casserole to Michael, who took a generous portion. Thanks to his upbringing—and a few months of deprivation—he had nothing against plain food.

"If we start talking now, we won't finish eating until midnight, and it will all be cold," Mrs. Dopso said. "So we will ... um ... skirt around the main topic and just fill our tummies. Then we'll ... yes." She smiled and placed a modest forkful of casserole into her mouth as an example.

They exchanged only light pleasantries until the meal was finished. Michael felt slightly apprehensive. Mrs. Dopso and her son were being politely mysterious, and that bothered him; they behaved as if they were privy to knowledge that he might find useful.

Robert cleared the table and brought out a bottle of wine. Mrs. Dopso bit her lower lip as he lifted and cradled the bottle for Michael's inspection.

The label was similar to that on the bottle he had found in the newly opened cellar. The double-shadowed sundial, the rose and the red grapes, the *fraktur* lettering.

"This is our last bottle. We thought we would open it tonight," Robert said. "Mr. Waltiri gave it as a gift to my father almost fifty years ago. You might have heard of the gentleman who provided it to Mr. Waltiri."

Michael raised an eyebrow.

"His name was David Clarkham. He was a friend of Mr. Waltiri's, although I gather they had a falling out before I was born."

"Yes, dear, a year or two before you were born," Mrs. Dopso said.

"My father met Mr. Clarkham several times and was very impressed by him. Mr. Clarkham was a connoisseur of wine. He tended to talk about unusual vintages, German wines mostly. Many of them my father had never heard of, and he was himself quite a connoisseur."

"But all this," said Mrs. Dopso, "is neither here nor there."

"No. Father last drank one of these bottles fifteen years ago, and judged it quite good, if unusual."

"Do you remember what he said?" Mrs. Dopso asked.

"Yes. 'A bit otherworldly, with a most unusual finish.'"

They seemed to expect a reaction from Michael. "I found several bottles like that today," he said.

"Good! Then this isn't the last. Notice there's no clue as to what kind of wine it is. Red, obviously—but what variety of grapes?"

Michael shook his head.

"What we're leading up to is that we're curious about that house. We've lived next to it for a very long time."

"One morning, very early," Mrs. Dopso said, her face warmly radiant in the candlelight, "I got out of bed and looked over the cinder block wall. It was foggy, and I wasn't sure I saw things properly. My husband was on a business trip, so I called out to Robert—poor, sleepy child—to confirm or deny."

"I confirmed," Robert said. "I was eight."

"The house was absolutely *covered* with birds," Mrs. Dopso said breathlessly. "Large dark birds with red breasts and wing-tips. Blackbirds and robins the size of crows."

"She means, with the characteristics of blackbirds and robins, but crow-sized."

"And sparrows. And other birds I recognized. They blanketed the roof, and they lined up along the wall. All silent."

"Hitchcock, you know," Robert said with a grin. "Scared the daylights out of me."

"And when the fog lifted, they were gone. But that's not all. Sometimes we'd see Mr. Waltiri and Golda—dear Golda—leave the house in their car, the predecessor of the one you drive now—funny-looking thing—and after they had gone, when the house must have been empty—"

"We'd hear someone playing the piano," Robert said, equally breathless now, leaning forward.

"Playing it *beautifully*, just lovely music."

Robert uncorked the bottle and poured the wine into crystal glasses. Michael sipped the deep reddish-amber liquid. He had never tasted anything like it. It was totally outside his experience of wines, which admittedly was not broad. The mellow, complex finish lingered long moments after he swallowed, succession upon succession of flavors revealing themselves on his tongue. The flavors stopped suddenly, leaving only a clean blankness. He took another sip. Mrs. Dopso closed her eyes and did the same.

"As wonderful as I remember it," she commented. "To my dear husband." They toasted the man whose name Michael did not know.

"I think perhaps the only person who was not aware that something was going on," Mrs. Dopso said, "was Golda. Arno protected her *fiercely*. Nothing would happen to dear Golda while he was around. But you know . . . after he departed, *died*, I mean, things became too much for her. A strain. She must have had her suspicions over the years. How could one not?" Mrs. Dopso sipped again and smiled beatifically. "We did not *volunteer* to tell her, because while we knew something was *odd*, we couldn't be sure . . . Other than the birds."

"Now that you're living there," Robert said, "what do you think?"

Michael stared into his glass and swirled the liquid reflectively. "Pretty quiet now," he said.

"Do you play the piano?" Mrs. Dopso asked.

He shook his head.

"*Someone* does," she said dramatically. "We've heard it after you've driven away. And the music is not quite so lovely now. It's angry, I would say. Robert?"

"Heavy-handed, skilled but . . . pounding," Robert said. "I'm not sure I'd call it angry. Powerful perhaps."

Despite himself, Michael shivered, and his arm-hairs stood on end. "I haven't heard any music," he said, putting the glass down.

"It's *so* familiar to us," Mrs. Dopso said, "over all these years. We wondered if Mr. Waltiri—Arno—or perhaps even Golda—had a relative who stayed with them."

"An old hunchbacked cousin," Robert suggested with a sly grin.

"No," Michael said, smiling broadly. "I'm the only one living there."

"Bring out the tape recorder, Robert," Mrs. Dopso instructed. Robert left the dining room and returned with an old Ampex reel-to-reel deck, the tape already looped and ready to play. He set it on an unused dining chair near the wall outlet and plugged it in. Then he turned it on and stood back.

Michael heard a piano playing. The sound was fuzzy and distant, but the music was indeed powerful, pounding. There was no melody, as such.

"When did you record this?" Michael asked.

"Yesterday," Robert said.

Michael raised a bushy red eyebrow.

"We're very curious," Mrs. Dopso said. "It's something of a mystery, don't you agree?"

Michael nodded, the dinner suddenly heavy in his stomach. "I can't tell you what's happening. I just don't know."

"The house is haunted by a spirit that loves music," said Mrs. Dopso with a firm nod, her expression again beatific. "How very appropriate. For Arno's house, I mean." She leaned forward, staring at Michael as if confiding or extending a conspiracy. "I do not think you're in danger in that house, young man." She took a deep breath. "But if you should find out more, do let us know?"

She went to bed shortly thereafter. Robert explained, chuckling, that his mother "Rises with the birds. She thought you'd like to . . . hear. Goal-oriented, you know. Having accomplished her goal, she goes to bed. Pardon our intruding."

"No intrusion," Michael said. "Has anybody complained?"

"We aren't complaining; please don't think that. And no, nobody else has commented."

"If you hear it again, will you record it for me again?"

"Of course," Robert said. They shook hands at the door, but Robert escorted Michael to the sidewalk anyway. Dusk hung deep blue above the rustling black outlines of the neighborhood trees. "Thanks for speaking with my mother. She won't pester me so much now."

"My pleasure."

Michael returned to the Waltiri house. He stood by the silent grand piano, tapping the rich black surface of the lid. "Arno?" he asked softly, the name again raising the hairs on his neck and arms.

No answer.

He hadn't expected one. Not yet.

A SHAFT OF late afternoon sunlight warmed the hardwood floor beneath his feet. He sat in Waltiri's music library, the old black phone in his lap, surrounded by tapes and records and books, and dialed Kristine Pendeers' home number. A man answered on the third ring, his voice deep and indistinct. Michael asked to speak to Kristine. "Who's this?" the man asked.

"My name is Michael. She'll know me."

"She isn't here right now . . . Wait. She's at the door. Hold on." In the background, Michael heard Kristine and the man talking. There seemed to be a disagreement between them. The man's hand made squelching sounds on the mouthpiece. She finally came on the line, breathless.

"I've found what you're looking for," Michael said.

"I was just coming up the steps . . . to our house. Wait a minute. I'm winded. I heard the phone. Tommy got it before I . . . I could. You've found what . . . 45?"

"I just opened a sealed basement door and found it among other papers below the house." He realized he didn't sound particularly happy about the discovery. Why was he calling at all? Perhaps to talk with her again, meet with her. Using the discovery as an excuse.

"That's wonderful. It really is. When can I take a look at it?"

He gingerly ran his fingers over the discolored, shimmering manuscript on Waltiri's desk. "It's not in very good shape. We'll need to copy it. Maybe a copy machine will work, and maybe not."

"What's wrong with it?"

"You'll have to see it." *Dangerous, dangerous!* Simply staring at the manuscript was enough to bend a person's view of reality.

"Can you bring it here, or do I come over there?" She seemed to catch on that he was playing a game, and she didn't sound comfortable.

"I think you'd better come over here," Michael said. "Not tonight. I'll be busy. Tomorrow. In the morning, perhaps?"

"I'll have to be there early. About seven-thirty."

"Fine. I'll expect you."

"You sound strange, Michael."

"I have a lot to do between now and then. We'll talk tomorrow."

"Okay." There was an awkward moment of silence and then simultaneous good-byes. He replaced the receiver and returned the phone to its niche on a bookcase. Then he held the manuscript up to his nose and smelled it. The sweet fragrance this time smelled fainter, like dried fruit.

Any world is just a song of addings and takings away . . . *The difference between the Realm and your home, that's just the difference between one song and another* . . . So Eleuth had informed him in the Realm.

Was it possible, then, to create a song—a piece of music—that actively contradicted the song of a world and subtly altered the world?

He wished he knew how to play the piano and was better at reading music. It was possible he had actually heard some of the music contained in the manuscript, when Clarkham's house and the replica of Kubla Khan's pleasure dome had collapsed in the Realm, but he couldn't remember what it sounded like now. The tune was elusive and the orchestration had faded from memory

He slipped the manuscript into a manila envelope and placed it in Waltiri's safe. After memorizing the safe's combination, written in Golda's hand on a piece of masking tape attached to the door, he removed the tape, burned it in a metal cup on the desk, and shut the door. Why the precautions were important, he wasn't sure.

(Perhaps it wasn't Arno—in any form—playing the piano when the house was empty . . .)

He had a lot to do this evening. He would not be back until early the next morning.

AT DUSK, AS the moon-colored streetlights switched on and a breeze sighed through the green leaves on the maples, Michael stood before David Clarkham's house. The air felt brisk and alive, playful.

He had not come to this place since his return from the Realm. The house was in worse shape than when he had last seen it. The lawn had gone to seed, a definite contrast to the green, well-kept grounds on both sides. Unruly hedges thrust themselves over the driveway of parallel concrete strips, branches like arms reaching out for the cracked white stucco walls. A FOR SALE sign still leaned at an awkward angle on the front lawn; either the realtors handling the property were not pushing it or the buyers were not enthusiastic, or the sign was a sham. There was no phone number attached, and Michael had never heard of the firm before: Hamilton Realty.

He closed his eyes and found the region nestled between his thoughts that controlled *evisa* and casting a shadow. It was not difficult to find, and the act was as easy on Earth as it had been in the Realm.

He left an unmoving and slowly fading decoy of himself by the curb. Anybody watching would soon lose interest and turn away; and if they didn't turn away, then the image would smoothly disappear among the shadows of the trees, and they would be none the wiser.

Michael approached the front porch with pry bar in hand. Best to begin at the beginning.

In four minutes, he had the door open. The house radiated something unpleasant; more than just unkempt, it was distasteful, as if the part of the world it occupied had been ill-used and now brooded resentfully. Michael didn't like the sensation, and his dislike went beyond mere association with the last time he had entered Clarkham's house.

He switched on his flashlight and closed the door to a crack behind him. The hallway before the living room stretched before him, dusty and quiet; the living room itself, empty and drained and faintly melancholy. Square samples of the streetlight across the way illuminated the back wall.

Despite the unpleasant sensations, there was nothing magical or supernatural about the place. Michael could feel no hidden power or lurking residue. He walked down the hall and checked the ground floor rooms sequentially, shining his flashlight into each. Dusty floors; emptiness. He returned to the middle hallway and played the beam up the flight of stairs to the second floor. The carpeted stairsteps exuded thin puffs of dust at each footfall.

At the head of the stairs, a hallway led past the three second-floor rooms, ending at the bathroom door. Clarkham's house in the pleasure dome had been laid out in just such a fashion; no surprise. Michael peered into the first bedroom. Nothing. The second bedroom was broad and empty, its windows draped with sun-tattered expanses of old cloth slung over bent curtain rods. Cupboards and file drawers covered the far wall, reminding Michael of a morgue. The cupboards and file drawers contained more emptiness.

"Nothing here," he said in a soft whisper. He was not afraid, not even particularly wary, but he knew that the preternatural sensibilities instilled in him by the Crane Women had brought him here for a reason and not just to satisfy old curiosities.

A thin layer of dust dulled the dark wood of the floor in the final bedroom. He took two steps into the room and played the beam back and forth across the dust. Footprints interrupted the grayness in the middle of the floor. The prints led to the hallway and passed beneath his feet, where they had been erased by his own shuffling. He knelt and examined them more carefully. The dust around the footprints was undisturbed. Only one pair of feet—wearing moccasins or sandals, since the prints were unbroken by an arch—had made the prints, and the owner had moved without hesitation, beginning his journey (*his* because the feet were large and broad) in the middle of the room

Michael touched the nearest complete print. There was something odd about the amount of dust disturbed. He walked beside the prints, noticing that near the center of the room, where they began, they were quite clear. Toward the end of the trail they became less distinct, disturbing the dust only slightly, as if the person had weighed much less.

He pointed the beam at the air above the floor where the prints began and saw nothing unusual. Felt nothing unusual. The house was otherwise undisturbed and normal. The sensation of earthly reality was seamless.

Still, Michael knew beyond any doubt that Clarkham's house had once again become a gate.

THE TIPPETT RESIDENTIAL Hotel appeared regal and desolate and out of place against the ragtag architecture of the Strip. Its sad, sooted, broken windows and the trash chute attached to its face gave it a painful air, as if it were a victim of patchwork surgery, of half-hearted and ill-guided attempts to bring it back to life.

Through the chain link, Michael saw that the main entrance had been securely boarded with big sheets of blue-painted plywood. Yet the former owner—if that was what the raggedy man was—had hinted that a few people still managed to get into the building, however foolishly. There had to be other ways inside.

He had looped the short pry bar onto his belt, hanging it down inside his pants. A palm-sized flashlight rested in his jacket pocket.

On the building's west side, a broad patio and empty, leaf-strewn swimming pool were visible through the trees and shrubs pressed against the fence. Steps rose from the patio level to a terrace on the south side, overlooking the city. All this was dimly illuminated by streetlights along Sunset, and the general sky-glow reflected from the broken cumulus clouds above the city.

Michael glanced over his right shoulder at the lighted windows in the Hyatt across and down the street. Two instances of breaking and entering in one night. Superstitiously, he thought that might make things twice as bad as they had been after the night of his first passage through Clarkham's house . . .

He couldn't enter from the front without risking discovery. He strolled east on Sunset until he reached a side street and then walked downhill and doubled back to approach from the rear.

An open-air asphalt parking area, still accessible from the street behind, abutted a blank concrete wall on the hotel's east side. No easy entrance from that direction.

On the west side, a garage in the lower depths of the building offered spaces for forty or fifty tenants. The entrance was blocked by a run of chain-link and a securely padlocked swinging gate. The iron-barred gate that had once rolled along a track on rubber wheels had been knocked out of place and set aside. Within, an old rusted-out Buick still occupied one space. Trash—cardboard, broken tiles, scraps of sheetrock—littered the concrete floor.

The rear doors and service entrances were also covered by sheets of blue plywood. He leaned back and looked up at the top of the building. More broken-out windows, dark and sightless in the night.

With a sigh, he stood in the shadows, thrust his hands into his jacket pockets, and closed his eyes.

How to get in . . . without noise, without drawing any attention . . .

No inner answers presented themselves. The mental silence of Earth prevailed; no Death's Radio, no supernatural clues. Just Michael Perrin, on his own.

He felt around the plywood sheets covering the rear doors. The pry bar would make a horrible racket pulling out these nails—would anyone notice?

"I thought you'd be back."

He tensed and immediately probed the aura of the speaker. Rotten vegetables—a supermarket full of dead produce, ancient thoughts, old dreams: the ex-owner. Michael could barely see him in the darkness; he stood inside the fence, at the south end of the footpath to the pool, little more than a gray smudge against the bushes beyond.

"I didn't think you were a reporter. You must have known them . . . the two women. But what would a young kid like you have been doing with them? I figure one was a circus fat lady, the other . . . Who knows?"

"I'm just curious about the building," Michael said.

"It gets to you, doesn't it? So pretty. Like a pretty woman, and you're all optimistic, ready to fall in love, then you find out she's a real whore. Well, she's not a whore, but she's not what you'd expect. She was built well. She still meets earthquake standards. Work of craftsmanship and art. Want to get in?"

"Yes."

"Just look around?"

"Right."

"You seem okay. Not the kind to set fires or worse. Why don't you follow me. I . . ." The blur rummaged through a pocket with an arm. ". . . have a key. Old key. Maintenance entrance. Go back around to the lot"—he pointed east—"and jump that short wall, then crawl along the fence until you meet me here."

"You're not afraid to go in?" Michael asked.

"You're not afraid to go in with me, are you? I'm maybe not harmless, but I'm clean. Took the bus to my sister's in Venice, showered, cleaned my grubbies out, and not with Woolite, either." He chuckled dryly.

Michael did as he was instructed and soon faced the man on the path. There was no menace in him, only a crazy kind of hope, but hope for what, Michael couldn't tell. Old dreams. Rotten produce stacked yards deep. Dead ideas.

"Journalism used to be an interest of mine, writing, all that. My name's Hopkins. Ronald Hopkins. Yours?"

"Michael."

"No last name, huh?"

Michael shook his head: no last name.

Hopkins held up the key, a gleam in the dim light, and waved for Michael to follow him around the south corner.

The maintenance entrance was a wide, heavy double door on the west side of the building, set flush against the wall. Michael hadn't even noticed it in passing. Hopkins inserted the key and opened one door, pushing it against a runnel of mud. "No power," he said. Michael held up the flashlight and switched it on.

"What do you expect to find?" Hopkins asked, his voice a low croak in the darkness.

"I don't know," Michael said. He shined the light against cinder block walls, water and sewage pipes on the ceiling, a flight of stairs at the end of the hallway. Through an open door on the right, he saw a huge hot water tank suspended high above the filthy floor.

"You looking for ghosts? A psychic investigator?"

Michael shook his head. While he was grateful for Hopkins' services, he much preferred acting alone in the darkness without having to take another's safety into account. (And did he think there would be something dangerous here? More red lights?)

"I should be quiet, right?" Hopkins asked. Michael turned the light on him.

"Right," he said. "Thanks for letting me in."

"Nothing to it. You going above the lobby level?"

"I think so," Michael said.

"I'll go that far. No farther."

"Okay." They climbed the stairs.

"Cops found the women on the eleventh floor," Hopkins said behind him. "I still won't go above the lobby."

Michael tried the handle on the door at the top of the stairs. Unlocked. They stepped into the darkened lobby. Hopkins eased the door softly shut behind them.

The air smelled sour and musty: mildew, dust, rotting carpet, stagnant puddles of water. Michael stepped over a pile of lumber and more fractured sheetrock and played the light around the lobby. A long upholstered counter ran along one wall, its faded red leatherette ripped and scuffed and stained. The countertop—probably marble at one time—was gone, no doubt salvaged. The walls around the elevator and near the entrance had also been stripped, leaving mottled plaster and gaping holes for bolts and electrical connections.

Just beyond the elevator, a grand-ballroom flight of stairs rose to the second floor. The once cardinal-red carpet on the stairs was now dirty brown and black, water-stained and torn, coyly revealing concrete floor and rotten padding.

Hopkins stood behind Michael, sadly surveying the ruin. "Brought it on herself," he murmured.

The half-open elevator doors smugly revealed a dark and empty shaft beyond. The elevator's gouged and hammered aluminum door panels reflected Michael's light with funhouse dazzle and glee.

He sensed nothing beyond the melancholy and careless decay. There was nothing supernatural about such destruction. It was characteristically human; that which is not viable and protected is soon eroded by the passage of the desperate and irresponsible, the opportunists and the destructively curious. Humans had passed through here like water in a channel, wearing and grinding. Still, he felt a need for caution.

The Sidhe, Michael thought, would never engage in idle destruction for its own sake. However evil the Sidhe might become, they were never petty, never so *unstylish* as to vandalize.

"I'm going upstairs," he said to Hopkins. "Will I need any more keys?"

"Nope," Hopkins answered.

Michael took the grand staircase, remembering Lamia at the top of her stairs, in Clarkham's first house in the Realm . . . a huge bag of flesh

Which did he prefer—humanity in its idle and destructive carelessness, or the exquisite cruelty of the Sidhe, who could condemn a dancer and lover of ballet to become an obese monster?

"Be careful," Hopkins admonished.

The second-floor hallways stretched in three directions from the landing at the top of the staircase. Michael's light traveled only so far in the muddy darkness; he could not see the ends of the hallways running east and west, but the south hall was short, with only one door on each side.

Water-stained walls, covered with markings, graffiti and scrawled names, random gouges and scratches. A smaller stairway opposite the elevator door led from one side of the landing to the next floor. Michael climbed again; no need to inspect every room.

On the fifth floor, he walked from end to end in each hall and found a broken, leaning door to one apartment on the east side. He kicked it open and grimaced at the destruction beyond. Anonymous green trash had drifted into the corners of the living room. The carpets had been shredded as if by ice skaters wearing razors for blades. Michael looked down at his feet and saw an ancient pile of feces. Nearby, yellow stains dribbled down one wall.

All of this, he thought, *from the descendants of those who struggled back to humanity—or something like it—across sixty million years.* The story was noble—yet as one of its end products, a human being had once defecated on this floor and urinated on this wall.

With a sudden flush of anger, Michael wondered to what extent human depravity could be blamed on the misguiding of the Sidhe acting in their capacity as gods—Tonn, who became Adonna in the Realm, portraying Baal and Yahweh, and how many other deities?

There was a puzzle here. He knew instinctively it was useless to blame others entirely for one's own failings—or to blame the Sidhe for the failings of his own kind. But surely there was some culpability. He had little doubt that the Sidhe had mimicked gods to restrain humans, to open a little more space for their own kind on the Earth they had abandoned thousands of millennia before.

He shook his head and backed away from the feces. Such profound thoughts from such miserable evidence.

And you, Michael? Withdrawing into cold intellectual splendor. Knowing you are superior because of your knowledge, knowing you would never be so unstylish as to crap on the floor of a deserted building . . . So you're superior to your own kind, more stylish; does that mean you have something of the Sidhe in you, then?

Suddenly, the crap on the floor and the piss on the wall became profoundly funny. In a way, that kind of fated animal indifference to the past had more style in it than any ordered Sidhe posturing. Michael's thoughts made a complete turnaround with dizzying celerity.

The Crane Women, seeing the crap on the floor, would have drawn conclusions quite different from his own. They would have seen human flexibility—not just lack of dignity, but lack of restrictions.

He backed out of the apartment and returned to the stairs.

On the eighth floor, he vaguely realized what had drawn him here: a sensation in the air, as of a loosening or an *opening*. It was so faint as to be almost non-existent, but he could feel it intermittently.

The higher he went in the Tippett Residential Hotel, the stronger the sensation became. Nothing out of the ordinary here and now . . . but there had been, and there would be again. A breach in the mind-silence and the stolid yet ever-changing and infinitely detailed reality of Earth. He felt a tickle in an area of his mind once touched only by Death's Radio—the voice of Tonn . . . and the voice of Arno Waltiri. Yet the tickle came from neither.

It was the spoor of another place, lying nearby, separated by a much thinner wall here in the neighborhood where once the Infinity Concerto had been performed.

Michael felt a sudden exultation. His need for the bite of adventure . . . Here, there was hope for more adventure, more tastes of the strange and dangerous and wonderful he had experienced in the Realm. Just a shadow away, across some sheer membrane . . . punch a hand through and bring back mystery, wonder . . . horror.

On the tenth floor, he felt an even stronger presence, quite different from that of the nearness of other worlds. He frowned, trying to analyze what the sensation was, draw it out from the back of his head and understand what it might mean.

Imprisoned music. Not the Infinity Concerto but something even stronger. How was that possible?

The sensation suddenly confused him. He temporarily forgot who he was and why he was here. He glanced around the tenth-floor landing and walked to the window overlooking the Strip. Wind brushed at him through a broken pane of glass. Somewhere in the building, a rush of air mourned for its freedom. Not remembering was exhilarating. Suddenly he could be anybody: murderer, vagrant, good Samaritan, saint.

Michael Perrin came back to him in a gentle, nonerosive flood. And with the returning memory, he could feel through his skin, rather than hear, the music that was not the Infinity Concerto. His neck hair stood on end. It sounded sad, fated, vibrant yet losing energy: the sound of a world getting old, and of a world young and full of life, whose *situation* was growing old and rickety and dangerous. Put them together . . .

He climbed the stairs to the eleventh and last floor before the penthouse. Here there were no apartments, but meeting rooms, game rooms, broad empty rooms only lightly littered, slightly decayed.

In one of these rooms, Michael surmised, the bodies of Lamia and Tristesse had been found, he could not tell which. If the police had drawn paint or chalk around the bodies, it was no longer evident, not in the fading beam of his flashlight.

He shook the light. No better; batteries dying.

The membrane between himself and *otherness* thinned more. Michael was certain that at some time in the recent past, Sidhe had been here. What they had been doing, and with what purpose, he could not tell.

Someone or something had returned through Clarkham's house, a solitary return, not likely to be repeated because the house had felt inert. The eleventh floor of the Tippett Residential Hotel did not feel inert.

Sidhe were emigrating to Earth. He had seen that much in his "dreams." Soon, a gate would open here, and many Sidhe would pass through this building, perhaps on this very floor.

Possibly, at the beginning, Lamia and Tristesse had tried to block passage to the hotel. The Sidhe themselves had cursed them to assume the roles of guardian and gatekeeper, but when they were no longer necessary, in fact an impediment, the sisters—Clarkham's former lovers—might have been killed and cast aside by much stronger forces.

The door to the staircase to the penthouse had been propped open with a crumbling rubber doorstop. Michael ascended from the eleventh floor to the twelfth, leaving behind the imprisoned music.

The penthouse apartment had once been surrounded by broad, floor-to-ceiling windows, fitted with heavy drapes. The drapes were gone, leaving only broken and despondent fittings. The glass windows had been shattered. Their shards crunched under his shoes. Wind blew through the empty suite, whistling but not mourning, for only the skeleton of the building restrained it on this level.

Michael stood on the open deck, hair flicking back and forth. He looked across the hills behind the Strip. Most of the lights in the Hyatt had been turned off. He walked around the deck to the opposite side and stared across the still-bright lights of downtown Hollywood and Los Angeles beyond. Dawn was the faintest suggestion of a lighter midnight blue in the east. The air smelled sweet and pure after the decay in the enclosed spaces below. He breathed deeply and stretched his arms, jaw gaping wide, neck bones cracking with tension.

"What a night," he said. His voice sounded flat and vague in the wind.

Something impressive was going to happen, and soon. Whether he was prepared or not, Michael didn't know, but he felt expectant, almost eager.

"Come and get me," he said, and then felt a chill. *But stay away from those I love.*

Even at this hour, the city lights were a wonder and a glory. Ranks of orange streetlights marched off to the horizon. High-rise towers, far off in the clear night air, offered random glowing floors as cleaning crews finished their night's work.

People.

His kind.

Shitting on floors.

Dreaming, growing old or sleeping in cribs with developing minds dreaming feverishly of vague infant things; working late into the morning or tossing restlessly, coming up out of slumber into an awareness of the imminent day; maybe somewhere someone killing a person, an animal, an insect, someone killing himself; someone being born; someone realizing inadequacies, or preparing breakfast for the early-risers; sleeping off a drunk or making early morning love; tossing through insomnia. Mourning a loved one. Waiting for the night to be over.

Just sleeping.

Just sleeping.

Just sleeping.

Unaware.

Having lived all their lives in the midst of mind-silence, in the midst of stolid and infinitely detailed reality. Never knowing anything of their distant past except perhaps through vague racial memories, bubbling up as fantasy or delusion.

Hoping for magic and change; hoping desperately for escape; or simply clinging, unable to imagine something beyond. Once in, never out, except through the black hole of death.

"Jesus," he whispered on the deck above the city and the hills. His mind raced toward a precipice.

Every little fractured emotion, every grand exaltation, all bred of Earth and nurtured by Earth and all without the compensation of what Michael had experienced: the true and undeniable awareness of another reality, another history and truth to match the grandest fantasies . . .

His neck-hair prickled again. Some of the music he had felt through his skin one floor below had searched through the building and found him again. A high, piercing chord of horns and strings blowing and bowing without relenting, a note of intermingled doom and hope (how was that possible?) conveying an
emotion unfelt for ages
Michael began to shake
the emotion that was the grandfather of all emotions, from which all human feelings had been struck like shards from a flint core.

Michael heard a voice in his mind, neither Death's Radio nor Arno Waltiri, a voice he did not recognize, very old, conveying the word *Preeda*—
that was its name, the emotion that burned inside of him, threatened to burn him hollow; the only true emotion, foreign to the Sidhe for sixty million years and almost lost to humans.

Michael reveled in the sudden breaking of the mind silence, and simultaneously a muscle-twitching terror infused him through the burning *Preeda*.

Soon we will meet, the ancient voice conveyed.

Earth's silence had been broken.

Michael saw mapped across the back of his brain an infinity of shining scales and dark, murky water.

"Enough!" he screamed out across the city. "Please! Enough!"

The building *lapsed,* as dead and silent as the rest of the Earth.

Michael gulped back saliva to soothe his raw throat and wiped the flood of wetness from his cheeks and eyes. He might be hoarse for a week. Certainly he would be hoarse when he met Kristine Pendeers to show her the manuscript . . .

Everyday was back. Thoughts, concerns, schedules, plans.

Preeda was gone, but where it had been, it left a clear track. And he had brought it on himself, by concentrating on the city and the people—the humans—living in it, by concentrating on their situation and breaking through to some sort of understanding.

The dissonant chord of horns and strings had also pushed.

Hopkins waited for him in the lobby, sitting on top of the counter, heels kicking at the torn upholstery.

"See any spooks?" he asked.

Michael shook his head.

"Find any more bodies?"

"No."

"Now do you see why no one will live here?"

He slipped one hand in his coat pocket, then nodded. "Yes."

"Thought you might. You look the type that might understand." Hopkins' Adam's apple convulsed in his long neck. "Thank you for that, and amen," he said, and led Michael down the stairs to the maintenance door.

They separated in the dawn with nothing more said.

6

He did not sleep. By the time he returned to the house, there was less than an hour before Kristine would arrive. He showered and changed his clothes, then decided now was as good a time as any to do a load of laundry. He did not feel sleepy; the old patterns could be retrieved without effort, apparently.

He hauled his clothes in a wicker basket to the service porch, across from the closed basement door, and stuffed them into the washer, then poured soap from a half-empty box of detergent. He hefted the box thoughtfully. Golda had used the first half.

Michael suddenly felt like an invader. Whether or not he had been invited, this was not *his* home; he did not have any real place on Earth now, and he had never found a place in the Realm. He had neither the achieved position of an adult nor the allotted circumstances of a child; what he had was an elusive, ill-defined but apparently indefinite sinecure.

Michael was hardly so naive as to believe that Waltiri had arranged for the sinecure out of the goodness of his heart. "You'll earn your place," he told himself, dipping his hand into the spray of warm water in the washing machine.

He entered the library and looked for things to straighten or put back in place, more out of nerves than necessity. The room was neat and quiet. Opening the safe, he removed the manuscript of Opus 45 and carefully slipped it into a manila envelope. The smell had dissipated, for which he was grateful. He carried the package into the living room and placed it on the polished black lacquer surface of the closed piano lid.

Letting everything take its course.

And when would he begin to *guide* the process?

At seven-fifteen, the door chimes rang. Michael answered expectantly and found himself face-to-face with a man in a brown suit, arms folded, carrying a zippered black folder tucked beneath one. The surprise on Michael's face must have been evident.

"Excuse me," the man said. "I'm Lieutenant Brian Harvey, LAPD homicide." He held the case under his elbow and produced a badge in a leather holder, which he suspended before Michael for several seconds, letting him examine it carefully. "This house belongs to—belonged to—Mr. Arno Waltiri?"

"Yes," Michael said. He suddenly felt guilty. The man's clear, steady blue eyes regarded him without accusation or any sign of emotion, but Michael's thoughts were already racing to find some explanation for the presence of a police detective.

"I'm sorry to arrive here so early, but I need to ask you some questions," Harvey continued. "Your name is Michael Perkins?"

"Perrin," Michael corrected.

"And you're in charge of Mr. Waltiri's estate."

"Yes."

"May I come in?"

Michael stood aside and motioned for the detective to enter. Harvey surveyed the hall and living room with eyebrows lifted. His receding fair hair had been cut to a close bristle on his scalp. His skin was pink and slightly puffy, but he appeared slender and in good shape. Michael did not even think of probing his aura of memory; it did not seem appropriate under the circumstances, and he was wary of what might happen if the lieutenant suspected he was doing something unusual.

Why so anxious? he asked himself.

He thought of Alyons, and of the Sidhe who had taken him into the Irall— his last brushes with appointed authority.

"We've encountered Mr. Waltiri's name under some unusual circumstances," Harvey said, standing before an easy chair. "May I sit?"

Michael nodded.

"Are you expecting somebody?" The lieutenant sat with the black folder resting on his crossed knees.

"Yes, actually," Michael said. "But if I can help you . . . "

"Maybe you can. I don't know. You made some visits to the Tippett Residential Hotel up on Sunset. Why?"

Michael's nerves suddenly calmed. He knew the direction the conversation was going to take. He immediately probed the lieutenant: a quiet, orderly room with stacks of paper awaiting methodical and concentrated attention. Michael liked the man; he was no Alyons. Harvey was smart and cautious and thoroughly professional. Michael had no reason to hide anything from him but no reason to divulge anything, either.

"I heard about the bodies," Michael said. "Maybe it was ghoulish, but I wanted to have a look."

"A very *early* morning look. Mr. Ronald Hopkins gave you access to the building about four hours ago."

"He said he was the former owner."

"Did he tell you the place was haunted?"

Michael nodded. "Something to that effect."

Harvey smiled pleasantly. "Just happenstance, whim, that you went there, then."

Michael returned the smile.

"Do you know anything about the bodies found in the Tippett?"

"Yes," Michael said. Harvey's eyes widened with interest, and he nodded encouragement to continue. "One was a very large woman. The other was a mummy."

"That's all?"

"Hopkins said they were named Lamia and Tristesse. Sadness."

"You found that intriguing?"

"Yes."

"Did he tell you about the note found with them?"

"He said there was a carved stone tablet with their names on it."

"He didn't see the tablet himself?"

"I don't think so. I don't know."

"Did you see the tablet?"

Michael shook his head.

"No, and neither did photographers from the papers, or anybody outside my department. I have photographs of the bodies. Could you identify them?"

Michael shrugged. "It should be easy to tell—"

"What I'm asking, Mr. Perrin, is whether you know of any connection between Mr. Waltiri and these women?"

"No."

"It's just coincidence that you're interested in the building at this particular time."

Michael said nothing. Harvey opened the folder. "You were missing for over five years. Your parents notified the police five and a half years ago. When you returned, you didn't offer any explanations. Could you have spent this time doing something in connection with Arno Waltiri?"

"He's dead," Michael said.

"Yes. He died before you . . . left the scene. Did he give you any instructions, any last-will-and-testament requests?"

"Yes."

"What were they?"

"I am to care for his estate and prepare his papers for donation to an institution."

"I mean, did he give you any instructions before you left?"

Michael shook his head. Let the detective interpret that whichever way he wanted.

"Did you know these two women?"

The simplest answer, Michael decided, was none at all.

Harvey waited patiently and, when Michael didn't reply, sighed and said, "Do you know of any connection between them and Waltiri?"

"No."

"Then why was Waltiri's name on the stone tablet, along with theirs?"

"I don't understand."

The lieutenant produced a glossy eight-by-ten photograph from the folder and held it out with fingers at the top corners for Michael's inspection. Michael took the photo and sat in the chair across from Harvey's. The photograph showed a block of stone about ten inches square and several inches deep, judging from the ball-point pen placed on the floor beside it for scale. On the tablet was carved

Lamia
Tristesse
Guardians past need
Victims of Arno Waltiri

"Can you see why we might be suspicious, why we think there might be a connection?" Harvey asked. "One of my younger officers knew that Waltiri was a composer and that he had died. I took it from there. Eventually, you made the connection seem much stronger."

"How did the women die?" Michael asked.

Harvey shook his head and lifted one hand. The other hand slipped the photograph back into the folder. "We don't know. The mummy had been dead for some time. If you're concerned about my not believing a very strange story, well, don't be. I'll listen to anything."

"I still don't understand," Michael said.

Harvey leaned forward. "The fat woman was shedding her skin. It was loose, like a sack. And the mummy ... " He cleared his throat and looked troubled. "Had a very odd affliction. Too many joints. Some sort of freak. The doctors told me freaks like that don't happen, not in this world. But you never know. The doctors could be wrong. We thought they might be circus freaks. Were they ever in the circus?"

"I don't know," Michael said.

Harvey took a deep breath. "There's stuff you'd tell me, but—"

The chimes sounded again.

"Your visitor," Harvey said.

"Yes."

"Was it murder?" Harvey asked, staring at him intently.

"I don't know," Michael said.

"You're not holding something back because you're involved?"

"No, I'm not," Michael said. "It would be difficult to explain. Perhaps later—we can talk? If you'll tell me more, I'll tell you ..." *No need to dissemble.* "I'll tell you as much as you'll believe. I don't want to hide anything. Their being in the building was a surprise to me. And to answer your question—yes, I did know them. Not well, and not ... here. But I knew them."

Harvey took another deep breath and stood up. "Later today?"

"Fine."

"Four o'clock this afternoon, I'll call you here."

"Fine."

"You're not leaving town, Mr. Perrin?"

"No."

"Better answer your door."

Michael opened the door. Kristine stood there, smiling and radiant and expectant. The contrast was so sharp Michael felt another brush with *Preeda.* Harvey stepped up behind him, said hello pleasantly, and glanced at Michael as he walked in an S around them and out the door. "Four o'clock," he reiterated.

"Who's that?" Kristine asked. Harvey crossed the lawn and opened the door to an unmarked sky-blue car parked in front of the Dopso house.

"The police," Michael said.

Kristine gave Michael a sharp, discerning and altogether intrigued look. Michael smiled and invited her in.

"Are you in trouble?" she asked lightly, entering the house. She absorbed the interior with a series of slow, entranced sweeps of her eyes.

"No," Michael said. "I don't think so."

"This place is *wonderful*," she enthused. Then she glanced over her shoulder and gave him an unconsciously beguiling Mona Lisa smile. "I hope you don't think I'm star-struck, but could I have a tour?"

"My pleasure," Michael said. He conducted her through the first-floor rooms, deftly avoiding the service porch and the library, then took her upstairs. She absorbed everything quietly, as if she were on a long-overdue pilgrimage.

"I know so little about him," she said. "There's not much biographical material available—some interviews with his colleagues, and what I've learned from Edgar Moffat. In some ways, Waltiri was the quintessential forties film composer—don't you think?"

Michael hadn't given the question much thought. "I suppose so," he said. Most of his attention was focused on her, with an embarrassing concentration he hadn't felt since he had been alone with Helena in the Realm. (And where was *she*, now?)

Kristine examined the framed prints hanging in the upstairs hall. "From Germany," she said. "They're old—they must have belonged to his family."

Did Arno Waltiri ever have a family, or a true human past? If not, he had assembled the evidence scrupulously.

"You only knew him a few months?"

Michael nodded.

"And he sort of adopted you?"

"We were friends," Michael said. "My father built furniture for him—his piano bench, that sort of thing. He came to a party at our house, and I met him there. Golda, also."

"Edgar tells me Golda was a darling woman."

"She was very nice," Michael said.

"Where did he do his composing?"

"There's a music library downstairs. Where the study used to be."

"And you mentioned a basement, where you found the manuscript?"

"Yes . . ." Michael said slowly. "I'd like you to see the manuscript first. And there's the attic—a lot of memorabilia is stored up there."

"You're being selectively mysterious, Michael." The glance she gave him was both intrigued and wary. It suddenly occurred to him that whatever childish pleasure he might derive from being mysterious could not possibly equal the pleasure of her continued company.

He would much rather be completely open with her. *Spill the beans to ev-*

erybody. To Harvey, to Kristine. Clarkham comes knocking at the door . . . spill the beans to him, too.

"I don't know where to begin," Michael said, looking at the carpet. They were near the stairs, and he took the first step down. "So I'll start with the manuscript."

He had left it on the piano. They returned to the living room, and Michael removed the manuscript from the manila envelope, handing it to her. She glanced at it with some shock and reluctantly took it from him, holding it on the tips of her fingers.

"It looks as if it's been soaking in something," she said. She rubbed a finger lightly across the shimmering surface. "This is the way you found it?"

"Yes."

"It *is* hard to read. What caused the paper to change?"

"Smell it," he suggested. She lifted it to her nose.

"Mmm," she said. "That's nice—I like that. Perfume? Soap or something?" She shook her head before he had a chance to answer. "No. Let me guess . . ." She sniffed it again, closing her eyes and almost hugging the manuscript to her. "That's really lovely. I could smell that all day."

"The scent was much stronger when I first found it," Michael said.

"Well, what is it?"

"It's the music, I think."

She gave him a hard look. "I'm not *that* star-struck."

Her reaction took him aback. "I don't have any other explanation," he said. "Have you ever smelled anything like it?"

She wrinkled her brow in thought, then shook her head. "Maybe he brought the paper from Europe. Before the war. And they don't make it any more. Were there any other copies—you know, performer's copies?"

"Just this one. After what happened, he may have had other copies destroyed."

"Okay. May I see the office and basement now?" With some reluctance, she returned the manuscript to him, and he replaced it in the envelope. Morning light through the arched front windows caught the envelope, and he noticed the faint beginnings of discoloration, influence passing from the manuscript to the envelope. "We can try to get it photocopied," she said. "If you trust me with it, I'll take it to the school . . ."

"I trust you," Michael said, "but I think I'd rather handle this copy. For the time being."

"I understand," she said.

The music library was dark and cool. Michael switched on the desk lamp and opened the shutters on the rear windows, admitting light filtered through green clumps of giant bird-of-paradise at the rear of the house.

"All of his master tapes and records," Kristine said in awe. "This is *wonderful.* There must be hundreds of scores here." She passed before the cases filled with tape boxes and old oversized lacquer master disks in bulky cardboard sleeves. "Have you listened to them?"

"Not to these, not yet," Michael said.

"Ohh . . . I wouldn't be able to wait, if I were you. This is priceless. We have to get them copied. These could be the only recordings."

"I've been thinking about buying new sound equipment and doing that," Michael said. "But I've really only just started getting organized."

"You're not a trained conservator," she said. "Are you?"

"No," Michael admitted.

"That's what this really needs. A musicologist and a conservator."

"I'll take whatever help I can get."

"I think I can convince the department this is important. What's in the basement?"

"More papers, manuscripts," Michael said.

"I'd like to see them, too."

"I'll show you anything you want," he said. "It really isn't mine to conceal . . . if you see what I mean."

"No," she said. "What do you mean? Is there something all that mysterious about old papers and records and tapes?"

"Do you believe the stories of what happened when the concerto was first performed?" Michael asked, deciding to adopt her point-blank style.

"No," she said.

"Do you believe music has a power beyond notes on paper and sounds in the air?"

She frowned. Her face was not accustomed to frowning, that much was obvious. "Yes," she said, "but I'm not . . . gullible. I'm as much of a realist as a music-lover can be."

She had been a beautiful child, not so long ago, Michael thought. *Her mother raised her after divorcing her father early, and her childhood was reasonably happy, and she developed rapidly both in body and mind. She was independent—* He closed his eyes when her face was turned and abruptly cut off the probe. He was ashamed for having begun it. But what he had found made her even more enchanting.

Kristine Pendeers was a genuinely good person, without a hint of guile.

"The basement?" she prodded, catching him with a blank and inward-turned look on his face.

He took a short breath and said, "This way."

In the service porch, Michael opened the door and switched on the light, then went to find the flashlight. When he returned, Kristine still stood at the top of the steps. She didn't look happy. "I don't like enclosed places," she said.

"We don't have to go down there," he said.

"I'll go. I just don't like the dark and the smallness. But I can handle it." She preceded him, and he shined the light between the stair railings to fill in their shadows and show her the stacks of papers and the armoire. She took a deep breath and turned in the cramped space between the boxes and cabinet. Michael remained on the stairs.

"May I . . . ?" she asked, touching the armoire's left door. Michael nodded.

She opened the door and examined the shelves within. "Wine bottles," she said with a grin, tapping one lightly with her knee. "You haven't read the letters yet, have you?"

"Not yet. I found the manuscript in there and left the rest for later."

She nodded and lightly riffled a tied bundle of letters on the shelf. Then she lifted up on tiptoe and tilted the bundle outward a few inches to see the topmost letter.

"Oh, my god," she said softly.

"What?" Michael descended a step, alarmed.

"This top letter . . . it's from Gustav Mahler. I only read a little German, but the signature . . . Can we open this and look at the rest of the bundle?"

Michael drew a Swiss army knife from his pocket and handed it to her. She sliced the string carefully and returned his knife, then lifted the letters away one by one. "They're all from Mahler . . . they're not dated . . . but some have envelopes. These are worth a *fortune*, Michael!"

"Who are they to?" he asked.

"The first one says 'Arno, *lieber Freund.*' And the next, '*Lieber Arno.*' They're all to Waltiri."

"He was only a boy when Mahler was alive," Michael said. *Oh?*

"Maybe so, but they're all addressed to him." She handed him the stack. The letters at the bottom had been sent from Wien—Vienna; farther up the stack, from New York; and then the rest from München—Munich—and Vienna again. There must have been two dozen letters, some more than five pages long.

"That's a find," Kristine said. "That's a *real* find. If that doesn't convince the department, I'll just give up. Boxes and boxes of stuff . . . Who knows how many correspondents, all over the world?"

"There's a manuscript of a Stravinsky oratorio in the attic," Michael said. "And letters from all sorts of people. Clark Gable."

Kristine's face flushed with excitement. "Okay," she said, raising and lowering her shoulders and arms like a fledgling bird. "Enough of this. This is too much all at once." She giggled and held her hand to her lips. "Sorry. It's just incredible. This house is *crammed* with treasure!"

"I really don't know why he put me in charge of it," Michael said, ascending the steps. "I don't know half what I should know. I only know of Mahler because Arno mentioned him to me."

"He chose you because he trusted you," Kristine said. "That's obvious. He knew you'd find all the right people and straighten everything out. When I hear what has happened to other estates, to the libraries and papers of people even more famous . . . Sold off, auctioned, broken apart, rejected by big universities for lack of space. God. It makes me want to cry. But this . . . It's all here." Suddenly, standing in the service porch, Kristine impulsively reached out and hugged Michael. "I have to go now. If you can get the manuscript of the concerto copied, perhaps I can pick it up this evening?"

"I'll try," Michael said.

"There's a U-Copy place not too far from here . . . three or four blocks."

Michael nodded.

"That policeman said he'd be back this afternoon." Kristine regarded him from the corners of her eyes. "What do you think?"

"About what?"

"Is he going to keep you busy very long?"

"No," Michael decided.

"Good. Then I'll call about six. Maybe we can have dinner?"

Michael's insides warmed appreciably. "That'll be fine."

He escorted her to the front door and watched her return to her car. Kristine's walk, like all her movements, was lithe and graceful, with an unaffected insouciance in the push of her legs and the angle of her shoulders.

Even after she drove away, Michael lingered by the door, reluctant to close it. He felt ridiculous, standing there with the morning well along, but now that she was gone, there didn't seem to be anything very important to do.

All of his training, all of his discipline, could not keep him from feeling empty and confused in her absence.

"You're a mess," he whispered to himself and shut the door with a decisive *clunk*.

7

Michael carried the manuscript of the Infinity Concerto into the U-Copy and waited in line behind a broad, short woman in a dark wool coat. She fidgeted impatiently and patted her thinning black hair with a plump hand. Ahead of her, a middle-aged man with a bulbous nose copied a tax form dozens of times. When he finished, he smiled as if he had just solved the problems of the world, paid the clerk and walked out the door.

The woman in the dark wool coat knew nothing about copy machines. The clerk, a raw-boned girl with an open and pleasant face, tried to explain the operation but met with an obstinate stare and finally did the job herself. She glanced at Michael and smiled wryly. "This'll just take a sec," she said. That commission completed, she took a quarter from the woman, who grumbled and shook her head as she left.

"You know how to work the machine?" the clerk asked. She wore jeans and a man's white work shirt.

Michael nodded. "This might not be an easy job, though."

"What are you copying?"

He removed the manuscript from the envelope. "It's been soaked in something," he lied, trying to avoid other explanations.

"Hope it wasn't toxic waste," the clerk said, eyeing the manuscript distastefully. She sniffed. "Smells good, whatever it was."

She dialed the machine to a new setting. "This might work." Michael removed the green-corroded paper clip from the music sheets.

However its eye was constructed, the machine saw none of the glistening, oily distortion. Each page emerged from the machine plain black and white, with faint edges of gray.

"Does fine, huh?" the clerk asked.

"Great," Michael said, surprised.

"Did you get the glass dirty?" she asked casually after he had finished the last page.

"I don't think so," he said.

"I'd like to know what it was soaked in, actually," she said, winking at him. "Might appeal to my boyfriend."

Michael grinned, thanked her and carried both sets to the Saab. *Simple enough,* he thought. But how long would it take the notes on the duplicate to transform the photocopy's fresh white paper?

He locked both manuscript and duplicate in Waltiri's library safe.

From the basement, he removed the open bundle of Mahler letters, found a German-English dictionary, and sat on a patio chair in the back yard—warming nicely now in late morning sunshine—to make an attempt at translation. It was slow going. How much easier if there was a German-speaker nearby; he could tap the knowledge, in-speak and translate effortlessly.

He closed his eyes and let his probe go out through the neighborhood. There was no way of knowing how far he could reach. Before last night, he had never probed beyond a few dozen meters.

He seemed to be suspended in a dense leafy glade with neither leaves nor light. In this glade he found . . .

An elderly man whose mind burned like banked coals, feverish with speculation on some topic Michael could not discern; the old man spoke only broken English and gutter Spanish.

A young girl home from summer school, in bed with a cold. She also knew rudimentary Spanish and was reading Walter Farley books stacked six high beside her.

A woman cleaning a large and elegantly furnished house, her mind filled with strikingly original jazz. Was she black, Michael wondered? There was no way of telling; her thoughts were of no particular color, and whatever voices he heard in people's heads betrayed no accents. She did not speak German.

Housewives, handymen, a late-middle-aged man with a mind like a musty bookstore typing on an old Royal, three young babies as selfish as three Scrooges, their thoughts incredibly sensual, nonverbal and as fresh as an ocean breeze . . .

He went back to the man at the typewriter. An article on guns was emerging from the antique upright Royal, an evaluation of a new Israeli automatic rifle.

This man spoke German fluently. He had <served as a guard at an American embassy in Europe during the fifties> <killed a dozen Asian soldiers in an empty grassy field> <married three times and shot his second wife on a hunting trip, but she recovered and did not prosecute, only rapidly divorced him, and he did not contest>

Michael pulled away from the middle-aged man as if stung. He did not wish to tap the man's language abilities if he had to face more of that sort of foulness.

Where did he live—and how far away?

He could not tell.

The shock of the man's frank evil had made Michael recoil drastically, throwing his probe out in a wide arc.

And he saw—for a brief moment became . . .

ELDRIDGE GORN, A horse trader. That was his euphemism for rounding up range horses and selling them to knackers. He had been in the trade for thirty years, starting in 1959, two years after he had been dishonorably discharged from the Navy.

He had come back to Utah and been received by his Mormon family with chilly aloofness. Eldridge Gorn had not lived up to his father's expectations. His father was a hard, unforgiving man, whom Gorn loved very deeply, and the rejection hurt.

He moved to Colorado, married and been divorced within a year. He tried to take his life with a twelve-gauge shotgun in a small motel room in Calneva. The gun jammed, and he spent twenty-five minutes laughing and crying and trying to get the gun to work. It wouldn't.

It appeared to Gorn that someone, at least, wanted him alive.

Shortly after, he went to work on a ranch in Nevada and learned the trade of rounding up wild horses and selling them to slaughterhouses. The money was marginal, and the last ten years—what with do-gooder animal groups and the ever-changing legal scene—had forced him to change his tactics, but he hung on. He knew he was a marginal man to start with, not worth much to anybody, the only sort of person who could seriously countenance turning range horses into dog food. He liked the work.

He even liked the horses. Sometimes they outsmarted him, and he would laugh as he had when the shotgun had jammed, and wave his battered felt hat at them and whoop.

Gorn sat on top of the cab of his pickup, a light afternoon breeze patting at his face and hair. Sage scrub to the horizon all around, a cinder cone of a centuries-old volcano off to the east, and nothing but silence and twenty or thirty head of wild horses about three miles away.

Today he would just drive around them, count and look them over. Just possibly he could drive through the scrub and herd them into a small box canyon a half mile west of the cinder cone; but tomorrow would be better, when he had an assistant or two on horseback themselves.

He lifted his nose and sniffed like a dog. He scowled and hawked and spat over the hood and sniffed again. There wasn't any storm or even a cloud in the mild blue sky, but he smelled something very much like cold and winter. He prided himself on his nose—he could smell mustangs from five miles away in a good straight wind—and what he smelled bothered him.

It didn't belong. It was out of season, that smell.

Winter. Snow and ice.

Something glittered by the cinder cone, like the flash from a circle of mirrors. Gorn began to feel spooked. His crusty burned-red arms itched, and his small hairs stood on end. He pinched his nose between two fingers and blew into his clean white cotton handkerchief.

The breeze became something out of a musty old refrigerator or freezer— not so much cold as having been kept still and confined for a long time.

Horses ran from the direction of the cinder cone—twenty, thirty, maybe as many as fifty, galloping from a direction where they couldn't possibly have been. What he smelled now was enough to send him into the cab of his truck, a scent fierce and electric and dangerous. He started the engine and watched the new herd through the windshield.

They were all gray, hard to see against the sage but for a quality of iridescence more at home in an oyster shell than on a horse.

And they were coming right for him, up the gentle scrub-covered slope, faster than any horses he had ever seen, gray blurs with long manes. Beautiful animals. If he could catch them (who could possibly own such beautiful horses and let them loose in this godforsaken country?) he could make a good deal more money by changing his tactics, avoiding the knackers and heading straight for the stock buyers in Vegas or Reno.

A quarter mile from his truck, the herd split in two. His sharp eyes told him the animals were sinewy, tight-muscled, oddly out of proportion compared to the animals he had known all his life. They looked flayed, but their heads were exquisite, more delicately featured than Arabians, wild and energetic and maybe scared by something behind them. Still running at full gallop.

Suddenly, the five or six horses in the lead lifted all their feet from the ground. They were barely fifty yards from his truck and Gorn clearly saw all four legs on each animal curl up and spread out like those ridiculous hunting paintings in rich men's clubs.

The lead horses grew long, leaned out, flew over the ground, not running, their hindquarters blurry and necks stretching until their heads seemed level with their shoulders.

"God *damn*," Gorn said under his breath.

Like bright streaks of Navajo silver, all five lead horses merged with the sky and simply vanished.

And then the five behind.

In ranks, all of the pearl-colored herd took to the air near his truck and vanished.

He did not see them come down again.

Gorn sat behind the wheel with the engine running for a quarter hour before he halfheartedly returned his attention to the ordinary animals still down in the middle of the sage scrub.

What he felt in his chest was something past all pain and feeling.

Loss. Bereavement. An agonizing sensation of beauty and one important thing long since fled from his life. Gorn did not know what it was.

But he knew he would spend the rest of that day, and perhaps the next, looking at the sky.

MICHAEL PUT THE packet of letters aside and pressed the bridge of his nose between two fingers.

His life was dividing in two, and the division was fuzzing rapidly. How long could he keep the parts separated—and how long could he observe and learn without acting?

The sky spread clear and bland overhead, an extremely self-assured sky, unlike the Realm's active and ever-changing blueness. Differences. *Contrasts are the direct path to knowing.*

He was becoming more and more aware of human variety; in contrast, the Sidhe had seemed almost uniform, lacking the physical and mental differences and distortions peculiar to humankind.

The Sidhe were like thoroughbreds; their lines had been molded across tens of millions of years, with who could tell what kind of strictures and impositions? Humans, however, had re-emerged from the condition of animals (were animals still), with all the riotous multiformity of nature.

They would not mix comfortably.

Michael returned the packet of letters to the armoire in the basement and fixed himself lunch, a cheese sandwich and an apple. Half an hour later, he returned to the back yard to practice *hyloka*. He squatted naked on the grass, skin glowing like a furnace.

"Salamander," he murmured, feeling the ecstasy of the unleashed heat subside. In such a condition, he realized, he could walk through a burning house unharmed; he would be hotter than the flames. He damped his discipline and got to his feet. Where he had been sitting, his legs and buttocks had left blackened prints in the grass. He was ravenously hungry again.

He ate a second lunch, much the same as the first, and replayed *The Man Who Would Be King* on the VCR. Halfway through, he found he was merely staring blankly at the TV screen, his mind elsewhere—with the horse trader on the rangeland, with the elderly woman in the old forest . . . Mulling over the Tippett Hotel and Lieutenant Harvey, but most of all, thinking of Kristine.

At four o'clock, the phone rang. Lieutenant Harvey was calling from downtown.

"I've had to put our mutual interest here, the Tippett Hotel case, on the back burner for the moment," he said. "But I'll want to talk with you in detail later. If it makes you feel more comfortable, you can have a lawyer present. I'm not looking for a confession, just information, you understand?"

"Yes," Michael said, aware the detective was telling the truth; learning more about Harvey perhaps than the reverse.

"I think you have some interesting things to talk about, don't you?" Harvey continued.

"If you have an open mind," Michael said.

"Uh-*huh*," Harvey grunted emphatically. "Keep me in the real world, okay?"

"No guarantees," Michael said.

"I have my instincts to rely on," Harvey said softly. "They don't fail me often. What they tell me now worries me. Should I be worried?"

Michael waited for a moment before answering. Eventually, Harvey would have to know. Dreams spilled into the real world. Divide between fuzzing all too rapidly.

"Yes," Michael said.

"I can see it's going to be a cheerful week," the lieutenant said. "I'll get back to you in a couple of days. Sooner, if anything new comes up." Michael deposited the receiver on the hook. Logically, Harvey should question him as soon as possible. But the lieutenant was postponing unpleasantness. Michael couldn't blame him for that.

He walked up the stairs, pulled down the ladder to the attic and climbed into the musty warmth. Once, sitting in the attic while Waltiri looked through boxes of old letters and memorabilia, Michael had felt as if time had rolled back or even ceased to exist; nothing had changed there for perhaps forty years.

The attic still seemed suspended above the outside flow. He idly opened the drawer of a wooden filing cabinet and leafed through the papers within. So much accumulated within a lifetime . . . reams of letters, piles of manuscripts and journals and records . . .

He pulled out folder after folder, peering inside. Several letters from Arnold Schönberg, dated 1938; he put those aside for later reading. Schönberg had been a composer, Michael remembered; perhaps the letters mentioned the concerto.

Then he found the Stravinsky oratorio manuscript. Stravinsky had composed *The Rite of Spring* early in the century, and Disney had set the work to dying dinosaurs. Every adolescent knew Stravinsky.

Holding the oratorio was like holding a piece of history. He lightly touched the signature and the accompanying letter, savoring the roughness of the fountain pen scratches.

1937, the letter was dated. He could almost imagine, outside, a calm bright spring day, the cars parked on the street and in the brick driveways all rounded and quaintly sleek, like the Packard in the garage; silver DC-3s and Lockheed Vegas flying in to Burbank airport, tall palms against the sky, everything more spread out, less crowded, almost sleepy . . .

Michael looked up from the manuscript with a glazed, distant expression. Before the war. Days of the late Depression, easing now that Roosevelt was rearming the country.

Days of comparative peace before the storm.

KRISTINE SEEMED TO regard Westwood as the center of the universe. She knew all the best restaurants there—"best" meaning good food on a slightly more than meager budget. This evening she had chosen a less crowded one. It was called Xanadu, which both discomfited and amused Michael. The decor was dark wood paneling inlaid with partly oriental, partly Art Deco scenes beaten into brass sheets. White silk canopies hung from the ceiling. Its fare was not Chinese food, but nouveau French, and Kristine assured him everything was very good despite the reasonable prices. "The chef here is young," she said. "Just getting started. He'll probably leave in two or three months; somebody else will hire him, and I'll never be able to afford his cooking again." They were seated at a corner table by a waitress dressed in tuxedo.

Kristine gauged his reaction as the waitress wobbled away on high heels. "So it's not consistent," she said, laughing.

"Xanadu's an odd name, isn't it?" he asked. "For a restaurant like this?"

She shrugged. "I suppose they intended it to mean . . . a pleasurable place, extravagant, not necessarily Chinese."

Michael felt a strong, all-too-adolescent urge to bring up his unusual familiarity with Xanadu, but he resisted. He would not impress Kristine by being any odder than he already was.

"Have you been reading about those hauntings?" she asked.

"Yes. In the papers."

"Aren't they strange? Like the flying saucer waves. Really spooky, though."

He glanced down at the side of his chair, where he had laid the envelope containing the copy of the manuscript. Time to change subjects completely, he decided. He raised the manuscript and handed it over the table to her. "I made a copy," he said.

She glanced at the envelope, obviously aware of the gingerly way he supported it on his fingertips. "How did it come out?"

"You can look for yourself."

She took it. "It's very clean." She pulled it halfway out of the envelope. "I didn't think it would copy."

"We're in luck," Michael said.

"Thank you." She riffled the pages, returned it to its envelope with a broad smile and slipped it in her voluminous canvas purse. Her smile changed to concern. "Are you feeling all right tonight?"

"I'm a little nervous," he admitted.

"Why? Is it the restaurant?"

"No. What will you do with the manuscript now?"

She shrugged, an odd reaction, as if it all meant very little to her. Then an excited smile broke through her nonchalance, and she rested her arms on the table, leaning forward eagerly. "I'll show it around the department. There are plans for a concert in the summer . . . July, I think. If we can get it prepared by then, perhaps we can perform it. And I'll show it to Edgar." The waitress returned for their orders. Michael chose poached halibut. There were no vegetarian dishes on the menu; he felt less uncomfortable eating the flesh of sea creatures but knew that a Sidhe would abhor even such nonmammalian fare.

Kristine ordered medallions of salmon. The waitress poured their wine, and Michael sipped it cautiously. He had drunk wine only once before, at the Dopsos' house, since his return, and he had reservations about how it might affect him in his present nervous state. He did not want to become even mildly drunk; the very thought bothered him. But the wine was agreeably sweet and light, and its effects were too subtle to be noticeable.

One evening, the soul of wine sang in its bottles . . .

Baudelaire. Why the line seemed appropriate now, he didn't know.

"I'm starting to have my doubts about this whole thing, about putting on a concert," Michael said, inching back into his chair.

"Why?" Kristine asked, startled. "Aren't you supposed to promote Waltiri's works? Isn't that what an executor does?"

"I'm not precisely an executor, I just manage the estate. I don't know." He shook his head. "I don't know what in hell I'm doing here. I'm giving you something you can't possibly understand—"

"Now wait a minute," Kristine flared.

He held up his hand, and pointed with a pistol finger to her bag, the corner of the envelope sticking out. "When that music was written on the manuscript I made this copy from, the paper was white and pure. It wasn't soaked in anything between that time and now. It just *aged*."

"I don't get you."

"No, and neither does anybody else." He felt his frustration suddenly rise to the surface. "I'm not in an enviable position right now. I'm pulled this way and that."

"How—"

"So—" He held up both hands. "Please. Just listen for a bit. You can say how crazy I am afterward. I know you're an expert on music, maybe even on Waltiri's music, but this is something else."

"I don't understand your doubts. You think—"

Michael's expression stopped her. She folded her arms and leaned back in her chair, glancing nervously at a patron walking past their table.

"You mentioned the hauntings. There's a connection."

"With this?" She dropped her hand to the envelope.

Michael nodded. "I don't know all the details. Even if I did, it wouldn't be worthwhile to tell you. Because you couldn't possibly believe."

"Jesus," she said. "What are you involved in?"

He laughed and looked up at the backlit white canopy overhead.

"That policeman. Is he part of it?"

"Not really. He's like you. And my father. And Bert Cantor."

"Who's Bert Cantor?"

"Somebody who knows. Whom do I tell? And how much? You all live in the real world."

"You don't?"

Michael sighed. "For a time, I didn't. I was missing for five years, Kristine."

Her brows knit. Then she leaned forward. "Because of the concerto?"

"It's part of the . . . experience. Yes." *And I ended up in a much better re-creation of Xanadu than this restaurant.* He severely edited what impulse would lead him to say. It was so difficult, wanting to tell the entire story and being constrained by practical considerations—belief, the impact the story might have on how she regarded him, his unease at what might seem self-aggrandizement.

"Okay. I'm listening." There was a look in Kristine's eyes then that only deepened his distress. She *was* interested. She was intrigued. He was something different in her life, and his attitude, his tone of voice, did not reveal him to be a nut or a liar.

Which compounded distress upon distress.

And stopped him cold before he could begin his next sentence. "I'm sorry." His face reddened.

"I said you were mysterious this morning," Kristine reminded him. "I don't know what I meant—"

"Okay," he said. "I'll tell you this much. I have been warned not to do any of this." He gestured toward the manuscript with an open hand. "I don't know by whom. I'm ignoring that warning, but I want you to be aware of the risk we're taking."

"Jesus," she said again, looking down at the table. The waitress in a tuxedo served their salads. "Why didn't you tell me this earlier?"

"Because I'm an idiot." He touched his fork to the salad.

"You are *not* an idiot," Kristine objected, raising her eyebrows not at him but at her salad plate.

"Then maybe it's because I'm way out of my depth."

She regarded him shrewdly. "Then why are you doing this?"

"Because I find you attractive," Michael said, discretion in tatters.

Kristine didn't react for an uncomfortable number of seconds. She would not look at him directly. Her lips worked, then she smiled falsely, lifted her eyes, said, "I'm living with someone now."

"I suspected as much."

"I'd like to think we're both interested in the music."

"We both are."

"And I'd like to think you wouldn't use all of this as an excuse, just to see somebody you're attracted to."

"I wouldn't. Not for that alone."

"How old are you?" Kristine asked. "I mean, really?"

"I don't know," Michael said. "I was gone five years. It didn't seem like five years to me."

"I thought you might be older than you said."

"If anything, I'm younger."

"I'm *really* confused." She removed her napkin from her lap and laid it on the tablecloth. "And I'm not very hungry."

"Neither am I."

"You don't want me to do anything with the manuscript?"

"On the contrary. I *do* want you to . . . take it to the music department, look it over, get it performed. But I think you should be aware there could be trouble."

"Do you always cause trouble for women you're attracted to?"

Her question stunned him. *Yes.* "Not like this," he answered. "It's not me causing the trouble."

"What I think you're trying to say is, if we play this music again, the same things will happen as happened in 1939. Supposedly."

"Or something even more important."

"And I could be sued, as Waltiri was sued."

"I don't know about that. That isn't what worries me most."

She seemed fascinated by the idea. "That would be . . . interesting. But you're right; I find it all hard to believe."

"You're only hearing the easy part," Michael said.

Again a pause as she bit her lower lip and searched his face intently. "Let's talk about how you feel about me . . ."

"It's embarrassing. I've said too much, and I've said it in all the wrong ways."

"No. I appreciate your honesty. You are being honest; that much is obvious. And you're not crazy. Believe me, I've gone out with enough crazy men . . ." She gazed off into the middle distance. "I like you, but there is this . . . situation."

"We shouldn't waste the food," Michael said.

"No." She picked up her fork, replaced her napkin and speared a leaf of lettuce from her salad plate. "I mentioned the Mahler letters to Gregory Dillman. He's our department expert on Mahler and Strauss and Wagner. He's fascinated—says that none of the letters have ever been published, which is obvious, I suppose."

"Yes," Michael said.

"He's advising a fellow named Berthold Crooke on his orchestration of Mahler's Tenth Symphony."

"Oh?"

"Mahler died before he could finish the orchestration. Deryck Cooke orchestrated a version about twenty years ago, but Crooke has a different approach. They—Dillman and Crooke—would love to see the letters."

Michael said, "Cooke and Crooke. That's funny."

"Right." She smiled. "Both with an e."

Their main course was served. They concentrated on the food for a few minutes, though Michael was not particularly hungry. The hollowness of want inside him had nothing to do with food. His mind raced ahead, speculating, seeing possibilities he had no right to even consider now.

Kristine, without realizing it, had set the hook by confirming Michael's suspicions. She was not yet available; she might even deny him. That made her infinitely more attractive. So it had been with Helena in the Realm.

"Your situation doesn't sound good," he said on impulse.

Kristine twisted her fork around a fleck of parsley in a small puddle of herb sauce. "Persistent, aren't you?"

"I'm just interested," he said. "Concerned."

"Well it doesn't matter. It'll work out," she said.

"I hope I didn't cause any trouble when I called. I thought I heard an argument."

Kristine sighed and met his eyes. "You know, I must want to talk about it, or I'd be angry with you now."

"I'm sorry," Michael said softly.

"I meet the strangest men. I really do. Maybe it's an occupational hazard, part of being a woman. My mother says most men are like wild horses. You can't expect all of them to be Lippizaners. But mostly I think I'm just too young to have much taste. You know. Can't tell the good wine from the bad right off."

"So what am I—Lippizaner or wild-eyed mustang?" Michael asked.

"I don't know." She finished her salmon and laid the fork beside untouched broccoli spears. Her eyes narrowed, and she appraised him. "I don't know you well at all, but you're no Lippizaner. You're not tamed, and you're not trained. Not domestic at all. I think you must be . . . wild but not a mustang. Some sort of fairy-tale horse."

Michael raised an eyebrow and grinned.

"Well, we're going to be frank tonight, aren't we?"

"Okay."

"A white stallion maybe. Something big and lean and out of a dream. I don't know whether you're benevolent or . . . I know you're not cruel, but—powerful.

Somehow. Oh, forget all this." She shook her head, hair drifting into her eyes. As she replaced the strands, the waitress asked them if they wanted dessert.

"Coffee," Kristine said. "I could have coffee. How about you?"

"Nothing, thanks."

"Flying horses, silver-gray and lean. Maybe that's what you're like. I had a dream about that last night. Maybe I was thinking of you."

Michael felt his breath stop, his insides tense, and then forced himself to some semblance of calm.

"Isn't that what a poet is supposed to be, powerful and ghostly inside, raise the hair on your neck?"

He had never heard it expressed quite so well before. He nodded. But—

. . . Once, poets were magicians. Poets were strong, stronger than warriors or kings—stronger than old hapless gods. And they will be strong once again. Adonna, Tonn, had told him that.

"So you're a real nightmare," Kristine said, smiling again.

"Better than being a nerd, I suppose."

"Tommy . . . he's the fellow I live with. We share a house with Stephen and Sue. A big four-bedroom place. We have a room and bathroom all to ourselves. Tommy's nice inside, but he doesn't know himself. He has no self-confidence. It makes him go off the deep end, like he has no real self-control." She held up both hands, one clutching her napkin, and leaned her head back as if looking for the right words to be printed on the silk canopy.

"If I left him now," she said, "he might just fall apart."

"Do you love him?"

To his distress, he saw tears in her eyes.

"Damn it," she said, touching the napkin to her cheeks. "You don't know me well enough to ask such questions. Let's get the check."

"I'm sorry. I'm just concerned."

"Oh, bullshit," she said, not unkindly. "You're on the make. No. I don't love him now. He's the albatross I get around my neck for having bad taste in men."

They split the bill, and Michael insisted he leave the tip. He expected Kristine to say good-bye and leave with the manuscript, but instead she began walking down Gayley toward Westwood, apparently expecting him to follow. He kept pace with her. "You know, maybe we could have a big concert in the summer," she said crisply. "Sort of the opposite ends of the early-twentieth-century German tradition—Mahler's Tenth and Waltiri's Infinity Concerto. Wouldn't that be an occasion? I'll mention it to Dillman. Maybe Crooke will have his performing version finished by then, and we can premiere it." She led them by a brightly lighted theater front. Michael automatically glanced at the movie posters on the side of the fourplex—a Blake Edwards romantic comedy called *Tempting Fate,* two theaters showing David Lynch's *Black Easter,* and a reissue of *Snow White.* The poster for *Black Easter* showed U.S. Army troops fighting demons around a city whose walls were made of red-hot iron.

Long lines of people waited behind ropes suspended from brass poles along the sidewalk. Michael feather-touched their auras automatically as he and Kristine walked past. The people were bright, expectant, full of the awareness that they were on a kind of social display; they were very much alive and enjoying themselves. Michael felt a fullness of love for them beyond immediate explanation.

"I'm an ambitious woman, Michael," Kristine said, walking ahead of him. "Or didn't you get that impression already?"

"I wouldn't use the word ambitious."

"Then I'm a dreamer. How's that?"

"That's a good word," Michael said.

"All these fantasy movies." She looked back over her shoulder and shook her head. "Won't they ever go out of style?"

"Maybe there's a reason everyone's interested in fantasy," Michael suggested.

"What?"

"Hauntings. Dreams of wild horses."

"What about them?"

"Never mind."

She didn't press him. They came to a bookstore and looked in the windows. "Wouldn't you like to see your books in there, sometime?" she asked.

"I would," Michael agreed.

"I'd like to go by Vogue or Tower and see my music all over the windows." She laughed, but Michael saw her eyes were still moist. She turned to him, blinking, suddenly very vulnerable. "I think it's time we went home. Tommy has the car tonight. I came here by bus. Can you give me a lift?"

"Of course," Michael said.

Michael drove east on Wilshire, following her directions. The night was warm and the air relatively clear, with a few bright stars showing through low, orange-lighted clouds. Kristine stared up through the open sunroof. "I'm not really a complainer," she said. "My life is going along. I enjoy my work." She glanced at Michael. "Even so, I want to get away sometimes. Have you ever had that feeling? That you'd like to go someplace far from everything, away from all the responsibilities and cares? That must be a common fantasy."

"I suppose," Michael said.

"You said you were missing—you were away for five years. Is that what you did?"

"I didn't go away from responsibilities."

"Can you tell me where you went? I've been doing all the confessing this evening."

He smiled and shook his head. "If I'm on the make, I shouldn't scare you away by making you think I'm crazy, should I?"

"All right," Kristine said ruefully.

"But I will confess one thing."

"What?"

"From what you've said about Tommy, I don't think I like him very much. He makes you unhappy."

"Michael, I'm the one who makes *him* unhappy. We make each *other* unhappy.

"Why don't you leave him?"

"That's the street up ahead—South Bronson. Turn right." They entered a neighborhood of old, large homes, most in the California bungalow style. Kristine told him to slow down and pointed out the house where she lived. Two stories high, fronted by a broad porch with low brick walls and pillars supporting a second-floor porch, it looked dark and ill-kept. Faded yellow paint peeled from the clapboard siding. An old black Trans-Am with gray patches of primer along its side and rear waited by the curb in front of the house, seats unoccupied, lights off and engine running. Someone stood in the shadow of the porch. Michael did not like the circumstances at all, but Kristine didn't seem alarmed.

"Tommy's back," she said, resigned. "You can just let me off here."

Michael stopped. Kristine opened the door and stepped out.

The figure on the porch descended the steps slowly, forced casual, with an exaggerated cowboy walk.

Michael clasped the Saab's steering wheel, quickly probed the man and found sullen anger, neat tidy rooms full of engine parts and tools, a flicker of light at the back of a long, dark hallway. The man crossed the street as Kristine shut the door.

She leaned into the window. "Thanks for the ride. I'll call you about meeting Edgar and coming to the department. We'll talk about having the library people take a look—"

"How cute," Tommy said, stopping several yards from the car. He was of middle height, black-haired, powerfully built and slightly bow-legged, his legs packed into faded jeans and his crossed arms revealed by a black T-shirt. "A Saab. Real powerhouse. College professor, right?"

"Tommy, this is Michael Perrin. He was kind enough to drive me home."

"I'm sure. Pleased to meet you, Michael."

"Same here," Michael said.

Tommy leaned his head to one side, squinted at Kristine. "I've been waiting."

"You were gone when I got home," Kristine said. "I couldn't leave you a message. And you had the car." She looked back at Michael as she touched Tommy's arms.

"Fine," Tommy said. "Thanks for dropping her off."

Michael could not believe what happened next. The man reached out casually with one arm, as if to embrace her. She stepped closer, and he made a half-spin, striking her cheek with his hand. Kristine dropped to the street in a half-crouch, one leg stuck out to keep from falling over. Her purse hit the pavement and the envelope slid out.

Michael put no thought into his reaction. He heard Tommy say something in a quiet voice to Kristine, and then he heard the Saab's door open. Michael stood on the street long enough to let the man know he was there, and then Tommy was on his back with his legs spraddled and blood pouring from his nose.

Michael had deftly lifted his leg and reached out with the toe of one running shoe to clip Tommy's face. Kristine had reached for the envelope and her big canvas purse and had not seen the blow connect. Now she scrambled across the pavement, dragging her purse, and knelt by Tommy.

"Bastard," Tommy said thickly. "Gib be a Kleedex."

"It isn't broken," Michael said with certainty, still calm but feeling the hot lava of angry reaction rising in a volcano tube to his head.

"Goddab," Tommy said, clutching Kristine's offered scarf to his face.

"Are you all right?" Michael asked Kristine. The print of Tommy's blow made a livid patch on her left cheek.

"I'm fine," she said. "He didn't mean to hit me hard. Oh, Jesus, what am I saying?" She knelt beside Tommy, saying softly, "You idiot. You poor, stupid bastard."

"Leabe be alode." Tommy pushed her away and she rose to her feet. "You dod't go out with subwud else, dot without by dowing," he said.

"It was a goddamn business dinner," she said. "Michael's in charge of the estate I told you about."

Michael probed Tommy as he stood, trying to predict what he would do next. Tommy's anger was now evenly mixed with shame, somewhere a small boy crying, light flaring red at the back of the dark hallway. Michael suddenly felt very sorry for the man, and confused.

Kristine confronted him. "You're my protector, are you?" she asked, her voice level, her stare glassy.

"I apologize."

"That was sharb," Tommy said, grinning through the scarf. Black smeared his jaw in the orange streetlight glow. "That was do college professor's trick. Dod't get bad at hib, Kristide. I pulled a stupid studt, and he showed be. He showed us."

Kristine looked between them as if they were both crazy. Then she shook her head and walked to the house.

"Okay, Bichael," Tommy said, backing off the street and onto the grass strip beyond the curb. "You showed us. So dow leave us alode, huh?" He turned off the idling engine of the Trans-Am and followed her up the porch steps into the dark house, keys dangling from his hand, the other still clutching Kristine's scarf to his nose.

MICHAEL STOOD IN the dark living room, having walked unerringly on a path between the furniture to the piano, and with his eyes closed wept for a time, his arms trembling and his chest heaving as he tried to subdue the sobs.

The real world.

How far away the Realm seemed now, and how cut and dried most of its problems. With every breath, every choked-off sob, the real world exploded behind his eyes. Growing up, trying to fit into society, trying to decide who and what he was: the immediate reality.

Making mistakes. Taking actions in which there was no apparent right or wrong.

Hitting a man who was already deeply confused, hurting.

But he struck Kristine.

Justified or not, what Michael had done this night simply tore him up inside. What made it worse was the knowledge that as a hidden part of what the Crane Women had taught him, he could have easily killed Tommy.

The impulse had been there—raw indignation quickly bursting into anger. He could still feel it in his gut: *The world would be better off without Tommy.*

Something in his memory tickled. Something about Kristine. From the Realm. How was that possible?

All his emotions seemed to retreat like a fast sea tide. He stood in the dark, made suddenly afraid by what he remembered, and wondering why he had not remembered before.

After the death of Alyons, Wickmaster of the Pact Lands, at the outer border of the Blasted Plain, he had encountered for the second time the hideous snail-like creature with the death's-head shell. With a woman's voice, it had implored Michael, *"Take me with you. Take me with you. I am not what I seem. I do not belong here."*

"What are you?"

"I am what Adonna wills."

"Who are you?"

"Tonn's wife. Abandoned. Betrayed. Take me with you!"

He walked in a wide circle around the creature. It made no further move toward him.

"You are a mage," it said. *"Take me where I might live again. And I will tell you where Kristine is."*

"I'm sorry," Michael had said. *"I'm no mage. And I don't know who Kristine is."*

He had crossed the border of the Blasted Plain, leaving the skull-snail—Tonn's wife—alone and trapped, a victim of Sidhe sorcery even more hideous than that used to transfigure Lamia and her sister.

His back crawled. Tonn's wife had referred to him as a mage. And by implication, something would happen to Kristine that Michael would have little or no power to prevent.

The Waltiri house seemed less and less a sanctuary and more his own special kind of trap.

8

I've opened that basement door," Michael told his father. They sat on the back porch of the Perrin house while his mother prepared iced tea and sandwiches in the kitchen.

"Oh? What'd you find?"

"A basement. It's crammed full of papers."

"John has something to ask you," Ruth said stiffly, laying a tray on the glass-topped table. She sat across from them, her face drawn. She had tied her long, dark red hair back in a bun.

"LAPD came by yesterday, in the form of a detective," John said. "He asked us questions about you, about your time away. We told him we'd rather discuss such things with you present."

"What did he say to that?"

"He smiled," Ruth said. "He said that was okay and that he had talked to you already. He said you were mysterious but seemed to want to cooperate."

"Then why did he come here?" Michael asked.

"I don't know," John said. "I suppose all this is linked with your disappearance."

Michael picked up a cucumber sandwich, examined it and then set it back on the plate. "I'm going to tell you everything," he said. "I don't care whether you believe me or whether you want to hear. I mean, I care, but I'll tell you anyway."

Ruth wrapped her arms around herself. John glanced at her. "I think it's about time, myself," he said. She sat beside him and nodded slowly.

"All right," she said.

Michael pulled a small cardboard box from his pocket and opened it on the table. There, embedded in cotton gauze, was the glass rose given to him by Mora, Clarkham's Sidhe mistress.

He told the story, much as he had spun it out for Bert Cantor, from the summer days he had spent with Arno and Golda to the few days in Clarkham's Xanadu; from the end of Xanadu to the opening of the basement and the discovery of the curiously altered manuscript of the Infinity Concerto.

The telling lasted into the evening, with a pause for dinner. There were many glasses of tea, and later of beer, and Ruth wept quietly once toward the end, whether for his sanity or in commiseration with what her son had experienced, Michael couldn't judge.

Twilight fell deep blue above the trees and hedges in the back yard. Michael sat with his father while his mother went for a sweater in the house.

"It was always twilight in the between-place," Michael said.

"Where Tristesse waited for travelers," John mused, eyes distant.

"It was odd in the between-worlds. Muddy. Peaceful. I mean, the sensation of reality there was thin. More like a dream, or a nightmare. In the Realm, everything was sharply real, but it didn't feel the same as this, now." Michael tapped the table.

Ruth re-emerged with a pink silk and angora sweater draped over her shoulders. "Do things like that happen?" she asked her husband, matter-of-factly.

John barked an astonished laugh. "Damned if I know."

"I've always thought myself the practical one in this family," she said, face turned toward the fading blue in the west. Michael detected a falseness in her voice, almost a posturing. He realized she was playing a kind of role, using this persona as armor against something that she felt threatened her. "John's the master at wood, and Michael . . . wordsmith, scattershot talents. I could never be sure what Michael would end up being." She glanced pointedly at her son. "This is the only evidence?" She touched the glass rose.

"I could show you the Tippett Hotel and Clarkham's house. Arno's basement."

"I suppose the rule is, you'll have to show us three impossible things before breakfast," John said, picking up the rose gingerly to inspect it. It retained a faint interior glow in the evening gloom. He sniffed it.

"Do you know what the hauntings in the newspapers mean?" his mother asked.

Michael shook his head. "I think I know what they're leading up to, though, which is why I'm telling you all this now."

"Is it why you're letting Kristine Pendeers get involved?" John asked.

"I don't know how I feel about all that." Michael stood and helped his father clear the dinner dishes from the table. When they were done, and the dishes had been stacked in the dishwasher and the table and counters wiped down, Ruth stood in the porch doorway with her arms folded.

She was crying. Her cheeks were shiny and drops beaded her sweater. "I just can't believe it," she said. "I've been saying this is all a nightmare for so long." Michael came to her, and she held him, running the fingers of one hand through his hair.

Michael started to say something, but John caught his eye and shook his head, no.

Later, after Ruth had gone to bed, Michael and his father sat in the back yard under the dim Los Angeles stars. "There's something she's going to tell us," John said. "She's had it inside her as long as I've known her. But it's never come out. Seems to me what you said tonight almost shook it loose."

"What is it?" Michael asked.

"I really don't know," John said. "It's scared me. I've never wanted to know. Sometimes . . ."

"Is it important?"

"To her, it sure is."

LIEUTENANT BRIAN HARVEY stood with Michael in the rear bedroom of Clarkham's house and peered at the footprints that began in the middle of the floor. "So there's no real estate company by that name," he said. "So there's no record of ownership for the house—no record of when it was even built. So this is supposed to be an empty lot. We're still trespassing."

"Are you worried?" Michael asked ironically.

"I suppose not," Harvey said. "It's a good trick, that." He pointed to the prints. "I can guess how it was done. Sprinkle dust around the floor—" He extended his jaw and rubbed his lower lip with his index finger.

"Your dad's an artist type, the kind that might enjoy this sort of thing, isn't he?"

"I suppose."

"You told them everything you've told me?"

"In more detail. There was more time. It took most of an afternoon and evening."

"Magic and ghosts and alien worlds," Harvey sighed. "Okay. So this Tristesse was transformed—is that a good word?—by the Shee."

"Sidhe," Michael corrected.

"I'll never get it right," Harvey grumbled. "They gave her extra joints and turned her into a mummy."

"She was a vampire," Michael said. "Did you look at her teeth?"

"No. Did you?"

Michael hadn't even seen her face. "What did her face look like?"

"I don't remember. A mummy's, I suppose. But you know, that is odd—I don't remember."

"Is she still in the morgue?"

"They were both cremated after nobody claimed them and the coroner's office couldn't prove homicide. I think they didn't want them hanging around. I always thought nothing would spook a coroner. I was wrong. But I have photos on file. And in my car."

"Why are you still on the case?"

"Because I go in for weird things, Mr. Perrin. And I wanted to know what your connection was. What Waltiri had to do with it. I'm a mystery fan. There're so many unsolved crimes and so damned few *mysteries* in my work. Do you understand?"

"I'd like to see the pictures," Michael said.

"I thought you would. Tit for tat. You tell me the story, show me around, and I show you the pictures. You've fulfilled your end of the bargain."

Sitting in the unmarked police car, Harvey handed a file folder to Michael. "They're grim," he said.

Michael opened the folder and took out the facial shots of Lamia. There was a coldness to the black-and-white photography, and the way her flesh had slumped after death added to the sense of unreality, of a poor cinematic makeup job.

He turned the picture over. The photo beneath it was ruined; an oily, varnish-like stain had obscured the middle of the print. Michael held it up for Harvey's inspection.

"Damn," Harvey said. "I'm sure there are other prints. We'll get new ones from the negative."

"I don't think you will," Michael said. "She must have been very beautiful, and very sweet."

"Why do you say that?"

"Because the Sidhe turned her into a monster and made certain no one would ever really see her face again."

Harvey sat silent for a moment, holding the ruined print in his hand. "Now you're spooking *me*," he said. "What in hell are we going to do?"

Michael shrugged. "Wait, I suppose. Do you want to investigate this case any more?"

"What's to investigate?" Harvey said. "There's nothing here that would mean anything to anybody in my profession. Only the end of the world."

"It may not be quite that bad," Michael said.

"I'd be scared stiff if I were you."

"Oh, I'm scared," Michael said. *But I can't just stop everything in its tracks.* There was a process under way, of which he was only a part—and how big a part, he had no way of knowing.

A mage. A face in the blown snow.

9

Kristine called late the next morning. He answered the phone in the master bedroom upstairs and sat on the edge of the four-poster.

"Michael, I'm sorry about the night before last." She sounded tired, voice flat.

"So am I."

"Things haven't gotten any better. I'm not sure whom I can turn to."

"He hasn't hurt you any more, has he?"

"He's taken the car. I don't know where he is. I've gotten this call . . . not from him. From an older-sounding man. He mentioned your name. And then he said terrible things were coming."

Michael looked down at his forearms. The hairs bristled. "Did he tell you his name?"

"No. Do you know anybody who would do that?"

"I'm not sure," Michael said, his eyes closed.

"I was going to talk up the concert before the department chairman today. Now I don't know what to do. Michael, this man said the manuscript should be burned. He didn't have to say what manuscript. We know what he means, don't we?"

"Yes."

"He's some sort of crank, right?"

"I don't know."

"He made me angry. Everything's making me angry now."

"I think you should move out of there," Michael said.

"Oh? Move where?"

Michael didn't answer.

"Yes, well, I've been packing. Some of my girlfriends are looking around for places. Rent is just crazy these days."

"You could move in here," Michael said, and immediately regretted it.

Silence on the other end for a long time. "It isn't that easy. You know why."

"Yes. But it's a large house, and—"

"I'll take a bus to the university this afternoon and try to do some work." She seemed to leave an opening.

"We should get together later," Michael said. "No talk about the concerto or about anything important. Just small talk."

"That would be nice." She sounded relieved. "Michael, what happened in the street—"

"I am sorry."

"No, it was stupid, it was all crazy, but I wanted to thank you. It was gallant, too. You thought you were defending me. I guess you were."

They made arrangements to meet in front of Royce Hall on the campus at five. Michael opened his eyes as he replaced the receiver on the old black phone.

The footsteps in the middle of the dusty floor. The message in the blank notebook. He could feel the presence at the very fringes of the probe he had made throughout the call. There was something foul in the air, a sensation that made his stomach twist and his muscles knot.

Michael stretched and practiced his discipline for several minutes on the bedroom's hardwood floor.

David Clarkham had not died in the conflagration that had consumed his Xanadu. He had managed to escape somehow and was now in Los Angeles, or at least on Earth, and he did not want the concerto performed.

Beneath the tension and the anxiety within him existed a calm place that Michael had only become aware of half-consciously in the last few weeks. The part of Michael Perrin that waited and grew in the calm place felt curious. How far would Clarkham go to prevent the performance?

THE BRICK FAÇADE of venerable Royce Hall dwarfed Kristine, who stood alone, hands clenched in the pockets of her brushed suede coat. Michael walked across the grass and concrete walkways toward her. She turned and smiled with a bare edge of sadness.

No doubt about it now. He was very smitten with Kristine Pendeers.

She hugged him briefly and then backed away. "I tried to call Tommy at the garage where he works. He quit the other day. They don't know where he is."

Michael damped the emotions Tommy's name conjured.

"I'm worried about him," she said. "He just has no control."

"What about your situation? I can help you find a place to rent."

"That would be nice. I have friends looking, too. I can't afford much on the pay of a teaching assistant." They walked to a bench and sat, Kristine crossing her booted legs and slumping against the back of the bench, leaning her head back until she faced the bright gray sky "You know who called me, don't you?"

"His name is—probably—David Clarkham. He's very old. He helped Arno compose Opus 45."

"How old is he?"

"Several centuries, at least," Michael said matter-of-factly.

Kristine straightened on the bench and half-turned toward him.

"I've told my mother and father, and I've told the detective, Lieutenant Harvey, about what happened when I was missing."

"I'm disappointed," Kristine said. "I would have thought you'd confess to me first." Her face was clear of guile.

"Do you believe what I said—you could be in some danger now?"

She nodded, staring at him. "Are you going to tell me?"

"Yes," he said.

"And we're still going to go ahead with the concert, if I can get it arranged?"

"Yes."

"I have a desk in an office in the music building. We can talk there. It's more private."

Michael agreed, and they crossed the campus, passing spare and modern Schönberg Hall. Michael began the story before they reached the small office.

He had become more practiced in the telling now. He could complete the story in much less time, with fewer unnecessary details.

THEY ATE DINNER in a small pizza parlor in Westwood, then went to see a Woody Allen movie playing in one of the smaller theaters of a hexaplex. Kristine was obviously absorbing and digesting what she had been told; she didn't seem to pay much attention to the film. Michael felt her touch his arm on the rest between them, then grip it.

"You must have been terrified," she whispered.

"I was," he said.

"You know what the hauntings are?"

"I can guess."

"I thought you were dangerous," she said. "I was right. I'm not sure I need this now."

"In your situation," Michael prompted.

A middle-aged couple in the row in front of Michael and Kristine turned their heads simultaneously and delivered stern looks.

"Let's go," Kristine said. Michael vaguely regretted the fifteen dollars spent on tickets. Back on the streets of Westwood, Kristine took him through several clothing stores, pointing out dresses she would buy if she could afford them. She was still digesting the story.

"You're not crazy," she said as they left a boutique specializing in Japanese contemporary designs. "I mean, I believe you—in a way. But can you show me something, maybe this *hyloka* or whatever it was?"

"I'd rather not," Michael said. "The last thing I want is for you to think I'm a freak."

She nodded, thought some more and then said, "I don't want to go home to the house on South Bronson tonight, and I'm not ready to make love with you. But I would like to go home with you. And maybe you could show me Clarkham's house? That might give me something solid to think about."

"All right."

"And when we're at Waltiri's house, I will not think you're a freak if you show me some magic."

Michael didn't answer. They doubled back toward the lot where he had parked the Saab.

MICHAEL LAY IN his small guest bed, arms crossed behind his head. The tip of his finger still ached from the trick he had performed for Kristine. Using as an example what Biri had done in the Realm, Michael had taken a boulder in the back yard, applied his glowing index finger to the rock's surface and split it cleanly in four sections. Kristine had jumped back and then quietly asked to return to the house.

She slept in the master bedroom now. Michael knew she slept without probing her aura. His awareness in many areas came without effort. He could feel the sleep-breathing of many people in the neighborhood; he seemed to hear the world turning, and the stars above were almost evident to him through the house's ceiling and the cloudy overcast. Rain fell in a thunderstorm far to the east, over the mountains; he heard its impact on the distant roofs of buildings and in the streets, on tree leaves and blades of grass.

How much of this was imagination, he could not say for sure; he thought none. Michael was simply coming into tune with his world. His inner breath seemed to follow the respiration of the whining molecules in the air itself. He felt he knew more about how those atoms operated than he had ever been taught in school.

He knew how each particle communicated its position and nature to all other particles, first by drawing a messenger from the well of nothing and sending it out, while the receiving particle dropped the messenger back into nothing once it had served its purpose. That rather amused him; no little scraps of telegrams lying about in drifts from all the atoms in the universe.

Yes, if he had designed this world, that would be an obvious asset.

Just before he let himself slide into sleep, he thought he felt the very singing of the vacuum itself, not empty but full of incredible potential—a ground on which the world was only lightly superimposed, from atoms to galaxies; it seemed as if it might all be swept away by a strong enough will. Or more probably, as if the ground of creation could be overlaid with another scheme, imitative but different in large details.

He composed a fragment of a poem, back-tracking over the words and editing several times before coming up with:

> Here makes real
> The weaver's weft.
> Lace-maker's bobbins
> Spin right, leap left;
> Lift time's thread
> Over atom's twist,
> Bind such knot with
> Death's stone fist.
>
> Weave of flower
> And twine of light

Must cross and thwart
By wilt, by night.

Michael mused for a time on how realities might be put together by those less than gods. Such thinking was so abstruse and farfetched, however, that he soon drifted back to more immediate concerns.

He was not disappointed that Kristine did not share his bed this evening. His affection for her—his growing love—made him patient. She already trusted him, though skittishly; she had given him an incredible gift by believing his story.

He smiled in his slumber, feeling Kristine's even, steady, sleeping existence. He would have gladly remained in that state forever, but he knew how fragile this contentment was.

Now he had told everyone who counted, who had the slightest possibility of believing him. If he had been secretive, if his courage had faltered and he had kept silent, he would have been playing along with Clarkham's plans.

Michael would not be isolated.

He suspected he had just purchased some extra time, at very little cost indeed.

Yet still, on the very fringes of his outermost perception: the foulness, the spoor of the Isomage.

Clarkham had one advantage over Michael still: a plan. Michael didn't have a clear idea of what he needed to do, or even of the nature of what was coming.

10

Downstairs, somebody banged on the door frantically. Michael broke out of a dream—dangerous, dreams, since they now pulled in his circle of awareness—and lurched out of bed, grabbing a robe and slipping it over his nakedness. In the hallway, he saw Kristine standing in the door to the master bedroom. She wore one of Golda's nightgowns, simple dark-blue flannel. "Somebody wants in," she said sleepily.

Michael extended his awareness as he thumped barefooted down the stairs. The aura of the person beyond the door, a man, was very familiar and very welcome, though there was something subtly wrong . . .

He opened the door. A heavy-set bearded fellow in his middle forties stood outside, dressed in skins and furs like a trapper, with a cloth bag slung over his shoulder. His short gray hair jutted out in all directions. "Nikolai!"

"Thank God," the man said with a mild Russian accent. "I have been looking all over for this place. I do not know Los Angeles now, Michael." He laid his cloth bag down on the step and hugged Michael twice, kissing him on both cheeks.

"How did you get here?" Michael was astonished; he had last seen Nikolai in the Realm, standing beside the Sidhe initiate Biri and Clarkham's mistress Mora at the outskirts of the imitation Xanadu.

"I walked," Nikolai said. Michael invited him in; Kristine watched them from the bottom of the stairs.

"This is a friend," Michael said to Kristine. "Nikolai Kuprin."

"Nikolai Nikolaievich Kuprin, Kolya to friends." He returned to the porch for his bag, grinning sheepishly.

"Nikolai, this is Kristine Pendeers."

"Beautiful, beautiful." Nikolai sighed, staring at her with embarrassing concentration. "My pleasure." He shook her hand delicately; Kristine, Michael noticed, extended her hand to Nikolai in the feminine fashion, allowing him to grasp her fingers. "I have not seen a human woman in . . . ah, if I think about how long, I'll weep. Here, I have been staying out of sight, walking at night, because I could be conspicuous, don't you think?"

"How did you cross over?" Michael asked.

"It is very bad in the Realm now," Nikolai said. "I think perhaps Adonna is dead. Everything is uncertain."

"This is *that* Nikolai?" Kristine asked.

"You've told her? Good. Prepare everybody."

"You still haven't answered my question," Michael said, too astonished and pleased to be exasperated.

"Because I am embarrassed," Nikolai said. "I took advantage of the Ban of Hours. I used the stepping stones in Inyas Trai." He crossed himself quickly as he said the name. "The Councils of Delf and Eleu have been dissolved—"

"You know about them?"

"Yes, yes—Eleu supports human participation in creating a new world, and Delf opposes . . . the Council of Delf sided with the Maln. But both are disbanded now, and even the Maln is in disarray. Tarax has disappeared. The crisis has divided everyone. Inyas Trai"—he crossed himself—"is full of Sidhe again, both sexes, all kinds. They are preparing the stepping stones for migration. Many thousands have left already. Exodus. And there are so many humans—more than I ever thought could exist in the Realm! Thousands. Where did they come from? I do not know! But I separated myself from those captured in Euterpe. I had to get back to Earth and warn you. I used a stone not yet open for the journey. I'm not sure I did the right thing." He looked around the house, face filled with wonder, mouth open. "So familiar. So beautiful. Like my parents' home in Pasadena."

"Why wasn't it right?" Michael asked, sensing again something wrong in Nikolai's aura.

"I don't feel very good. Sometimes everything seems like a painting on glass. I can see through. Perhaps the stone hadn't been . . ." He shrugged. "I am tired. May I sit?"

They entered the living room. Nikolai lay down on the couch, then leaned back and twisted his head to look at the piano. "A beautiful instrument," he said. "Is it yours?"

"It belonged to Arno Waltiri," Michael said.

Nikolai stiffened despite his exhaustion. "Do you know about Waltiri?" he asked.

"He was a mage," Michael said. "I know that."

"Mage of the Cledar." Nikolai returned his gaze to Kristine, and his drawn, dirty face seemed to light up from within as he smiled. "Birds. The musical race. He worked with the Council of Eleu, on Earth mostly. There was a rumor that the Maln collected humans from Earth, like Emma Livry . . . so much confusion, so many rumors."

"I haven't told Kristine about that, yet," Michael said. "Where are the Sidhe migrating?"

"I attended the last meeting of the Council of Eleu," Nikolai said. "The Ban requested the presence of a human, and I was the most convenient. The Ban became part of the Council, but what her intentions are now, I don't know. I have no idea what is happening in the Irall. The Maln do not enter Inyas Trai."

Kristine shook her head, completely lost. "He's talking just like you," she said.

"Do not doubt my friend's word," Nikolai advised solemnly, leaning toward her from his recumbent position. "However crazy he might seem. Michael is a very powerful fellow. He bested the Isomage and destroyed him."

"Clarkham isn't dead," Michael said. "Where are the Sidhe migrating? Answer me, Nikolai. It's important."

"Back to the Earth. They have not the power to go anywhere else. Adonna built the Realm close to the Earth on the string of worlds. They can only return."

"The hauntings?" Kristine asked, looking between them, eyes wide.

"I thought as much," Michael said.

"The stone I took is a direct route to Los Angeles," Nikolai said. "Nobody explained why. It was certainly convenient. If I haven't done myself a mischief . . ." He fell back on the couch pillow and closed his eyes. "Do you have aspirin?"

Michael brought a bottle of aspirin and a glass of water. "Where did you arrive in Los Angeles?" he asked, stooping beside the couch and dropping two tablets into Nikolai's hand.

"Hollywood," Nikolai said after swallowing the tablets and draining the glass. "A tall building on Sunset. Very bad shape, filthy. Worse than Ellis Island."

"Are you hungry?" Kristine asked. Nikolai regarded her as if she were a saint.

"Very hungry," he said.

"Then let's have breakfast." She went into the kitchen. Nikolai smiled weakly at Michael.

"She is very nice," he said. "You have been well since your return?"

"Healthy, getting stronger," Michael said.

Nikolai appraised him shrewdly. "Stronger, as in arm-strong, leg-strong?"

"That, too," Michael said.

"I surprised you, no, by coming back? I'm not a great magician, not even of much concern to the Sidhe, yet I made it home. What year is it—truly, I mean? I look at the city and think perhaps centuries have passed."

"It's 1990," Michael said. "May the twelfth."

Combined grief and dismay crossed Nikolai's face. "Not as bad as I expected. So many changes! I am Rip van Winkle now, true?"

Michael nodded. "There doesn't seem to be any link between time in the Realm and here," he said. "I was gone for only a few months, yet five years passed on Earth. And you . . ."

"It is good to see you, very good," Nikolai interrupted. "My brain swims. I cannot think clearly now. Perhaps some food."

Michael spread his hands out beside Nikolai and frowned. The man's aura was extremely weak, almost undetectable. The way the morning light from the front windows played on Nikolai's eyes was also subtly wrong—the reflections seemed bland, lackluster.

Nikolai got to his feet and wobbled, shaking his head. They joined Kristine in the kitchen and sat at the small table. She complimented Michael on the larder he had stocked. "You're pretty self-sufficient. Most bachelors act as if their mommies were still around to do everything for them."

"Most women I know would have freaked out long before this," Michael said.

"'Freaked out,'" Nikolai repeated, chewing on a slice of toast he had slathered with butter and marmalade. "That means go crazy, perhaps?"

"How long has he been gone?" Kristine asked.

"Sixty, maybe seventy years," Michael said.

"Sixty-seven years," Nikolai said. "You would have made a fine dancer, Miss Pendeers."

"My legs and hips are too heavy," she said.

"Not at all. It is strength that is important, and grace. You have grace, and the strength—" He slowly lowered the last scrap of toast to the plate and paled, as if ill. "Oh, Michael, it is not good. It is not working."

Michael could not detect Nikolai's aura. Instinctively, he reached out to hold Nikolai with both arms.

"I am going back!" Nikolai bellowed, standing and rocking the table. He held his hands up to the ceiling and moaned, clutching at the air. "Please, not—"

His last word ended in a high-pitched squeak. The table rocked on its pedestal, upsetting jars of jam and cups of coffee. Kristine screamed and backed against the sink. Michael had taken hold of Nikolai's skin jerkin and felt the material squirm between his fingers as if alive.

The table settled, and a cup rolled to the floor and shattered. Where the man had stood, the air was wrinkled by a heat mirage. That also faded. Nikolai was gone.

Kristine began to cry. "Michael, what happened to him?" She wrapped her arms around herself, leaning backward over the sink.

Michael stepped away from the table and stood with his arms hanging by his sides, clenching and unclenching his fists helplessly.

"What happened?" she asked again, more quietly.

"I think he's back in the Realm," Michael said. The eggs that she had begun frying now smoked in the iron skillet. He lifted the skillet from the stove and carried it carefully around her, lowered it into the sink and filled it with water. She watched him as if hypnotized.

"Nobody's joking, right?" she asked. "This is serious?"

Michael nodded and took her hand, sitting her down in the chair he had occupied. He righted Nikolai's chair and ran his hand over the seat as if to search for a trace of the vanished friend. Kristine sat in silence for several long minutes, not looking at him. Her breathing slowed, and she swallowed less often.

"Do you still want to go on with it?" he asked.

"The performance?" She shrugged with a sharp upward jerk of her shoulders. Her arms shook. "This is frightening. It's . . ."

Michael squeezed her hand and looked at her intently.

"It's not like anything I've experienced. I mean, that's obvious, but . . . It's incredible." She was high from terror and excitement. "I want to go on with it. Oh, yes!"

"Why?" Michael asked, his tone close to anger. "You saw what happened to Nikolai. It's no game."

"What do you want me to say, then? That I'm going to give up? I don't understand you."

"I'm angry at myself," Michael said.

"That's your privilege," Kristine said, drawing herself up. "I think I'm doing rather well."

Michael laughed and shook his head, then sat in Nikolai's chair. "You think it's an adventure," he said.

"Isn't it?"

"Do you understand the danger?"

"Is Nikolai dead?"

"I don't think so."

"Will someone try to kill me? Us?"

"Very likely," Michael said. "Or worse. The Sidhe can turn people into monsters, or they can lock them away in limbo."

Kristine's face was bland, seemingly peaceful, as she considered. "When I was nineteen," she said, "I thought about committing suicide. Everything seemed cut and dried. Art and music were fine, but could they explain anything? Could they tell me why I was alive or what the world was all about? I didn't think so. And ever since, I've lived a compromise: I wouldn't try to kill myself, because there was always a chance something would happen to explain everything."

Here was a depth to Kristine he hadn't begun to reach. He could feel, without probing, a melancholy and rootlessness in her words that shook him.

"When I listened to your story, I had a crazy hope that it was true and you weren't just crazy or putting me on. Even if the world was a wall of paper and everything I had learned was wrong. Because it meant there was something behind everything, some purpose or greater . . ." She gestured with the fingers of her right hand. "Something. Life is such a mess most of the time, and everything that's supposed to be important—love and work and all of it—can be so petty and senseless. Now I've seen a man just vanish, after confirming your story. And . . ." Tears on her cheeks. "God damn it," she said, wiping them away hastily. "I'm so goddamn *grateful,* and scared, and excited. There *is* something else, and maybe I'll be really important."

Michael smiled. "You have real courage," he said.

"Why do we *have* to perform the concerto?" she asked, expressing no doubts about the project but simply requesting a reason.

"I wish I knew."

11

Kristine stayed in the Waltiri house only two nights. She then found a small studio apartment, splitting the rent with an older geology student who spent most of her time on field trips in the Mojave Desert. No mention was made of Tommy; there seemed to have been a clean break. Nor did Kristine speak of Nikolai again; her panicked enthusiasm of that day had subsided.

She kept up a feverish activity arranging for the concert, but whenever the possibility of something more came up—something more intimate—she backed away. A look came into her eyes. As tempted as he was, Michael did not probe. His own emotions seemed to have slipped into neutral. The times they met and discussed the performance, he felt more relaxed and open, unpressured. But as interested as they were in each other, their relationship did not advance. It was necessary for Kristine to reevaluate, and for Michael as well.

Students from the university came to the Waltiri house and carted away truckloads of papers. For a week, Michael simply kept out of the way of a group of musicologists and librarians who spent the hours from eight in the morning to six at night cataloging, re-recording and safeguarding Waltiri's masters. They worked mostly in the music room.

Two weeks passed. He experienced no further visions or revelations, and there was nothing overtly unworldly in the news. Twice Michael inspected the Tippett Residential Hotel, and once, late at night, he revisited Clarkham's house, but all was quiet.

The quiet times would end soon.

He began sleeping in the master bedroom in late May. Kristine's occupation of the room had dispelled some of the groundless taboo Michael had felt about the marital bed of Arno and Golda. He found he slept more peacefully there; it was quieter even than the rest of the house. His sleeping awareness felt sharper in that room.

On an overcast, drizzling night in early June, Michael dreamed of the reoccupation of Earth's oceans by the Pelagal Sidhe.

He floated just above the level of deep-ocean waves cresting at thirty and forty feet. On the horizon, a wickedly glorious sunset came to its climax, tipping each wave with red and gold. Columns of clouds advanced east from the squat red sun, each wearing a cap of fading glory and resting on a base of shaded slate-brown. Rain fell in sheets to the north. Michael could feel the freshness of the ocean wind and the cold of the sea spray; he could smell the salt and the fresh rain. He had never felt more alive, and yet he knew he was asleep and that his sensible body was nowhere near.

The west darkened. The clouds lost their glow, became gray and dark brown with edges of green. He seemed to look up at the zenith, rotating his nonbody somehow, and sensed a discontinuity in a massive gray cloud high overhead. Water began to fall, not fresh rain but salty and brackish, copper-colored like the sea beyond Clarkham's Xanadu. Michael thought of water breaking during birth. A radiance of night ate away the bottom of the cloud, and out of the blackness, an entire ocean fell, not in drops, but in solid columns dozens of yards wide. In the columns, Michael saw deep-sea-green male and female Sidhe ride the fall with webbed feet pointed down, arms held high over their heads and fingers meeting in a prayer gesture, eyes trained down, huge bubbles flowing around them from air trapped between the columns and the Earth sea below.

The ocean seethed with foam for miles around, and the air filled with a noise beyond the capacity of ears to hear, even had he listened with ears. Waves surged outward from the fall in immense rolls.

The sky closed and the cloud dissipated.

Michael's point of view shifted. He now looked down on the roiling Earth sea, its surface lime-green with breaking bubbles. Fog and salt mist hid the horizon on all sides.

A dozen, then a hundred, a thousand, a myriad of the Sidhe breached the surface in graceful lines, ordered themselves in cylindrical ranks beneath the waves and swam from the site of the fall.

Michael came awake abruptly and lay on the bed, his body cold as ice. After a few moments of *hyloka*, he warmed again.

The mass migrations had begun.

KRISTINE PARKED AT a lot across from the studio's tan and gray Gower Street gate. "Edgar's very busy now. He's doing sessions on the score for Lean's new picture— a real break for him, you know. Lean has always used Maurice Jarre."

Michael nodded, more intent on examining the studio than the names. The bare tan outer walls seemed more appropriate for heavy industry than a dream factory.

Kristine crossed the street and opened the glass door for him, pointing to a reception desk on the left side of a small sitting room. Behind the desk sat a woman in a blue and gray security uniform, appointment book and computer terminal before her. She smiled at Kristine.

"Betty, this is Michael Perrin," Kristine introduced. "Betty Folger. She keeps out riffraff like us most of the time, but . . ."

"Mr. Moffat?" Betty asked, smiling. She referred to the screen, then to the book. "He's logged you in for eleven fifteen. It'll take you five minutes to get to recording studio 3B. If you start now, you'll be right on time." She held up a map, but Kristine waved it off.

"I know the way," she said. "Thanks."

Michael followed, impressed by the quiet and sense of order within the studio. Kristine led him down a corridor lined with offices and out of the building, across a small grassy park shaded with olive trees and then between two huge hangar-like sound stages. Beyond one rank of sound stages and before a second, nestled between backdrops imitating sky and rocks, was a quaint western town, quiet now except for a repair crew and a blue Ford pickup loaded with paint and supplies.

"It's magic, isn't it?" Kristine said.

Michael agreed. He had never visited a studio before, not even on the déclassé Universal tour. He knew the basics of motion picture production—location shooting, interior sets built within the sound stages, special effects and opticals, but the actuality was still magic.

They skirted a shallow, dry concrete basin covering at least two acres, with a rough-hewn wooden pier jutting out to the middle. On the sound stage immediately behind the basin, a monumental blue sky and clouds had been painted. A line of painted dead palm trees hid the foundation of the sound stage.

"3B is back around that way," Kristine said. "We're taking the long route. I wanted you to see the sets. No tour complete without them."

They entered a long, white two-story building across from the studio fire department, passed down yet another cool, darkened hall lined with framed photos of studio executives, composers, and movie sets, and stopped before a door marked "3B—Authorized Only." A red light above the door was not glowing. Kristine knocked lightly on the door, and a dark bearded young man in a *Black Easter* T-shirt and jeans answered.

"Frank, this is Michael Perrin—Frank Warden."

Warden shook Michael's hand and returned to a bank of sound equipment covering an entire wall. 35mm spools unloaded their tan recording tape through a maze of guides and heads, while rows of lights blinked nearby and dB meters bounced their needles in reaction to sounds unheard. "Edgar's listening to the playback now. Might as well go in. We're about to dump a flighty saw man and do it all digital." He gave them both a stern, meaningful look: *rough session.*

"It's a different world from Waltiri's day," Kristine commented softly as they took the right-hand door into the control room. Edgar Moffat—in his early fifties, balding, with a circlet of short-cut gray hair—sat in a leather swivel chair before a bank of sliding switches, verniers and three small inset computer screens. Compact earphones wrapped around his head played faint, eerie music. Through the glass beyond the controls, Michael saw two performers in a soundproofed recording studio, one clutching a violin and the other an elongated band of flexible steel. They were exchanging bows with each other and trying them out, in complete silence, on the bandsaw and the violin. Moffat removed his earphones and shook his head, then punched a switch. A squeal of vibrating metal invaded the control room.

"Gordon, George, it's still off. Take a break and get your shit together. We'll want it right next time or we synthesize it. One more blow against live performers, right?"

The musicians nodded glumly and set their instruments down.

Moffat swiveled to face them with a broad smile. "Kristine, good to see you again. It's been weeks since you last slummed from the heights of academe."

"It's been busy. Very busy. Edgar, this is—"

"Your new boyfriend. You dumped that Tommy bastard, right?"

Kristine gave him a pained look. "This is Michael Perrin. He's executor for the Waltiri estate."

Moffat's expression intensified, and he stood up. "Sorry, but he wasn't worthy of you, and you know it. Michael, glad to meet you. Kristine told me about the situation. I worked with Arno in the fifties and sixties. You might say he gave me my start. Tough old bird." He raised a bushy white eyebrow as if hoping for a reaction.

Michael calmly shook his hand.

"Kristine says you've found 45."

"We're going to perform it, if I have my way," Kristine said proudly.

"Christ, I always thought it was a myth. I talked with Steiner once—he said he was there, at the Pandall. He plugged his ears with cotton. Now I ask you, is that to be believed? Others weren't so lucky, he said. Friedrich, Topsalin—where are they now? Topsalin sued, so the legend goes."

"It's all true," Michael said. "That's what Arno told me."

"Well, Arno never talked about it to us. Not even to Previn, and he was really intent on making Previn a protégé. Previn resisted, unlike me, and look where he is, and look where I am." He held out his hands, smiling ruefully. "Arguing with a man playing a blunted cross-cut saw."

"I brought a copy along," Kristine said, unzipping her bag. She handed Moffat the manuscript. He motioned them to sit in worn but comfortable chairs crammed into a corner, then put on a pair of glasses and peered at the pages.

"Mm," he said on the third page. "I heard once that Schönberg liked this better than anything else Arno had done. Heard that from David Raksin. More legend. Arnold and Arno. Arnold kept accusing Arno of doing nothing but Hollywood." He briefly assumed Schönberg's Viennese accent. "'45 is not Hollywoody. Finally!' I can see why he said that. I wouldn't dare put a score like this in front of a bunch of union musicians. This is difficult stuff. The piano . . . Jesus, how to mangle a good instrument. Brass bars on the strings, a microphone hookup . . . hell, he was asking for an electric piano. Cosmic honky-tonk." He spent several minutes leafing through the first third of the concerto, then closed it and sighed. "Absolutely insane. You can't even call it discord. It's wonderful. So who'll perform it?"

"I was hoping you could make recommendations. We have a good orchestra, but—"

"You need seasoned folks. You know, a lot of pros would give their perfect pitch for a chance to perform a legend like this."

"You have the contacts," Kristine said. "If you could put out the word . . ."

"Have you tried to reach David Clarkham?" Moffat asked.

"He disappeared in the forties," Michael said.

"Why should we talk to him?" Kristine asked, tensing.

"If he's still alive, he might have something to say about this. He's almost as legendary as 45. The dark man of Los Angeles music. I could tell you stories . . . secondhand, of course . . . the man was certifiable. Why Arno worked with him I'll never understand, and of course he never told me, except to shake his head once or twice and wave away my questions."

"What kind of stories?" Kristine asked, forcing herself to relax with a small shiver.

"Steiner told me once, before he died, that he met Clarkham. Clarkham confessed to Steiner that he was the figure in gray who commissioned Mozart to write his requiem. Hounded Mozart."

Michael's eyes widened. "He might have been," he said simply. Moffat narrowed his eyes and cocked his head to one side.

"Don't mind Michael," Kristine said. "He's full of mystery, too."

"At any rate, combining both of their talents in one work . . ." Moffat returned the concerto score with some reluctance to Kristine. "It'll need reorchestration. I can already pick out passages that simply can't be played."

"Arno would want it exact," Michael said.

"I'm sure he would," Moffat replied, lifting his eyebrows. "He could be as bitten by the serial bug as any of us. But he knew as well as I that a score has to be looked at realistically. Some things inevitably have to be changed. And I think we can do it *better* than it was done in 1939. The notation here . . ." He reclaimed the manuscript and opened it to the middle, pointing out long black jagged lines, half-circles and Maltese crosses. "I may be the only person who can decipher some of this now. Arno's special symbols. I decoded from his four-staff scores when I orchestrated for him."

"I knew we'd need you," Kristine said.

"Okay, but where's the funding?"

"I'm working on that. When will you have time to rehearse?"

"Starting on the thirty-sixth of June," Moffat said ruefully. "Depends on whether or not Lean and I see eye to eye on this. He insists on waltz beats in the strangest places. I love David dearly, but he and Maurice have worked together entirely too long." He reached his hand out and gripped Michael's shoulder. "You know music, young man?"

"Not very well," Michael said. "I've been teaching myself for a few months now."

"Not the way to go about it, believe me. You seem concerned about . . . what? Duplicating the effect of the original performance?"

Michael nodded.

"You want to get us all sued?" Moffat smiled wolfishly, knitting his gray brows. "I'll take the risk. There's not much adventure in this business. I'll need all the notes and journal entries you can find on this . . . and correspondence, anything where Arno might have revealed his intentions. He was never the most precise composer. It'll be doubly difficult not having him here to make final decisions."

"There's a special study crew from the UCLA music library going through all his papers now."

Moffat released Michael's shoulder and patted it gently. "I will await further instructions, then. Honestly, I should have the recording wrapped up in three weeks. I can start rehearsal after I get back from Pinewood. Shall we aim for something in a month and a half?"

"Not unreasonable," Kristine said.

"Good. Now go away and let me harass my sessions people. Michael." He held out his hand, and Michael shook it firmly. "Far be it from me to nudge, but this woman . . ." He indicated Kristine with a nod and a wink. "She's special. You could do much, much worse."

"Edgar . . ." Kristine warned, lifting a fist.

"Out! Work to do." Moffat opened the door and showed them back through the recording room to the hallway, then shut the door abruptly. The red light came on.

Kristine and Michael regarded each other in the hallway for a moment. "All right," Kristine said. "Now you've met him. I think he's essential. Don't you?"

"Yes," Michael said. "Especially since Arno didn't leave many instructions or clues. I've looked through a lot of papers and letters in the past few weeks. The manuscript is all I've found."

"Can't hurt to look again, though," Kristine said. "Now. If you'll drop me off at the campus . . ." She marched down the hall ahead of him, turned and cocked her head. Michael remained by the door smiling at her.

"Coming?"

He caught up, and they left the building. "Moffat's a touch pushy, isn't he?"

"More than a touch," Kristine said. "He only met Tommy once, for just a few minutes, and—well. Not worth talking about."

"We haven't had lunch in a long time," Michael said hesitantly.

"No time, not today," Kristine answered crisply. He did not persist. Even without a probe, he could sense her uncertainty and pain. She glanced at him as they climbed into her car. "Patience, Michael. Please."

He agreed with a nod and put the car in gear.

MICHAEL WATCHED AS a librarian and a team of students hauled the last papers from the garage into a campus van. The attic was empty; the music room had been processed the week before, leaving little more than the furniture. With the removal of the last of the material from the garage, the house seemed less protective and himself more vulnerable, but vulnerable to what he couldn't say. Clarkham's inroads, perhaps.

But Michael couldn't believe Clarkham was the greatest of his problems.

> I am dark!
> Awaiting sight

Formless wave
Guiding light

Again his poems were short and enigmatic, as they had been in the Realm, but they offered no answers to his questions; there was no Death's Radio infusing his art.

He was on his own, whatever he had to face.

The van drove away, and Michael shut the garage door on the aisles of empty metal shelves and the old Packard. He paused at the latch and lock, frowning.

Confusion. Carpets of dirty car parts arrayed in dark halls. And over all—a sickening foulness.

"That's a beautiful old car."

Michael turned and saw Tommy at the end of the drive. "Isn't it?" he said. "Pity it's too expensive to drive."

Tommy shrugged that off. "Belonged to your friend, didn't it? Waltari? Martini?"

Michael nodded. "What can I do for you?"

Tommy crossed his arms. "Leave her alone."

"I haven't heard from Kristine in two days." He swallowed. "Besides, you split up weeks ago."

"Just two days. Great. You're right. She left me weeks ago. I'm partly to blame. You're the main reason, though."

There was a repulsive foulness in the man's aura that Michael found all too familiar. He began walking down the brick drive toward Tommy, acting on instinct again. The situation felt dangerous.

"You know a fellow named Clarkham?" Tommy asked, backing up a step and then standing his ground as Michael approached.

"Yes."

"He knows you. He's been watching you and Kristine. He told me all about you. How you badmouth me. A poet." Tommy laughed as if he had just seen a pratfall on TV. "Jesus, a poet! You look like a goddamn athlete, not a poet."

"Looks deceive," Michael said, sensing that Tommy had a gun, knowing it was behind the jacket, held by the left hand stuck through a hole cut in the fabric of the side pocket. The jacket could open, and he could fire in an instant. Michael stood five yards from the gun.

"He said you're as bad for her as I was. You hit her more than I did. He says you take her to . . ." His free hand swung back and forth, and he nodded his head deeply, twice. "Parties. Get her in that scene. Do lines of coke. Shit, I would never get her involved in that." The hand stopped swinging. "Hollywood shit."

Whatever native intelligence Tommy had once possessed had been corroded by Clarkham's discharge of foulness. Michael could feel the Isomage near, if not in space then in influence, watching through this pitiful and extremely dangerous intermediary.

"He's a liar," Michael said. "You can't believe him."

"No, I don't, really," Tommy said. "I didn't know she was like that. I was bad enough for her. I just loved her too much, and I'd get jealous, you know?"

Soon; it would be very soon. Two and a half strides. He could judge the size of the gun. It was a .45 automatic loaded with hollow-core bullets. It could cut him in half. Clarkham had sent him a missile loaded with death, much as the Sidhe had sent Michael to Clarkham.

It would be useless trying to stop Tommy. If Michael cast a decoy shadow, to give himself time to find shelter, it was entirely possible that Clarkham would have prepared the man for such an eventuality, even equipped him with a means to see through the deception. Michael's thoughts became sharp as razors, cutting quickly at this hypothesis, then at that.

He felt Robert Dopso nearby—a definite complication if Dopso or his mother came out of the house now. Michael's senses rose to a higher level of acuity.

"It's not that I hate you," Tommy said, smiling, the arm in the jacket pocket twitching. "You're just like any other son-of-a-bitch. Her body." Pain crossed Tommy's face. "That's all you care about. Me, I really *cared*. I wanted her to be everything she could be." His voice grated. He shook.

"We're friends, that's all," Michael said calmly. "No need to be upset."

"My needs and your needs aren't the point, are they?" Tommy said. "Don't come any closer. He warned me, but he didn't need to warn me, did he? I remember." He touched his nose.

"Clarkham is a liar," Michael reiterated. "He filled you full of bad things . . . didn't he?"

A light of recognition appeared in Tommy's eyes. "He touched me when we were talking."

Something built rapidly in Michael, a shadow different from the ones he had cast before, different even from the one he had finally sent spinning to trap Clarkham in Xanadu. This was a variety of shadow he had not been told about, and finding it within him frightened him almost as much as Tommy did. He tried to hold it back but could not; his augmented instinct told him there was no other way.

But Michael did not want to believe that. He did not want to believe he was capable of defending himself in such a way.

The part that thinks death is sleep. Lose that part. The part that seeks warm darkness and oblivion. Lose that self. He will embrace it. He desires rest and escape from the pain.

The voice telling Michael these things was his own.

Dopso walked down the sidewalk before the driveway, saw Tommy and Michael and smiled at Michael. "Hello," he said. Then he frowned. "What's—"

"No!" Michael said. "Go back!" Whatever choice he had was now taken from him. Tommy would kill Dopso and anybody else who walked by. Clarkham's missile was not precise, could not control itself, could not discriminate.

Across the street, a middle-aged woman in a pink dress sauntered by, taking her chain-tugging schnauzer for a walk.

Tommy jerked the jacket open, revealing the dull gray gun.

Michael *sent*. The shadow that went forth was not even visible. It did not mimic Michael's form. It simply carried another self away, a self he did not need and could use to advantage.

Dopso and the middle-aged woman saw Tommy lift the gun, turn halfway, twitch and apply the gun to his own head. He had a sleepy look on his face; this would have happened anyway, but nevertheless—

Michael screamed inside.

The gun went off.

Tommy's hair lifted obscenely on the opposite side of his head, and he dropped as if kicked by a bull. Michael closed his eyes and heard the dog barking and the woman shrieking. He opened his eyes and saw the dog dragging the woman back and forth in a space of a few yards. Dopso had turned away, arms held up against the sound of the shot. Splashes of blood covered the sidewalk and grass by his feet.

Even knowing there had been no other choice, Michael felt sick. He forced himself to look at the body. Clarkham's deposited foulness had eaten away the dead Tommy almost instantly. What was left was not recognizable. It was covered with a shining blackness and had slumped inward, wicked-witch style, only the gun unaffected. In seconds, there was little more than a pile of tattered clothing and evil-smelling dust.

The woman stopped shrieking. The dog sat on the sidewalk, tongue hanging. "Are you all right?" she called out to Michael, her voice hoarse. Michael was too stunned to answer.

"God," Dopso said, eyes wide, staring at the dust.

"What happened to him?" the woman asked sharply, her voice on the edge of a scream again.

"He's dead," Michael said. "I'll call the police."

"He shot himself," Dopso said. "But he's . . ."

Michael nodded and looked at the ridge of the roof on the house directly opposite. A large crow-like bird with a red breast perched there.

The woman crossed the street, dragging the dog on its leash behind her back, her eyes glazed with anticipation of disgust. She stepped up on the curb, staring fixedly at the pile of debris. "He's not there," she said, amazed. "What happened to his body?"

"Please go home," Michael said. Gently, he gave her a forgetfulness, hardly even aware that he used an ability for the first time. He extended the forgetfulness to the dog. The woman walked off, silent and calm.

The bird on the roof had flown away.

He did not want Dopso to forget. He was close enough to the action to need to remember and understand.

"Michael . . ."

"Do you want to know what happened?" Michael asked.

"I don't think so," Dopso replied, his voice fading. He shook his head.

"You'll have to know sooner or later."

"But not now . . . Where did he go?"

"He was sent here by David Clarkham."

"Yes . . . ?"

Michael could tell now was not the time to reveal all to Dopso.

"I'm going to call the police," Michael said.

He entered the house and walked into the kitchen, slumping into a chair. He picked up the phone receiver and dialed the number Lieutenant Harvey had given him. Harvey's assistant, a young-sounding man, answered. Michael gave him few details, just saying that the lieutenant should call him immediately.

"I'll tell him when he comes in," the assistant said dubiously.

Michael hung up and returned to the clothes and the gun. No other people had stepped out of their homes to investigate. Dopso had gone back into his house. Michael could feel him sitting in a chair inside, ignoring his mother's questions.

The woman and her dog had walked out of sight. Everything was quiet again.

The clothes themselves had disintegrated. The gun's grip had turned rusty brown and ash-gray. Michael held the gun butt between two fingers and carried it into the house.

The wind was already blowing what was left of Tommy down the sidewalk, onto the grass and the bushes at the edge of the driveway.

12

I think I'm more upset than you are," Michael said, sitting across from her in the cramped apartment. Rock-climbing tools hung on the small dining nook wall like pieces of art; knapsacks, tents and metal shelving covered with rocks filled the hall to the bathroom and bedroom. Kristine's living there seemed to have hardly made an impression. Aside from a three-tier fold-up bookcase beside the couch and a stack of blank ruled composition sheets, the roommate's presence dominated even in her absence.

Kristine looked at him sharply, turned away, and did not speak for a long time. She took deep, even breaths, gazing past the hide-a-bed and through the sliding glass door at the courtyard beyond. "You're sure he died. He didn't just disappear."

"He died, and then he decayed," Michael said bluntly.

"I don't know why *you* should be upset," Kristine said, still not looking at him. "He threatened you, and you lived. You won. Poor bastard."

"He was used," Michael said for the third time.

"Did he feel what he was doing—did he know?"

"I think so," Michael said. "I can't be sure, though."

"This fantasy of yours is really ugly, you know that?"

Michael didn't understand.

"This macho fantasy world. Men do so like to kill each other." Her soft voice dripped venom. "I *do* care. I loved him. I said I didn't, but . . . I didn't need you to protect me from him. I don't care what I said."

"No. He didn't go to you after Clarkham—"

"Just shut up about Clarkham. About everything. Jesus, Michael, it's so convenient. He didn't even leave a body. What did your police lieutenant think about that?"

"I haven't talked to him yet. It's only been two hours. He's supposed to call me back."

"Trying to be legal and above suspicion. Good move." She had not cried at all, but her eyes appeared puffy. "I'm not excited now about the strangeness. I was. It seemed fantastic, people disappearing, fairies coming back to Earth, old sorcerers battling it out with music. Now it just seems like maybe the Middle East. Terrorists. Murder. No different."

"It's not a fantasy," Michael said. "It's deadly serious. Nobody escapes for long." His last four words sounded ominous even to himself. Kristine looked at him directly and squinted, as if about to cringe away.

"Are lots more people going to die?" she asked.

"I don't know."

"You're talking about a war, aren't you?"

Michael shook his head.

"But you didn't really kill . . . Tommy."

"I made him kill himself. That's close enough."

"You didn't murder him because he would have killed you. Self-defense isn't murder. Clarkham filled Tommy with lies. That means *he* killed Tommy. What do you think about that? Don't you hate Clarkham now?"

Michael considered for a moment, then shook his head. "Does me no good to hate him, or anyone."

"But you'll kill him if you get the chance?"

Michael considered some more, then said, "Yes."

Suddenly, everything about Kristine seemed to soften and relax. She closed her eyes and drew in a shuddering breath, letting it out with a moan. "I cut him out of my life weeks ago. Isn't that strange? When you build up a dependence on people, knowing you can't possibly ever see them again—because they're dead—that's like having it shoved in your face. It means you'll die too. Am I making any sense?"

Michael nodded. Alyons, Eleuth, Lin Piao Tai, and now Tommy. Directly or indirectly, four deaths. That wasn't what Kristine meant, but the sensation was the same—he felt his own mortality acutely.

"I'm supposed to be on campus at two," Kristine said. "I'll wash my face." She stood.

"Kristine, if I could have done it any other way, I would have."

"I don't blame you, Michael," she said, two steps from the table. "I'm glad you're alive. I don't . . . I just don't believe some of it. Tommy with a gun. He's gone. And you."

A manic voice inside Michael: *Tommy gun gone, Tommy's gone with his gun.*

Kristine shuddered. "I don't know what to feel or think now."

Michael felt his insides knot. What he had suspected, when he thought about telling her. It was finished. He had killed or caused to die or *something fatal* her ex-boyfriend. How could she accept him now, in any way? "There should be something more between us. Don't you feel it?" he asked.

"Yes."

"It's just not working out."

"That's putting it mildly."

"I'll go, then." He walked toward the door.

"Not that I don't want it to work out," Kristine said, her voice stopping him. "We're partners in something else, aren't we?" She primmed her lips in a defiant, hard line.

"Yes?"

"We're partners in the concerto. Clarkham doesn't want it performed. If you don't hate him, I do. He's the one who killed Tommy. That's enough to convince me to keep on. And you?"

"Yes," Michael said. "That's enough."

"Let's do *anything* that displeases Clarkham. Let's move on and let the other stuff work itself out in due course."

"Okay."

She walked with him and they parted outside the apartment's main gate.

Michael returned to the Saab. He sat in the car with his hands on the wheel, certain about nothing and guilty because he was hurting, not for being a murderer, but simply because he was no longer in Kristine's presence.

In truth, everything had been so much easier in the Realm, so much more clear-cut.

HARVEY LED MICHAEL down the hallway, his scuffed brown Florsheims clacking, echoing from the ranks of stainless steel doors. An assistant coroner in a pristine white lab smock followed a few steps behind.

The unofficially-named Noguchi Wing of the Los Angeles County Morgue had been added three years before, after years of overcrowding, and was seldom filled to capacity. The last tagged stainless-steel door was on a corner with an as-yet unfinished corridor stretching to the left for another dozen yards.

Harvey pointed at the door. The assistant coroner placed an electronic key against the code box. The door popped open with a slight hiss, and the chamber bed slid smoothly out. On the bed, within a translucent bag, lay a blue-green body at least six and a half feet long. The assistant unzipped the head of the bag and pulled the material wide for Michael to see.

"Do you know what she—it—is?" Harvey asked.

"It's an Arboral female, I think," Michael said.

"And what is an Arboral?"

"A Sidhe that lives in forests. Controls the wood." The Sidhe's face appeared composed, peaceful. Michael intuited a kind of after-death discipline at work.

"Okay," Harvey said. "I've never seen a human being with skin that color. Even dead. Or with a face that long. Do you know her?"

"No," Michael said. "I never knew any Arborals." He had only seen Arborals twice, the first time when they had delivered the gift of wood to him near the Crane Women's hut in the Realm. That had been at night, and he had not seen them clearly. The second time had been in Inyas Trai, just a glimpse of them tending the Ban's library-forest.

"Now after this, I ask you, should I be surprised by what you've told me about this Tommy fellow?"

Michael could not turn away from the blue-green face. "I suppose not."

"Because I believe you." Harvey nodded to the assistant, and he zipped the bag up and sealed the chamber. "Thank you." The assistant walked back up the hallway without a single backward glance. "He may not look it, but he's scared. Twelve years in this office, and he's really spooked. Everything's changing now.

We found this," he indicated the body, "in Griffith Park, not far from the observatory. It was backed up against a tree. Somebody had shot it. Her. Just once. This is the third unexplainable body found in Los Angeles in the last month. I'm going to ask you a question." Harvey stared up at the fluorescent fixtures on the ceiling. "What in hell are we supposed to do to prepare for this? Wetbacks from beyond. Christ."

"I don't think you *can* prepare," Michael said.

"There are going to be more?"

"Yes."

"How many, and where?"

"I don't know how many, and I don't know exactly where they'll arrive."

"The Tippett Hotel?"

Michael nodded. "That's going to be a major gateway."

"And if I tell my department we have to surround the hotel—if they believe me and don't let me out on a stress-related discharge—will that do any good?"

"No," Michael said.

"They can be killed, though."

"Arborals, maybe even some Faer, but I don't think you could kill some of the other types that will be coming through. I wouldn't advise you to try."

"'Wouldn't advise me to try.' Maybe I should resign and take up throwing ashes over my head and wearing hair shirts?"

Michael smiled.

Harvey looked disgusted. "You're not doing me any good at all," he said. "And it wouldn't do either of us any good to have you arrested. There's a witness who says Tommy committed suicide. This Dopso fellow. Whatever you say about self-defense, that's all that matters. I presume there's going to be a missing persons report. I'll try to take care of that. But what are *you* going to do?"

"Wait. Try to be patient. I'm not in control, Lieutenant."

"Is anybody in control?"

"Perhaps."

"Anybody human, I mean?"

Michael hesitated, then shook his head, no.

13

He walked for miles along the fire trails through the hills, feeling the growth within him and trying to come to grips with what he was, and what he was becoming. This time, the development was internal; it had been triggered by the Crane Women's training but was not now controlled by anybody. He had no specific assigned task. If anything, Michael Perrin was a rogue, an unexpected product of Sidhe and Breed ingenuity.

Somehow, he was able to work powerful magic on Earth. Forcing a man to kill himself had to be very powerful magic or the word lacked any meaning.

The sky was clear and hot and dusty blue. Sparrows and mockingbirds sparred through the scrub bushes. The hillsides had already turned brown and gray after less than two weeks of no rain and only a few hot days; they reverted so easily to their accustomed state, as if uncomfortable in the luxury of a wet spring. Michael wished he could do the same. His last faint hopes of normality and a reasonably peaceful life had fled.

He would never sit in a fine old house in Laurel Canyon and write poetry and worry about brush fires. That dream had never been particularly well-thought-out, but he had recently been placing Kristine in the middle of it nevertheless. He was still an adolescent in many respects. His visions had not yet been completely tempered by reality.

And why should they be? Which reality?

Such considerations made maturing all the harder.

How much magic could he do, and how ambitious could he be? He hardly wanted to test the abilities (not yet skills) he felt within him, but he was impelled to do so. More important than knowing how he had acquired or developed these abilities was deciding how to use them in the coming exodus and the merging of the Realm and Earth.

He stopped and shaded his eyes against the sun, looking south over the city, the tall skyscrapers of downtown Los Angeles faint in the hazy distance. Then he hunkered down and picked up a stick, using it first to break the crusty dry soil of the fire trail into a finer powder, then to write in the powder: "Protect this city from harm."

He had no idea whom he was addressing, or what. He scratched out "city" and replaced it with "land," then scratched that out and replaced it in turn with "world." He would have to start thinking on a much broader scale.

MOFFAT'S STUDIO OFFICE resembled an especially broad hallway, about three times deeper than it was wide. Moffat had placed his desk at the end opposite the door. An electronic keyboard and computer on a stand occupied one corner near the door; propped beside it stood a cello in its black leatherette case. On the carpeted floor, under a broad glass window showing the false-front tops of the Western set buildings, Moffat had spread printouts and sheet music and scribbled notes on tiny squares of adhesive-backed yellow paper. More printouts had been pinned to the opposite wall, with copies of storyboard sketches taped beside the appropriate sections. Next to his desk was a small laser audio disk recorder on a rolling cart. Wires trailed from the unit to a jury-rigged stereo system.

"Welcome to confusion," Moffat said. "The Lean score's recorded, and I am free to contemplate this monstrosity"—he pointed at the copy of Opus 45 on the desk—"at some leisure. I've already worked some of it through on the Synclavier."

Kristine wore a gray silk dress with billowing sleeves and silver-gray nylons. Michael had never seen her so formally attired. Her behavior was also strictly business. He took the second chair at Moffat's invitation. Moffat sat in his black leather executive seat behind the desk and looked from one to the other.

"It's in five movements," he said. "I'm sure you're both aware of that. Clarkham's instructions—they must be his, since they're in English and are not in Arno's handwriting—say that the movements should not be rehearsed together, that movement four should be left out until the actual performance. Rather like assembling the bomb without the explosives." He smiled, but Kristine and Michael did not. Moffat's smile faded, and he shook his head. "Bit chilly in here, don't you think? Maybe we should open our mouths and let out some air, warm the place up?"

"I'm sorry," Kristine said. "We've got other things on our minds."

Moffat swiveled on the chair to look at Michael. "No comments?"

"No," Michael said. "But I think you should follow Clarkham's advice."

"Oh, I will, if only for authenticity's sake. The game is part of the pleasure, don't you think? Do it just as they did it fifty years ago. Now. I've managed to put together a fair string section. I have the two pianos required and a fellow I trust to play one of them. I think I can get another pianist within the week. Two oboes, two bassoons—a celeste. That might be considered overkill, three percussion keyboards, but I'm going to be authentic. In 1939, Clarkham suggested a theremin. I'll substitute something that seems to suit Waltiri's requirements better—my digital synthesizer. That makes four keyboards. Since overkill is what this piece is all about, who will complain? Not I. The other instruments I can get out of the sessions pool in a couple of weeks. No problem. Now, as for *paying* these people—"

"The university is going to pay scale for a week of rehearsal and two performances," Kristine said.

"Labor of love, is it? Well. It's not the busiest season now. Everybody needs work. Okay. We'll manage. My agent will wince, but we'll manage."

"You're doing it for the challenge, aren't you?" Kristine asked.

Moffat looked pained. "Challenge isn't the word for it. Arno was always the type to ask for sixty-fourth notes out of the French horns. But in the time I worked with him, he was positively *restrained*, compared to when he wrote Opus 45. Some of it is clearly impractical. Nobody human could play a few of the measures, so to accomplish what the score demands, the synthesizer will be programmed to do some of what he's asking for. Not exactly live, but then, neither is most music today. I want to go over the movements with you—you, too," he added, glaring at Michael, "and see if my plans match your expectations. Remember, this is very humble of me."

"We'll remember," Kristine said with a hint of a smile.

"That's it. No gloom. This is a lively piece."

He handed copies of the manuscript to both *of* them and went through the movements one by one. The first movement began in A minor, crossed into C major, then returned to A minor. It was labeled *allegro con brio*. "A quick intro, with six very odd half-notes tacked on just after it should end." Moffat said. "Beat of eight to the measure. Fast, fast. First piano does most of the hard work here, *mezzo forte*. That's good. Mutilated piano comes into its own in the second movement."

"We have a campus engineer building the brass piano baffle," Kristine said.

"I'm anxious to hear it. I can't make anything out of the instructions—what is it supposed to do to a piano?"

"We don't know," Michael said.

Moffat raised an eyebrow. "Oh, good. I like surprises."

The second movement in C major-minor was in common time and introduced entirely new themes, which gradually blended into a much slowed and much softened reprise in A minor of the first movement. The third movement was a dialogue between an unspecified but closely described instrument—originally a theremin, now to be the synthesizer—and the "mutilated" piano. "Not easy," Moffat commented. "Full of traps. It would take a small army of spiders to play some of the passages."

The fourth movement was a torturously slow *adagio* in F major, again blending at the end into a reprise, transposed to B minor, of the original theme. This was the "explosive," Moffat reiterated, not to be rehearsed with the other pieces, not to be played together with the other four movements until the actual performance. The fifth movement, in A major-minor, was a sweeping, romantic *ländler*, a country dance. "Very Mahler. Brisk, not as fast as the first movement, but coming to a cheerful conclusion—and *then*—" He shook his head. "An abrupt switch to C minor. I cannot 'hear' the last hundred measures. I've been reading scores for four and a half decades now, but I can't hear those notes. That's odd, and maybe it's magic, too. But I've played them on the keyboard and on a piano, and they're quite interesting."

"It sounds confused," Kristine said. "All those abrupt key changes."

"Oh, it's worse than that," Moffat said. "It's downright chaotic. There's no way in hell it should work. Psychotropic tone structure or not, it reads like Korngold and Mahler take a vacation with Schönberg and end up on Krakatoa with a gamelan."

"You mean, it's bad?" Michael asked, feeling as if the last firm foundation was about to be pulled from beneath his feet.

Moffat smiled up at the ceiling and closed his eyes. "Not at all," he said. "It's impossible, but it's wonderful. The few sections I've played—masterful. Demonic, but masterful. Liszt with his hair in braids and on LSD."

Kristine laughed, the first time Michael had heard her laugh in weeks. She glanced at him and pursed her lips primly, then shook her head. Serious. Subdued.

"I'm sure you two are keeping things secret from me," Moffat said. "I wouldn't want to guess what. Scandal? The Society of Musicians is about to picket us for trying to play this piece again?"

Kristine leaned forward. "I couldn't have chosen a better conductor," she said.

Moffat sighed. "What makes you think you chose me?" he asked. "Maybe there are forces at work here of which you wot not of, or whatever." He was puzzled by their silence. "That was a joke."

"A stunningly bad one," Kristine said softly. "There are a few more details to arrange at the university, and then we'll get the hall scheduled for you—"

"Which hall?" Moffat asked.

"Royce Hall."

"That fossil?"

"It meets the requirements perfectly," Kristine said. "It's about as close to the old Pandall Theater as we could possibly come."

Moffat smirked and then held up his hands. "So be it. We're still on for a double bill with Mahler's Tenth?"

"I'll be firming that up this afternoon," Kristine said.

"What a night," Moffat said, rubbing his hands. "We'll knock 'em dead."

Walking to the main gate, Kristine looped her arm through Michael's and squeezed his hand. "It's really going to happen," she said.

"You didn't think it would?"

"I had my doubts."

"Why?"

They passed the guard and waited for traffic before crossing Gower to get to their cars. "Because I've been getting phone calls," she said. "Someone's still trying to stop us. He's not succeeding, but he's trying."

"Who?"

"Clarkham, I presume," Kristine said almost lightly. She glanced at Michael. "He's been talking to you directly?"

"He hasn't called you?" Kristine countered.

"No," Michael said.

"Maybe he's afraid of you."

Michael snorted. "I don't think so."

"You say you beat him once."

"Yeah, with all the Sidhe behind me."

"But you *did* beat him."

"And he survived. Apparently."

"Why does he feel threatened by this performance?"

"I'm not sure he does. He hasn't been able to stop it, and he must be a hell of a lot more powerful than . . ." Michael shrugged. "Than my beating him would lead you to believe."

"You think he *wants* it performed?" Kristine asked. "He's running all this interference just to make us follow through?"

"I don't know."

Kristine unhooked her arm from his and backed off a step. "I don't know any magic," she said. "What will I do if things really get rugged?"

Michael had no answer. That made him acutely miserable.

"I suppose you'll protect me?"

Michael felt his eyes smart and then a rising warmth behind them. Whether she was baiting him or not, he decided to give a completely serious and sincere reply. "I'll try," he said. "I'll do my very damnedest."

"You know, I'd like to be self-reliant, but failing that . . ." She smiled at him. "You'll do. I have to go now—I'm meeting Berthold Crooke at two. The fellow with the new orchestration of the Tenth."

They stood awkwardly two steps apart. Kristine moved in quickly and kissed him on the cheek. Michael blushed as she backed away. "You'd think we could talk about normal things sometime," she said.

"I'd love to."

She cocked her head to one side. "It'll happen, Michael. I'm pretty sure of that."

"I wish I was," Michael said.

"Got to go. You'll be at the library tomorrow?"

"Signing papers. Yes."

"We'll talk then." She walked to her car.

You can spend the most important parts of your life on a street, Michael thought, and unlocked the Saab's door. His whole body seemed to be breathing in and out, restless and ebullient at once.

14

The next day, at eleven in the morning, two Jehovah's Witnesses came to the door of the Waltiri house, and Michael did not have the heart to simply send them on their way. The elder of the two was middle-aged, gray hair carefully groomed, dressed in a brown suit with a narrow gold tie; the younger, a trainee about twenty years old, wore a black suit and a red tie. Both carried satchels.

Michael listened wearily to their prophecies and Bible quotations, and they kept him at the door for half an hour. When he managed to convince them he was not really interested, he shut the door and stood with his back against the dark wood, eyes closed, almost sick.

They preached the Apocalypse. He knew it was coming—but not as they visualized it.

He could practically smell the poisoned Sidhe-imposed ignorance, the most modern incarnation of the thousands of years of Tonn's attempts to play God for humans. Some of the poisonous philosophies had been transmuted by humans despite the best efforts of the Sidhe—but how many hundreds of millions of humans still wholeheartedly embraced the blindness and cruelty and the shackles? He stood up straight but kept his eyes closed.

"No way," he said softly. "I'm just a kid. No way I can understand how to lead so many different kinds of people. I don't want it. I reject it." He opened his eyes and blinked at the framed prints in the hallway.

The silence demanded, *Who asked you to lead?*

But Michael could feel it as surely as he could hear the ticking of the grandfather clock. That was what it was all moving toward: his growth, his maturation, the challenges and the apocalypse.

He shivered and then convulsed, dropping to his knees on the tiled kitchen floor. His arms shook until he clenched his fists and he felt the inner abilities—*nothing from outside all inside all from within*—course through him like power through an electric line let loose for a moment, set free and exulting at its lack of restraint. It was all he could do to keep his skin on his body, to stop muscle fleeing from bone and his brain from popping through his skull.

The trembling slowed. He lay flat on his back on the floor. Beneath him, the tiles lay cracked and powdered. His clothes smoked; he reached down to pick scraps of burned cloth from his legs. Still, the potential pulsed through him.

Even after he had regained control of the power and had wrapped thick steel bars of his will around it, it took him hours to stop trembling, and he realized how close he had come to simply disintegrating, much as Tommy had done, but for different reasons.

He walked slowly upstairs and lay down in the Waltiri bed. not tired but stunned, for the first time fully aware of how sensitive he was and how dangerous his sensitivity could be.

Tiger by the tail.

Michael—and what he contained, generated, not by his conscious self but by something within him that didn't have a name—Michael was his own tiger. Losing control, he would eat himself alive.

"Who in hell am I?" he whispered harshly, wiping sweat from his eyes.

IN MID-JULY, KRISTINE drove Michael to Northridge to meet Berthold Crooke. Crooke lived in a complex of condominiums at the edge of a broad empty field of dry yellow grass. He taught music in a local junior college and had received little attention until the publication of his orchestration of Mahler's unfinished Tenth Symphony.

Crooke was a lanky, hawk-faced man with blue-black hair and a perennial shadow of beard. His eyes were his most remarkable feature, large and vaguely horse-like. His teeth were also large and prominent. He was slow of speech and quick to smile, pulling his lips back over his broad white teeth in a way that would have seemed menacing but for the obvious gentleness of his eyes. His manner was self-deprecating but also obviously confident. Michael liked him immediately and felt no need to read his aura; however, to his mild jealousy and chagrin, he saw that Kristine also liked Crooke.

They sat at Crooke's kitchen table and went over the arrangements point by point. After an hour of discussion, Crooke served coffee and doughnuts and stood behind Kristine, looking over her shoulder as she compared the orchestral requirements for the concerto and the symphony.

"They're not really all that different," she said, shaking her head in some surprise. "We can use practically the same players. Edgar told me the concerto was lush with orchestra, but . . ." She glanced at Michael. "Mahler isn't known for his spareness."

"No indeed," Crooke said. "You mentioned Moffat had the orchestra assembled—I don't need to approve them or anything, but—"

"You'll have equal time for rehearsals," Kristine said. "The university hasn't done anything this ambitious in years. I think it's starting to catch on. Nobody in the department is complaining about costs, and *that's* a miracle."

"What I meant," Crooke said, smiling sheepishly, "is that I haven't conducted that large an orchestra. Only college orchestras. I'll need the rehearsal more than the musicians."

Kristine patted his arm reassuringly. "We have faith," she said. "It's going to come together just fine."

Crooke made a face and slumped in his chair with a sigh. "Makes me almost wish I didn't start the whole thing . . ."

"How did you start it?" Michael asked.

Crooke knitted his fingers together. "When I was sixteen, I heard a recording of Rafael Kubelik conducting the only portion of the Tenth orchestrated at the time—the *adagio*, the first movement. I was playing the record in my room, away from the rest of the family. We had a huge ranch house in Thousand Oaks, halls and bedrooms all over—like a maze. Even six kids rattled around in it. The music seemed very sad, a slow and discouraged dance, and then toward the conclusion of the movement, there is this discord—trumpets shrilling in A, the orchestra seeming to scream or cry out . . ." He shook his head. "It devastated me. I had never heard anything like it. It was . . . all the oppressed, all those in pain, breaking their bonds and looking up. It was revelation, and it was death, too. It really affected me. I started to shake and cry." The sheepish smile returned. "I knew there had to be more. I found Deryck Cooke's orchestration and listened to that—Eugene Ormandy conducting. It was beautiful, but it seemed to be missing something. The symphony became an obsession for me. I thought if only the piece could be orchestrated the way Mahler would have done it, had he lived, then . . ." Crooke lifted his hands. "Bingo. How to express it? It would be the greatest piece of Western music ever written, or at least the most powerful. There were times when I simply couldn't listen to the pages after I finished orchestrating them. I couldn't even play parts of the four-staff score on the piano."

"Some people say you've succeeded in doing it just as Mahler would have done it," Kristine said. "How do you feel about that?"

"Oh, yes," Crooke said, his expression suddenly stiff and serious. He straightened up and cleared his throat. "That's the way it had to be. This sounds silly . . . perhaps even a bit insane . . ." His index finger tapped on the table top nervously. "But sometimes I felt I had Mahler helping me." He laughed nervously, shaking his head. "Have you heard it before?" he asked Michael. "Any of the other versions?"

"Not all the way through," Michael said.

"It is sublime, even incomplete."

Michael nodded. The discord, the trumpets sounding a shrill A, all that was very familiar to him. He had heard it while exploring the top floors of the Tippett Residential Hotel.

LATE JULY IN Los Angeles was a procession of cloudy days held over from June, broken by a week of the more usual summer weather, the temperature climbing into the eighties and the sky clear of overcast, if not of haze.

Michael did not attend the rehearsals. Kristine reported on the progress to him every two or three days. Otherwise, they did not see each other.

He spent most of his time exercising in the back yard or jogging. Dopso no longer ran with him. Since the incident with Tommy, Michael had heard nothing from the Dopsos. The mystery had become all too specific for them, apparently.

At night, in the house, Michael sat before the fire in the living room, practicing his discipline.

On July 16th, at one in the morning, after six hours of steady concentration, Michael reached into the Realm with one hand and brought back a leaf and a translucent red insect, much like a ladybug. The insect quickly died, and the leaf shriveled into a brown husk.

He had barely reached the level of Eleuth. But with just his hand in the Realm, he had sensed a discontinuity that was most unsettling.

If reality could be described as a kind of heat or warmth, then his body—sitting on the oriental rug in Waltiri's house on Earth—was in the middle of a kiln, reality invading everything with a bright white glow.

In the Realm, everything felt cold. The fire was going out.

The real fire before him was dying into embers as he thought about this. His eyes closed, and almost of their own volition, his arms rose from his sides, and he spaced his hands some five inches apart. His palms tingled, and something passed between them, a silvery extension of his discipline and of the primal emotion *Preeda*. He tried to bring them together and could not; startled, he opened his eyes and saw a pearly thread stretched between, and strung on the thread, a glowing sphere. He could feel the sphere's qualities through the skin of his palms and along his arms; it was *enfolded*, and it embodied some of the requirements he had outlined in his poem about reality knots.

But what was it? He slowly pulled his hands apart, and the thread snapped. The sphere swung to his left palm and clung there for a moment before vanishing.

IN EARLY AUGUST, the rehearsals neared completion on both the concerto and the symphony. Advertisements were placed in the Sunday *Los Angeles Times* Calendar Supplement, four days before the first of the two scheduled performances. Flyers were mailed out and posted on bulletin boards around the campus. Kristine did much of this work herself.

On Thursday evening, she appeared on the front porch of the Waltiri house, dressed in an exquisite dark blue-black gown, smiling, holding two tickets in one gloved hand.

"An occasion," she said. "Shall we go, partner?"

THE DUSK SKY above Los Angeles was a cloudless, clear sapphire blue, complete with evening star. Kristine drove down Wilshire toward UCLA, talking about the last-minute preparations, why she had been a few minutes late—having to reassure a nervous Crooke by phone that all would go well—and generally expressing her own reservations about the evening. She became quiet as they approached Westwood, glancing at him with one eyebrow raised slightly, lips drawn together.

"Something wrong?" he asked.

She laughed and shook her head. "My whole world has changed since I met you, and you ask if something's wrong. I don't know how I've managed to lead a normal life after . . . Your friend disappeared. What happened to Tommy. I should be terrified. I really should."

"Why aren't you?"

"Because you're with me."

"Not much assurance there," Michael said softly, turning away.

"Clarkham called again this evening," she said, "just after I got off the phone with Berthold."

Michael felt a deep barb of anger and quickly buried it under the rising inner warmth of *hyloka*. "What did our ghost have to say?"

"He says if the performance takes place tonight, he'll be seeing you. You, Michael."

"That's all?"

"Yes. I'm not afraid of him now."

"You should be. We should be."

"Don't you feel it, though? Tonight is going to be a fine night. Because of us."

He shook his head. "I just feel nervous."

"I'm the one who should feel nervous, but I don't. I don't even believe I'm awake now. I think I've been dreaming all the time since I met you." She swung the car into a reserved space, pointing out Moffat's BMW and Crooke's ancient, battered Chevy Nova on either side. "Everybody's here. The cast is assembled. Let the dream reach its climax." She shut off the car motor and twisted in her seat to face him. "This has been difficult for us, especially difficult for you, I think," Kristine said. "You've been . . . not 'patient.' That sounds so prosaic. You've been . . ." She shook her head vigorously. "Tonight, after the performance, we have to go out with everybody to Macho's and celebrate."

"Macho's?" Michael asked, incredulous.

"It's a Mexican restaurant in Westwood. We have reservations. And afterward—listen carefully, because this is important—we are going to go back to the Waltiri house, together, and make love." She stared at him intently, biting her lower lip. "If you want to."

"I want to." His need mixed with the warmth of *hyloka* and made an indescribable echo through his abdomen.

"That is as important as anything else that happens tonight," Kristine said. "To me, it is. Being involved doesn't come easily for me. I'm cautious, too cautious. You've noticed."

He didn't answer, simply returned her stare.

"You are so *unreadable*," she said, smiling faintly. "Let's break through it all tonight—the music, this world, all the walls and the shams." She opened her door and got out, and they walked side by side across the grass, heading toward Royce Hall.

UCLA at night was more attractive than by daylight. Floodlights and the lighted windows of buildings produced magical areas of brightness and pitch-dark. A few students walked quickly between buildings, on breaks from their night classes or hurrying to the library.

In front of Royce Hall, the crowd standing in line before venerable pillars and brick Romanesque arches was encouragingly large. Michael spotted his parents in the line and introduced them to Kristine. Ruth was very pleased with her but kept glancing at Michael with unspoken questions. John became debonair and witty and inquired whether they would all be able to get together after for a celebration. "If we're still here," he added ominously.

"We have an appointment for a kind of orchestra party," Michael explained. "But maybe tomorrow . . ."

Ruth held John's elbow and said that would be fine. "Go on now. This is your night." John raised his eyebrows. "Don't mind him." Michael smiled and hugged them both.

Kristine then led him around the side of the building and up a flight of concrete steps to a double door, where a male usher in a crew neck sweater and white pants examined her pass, gave them programs and let them in. They took seats in the center, fifth row back.

Michael cleared his throat and opened the pamphlet. "Do you think we should be sitting this close to the orchestra?" he asked, only half joking.

"All the better," Kristine said, "that the perpetrators should take the brunt, don't you think?" She patted his arm and opened her own program.

"They've got this wrong," Michael said, pointing out a passage on the second page. "Clarkham didn't get sued—he left before the lawsuits began. Arno faced the reaction alone."

"Let's hope our audience isn't litigious."

The curtain rose, and the players whose instruments were not already on the stage carried them to their seats. In Clarkham's instructions, the orchestra was enjoined to make itself conspicuous and to exhibit the process of the performance as openly as possible. That instruction was reproduced in the program booklet, in Clarkham's original handwriting.

The crowd grew quiet as the lights dimmed. Mahler's Tenth, the giant of the evening, was to be performed first, followed by an intermission of only five minutes, then finally the concerto.

Berthold Crooke came to the podium, with the orchestra already assembled and waiting. Crooke tapped lightly on the podium and motioned for an oboist to play an A-sharp. The orchestra tuned to that note and then went off on its own, instrument by instrument. Again the oboist played an A sharp, and again the orchestra tuned. Finally—on the verge of overkill—the digital keyboard performer produced a perfect A-natural, and the orchestra tuned to that.

When the pleasant cacophony was over. Crooke tapped again, and silence fell.

He raised his baton.

The first movement of the Tenth was an elegiac *adagio* in F sharp major-minor. Michael fell into the music despite its intense anxiety and sadness. The weave of the music swung hypnotically from domestic tranquillity to ominous warning. What ensued was almost painful in its intensity—a dissonant clash of the orchestra, topped by a solo trumpet blaring a high A note—death and destruction, shock and dismay. The *adagio* now concluded, seemed complete in itself, and it left Michael almost empty of feeling, drained.

The second movement, a *scherzo*—the first of two—was a complete contrast, beginning with a heavily satiric taunt in changing rhythms and tempos and then transforming the theme of the first movement into a happy country dance. It concluded joyously in the major key, leaving Michael with an overwhelming sensation of hope.

That sensation was tempered by the third movement, titled *Purgatorio*. In B-flat minor and 2/4 time, it drew its own conclusions after seesawing between anxiety and hope, sun and cold shadow . . . and those conclusions were dark, declining.

" 'Oh God, why hast thou forsaken me?' " Kristine whispered.

"What?" Michael asked.

"That's what Mahler wrote on the original score."

The beginning of the second *scherzo* nearly lifted him from his seat—a shrill blast from horns and strings and then back to the dance with life and hope, decline and death.

The *scherzo* brought to mind a long-past snippet of conversation between Mora and Clarkham under the Pleasure Dome.

"The poor, sad German."

"I was not responsible for Mahler. Or for his child. That was not my work at all."

"Did Mahler lose one of his children?" Michael asked Kristine.

"A daughter," she whispered. "His other daughter was incarcerated in a concentration camp during World War II," Kristine added softly, leaning to speak into his ear.

"He was dead by then," Michael said.

"Maybe he could tell what was coming. Saw what the old world would bring."

Michael felt a thrill run up his spine. *Yes* . . . Old world passing into new.

More anxiety after a rich, romantic interlude. Horns, xylophone accents, clarinets and French horns—that hideous solo trumpet again, intruding into the anxiety, presaging a delicious, horrible revelation.

Michael sat frozen. He could hardly think about what was shaping itself within him. *Old world into new.*

Yet all this was accidental—the matching of the Tenth—

Unfinished. Interrupted by death.

—with the Infinity Concerto.

Uplift, again the anxious strains, and back to domestic normality, the world and social life and children—

Mixed with a foreboding of disaster to come—

Of change and trauma and anticipation, foresight—

Harbinger of a new age, of fear and even disaster—

Then quiet, skeletal strings, thinning out the fabric of reality, extending the cold from his stomach to his head. Drums pounded unobtrusively, ominously.

On the stage, the largest drum—an eight-foot-wide monster—was assaulted by the drummer with one shattering beat.

The coldness vanished, leaving him suspended in the auditorium, hardly aware of seats, orchestra, walls, ceiling. He could feel the sky beyond. In his left palm lay a pearly sphere. He closed his hand to conceal it.

Camouflage. Everything had been camouflaged to mislead, misdirect. The Infinity Concerto was not by itself a song of power. The similarities had seemed merely coincidental.

Mahler's Tenth led the way, closing out the old world, describing the end of a long age (sixty million years! or just the end of European peace—or merely the tranquillity of one man's life, blighted by the death of a daughter . . . perhaps feeling what the second daughter would have to suffer in a new world gone twice mad) and expressing hope for a time beyond. Rich, anxious, neurotic, jumping with each tic and twitch of things gone awry, trying to maintain decorum and probity in the midst of coming chaos.

The beats of the huge drum accented a funeral dirge. Again the skeletal tones, this time from muted trumpets . . . and then heralding horns, a light and lovely flute song of hope developed by the strings . . . becoming strained again, over-blown, life lived too hard, tics and twitches—

Drum beat. A tragic triad of notes on the trumpet.

Drum beat. Low bassoons vibrating apart the seconds of his life. Michael still could not move.

(Deception. Camouflage. Misdirection.)

The tempo increasing into a new dance, new hope—recovery and healing—and yet another decline. Michael was growing weary of the seesaw, but only because it came too close to the everyday pace of his life. Life in this world, world passing.

Rise to triad and . . .

Disaster. The entire orchestra joined in a dissonant clash, trumpet holding on the high A again, echoed by more horns, another clash that made his head ache, reprise of the theme of everyday life . . . And then the trumpet, released from its harsh warning role, allowed a small solo. The triad on other instruments, in a major key and hopeful, not shattering. Then domesticity.

Segue. Connective tissue, old to new.

How much like what had happened recently, weirdness mixed unpredictably with Earth's solid reality and inner silence of mind. There seemed to be a rise in intensity to some anticipated triumph, thoughtful, loving and accepting . . . but not acceding. Quiet contemplation.

Michael could move again. He glanced nervously at Kristine to see if she had noticed. The symphony was coming to a conclusion, and he felt his inner strength surge.

Triumph. Quiet, strong and sure—overcoming all tragedy.

Triumph.

The last notes of the Tenth faded, and Crooke seemed to reappear on the podium, and the orchestra seemed to become real again.

The audience sat silent for an uncomfortably long time.

"You're sweating," Kristine said, handing him a handkerchief from her purse.

"Thanks." Michael wiped his forehead. Sweat had dripped into his eyes, stinging. The hall seemed stifling. He glanced at his hand. The pearl was gone.

Finally the audience reacted with strong but not overwhelming applause.

They had heard, appreciated, but they had not felt, or had ignored what they felt. A few stood and applauded vigorously, as if to make up for the rest. Michael glanced back but could not see his parents.

Crooke appeared exhausted but happy. He bowed and then continued with the structure of the program by taking a microphone handed to him and announcing that the interval between pieces would be very short. Some in the audience grumbled.

"Stand, stretch our legs?" Kristine suggested.

Michael stood beside her and discreetly windmilled his arms, tensing and untensing his legs. His lungs felt as they once had when he had accidentally breathed dilute fumes from a spill of nitric acid in chemistry class—tight, but not constricted.

"That was wonderful," he said, sounding doubtful even to himself.

"I'm very proud," Kristine said softly. "Everything's turning out fine. Even the audience."

The air seemed much improved. He felt calm again, prepared.

Mahler's Tenth, properly orchestrated, was itself a song of power. It codified the old world, harsh and demanding, lovely and lyrical, unyielding and fickle.

An old rose, fading and growing thorny. How had it avoided being pruned by the Sidhe? Then again, it had not—Mahler had died before finishing it. Other attempts to fulfill the promise had not succeeded . . .

Edgar Moffat came to the podium. Michael, on impulse, kissed Kristine lightly on the cheek, then caressed her bare shoulder with one hand. She smiled uncertainly at him, then sat and focused her attention on the podium.

The baton went up and lowered slowly . . .

The first movement began rapidly, the unmutilated piano jumping in almost immediately. As it played, a deep, resounding tone came from the double basses, ascending in pitch through the strings, almost harsh, moving from cello to viola to violin to be drowned by drums, low and rumbling. A sharp rise of French horns glared and did battle, fast, fast, dancing, dissonant and yet perfect, a rousing gallop of ghost horses that faded into whispering strings.

Sea-grass propelled by moonlight.

Horns sketched out a vast unease, brooding. They lost all musical tone and *whooshed* like the wind, a soft winter storm coming.

A passage of unfilled graves, herald of change and nightmares from unlived childhoods, from an infinity of lives never occupied by the moving strands of an infinity of souls.

Michael blinked back tears and held Kristine's hand. She, too, was responding, and her cheeks were wet.

Lives lived and lost. *Tommy.* The others.

Eleuth.

If they let go, he seemed to understand, they would lose each other. She moved against his shoulder and shivered.

"Is this what they heard?" she asked.

Michael swallowed. "No. Everything was different then. It's the same music, but it's in its proper time now."

"How do you *know* that?" she asked.

He shook his head. "It resonates."

"Will people vanish tonight, or later?"

"Not from hearing this," he said.

The music increased tempo and surged forward on horns, harp and strings, the second rank of violins plucking furiously. The musicians seemed obsessed, and Moffat directed them with a minimum of motion, baton describing the beat and left hand barely indicating emphasis; he gave them their lead and let their concentration carry them through.

At no point did the music let up. When the piano rejoined the flow, the beat, the pulse, changed to a fractured and disjointed waltz time. The pulse became even more ragged, jazzed, with unpredictable and violent bursts from the drums and horns. Then it smoothed and mellowed.

Gentle, lulling heart-beat sounds, ragged dances fading, recurring but polished, then slowing.

As gently as could be imagined, the prelude ended. Without a moment's pause, the second, mutilated piano began a quiet and persistent solo, staying in the middle register, its tone odd and almost harsh, yet not disturbing, simply biding its time. And the music did something Michael had never heard before.

It described waiting. While not long in itself, the piano solo covered thousands, perhaps millions of years.

He glanced at Kristine. Her eyes were wide. She was enchanted, uncritical. Absorbing all. Waltiri's magic—evident in his movie scores—was here unbridled.

The orchestra leaped in behind the piano. Time was still at issue—and growth. Michael no longer paid attention to the mechanics, the key or the structure or the way the sounds were created.

He had caught on to the underlying beauty of the piece. He saw it in relation to "Kubla Khan," to the pleasure dome even in its incomplete. unsuccessful form; he saw it in relation to the symphony just played. They were all similar songs played in different worlds, to accomplish similar purposes. Subtle variations in the underlying patterns could lead to widely disparate results.

Mahler had once written a song-cycle/symphony called *Das Lied von der Erde*—the *Song of the Earth*. The name had been applied, perhaps, to the wrong piece. His Tenth was a song of the Earth, of Earth as it had been.

The Infinity Concerto was heralding the Earth to come.

And Michael felt himself in it. He was described there—not personally, but in his role. Growing, mutating, uncontrolled, all potential and little achievement. It frightened him. The music was not gentle now. It was complex, demanding, full of discord.

Discord.

Discard.

Start again.

Renew.

Unite. (How?)

Create. Create what?

The audience was becoming noisy, even above the now-loud music. Something had not been resolved, and they sensed it almost *en masse.*

Decline to quiet, persistent but soft, demanding but muted . . .

Strings played on their bridges—skeletal—horns muted—breaking time down. The celeste tinkling behind all. Apprehension . . .

What happened next, Michael could not describe, nor could members of the orchestra. The music suddenly depended on the fourth movement, *adagio, which had not yet been played,* and that fore-reference *worked* because he—they—understood what would happen in the fourth movement.

Kristine smiled ecstatically. The audience fell silent. The tension had been impossibly resolved.

The second movement ended. The third began without more than a few seconds' pause. The digital keyboard and the mutilated piano involved each other in a philosophical discussion. The third movement passed, and Michael did not remember its passing, or even what it was. It was played, but it added a non-memorable subtext to everything around it. It was a movement and a bridge in itself, effective only as a commentary.

The fourth movement was upon them. Kristine's face showed irritation or pain. The pain changed to dismay.

The fourth was not the same movement referred to in the second. There were in fact two *adagios,* but only one was being manifested. The other existed as a creation solely in the minds of the audience, a phantasm of music, yet Michael had no doubt that both movements had been minutely composed and scored by Waltiri.

He began to fear what the fifth movement might bring.

The fourth, as played, was slow, primitive, spare, even deliberately inelegant. It was a new world unresolved, the shape undefined, though with all the elements present, coalescing. Instruments played to different rhythms, slowly coordinating, then fading, then coming to agreement again; themes weaving in and out, with then a reprise of the original theme transposed to B minor. Moffat had called this the "explosive," yet it seemed anticlimactic.

The normal piano began to dominate, with its precise laying down of individual notes and chords, no glissandos, no slides, simply sketching what was to come.

Then, entirely unearthly, the digital keyboard mocked the piano. It created the slides and linked the sketched-out harmonies. It played them back upon themselves and created canons and reversed them in ways only a machine could manage.

This was the human contribution to the music. The Sidhe would never have countenanced an electronic instrument—not even a simple theremin. What Waltiri had requested was something only humans could add to music. Through technology, they made music the Sidhe could have created only through magic.

Humans had found their place in the world to come. They had lived in this universe long enough to master it not with magic, but on its own terms. Not with outside skill, but with skills taught by the hard, unyielding nature of reality.

And they had turned those skills into devices for creating wonderful, impossible music.

But this isn't music any more, Michael thought.

"What is this?" Kristine whispered.

The keyboard had made its point and did not belabor it. Sounding almost abashed, the orchestra resumed its dominance, but the normal piano was done for. It played no more in the fourth and not at all in the final movement. The final movement was home for the mutilated piano and the keyboard.

Michael shut his eyes. It seemed as if all his hopes and concerns were about to be examined. The fifth movement would be *himself.* And he knew Kristine was feeling the same—that it would be about herself.

The music, a sweeping, demanding dance, was now a training ground for a new world.

In 1939, before its time, Opus 45 at this point in the score would have sown the seeds for a translation into the Realm. Other music had accidentally achieved this effect; Clarkham, and perhaps Waltiri as well, had deliberately designed the Infinity Concerto to work in such a way.

But Waltiri had woven in something else. With time, the effect of the music would alter. It would not translate; it would prepare. The audience was being made aware of the world they would ultimately have to face.

The music vanished into its own purpose.

Only in the last part of the fifth movement did the adjunct song of power rise up and show its medium again. The music became light and beautiful, consciously showy and rich with melody. The melody switched to C minor.

"Jesus Christ," said a man behind Michael, loudly.

Out of the last hundred measures—the measures Moffat had confessed he could not "hear" while reading the score—came quiet assurance, not disturbance. The bomb was being carefully, elegantly defused. The worlds would meet, pass into each other . . .

They would not destroy each other.

The concerto reached its conclusion. (But the unplayed fourth movement echoed; perhaps it would never stop: *Das Unendlichkeit Konzert.*)

The music faded.

The hall was as quiet as empty space.

Kristine shut her eyes, folded her hands as if in prayer. "They're going to like it," Michael reassured her.

The audience exploded. Everyone stood at once. Applause, shouts of "Bravo!" and exclamations of amazement both crude and ecstatic. Michael stood and looked around anxiously, seeing a few people still in their seats, limp, eyes glazed. But gradually they, too, stood and applauded, returning to the hall from wherever they had been. Moffat took his bow and called Crooke out from the wings. The applause redoubled and did not diminish as the soloists were brought forward. Michael glanced around apprehensively.

He didn't know what he expected next. Whether the sky would come crashing down and the air would be filled with flying Sidhe, whether Clarkham himself

would appear ringed in fire, whether Waltiri and his birds would fill the hall . . .
Anything seemed possible. The song had been played through. How long would
it take to accomplish its task?

The crowd surged out of the hall, forcing Michael and Kristine with it. It
stood on the grass and sidewalks outside, shouting and arguing. Kristine beamed.
"It's like when they played Stravinsky and Milhaud," she said. "It's really happened!"

"I thought they threw the seat cushions around for Stravinsky," Michael said.

"Our crowd is much too *with it* to do that," Kristine said. "Let's find Berthold
and Edgar."

THE GATHERING AT Macho's was crowded and noisy. Michael stayed on the side-
lines, letting others enjoy their triumph; he had really had so little to do with it.
Flushed, Crooke carried a beer in one hand and a glass of sparkling water in the
other, sipping from them alternately and smiling at a short, very shapely woman
who had attached herself to him. Moffat held court from a large round table,
regaling his audience of students and formally dressed alumni with tales of Hollywood in the fifties.

"Maybe everything's going to be all right, hmm?" Kristine suggested as she
passed Michael in one of her orbits. She made frequent eye contact with him,
smiling reassurance. It suddenly occurred to Michael that *she* was uncertain about
him, a little afraid he might leave without her.

Little chance of that. Even Songs of Power and the sway of dying and birthing
worlds seemed pale compared to what he anticipated.

He ordered and drank a beer, enjoyed it immensely and almost immediately
regretted it; his *hyloka*, held at a constant simmer under all his careening emotions, fluctuated wildly under the influence of the alcohol. He felt excessively
warm—as he had for a time during the concert—and looked for ways through
the crowd to a restroom in case things got out of control and he had to doff his
clothes.

But the *hyloka* settled down, and he felt a simple, direct sensation of well-
being. Everything had gone beautifully. Clarkham—wherever and whatever he
was now—had failed again.

Kristine hooked her arm through his on her next orbit and took him with
her. "Let's find a door," she said. "It's getting late."

They went to the Waltiri home, and Michael took Kristine into the upstairs
bedroom. As he held her warmth closely, still fully dressed, he felt that nothing
could possibly go wrong, ever.

He could feel her nervousness, her tension, and he eased it away expertly
with his fingers, drawing a line down both sides of her spine, searching for and
finding the physical centers of her anxiety and releasing them.

More things he had not known he could do.

More growth.

She started to undo the eyes and zipper of her dress, and he finished the task
for her, pulling it away from her shoulders, letting it slide past her hips. He

lowered her half-slip a few inches with his index fingers and kneeled, rubbing his cheek against her stomach, feeling the warmth and softness of her skin.

They made love as if lost deep in woods, and nothing mattered or could interfere: nothing improper or suspect, nothing to hold him back or bring an edge of dismay to his enthusiasm, nothing tragic.

Michael found the crescented outline of Kristine beneath the sheets more beautiful than anything he had ever hoped to see, much less have. He propped himself on one elbow and stared at her as she lay in the ghost-glow of the window. Her eyelids fell half-closed, drowsy; she was content as a tree is content after a day full of sun. He probed her aura gently and found a smooth continuity, near slumber, mellow.

He lay back on his pillow. He would sleep with her tonight. They would dream beside each other. For the first time in a great many months, he would be merely a young human being, not in the least important.

The unplayed fourth movement came back to haunt him just before sleep, making a cold, hard circle at the center of his contentment. In the silence of the old house, in the darkness, the music was almost audible.

The bomb had not gone off.

Not yet.

But

15

Michael.

A voice in his sleep. He cannot struggle up out of slumber, and he feels as if all his senses have been smothered in thick clouds of wool. He struggles without moving or waking.

I've been right here for weeks.

He feels the hidden foulness. It fills his mind like a mist of sulfurous gas and ammonia.

Waiting.

The wool lifts but not enough to allow him to awaken or put his discipline to use. He cannot sense Kristine beside him.

I've taken her. But that isn't enough. You must go as well. You've become entirely too dangerous, too skilled. Look to your ancestry, Michael.

The words fade.

Look to your ancestry. And calm, assured laughter.

Downstairs, a few sharp measures from the second movement of the Infinity Concerto are pounded out on the piano, then more laughter. Michael tries to struggle up out of sleep, but he knows he is much too late. He has let his guard down; he has been happy, and he has let his happiness and his wish to be normal obscure all the defenses the Crane Women had instilled in him, overtly and otherwise.

Clarkham has been in the Waltiri house, or very near by as worlds are concerned, for weeks. Has played the piano when Michael was out; has perhaps even used the house phones to call Kristine. The house has been Clarkham's base of operations.

Michael feels all of these realizations blur, break up, scramble. He opens his eyes in time to see everything in the bedroom suffused in sepia. When the sepia brightens, he—

16

—felt a pang of grief so sharp it made his stomach twist. Another morning. Another day of living with the loss and the sheer misery of his aloneness and vulnerability.

He closed his eyes and silently rolled his face into the pillow, trying not to weep.

No.

He rolled back and took a deep breath, letting it out slowly. Through the still curtains over the open window he heard nothing outside, no cars, no birds, only a steady low whine of wind. The sounds of a desert. Sun faded in and out in the room as if clouds passed overhead. He glanced at the opposite side of the bed and saw pillows still wrapped in the comforter, sheets and blankets undisturbed except by his tossing.

Michael Waltiri

—no—

got out of the bed and slipped on his boxer shorts and pants, white Arrow shirt with button-down collar, slinging the suspenders over his shoulders with both thumbs. Wide-cuff baggy pants rode high on his hips. Wool socks and black patent leather shoes. Sports coat hung over the back of the chair before the vanity, the chair where just weeks before Kristine had put on her makeup, her rayon stockings, her dress and hat.

NO!

And taken the Packard to the bank. Wifely errands.

He parted the curtains and leaned out the window. Warm yellow sun fell on him. Round and puffy clouds drifted in the Wedgwood sky, regular and sheep-like.

Taken the Packard to the bank and . . .

He shut his eyes and bent down to tie the flapping laces on his shoes. Everything was wrong. The world was topsy-turvy.

She was gone. Quick as that. Just as his parents were gone. They crashed in a Dakota near Guam, along with other entertainers, all out to

—the war's over, Michael; it was over before you were born—

give the troops a little amusement. And here he was. 4F. Useless. An orphan and a widower. Dead to the world, whatever world there was outside.

He went downstairs and made himself a pan of oatmeal, mechanically lacing it with oleo and Karo syrup. He ate it mechanically, mind blank and uncritical simply to avoid the pain.

As he finished, slowly pushing the last dollop of oatmeal into his mouth, the hall chimes clanged. Still chewing, Michael went to the front door and opened it. His father's partner, David Clarkham, stood on the porch with hat in hand, wearing a very natty camel hair coat and matching pants, wide sky-blue tie covered with regular puffy clouds, sheep-like. Michael stared at the clouds and watched them move across the tie.

"Come to see how you're doing, Michael," Clarkham said, concern crossing his smooth, young face.

"As well as can be expected," Michael replied. "Want to come in? Can I offer you a drink? Some wine?"

"No, thank you. You shouldn't be drinking, anyway. There's a lot of work to be done. Organizing your father's papers, settling things down at the studio. I spoke with Zanuck yesterday. He wishes me to pass along his condolences, both for your parents and . . . Kristine."

"Fine." Numb. Pain pushed back by an effort of sheer forced blankness. "Thanks. Tell him . . . yes."

"I'll take over the work on *Yellowtail*. Your father would have wished that."

"Fine."

"Is there anything I can do for you, Michael? At the studio, perhaps? Need legal matters resolved?"

"The lawyers are taking care of all that."

"Your parents were fine people, Michael. They would have wanted to go together. But there is nothing sensible to be said about Kristine. So much death overseas . . . it seems doubly senseless here."

"I know." He wanted the man to go away. He wanted to shut the door again and block out the sun and the sky and the regular sheep-like clouds and the faint whine of the wind.

"I'll go now. Just checking." Clarkham smiled, and for a moment Michael felt a black depth of corruption behind the smile that made him dizzy, that almost brought back—

"Thanks for your concern." He shut the door and returned to the kitchen, where he poured himself another cup of tea. As he sipped it, he frowned. Why feel such antagonism toward his father's partner? Just a symptom of his general condition: a wreck.

He considered exercising in the back yard and decided it was not worth the effort.

A blackness descended over Michael Waltiri then, numbing his senses even further, discouraging him from making any plans or thinking too deeply about anything. He loved Kristine very, very much, and they had had so short a life together (How long? Hours? Nonsense) that his own youth and upcoming three score and ten years of life seemed to conspire against him, offering a bleak desert of endless and unfilled hours, days, years.

Michael Waltiri felt as if he had been sentenced to prison. He would live it out; that was all he could do.

17

Days and weeks passed, and he ate and slept and worked in the garden in the back yard, keeping the roses trimmed. He patched and rehung the Chinese paper lanterns strung from the trellis to poles in the back yard, and he wiped down the white-enameled wrought-iron table on the brick patio. He disliked the back yard—it gave him the creeps—but he worked there nonetheless, making sure it was tidy, because (it must have been so, though he couldn't remember specifics) he and Kristine had spent time there.

He remembered someone wearing a fancy dress sitting behind the white table at one time. That must have been Kristine. Not her style (certainly not Golda's— his mother's—style), and why was he so aware of having been frightened by her in the dress? Everything was jumbled by his grief.

Days and weeks. He shaved with a French razor and played records on the Victrola, Toscanini and Reiner and Strauss and Stokowski conducting, on 78s. Endless hours of music, over and over again.

The grief and numbness refused to fade.

He never saw anyone, and nobody called him on the phone. He read the newspapers and occasionally listened to the radio. None of it seemed right, but what could he do?

Michael felt as if he were in hell.

18

H e finally gathered up enough energy to take a long walk. He started out at dusk, as the empty sky turned a dark and dusty blue, when the twilight seemed willing to last forever, and walked along the empty streets, past the white plaster and stucco Spanish-style houses the neighborhood favored, past the ranch-style houses and the California bungalows. He stopped with a frown and watched an electric streetlight come on with the deepening of dusk. A brown-leafed maple drooped its branches over the light as the wind whined. The stars came out and whirled like fireflies on strings and then settled. The sky became a gelatinous black.

Michael walked to La Cienega and followed its course, seeing people on the other side of the street, or walking some distance ahead or behind him, but never passing them or seeing them up close. All the shops and restaurants and even the bars were closed. The war, he decided. Not enough to go around.

Not even enough people.

The street narrowed as he approached the hills. He looked both ways on the corner of Sunset, at the houses on each side and the shops, all closed and dark, and then at the old theater rising above the roofs to his right. He headed toward the theater.

In round neon letters, the neon turned off, the name of the theater stretched around the marquee and up a tall radio tower mounted on a silver plaster sphere.

P
A
N
D
A
L
L

P A N D A L L

The doors were boarded over. The wind whispered between the plywood and the locked glass beyond.

The place was dead. Its hold on reality seemed tenuous, as if it were merely a memory. He didn't like it. He walked away, glancing over his shoulder. Someone dark followed and that frightened the wits out of him. He turned onto a side street and tried as casually as possible to shake the pursuer: a tall white-haired figure in a black robe.

Michael came home and shut the door.

He felt as if he had been suspended in a jar, some museum specimen, all life drained, time and blood replaced with formaldehyde.

19

At some point he began to write poetry, though he had no memory of having ever written poetry before. He wrote about what was on his mind all the time: Kristine.

Who goes in me
The one who pulls my
Lost mind into dawn is
Innocent of guile

From cold dreams to fire at
End of day she crowds a zoo
All my animal thoughts She

Is innocent of guile Does
Not see my labyrinth More
Than flesh in space words on paper

In me she lives Once
She lived her own

Now alone in me she goes.

And after a day sitting quiet in the dark upstairs bedroom, he took out a pencil and wrote on a paper napkin:

Watch him developing!
But where's his knowledge?
See that bright little pinpoint? That's it.
And his maturity?
Coming along slowly.

I see a dark spot, too. Someone missing?
He's lost someone.
Looks like he's trying to replace the dark spot with the bright.
He thinks he may be able to bring back the lost.
Can he do it?

No answer; the pencil stopped at the end of the napkin. The next day, he could not find the napkin, or any of the poems he had written, and an odor like ammonia and sulfurous gas crept through the house and drove him outdoors.

He sat before a clump of gladioli, squatting on the sidewalk with nobody to see him—nobody visible, anyway—and held a leaf in his hand, concentrating on it.

Focus. Detail. Clarity. Sharpness.

Detail.

He could not concentrate on the leaf. It seemed to shy away from him, all its innermost details fuzzing and his attention drifting. That was not right.

The anger he felt was quickly damped by his dark mood.

Have to get over this. Can't think straight.

He stood and wiped his hand on his pants for no particular reason. He was always clean; he did not sweat and had not taken a bath since

When?

He looked down the street and saw the white-haired figure in black watching him. It raised its arm. Michael ran back to the house. Even behind the door, however, he knew he could not escape this time.

Mixed with his horror was an inexplicable spark of hope. If what he saw was death coming for him, then it would take away the burden of this dreary life, this grief-bound hell.

He stood two steps behind the door, waiting.

A light, almost casual knuckle-rap sounded on the thick dark wood.

Michael swallowed a lump in his throat and reached for the doorknob. Before his hand reached it, the lock clicked. The deadbolt slid aside and the knob turned. He retreated three steps.

The door swung open. He recognized but did not know the man standing on the porch. He was tall, slender but very strong-looking, of indeterminate age, face long and somber, hair white and fine as mineral whiskers from a cave. The collar of the robe was the color of old dried roses, cut from dusty velvet woven with floral details that seemed to blow in a wind quite different from that whining even now outside. The man's eyes were the color of pearls, his skin pale as the moon.

"Michael Perrin. Do you know me?"

His voice hissed like a sword drawn across folds of silk. Michael shook his head, then nodded. He could feel power radiating from the man.

"Do you know where you are?" A stinging pity came to the man's face, mixed with mild contempt.

"I'm not at home."

"You are *loghan laburt*, loss-cursed. You cannot see through your pain. You have been wrapped in a large but poorly conceived *almeig epon*. A bad dream."

"Your name is Tarax," Michael said, feeling something rip in the back of his head, a shroud around his thoughts. But the name brought him no comfort. He began to shiver.

"I am Tarax. I can bring you out of here, but you must do something for me."

"I don't remember clearly. I can't think straight."

Tarax narrowed his pearl-silver eyes, and Michael felt another rip in the shroud, releasing more memory. "Music," Tarax said. "The songs of worlds breathing in and out."

"Before I was here."

"Yes?"

"Nothing is *right* here. Where is Kristine?"

"She can be part of our bargain."

"Is she dead?"

"She might as well be," Tarax said, "unless you pull yourself free of self-pity and think clearly."

"She's not dead." The veil lightened and dissolved. The grief withdrew its dark wings and flew up and away from him.

"You were trained by the Crane Women," Tarax said. "They are gone now, and nobody replaces them. I need their function. You can fulfill that function." Tarax's smile curled distant and ironic; that he should come to a mere human child with such a proposal . . .

Michael said nothing, simply reveled in the clarity of his mind and the relief he felt. He listened closely.

"I have a daughter," Tarax said. He stepped inside, and the door swung shut behind him without a sound. "My only offspring. She is of age for training in the discipline. She will attend me as a priest of the Irall, so long as it lasts, and on Earth after that."

Mention of the Irall drove away his relief and brought back an old dread.

"You have the heritage of the Crane Women within you. You can—you must—train my daughter in their ways. If you agree to that, I will tell you how to leave this dream and return to your world."

Michael nodded, signifying not agreement but only that he was still listening.

"If you succeed in training her, I will reveal to you where this female called Kristine is trapped, much as you are trapped here."

"You and I are enemies," Michael said. "You hate me."

Tarax raised his hand, long fingers pointing, and tossed those words away. "I hate nobody. We have cooperated in the past, and you have been aware of that. And there is the Law of Mages, which must be observed."

Indeed, they might have cooperated; Tarax might have been part of the conspiracy to nullify Clarkham. But what was the Law of Mages? "We failed. Clarkham is still alive."

"Not precisely alive," Tarax said. "The struggle isn't over."

"I've been warned never to trust a Sidhe," Michael said.

"Do you have any choice? At the very least, you will return to your world."

Michael considered. "What could I possibly teach your daughter?"

Tarax betrayed his only sign of uncertainty at this question. "What the Crane Women have willed, I presume."

"You'll take the risk that I might not be able to pass on the discipline?"

"Yes."

Michael faced the Sidhe and stood erect, saying, "Then I agree."

"Take yourself back to Earth now. Simply use what you know. Ask yourself where you are." Tarax turned, and the door swung open. The Sidhe reached out with his long fingers and ripped the door apart, letting it drift in dusty shards to the floor. The wind ceased its whine.

"How?" Michael asked, frightened again.

Tarax faded, and then he was gone.

Michael trembled and stared at his hand. Already he could feel the memory of this experience slipping away and the dreary grief returning. He looked upon the house as a refuge, a place where he could grieve in comfort; it seemed suited to him, since he had lost everything.

He bit his lip and wriggled his fingers. "Where am I?" he asked. He thought of the floorplan and the

No piano in the house. This was not Waltiri's house, and Waltiri was not his father.

brick patio and white wrought-iron table, which Kristine had never seen, much less sat behind, and the figure in the flounced dress, Tristesse, that had been somebody *something* else.

It was so simple. He reached his hand through the air—not across but through the intervening space—and tore aside the dream. Then he stepped through the descending ruins of Clarkham's trap.

And stood (shadows slipping away from him)

In the middle

(dust on the floor, a single track of footprints)

Of the upstairs room in Clarkham's house.

Rare summer rain fell on the roof, a sound so simple and soothing that he closed his eyes and listened for almost a minute before walking down the stairs and out the front door.

HE HAD NOT been trapped in Clarkham's house; that much he knew almost immediately upon returning. Clarkham had created a crude and simple world for him and held him there. The house had not even been an integral part of it; where he had lived had seemed a mix of the Waltiri house, Clarkham's, and even parts of the house next door to Clarkham's.

Michael walked slowly up the walk to the Waltiri home, exhausted but inwardly reveling, each breath he inhaled like an intoxicating liquor.

How long had he been away?

"Finally home!" Robert Dopso stared at him from his own porch.

"How long have I been gone?" Michael asked.

"Just long enough for everything to go to hell. Your folks have been by here several times, talking to Mom and me . . ."

"Kristine? Have you heard from Kristine Pendeers?"

Dopso frowned. "Nobody else . . . Your parents mentioned a somebody-or-other Moffat. No women. I've got your newspapers here—those that have been delivered. The city's a shambles. Nothing's on time or reliable now."

"Why?"

"Haunts," Dopso said, shaking his head. "It's been at least a month since we saw you last."

Michael unlocked the door and entered, hoping vaguely that Kristine might be waiting, but the house was empty. Forearmed now, he probed deeply for signs of Clarkham, physical or otherwise, but found no evidence of him.

Dopso came up to the open doorway with an armful of newspapers. "Where should I put these?" he asked. "And your mail, too. Not much of that."

Michael indicated the couch. Dopso deposited the pile and stood, brushing his hands on his pants. "I've been thinking," he said, "that maybe it's time you give Mom and me the full story. I've had time to sort a few things out—that fellow who shot himself and disappeared. We both decided that if anybody knows what's going on, it must be you. We'd be very grateful if you'd let us know."

"All right," Michael said. "Let me catch up, and I'll come over this evening. What time is it?"

Dopso checked his watch. "Five-thirty."

"Make it eight."

Dopso nodded, stood for a moment with his hands in his pants pockets as if waiting to say more, then shrugged his shoulders and walked through the front door.

"Oh." He stopped halfway down the sidewalk, raising his voice so Michael could hear. "You might want to clean out your refrigerator. The electricity isn't on all the time now."

20

ichael read the papers voraciously; there had been no news at all in Clarkham's dream-trap, of course. What he read both horrified and exhilarated
him.

The Sidhe were reappearing all over the world, in the hundreds of thousands,
if not millions. Apparently, large migrations from the Realm had resumed just
days after the performance. He thumbed through the papers, tearing pages in his
haste. England, of course—and Ireland and Scotland—appearances by the hundreds. Whole sections of Ireland were now closed off by impenetrable and immaterial barriers, erected by the Sidhe; there was no way of knowing what kind
of Sidhe. The editorials and reports he barely glanced at; they were, of course,
not informed, and their guesses were ludicrous, if very twentieth-century: aliens
from space, high-technology terrorist actions.

They had no idea.

In other areas—India, China, the Soviet Union—news reports had stopped,
and all travel had been banned. There were hints of enormous disruptions and
even battles.

In Los Angeles, the "invasions" had centered on the Tippett Hotel, through
which hundreds of "tall, strangely dressed" individuals had passed in just the last
two weeks. The building was now surrounded by National Guard troops, but
(Michael whooped and shook his head) that did not stop individuals from flying
off the roof, some riding gray horses and others without apparent aid, vanishing
into the sky.

The Sidhe were returning to find Earth a hornet's nest. How many had died,
both Sidhe and humans, so far?

There was an enormous amount of work to do. First, he had to meet with
his parents.

And then—Kristine. He had no idea how to find her. He wanted to pound
the walls with frustration; his fingers gripped the pages of yesterday's *Times*. The
paper curled up as if in pain.

When would Tarax send his daughter—or could he believe anything from
Tarax's lips? Michael had found his way back—that part of the bargain had been

carried through. But anything else . . . "I am so goddamn *ignorant!*" Michael yelled, throwing the papers from the couch. He walked stiffly into the kitchen, face red, and tried to comb his hair back in place with his fingers as he punched out the number of his parents' phone.

RUTH STARED OFF across the living room, eyes focused on something far beyond the opposite wall. John regarded his son directly, his face slack, eyes tracking with little jerks.

"Everything that's happened here since you left, it's been more than a nightmare for me," she said. John leaned forward and took her hand. "The world is real," she continued. "These things don't happen. But once they did, and now they do again."

Look to your ancestor. Michael sat stiff as a wooden dowel in the familiar chair, in the familiar living room. His father's maple, oak, and rosewood furniture surrounded them, and from the TV and stereo stand, the VCR clock blinked on and off in bright turquoise numerals, 12:00, 12:00, 12:00. It had not been reset since the last power outage.

"She's never told any of us," John said softly. "I tried to get it out of her over the years."

Ruth said, "Look at your hair, Michael."

"That's rather hard to do," John said, smiling. "You'd have an easier time of it, sweet one."

Ruth tapped his extended hand with her fingers but did not grasp it. "It's the color of my great-grandmother's hair . . ." She sighed. "In West Virginia, back when it was still old Virginia, before the Civil War, my great-grandfather took a Hill wife. That's what he called her. In the family Bible, her name is Underhill. Salafrance Underhill."

Michael had read the family names and always thought that one strange and beautiful, but he had never been told anything about his relatives so far back.

"She was a tall woman. Some said she was a witch. My grandfather always said she died, but my grandmother said she just went away, around the turn of the century. Great-grandfather never married again. And my grandfather, before he caught sick and died, asked that my parents keep my hair cut short always, and when I was grown, marry me off right away, because 'In our family a woman is a curse.' That's what he said. And my father always obeyed his father without question.

"I would dream things at night, and in the middle of the night, Father and Mother would come into my room, and Father would tell me what I dreamed was bad—he *knew* what I was dreaming—and he would beat me."

Her face softened and her eyes grew large. She looked as if she were crying, but no tears came.

"I would dream of forests, and of Salafrance Underhill living in the Virginia woods, deep back where the great maples and oaks could sing their own songs when the wind blew through them. And her eyes were the color of old silver dollars. That's what I would dream of, and when I dreamed, I knew she was still alive . . . but not on Earth. She had gone back with her people. She had left my

great-grandfather with two babies to care for, one a girl that died young. I think
he killed her. And one a boy. My grandfather. And they beat the dreams out of
him early."

John patted the chair arm rhythmically with one hand.

"So from what *you* say," Ruth went on, "my great-grandmother must have
been a Sidhe and that makes you and me Breeds."

"Lord," John said hoarsely. He cleared his throat. "This *is* a day, isn't it?"

"I left Virginia when I was fifteen and went to work in Ohio. I met your
father in 1965, and it took me three years after we were married to decide to
have a child. Your father pestered me year after year, but I was afraid, and I
couldn't tell him why. I didn't know what I'd do if I had a girl. What I'd tell
her."

"Do you have powers?" John asked her matter-of-factly.

"I've never tried to find out," she said. "Outside of what could get away with
being called intuition. But Michael . . . he's always had a way of seeing, a sensibility. Even though he's male, I've feared for him. All his poetry and his thinking.
He has something. So now there's this. Now people might believe about Hill
women and fear and cutting hair short to stop something not right, not Christian.
When he went away . . . I felt where he was, and I couldn't tell even you, my
husband. I couldn't believe it myself because so much time had passed, and
everything was hazy. I'd blocked it for so many years—the beatings and the
dreams. My mother looking so scared and not knowing what to do."

She lifted both her arms, and Michael came to her, and she enfolded him
and asked, "What are you going to do?"

"I don't have any choice, really," he said, voice muffled against her shoulder.
She opened one arm and motioned for John to join them, and they sat on the
couch, as they had after Michael returned, all together, silent for a moment.

"Will they ever go away ?" Ruth asked. "The Sidhe?"

Michael shook his head. "I don't think they can," he said. "They wouldn't
be coming back to Earth if they could avoid it."

"And you love this girl, this woman, Kristine."

"Yes," he said.

"She loves you?"

"Yes."

"She's a hostage, then."

"I don't know why he's keeping her."

"Can he hurt *you*?" Ruth asked.

Michael leaned back and looked into her eyes. "Not any more," he said. "I
don't think so."

"Be very, very careful."

"Whatever happened to your grandfather?" he asked. "And to your father?"
He could not simply ask if they had been immortal.

"Grandfather was killed in a wagon accident," Ruth said. "Father just disappeared a year after I ran away from home."

Michael left the house, stunned and thoughtful. How many times would
everything cast itself in a new light? Had anybody else besides Clarkham—

apparently—known he was a Breed? The Crane Women, or Waltiri himself? *How many Breeds were there on Earth now?*

Theoretically, because of Aske and Elme, most of the human race could have some Sidhe blood; he had accepted that much months ago. But to be so close to the Sidhe himself—almost as close as Eleuth—was a shock he was not prepared for.

It explained a great many things, however.

MRS. DOPSO SAT in her overstuffed chair, the light of the reading lamp missing her face and casting a warm glow on her lap, which held a Bible opened to Revelations. Robert sat on a dining room chair next to her; Michael sat on the couch.

"Then the house *was* haunted," Mrs. Dopso said, seeming to derive satisfaction from the confirmation.

"In a way, yes."

"But it doesn't matter much now," she went on. "The whole world's haunted."

Michael nodded.

"I've been reading the Good Book," Mrs. Dopso said. "I'm afraid it doesn't give me much comfort."

Michael, remembering the debate with the Jehovah's Witnesses, said nothing.

"Will there be a war?" she asked. "I mean, will we drop bombs on them?"

"Not that kind of war, I don't think," Michael said. The old woman nodded. Dopso moved his chair forward.

"Should we move out of the city?" he asked.

Michael shook his head. "I don't recommend it."

"What are you going to do?" Robert pursued.

"I have a lot of . . . tasks. Jobs. I'm not sure where I'll start."

"Maybe you'll be a diplomat," Mrs. Dopso suggested.

"Maybe."

"Everything has become serious, so serious for somebody so young." She closed the Bible. "Will Christ come to Earth again?"

"Mother . . ." Robert said with only mild disapproval.

"I need to know. Is this the Apocalypse? I don't think you could be the Antichrist . . . but is it Clarkham, then? Or one of the . . . what did you call them . . . the Shee?"

"I don't think so," Michael said softly.

"But everything will change," Robert said.

"Everything will have to change."

"I don't believe it." Robert stood up and stretched his arms out. "The world doesn't work this way. It's a delusion."

"I owed you an explanation," Michael said after a silent moment went by. "And I'm telling you what little I know. I presume I'll have to tell others also. I don't know how many will believe me. There are probably thousands of people out there trying to cash in on what's happening. My story won't be any less crazy than theirs."

Robert shook his head. Mrs. Dopso simply placed her hand on the Bible in her lap.

"Godspeed," she said.

THAT EVENING, LYING in the downstairs bed but not sleeping—he might never sleep again—Michael wondered if he should offer his help to those dealing with the Sidhe. As a mediator, a diplomat. Or simply an advisor. Lieutenant Harvey might appreciate such guidance.

But it was immediately obvious to him that he could not. Becoming involved in the confusion might be brave, even noble, but it would ultimately be futile.

The *enormity* of the confusion was awesome. Billions of people becoming aware of a new reality almost overnight . . . He could not encompass such an upheaval. Some would welcome the change, taking it as an adventure—the disenfranchised, the disillusioned, those who yearned for apocalypse, whether it be Christian, nuclear or any combination thereof. Others would opt out, ignoring it or simply drawing up their barricades; in effect, becoming crazy, unable to face a reality they had never been prepared for. Facing the change realistically, Michael realized, would be almost impossible, for the humans of his time had been enmeshed in status reality for so many thousands of years . . .

If he tried to involve himself directly, he would be swept away in the hurricane of disruption, no matter what his powers.

But there was another less overtly courageous approach. He would go behind the scenes, doing what he had to do—finding Kristine, fulfilling his pact with Tarax, finding and eliminating Clarkham—and at the same time, he would work toward an understanding of the major problems.

When he was prepared, he would take whatever role was best suited for him.

"Coward," he whispered in the darkness. He unfolded his senses then, impetuously answering that self-accusation with an immediate act.

And felt:

The city, spread across its hills and shallow, wide valleys, vibrating, moving like a sluggish river this way and that in its tide of individual thoughts, disturbed like an anthill by a stick brought down from some direction it could not comprehend. Children having nightmares, having seen not airplanes, not kites or gliders, not even flying saucers, but Amorphals, wraiths and ghosts, or having been told about them not just by other children but by grownups on *television* with pictures and video.

Thousands contemplating their sins and the inadequacies of their lives, their inability to face unforeseen change; considering suicide.

He focused:

On a pregnant woman not more than five blocks away, radiant with health, holding her full abdomen as she lay in bed next to her sleeping husband, wide awake, mind suffused with a shadow. *I decided to have it and now look now look what it will be born into.*

On:

A boy, fourteen or fifteen, mind twisted like a wrecked ship, thoughts caroming without pattern, full of anger, trying to feel his way through instinctively to a method of dealing with the little he did know, wondering if his dead father would return with the ghosts to punish him. Walking a city street—Santa Monica Boulevard—alone, armed with a small pistol, daring something weird to pop up in front of him yes he could deal with *that* images of a dozen movie screens and big guns and Max Factor blood, flying acrobatic martial artists, and finally of drawn-faced priests pulling forth huge crosses and *losing* to the devil.

On:

Faer, huddling beneath a city bridge, weak and exhausted, waiting to cast shadows should they be discovered, their magic much weaker here; their horror and confusion matching if not exceeding that of the humans they had met.

Umbrals, dark and brooding and powerful; they had dug holes for themselves in the ground beneath the trees in Griffith Park and waited for the night; or they had lingered in shadows, dazzled by the sunlight, whispering softly to each other as the long day passed. Now they were abroad, trying to find a niche for themselves in this unfamiliar world.

The Pelagals had already set up liaisons with the creatures of the sea and swam with whales and sharks and huge wide-finned mantas in the sparkling moonlit waters beyond San Pedro harbor.

He extended his range and focused once more on humans. There was something he had to acquire, a *sense* about the world. The sweat started again on his skin. The effort was almost painful, but he stretched the range of his probe and the breadth of its sweep until he could feel himself reach high into the sky, and deep into the Earth and across the city for miles around. Then he drew in the height and depth and seemed for a moment to cup the land in his hands, touching lightly upon a million, two million, five million minds.

The richness of flow overwhelmed. He drew back and became selective again, but over a much wider area.

sleeping city dark and nervous

This is what humans are

to work all day work for wages hope for gain and all this comes this nonsense fall behind expected expected this is the way life is it gets you you don't watch it and it creeps up on you Oh yes Daddy says Mommy says meanness meanness don't touch the cat that way I should have listened and not taken that position before the board Satisfaction in that the world is falling apart and still I have peace in the garden with the thick crumbling soil works into my fingers and sprinkle the bone meal think this was an animal once a cow I suppose now it's garden that's what we'll be garden stuff walking meat and bone meal for Earth's garden Yes it was sex and I don't

know what to do it comes up it sneaks up I must answer like an animal not an angel ape not angel wish for self-control but what the hell Pills and such death and simple joy in a bottle so hard so hard to be good when what feels good to me kills me a bit at a time *what did she say in sleep she comes to me just stares with that look she always had when she was alive I wonder is it really her and she's talking in my sleep to me?* Shot strategy all to hell all that work all that dedication and now it doesn't mean shit well I'm free (tomorrow back to the struggle act like it's all the same but it isn't it's a nightmare out there) *Thick waves oily and blue-green up around my sleeping ankles I can wake up before it covers my head I know I can but what if I'm not asleep same dream this has happened before but I can feel it cold and know it's rising I can see the moon overhead full drawing it up over my head and those people on the shore, they see the seaweed around my ankles, they know the knife is dull* Ceiling blank and dark spackle landscape it's like a joy that doesn't let me sleep he loves me and it doesn't matter all else Stupid goddamn kikes every year stronger hate them so much liars and niggers and their women breeding and the brownies from the south and now *this* shit who can take care of it maybe they'll all kill each other and what's left over will be mine ours

Take it then take it and be damned CROSSING OVER yes God is with me and I can cross over swift river river of sinners *Listening!* Must pray Jesus for a drink Wait for the sun stretch out my outrageous arms and warm them in the *sun* sleep in the dumpster tonight listen for the trucks in the morning mustn't drink all this tonight or I'll sleep through the truck will get me eat me What can I teach them now it's all changed have a hard enough time anyway who wants to take a test when ghosts walk the streets and oh God I'm scared what must they be feeling just young kids faced the bomb now this

Kill him Shouldn't have eaten that Kill him Damned dog cleaned it up Pray Pray *Prey* Walked all over Like frogs on lily pad staring at each other oh it hurts I want to love Lust for nirvana that's it make them lust for enlightenment Breaking down everything Can't say it what I feel it's been twenty years we're together and she's everything and I'm so afraid of her for her for me Tomorrow I might be dead and no worries then it's getting close what can I expect five years maybe six

The grownups don't know nobody knows what do I tell my sister *Growling stomach* Filth filth and degradation Kill them Kill them *Whistling* I can't go on just being hungry and the children that bastard kill him Why won't they let me be *Listening! Somebody listening! Feel—*

He expanded the range of his probe. It seemed an effortless maneuver, but he scrambled to become more selective—

And nowhere Kristine

Beautiful women in bed making love and not thinking of love and the men not thinking some thinking of cars High glass and steel Lord could use a sniff a line how much I wonder call Marge no turn in script tomorrow Kill them Meeting Immigration car lawyer card car card lawyer My baby my baby (Emptiness, hollowness, grief close to bliss it has burned so deep) The way the paint muddies when you use those colors Bad mix Station nulls out that way six antennas got to save Utah from 50,000 watts I'll remember and tomorrow River flows river deep moon wide in my loins the blood dances with the moon I hate her for what she did but I hate everybody they hate me I know How do I convince them they are so bored they might as well be dead

(Pain so intense and prolonged it makes him flinch)

Interruption.

Something searching *for him* not Clarkham not Tarax, long and dark plying the waters of the Earth, a huge and ancient sinuosity, inwardly human.

He tried to withdraw but it was upon him, gripping him with unbreakable gentleness, leaving a message:

Soon we must meet. Our time is coming.

Then releasing him.

And Michael, still and cold in the downstairs bed, eyes stinging, deduced, knew, what it was that had reached out several times to touch him: the oldest living being on Earth, even now that the Sidhe were returning; the only representative of the first humans, alone of his kind cursed by the Sidhe to remain sentient after all the rest had been transformed into shrew-like animals. Alive and thinking and remembering for sixty million years under that curse.

The Serpent Mage.

He pulled back within himself, head aching, and struggled to reduce the pain with his discipline. He had overextended; he had been met, matched and exceeded.

21

The Tippett Residential Hotel now stood at the center of an evacuated no-man's-land about three long blocks square. Helicopters patrolled above the Strip and the Hollywood hills in the early morning darkness, spotlights searching the curfewed streets. Soldiers waited nervously beyond their sandbag and brick barricades. They had been awake, most of them, all night.

Michael walked casually down Sunset toward the barricades. Police cars parked diagonally across the street before the Hyatt. Highway patrol and LAPD officers stood with arms folded, talking. They paid him little attention. Gawkers had been around for days.

He reached out and skimmed their thoughts, taking in all that had been happening—all they thought had been happening—and distilling from the different viewpoints a reasonably clear picture.

The hotel had become particularly active about two weeks before. Hundreds of Sidhe had appeared in the building and exited, most from the ground floor, vanishing into the city. A few had flown from the roof on *epon*, the Sidhe horses. Amorphals and Faer, at least, had joined in the exodus through the Tippett. Other varieties of Sidhe—the Pelagals in his sleeping vision, for example—had taken other routes, used other gates.

It would not be difficult for many of the Sidhe to doff their clothes, find or steal or even buy others and merge with the human population. With a few simple illusions—cosmetic touchups in their appearance—the Faer, at least, could pass.

Now, however, the gate through the Tippett was blocked, at least on the ground. Michael had to go back into the building and learn what the situation was. If an accumulation of refugees was building up, something would have to give, and that meant more people—and perhaps Sidhe—would be hurt or killed.

But that was not his main purpose. It was possible the gate was two-way—or that he could use the presence of a one-way gate to enhance his own abilities and cross over into the Realm. And perhaps there, someone could tell him where Kristine was . . .

Tonn's wife.

He did not feel easy relying on Tarax, at Tarax's leisure, to regain Kristine.

The line of squad cars and police was easy to penetrate. He threw a shadow of himself walking back up the street and moved casually past them, unnoticed. A sandbag emplacement blocked the street a dozen yards beyond, with three armed National Guardsmen sitting behind it, weapons aimed toward the Tippett Hotel. They had their backs turned to Michael. He suggested that if and when they turned, they would see—and recognize—another guardsman. None of them turned.

The side walkway of the hotel was hidden from view. Michael climbed the battered front fence quickly and found the side door open a few inches. Pausing to close his eyes and concentrate on the service hallway beyond, he took a deep breath. Nothing. The hallway was empty, as was the first floor—empty, that is, of anybody or anything he could probe. He knew he could not necessarily locate Sidhe.

The lobby of the hotel had changed little since he was last there. The elevator doors reflected a muddy, distorted view of the light coming through cracks in the freshly-boarded entrance. Bullets had penetrated the wood and left the remaining glass in diamond scatters on the faded and torn carpeting.

Michael walked up the stairs slowly and paused on the landing, glancing over his shoulder at the lobby now half a floor below. Indefinite emotions, memories, hung in the air like evidence of a passing cigarette: not good emotions, and not human.

It took him a moment to recognize the mental spoor of frightened Sidhe.

On the second floor, he saw a piece of fabric cast aside in a corner opposite the elevator door. He bent and picked up the cloth, holding it loosely in both hands: a dark amber jerkin embroidered with vivid brambles and unfamiliar thorny flowers. The jerkin smelled like a winter forest. He laid the fabric down, disturbed by it, and saw another piece of clothing and a wooden staff on the stairway, the staff lying along one step.

The higher he climbed, the more discarded articles of clothing and accessories he found: bits of polished and engraved rock, even viewing crystals similar to the ones he had peered into in the Crane Women's hut, but dark and empty; a long full robe the precise color of a thunderstorm; several pairs of slipper-like shoes; and gems that would command a fortune in normal times.

On the fourth floor, Michael stopped. The spoor was strong enough here to tighten his stomach. The thought of powerful and noble Sidhe knowing such fear, almost panic, was frightening in itself.

On the fifth floor, he felt rather than heard a movement in the shadows. The dawn light did not relieve the gloom. He walked between a thin forest of creeper-like electrical conduits hanging from the ceiling. The interior walls had been torn out long ago, leaving the entire floor open but for the elevator and stairwell.

The floor undulated and crawled as Michael slowly approached the rear of the building. His feet brushed soft objects, and he stopped; the objects soundlessly huddled and bunched away from him.

His vision adapted with uncanny quickness.

"Birds," he whispered. The floor was carpeted with sparrows, pigeons, robins and blackbirds. They all watched him without menace but also without fear, and silently: not a single coo or chirp among the thousands.

On the porch, beyond shattered and leaning sliding glass doors, a single much larger bird about two feet tall perched on the edge of a concrete rail. Its feathers ruffled in a passing breeze, and it turned to face him. It appeared corvine, but with a blood-red breast and beak; its eyes were small black jewels lined in white. Michael thought it might be the same bird that had watched from the roof when Tommy came.

The large red-breasted bird stabbed its beak toward the upper floors and nodded three times, making a tiny *gluck* sound in its throat.

"Arno?" Michael asked. The bird preened itself, ignoring him. Then it smoothed its feathers and pointed to the upper floors again.

Michael backed away from the carpet of silent birds and resumed his climb. There were no more abandoned articles of clothing; if anything, the stairway and halls of each floor seemed less cluttered than when he had last been there, as if a group had made some pretense at cleaning and inhabiting the empty rooms.

As he approached the eleventh floor, he could feel the presence of an intrusion quite strongly. The gate was still open. And someone stood before it . . . That much he could sense but no more. He paused by the elevators, staring down a long, dark southern hall, all its doors closed. The end of the hallway was darker than it should have been—a rectangle of subterranean blackness. A white-haired figure in dark clothes stood before the blackness.

Michael's heart was subjected to two separate moments of alarm and shock. The first came when he thought the figure was Tarax. He had half-expected to find Tarax here, and perhaps his daughter as well, but this individual was neither. As his eyes probed the gloom, he saw that it was long of arm and leg and short of trunk, which gave him his second shock; he thought it was one of the Crane Women. Then it approached him.

It was indeed an old Breed female, but it was not Nare, Spart or Coom. Her long white-blond hair hung down to her shoulders. Her lips were full, pink, even luxurious, but her skin was nearly as pale as her hair. She regarded him suspiciously with small, bright blue eyes sighting along a thin nose. She wore a man's black suit, which hung loosely on her, a stiff, starchy white shirt (also baggy) and a narrow black tie. "I've been here two days," she said with a mild Scottish brogue. She did not touch his aura to learn what language to speak. "The Serpent told me to wait for you and bring you back with me."

"Who are you?" Michael asked. Why did such a simple question seem so clumsy? Because he already knew the answer, had known without even asking. "You're his attendant," he said.

She nodded. "The Serpent expects you. You are a candidate."

Then she motioned for him to follow. "This is not the path the Sidhe take from the Realm," she said, waiting for him to approach only two steps behind her before she reached with one hand toward the cavern-dark rectangle at the end of the hallway. "That is closed temporarily, but its power is here, waiting for those who know how to hitch on." The Breed pushed her hand into the blackness and passed through, briefly filling the hallway with blinding daylight. The blackness closed around her, leaving only her left hand suspended in the gloom, long finger curling, curling, urging him on.

The daylight flashed around him this time, and he stood on the barren shore of a broad slate-colored lake. The time was early afternoon. Thick clouds hovered over the lake and the adjacent brown hills. Near by, gnarled pines encroached upon the rocky shore. A mist drifted across the far shore, obscuring more hills and a small peninsula sparsely fletched with more pines. The air was chill and moist but not cold.

The Breed female stood near the still edge of the lake a few yards away. "Do you know where you are?" she asked.

Michael sniffed. "East," he said. "England . . . or Scotland."

"Have you been here before?"

He shook his head.

"Do you know why you have been called here?"

"No, not exactly."

"You've heard the tale . . . of the war, and the fall, and the loss, and the rise again, the flight and the return?"

"Yes," Michael said.

She nodded, and then she was gone. In her place stood a tree stump, its roots covered with algae below the water's murky line. "Thank you," he said with mock brightness. Then he sat on a rock and waited, feeling curiously patient. Only the gnawing thought of Kristine's captivity disturbed an extraordinary peace that settled over him.

This was finally the time, and it was sufficient in and of itself. What he felt was akin to pride, but he was not prideful. He was worthy to meet the Serpent Mage, but did that convey any honor? Yes, and no. If Michael thought as a human might think, then yes. If he thought as a Sidhe, it conveyed something else entirely. A fitting into the flow, a final integration into the overall story.

Late afternoon lengthened imperceptibly into dusk. He was neither bored nor anxious. He simply waited, his *hyloka* throbbing, heating and cooling him like another kind of breathing. Michael did not think much, nor did he daydream or doze. The hour approached. He would feel apprehension and even terror when it arrived; he was not above his origins. Transcendence, perhaps, but not aloofness.

He had come a long way to be here. Distance in space was the smallest component of that long, difficult vector. He had learned many disturbing things about himself, about the world and about his family. He was no longer the same Michael Perrin he had been when he had first entered Clarkham's house, passed through and around and entered the house next door, to find Tristesse's backyard and alley and the gate that gave access to the Realm.

The water of the lake—the loch—rose in a glassy, swelling hump in the middle distance, then smoothed again without waves. The hump reappeared halfway toward the shore, this time disturbing the water with the faintest iridescent ripples. Night was falling rapidly, and the mist was thickening, beading his shirt and light jacket.

The oldest living creature on the Earth, or perhaps anywhere else. Older even than Adonna called Tonn.

The air warmed. Michael surveyed the nearby waters. A very long black shape—perhaps twenty yards from beginning to end—lay curled just below the surface of the loch about ten yards offshore, taking advantage of the decline and deeper water beyond.

Slowly, it unwound and moved toward the shore, sinewaving from side to side, sending out oily ripples in beautiful whirlpool patterns. Its head broke the surface in the shallows, and Michael felt its dark gaze on him.

Ugly: the Serpent Mage was ugly. It looked dangerous, its smooth black skin dimpled all over like a very old catfish or electric eel, its filmed eyes tiny, its fins small and barbed, dorsal fin little more than a ridge of thorn-like stickles in the middle of its back. It was a yard wide and squat in cross-section, as if oppressed even in the water by its freight of time.

Michael shivered. The huge head slithered up the shore, cresting sand and gravel before it. Then it rested, careened slightly to one side, still watching him, silent on all levels.

Its mouth was a wide, round-gummed crescent recessed behind the blunt two-lobed snout. The mouth opened an inch or two and shut, then again. Recessed deep behind the gums were crescents of sharp, tiny teeth, no larger than Michael's, but far greater in number.

Michael dropped his legs over the side of the rock and approached the Serpent, hands held out before him. His fingers trembled.

But for a tiny, final thread of noctilucent cloud, the last light had gone out of the sky, He was seeing the Serpent by all of his new senses, and in that seeing, the Serpent was suddenly wrapped in cold fire. Mother-of-pearl stripes retreated down its length from its snout. Its eyes became sullen blood rubies. Then the decorations passed away, and it lost all character but its length and its width. It sat on the shore as black as polished obsidian, blacker than the turbid loch water and the mist-shrouded night air beyond.

"You called me," Michael finally said.

"Yes, I did," a voice issued from the long form. It spoke human words but hardly sounded human. There was too much age in it, too much time wrapped in solitary contemplation.

"I don't know why you called me."

"We must discuss what you're going to do," the Serpent said. "The world is remaking itself."

"I'm ready to listen," Michael said, stopping three strides from the Serpent's head.

"I am not here to give instructions," the Serpent said. "The most I will do is suggest. The rest is up to you. Do you know what you are now?"

"The Breed woman who brought me here said I was a candidate. I assume that means I'm a candidate to be a mage."

"And how do you feel about that?" The Serpent rolled slightly and inched back and forth on the pebbles, as if scratching.

Michael shook his head. *Not much different from any other job interview,* he thought. "It seems ridiculous. I'm weak and ignorant and unprepared."

"What is required of this new mage?" the Serpent asked.

"I'm not sure," Michael said. "I assume to offer leadership and help bring humans and Sidhe together to live in peace."

"Do you know that such a thing is possible?"

"No. But I know it's necessary, or we will all die."

"I have been listening to humans for sixty million years, give or take a few million, and I've listened to the Sidhe also. I've reached around the world, and beyond the world, and felt lives. When our kind was incapable of thoughts much deeper than planning for the next meal, or the next coupling, I waited. I saw their dreams increase in subtlety and power and watched them struggle back to awareness. The seed of rebirth I planted in them began to bear fruit. But time still dragged.

"I have been alive and imprisoned in this body much too long. I have lived so long that I have gone crazy, and outlived my insanity, thousands of time. Each time I slipped back to savagery, I fought my way out of the tangle, even though savagery and insanity were more comfortable, because I knew this time would come. I suspect other mages have also known. But unlike other mages, I could not participate in the preparations. And during my lucid moments, I planned what I would say when a new candidate appeared."

Rain started to fall. The loch sang and hissed under the passing storm.

"I swam the oceans of the world and found deep passages beneath the land and came to these inland bodies of water to rest. Once, not long ago, Elme brought me to her garden, and for a time I taught the children she had made with Aske, and the others who had gathered there. When Tonn reigned as Yahweh, our time in the garden became a legend, then a lie, and I swam the deep reaches for a thousand years, sick at heart and crazy again. I hated all living things. I thought the past, before the War, was lost forever. Even now, human life seems to me largely a dance of ignorance and hunger. What light there is, is rare, and when discovered, usually snuffed. Do you know who most often does the snuffing?"

Michael considered for a moment, water dripping from his face and steaming from the heat of his body. "Tarax and the Maln," he finally answered.

"They are the latest, yes. Do you know why humans have had to struggle against such odds in the past thousands of years?"

"Because of interference from the Sidhe."

"Yes. Do you hate them for their interference?"

Michael considered again, then shook his head. "It wouldn't do any good," he said.

"Wouldn't it be best to free us all by destroying the Sidhe?"

"We need them."

"Do they need us?"

"Even more."

"You know of some of the actions taken by the Sidhe. But the conspiracies have gone much deeper than you suspect. When you think of the finest human achievements, practical and artistic, names occur to you. Whom do you think of immediately?"

"Leonardo da Vinci, I suppose," Michael said. "Shakespeare, Beethoven. Einstein. Newton."

"In the west, yes, and hundreds of others, east and west, most lost to history. I hope you do not leave out Bach ... not very long ago, listening to his music helped me return to my present clarity. In your culture, these giants seem preeminent, do they not? But they are not the peak of human potential. They were *safe* enough to be ignored by the Sidhe. Some were ignored for a time, and when, unexpectedly, they began to worry the Sidhe, their lives and careers were plagued or cut short. But the finest, the preeminent—the ones I could feel even in the womb, radiating their genius—were snatched away by the Sidhe before maturity, or before they could accomplish their work. Almost all of the finest have been stolen away for ten thousand years, and *still we have matured and progressed.* The Sidhe have failed again. But they have come close to crippling us."

Michael said nothing, simply listened and waited.

"Only in the past few centuries—the wink of an eye—have some of the Sidhe come to their senses. Plans have been made, and factions have struggled with each other. And you have survived and come here to listen to me. So listen closely, for this is the most important information of all.

"The worlds are coming together. Adonna's Realm has failed. It lacked the mastery of prior creations. And here, in our universe, all have forgotten the art of making worlds. The true masters died during the War or were turned into animals and died not long after. Since that time, this world—our world—has not been maintained. Few even remember that once, making worlds was the grandest craft of all—and the most necessary."

"Somebody made this world—the Earth?" Michael asked, incredulous—yet it felt so right! Answered so many inner questions ...

"Not just the Earth. The universe."

"But it's *huge,*" Michael said. "I don't see how humans or even Sidhe could have made something so enormous, so complex."

"Complexity is not always desirable. Enormity ... yes. It always had a potential for growth. But it has gotten completely out of control. Hundreds of creators, dozens of mages, worked to make this the grandest world of all ... and succeeded. But the War ended cooperation. Now only I remember those times."

"People once lived only in universes they had made?"

"Why should it be otherwise?" the Serpent asked. "You are a child of your times. Do you not build your homes and live in them, in preference to staying out in the wind and the rain?"

"But that can't be quite the same thing. I thought that the Realm was like a growth, a polyp or something, on our universe."

The Serpent growled. For a moment, Michael began to tremble again, until he realized it was laughing. He did not expect such a human response from the monster stretched out before him, but then he realized how ridiculous that was.

The Serpent was *more* human than he was. Age and transformation did not cloak its humanity.

"That was all Adonna managed," it finally said. "An admirable effort, but ill-conceived. The Sidhe had destroyed or transformed all the mages and peoples who might have helped Adonna succeed. His was the ultimate conceit."

"How can this universe be controlled again?"

"It can never be controlled again. If you leave a garden untended long enough, it is no longer a garden but a wild forest or a jungle, and it cannot simply be trimmed back and weeded and replanted. Our world has grown far beyond our power to control. It has merged with other worlds, cross-pollinating and taking on their qualities. That is part of the enormity you see—we are now a polyp on the worlds of creators beyond our reach or understanding.

"Besides, your people—my children—have evolved in this garden-turned-jungle. You have learned some of its ways, and you are attuned to its character, however much you struggle against it. The world has turned cruel and harsh against you and made you tough and creative and resilient. The Sidhe cannot hope to match your creativity, whatever magic they wield.

"Human discipline, on Earth, is now stronger than theirs. And strongest of all, in potential, is the discipline of the Breeds. Those who cross the barriers between Sidhe and humans hold the heritage of both peoples."

"I'm a Breed . . ."

"You are still more human than Sidhe. You are not immortal, and you have that miracle called a soul."

"What . . . what is that?" Michael asked.

"Curious that you think I would know," the Serpent said.

"You don't know?"

"I only discovered how to destroy the soul, not to understand it. It is perhaps the final mystery, forever closed to those who live in universes. Those who do not need to dwell in shells, who stand out in the final sunlight and the final rainstorms, the weather beyond all worlds, perhaps they understand souls. Or perhaps that is what our souls mature to become . . . independent, free."

"The Sidhe will never have souls again?"

"My work was final."

"No wonder they hated you. You were worse than they."

The Serpent rolled back again, and Michael felt its clouded eye on him. "More evil, more willful, and more creative. I have had long enough to contemplate my excesses."

"Then they're doomed."

"No. There is a way to save them. Not in the individual—only in the race. And they must sacrifice their racial purity to do so."

"They must join with humans."

"Yes."

"But they hate us."

"Many of them both hate and fear us. We are the vital ones now. They are the elegant and stylish ones. They have maturity and experience. We have anger and compassion and creativity. Now they come to Earth and hide. They feel hunted; they feel lost. They fear retaliation when humans discover what the Sidhe have done to hold them back."

"Humans will take a long time to accept what I've learned," Michael said. "It wasn't easy for me, and I saw things with my own eyes."

"Now they see things directly, too. The Earth will not be the same. The Realm will not just vanish—it will leave its mark when it finally disintegrates. And no one surviving that cataclysm will doubt the new reality."

Michael squatted on the sand, then sat back on his butt and took a deep breath. "Why always disaster?"

"Because our universe has lost its safeguards. The garden has become filled with lions and scorpions. The gardeners are dead or, like me, ineffective, most of their skill sucked away."

"I had a safe and peaceful life until just recently," Michael said. "I still wonder about being a candidate for anything as important as a mage. I suppose I'd be asked to tie worlds together and to help create new ones."

"Ultimately," the Serpent agreed, "that would be your task. Why do you think you are inadequate?"

"I've done silly things," Michael said. "I've gotten people killed. My magic is comparatively weak. I'm young, and I feel very stupid most of the time. And . . . I don't want to be powerful and important." So he had finally said it.

"No person in his right mind ever wants to be a mage," the Serpent said. "It is a greater sacrifice and a harder life than any other you could choose or have forced upon you. No, those who want to be mages can never be true candidates. Clarkham, for example. His desire corrupts him."

"But I have been *stupid*," Michael cried out. "In the Realm, there was a Breed woman who loved me. She sacrificed herself for me—for nothing—and I . . ." He stopped, gulping rapidly, and found he couldn't say any more. He shook his head and wiped tears from his eyes.

The Serpent watched him without responding.

"Now, I've put another woman in danger. I have to find her. I don't know what I'll have to do to save her."

"You'll do what you must, obviously," the Serpent said. "Conflict is part of your existence. Why are you ashamed of your mistakes?"

"There's no excuse for being stupid. I was blind. Ignorant."

"Do you think you committed a sin?" the Serpent asked.

Michael was a little shocked to have the word he had been avoiding brought forward so abruptly. "I suppose I have."

"Do you know what a sin is?"

"Doing something stupid you can avoid. Being vicious or selfish. Not thinking of others as living, thinking beings."

The Serpent growled. "Sin is refusing to accept things as they are and refusing to learn from them. Sin is acting out of deliberate ignorance. Did you act out of deliberate ignorance?"

"No," Michael said. "But I was acting in my own self-interest. I didn't think about Eleuth . . . I used her."

"That is a very youthful thing to do."

"It was still wrong."

"She chose to sacrifice herself, did she not?"

"Yes, and she didn't tell me it would kill her, but I should have known."

"Adonna, when he play-acted as God, implanted a very inadequate and corrupt notion of sin in human minds. He said sin was a violation of god's law. That is the philosophy of a tyrant, not a creator. He wished to keep all humans subjugated and ignorant. Human growth was anathema to him. He wished to keep us in ignorance and darkness. There is no god's law. Why should a god impose arbitrary limits? There is only growth and understanding. Through growth and understanding, there is love. Where there is no understanding and no growth, only ignorance, there is no love. That is sin. But to grow is to commit mistakes. To learn sometimes requires trial and error. It should be apparent to you now that all sins are youthful transgressions. All evil is youthful. After a few thousand years, thoughts of evil become ineffably boring, like the posturing of ill-mannered children."

"But *I've felt* evil. In Clarkham . . ."

"Poor Clarkham. Ambitious, inadequate, very talented but flawed clear through. Adonna was once like Clarkham. And that is how Clarkham was ultimately defeated, by those who could reach into their own pasts and understand him. Clarkham is only a few hundred years old. Adonna and the members of the Maln and the Councils of Eleu and Delf are tens of thousands of years old."

"But what they did to him—filling him with evil?"

"Clarkham brought that upon himself. He made a trade when he was young. Magic for corruption. It is a way to gain power—a short-sighted and foolish way. When he had his power, he wished to stay the way he was, forever. And that means he cannot grow or learn. Such temptations are often placed before candidates. If they succumb, they are marked forever and easily detected."

"I haven't been tempted that way."

"Not yet," the Serpent said.

"And even if I should become a mage, it would still be possible for me to sin, wouldn't it?"

The Serpent rolled and rubbed itself on the stones

"I mean," Michael continued, "you sinned . . . in the War."

"I fought. We all sinned."

"But you took away the souls of the Sidhe."

"And it was not enough. I would have destroyed them utterly if I could have."

"Why?"

"Because they chose to destroy my people. I was a mage, and I was sworn to protect my people."

"Then evil breeds evil."

"Around you is the result. Conflict. Confusion. Horror. And also . . ."

Michael waited, but the Serpent's voice had simply trailed off. It did not continue.

"Beauty," Michael finished for it.

The Serpent growled. "I have listened and watched for so long that I am beyond weariness or astonishment. I have lived far too long, but I cannot die. If you succeed, then perhaps I can be released."

"But you still haven't told me all that a mage does."

"A mage cares for his people. He—or she, for some mages have been female, though not many—smooths the path. A mage must understand his people. Do you understand yours? Humans, I mean."

Michael shook his head.

"Now think deeply, don't answer quickly. Do you know the character of humans?"

"They surprise me all the time. How can I know them?"

"Then you already understand that humans are surprising. Sidhe rarely are; Sidhe are deliberate. How else do humans and Sidhe differ?"

"Humans don't have magic," Michael said.

"But some can work magic, no?"

"Breeds."

"Michael, you are mostly human; what Sidhe there is in you is not enough, by itself, to convey magic if magic was the talent of the Sidhe alone."

"Then I was lied to."

"If you do not believe you can work magic, then you cannot work magic. Simple and effective; another link in the chain the Sidhe forged thousands of years ago. Adonna taught humans that even if magic can be worked, it is evil, a sin. How have humans compensated?"

"By working with matter. Science and technology."

The Serpent seemed to purr deep in its throat. "Yes. A surprise. Using the wild fruits of the untended garden. Adapting to a universe, rather than tailoring a universe to fit them. Listening to the echo of the long, complicated song the world has become and accepting it, not circumventing it. A novel idea. The Sidhe have not done it; they have worked their magic, but in a way, magic is a denial of reality, not an acceptance.

"So humans are makers of tools, forgers of iron, builders of metal wings and artists of plants and animal flesh. Such work seemed a crude and futile quest to the Sidhe, thousands of years ago; they were much more worried about your artists and musicians. They did not discourage your scientists. They could not understand them. Now, the quest of human science has been so successful, it is often more powerful than its masters. And in the twentieth century, it has become more powerful than the Sidhe."

"But scientists can't make universes."

"Not yet," the Serpent said. "Given another hundred years or so—a very small amount of time—they will. If it is necessary. It may be necessary. But they will not do it through magic. And really, even the Sidhe can no longer create successful worlds. Adonna was the best, and his Realm is failing even as we speak. But we have gotten away from my question. *What are humans?*"

"Humans are animals," Michael said. "They think they aren't, but they are."

"True, but not in the way you mean. Humans are like animals, because many animals—even cockroaches, Michael!—were once *people*, long ago. The Sidhe forced me to turn my own kind into animals. And they transformed all their past enemies. You know of the Cledar and of the Spryggla. Their descendants are the birds and the mammals of the sea."

"I mean, so few humans can think beyond their immediate concerns."

"That may lead to tragedy, but could they have survived with any other attitude? The universe is no longer kind and nurturing."

"But some of them are cruel."

"And some Sidhe are cruel. How are they different?"

Michael was confused. "I don't understand what you want me to say."

"Do you detect similarities between humans and Sidhe, at the very bottom? Similar capacities for evil?"

"Yes," Michael said.

"Our kind and the Sidhe and the others were all one, once. Have you thought about the origins of those who lived in the original tailored worlds?"

He hadn't. "Where did they come from?"

"They had no beginning. They were never created."

Michael wrinkled his nose. "That doesn't make sense."

"We are eternal. We change, we die, we return, and the combinations and permutations go on forever and ever. And slowly, we progress. Ever higher and higher. I imagine that long ago, we were simple vibrations in nothingness, small songs, each individual differing only in subtleties. How long the simple songs lasted, who can say? But they became more complex and more involved with each other. The songs joined and withdrew. Again and again they found patterns together, and the patterns broke down to make new patterns. New collections of songs, new styles, new addings and takings away. At times, what might seem setbacks—even disasters—happened, but across the greatest spans of time, there was progress. You must draw back before you can leap.

"And finally, that progress has come down to us. There was no beginning. There shall be no end. Only variations on a theme, never repeating, always improving."

"Sidhe and humans were once one people?" Michael asked, still incredulous.

"It must have been so. One comes before many. And there are similarities."

"Yes . . ."

"Deep similarities. Though thousands of millennia have passed, the descendants of the original Sidhe can still mate with re-evolved humans. The songs even now beckon to each other."

"Why all the fuss, then?" Michael asked.

The Serpent growled quite loudly and rolled back and forth on the rocks. Michael backed away in alarm.

"Why all the fuss, indeed! Do you imagine I have all the answers?" it finally said when it could control its laughter.

"You should," Michael said resentfully. "You're old enough."

"I should indeed. But my life as a serpent has not been an unbroken and rational continuity. As I said, I've spent much of that time being little more than a senseless sea monster, loving shadows and deeps, only rarely stumbling back into something like sanity. Fortunately, this season I am reasonably lucid. But . . . not entirely. Once I knew much more than I do now. Perhaps even the answer to the profound question, 'Why all the fuss?' "

"Maybe I shouldn't ask any more questions," Michael said, disgruntled.

"Not at all. Continue. There is much more to talk about . . . But I should warn you. Even the answers I have given to you—*they are not certain*. They may not be entirely true. I am too old by far to be sure what the truth is. My own fantasies and dreams. They could be more real to me than memories."

They continued talking until morning light suffused the mist. The Serpent withdrew into the water for a time, leaving Michael alone on the shore while it made a circuit of the loch. Then it asked him to swim, and Michael stripped down and waded into the murky water. Not once did he touch the serpent but simply treaded water while it slithered in wide circles around him, head breaking the surface like the end of a weather-smoothed log.

Every few hours, the Serpent would illuminate itself with some fabulous design—lines of jewel-like swellings along its body, large and ornate fins, shimmering scales. But usually it was black or mud-colored, dimpled and ugly, ugly and ageless.

With the sun high, directly overhead, and the mist burned away, the dreary landscape around the loch took on a bright, desolate beauty. Michael lay on the rocks and sand to dry himself. The water had tasted sharp, like weak tea.

The Serpent crawled half its length up on the shore and rolled on its back, revealing a pale blue stripe running the length of its belly. A series of rune-like symbols were carved in the stripe. Michael crawled closer to the Serpent to examine the symbols. "What are those?"

"The terms of my imprisonment. The list of my crimes."

"I thought the Sidhe abhorred writing."

"They abhor the casual use of writing. They abhor bookkeeping or the pinning-down of history. For poetry, or for magic, writing is sometimes essential. These symbols are my prison."

"What do they say?"

"I don't know," the Serpent replied. "I can't see them. If I knew, I could free myself. And no one can reveal them to me."

They lay silent in the sun for minutes.

"Who was the last human you spoke to?" Michael asked.

The Serpent became a volcanic line of glowing red and then darkened into dying embers. "I haven't conversed with a human, face to face, for almost two thousand years," he said. "It is not pleasant to discuss."

"Why?"

"Because the last human candidate was deluded into thinking of our conversation as a temptation. He was extraordinary. He could have been a mage of the highest order, but he had attracted Adonna's attention as a youth. He had something else within him . . . something that went beyond the limits Adonna had set for him. Something above and beyond all these conflicts, very beautiful, without hatred, without greed. Still, he carried Adonna's mark . . .

"When his philosophy touched people on a large scale, it perverted and destroyed as much as it comforted and enlightened. There have been others like him since, but not nearly as strong. I have spoken with none of them."

Michael was tempted to ask more, but the tone of the Serpent's voice dissuaded him. After a while, when his clothes had dried, he stood and stretched. "I don't have much time," he said. "I have to find Kristine."

"We have wandered far with words, haven't we?" the Serpent asked. "How much have you learned?"

"Some. Not a great deal," Michael said.

"Then you know that what must be learned cannot be taught with words." Michael felt a chill.

"You must sacrifice yourself now."

"I don't understand."

"You pride yourself in your individuality, your personal memories and accomplishments. But if you were to place all you have thought and been and done on top of what I contain, your mere two decades on my millions of years, you would be lost."

"Yes. Probably."

The Serpent growled softly. "That is what you must do."

Michael stared. "Why?"

"You cannot be a mage as you are now. You must have experience. You must learn."

"I don't want to be a mage," Michael said softly, shivering again.

"Do you have a choice?" the Serpent asked.

"Is this what you offered the last man you spoke to?" Michael asked. The Serpent did not answer. "Is it?"

"Yes."

"And he refused?"

"He had the mark of Adonna."

"Do I have the mark of Adonna?"

"You do not," the Serpent said. "You shed the mark in the Realm."

"And you want me to carry your mark?"

Again the Serpent burned lava-red, and the water around his submerged length bubbled and steamed. "You must combine worlds. You must create new worlds. You must unite the races."

"Yes, yes, somebody has to do that! I know."

"And you are a candidate. Perhaps the best candidate."

"But why must I submerge myself in . . . in you?"

"I have the experience. The memories. I cannot use them. You can."

"You have something else," Michael said, hardly believing what he was feeling, what he was about to say. A voice inside him fairly screamed that he was being childish and stupid. Who was he to challenge the oldest living human? But another, stronger voice compelled him. Both voices were purely his own. This choice was his. "You carry the horrors of the past. If I absorb you, and lose myself, then I *become you*. And you were as evil and willful as Adonna."

"I have contemplated my excesses," the Serpent said again, its length obsidian-black.

"But would you commit those excesses again . . . to save your people?" Michael put on his clothes.

The Serpent withdrew a few yards into the water. "If I were given no choice, I would."

"When you tried to destroy the Sidhe, did you really have no other choice? Or did you hate them?"

"I hated them," the Serpent admitted.

"Would you try again?"

"They are weak now."

"Would you try to destroy them?" Michael felt a surge of defiant horror. "You could, now that they're weak. You could finish what you started."

Only the last three yards of the Serpent's trunk and head protruded onto the shore now. "I hope I would not do that."

"But you might . . . anyway."

"I might," the Serpent conceded.

"I can't become you," Michael cried. "I can't be the kind of mage you were. If I can be any sort of mage at all . . ."

"You are very young."

"I wish there was a way I could learn from you, learn what is necessary, without the risk. If that is possible . . ."

But the Serpent withdrew into the loch without another word. The ripples stilled along the shore, and Michael was alone. He turned toward the tree trunk where the Breed female attendant had faded away.

She stood there again, white hair dazzling in the sun, baggy black suit and starchy white shirt and narrow black tie just as he remembered them.

"Follow me," she said. She tore away a part of the landscape beyond the tree trunk and stepped into inky darkness. Michael crawled through the hole after her.

And returned to the eleventh floor of the Tippett Hotel.

The Breed woman was a translucent shadow ahead of him, halfway down the hall. "You failed," she said, her voice as weak as her image. "You are no longer a candidate. Go home and weep for your people and your world."

22

Michael stood in the hallway, alone and angry and as still as the marred plaster walls around him. *Why did I do that?* he asked himself, relaxing his clenched fists and arm muscles. *Because I am a coward? Afraid to submit to a higher personality?*

"No," he said. He felt his strength returning—that strength which had been growing, unaided, since he had returned from the Realm, since he had dropped out of the complex picture of machinations between the Sidhe and Waltiri and Clarkham. The strength returned, but not his confidence.

The talk with the Serpent Mage had been so *interesting*. For it to come to such an unexpected and painful end, because of his own rebellion, was agonizing.

In a way, he had been waiting for just such a conference for months.

"I'm a renegade," he said. If he was out of the picture completely, with no hope of returning, then he was free to act as he chose . . .

Which was what he seemed to be doing anyway.

He turned to look at the rectangle of darkness. When he had first passed through, following the old Breed female, he had felt the nature of the region beyond as a kind of tingling against his palms. He could feel that same tingling now. The nonspecific gate led to nowhere in particular—it was an open exit with no fixed destination. To someone with no training whatsoever—the soldiers and police in the streets below, for example—it would be simply a blank wall, darkened as if by a polarized filter. For someone with inadequate training, it could be very dangerous. It could put Michael into a between-world as complex and delusive as a nightmare . . . Or it could take him where he wished to go.

To the Realm.

To seek out Tonn's wife, the skull-snail, if she was still alive.

Toh kelih ondulya, med nat ondulya trasn spaan nat kod . . .

So Eleuth had told him in the Realm, before bringing back a beetle from Earth. "All is waves, with nothing waving across no distance at all."

"*The Sidhe part of a Breed,*" she had explained, "*knows instinctively that any world is just a song of addings and takings away. To do grand magic, you must be completely in tune with the world—adding when the world adds, taking away when the world takes away."*

Did he feel that instinct clearly? When he had last stood on the top of the Tippett Hotel, looking out over the city, he had felt in touch with the inhabitants of the Earth for miles around—and he had felt even more in touch later, lying in bed in the Waltiri house. But the inhabitants were not the world itself. He needed to make that final link.

It was certain no one else would do it for him. He was working alone now, without support from any faction or quarter. He had to lift himself up by his bootstraps.

For an instant, he felt a sense of despair and defeat that left him dizzy. How inadequate he was, how ill-trained and ignorant.

And yet . . .

And yet, he was capable. He had the means to do what needed to be done. Clarkham, the Serpent Mage, Adonna, Tarax, even Waltiri aside, Michael felt the strength within him. The product of a long year's discipline.

For a moment, the hallway ahead of him seemed to vanish, and he saw nothing but waves of darkness shimmering against each other. Addings and takings away—risings and fallings. Peaks and valleys. He felt the hum in his palms, the singing of all reality, and closed his eyes to tune himself to that.

With Tarax's suggestion, he had broken free of Clarkham's weak trap-world. Now—

He turned to the dark rectangle. He remembered the *tune* and *timbre* of the Realm. He made the distinction between Earth and the Realm. Their wave-trains separated, and he could feel the distinct hummings. He reached out with one hand, feeling the buzzing in his palm, and pressed against the darkness.

Adding.

Taking away.

The darkness became potential. For a moment, he felt a hideous between-world beyond his fingers, and he wanted to pull back, but he held himself there and tuned an interval higher. Closer. Another interval.

His index finger drew a gash in the darkness, and sunlight beamed through onto his feet. He clawed the opening wider and felt it resist him, trying to close again.

The Realm glistened distinct and real beyond the darkness, but hardly stable. The tune and timbre were in fact fluctuating even as he tried to break through. He ad-libbed a tremolo to the song. The darkness faded.

He stepped through.

And stood on a grassy dell, with thick, green forest beyond. Overhead, in the dusk of a failing day, stars twirled like fireflies on short leashes, and the moon cut a trail of crescents in a pearly band across the sky.

The Realm.

FOR THE FIRST few hours, Michael reveled in the clean, cold sensation of air that had blown across scattered patches of snow and through miles of uninterrupted forest. He reached out to the auras of any within his range and found only a few lone Arborals—and a hint of others in the direction of the setting sun. He then settled into a cold evening, warmed by his *hyloka.*

Wherever his probe extended, it met an undertone of disruption. In one direction, he actually felt a cutting-off of the Realm—an edge, beyond which lay something distastefully like the Blasted Plain that had surrounded the Pact Lands. As the evening lengthened, he felt more such edges. Swaths of decay now cut through the Realm. He did not know whether he could cross such a discontinuity or whether the Realm would last long enough for him to find Tonn's wife, but he felt a nervous contentment nonetheless. He was actually doing something to locate Kristine. For the time being, it was all he could do.

Until, of course, Tarax came forth to present his daughter. When—and if—that happened, Michael would change his plans accordingly. But the thought of waiting for Tarax's move had eaten away at him. This was much better, if no more certain.

Michael had never suspected himself to be such a rebel. He had trained under the Crane Women with a bare minimum of argument, accepting the situation and the necessity of their discipline. Now he was ignoring Tarax, who was almost certainly more powerful, and he had defied the Serpent Mage, who was beyond doubt wiser.

But tainted. If the wisdom of the past came with all the patterns and mistakes of the past built in, then surely there was another and better way.

He ruminated on these thoughts until dawn, which came much sooner than he had expected, even given the Realm's erratic time scales. Everything was shifting.

Then he set out in the direction of the murmuring crowd of auras, more certain with each mile he ran and walked that there were humans among that group—a great many humans. This gave him another hope, that he could rescue the humans he had left behind in the Realm. That was something he had never felt right about. However weak he had been, he should have tried to help them . . . But he had not been his own individual then. He had been carrying out somebody else's mission.

And if that's what you're doing now, and you don't even know it? The nagging doubt was his own; it came from no outside source. He was of so little importance now, so rejected and ignored, that nobody in all the Realm felt it necessary to cloud his mind with messages.

Not even Adonna, who might be dead . . . though that was hard to believe. What could kill a god-like Sidhe? Nothing, perhaps, but the end of his greatest creation. If Adonna had fashioned the Realm out of himself, then the Realm's death might be his own.

Within two of the irregular days and nights, he stood on the inner edge of the forest that had once surrounded the Blasted Plain. Nearby, the river still flowed, and the bitter, corrupted circle of the Blasted Plain itself still stuck out like a festering sore. But where the Pact Lands had been, where the villages of Euterpe and Halftown had stood and the mansion that had once belonged to Clarkham: desolate emptiness. The Blasted Plain had half-heartedly moved in to fill the void.

Here no humans, no Breeds, and certainly no Sidhe lingered . . . with one exception. Michael probed cautiously, unwilling to intersect with the minds of the Children, if any still existed.

But the Children had gone, too. They had been expunged by the Sidhe who had carried away the humans and Breeds and resettled them, perhaps in the direction where Michael sensed a large group of humans.

He thought of Lamia, the last inhabitant of Clarkham's house. The house and the decaying field of vine stumps behind it, on a bank above the sluggish river, had vanished without trace.

Michael blanked his thoughts of all cross-connections and associations, searching for one aura: Tonn's wife, transformed into the skull-snail.

He found nothing. Concentrating, reaching out again, he refined his sweep. Again nothing—and still no sign of the Children or anything else alive—or quasi-living—in the Blasted Plain.

And then he came across a wavering pinpoint of awareness, almost too weak to be perceived.

Without hesitation, he stepped from the forest into the Blasted Plain, his feet raising puffs of bitter dust.

Within an hour, he came upon the hulk of the skull-snail, its hideous shell stuck fast between two leaning pillars of rock the color and texture of clotted blood. In the orange light of the dusty sky, he walked around the hulk, examining the desiccated remains of the beast within the shell. The skin had hardened to tough leather on the trunk and tentacles; the lantern-like protrusions at the ends of the arms were dim and opaque.

Yet Tonn's wife was not dead. He reached deep into the hulk, touching the weak aura directly.

Sun. He kills me finally.

—I've returned, Michael signaled.

The boy . . . Seeking now?

—You said you knew where I could find Kristine.

You did not even know who Kristine was then.

—No, I hadn't met her. How did you know?

A mage's wife has many skills. I taught Tonn a great deal. Magic is transferred through the female.

Michael wondered about that but decided to let it pass. He did not think Tonn's wife would live much longer.

—Where is she?

I knew then. I knew where she would be . . . But you have changed things. The answer is less clear now.

—How did I change things?

You did not concentrate on Clarkham. You thought he was defeated forever, when he was only removed from the immediate concerns of the Sidhe. What I saw was that Tarax held her, to force you to train his daughter as the Crane Women would have. But Clarkham may also have taken her now. The picture is not clear.

The leathery appendage emerging from the "nose" of the skull-shell twitched and slid a few feet in his direction. Michael did not move to avoid it. She had no power to harm him.

Please. You must call the Arborals. I am dying.

—There are none close now. The Realm is being evacuated.

Then it is over. I will be released even from memories.

—If Clarkham has her, where would he keep her?

Practicing. Mock-ups, dreams, failed attempts to be a mage.

—He would keep her in another incomplete world, as he kept me?

No answer.

—Which world? Please—describe the song, the timbre.

A world built to contain his evil. A slippery, hardsided world, a trap for all, even him. She does not know.

—How will I find it?

By teaching Tarax's daughter. Or by . . . you are strong now, much stronger.

The hulk shifted between the rocks.

If the Arborals cannot come, then I will not wait. The last pinpoint of awareness winked out, suddenly and finally. The hulk slumped, empty and useless.

Michael stood for a few moments by the remains, filled with an emotion between pity and indignation. From what he had felt in his probe, he could tell that Tonn's wife—he didn't even know her name!—had once been nearly as noble a Sidhe as the Ban of Hours. What had she done to deserve such punishment? What had Lamia and Tristesse done? He could understand the action taken against the Serpent Mage, but why so much undirected and senseless cruelty?

As he recrossed the border of the Blasted Plain, Michael saw the sky and the sun slew to one side, then spin. He fell to the ground and crept toward a tree. The shadows of the forest recessed wildly, then steadied. He looked up, eyes wide, and slowly rose to his knees. All the directions had changed.

His skin itched, and his hair stood on end. Fundamentals in the construction of the Realm were decaying, that much was clear.

But which direction would he take now? He couldn't follow the sun—it seemed to have been smeared into a constant glowing haze above the land. He walked into a clearing and shaded his eyes against the warmth and glare of the entire sky. He would have to travel rapidly. There was very little time left.

Calling upon all his discipline, he took several deep breaths and began to run through the forest and across the open fields, following now the much weaker and confused beacon of that mass of human minds. He did not run far.

The land ahead had abruptly separated, leaving a chasm several miles wide. Michael slowed to a walk, frustrated and more than a little frightened. He had never seen such a feature in the Realm before; it was new, and it looked very dangerous, certainly uncrossable without aid. The edges of the chasm were crumbling away, the clumps falling off into nothingness with majestic slowness.

Michael came as close to the edge as he dared, crawling out on a lip of solid rock, fingers seeking any sign of tremors or instability. Far below, he saw the foundation of Adonna's creation roiling and rainbowing in opalescent mist.

The chasm appeared to extend in both directions forever. It cut him off from the human murmurings. It even separated him from the distant sensation of Inyas Trai and the Irall.

If he could not cross, then he could do nothing more in the Realm. He retreated from the lip of the precipice and walked back into the forest a safe mile or so, to rethink his plans and see if another way presented itself.

"Why do I feel so *good?*" he asked himself, standing beneath an enormous conifer, at the center of a circle of half-melted snow. "Everything's going wrong . . ." But he already knew. It was because he was back in the Realm. The Realm had a beauty, even now, that he had deeply missed after returning to Earth. Beauty—and horror and sadness, much more concentrated than on Earth. Every sensation felt here was at once more intense and more stimulating.

The inexplicable horror of Adonna's wife; the surreal nastiness of the Blasted Plain; the ever-changing days and seasons. The lushness of the forest, with its wild orchards. Inyas Trai. The cursed territory of Lin Piao Tai. How would the Sidhe feel, forced to return to Earth after their centuries here?

How could a mage take the demanding variety of Earth and mix it with the intensity of the Realm?

He closed his eyes and spread his palms. He could *see* everything through his skin. The Realm vibrated and sketched itself across his eyelids. He could almost feel its deep structure, catch the secret of Adonna's creation . . .

"Man-child."

Michael opened his eyes and saw a Sidhe horse approaching him. An image of Tarax—clearly not the Sidhe himself but a shadow—guided the *epon* through the trees with one hand cupped under its chin. The shadow smiled. "Play-acting at magic?"

Michael stumbled over his words and finally, face flushed, just nodded.

"We have an appointment," the shadow said. "You obviously can't make your way across the Realm unaided. Even most Sidhe have difficulty now. Adonna can spare one of its *epon* for your journey. We will meet beneath the Testament of the Irall."

The shadow faded. The horse stood, tail flicking, long foreleg pawing the grass and humus, with its eyes fixed patiently on Michael.

"Hello," Michael said.

The *epon* tossed its head and turned sideways to allow him to mount.

23

The Sidhe horse, eyes blank as ice, silver-pearl skin blinding in the diffuse sky-glow, leaped from the crumbling edge with legs extended fore and aft. Michael clung to the mane, his heart racing, and cried out, *"Abana!"*

The chasm, the separated sections of the Realm, the mist of Adonna's creation far below, all skewed and tumbled. The horse screamed and was surrounded by a coma of fire that broke away like shards of glass behind them. The cold was so intense that Michael nearly froze before he could increase his *hyloka*. The horse's lips curled back from its teeth, and its muscles tensed hard as stone between his legs. Michael's head seemed about to explode.

The journey was an agony. It hadn't been this way the last time. The Realm no longer accommodated such rapid travel without protest. They skimmed the ragged, bleeding borders of the Realm and the Earth and a thousand between-worlds. The Realm was an open wound, and the Earth beyond cut deep as a knife, defending itself. Michael could stand no more when the journey ended, and the horse threw him and fell on its side, kicking and shrieking.

He rolled across a flat, abrasive surface and leaped to his feet instinctively, bruised, knees and arms scraped, but otherwise intact. *That's more like it*, he thought. He had seldom spent more than a few hours uninjured during his last visit to the Realm. The horse, shivering but also unhurt, clambered upright and regarded Michael resentfully.

They stood on a dark stone road flanked by shiny black pillars, each pillar filled with tiny flaming glints like eyes around a campfire, watching, enjoying their predicament. At the end of the road, squatting under the brilliant, hot, milk-white sky like a monstrous gray seed-pod, was the Irall. At the opposite end of the road, behind them now, the color of incandescent marble, rose Inyas Trai, the city that the last of the Cledar had designed for the Sidhe ages past.

Michael was alone on the road. The horse calmed under his caressing hands and allowed him to remount.

His enthusiasm for the Realm had declined considerably. The sky was hotter here, abusive in its brilliance. The Irall stood in sharp contrast, its inward-leaning outer towers rising black as coal from a dome of silky gray. Its black central spire climbed to a haloed needle point that could hardly be seen against the dazzling whiteness.

The last time he had entered the Irall, it had been involuntarily, surrounded by Sidhe coursers. He was not so sure that this time was much different.

Michael stopped the horse and surveyed the land around Inyas Trai and the Irall. The city seemed empty—a quick probe found no sign of Sidhe, Breeds or humans. Perhaps most of them had been evacuated through the customized stepping stones Nikolai had mentioned. Another probe into the Irall itself, cautious and tentative, revealed that it was also deserted.

He tried to find the direction of the massed human auras again, and when he did, he sensed a great body of water and mountains between. The humans had been taken to the other side of *Nebchat Len*, in the mountains where the Sidhe habitually trained their initiates. Michael received some of the captives' emotions—and made his first good guess as to their number.

There were far more than Euterpe had ever contained; as many as five thousand. Some were fearful, others calm and expectant. He did not have time to find the individual auras of people familiar to him—Nikolai or Helena. If he did not take Tarax at his word, perhaps even Kristine waited there.

Michael urged his mount forward into the gate of the Irall, barely wide enough to allow three horses entry abreast. He remembered the cupped dark walls beyond, like a glacial cave suddenly converted to stone. The floor was littered this time not with dried flowers, but with the leavings of panic and flight— shreds of clothing, muddy bare footprints, broken and powerless wicks; not unlike the stairs of the Tippett Hotel.

The tunnel broadened but remained dark, without its prior greenish luminosity. The walkways stretched empty on each side; there were no longer enslaved Breeds in the Irall to serve Adonna, or Tarax and the Maln.

The walls spread into an immense chamber, its limits lost in darkness. Where before there had been smoke rising to its heights, now there was only cold, stale air. The beehive chamber beyond was flooded to the horse's hocks with rusty water, hiding the sunken amphitheater at its center. He rode the horse around the perimeter and into a tunnel carpeted with swaths of electric blue mist. That, at least, was the same; they were nearing the Testament.

Thus far, they had only passed through chambers within the wall of the temple. They emerged from the tunnel into the central hollow of the dome. The air smelled of dust and decay and sour, poisonous blossoms. Yet Michael was not afraid. He had been more nervous meeting the Serpent Mage.

Long minutes passed while they crossed the interior. All around, the blue mist mocked them, rising in animated whorls and snake-like curls, beckoning and striking, reminding Michael of the blueness that had emerged from a single flower to destroy Lin Piao Tai. (Was all magical power simple and interrelated, like combinations of letters in a remarkably small alphabet?)

Finally, before them appeared the stone table flanked by tall stone chairs. No amphitheater crowded with Sidhe appeared out of the mist this time to surround the table, and the chairs were empty.

"Where do I go?" he asked nobody in particular, except perhaps the horse. He patted its shoulder. It glanced back at him, eyes unfathomable but calm, and flared its nostrils. Then it led him past the table, and Michael knew where he was going. The horse would take him to the pit at the center of the Irall.

They would fly to the spinning brass cylinder above the mist and beneath the Realm proper.

And so it was.

Down the rocky shaft, past the thick upper layer of rock and the lower layer of blue translucent ice, now cut through with milky fractures, toward the spot of rainbow-colored light and finally out the bottom of the shaft, the horse's hooves straining for solid ground and finding none, its mane and tail streaming, lips revealing tiger teeth biting the empty air ahead—under the rugged ice belly of the Realm, above the chaos of the mist—

Toward the spinning brass cylinder, perhaps a mile wide and two long—

And into the hole at the center. The last time, he had been struck unconscious by the errant hoof of a horse. Now he saw it all. And still he was not afraid.

The horse flew him past bent and twisted platforms mounted on girders that vanished into dusty darkness. The cylinder did not seem designed for any practical habitation; it might have suited a community of anchorites, each sitting on a platform separated from the others, contemplating verdigris decay and endless rotation about the hollow axis. Michael probed ranks upon ranks of platforms revealed to his dark-adjusted eyes, the ranks half a mile deep to the wall of the cylinder, each platform empty, collecting only dust. *Why all this?*

He thought of the graveyard near the opposite end of the cylinder, thousands of Sidhe and Breed and human skeletons chained to a free-floating network of brass bars. Had Adonna truly demanded so many sacrifices? Or had the corpses been criminals captured and executed by Tarax?

The horse shuddered, and Michael turned it away from the center as they saw the graveyard ahead, still filled with dust and captive dead. They flew in a spiral around the cluster of bones. He saw the platform from which Tarax had addressed him when Michael had found himself chained among the corpses. The horse stretched and flew around the platform and then moved inward toward the axis again as the graveyard receded into a lattice of brown points.

Repeating journeys. Ringing changes on the same themes.

This time, however, Michael knew he had some measure of control. Tarax needed him—or at least behaved as if Michael were necessary.

The solid, closed end of the cylinder loomed, streaked with black and green stains radiating from the center to the edges. Then a pinprick of light appeared in the center, widening, its edges glowing and sparkling. Beyond, an unknowable distance below—if distance meant anything there—was the mist, chaos and potential, a vortex of pastel rainbow colors run through with painful ambiguities. Michael would not allow himself to turn his head away. He would have to face such—

If he wished to become a mage. Did he? What sort of mage, without the support of the Serpent? Ignorant and weak? A renegade mage. Something young and powerful and unexpected.

He shook his head slowly and grinned. His every thought betrayed how foolish he truly was.

The hole stopped growing, its edges solidifying into fresh-polished brass, as if a giant drill bit had recently pushed through. Two figures floated at the center. Michael recognized Tarax. Beside him hovered a Sidhe female, tall and slender. The horse shivered and accelerated, neck muscles writhing.

From a hundred yards, Michael could see Tarax's patient, weary face surrounded by a drift of fine white hair. He wore the same robe he had worn when he had last sent Michael into the mist to meet Adonna: gray stripes floating above black fabric, intertwining to form knot-like designs.

You don't even have the necessary clothes to be a mage, Michael admonished himself. Tarax observed the faint smile on his lips. The horse turned and slowed barely five yards from the Sidhe father and daughter. They all might as well have drifted in emptiness above the mist; without looking back or toward the distant reflecting edges of the hole, the only sign of the cylinder's presence was a sensation of vast silent motion.

"You've matured, man-child," Tarax said. "You're no longer a mere tool, an aimed weapon."

Michael examined the daughter. Her face was sternly beautiful, in the way he had never quite grown used to among the Sidhe: long, sharply cut, with large pale eyes and dark red hair. He could not tell how old she was; her figure betrayed some maturity, but was by no means voluptuous. She wore a white blouse with the sleeves rolled and tied back above her elbows, and knee-cut riding pants. Her boots were long and black and came to mid-calf. Her gaze was steady and calm. Beyond the Sidhe resemblance, Michael could detect neither Tarax's nor any other heritage in her; she could even have passed as a Breed. She was taller than Michael by three or four inches, if height could be judged in the weightlessness above the mist.

He thought of walking beside her on an Earth boulevard, through a human crowd. She would pass—but barely.

"I'm puzzled," Michael said. "This is your daughter?"

Tarax nodded. He had not even bothered to probe Michael, nor had Michael tried with him. Mutual respect. "Her name is Shiafa." That, Michael knew, would be the extent of the introductions. "What puzzles you, Man-child?"

"The last time we met, you wanted me dead. You were very disappointed when Adonna spared me."

"I was even more disappointed to learn you had survived your encounter with the Isomage."

"Then you saved my life, and now you bring me here on one of Adonna's horses—which I presume I will not be arrested for stealing—and treat me with civility and even respect, though you keep calling me man-child."

"All humans are children to me. Shiafa is a child, and she is three times older than you, by Earth time."

Michael shrugged. "I don't understand why your attitude toward me has changed."

"Sidhe take advantage of fortune and misfortune alike. My misfortune—that you have survived and matured—is also my daughter's fortune, for the Crane Women are gone—"

"Dead?"

There was a hint of the old Tarax in the Sidhe's long, patient silence and slow blink. "They are gone," he repeated, "and my daughter needs to be trained. Only you can pass along the discipline of the Crane Women."

"What about Biridashwa—Biri? He was trained by the Crane Women."

"He is a Sidhe. You are a Breed. It is necessary that Breeds train."

"Why?" Michael asked.

Shiafa had hardly moved during this exchange. Now she pushed away from Tarax, swam forward with peculiar grace in the weightlessness, and, without a word, mounted behind Michael.

"There is subtlety in Breed discipline," Tarax said. "That subtlety is necessary for an initiate to the Maln." Michael sensed this was not the complete truth.

"Is there still a priesthood? I've heard Adonna is dead and the Councils are dissolved."

"Adonna is dead," Tarax said. "The creation is sundered and will soon die. But there is still need for a priesthood. Train my daughter, and you will learn where the Isomage keeps your woman."

"What will I teach her?" Michael asked, glancing over his shoulder at Shiafa.

But Tarax was already fading. The Sidhe's black robes smeared like paint in water. His face and hands and feet lengthened into blurred lines. A billow of mist flashed and danced around him, and he was gone.

"I will be first priestess to the new mage," Shiafa said, her voice husky and musical and enchanting. "My father." She gripped Michael's hips with her long-fingered hands. "You will train me on Earth—"

"I'll train you where I damn well please," Michael said, reacting with anger to his arousal at her touch. "Whatever I'm going to teach you, I'll start in the Realm. We have work to do."

The new mage. Michael brought the horse around and urged it back along the cylinder's length.

"Our first job is to undo all your father and the Sidhe have done with humans in the Realm," he said. "If you refuse to help, then I'll cut you loose here and you can return to Tarax."

"I will help," Shiafa said without inflection. Michael glanced back at her with some surprise. Her eyes were closed to slits. "You are the master of discipline. But we will not have much time. My father could dissolve the Realm any day now."

"Heir to Adonna, eh?" Michael asked, as the dusty wind beat at them from around the floating graveyard. Shiafa said nothing.

The ice beneath the Realm was cracked and veined and calving into huge, drifting spikes and bergs. With some difficulty, Michael found the shaft leading back to the Irall, and they rose to the surface of the Realm.

24

The night of the failing Realm was impenetrably dark. The ribbon of moon that had once stretched across the sky, and all the twirling stars congealing into a fixed night canopy, had gone. There was nothing but cold wind and the soughing of the dry grass around their campfire.

Michael had started the fire by extending his *hyloka* to one finger and igniting a small pyre of dried wood and leaves. Shiafa watched him with some interest and then experimented on her own pile of leaves. She, too, was able to light a small blaze, which she then heaped on the bigger fire. She turned her large pale blue-green eyes on Michael and blinked.

"I'm not sure there's anything I can teach you," Michael said. "My skills are crude."

She went to the horse and removed a comb from her pack, then began currying the animal's short, tight-packed fur swiftly from neck to withers.

"There are people here—humans," Michael said. "I know some of them. I'd like to get them out of the Realm before it collapses."

Shiafa nodded once.

"Do you have any suggestions?"

"The Ban of Hours defies my father," she said. "You might consult with her."

"Is she still in Inyas Trai?"

"No. The city is empty."

Truth so far, he thought.

"She's protecting the humans?"

Pulling back from a long stroke that made the animal shiver with pleasure, Shiafa shook her head. "I do not know."

"You speak English well," Michael said. Neither Tarax nor his daughter had resorted to in-speaking. "Where did you learn it?"

"From my *Mafoc Mar,*" she said. "My Bag Mother. She attended the Mab on Earth before the final flight to the Realm. The Mab had dealings with English and Irish and Scots. And my father has been to Earth since."

"Your father still hates humans."

"Yes," she answered matter-of-factly.

Michael sighed and stared into the crackling flames. "If he becomes mage, the new world he makes won't be suited to my people, will it?"

She did not answer. That much was self-evident.

"This is crazy," Michael said. "You're probably a better magician, purely by instinct, than I am."

"No," she said. "That is not so. You defeated the Isomage. My father could not do that."

"I had some guidance," Michael said. *And an element of surprise.* "What does your father plan to do with the humans here?"

"I do not know."

"Is he at war with the Ban of Hours?"

"I do not know."

Michael wrapped his hands together and cracked his knuckles, something he hadn't done in years. Shiafa's voice affected him in a way he did not enjoy. He increased the level of his discipline and fought back the attraction.

"You don't sleep, do you?" he asked.

"No."

"Do you eat?"

"I eat what food the teacher thinks necessary."

Now was the time for the big question. "If your father is unhappy with the way I train you, he won't tell me how to find the woman I'm looking for, will he?"

"I do not know," Shiafa said.

"Are you keeping track of me for him? Spying?"

"I will not communicate with my father until the training is finished."

"Honestly?"

Shiafa betrayed her first sign of irritation. "Humans may find Sidhe untrustworthy," she said. "But I have never lied in my life. Neither has my father."

"Some Sidhe haven't been allowed that luxury," Michael said, thinking of Biri and Clarkham's Sidhe woman, Mora. "Do you hate humans?"

"You are the first I've ever met."

"Do you sympathize with your father?"

"I have had little contact with my father."

"And your mother?"

"Since my birth, I have never met her." Not knowing one's mother was the reverse of the usual situation for Sidhe, Michael thought.

"I'm going to close my eyes and rest," he said a moment later. He lay back and banked his *hyloka* until warmth enveloped him. After some hours had passed, he opened his eyes and saw Shiafa sitting on her slender haunches by the fire, face peaceful, staring into the darkness.

Wary thoughts tickled him. *Magic is passed through the female.*

DAWN CAME AS a sudden steely grayness and a teeth-grating vibration that set the grass shivering. The vibration passed quickly, but it left Michael disoriented and uncertain of what he was doing. Shiafa was also discomfited.

"Morning has never been that bad," she said. "We must hurry."

Michael had composed another string of questions, but thinking about what he had learned last night—not much of any use—he kept his silence. They mounted the horse. He spread his probe out across the land and felt for the human sign, but his disorientation persisted.

"Everything's changed location," he said. "Nothing is where it was yesterday."

"Dead gods have bad memories," Shiafa said behind him.

"I thought your father was taking Adonna's place."

"He is not stronger than Adonna was," she replied. "And he would have to be much stronger and more clever to hold the Realm together."

Michael concentrated all his effort and fanned his probe in a broad circle, as he had done on Earth. The result was remarkable. For the first time, he felt the *edges* of the Realm—not the chasms paring it like a badly cut pie, but the borders it shared with the between-worlds and the Earth. They were not linear borders, nor even areas of boundary—they were spaces of demarcation, hard to visualize and even harder to think about. *I can learn from witnessing a world falling apart,* he thought. *Learn what, though? How to be a mage?*

Within the borders, still at about the same distance but in a new direction, he found once again the massed human auras. Overall, they seemed little changed from the day before. He bent over and whispered in the horse's ear, then jerked back with astart.

"Is this your horse—the one you'll have to—?"

Shiafa shook her head. "Tarax will bring that one to me. A special horse."

"I can impress myself on this horse?"

"You can try," she said. "Not all of Adonna's mounts are so cooperative."

He frowned and reapplied his lips to the naked, warm interior of the horse's ear. "You are my soul, I am your body." The horse shook its ears and twisted its head to stare at him. Again there was that icy, resentful, half-lidded eye, filled with light like a frozen man's dream of fire. "Okay," Michael said. "Unimpressed."

Shiafa smiled, and Michael quickly looked away from her. Very dangerous, a smile on that long, lovely face.

"So we only *borrow* this horse," Michael said. He stroked its neck and then felt under its ear, along the deep line of its jaw. Through his fingers he passed a kind of out-seeing or *evisa* for the beast. The horse trembled, then trotted across the grass in the direction he had requested.

Michael had decided against any more precipitous *abana*, at least for the time being. The last such journey had not been pleasant; he thought it best to rely on the horse's higher talents only in an emergency. He was even wary of prodding the horse into the spectacular flying gallop its kind could execute so easily. So they moved at a measured pace across the inconstant landscape, passing within hours through areas where both spring and winter ruled.

They found another chasm when they crested a hill and looked across a broad, sparsely forested savanna. Within the chasm, an island tens of miles long—carrying a mountain on its broad back—had pulled away and wobbled ponderously. Chunks of ice several hundred yards wide hung without support near the island.

"Were you born in the Realm?" Michael asked.

"Yes," Shiafa replied.

"But you've never been to Earth."

She shook her head when he glanced back at her. "My father has been telling me about it."

"What do you know about magic? About *lengu spu*, for example—in-speaking."

"I know only the basics," Shiafa said. "Only from one to one. Not to spread wide."

"Can you feel me broadcasting?"

He allowed her to draw the meaning of that word from his own memory. "Yes," she said. "Like standing before the sun."

"Do you know the three disciplines of combat—*isray, vickay, stray?*"

"I know of them," she said. "Sidhe females are not always trained in those things. The *Mafoc Mar* have other defenses for us to learn."

Michael suddenly realized that he could not train this female the way the Crane Women had trained him. He could use very little of their instruction, in fact . . . because they had trained him as a male. He had no idea how to train a female Sidhe. Shiafa would have to guide him . . . student leading the teacher.

"Do you know how to throw a shadow?"

"Yes. We have many kinds of shadow. There is the shadow preparatory to birthing—given out before we are born, to carry away all illness and malformation. That shadow is taken and disposed of by the *Ban Sidhe*. We do that instinctively. And there is the shadow before mating and the shadow of motherhood."

"That's *all* you know?" Michael asked facetiously.

"It is not," Shiafa said, slightly indignant. "When women fight, we spin shadows like webs to confound our foes—"

"And you know how to do that?"

"No. That you must teach me."

Jesus, Michael thought. "I'm not sure why your father thinks I can train you."

"Nor am I," Shiafa confided. "But he does, and you must."

So be it.

They rode until the quick evening, then set up a temporary camp. In the darkness, they ate a few pieces of overripe fruit from a withered copse of trees.

As the evening lengthened, there was once again a discontinuity, and all locations and directions changed—but this time to their advantage. Michael sensed that the humans were much closer. The next morning, he directed the horse again, and they traveled across another, much wider savanna of emerald grass.

"I think we are near the *Chebal Malen,*" Shiafa said. "Can you smell the snow?"

Michael sniffed the air but could not. "It's a little colder," he said. "That might be the seasons changing again."

"I don't think so," Shiafa said.

At the end of that day, they came across the nearly empty basin of what had once been a huge lake, perhaps fifty miles wide and as much as a mile deep, with scattered ponds of water glistening green and stagnant at the basin's bottom. "*Nebchat Len*," Shiafa said.

"Someone once described this to me as a sea," Michael mused, rubbing his cheek with one finger. "I wonder what drained it . . . ?" Then he shook his head and grinned "I think I know. The Pelagals lived here, didn't they?"

"Here, and in the brazen ocean at the edge of the world," Shiafa said.

"Most of them are on Earth now. They crossed over in a cataract."

"You saw that?"

He nodded. "Why haven't all the Faer left the Realm yet? Many are already on Earth."

"You are the teacher," Shiafa said quietly.

"That means you don't know."

"It means I don't know."

"All right. We travel around the lake, across the forest called *Konhem*—am I right?—and after that we'll find the *Chebal Malen*, the Black Mountains. And somewhere in the *Chebal Malen* is the Sklassa, the fortress of the Maln." He drew his brows together and reached out again to feel for the humans. His heart sank. Beyond any doubt, that was where they were being detained. "We'll have to go there," he said.

"There may not be time, and it is very difficult to reach the Sklassa. It is protected." The emotion in her voice went beyond caution. For the first time, Michael detected unease in Shiafa.

"That's where we're going," Michael said. "That's where all my people are being held. Have you been there?"

"No," she said. "I was raised in Inyas Trai and the Irall."

"What sort of difficulties can we expect to find there?"

"You are the teacher," Shiafa said, somewhat forcefully.

"But you *do* know," Michael persisted.

"I am not supposed to know."

"What does that mean?"

Shiafa averted her eyes, and an odd, defiant expression—chin outthrust, eyes narrowed—crossed her face. "When I was a child, I listened to the *Mafoc Mar* when I was not supposed to. They talked about the Sklassa. It is not a place for young Sidhe."

"But you're Tarax's daughter," Michael reminded her.

"It is not a place even for me."

"Somehow, I doubt that," Michael said. "What are the difficulties?"

"I cannot tell you."

"I am your teacher," Michael prodded.

Shiafa's eyes widened, and her mouth became a tight, thin line. "We will learn together, then," she said.

Michael shook his head and smiled. Beginning of the discipline, he thought.

Rattle the student, the initiate, and strip away preconceptions. Ultimately, terrify her. That's what the Crane Women had done to him. But who was rattling whom?

If Tarax's daughter was worried by the thought of going to the Sklassa, then what should his own attitude be? Michael started the horse on the long journey around the drained basin of *Nebchat Len,* uncertain now whether they could keep up such a torturously slow pace—or whether they would have to use the horse's erratic talents again.

"Perhaps we should hurry," Shiafa said an hour later.

He sighed, then squinted at the empty blue sky. "I agree," he said. "Are you prepared to *aband?*"

"Anything," Shiafa said nervously. "You are the teacher."

"The teacher asks you not to say that any more." Michael leaned forward. "Hang on." He whispered in the horse's ear, "*Abana!*"

This time, the ride was much worse.

They rested in the shadow of a rock overhang, the horse gasping and trembling, its eyes half-closed. Shiafa had collapsed on her side. Michael sat down heavily beside her. They did not move for an hour. "Next time, we'll just try the gallop." Even speaking was a chore. With an effort of will, all his muscles protesting, Michael finally stood and walked out into the glare. Shading his eyes with both hands, he turned toward the black rock of the lower slopes of one of the mountains of *Chebal Malen.* No foothills, no gradual ascent to the peaks beyond; the *Chebal Malen* began abruptly as huge, jagged black monsters, mottled with snow up their sides and capped with solid sheets of snow and ice, partly hidden in clouds dipping and wheeling like huge gray and white birds.

"The Sklassa is on the opposite side of the *Chebal Malen,* isn't it?" Michael asked, as he stepped back under the overhang.

Shiafa rolled over on her side, head weaving slightly, and said, "Yes."

"We're closer to the Stone Field on this side, aren't we? Where male initiates are taken to be trained."

She nodded.

The Sklassa was where he had instructed the horse to go; obviously, it had been unable to comply. So one could not simply *aband* into the fortress of the Maln. He doubted that the horse could make such a climb by galloping, however miraculous an *epon's* gallop could be.

Worse, he could not feel the human auras; he had lost them totally since the last *abana.* "We don't have time to climb the mountains," he said. "And we don't have time to go around them, that's for sure. I don't think we should try to *aband* again."

Shiafa sat up and crossed her legs. "No."

"Any suggestions, then?"

She simply looked disgusted.

Her reaction dismayed Michael. "I've never been here, either," he said. "It's obvious we've run into one of those barriers you mentioned. If you can't tell me what the barriers are, then—" He shook his head vigorously. "This whole stunt is ridiculous. Your father must be a fool."

Shiafa continued to stare at him.

"So how do the Maln get there? A password, specially bred horses? A secret path? A stepping stone?"

Still no reply. Michael paced angrily, then kneeled and closed his eyes, feeling, thinking, reaching out to their surroundings. Again he could sense the borders of the Realm inexorably closing in. They had a few days, at best, and toward the end, time would be uncertain.

"All right," he said. "Now is as good a time as any to begin your training. Come with me." Shiafa followed him onto a patch of snow that had filled a shallow, narrow canyon. The black rock reached to twice his height above the snow on each side; at the end of the canyon, about a hundred yards beyond, the walls met in a V.

"What do you think Sidhe magic is?" Michael asked her, taking a stance two paces in front of her, arms folded.

"It is putting yourself in sympathy with the Realm. When your thoughts breathe in, they should match the breathing of the world."

"What if the world isn't so cooperative?"

"You mean, the Earth?"

"Yes."

"Then magic is more difficult, but not impossible."

"Is it impossible for humans to work magic?"

"They are not known for being magicians."

"I'm mostly human. There's some Sidhe blood in all humans by now. So is it necessary to be a Sidhe?"

Shiafa shook her head, unsure.

"Obviously not. But Sidhe, even Breeds, would like to keep humans in their place. And the humans who come here—or who have been brought here—are deliberately kept in the dark. I've come to the conclusion that it doesn't matter what you are. Concentration is the key, and seeing without preconceptions. Do you have preconceptions?"

"I must," Shiafa said, all too reasonably. He had expected some youthful bravado, but then he remembered: she was three times older than he was.

"I certainly do. I believe I'm weak. That makes me weak. I believe in things being a certain way, and they are. Each time I truly break through . . ." He smiled. He was formulating thoughts heretofore scattered and unorganized. Teaching was also learning, or at least *realizing*. "Each time I break through my preconceptions, I dare something new. Sometimes I succeed. I gain a new ability." There were no flowers nearby. He stooped to pick up a rock the size of a golf ball. "Sidhe dislike casually written words. Writing fixes reality and creates stronger preconceptions. It's dangerous. But any language involves preconceptions. Any communication. That's why words are powerful—they convey the thoughts *of* others. And the thoughts of others can get in your way." He opened his palm. "What is this?"

"A rock," she said.

He closed his palm . . . trying something he suspected the Crane Women had used on him . . . and opened it again. She smiled at his legerdemain. The rock was a butterfly.

"And what now?" He opened and closed his palm again. His powerful *evisa* seemed to impress her no more than a child's toy.

"A rock," she said.

"Do you know how to be a butterfly and remain a rock?"

"I cast a shadow."

"I'm going to attack you," Michael said abruptly, stepping back from her half a dozen paces. It was time to discover what she was capable of. Shiafa was starting out substantially more sophisticated than Michael had been. "Prepare yourself."

Shiafa stood, hands hanging at her sides, head lowered slightly, still a little woozy from the *abana*. *Fine,* he thought. Jerk her up out of her uncertainty, just as the Crane Women had done to him.

Suddenly, five Michaels surrounded her. She looked from one to the next, turning, raising her hands. One Michael moved in toward her; the next seemed ready to send a sharp probe in her direction; and the next began to circle, grinning. "You can't predict humans," all five said. Then, one by one in the circle, "They're dangerous that way." "They don't know the discipline." "They don't know magic, and they have all the guile and unpredictability of the weak and fearful." "They have emotions even they are not aware of." "They can become angry in a flash. Some are ill-trained and ill-educated, and because of that they are under-privileged, and that makes them vicious." "They can turn on you without warning. I imagine even a few Breeds won't miss a chance to take revenge on you." "And some Breeds know the disciplines. They can assault you with magic." "Humans and Breeds may join forces to hunt you down. When you go to Earth, that's the way it could be—hard and bitter times." "Especially when humans find out their real history. No mercy. No style, no dignity. Just revenge." "Are you ready for that?"

"No," Shiafa said, facing the shadows one by one. They closed in.

"Which one of us will you fight first?"

"The real one," Shiafa said.

"How will you know the real one?"

She shook her head, agitated.

"*Think,*" the shadows intoned together.

"What purpose?" she demanded. "I have told you I do not know how to defend myself."

"I think you do," Michael said.

She frowned and bore down hard with a single probe—aimed at a shadow. The effort seemed to exhaust her. She shook her head and made a weak probe at another shadow. She had wasted her energy by making the first probe too strong. She should have feather-touched the entire circle in one sweep, as if politely in-speaking for an item of information, something Sidhe did all the time by instinct. Instead, she had panicked.

Michael considered probing *her* at this weak moment, breaking through whatever personal barriers she might have set up and taking the information he needed about the Sklassa. He would have been justified; a great many lives were at stake, and as Shiafa had stated repeatedly, they had little time. But he did not. The shadows continued to move in, a step at a time, menacing her.

There was something deeper, stronger, far below the surface of her exhaustion and youthful inadequacy. He could sense it without probing. She was Tarax's daughter . . . and if he could get her to reach that far down, *he* might be the one to learn a lesson.

She straightened. "You are not going to hurt me," she said. "You are a teacher, not an enemy."

There! He had it. A strong preconception. One of the shadows turned black as coal and swung a long, night-colored swath at her from shoulder-level. The swath wrapped around her head. She struggled to tear it away. It soaked up her breath. Michael could feel her discomfort. It was not wrong for a teacher to inflict discomfort on a student; it was wrong, however, not to share the discomfort. *The Crane Women felt all my pain when they trained me, and all my confusion and fear,* he realized. *They did what I am doing now when they left me under the path of the Amorphal Sidhe.*

Shiafa was genuinely afraid. She could not breathe and she was close to fainting. "Come on," Michael said under his breath. "Dig deep."

She cried out, her voice muffled. Michael felt faint himself and had the urge to run to her and tear away the veil. Then something snapped within her. There was nothing animal within the Sidhe to be unleashed, since they had never been animals, but there were deeper and more primitive layers of Sidhe-ness. Shiafa reached into one of those layers to perform instinctive magic that—he now knew without doubt—had once been the common heritage of all peoples.

She left a shadow-self wrapped in the black veil and stood outside the circle of Michael's shadows. Lightly, swiftly, she probed the remaining figures and located him. She then reversed the black shadow's net and shot it toward him, tinged red with her own anger.

Michael dodged the veil—but just barely—and dissolved his shadows. They stood facing each other across the snow. "Your feet are cold," he said. "Bring up your *hyloka.*"

She fell to her knees. Her cheeks and neck were flushed. "Why?" she asked, voice harsh.

"Did you feel your strength?" he asked, reaching out to help her stand again.

She did not look at him for a long moment. He had given her a scare. "I felt something . . ."

"That's where we have to begin. You have it in you. It's closer to the surface than it was in me. You have to find it and make it yours. It's like an *epon.* You must impress it."

He led her back beneath the overhang and watched her closely as she sat and controlled her energy levels. Her normal skin color returned.

There was hardly any time to bring out her talents and train her, even less time than the Crane Women had taken with Michael. He had to play with an even more delicate balance, between the trust, or at least respect, necessary between teacher and student and the harsh techniques urgency required.

"Since you won't tell me how we can get into the Sklassa, we'll go to the Stone Field. We'll try putting the horse into a gallop. We'll leave as soon as you've recovered."

"I feel it now," Shiafa said, looking at him with wonder. "It's within me. It burns. I wonder I never knew it before."

"Good," Michael said. At the center of his stomach, he felt slightly ill.

AT A GALLOP—if it could be called that—the Sidhe horse was much slower than during an *abana*, but the effects of the Realm's disintegration were much less apparent. They half rode, half-flew through the passes of the *Chebal Malen*, looking for the trail that would take them to the Stone Field. The horse could not simply scale the tall peaks at a single bound; its flight relied on stable ground in a way Michael could see but not yet understand. The Sidhe horses had flown away from the Tippett Hotel on Earth; they had lifted from the prairie before the startled horse trader. But they could not simply rise tens of thousands of feet up sheer rock precipices.

Shiafa genuinely did not know where such a trail was, or even if one existed. Michael tried again to search for the human or Sidhe auras, but the mountains from this angle seemed absolutely barren. There was only monotonous black rock and snow, under the pale sky gone curiously cold in this region.

During their pauses to rest. Michael instructed Shiafa in the proper fine control of her *hyloka*. At the end of the second day, when they had traversed thousands of miles through and around the *Chebal Malen* and still had not found a trail, he guided the horse to ground beside an ice-glazed stream of snow-melt. "Get off," he told Shiafa. His patience was at an end.

She dismounted and stood beside the horse.

"Something has to give," he said, squinting up at the sky. "*Someone* has to give. We're all carrying honor and honesty a bit far. And we're getting nowhere. We can't even reach the Stone Field. I've lost the sense of human auras I felt from far away."

Shiafa looked down at the undisturbed snow around her feet.

"Do you have any suggestions?"

She shook her head.

Michael swore under his breath. "Then that's it," he said. "We go back to the Earth. You've defeated me. We leave the humans here; I doubt the Maln will bring them to the Earth with them. So they'll die in the Realm. All because of a young Sidhe's honor." He thought of Nikolai, of Helena and Savarin and all the others in Euterpe. And he thought of the thousands of humans selected from Earth over millennia, kept in the Realm—humanity's finest. Not even his discipline could quell his anger and frustration. He leaned over to bring his face closer to Shiafa.

"*Damn* you and your father," he said. "I was an idiot to think there was any possibility—" He couldn't express himself through his anger.

"You will not teach me?" Shiafa asked evenly.

"Hell, no. You can stay here and freeze. I'm going back to Inyas Trai. Maybe I can find a stepping stone there . . . in the few days I have left."

"There is a stepping stone here," Shiafa said.

Michael stared at her.

"You cannot get into the Sklassa or the Stone Field from the passes below. You must return to Inyas Trai through the stepping stone, and then you can take a stepping stone to the fortress. Now there is no other way to enter Inyas Trai. The city is forbidden."

"Why are you telling me this now? Why not earlier?"

"Because I need to be trained," Shiafa said. "Whether I die or not is unimportant, but I need to be trained by you. Your training me is more important than my betraying knowledge I should not have."

Michael sniffed and rubbed a sudden itch in his nose. His anger had not yet subsided; he still had half a mind to leave her and go off on his own. Another idea formed in his head: they might not need to go to Inyas Trai. "Will you give the horse directions to the stepping stone?"

"I will," she said.

"Then do it and climb back on."

She stood by the horse's head and touched it behind its jaw, as he had done, out-seeing the location of the stepping stone. "It is at the edge of the *Chebal Malen*, below the Sklassa," she told Michael as she remounted behind him. "It was used long ago, but not recently."

WITHIN HOURS, THEY stood before the largest stepping stone Michael had ever seen, black as night, circular, and fully a hundred yards wide. Two obelisks jutted beside a slab of white marble at the center, featureless and ancient. Drifts of snow formed crescents on the surface of the larger stone.

The stepping stone rose from the floor of a broad rocky valley, at the head of which glowered an immense wall of ice; he could not tell if it was a glacier or something else unique to the Realm.

They crossed the black expanse on foot.

Michael climbed the steps to the white slab and stood there with hands extended, hair blowing in the freezing wind. He advanced slowly, feeling for the gate. He passed between the obelisks and turned to look at Shiafa, who remained by the steps. "Nothing," he said. "It's closed."

"I did not know that," she said. "Though perhaps I should have. If the city is forbidden . . ." If she had been human, Michael would have predicted she was about to cry. But she did not cry.

He balled up his fists and kicked aside a limb of snow from a perfect crescent. More time wasted. *Dig deep.* He let his hands relax. *No sense even thinking about it. Just dig deep and do it.*

He stared down at his hands. The limits of the possible, of his ability . . . What were the limits? In the palms of his hands, he could feel the quality of the Realm as a singing tingle. With the exception of his unsuccessful first attempt to reach into the Realm and his escape from Clarkham's near-Earth nightmare,

he had used gates made by others, or adapted pre-existing gates for his purpose. Now ... to simply create an opening between one spot in a world and
another ... he had never done that.

*Not the greatest task ever performed. Simple for a very accomplished Sidhe or
Breed. In a way, the horses do it when they* aband, *and they're just animals. Don't
even think about it. Dig deep. Last chance. Do it.*

"Come up here," he told Shiafa. "Bring the horse."

She obeyed and stood beside Michael between the obelisks. He closed his
eyes, listening with his palms, feeling the different parts of the song that was the
Realm, now discordant, its melody weak and wandering.

Just what you forced Shiafa to do. Find the resources within.

But he had never dug so far into his dark, untried potential. He had never
thought it necessary; indeed, he had never known there were such depths to be
found. "I'm learning a lesson," he told Shiafa.

"What lesson?"

"Whether you succeed or fail, you are what you dare."

And if I dare to be a mage, against Tarax and Clarkham and all the others?

For an instant, no more, he had absolutely no doubt that he could open a
way to the Sklassa, completely avoiding the Stone Field, whatever the barriers
and defenses. He would simply invert the song, play it back upon itself, add
where normally one would find a taking-away, and then take away during the
adding ...

Nonsense.

But it worked. He tore aside a piece of empty air and widened it for the
horse. Shiafa stared at his face, radiating heat and power, then at his hand, glowing like a white-hot iron, and passed through after the horse. Michael stepped
into the rent and closed it up after him.

As when he had let his *hyloka* run wild, he felt a sense of giddy exaltation.
He wanted to skip and dance and shake his hair in the breeze. But their surroundings immediately sobered him.

"The Sklassa," Shiafa said, her voice filled with wonder and fear.

25

There was the Spryggla touch about the fortress of the Maln. Michael and Shiafa stood on top of a broad, thick wall of polished black stone, like the petal of a huge, squat obsidian flower blooming from a mountain peak. No snow sullied the Sklassa's perfect surfaces. Although their reflected images showed in the stone beneath their feet, the hot-milk sky did not, and in the depths of the wall, stars gleamed. The flower-fortress might have been carved from a block of space itself.

Between two huge petal-walls hung a spider's bridge of silvery lace. It began barely ten yards from where they stood and ended at a single small wooden door. "This is incredible," Michael said. "It looks simple from here."

"We are not inside yet," Shiafa reminded him.

He could feel the presence of humans very close, but he could not tell how many. "Did Adonna build this?" he asked.

"My father built this," Shiafa said, without pride or any other emotional inflection. "A Spryggla designed it, and Adonna approved the plans, but Tarax supervised the construction."

"A multi-talented Sidhe, your father," Michael said lightly. "I assume the only way is across that bridge."

Shiafa nodded. "From what I heard, even that is uncertain."

Michael was feeling very assured now. He walked toward the near end of the bridge and motioned for Shiafa to follow. "We'll leave the horse here. It's on loan anyway; presumably someone will take care of it if . . ." He smiled at her. "If. I'll cross first. You follow after I've made it through the door."

The span, Michael realized as he touched the guy rope on his left, was a taut and very fancy rope bridge. Its strands, woven into intricate patterns of starbursts, leaves and flowers, gleamed with an inner light, combining the qualities of silk and milk opal. He pushed one foot forward and tested the tension. To his surprise, there was no give; the bridge might as well have been made of iron. Cautiously, he rapped on a guy rope with his hand to see if it would shatter. It did not.

"Nothing ventured, no pain," he said, mixing adages. He put his entire weight on the bridge. Then, slowly at first, he made the crossing. When he stood before the wooden door he examined it closely, bending to run a finger along its intricately carved surface. The wood was dark and well-worn, polished by centuries of touch. The carvings, contained in four panels forming a compacted Maltese cross, were of mazes and whorls. At the center of each panel appear a schematic flower representing the Sklassa. There was no knob or latch.

"Open sesame," he muttered. He tried to grip a panel and pull the door outward, but it was fixed. His palms tingled faintly, and he heard a tune playing under the rhythm of his breath. He brought the tune forward to his lips and whistled it softly. The door recessed a few inches and swung inward. Beyond lay a corridor illuminated in a wedge by the milky daylight outside.

Michael entered the corridor, then turned and called for Shiafa to cross. She did so without mishap. "We need some light," he said. "Do you know how to turn up your *hyloka* and make your hand glow?"

She shook her head. "But I know how to see in the dark."

"Good enough," Michael said.

"Can you?" she asked.

"I can certainly try." He tried and found that with some effort, he could indeed see down the hall as if through a night-vision scope. The hall's green, ghostly image shimmered like a heat mirage. "Will wonders never cease?"

"You do not seem serious," Shiafa observed.

"I do not *feel* serious," Michael said. "I have had just about enough of Sidhe wonders and portents. This place is incredible. It's beautiful, it's weird, it's powerful—and I don't really care any more. I want to get my people out of here and return to the Earth. And I'm hungry. I'd love a plain old hamburger right now." He glanced at her apologetically. "Pardon my savage heritage."

"Flesh of beasts?" she inquired.

"You got it."

She shuddered. "Will humans stop eating meat if the Sidhe live among them?"

"That's a good question," Michael said. "I don't know the answer."

"That will cause . . ." She touched his aura lightly. "Friction."

He grimaced and chuckled. "I'll worry about it later." The presence of humans was much stronger. "I think we're very close," he said. "I can feel my people everywhere, all around." The hallway ended at a circular shaft about twenty yards across; a spiral staircase wound around its walls into the depths. "Down," Michael said. But he held her shoulder before they descended. "If push comes to shove, are you still committed to your teacher—even against Sidhe?"

"Do not doubt me," Shiafa said in the dark. "Without discipline, I am nothing, and you will teach me the discipline."

They came to the bottom of the shaft. Throughout their time in the Sklassa, not once had Michael felt any sign of Sidhe. This lack of sign conveyed no reliable information; the Sklassa was a place of unknown qualities, and the Sidhe within it were bound to be watchful, protected—as Shiafa had told him, without being specific. And they would have good reason for protecting the humans now held prisoner within the fortress and for wanting to keep them away from Earth. *There might be hundreds of potential mages here,* Michael thought, not without a tinge of worry. His newfound desire to be a mage rankled like a burr. *Why a mage? Because of the challenge. Because the alternate candidates are so undesirable. And is that all?*

Because of the power. Wouldn't it be something?

The hallway ended abruptly. One moment, Michael looked at what appeared to be a bend in the hall, and the next, it was a blank wall. He touched the wall tentatively—cold stone. Nothing more. He turned. Behind Shiafa was another wall.

"No," he said. "This will not do." He extended his palms and squeezed around her in the cramped space. "This is one trap you didn't know about?"

She shook her head, her breath coming faster.

"Control yourself," he said. "The air might give out." And *it might not.* Everything . . . *vibrated* suspiciously. He smiled and felt his power again, like stroking an internal dynamo. It seemed to expand within him, taking its own kind of breath.

"If I were to design the Sklassa to be impregnable," he said, turning back to the other wall, "with the power of the Sidhe at my disposal, how would I do it? Would I build physical traps? That seems too obvious. No, I might go for something more ornate, more devious. More a credit to the style and ingenuity of the designer." Concentration was the key to this prison. Shadows could take many forms.

Blue flower, yellow flower. Black flower.

The flower fortress was not real. "We have to close our eyes and clear our thoughts," Michael said. They did so. After a few moments, Michael opened his eyes and touched Shiafa's arm.

They stood at the end of the hard silk bridge, on the flower-petal parapet. The horse blinked curiously at them. The black flower-fortress lost definition, powdering in the air, the powder swirling and assuming a new shape.

This new shape was less artistic but much more ominous. They now stood on a cliff edge, with the same bridge before them, but the Sklassa had become a broad, many-leveled castle. Its walls were rounded like water-worn rocks, and its towers were blunt, squat and featureless, upper surfaces polished gun-metal gray, vertical surfaces streaked with black and rusty brown.

The bridge led to the same wooden door, now embedded in a metallic wall below one of the faceless towers. Michael squinted, his palms still tingling. Shiafa said nothing, watching him with a studied patience he found irritating.

"Why is the door made of wood?" Michael asked.

"I do not know," Shiafa said.

He frowned at her briefly. "Do you believe this shape?" he asked, pointing to the castle.

"I have my doubts," she said.

"So do I." Concentration. Palms extended. The designs could be arrayed like bars, bells and fruit on a wheel inside a slot machine. Any one of them could be real. Choosing one that was not real could result in their being lured into a dream of imprisonment and even death. They might or might not be able to escape from the trap of each false design.

And, of course, it was just as possible that the true Sklassa would have traps of its own.

"Adventure," Michael said under his breath. "This part's like a game of Adventure. I never liked that game."

Think it out.

"Here's an exercise for you," Michael said. "I assume you're as ignorant as I am about which design is the real one."

Shiafa said, "I have nothing to conceal now."

"If you were building a fortress that could withstand a hundred or more different kinds of assault, what design would you choose for the actual structure? Thinking like a Spryggla—or a Sidhe overseeing a Spryggla."

Shiafa stared at the gun-metal castle. "In the Realm, the only purpose fortifications would serve would be to defend against a mage. No Sidhe or Breed— much less a human—would think of acting against Adonna."

"That's—" Michael stopped. "No mages here but Adonna and possibly Clarkham. Did they fear Clarkham? I don't think so. But they must have feared somebody. Who? Waltiri? The Serpent? Did they think their magic would fade?"

"It has," Shiafa said. "The Realm is failing."

Michael was confused. He brushed the confusion aside. In the time remaining to them, they could not afford to speculate endlessly. "No physical barriers would prevent a mage from entering a fortress. These walls and towers are ridiculous. Any other fortress design is equally ridiculous. I don't believe there's a fortress here at all. I think . . . it's a place pleasant to the Sidhe of the Maln. It's the opposite of the Irall, the opposite of cold and dank and hard."

He took his hand and spread it against the image of the castle and then smoothly, with substantial mental effort, wiped the image away like so much dust on a sheet of glass. Shiafa stepped closer to him, and he passed on to her what he saw through gentle *evisa*.

The shining silk bridge now crossed a rushing stream of clear water and green, flowing reeds. Across the bridge lay a meadow of tall blue-green grass and flowers. At the center of the meadow rose a Boschian tower seemingly carved from red coral. The tower was at least as tall as a good-sized skyscraper, ornately embellished in a style Michael could easily recognize. A Spryggla had designed that tower; it seemed obvious that a Spryggla had sketched all the illusory forms of the Sklassa as well.

He crossed the bridge. Shiafa followed. The horse again remained behind, but this time there was some grass on the cliff top for it to crop.

At the sprawling base of the coral tower, covered with vines bearing huge red berries, they found a broad gate carved from transparent crystal and flanked by what looked like ivory posts. Michael pushed gently on the gate. It swung inward. Between the posts poured a virtual flood of human sign; thousands of humans, and only a few Sidhe.

But among those Sidhe: no mistaking the aura of the Ban of Hours. He began to have a glimmer of understanding; the Ban's opposition to the Maln continued, even after the Maln's dissolution. As Shiafa had said, she must be in the Sklassa to protect the humans the Maln had gathered over the centuries, and perhaps the humans of Euterpe and the Breeds of Halftown. But where were the other Sidhe of the Maln? Surely there were more than a handful . . .

Overhead, the sky changed abruptly to anthracitic blackness, overlaid by an oily smear of spectral red, green and blue. It was more than a precipitous nightfall; it was the end of the Realm's sky.

The meadow and tower were wrapped in penumbral gloom. All around, flowers withdrew and grass withered. Then, just as the darkness became oppressive, the tower began to gleam from within, a warm and welcoming glow that belied all Michael had heard about the Maln and made him wonder if he had stumbled into yet another illusion.

Even villains would enjoy paradise, he told himself.

"I never knew of this," Shiafa said. They stepped through the crystal gate, between the ivory posts, and stood on a white-tiled floor beneath a broad blue dome mimicking the night-skies of Earth. Each star was a glittering jewel, and thousands of stars were set within the lapis firmament.

Michael looked down from the jeweled sky. A young male Sidhe stood before them, wearing the full black and gray of the Maln, with a red robe beneath. His face was a mask of discipline. For a moment, Michael didn't recognize him.

"You are not expected, man-child," the Sidhe said, smiling faintly. "We thought your work was done here."

"Biri!" Michael said, startled. Biridashwa—with whom he had shared the Crane Women's training, who had attempted to infuse him with poisonous Sidhe philosophy, and who had then contemptuously watched Michael be jerked back to the Earth after the destruction of the pleasure dome. The one-time initiate's red hair had been cut to a skullcap, and his eyes seemed hollow and haunted.

"We have no need for you," Biri said, advancing a step. He held out his right arm, and a wick grew into it, starting as a green branch and ending as a sharp-pointed pike.

Michael looked over the haggard Sidhe with a touch of sadness. "I bring Tarax's daughter—"

"Tarax is no longer of the Maln," Biri said. "He is in the isolation of becoming a mage. His daughter is not our concern."

Michael glanced at the wooden doors set into the circled wall of the chamber. "The Ban of Hours is here. She is protecting some of my people."

"You are a Breed. You have no people but Breeds," Biri said. Michael could almost smell his desperation—and his fear. Stronger than both, however, was the acid hatred that etched the depths behind his blue eyes.

"Nonsense," Michael said almost casually. His assurance was seamless; he might soon cross the border into arrogance. Catching himself, he backed away from that danger and smiled politely. "I'm here to take my people home."

"Their sentence is absolute," Biri said. "We will not allow you to return them to the Earth."

"Why?"

"You are still a man-child if you do not see."

Michael folded his arms. *Arrogant gesture,* he warned himself. *Don't underestimate this Sidhe. He's fooled you before.*

"I'm sure the Ban of Hours wants to speak with me," Michael said. "Surely you wouldn't deny her that?"

"She is here by pact. She remains with the humans until we all die."

"Who ordains this?"

"I do. I have replaced Tarax as Chief of the Maln."

"I didn't know the Maln still existed."

Biri's face paled ever so slightly, giving his skin a mother-of-pearl iridescence that was quite beautiful. "It exists in me," he said. "The Councils are dissolved. Their work is done."

"Now that Tarax is going to be mage."

"Now that the succession is assured."

"They opposed Adonna?"

"In the end, Tarax opposed Adonna. The Councils agreed with his judgment that Adonna was failing."

"So whom are you sacrificing yourself for?" he asked.

"For my people," Biri answered.

"By letting all these humans die—and Breeds, and yourself—you think you'll make the Earth safer for Sidhe?"

Biri's jaw was outlined by clenched muscles.

"It's a useless gesture," Michael continued. "The Sidhe are overpowered on Earth. Their magic can't win them dominance. They'll have to parley. Killing these humans won't affect that outcome—because my people have already won."

Shiafa stood a step behind Michael, stiff and silent. He could not detect her emotions without lifting his concentration from Biri, which he did not dare do. The wall of discipline behind which Biri stood was strong and only grew stronger under Michael's pressure. He did not want to fight Biri—not yet. *But you'll ultimately have to defeat Tarax, defy the Serpent, deal with Clarkham . . .*

"Is this true?" Biri asked Shiafa.

"As far as I know," Shiafa said.

"There are no strongholds on Earth?"

"Science beats magic," Michael said. "Not for subtlety, perhaps, and not at magic's highest levels—but in the long haul, and with my world as it is now . . . That's why the Sidhe finally withdrew from Earth."

"There is war on Earth?" Biri's dignified demeanor slipped a little. Clearly, he did not relish the thought of dying—especially without good reason.

"I don't know what's happening on Earth now, but yes, very likely Sidhe and humans are dying. I would like to prevent more deaths. I can't if I'm stuck here."

Biri considered this at some length. "You must leave," he concluded. "The decision is not mine to make."

Biri's defenses, from the moment of his appearance, had been focused on Michael. They were weak in Shiafa's direction. Michael took his own arrogance and frustration and drew from the center of his *hyloka* as much power as he could spare and remain alive. He held this mix for as long as he dared and then echoed the virulent shadow off Shiafa. Shiafa reeled and barely kept her footing. Biri's eyes widened as the darkness oozed through his defenses and enveloped him. He struggled, but Michael's strength seemed to reverberate through him; the more anger and frustration Michael felt, the more stymied and impatient, the stronger the shadow became. Within seconds, Biri fell to the tiles.

Michael probed the Sidhe, not knowing precisely what to look for, but knowing it was there. A glowing thread. A cord that held together Biri's discipline.

Someone buried deep within Michael was almost hysterical. *Jesus! Stop this now, before you eat yourself alive!* But he did not listen. He cut Biri's cord of discipline.

Michael glanced at Shiafa, who had slipped to her knees, and then at Biri, who lay on the tiles as weak as an unstringed puppet.

"My apologies," he said to Shiafa.

She did not bother to use English. "*Yassira bettl striks,*" she hissed. "You fight unfairly."

"I suppose there's fairness in smudging out thousands of innocent lives?" Michael asked, shaking his head. "The hell with Sidhe honor. I apologize for using you without asking. There wasn't time."

She stood and looked down at Biri with wide eyes. "He was Chief of the Maln. He had great power . . . Hidden ways of discipline are given to the chief."

I am a bomb again, Michael thought. *More powerful, more of a wild card, every minute. Someone will have to stop me before this is finished, or I'll—*

He shook his head slowly and probed for more Sidhe. There were two others, and one of them was the Ban. He did not think there would be any more opposition. The Sidhe of the Maln had deserted their own fortress, probably to return to Earth—leaving behind only Biri. They had not expected anyone to reach this far into their defenses.

Michael delved into Biri's aura for knowledge of which door to take. The Sidhe rolled over on the tiles and gasped, still in the shadow's grip. Michael considered lifting the shadow, then decided against it. *Don't press your luck.*

He walked across the chamber toward the proper door. Shiafa ran to catch up with him.

"I am afraid of you, Teacher," she said in a harsh whisper. "You do not know all that you do."

"Amen," Michael said. After so many months in the Realm as a helpless pawn, he felt fierce joy at being able to convert his uncertainty and even his fear into weapons. How far could he just glide, stacking victory upon accomplishment? "It's about time the Sidhe face a real challenge on their own territory. I am sick of duty masking cruelty and of hatred and envy disguised as Sidhe honor and purity. The hell with all of you."

He felt a hint of the Serpent's deep rage there and, to negate that, touched the door with unnecessary gentleness, as if caressing Kristine. The wood felt rough and unvarnished. As he had half-expected, it spoke to him. "Welcome, Manchild." The voice was familiar to him; it belonged to the attendant of the Ban whom Michael had met in Inyas Trai while traveling with Nikolai.

"Ulath?"

"I am honored you remember. The Ban awaits you. She is in her chamber."

"Are you dead?" In his experience, only dying Sidhe had their thoughts pressed into wood.

The voice laughed. "No! This door carries only a shadow. There are so few of us here and so much to be vigilant against. Enter, Man-child."

26

The door swung inward and Michael passed through. Shiafa did not. "She stays outside," Ulath explained.

"Why?" Michael asked, though he was relieved not to have her tagging along.

"Please, no questions. You must move quickly."

The floor-plan of the dark, quiet rooms beyond the domed chamber was like a cross section through a lump of pumice. Ulath's voice guided him from one round bubble-room to another, and it took him some effort to remember the path and keep track of where he had been. Resilient carpets covered the floors in brilliant sun-yellow and coral-red tessellations. Throughout the rooms, translucent silken curtains dyed in leaf, floral and geometric patterns hung from bars reaching wall to wall.

This was not at all what Michael had imagined the fortress of the Maln to look like. There was a feminine sensibility and elegance to the place that completely contrasted with the Maln's age-long activities.

"Stop," Ulath's voice gently commanded when he stood at the center of another large, domed chamber, very much like the first. Overhead, however, soft clouds wove back and forth across a sophisticated mimicry of day. At zenith, a gold-leaf stylized sun spread its rays like the branches of an incandescent tree.

Through a door on the opposite side, a Sidhe female in a cream-colored robe with red trim entered. Michael recognized the warm brown skin and black hair, the full lips and eyebrows wryly askew: Mora, who had once been Clarkham's consort. She smiled warmly, but with an edge of guilty tension, and approached Michael slowly, her gown trailing.

"You surprise us all," she said. "The Sidhe thought they were done with you. Even the Ban."

Michael nodded. "I had to fight Biri to get in here. Subdue him."

She did not seem distressed. "Then you've grown remarkably strong. Biri is not easily overcome." She sensed Michael's unease at her lack of sympathy. Biri, he had learned during his last few minutes in Clarkham's Xanadu, had been her lover, and she had served Clarkham only in the interests of the Sidhe. "I have

been sequestered here, away from Biri, that I might not endanger his accession."
Her eyes searched him for any further response, but he kept his reactions under
tight control. "Why have you returned?"

"To bring the my people back to Earth."

"If you can do that, you will have our cooperation. The stepping stones to
Earth have been closed; we are not sure by whom."

"Tarax?" Michael suggested.

"Perhaps. At any rate, Ulath tells me we should arrange a meeting with the
Ban, and with Mahler, with whom you are, I believe, familiar."

"I've heard some of his music," Michael said. "Waltiri met him . . . knew
him, once. They corresponded." His eyebrows lifted. "He's *here?* Alive?"

"We also have a human named Mozart . . . He and Mahler have quarreled
some in the past. Debated is perhaps a better word. Mozart was astonished when
the Ban allowed Mahler to confer with a human on Earth."

"When was this?" Michael asked.

"Recently. Days or weeks or months past on Earth. The conspiracies have
not even begun to spin themselves out, Michael. Plays of power and flights of
intrigue. Mahler can convey your plans to the others kept here."

"How many are there?" Michael asked.

"Five thousand and twenty-one. Artists, writers of poetry and fiction, sto-
rytellers, composers, potters, dancers, dreamers . . ."

"All . . . recent?" *Days, months . . . centuries?*

"Heavens, no," Mora said, laughing lightly. "The Maln has been collecting
them for ten thousand years, ever since the end of the *Paradiso.* The Ban was
appointed by Adonna to watch over them."

"Then . . . Emma Livry was not the only one brought here."

"Not at all. She was a special case, because of her suffering. The Maln allowed
the Ban to bring her to the Realm, even though she was no longer a danger to
them—and of no use to Clarkham. Other humans whom the Maln ignored until
they proved to be a threat were the most unfortunate . . . Mahler and Mozart
among them."

Michael shook his head in wonder. "And the prisoners from Euterpe?"

"They are here."

"Nikolai?"

"After his brief venture on Earth. His journey alerted Biri, who may or may
not have acted under Tarax's orders in shutting down the stepping stone in Inyas
Trai reserved for humans."

"Then the Ban was going to return them to Earth."

"Of course. They cannot stay here."

"So you're all prisoners . . . and Biri is your guard?"

"There are other guards," Mora said with a delicate shudder. "The Realm
has become much more . . . creative, let us say, since Adonna's passage. The Maln
has taken advantage of this. Leaving will be much more difficult than getting in."

I should have thought as much. "I'd like to see the Ban now," Michael said.

Mora nodded once and withdrew. Michael took a deep breath and prepared
himself; at their last meeting, the Ban had been in complete control—time had

seemed to stop, and his memories of her had emerged only after hours of contemplation, emerged in just the right order to convey what the Ban had wished
him to know: that he was a pawn.

Her magic was of a peculiar kind, he could see from this more experienced
perspective. It was passive, not active magic. It did not assert and create and
destroy; it nurtured and cherished and allowed development. She was none the
less powerful for that.

And she had not followed her sister, Elme, in defying their father, Tonn. She
had remained loyal to Tonn—later Adonna, God of the Realm. In return, Adonna
had granted her a place and position in Inyas Trai and had supported at least
some of her efforts to help the humans in the Realm. *Then had she really differed
from Elme? In tactics, perhaps, but not intent?*

He heard and felt her approach. Her aura was broad and comforting—and
also, more than a little deluding. He penetrated the delusion and found warmth
beneath. He also found something that drew tears to his eyes and a fullness to
his throat.

The daylight dome came alive with a greenhouse heat. The Ban of Hours
stepped through the doorway, followed by Ulath. She was tall, dressed in a gown
the color of clouds covering the sun, with silver and gold trim on sleeves and
hem. She glided silently across the floor with the ease of a dancer—*Kristine is
almost that graceful*—and smiled at him. Her eyes were the only cold thing about
her, as dark and intensely blue-green as the ice beneath the Realm, but the coldness enhanced by contrast rather than detracting. She was nurturing, but not to
be trifled with, her eyes said.

She used none of the tactics she had used on him during their last meeting.
She was not greeting him as a pawn or a weak supplicant.

Her gold-red hair was restrained by a white scarf that trailed down her back.
She held her hand out to Michael, and he took it, bending automatically to kiss
it.

"Welcome," she said. "Friend of Nikolai and one-time weapon of the Councils, now burst his bonds and turned rogue." Her smile dazzled, conveying gentle
humor and no hint of superiority.

She's treating me as an equal . . . or an ally, Michael realized. *Even though I
don't yet deserve it. She nurtures what is in me.*

"Thank you," Michael said quietly. "I am honored to be in your presence
again, Mother." The honorific surprised him some, but it seemed completely
appropriate.

"Unfortunately, there is little time to discuss matters, and not even we can
hold back the death of my father's creation. Not even if we join hands and
concentrate all our combined power." Even so, she held out her hands, and he
took them. The sensation that passed back and forth was stunning, an echo of
some of the abilities he had felt springing unwilled and unknown from within
him. In the Ban, however, these abilities, though weaker (!), were controlled, fully
realized. "Not even then," she added softly. "How will you save our humans and
Breeds?"

"I'm not sure," Michael said. "I have to know what guards the Sklassa and whether I can open a path to Earth big enough, or for a long enough time."

"You already advance beyond me, if you contemplate such acts," the Ban said. "Only the tribal sorcerers—and my father, of course—could do such things, and they are nearly all on Earth now, with their people."

"What I have . . . what I am . . . is not developed, Mother," he confessed. "I don't know my limits. I might be dangerous."

"Oh, yes, you are that. But you are the last chance we have. You have seen the true Sklassa, I assume?"

He nodded. "It is not what I expected."

"The illusions of fortresses and horrors . . . something of a joke for my father, I fear. He ordered Tarax to create this refuge that he might bring Sidhe males and females together in harmony. The Maln administered this fastness. Here they brought Sidhe of all races from around the Realm, to reconcile . . ." Her voice turned suddenly sad. "We have declined for millions of years. The Sklassa was kept secret because it was not a center of raw power, but only of hope. And the hope was not fulfilled. Few children were born here. Not even Tarax's daughter, though he took a wife in the Sklassa. Shiafa's mother is dead now. Most of the women who came here did not live, or wished they might not . . ."

A darkness shaded the Ban at that moment that chilled Michael to the bone. The Sidhe were a dying race. Even the Ban had given up hope for them.

"You have brought her with you, have you not?" she asked. "Tarax's daughter, Shiafa?"

"Yes."

"And she will come with us to Earth, should you succeed?"

He nodded. "I'm her teacher, for the time being."

"And she will teach you much," the Ban said. "Now it would help you, I think, to see the quarters of your brothers and sisters, to look over our preparations for the end and to meet our Mahler. He can tell you more."

The Ban dismissed him with a distant smile. Ulath took Michael's hand and led him through another door. "The Ban is very tired," she explained. "Adonna's death and the difficulties since have drained her of more than even she can give."

"How did you come to be here?" Michael asked. "And where is the rest of the Maln?"

"The Ban insisted that she stay with the humans when Tarax brought them here from Inyas Trai and other refuges in the Realm. Adonna was still alive then and had some influence, though waning. The Maln disbanded shortly thereafter, that the tribal and racial sorcerers might focus on the problem of the dissipation."

They walked through a sinuous corridor, passing many wooden doors with names scratched on them in Roman and other alphabets.

"Dissipation?"

"When the Realm finally breaks up, it must dissipate. Since the Realm is not far from Earth as worlds go, its end will have an effect."

"I haven't given much thought to that."

"It will change Earth. Much time will pass before the influence of the surrounding reality of Earth will stabilize things."

At the end of the corridor, Ulath held open another thick wooden door for him. Beyond lay a vast ruined garden, rising to hills crested by dying trees and rugged upthrusts of black rock and falling into what might have once been leafy glens. Michael experienced a sharp disorientation; where was the tower? Behind them was only the door in a low cylindrical brick structure like a squat silo. And the sky was not oily slate but a dusty dark gray-blue, like the twilight of the between-worlds.

Across the garden, men and women dressed in Sidhe garb, white *seplas* and long gray robes, strolled singly or in groups. The nearest man, a middle-aged oriental, looked on Ulath and Michael with some interest but did not approach.

"Our humans," Ulath said. "The Ban has come to think of them as her children—and indeed, she is in a way their aunt."

"Where are we?" Michael asked.

"Still inside the tower. The walls themselves have out-seeing pressed into their fabric. The Ban and Adonna designed this thousands of years ago, that Sidhe might court and find peace. It has not been tended of late."

"I see that. It's sad."

"We are a sad race," Ulath said. They followed a stone path weaving through the hills. Here and there, houses much like the hut of the Crane Women rose in the middle of spinneys of skeletal trees. "Some have chosen to live here, some in the tower's upper reaches."

"And outside the tower?"

"Biri gathered Adonna's abortions and placed them in the grounds. No one goes there."

Ahead, a house unlike the others, small and square, surrounded by a rickety porch, stood alone on a hill overlooking a lead-colored lake. The house had apparently been recently assembled in some haste and lacked the ancient stolidity of the other buildings.

A door stood half-open on the side facing away from the lake. Ulath knocked lightly on the frame. A small man, thin and slightly stooped, pushed the door open all the way and stared at Michael and Ulath over pince-nez glasses perched on a blade-sharp aquiline nose. His gray-unto-white hair flowed back from a high forehead, topping almost emaciated features; he radiated an intensity Michael found fascinating.

"This is our savior?" the man asked in English with a soft Viennese accent.

"This is Michael Perrin," Ulath said, opening her hands between them. "I believe you are acquainted with Gustav Mahler."

Michael hesitantly extended his hand.

Mahler looked down on it with a frown, then grasped it with both hands and shook it vigorously. "Please come in," he said. The room beyond was sparely furnished with wicker and wood. There was a small writing table and chair beneath a piece of tattered gray and black floral-patterned Sidhe fabric. The table held layers of dozens of sheets of handmade paper, creamy and rough-edged, covered with hastily scrawled musical notes and blots of watery ink. A goose-quill lay near one of the fresh blots. On the opposite side of the room stretched a narrow wicker cot covered with a richly woven red rug. The walls of the room were bare but for dead branches strung up in the corners, reaching out like withered hands.

Michael hardly knew what to say. Mahler had supposedly been dead for eighty years. This man matched the pictures Kristine had shown him, though some years older.

When Michael had stood before the Ban of Hours, he had felt a magical presence, an age-old personality enhanced by inhuman power and the mystique of the Sidhe. Mahler was human—not even measurably a Breed, as Michael was—and his accomplishments had been purely human, and mortal. Yet Michael's emotions were much the same. He vividly remembered the extraordinary music in Royce Hall.

"Did it go well? Were you there?" Mahler asked.

"I'm sorry?"

"The performance of my symphony, my Tenth."

"It went very well," Michael said.

Mahler rubbed his bony hands together. "Ah! Good," he said almost as one word. "Ah yes good. The *jungling* Berthold Crooke was skillful. I came to his dreams. I hinted, pushed, and he was kind enough to listen. It was frustrating not to be there *incarnatus*, but then, I am a ghost, no? A muse.

"I don't know much about the Earth now. What I was shown in the past discouraged me. But it still has music. My music is still listened to. More . . ." He took a deep breath. "More popular than when I was alive, I understand. And all the ways you have to listen to it . . . !" Abruptly his face, which had assumed a mask of angelic enthusiasm, paled and stiffened. He glared at Michael and gestured for him to sit on a second wicker chair. He then pulled out the desk chair and sat on it, hunched forward with elbows resting on his knees, hands clasping each other. "Can you return us to Earth? Bring us all to life again?"

"I came here to try," Michael said.

"Is my . . . is my daughter still alive? Is Anna still alive?"

Michael glanced at Ulath. "I don't know."

"After I was taken, after I *died*, they put her through such *hell*." Mahler shook his head furiously, face flushing. "I vowed I would never have anything to do with Earth, after the Maln . . . Tarax, the damned son of a whore, after he showed me."

"I don't understand," Michael said.

"They convinced me to work for them," Mahler said. "The Maln let me see what was happening on Earth. Alma! She I could understand and forgive, though that Werfel fellow . . ." He shook his head sadly. His emotions flashed like shadows of clouds passing over a landscape. "But my daughter! My last daughter!"

Michael was still puzzled.

"You do not know about the labor camps, the death camps, the guards, the ovens? They made my daughter conduct music for human monstrosities. They made her play music to entertain the ones who could have killed her, who were killing all those around her. I saw this, and I *hated. I hated* my own countrymen. I swore I would never . . ." He stood up and leaned on the desk, facing away from Michael. His gestures were stage-dramatic, but the sincerity and strength of his feeling was beyond question.

Michael gently probed the man and emerged with a confusion of horrifying images: the camps constructed by Germans in Europe during the Second World War. Bodies stacked like shriveled logs, ready for burning. Human skeletons still alive, eyes haunted for eternity. "The Maln showed you these things?" Michael asked, incredulous.

"Yes. Jews. Christians. Women and children. Infants. Old men and old women. My entire *world*, consumed by wars! I blessed the day I was taken from the foulness of the Earth."

Mahler's cheeks shone with tears. He straightened abruptly, pressing his hands into the small of his back, and stared at Michael with a sad, dreamy expression. "They wanted songs from me. Songs I wrote for them. But nothing like the symphony, my Tenth. I am not of Earth now, and my strength has always been in the Earth. *Erde.* My mother, mother of skies and fields and woods." He held up his hands and nodded forcefully, thrusting his long chin forward.

"All right. Here is what they told me. They said my Tenth was a song of power. They said if performed properly, it could let this Realm die gently and pass into the Earth without destroying it. It could harmonize the two worlds. So I worked in the dreams of this young man, this finisher of a symphony I was not allowed to complete because of the Sidhe *in the first place!*" He smiled ironically, and despite himself, Michael smiled along with him. "I am a bastard to work with. Not unreasonable, but demanding of perfection. I could not expect perfection, directing the young man like a puppet master with half the strings cut. But I could expect *power,* and apparently . . . that is what I have gotten. Without my music . . ." He threw his hands out, fingers spread. "Without that, the Sidhe would return to our world and find themselves crushed not long after by the death of the Realm."

"The Maln explained all this to you?" Michael asked. He was piecing together an impression of the Maln very different from the one he had picked up on his first visit.

"They never lied to me," Mahler said solemnly. "They have treated all of us well . . . Once we were brought here. Better than my own people would have treated me, no? Their only torture was to show us what was happening on Earth. Madness and madmen. 'This is your humanity,' they said."

Michael felt a sharp tickle of anger. "Did they show you other things? Liberating the camps, rebuilding after the war . . . Humans conquering disease, trying to work against plagues and famine? Going to the Moon?"

Mahler shook his head as if that did not matter. "What they showed was the truth." He gave Michael a hard look

Ulath spoke. "Your people were shown only what the Maln considered appropriate, and only in special cases."

Softly, dreamily, Mahler said, "They claimed Sidhe had been to the Moon, and beyond, by magic . . ." He sat again. "I was shown machines that play music, writing it down—recording it. The Sidhe can do that too. They can conjure an entire orchestra out of thin air . . ." He snapped his fingers. "They wanted me to understand that everything on Earth, everything done by humans, they could do as well."

Michael pushed back his anger and followed an inner thread of thought, unwinding so rapidly he could hardly keep up. He saw things rather than traced their progression: the Realm's edges meeting the boundaries of the Earth and smoothing out across the landscape—the mental landscape, the physical landscape.

Even with Mahler's song of power in effect, the Realm's death would change the Earth's reality. Everything remaining in the Realm would be destroyed. But there was no way he could open a gate for five thousand people. That might not be the best method, anyway.

Again Michael felt the cold dagger-twist of uncertainty. He closed his eyes for several seconds and fought back his fear.

What I am thinking of doing . . . not thinking, seeing myself do . . . You are what you dare. Succeed or fail.

He stood and gripped Mahler's extended hands. "Can you improvise a composition?"

A large black man entered the cabin, saw Ulath and Michael and bowed deeply toward the Ban's attendant with hands folded before him. "Excuse me," he said, his voice deep as a drum. "Gustav, the committee is meeting in the tower. Bes Amato and Hillel ask that you be there. Again they want to move *Die Zauberflöte.*"

Michael easily read the man's aura. He was—or had been more than two thousand years ago—a soldier in the army of the Mauretanian King Bocchus. He seemed to have been a storyteller, a singer and an archer.

"This is Uffas," Mahler explained. "He is superintendent of our pageant."

"What pageant?" Michael said.

"Music, drama, dancing," Mahler said. "To celebrate our release by death from captivity. Uffas, the committee should know we may not have time to put on the pageant. This man is here to save us."

Uffas regarded Michael with a mild, almost placid suspicion. "We've planned for many months," he said.

Mahler placed his arm on the huge black's lower shoulder. "Uffas, how long have you been here?"

"Centuries. I do not know."

"And what did you do?"

"I sang and told stories for the Sidhe."

"Like my daughter," Mahler said quietly, eyes on Michael. He looked at Ulath, tall and still. "Like Anna, playing for the monsters. Tell the committee nothing. Let them plan. Perhaps there will be time, and we will celebrate something else. Living."

Uffas left, and Mahler closed the door behind him. "I am sorry. What were you asking me before Uffas came?"

"Can you play music on a piano, new music, without a score, without composing ahead of time?"

Mahler's eyes became languid. "Not well," he said. "But I know one who can."

"Who?"

"Wolferl," Mahler said. "Mozart. He excels at that sort of display. Why is this talent necessary?"

"I'll need music to save us," Michael said. "An extemporaneous song of power."

Mahler smiled broadly. "Mozart has been bored, you know. He prefers the drama and pain of Earth to this limbo. I hope the Ban does not think us ungrateful . . . Mozart and I have argued much in the past. But I think he will agree to try."

Michael told Ulath what would be necessary. "And bring Shiafa here," he added.

"The Ban does not want her in the Sklassa," Ulath said.

"Tell the Ban I will need her," Michael said firmly. His *hubris* led him to defy even the Ban of Hours! He turned again to Mahler. "Where is Mozart now?" he asked, the back of his eyes again warming with an inexpressible wonder. *Mozart!*

"Follow me," Mahler said. "If he is not talking or playing music, he will be in his room in the tower."

27

Wolfgang Amadeus Mozart, who had allegedly died of typhus on Earth at the age of thirty-five, had left the wooden door and curtain of his chamber open. Mahler knocked lightly on the coral wall and then held his hand to his lips and turned to Michael. "He is napping," he said, almost reverently. "We will not—"

"We don't have a choice," Michael said. The three of them entered the room. Mozart lay on a wicker couch covered with a single brown blanket. He wore a gray robe embroidered with black leaves. The robe was obviously meant for a Sidhe and fell below his feet. The finely woven cloth clearly outlined his paunch, rising and falling to the tune of faint snores. Michael stood over him and bent to touch his shoulder.

Mozart opened his eyes and glanced up at Michael, then turned his head to see Mahler standing in the door. "Ah, God, Gustav, not now," he said in German. "I'm sleeping. We'll talk about the pageant later." He returned his gaze to Michael and half-sat in the bed. "You're in *my* room," he said shortly. "Don't gawk."

Mozart resembled a very wise, sad child. He might have been thirty, or he might have been forty—his apparent age had settled at some indefinite point, leaving him suspended between middle age and late adulthood. His large eyes protruded slightly but seemed sympathetic even when he was irritated. His thinning brown hair had been cut short and carefully combed back.

No wig, Michael thought. "We need you," he said. "We're going back to Earth."

Mozart blinked and then smiled. "Mahler, too?" he asked.

"All of us."

"If Mahler's going back, I don't want anything to do with it."

"Wolferl, don't be churlish," Mahler chided. "We argue," he said to Michael, "but we are friends."

"The hell you say." Mozart kept his gaze on Michael, exploring his face as if it were a landscape. "Who are you?"

"I'm from Earth," Michael said. "Recently."

"Yes, but *who* are you?"

"My name is Michael Perrin," he replied. "If that's any answer."

"It isn't," Mozart murmured.

"We must hurry."

"Is this true?" Mozart asked Ulath, who nodded once. "All right," he said grudgingly, sitting on the edge of the couch. "Good riddance to this *Ort*. Any way out. It's all been a mighty pain in the arse."

Michael turned to Ulath. "Is there a large hall where everyone can be assembled?"

"At the top of the tower. The arena of the skies."

"It's reserved for the pageant," Mozart said. "Is the pageant canceled?"

"Please tell the Ban that everybody in the Sklassa who wishes to return to Earth—who wishes to live—must be assembled in the arena soon," Michael said. "You have a piano, don't you?"

"Yes," Ulath said. "And other human instruments—we brought them with us, with the Maln's permission."

"For the pageant. Such singers assembled for my opera! The Ban herself to play the Queen of the Night, and Uffas—did you meet Uffas? To be Monostatos—"

"Just a piano. Please have it placed in the arena."

"What *is* all this?" Mozart asked indignantly.

"You know that music can send humans to the Realm?" Michael asked.

Mozart smiled, baring uneven teeth. "I wrote quite a bit of that sort of music. So I'm told." He favored Ulath with a wink.

"We're going to try the reverse. You must play music that will transport us to Earth. You must play the finest and the most enchanting music you've ever played."

Mozart gaped at Michael. "You put him up to this," he accused Mahler.

"Can you do it?" Mahler challenged.

Mozart shrugged. "No rehearsals?"

"There isn't time," Michael said.

"Of course I can do it," Mozart grumbled. "I'm surprised nobody asked me earlier. '*Wir wondeln durch die Tones Macht / Froh durch des Todes düstre Nacht.*' Do you know that?"

Michael said he did not.

" 'We walk with music as our might / In cheer through Death's own darkest night!' Pity, if the pageant is canceled, you won't hear that sung. We have the most *engelgleich* voices here. But despite that, I've spent some very dull decades in the company of nothing but Faeries and arsehead geniuses. Very trying." He swung his legs off the cot, stood, stretched his arms out and spun around. "What shall I wear?"

"Formal attire, I suggest," Mahler said.

"Of course. My best. Now please leave, all of you."

MICHAEL RETURNED TO the outer courtyard to check on Biri's condition. He found him as he had left him, still helplessly bound by the shadow. Biri regarded him through the shadow's dark strands with the calmness of a trussed pig, resigned to slaughter.

"What are we going to do?" Michael asked him. "Do you still oppose me?" Biri said nothing.

"You told me never to trust a Sidhe. But I've been told by the people here that the Sidhe never lied to them. I think . . ." He knelt to bring his face closer to Biri's. "I think you've been used as much as I have by the Maln and all the others. Mora was used, too. You've been sacrificed. That much should be obvious to you by now. They left you here to die."

Biri turned his face away and stared at the tiles.

"Well, you've failed. But you shouldn't have to die. One way or another, if we succeed, you'll be coming back with us. I'll ask the Ban to watch over you. I may keep you wrapped in this shadow. But you're going to Earth."

"I am disgraced," Biri said. "Better by far to kill me."

"Nonsense," Michael said. "There's too much work to do. We have to help your people on Earth. I'll certainly need assistance. I think the time for lies is over. Will you help?"

Biri's face had gone pearly-ashen. "You say we are all pawns."

"And we're moving into the end-game. Most of the powerful pieces are gone. Pawns are very important. We're marching across the board. Do you play chess?"

"Sidhe do not play human games. I am aware of its rules."

"Then you know that a pawn can become a very powerful piece if it crosses the board."

"It cannot become a king."

Michael shrugged. "Rules change. Would I be stupid to trust you now?"

Biri looked directly into Michael's eyes.

The shadow dissipated at Michael's touch. "We're gathering in the arena," he said.

At the top of the tower, they could see across all that was left of the Realm. Chasms had absorbed huge sections; the territories around the *Chebal Malen* had been pierced by upthrust needles of ice. All around, the land seemed in constant motion, heaving and quaking in a slow, spastic dance.

Michael stood at the edge of the arena, beneath the glistening black sky, watching the five thousand humans file through the central doors around the stage. The arena had been designed to hold perhaps four thousand; the performance would be crowded, but all would get to hear.

Shiafa approached him along the walkway. Her hair had grown unkempt and stringy. Michael thought she had the aspect of an ill-treated human adolescent; he realized, with a pang, that she was as frightened and unhappy as any Sidhe he had ever met. She thought they were all going to die soon, and she no longer trusted her teacher. "Why do you need me here?" she asked. "I am not welcome. They think my father has tainted me."

"Magic is passed through the female," Michael said. "I don't want your magic for myself, but to help us go to Earth. There's no time to do it subtly, so I'll have to . . ." He shook his head. "I can't even describe it. When we're done, you'll know your potential, and your training will almost be finished."

"Do you know what you're doing?" she asked.

"No," Michael said. "Not exactly." *It might kill us all.*

She looked out over the mountains. From where they stood, they could see the deserted Stone Field and the empty basin of *Nebchat Len.* "My father does not know you," she said. "You do not think like a Sidhe. Nor do you think like a human."

Michael nodded, not really listening. He was absorbed in some inner dialogue that he could only follow in part; a dialogue between the various parts of himself, all his voices coming together. They could not stand apart within him now. When this was done, he would no longer be able to isolate a part of himself and sacrifice it as a shadow; the only shadow he would throw would be the one attendant upon his death. He would lose this neophyte ability. *You've already lost Michael Perrin. Where is he, amid all these voices?*

"I don't think the Realm has more than an hour remaining," Michael said. He could feel an almost nauseating vibration in his palms.

Three people pushed their way through the crowd in the upper tiers of the arena. They broke into the clear and climbed the steps to the walkway, approaching Michael and Shiafa. Michael saw Nikolai first among them and smiled broadly, then hesitated as he saw Savarin and Helena trailing him. But there was no bitterness left in him now. He had sacrificed those shadows long ago.

Nikolai ran toward Michael and hugged him vigorously. "We're all here!" the Russian enthused, his face red from exertion. "Ah, all that has happened since I tried to escape! But we're here, all of Euterpe . . . Emma Livry and the others . . . and you!"

Helena smiled nervously, hanging back. Michael extended his hands to them as Nikolai stepped aside. "Friends," he said. Helena swallowed hard and took his hand firmly in hers. Savarin nodded solemnly and did likewise. Nikolai removed a handkerchief and loudly blew his nose. There were tears in their eyes, he saw with another pang. In the middle of his interior preparations, he could not feel such strong emotions.

"So wonderful," Nikolai continued. "We will all be together when it ends."

"It isn't ending," Michael said. "We're returning to Earth. We're going back the same way you came."

"There was a rumor . . ." Savarin said. "Mozart is going to play . . . And the pageant is canceled. Is that true?"

Michael nodded.

Helena glanced over Michael's shoulder at Shiafa, her eyes narrowing. Helena had aged noticeably—she appeared to be forty or older. Michael doubted that so many years had passed in the Realm.

"You should find your seats now," Michael said.

"You will not believe who is here with us!" Nikolai enthused. "Besides Mozart. People we've never heard of, but wonderful artists and—" He saw Michael's concern and clasped his own hands together before him. "Later. We talk later." He ushered Savarin and Helena down the steps to seats below the walkway.

The faces of the crowd filling the arena were as varied as the leaves on an autumn tree. Michael saw all races represented, and with some surprise—would he ever be beyond surprise?—he realized that more than half, perhaps three out of four of the humans assembled were women.

These were the best, the ones the Sidhe had thought the most likely to imperil their position as the supreme people on Earth. They had been gathered by the Maln across thousands of years and brought to the Realm . . . and most of them were women.

Magic is passed through the female. Was that adage, or something like it, true for both Sidhe and humans? And did the proportions of the crowd filling the arena explain a major curiosity about the arts on Earth—the predominance of men?

A single broad aisle without seats was left mostly clear. Michael and Shiafa descended the steps between a few standing humans dressed in Sidhe garb and makeshift styles from their own eras. They watched Michael and Shiafa pass without a word, and from them Michael felt that thing he had always assumed was the difference between humans and Sidhe: a strong sense of reserve and style, of discretion. He also felt the strength of their personalities and saw the clarity of their eyes, whatever age they had finally settled on in the Realm's odd scale of time, and the expressions of calm anticipation. There was fear, but no panic; concern, but no hysteria. They all fully expected to die soon, but they were prepared and self-possessed.

Michael and Shiafa came to the center of the arena, an elliptical stage about sixty feet wide in one direction and thirty feet deep. The ponderous black grand piano was already on stage, its lid opened.

Could the song of power be played with just a piano? Waltiri's concerto and Mahler's symphony required complete orchestras . . . but then, they had been patterned for many instruments. Mozart's playing would not be so patterned. Scale was not the secret—it was the subtlety of design. And if the music was not enough . . . Then Michael would engage his own power, and Shiafa's.

But there had been an expression in Mozart's protruding eyes . . . There was more to magic than could be encompassed in Sidhe disciplines.

Michael looked around the inner circle of benches and saw Ulath and the Ban of Hours seated nearby. Ulath regarded him with calm expectation. Beside the Ban sat the delicately beautiful dancer Emma Livry and her odd, thin woman companion. Emma did not look in Michael's direction; she waited for Mozart, her rapt attention fixed on the stage.

Mahler was nowhere to be seen.

Michael's impatience grew. He probed for Mozart and found the composer waiting in a small dark room beneath the stage, talking quietly with Mahler. Mozart's mental state was unperturbed, casual, but the energy pent up within him was enormous, and his confidence was a wonder to feel. *He doesn't doubt he will succeed,* Michael realized. *You are what you dare.*

Already, time was beginning to play tricks. As the Realm condensed and collapsed, fragments shredding and rotting away, even within the Sklassa he could feel the deep tremors of each moment straining to pass, each second shuddering with a kind of pain.

Mozart took a deep breath and left the small room, climbing a short flight of steps onto the stage. He wore a sky-blue coat, short white kneepants and high stockings, and a powdered white wig. The Ban smiled upon seeing him, and Michael realized that Mozart, like Livry, had been one of the Ban's favorites.

Michael probed his memories, saw the ghostly figure in gray commissioning Mozart to write a requiem . . . and the Maln moving in to end his career on Earth before he could finish.

Clarkham. The figure in gray, as Moffat had heard, could have been no other. Mozart had almost certainly been Clarkham's first victim, even before Coleridge.

Once again the emotion he felt toward Clarkham lay rich and heavy in him, not precisely anger, but a kind of necessity.

Michael's thoughts came to an abrupt dividing line. He looked across the stage, where Mozart was even now sitting at the piano, as casual and relaxed as if he were alone.

Beneath the oily black sky, with time's heartbeat fluttering in his palms like a wounded dove, Michael felt tears running down his cheeks.

Say good-bye to everything you've ever been. There's a sixteen-year-old boy still buried in you who wants nothing more than a normal adolescence. You'll kill him; he is you. A new person starts here, not normal, weighed down with impossible responsibilities. He thought of the key and Waltiri's note and the door through Clarkham's house. If he had simply left that avenue untraveled, would any of this have happened? Would he have involved himself in this incredibly convoluted, beautiful, horrible nightmare? It seemed that all of reality had changed when he entered that door.

The Jehovah's Witnesses, with their crazy and unshakable convictions about history and prophecy, about the way the universe was . . . Were they any crazier than he, with his new knowledge? Perhaps not.

But they were weaker.

The most frightening realization of all was that *he* could be master of this particular nightmare. He could swing worlds one way or another, create paradise or hell or simply continue the monstrous progression of the past.

Mozart applied his fingers to the keyboard.

I am the key. A few realize that now. But I am not even sure who I am or what I am going to do. Michael tried to recall the self-confidence he had felt earlier, the undoubting assurance of what had to be done. He could not. Something like that assurance was necessary, but he had disliked himself, feeling thus.

Still, he did not have the luxury of long introspection.

Mozart sat at the piano with head cocked to one side, listening to the music before his fingers drew it from the keys. Then he began to play, slowly at first, with implications of unease, fear, in the key of G minor. But he quickly moved to the major, and the music began a climb to exaltation.

For a moment, Michael tried to analyze that music. Then he simply shut his eyes and let the music penetrate him. Without analysis, without the feeling that there was a score behind the sounds—there wasn't, of course—the music could do what it was meant to do. It could define and create a language of worlds, not words or thoughts, guiding Michael at the same time that it put the audience in a spell. They would learn the differences between worlds, and they would discover they had a choice . . .

For Mozart's playing was virtually a definition of sanity and peace and order. It was not lacking in conflict; it did not sugar-coat. It calmly and confidently outlined a place in which it would be wonderful to live.

From what Michael remembered of Mozart's music in Waltiri's collection of records, that was what virtually all of his music had done. In a world of people adapted to hard times and social infighting and inhospitable realities, it had gracefully outlined an alternative.

The best that we can be.

Michael looked down at his hands, folded before him.

Something glowed between the intertwined fingers. Ulath watched him, apprehension in her eyes. The Ban of Hours, listening to Mozart's music, clasped her own hands before her breast and lowered her head as if in prayer.

"Shiafa," he said softly, raising his hands. "Will you join with me, this once?"

She trembled. "We will die," she said. He thought of Eleuth, trying powerful magic before she was ready.

"If we don't try, we'll die anyway, and everybody with us."

"My father will protect me," she said. "He is the God of the Realm."

"He has left you to me," Michael reminded her. *Would Tarax interfere?*

"What do you want from me? That which I will give only in mating? I don't even know what that is."

"No mating," Michael said. "No loss. I need what you have inside you, but I cannot take it. You can only give it to me—to us—and I *will not keep it.*"

Shiafa lifted her eyes to the sky. The music was not so much heard as lived, now. Mozart was succeeding. "I am so afraid," she said.

"So am I." Michael unclasped his hands, and the light between them went out. He held his right hand out to her. All around, save for Ulath, the audience paid them no attention, entranced by the music. "There isn't enough time to train you and give you all the discipline. I cannot make you what your father would have you be. The old traditions are inadequate. Help me forge new ones."

Shiafa took his hand and grasped it firmly. White light escaped from between their fingers.

In the palm of his other hand, Michael felt time come apart like a squeezed clot of dust. The sky went from uncertain blackness to the nonexistence and nonquality of death. The arena skewed and bled upward, all of its coral redness fragmenting and smearing.

Now we begin, Michael told Shiafa through their joined hands. The humans in the arena had been enchanted by Mozart's music, but they had not had time to transport. It was necessary for Michael to make his first small world and wrap them in it.

Where are we? Shiafa asked.

We are dead, I think, Michael said. There was no seeing, no feeling, only their thoughts and joined energy. Around them—if "around" could be used to describe relations without space or coherent time—were the people who had been in the arena and Mozart's music, pure pattern without sound. Michael used the pattern as a model.

There was no time to lay solid underpinnings for the world. Instead, he began a "gloss"—warmth, sustenance, distance, some semblance of time. What else did a world need? Limits. He established a size.

And saw three hands. His hand and Shiafa's, joined, and his other hand. In his free hand he saw a pearl the size of a walnut. The pearl blossomed and became a coral-red rose. The edges of the rose's petals spread out as red lines, vibrating to Mozart's pattern. The red lines marked out a space, twisting to meet and close off the space. The lines then vanished. Again, in his free hand grew a pearl, this time the size of a baseball. He closed his fingers around it and pushed it back— not necessary. He would save it for another time.

Space and warmth surrounded the five thousand. Michael listened for the Earth. It was, of course, quite close, singing its complex, steady, but somewhat out-of-tune melody. *Do you feel the Earth?* he asked Shiafa.

Yes.

This is what war between Sidhe and humans left behind—a Garden gone to seed. Hatred and pain and deception.

Yes.

Our people are more alike than either would suspect.

Yes.

I need you to help me bring all of us to the Earth. Do you feel how it must be done? Training through necessity . . .

She replied that she could feel the necessity but not yet the method.

Just listen . . . he suggested. *Feel the addings and takings away. We must come to the Earth when it is neither adding nor taking away, and then we must synchronize.*

She was no longer afraid. He felt in her some of the confidence he had experienced earlier.

Dare, he said.

Together, they dared.

He saw the between-worlds arrayed beneath them like nightmare relief maps, all the shadows and discarded possibilities. He veered away from them, toward the song of the true and finished Earth.

The limits of his little world were fading. His first creation would hold together only briefly.

The Earth unfolded, and around it, all the possible points of space and time. He disregarded those possible points—*how the Sidhe felt their way between the stars, back when the world had not joined with so many other worlds and was so much smaller*—and concentrated on the familiar.

Young, homesick Michael Perrin rose up and asserted himself. Shiafa did not object. Neither did the newer, more powerful Michael. Los Angeles spread its night tapestry below them.

They needed a place to let the bubble burst, a place that could accommodate everybody, an empty place . . .

Dodger Stadium, dark and deserted under the warm night skies
Accepted them, and Michael's first world died.

28

Five thousand people, some of whom had not seen the Earth for millennia, stood on the turf and soil, spread out over the diamond, infield and outfield, all the way to the fence.

Moon and sun briefly arced with shadow and fire in the sky as the dead Realm fell across and through the Earth. Everybody dropped to their hands and knees as the ground shook. The noise and quaking went on for a very long time; Michael wondered if Mahler's symphony had been enough to cushion the fall. Then the noise subsided, and the ground became still.

Michael released Shiafa's hand in the silence. "Thank you," he said.

Shiafa sat up with her legs crossed beneath her. "This is Earth?" she asked, staring up at the dark seats arrayed in concentric rows and the few scattered security lights.

"It is," Michael said.

"It doesn't *feel* right," she said. "It feels harsh." He did not disagree.

29

Morning light touched cirrus clouds high above Los Angeles. Michael, Shiafa, Nikolai and Ulath walked through the people sitting, standing, conversing or just staring—at the sky, the walls, the tiers of seats—while Michael tried to assess the extent of their problem.

Five thousand people. Frightened, most of them unfamiliar with the Earth. Soon to be hungry. Brought abruptly into a world already upset and confused. Most of them illegal aliens.

"I need some organization," he said. "How did the Ban administer them all in the Sklassa?"

"They have speakers—one for every fifty—and a knotmaker for every ten speakers. The knotmakers address the assistants of the Ban," Ulath explained.

Michael pursed his lips, thinking rapidly. "Where is Biri? The other assistants?"

"I saw Biri inspecting the walls around the field," Nikolai said. Michael probed for him, found him and sent a dubious Nikolai to bring him into the center of the group, near second base.

"Nobody should leave the stadium until I've learned what conditions are like outside. I think"—he knew, actually, but the feeling was unfamiliar—"that Biri will cooperate with us. Together, we can keep order—where is the Ban?" He could feel her presence but could not pinpoint her location.

"She has chosen to spread herself among her children," Ulath said.

"What does that mean?"

"She is diffuse now. She will attend to us all and to the Sidhe of Earth."

"How do we communicate with her?"

"I speak to her," Ulath said.

"Yes, but why did she do this now, when we need her?"

"Because Tarax is here. He has brought the Realm to its end and now begins his rule on Earth. She protects us best by spreading herself."

Michael closed his eyes briefly to feel for her. *What has happened to you now? Are you dead?*

"The Ban is not dead."

"I still have a lot to learn about the Sidhe," he said.

"Perhaps about the Ban only," Ulath suggested, smiling.

Nikolai and Biri approached, Biri trailing the Russian by several steps. "This is a foul place," Biri said. "It is dirty and painful."

"There's no place like home." Michael told him they would need a perimeter of protection to prevent people from entering the stadium and to discourage the captives from leaving.

"That is simple enough," Biri said.

"Ulath will help you."

"I can do that alone."

"Fine. I have to leave to make arrangements outside. Is everybody here except the Ban?"

"The Ban is here," Ulath reiterated.

"Yes. Well?"

"I think so," Nikolai said.

"Where are Mozart and Mahler?"

"I will find them," Nikolai said, running off between the crowds of people.

They're still remarkably well-behaved, Michael thought. *No clamoring, no confused milling about. And it's not because they're dazed, either.* Perhaps there would be fewer problems than he had imagined, at least among the five thousand inside the stadium.

Savarin approached Michael alone. His robes were stained green with grass and smudged with dirt. "This is truly Earth?" he asked.

"Yes," Michael said. "You aren't by any chance a speaker or knotmaker, are you?"

"Henrik is a knotmaker," Ulath said.

Savarin grinned sheepishly. "I am always the organizer," he said.

"Good. Then you'll help us—" He spotted Nikolai returning with Mahler and Mozart. "Excuse me."

Michael hugged Mozart firmly and shook Mahler's hand. "You've done it," he said to them.

"Wolferl played magnificently," Mahler said.

"Yes, well, such an audience, *nein?*"

"Would both of you be up to accompanying me?" Michael asked. "I'll need help outside. Nikolai, you too . . ."

"Gladly," Nikolai said.

Mahler inhaled deeply and shook his head. "The air smells bad."

"There's lots to get used to. But there are people—friends of mine—who would very much like to meet you. I have to make some phone calls—talk to them." *If phones are still working.*

"I will go," Mozart said. "This is exciting, really." He sounded more willing than he looked. Mahler rubbed his hand back across his high forehead and gray hair.

"*Ja,*" he said. "But be careful with us. We are not young men, you know."

"Speak for yourself," Mozart said.

In a group, they made their way off the field and down a ramp. Michael searched for a pay phone, though he didn't have any money in his ragged clothes.

"There is a frightened man ahead," Shiafa said as they passed the door of a locker room. Michael had felt him also—and he was armed.

"A security guard, probably," Michael said. "Best to be open." He cupped his hands to his mouth. "Hey! We need help."

A portly, middle-aged man in a gray uniform came out of the shadows with his gun drawn. "Who in the hell are you?"

"We need help," Michael said, holding his hands in the clear and nodding for the others to follow suit. "I need to make a call. There're a lot of people on the field—"

"I saw them. They're like those freaks coming out of everywhere."

"No, no they aren't," Michael reassured him. "They're people, most of them, and so am I. But they need help. We have to call the police, the city. They're going to need shelter, food, clothing."

"What in hell is this?" the guard asked, clearly out of his depth. He was close enough now that Michael could see his sweating face and the wicked gleam on the black barrel of his service revolver.

"I need to get to a phone," Michael said.

"The phones aren't working. I mean, they're only working some of the time. Who are you?"

Michael approached the guard slowly, hands extended, and gave him his name and street address. The guard finally acquiesced and took them to a pay phone near the end of the corridor. He did not put away his gun, however, and he stood well back from them.

Michael smiled his thanks and dialed for the operator. He got a beeping noise and then a recording: "All phone connections are for emergency use only. An operator will be on the line soon. If this is not an emergency, please hang up. Penalties may be levied for abuse of emergency services."

Half a minute passed, then a weary male voice answered. "Emergency service only. May I help you?"

"Yes. I need to reach the office of the Mayor."

"You're whistling in the wind, buddy," the operator said. "You're on a pay phone. Unless you need the police or are reporting an accident with injuries, we don't service pay phones."

"Fine," Michael said patiently. "Connect me with LAPD Central."

"It's your head."

Several minutes passed before he was able to get a line through, and then an even more weary female voice answered.

"I'd like to speak to Lieutenant Harvey in homicide," Michael said.

"Lieutenant Harvey is no longer on homicide. He's on Invasion Task Force."

"Wherever he is, I need to talk to him."

"Is this an emergency?"

"Yes," Michael said. He glanced at the guard. "I'm talking to the police now," he said, cupping his hand over the mouthpiece.

"Invasion Task Force, Sergeant Dinato."

"My name is Michael Perrin."

There was a sharp intake of breath and then a quick, stuttered, "Hold on. I'm transferring you to Lieutenant Harvey's office now."

"Thank you," Michael said. He banked his *hyloka* carefully, realizing how tired he was. The guard held his ground, but he had lowered his pistol a few inches and was mopping his forehead with a handkerchief. He inspected them closely, eyes darting from Mozart's blue silk jacket and white breeches and hose to Mahler's dark robe and Shiafa's ragged pants and loose blouse. "Where all did you come from, anyway?" he asked nervously.

"From Dreamland," Mozart said. "We've just awakened."

"You're all German?"

"I'm Russian," Nikolai said.

"All of you?"

Michael recognized Lieutenant Harvey's resonant voice immediately. "Where the hell have you been?" Harvey asked. The lieutenant sounded exhausted.

"Not far. I'm calling from Dodger Stadium. I have something of an emergency here."

"Oh?" Harvey asked cautiously.

"I'll need food, supplies and shelter for about five thousand people. Human beings. There are a few Sidhe here, as well."

Harvey's silence was prolonged. "That will stretch us a bit," he said. "Dodger Stadium. Where?"

"On the field."

"I mean, where did they come from?"

"The Realm," Michael said.

"All at once?"

"All at once."

There was a sharp edge to Harvey's laughter. "You know," he said, "I'm almost used to this crap now. I guess I owe you. Are these people dangerous?"

"No," Michael said. "Mostly, they're frightened. Some have been away for a long time."

"I'll see what I can do. Are you going to stay there?"

"I don't think so," Michael said, thinking rapidly. "I have a lot of other work to catch up on. We'll have a committee here to meet your people and work with them."

"I'll put together a team now. I feel silly asking you this, but when will I hear from you again?"

"I don't know," Michael said. There was simply no way of telling how much time his next few challenges would take. "Can you get me an open phone line? I need to call my parents."

"Sure," Harvey said. "Hold on for a sec."

"Thanks," Michael said.

30

The taxi driver—a portly Lebanese with a well-trimmed mustache and curious, darting eyes—took Michael, Shiafa, Mahler and Mozart from the stadium parking lot to the Waltiri house in record time. The streets were almost deserted. "I'm the only one out this time of day. Everybody else, they stay home," he said. "I'm not afraid of these spooks. It's fear hurts people." He glanced nervously in his mirror at Shiafa. "Don't you think that's what hurts people?"

Nobody answered. Mahler and Mozart seemed lost in shock. The modern buildings and sprawled clutter of Los Angeles were completely contrary to their experience. "Ugly," Mahler said under his breath again and again, but he did not turn away. Mozart, sitting between Shiafa and Mahler in the back seat, was frozen, his hands folded and clamped between his knees, only his eyes moving away from the cab's center line.

Michael was too tired to do more than broadcast a light circle of awareness tuned to Tarax or Clarkham. His more experienced eye—helped by the driver's occasional observations—was already picking out the city's new incongruities.

The late morning sky over the city was cut through with wildly tangled clouds on several levels. Michael had never seen their like before. The air smelled electric, and his palms tingled constantly, telling him that the song of Earth had been disturbed by the Realm's death. Some of the Realm's qualities had been passed on to the Earth, perhaps by Tarax's design. Michael wearily realized that magic would not be so difficult on Earth now.

"No people at all up and down Wilshire. On a Wednesday!" the taxi driver said, waving his free hand out the window. "You're my first fare today. God knows why I work, but I got no wife, no kids, this cab's my life."

"We appreciate your working," Michael said.

"Take my advice. You all look very tired. You belong to some rock band, some group? I notice your dress. That's a fine wig. You look all rumpled, like you've been playing a concert all night . . ." He shook his head.

"We're musicians," Michael said. He found his head nodding as if to some inner beat and had to stop it with an effort of will. "Hard couple of days."

Mozart laughed abruptly and without explanation, then grabbed the front seat and leaned forward. "Is it all this bad?" he asked plaintively. "Is there no place the eye can rest?"

"Sorry," Michael said. "We'll be home soon." He glanced at Mahler. "Arno Waltiri's house."

Mahler's eyelids assumed that languid expression Michael had seen before. "Waltiri. Brilliant youth. He must be very old by now."

"He's dead," Michael said. Time enough to explain the details later.

John and Ruth were sitting on the front steps of the Waltiri house as the cab drove up and deposited the four of them on the sidewalk. John paid the fare, and Ruth hugged Michael as the others stood on the concrete and grass, squinting and blinking in the bright sun.

"Everyone has their own tiny estate here," Mozart said, gazing at the neighborhood.

Michael and John embraced peremptorily. "Welcome back," John said. "You've been gone during the worst of it. Ruth and I thought you'd choose this morning to come back. It just . . . seemed appropriate."

"After the earthquake," Ruth said. "After the false dawn."

Michael introduced them as they walked to the house. He reached into his pocket and produced the key, still there after all he had been through, and opened the door.

A warm wind blew out of the house, redolent with jasmine, honeysuckle and tea roses. The interior of Waltiri's house was overgrown with flowering plants and vines. They ascended the walls to the ceiling, forming an arch, and covered all the furniture, leaving only the floor and a narrow passageway clear. On every branch and twig, peering from every tiny hollow, birds blinked at him through the foliage. Pigeons and sparrows rustled and milled on the floor as the door opened wider; others regarded the intruders with sleepy black eyes, unperturbed.

"All right," Michael said slowly, stopping in the hallway and spreading his hands.

"I feel a power," Shiafa said. Ruth regarded her with frank worry, obviously thinking of the Hill wife her great-grandfather had taken.

Mozart sat on the front step and leaned his head on one hand, staring at the street, too jaded by marvels to care much about a house full of forest and birds. "Where do we sleep? In there?" he asked, poking his thumb behind him.

Michael, Shiafa and Mahler walked down the flowered passage until they came to the stairway. The birds calmly made way for them. "Surely this is magic," Mahler commented. "All these birds, yet the place is so *clean.*"

"Do you feel anything?" Michael asked Shiafa.

"It feels powerful. Someone important is here."

A large black crow with red breast-feathers and white-rimmed eyes hopped down the stairs, intent on its descent until it reached the bottom. Then it turned its attention to Michael, beak open and thin black tongue protruding, angling its head this way and that.

"Arno?" Michael inquired softly.

The crow lifted its head. "Arno is dead," it squawked. "Now is the time of marvels. Boy become man. Death of worlds. Gods die too."

Michael kneeled to be closer to the bird's level. "Were you Arno?"

"Helped be him. Arno was man. Gone where dead men go."

"Are you . . . ?"

"Am feathered mage," the crow said, strutting. It spread its wings, revealing iridescent black plumage and, under both wings, the lettering of its bondage.

Mahler shrank back. A sparrow landed on his shoulder and chirruped, the first actual bird noise they had heard since entering. Mahler did not attempt to brush it off, but he was clearly enchanted and unhappy at once. "What does this mean?" he asked.

"It means we'll be sleeping at my parents' house," Michael said. "Doesn't it?" he asked the crow.

"Come back. Time to confer. The bonds soon will break. We choose you. Come back."

"All right," Michael said, standing. "I'll be back."

Outside, as they walked the few blocks to his parents' house, John asked, "Pardon the cliché, Michael, but what does it all mean?"

"There's magic on Earth again, and the Sidhe are no longer its only masters," he said.

"That sounds suitably portentous, son," John commented dryly. "Bring it down to my level."

"I think I understand," Ruth said. "Fairyland is dead. We have to live with each other."

"We will share the rent," Mozart said muzzily. "Do we have to walk much farther?"

They did not.

31

John seemed dazed. He followed Mozart, Mahler and his son up the stairs to the second floor. Mozart peered into the bathroom while Michael pulled towels from the linen closet.

"There's plenty of room," John said. Mahler squared his slumped shoulders and yawned. John suddenly seemed to focus on the two men, and his eyes grew wider as he stared at them. Michael walked past him with the towels. "They can stay in the guest room; there are two beds in there," John suggested.

"One can stay in my room," Michael said. "I don't think I'll be sleeping."

"Right. Michael's room."

Mozart inquired where that was, and John opened the door for him.

"Good. Crowded and busy. I'll stay here." He thanked John and shut the door behind him. John stood in the hallway, hands in pockets, blinking owlishly.

"We are very appreciative of your hospitality," Mahler said. "I do not know why your son brought us here."

"I don't either," John said. "But we're glad . . . to have you."

Michael emerged from the bathroom. "There. All set. Do you sleep?" he asked Mahler.

"I haven't slept in many years, but today . . . yes. I'll sleep." He entered the guest bedroom and swung the door shut, smiling at John briefly through the crack before the latch clicked.

Michael put his arm around his father's shoulder. "I'm sorry to upset everything on such short notice."

"Don't mind me," John said. "I just can't accept what's happening. Those two—they're *really* Mahler, Gustav Mahler, and Wolfgang Amadeus Mozart?"

"They are," Michael said.

"They were held by the Sidhe . . . for all this time?"

"However long it was for them," Michael said. He paused at the head of the stairs. Ruth was in the living room, busily making up the couch, apparently intending it as a bed for Shiafa, who stood near the front door watching her. "I don't think Shiafa sleeps, either," Michael said.

"Who is she?" John asked softly.

"Where are you from?" Ruth asked her in a high-pitched, nervous voice clearly audible on the stairs.

"She's the daughter of a Sidhe named Tarax," Michael told John, too low for his mother to hear.

"I was born in the Realm," Shiafa said to Ruth.

John glanced at Michael. They stopped halfway down the stairs, eavesdropping by silent and mutual consent.

"Oh? That's what we called Faerie, until now, isn't it?"

"I do not know."

"You know, you remind me of . . . Well, never mind that. Have you known my son long?"

"Not long," Shiafa said.

"Is he important to you?"

"Yes."

"Oh," Ruth said breathlessly, fitting the top sheet and blanket over the couch cushions. She kept a constant watch on Shiafa from the corner of her eye. "Will you be staying with us for some time? I'm sorry. That's not polite." She stood, smoothing her hands down her legs, and tossed a strand of hair back. "This is not easy for me to accept. Are you and Michael, my son . . . lovers?"

"Jesus," Michael breathed, immediately resuming his descent.

"No," Shiafa said. "He is my teacher."

"Mother, no time for this now," Michael interrupted. "Shiafa probably won't be sleeping. She may want to clean up—"

"Good . . . *God*," Ruth said, staring at Michael with a fierce expression. "John, is any of this happening?"

"You know it is," John said.

"She looks just like my great-grandmother. She could *be* my great-grandmother!"

"No, she couldn't," Michael said.

"They're all over the world now, aren't they? Just like her?"

"And like us, Mother," Michael said. He gripped her shoulders tightly with both hands. "Listen. You're better prepared to accept what's happening than most people. Shiafa is a pure Sidhe. I'm training her, or at least going through the motions. The men upstairs—"

Her expression changed from anger to pain. "Michael," she interrupted, "what can we say to those men? John, what can we say to them? To Mozart! Famous dead people?"

John shrugged.

Michael grinned despite himself. "I'm sorry," he said. "I should have called ahead."

"Damn you!" Ruth said, but she was beginning to laugh and cry at once. "Damn everything." She turned to Shiafa. "I'm sorry. We don't know how to react to all this."

Michael could feel tension radiating from Shiafa. If he didn't isolate her soon, he wasn't sure what would happen.

"We have to leave now. I'll be back in a few hours. There are people I have to call—but the phones are restricted. So I may have to talk to them in person. Mahler and Mozart are just the beginning. I came back with many others—about five thousand of them."

Ruth's face went white. "Here?"

"They're in Dodger Stadium. That's where I called you from. I have to make arrangements for them. They've been in the Realm for a long time, some of them thousands of years."

"All right," Ruth said. She pointed with a nod of her chin at Shiafa. "Will she go with you?"

"Yes," Michael said. "This is difficult for her. She can't go home."

"There is no home," Shiafa said distantly.

"So please, bear with me, with us," Michael said. "If I'm not mistaken, Mahler and Mozart are going to sleep for hours. I hope to be back before they wake up. I don't have much time."

"We'll manage," John said, hugging his wife to him with one arm. "Won't we?"

"We'll have to," Ruth said. "What do they eat?"

"Go easy on the meat," Michael advised. "They haven't had much of that where they've been." Shiafa's skin grayed noticeably at the mention of meat.

"You look very tired," Ruth said. "Both of you. I'm sorry about reacting badly . . ."

"No time to rest. And no self-recriminations. We'll be back soon."

"Why was the Waltiri house full of birds?" Ruth asked.

"Please, Mother."

"All right. Go."

MICHAEL REACHED OUT to feel for Edgar Moffat and found him sitting in the recording room in the studio where they had first met. His probe seemed to be surrounded by razors, the harsh reality now that the Realm had beached itself on Earth's shoals.

"Will we take the machine again?" Shiafa asked.

"It's the easiest way," Michael said. "I think my car is still full of gas."

They walked back to the Waltiri house under the gray, overcast afternoon.

"This place smells horrible," Shiafa said sharply. "It smells like death."

"Right here?" he asked, glancing at the sidewalk where Tommy had shot himself.

"Everywhere. The entire city."

Michael shrugged. "I've gotten used to it. I don't notice."

"It smells like dead forests," Shiafa said. "Like one of Adonna's abortions."

He realized that what she was objecting to was not just the smell of smog—very light this day, he thought—but of technology and human habitations in general. The houses around them, including Waltiri's, had been made from un-consecrated wood. The power lines overhead could upset a Sidhe's sensibilities. If other human technologies still worked, the air would be full of beamed energy—radar and television and radio. How were the tens of thousands of other Sidhe reacting to this sudden change in their surroundings?

Shiafa's mood was upon *him* now. He brushed it aside with a small shudder and told her to stand away from the driveway. He unlocked the Saab and got in.

The engine caught quickly and rumbled to life, murmuring with twin-exhaust throatiness. As he backed the car down the driveway, he glanced through the opposite window at the wall of the house and the entrance to the crawl space.

The wine bottles in the basement.

During the first few minutes of his first visit to the Realm, Michael had crossed a decaying vineyard behind the ruined Clarkham mansion, covered with the twisted, blackened and thick-boled stumps of thousands of dead vines. Nothing Clarkham did was uncalculated.

Clarkham brought Waltiri bottles of wines as a gift. Waltiri passed some of them on to his neighbors.

He almost stopped the car. *One thing at a time. Priorities.* Reaching over to open the car door for Shiafa, Michael felt a buzz of excitement. Clarkham had failed at creating a personal song of power; he had always relied on the genius of others, even at the height of his sorceries. He had interfered with poets, composers, dancers . . . He had failed at architecture. Had he cultured vines simply to please himself—and perhaps anger the more abstemious Sidhe . . . or had he an ulterior motive?

Shiafa sat reluctantly on the seat. "Close your door," Michael instructed her. She stared at him, eyes burning. He sighed and reached across. "Like this," he said, grabbing the handle to pull it shut.

"There is too much iron," she said quietly. "It kills."

"You can stand it. The Sidhe use iron for their own purposes."

"Not like this."

He drove out onto the street. The trees cast long shadows. Time was passing too quickly; the Realm's chronometry was evident on Earth now. What that ultimately meant, there was no way of knowing. Was it a temporary effect—no pun intended, he thought wryly—or a permanent distortion?

He frowned as he guided the Saab through the empty streets of the city. Other changes: leaves on the trees seemed darker and the streets and buildings less hard-edged, as if viewed through a fog.

"Your world is sick," Shiafa said as he turned onto Melrose.

"How do you mean?"

"It is suffering."

"Because of the Realm?"

She nodded, staring at him with an expression he had never before seen—a mix of barely subdued greed and deep concern. It shook him.

"How do you know?" he asked, arguing more out of pique than disagreement.

"Even beyond the dead smell, it is afflicted."

He pressed his lips together and shrugged. Now he was really worried. Who was working to set things right again—Tarax, who had plowed the Realm onto a reef and perhaps started the disintegration of the reef? Clarkham, hiding somewhere . . .

in a bottle of wine

"Jesus," he whispered. *A wine of power. Flavor that seduces, a finish that lasts forever.* It seemed quite possible that Clarkham had kept that art as a backup, almost inaccessible to the Sidhe, who—as Clarkham had stated—"love human liquor entirely too much." What they loved, obviously, was not the flavor but the numbing effect. Because of that, the best of the Sidhe—those who might be interested in Songs of Power—would fastidiously avoid alcoholic beverages.

What was the word for the art of wine-making? The study of wines? *Oenology.* Having failed at everything else, Clarkham could have hidden himself, biding his time, waiting for the proper moment. Preparing to spring a surprise.

In the Realm, Clarkham had served not wine but brandy . . . hiding his craft for decades in Waltiri's cellar, where not even the mage of the Cledar would suspect chicanery.

Michael was so excited he had to bank his *hyloka to* keep from flaming his clothes and the car seat. Shiafa regarded him with that same new hungry, greedy expression . . . and he felt himself responding. He had used her magic. That had somehow bonded them, and it could draw them together . . .

Shocked, he avoided Shiafa's gaze and focused his attention on the road.

The studio's Gower gate was open. The guard blinked passively at Michael and Shiafa as they walked through the door, leaning forward to say, "Hey. Nobody's here. Everybody's home."

Michael smiled at her and nodded. "Edgar Moffat's here."

"Yeah," the guard said. "Edgar's here. Is he expecting both of you?"

"No," Michael said.

"But he knows you."

Michael nodded again.

"I remember you, but not her. Where's Kristine Pendeers?"

"I don't know," Michael said. "I'm looking for her, and I thought Edgar might help." That was a minor fib, but he hoped it would play. It did. The guard shrugged and leaned back in her seat.

In the hallway of the music building, Michael knocked on the recording-studio door. Moffat himself answered this time, wearing gray slacks and a rumpled white business shirt. His crown of hair stood straight up, stiff and dark with sweat, as if he had run his hands through it all night long. He hardly reacted when he saw Michael, but his expression changed to nervous anxiety as he stared at Shiafa.

"We need your help," Michael said.

"I'm the only one here. I think Hollywood packed up its bags and went to hide in the hills. Did you feel the earthquake?"

"Yes. We need you to organize things for us. You and Crooke."

"I haven't talked to Crooke for days. I don't even know where he is."

"This is important. Did Kristine tell you what she knew?"

"You mean, about you and the man who disappeared in front of her?"

"Yes."

"She told me a little. Enough to make the rest of this a real nightmare. A little knowledge is worse than none at all." Edgar opened the door wider and motioned for them to come in. "Who's your designer?" he asked Shiafa. "You could be the toast of the garment district."

"I have some men I want you to meet," Michael said. "And when you've met these men, I'll need you to organize a rescue operation. Get together all the artists and musicians and writers you know. We'll need houses—hundreds of houses—and we'll need them in the next couple of days."

"Why?"

"Refugees," Michael said.

"Who am I going to meet?"

"Gustav Mahler and Wolfgang Amadeus Mozart," Michael answered.

Edgar smiled warily. "Napoleon, too? Maybe Christ?"

Michael shook his head. Edgar's smile vanished. "Jesus. Crooke said he'd dreamed about Mahler, just as if he were still alive." Edgar swallowed convulsively, and his hands fluttered. "The real McCoys?"

"And five thousand others."

"Brought back by the concerto and the symphony?"

"In a way. Are you up to it?"

Edgar glanced at the banks of electronic equipment and ran his fingers through his hair again. "Just one more question. Is the world coming to an end because of what we did?"

"No," Michael said.

"All right. I'm just wasting my time here anyway. Nobody's going to be making movies for some time. Who needs fantasy? The world's full of the real thing."

32

One thing at time. Michael had located Crooke sitting on a bench near the Griffith Park Observatory—simply sitting and staring out over the city. Griffith Park, Michael sensed, was full of hidden Sidhe. The police and National Guard had unofficially made it off-limits. Michael and Shiafa, working their discipline together, had penetrated makeshift barricades and driven up the winding road to the observatory, where they spoke with Crooke and persuaded him to come with them.

Moffat waited in his car in front of the Perrin house. Moffat and Crooke followed Michael up the steps and through the front door, held open by his father. Michael then introduced them to Mahler and Mozart. Crooke gaped.

"You did well," Mahler said to him. Mozart hung back, frowning. His frown changed to consternation when Moffat approached with an almost worshipful look on his face.

"You *are* Mozart," Moffat said. "Everybody said the portraits were bad, but I recognize you. I know you through your music."

"Well," Mozart said, still edging away. He shook Moffat's hand quickly. "All this. What is it for?"

"You came back with how many, again?" Crooke asked. Michael had given him a brief explanation in the car.

"Five thousand, approximately."

Crooke took Moffat aside, and they conferred for a few minutes. When they returned, Moffat said, "I think this is a job for Mrs. Pierce-Fennady."

Crooke agreed. "She raises money for the Huntington. She knows lots of people."

"We'll introduce her to Mahler and Mozart."

"*Mein Gott,*" Mozart moaned. "Society women!"

"She's much more than that," Crooke said. "She's a real mover and shaker."

"Does she keep her rooms warm?" Mozart asked, but he did not explain what he meant.

One thing at a time.

"I'm leaving now," Michael said. "Shiafa's going with me. We may or may not be back soon."

"What are you going to do?" Ruth asked, her face pale. She kept glancing at Shiafa with anything but approval.

"I'm not sure," Michael said.

You are what you dare.

Dusk formed a wall of fire above the treetops. The air was cool and sharp, electric. As Michael and Shiafa approached the Clarkham house on foot, he saw little streaks of darkness shoot inches above the black grass of the nearby lawns. Roses in a well-tended garden glowed in unnaturally bright pinks and blood-reds.

The two-story Clarkham house seemed covered by a shadow darker than the evening around it. Michael edged the door open slowly. Behind him, Shiafa kept her eyes on his back, as if willing him to do something. He could feel her attention, but he could not riddle her thoughts. Still, he felt he might need her; his own magic might not be strong enough for what lay ahead.

And if he resorted to using her buried power one more time . . . What then? What commitment would he feel, and what would she demand in return?

He ignored the stairs and looked through the service porch and kitchen for the doorway he knew must exist. Shiafa sensed the unspoken object of his search; she summoned him to the back of a walk-in pantry and pointed to a small door sealed with an ancient brass padlock. Michael drew a small percentage of his strength from his center and melted the hasp, singeing the wood behind it. A small, ghostly curl of smoke rose and spread under the low ceiling. Shiafa breathed deeply. He glanced at her and turned away quickly. Her face glowed like the moon in the dark confines of the pantry.

The door opened easily and silently. He descended the narrow steps after asking Shiafa to remain above. The basement spread under the length and breadth of the house, broken only by dark outlines of vats and racks and large square supporting beams.

In one corner, a large Archimedean screw nestled at the bottom of a metal trough—a grape crusher. Wooden boxes in the opposite corner held the dried and dusty remains of crushed grapes and their stems—looking not unlike Tommy. Michael peered closer at the remains and saw a faint rainbow-hematite-oil sheen hovering about them.

"Vintage," he murmured. Their smell was sweeter than any grapes he remembered, as sweet as the perfume he had exuded in the Realm whenever he had come in contact with water, or the fragrance of the manuscript of Opus 45.

The racks were empty of bottles. He searched the corners of the cellar meticulously and found no evidence of hidden caches. The cellar had not been used for some time—perhaps fifty years.

There was no choice but to return to the Waltiri house and disturb the birds—the Cledar—again.

Shiafa blocked him at the top of the stairs. Her face was a cool, mellow beacon, lovely in the darkness. Her lips parted expectantly, the teeth behind them like white mother-of-pearl. Her red hair spread like feathers around her head, loose and fragrant. "Nothing?" she asked.

He shook his head, regarding her steadily.

"We can join to search," she suggested.

"I don't think that's a good idea."

"You've taken my power from me once already," she said. "It's not as if we'll be doing anything unfamiliar. Isn't that why you brought me with you?"

He nodded. "It is. But I don't need help just now."

"Perhaps I need yours," she said.

Kristine suddenly seemed far away and not very well-suited to be the partner of a mage. How could he live with a purely human woman, who had no idea of his problems and abilities?

Michael took another step up, and Shiafa backed out of his way reluctantly. "I know where we—I need to go," he said. She followed him out of the house.

In the darkness, the leaves on the trees sparkled like crystals. Stars overhead wobbled almost imperceptibly. The cold had intensified and chilled him even with his *hyloka* in effect. Reality was becoming most inhospitable—why? Because of the weight of the Realm's demise? Or by plan . . . Tarax's plan, or Clarkham's?

Even from a distance of half a block, Waltiri's house radiated an aura of life and energy. It seemed filled with anticipation and joy. Michael's spirits took an abrupt upswing as he approached, and Shiafa seemed less enchanting and menacing. He removed the key from his pocket on the front step and opened the door.

"Life for you is opening doors," said the mage of the Cledar, who stood surrounded by pigeons and swallows in the hallway. His white-rimmed eyes flashed at Michael with an inhuman but not unwelcome (and not unfamiliar) humor. Michael could feel the connection clearly now. This creature had once been part of Arno Waltiri, a buried but considerable part.

Shiafa chose to remain outside, standing in the chill night air at the end of the front walk. Michael did not think about her now. He walked through the birds, who parted without complaint, to the service porch.

The birds had not occupied the basement. The armoire had not been disturbed since it had been emptied of its papers, months before. All that remained were a few odds and ends—stone paperweights, an andiron in one corner, and at the bottom of the armoire, the little rack of three wine bottles, each bearing the label, "Doppelsonnenuhr, Feinste Geistenbeerenauslese, 1921."

Drink me, Alice.

He sensed the Cledar mage's presence above him, waiting patiently for his decision, tendering neither judgment nor advice. Full of life, full of joy. *They feel something beyond the edge of harsh, sickened reality, beyond the razor cold and the night.*

They feel me.

They trust me.

If this wine did indeed take him to Clarkham's hidden experimental reality, his embryonic attempt to replace this world with another, then it was likely Kristine would be there, or accessible once he was there. His agreement with

Tarax would be unnecessary. Michael had never been comfortable with Shiafa; now he felt a kind of dread at the thought of her. She could demand so much of him, and he did not know if he could resist. Easy paths to—

What? Damnation?

Away from Kristine, at the very least.

Away from honor and self-trust. Michael could feel the tiny Sidhe part of him struggling to go to Shiafa and unite with her.

The easy path, finally offered—similar to the path Clarkham might have taken. And Clarkham was filled with ever-regenerating evil. There were so many things Michael did not know, so many things he had to puzzle out for himself . . .

And still, he had made it this far.

He removed a bottle of wine from the rack and examined it in the cellar's dim light. The cork had disintegrated beneath the lead cap, and the wine inside had long since dried to black paste. Putting the first bottle aside, he lifted the second; liquid still shimmered within.

His father had taught him something about wines; he did not shake it nor in any other way disturb the sediment cast off to the side of the reclining bottle. Sediment could take days to settle out again. Spoil the purity.

The contents were a deep, rich green-brown through the green glass, as clear and suggestive as the depths of a gemstone. All summer and winter caught in a swallow, fogs and soil, earth and sky and sun, distillations of time and reality. A core-sample of a universe, not the cultural universe of books and music and art, but of the world itself as shaped by humans.

Oenology. The one art the Sidhe would almost certainly ignore. The one art the Sidhe had not passed on to the re-evolved humans.

His respect for Clarkham grew. *Never underestimate your enemies.* He took his knife from his pocket and contemplated removing the lead wrapping, but found himself paralyzed with indecision. Drink it here, or elsewhere? Share it with Shiafa? That idea particularly disturbed him.

Swallowing this vintage might do more than transport. It might teach, give clues. He did not want Tarax's daughter to be more powerful than he was.

He pushed the knife blade into the foil around the lip of the bottle. Pulling the lead and impressed wax away, he unfolded the corkscrew from the base of his knife and pushed the tip into the dark cork. The cork seemed brittle. The screw finally found purchase, and he twisted the knife handle. With less dexterity than he might have wished, holding the bottle between his knees and glancing up the stairs to see that nobody was watching, he pulled the cork free of the neck.

The base of the cork showed a dark reddish-purple glaze. He sniffed the cork and smiled—his father's ritual—and then smelled the open bottle. The odor was not strong; it reminded him more of dust than flowers or fruit. Should he let it breathe for a while for maximum effect? How fastidious should one be, uncorking a wine between worlds?

He lifted the bottle to his lips. In other circumstances, he might take days to make this decision and follow every little precaution—including his father's wine rituals.

The liquid met his lower lip, cool and slick. It spilled across his tongue in a thin dribble, and he swirled the small amount of wine across his palate and over the full surface of his tongue.

His eyes widened.

With a barely controlled gag, he spit the wine out onto the dusty floor and wiped his lips hastily. Sour and bitter. He held the cork up to the light; brittle and crumbling. The wine had turned.

But even so—

For a moment, he felt his skin warm and his hair stand on end. The basement's outlines seemed to change. With a blink, the effect vanished. He might have imagined everything.

Michael recorked the bad bottle. The wine the Dopsos had served had been very good but certainly not a wine of power. Perhaps he was on the wrong track after all. Or Clarkham had reserved the finest bottles for his own use, giving the Waltiris only *vin ordinaire.*

He returned the corked bottle to the rack and removed the last. This one seemed dustier, less clear behind the glass. The sediment lay thick within, covering almost a quarter of the bottle's circumference. He removed the foil and the cork and lifted the bottle to his nose. Eyes closed, he inhaled.

When he opened his eyes again, the light bulb sang like an insect. The walls flexed outward. He smelled the sweetness deep in his nose and all down his throat, into his stomach and down into the center of his being. His eyes felt encrusted with rainbows. Curiously, he examined the cork's bottom and saw that the varnished darkness there was absolute.

He took a swallow from the bottle.

The sweetness was that of a season—late summer.

The tickle in his nose hit like a burst of sunlight, drawing him closer to a sneeze.

The rounded, almost oily sensation was a distant lake slowly rippling under hazy sun. In the lake, the Serpent wallowed. In the Serpent's memories, a mix of dangers and opportunities.

The smell of distant raspberries: a vine on a trellis in a garden with no guardian, no Tristesse to menace and frighten. The way is open.

Choose.

From a multitude of possible places to go.

The wine was not a passkey to a distinct world. It was

as he had barely suspected

a skeleton key

Clarkham being far more powerful than Waltiri or even the mage of the Cledar, and in his own way far more subtle, an instigator of unrest and trouble and a prompter of actions

a skeleton key to the dozens of worlds or more that Clarkham had created; an open invitation, for the wine would not have been left here had Clarkham wished otherwise; a challenge—*find me in my creations*

Michael saw the Isomage's house as a kind of skeleton on a background the shade of the cork's varnished bottom. He also saw the pleasure dome and the house in Los Angeles. These were the shadows of Clarkham's creations, no longer

accessible. The taste of the wine continued to quietly massage his tongue, revealing layer after layer of finish.

Here was the primitive, stark world in which Michael had been imprisoned.
Beyond it was something more complex but difficult to distinguish; the taste
seemed muddy. At another level, Michael saw a city stretching across a valley, a
sprawled and sunny place . . . not unlike Los Angeles in the 1930s and 1940s, he
realized. The Hollywood hills and Griffith Park seemed to stand out, as well as
the large barn-like studios and great stretches of empty fields where more of the
city would lie in Michael's time. A derivative creation.

He probed that world and felt his energies spread from end to end of the
tiny creation, barely twenty miles wide. The world felt empty; like Michael's
former prison, it contained only pale shadows, architectural mannequins indicating where people might be.

The next layer of taste unfolded across his tongue. He saw a field of yellow
grass with an intensely blue, almost purple sky rising above the field and the low
golden hills beyond.

David Clarkham stood under the hot sun in the field. He appeared younger—
in his thirties perhaps—with thick brown hair and a wide mustache. His face
was narrow with a narrow hawk nose and high cheekbones, and his eyes were
languorous, relaxed. His lips curved in a faintly bemused smile. Michael swallowed the wine and felt the grass part around his solidifying body. His shoes sank
into the dirt as he took on substance.

"Hello," the young Clarkham said.

Michael shaded his eyes against the glare and built up all of his *hyloka* for a
defensive surge. But Clarkham's assault did not come. Michael probed quickly,
and Clarkham allowed him to sample his reality and character before blocking.

It was indeed Clarkham, but not quite real and not quite a shadow; this
Clarkham was almost as much a creation as the prairie around them. Even so,
behind the image lay the merest hint of Clarkham's inescapable foulness.

"Hello," Michael replied, feeling the sweat start out on his brow. The sun
glared, almost unbearably hot. Clarkham, dressed in a dark corduroy suit with a
white linen shirt, appeared to mimic a Western pioneer. He wore scuffed leather
boots, cuffs pulled down over them.

"I'm surprised," Clarkham said, hitching his thumbs in the pockets of his
coat. "You're much more resourceful than I thought. More powerful, too."

"I'm looking for Kristine," Michael said.

"She's not here. I can't return her to you. I took her for just such an eventuality."

"Why? That's the only reason I'm here." Michael realized the shallowness of
that particular untruth; and yet, as he said it, he believed it. Part of him would
have forgiven all, just to have the Earth return to normal and Kristine back.

Clarkham's smile broadened. "You have no other ambitions, after making it
this far? Surely you've faced . . . let's call them opportunities, if not temptations?"

Normality was as impossible now as a peaceful settlement of the disputes
between them. Michael could not have a normal life; Clarkham had never had
one. Michael threw aside that especially tenuous shadow-self's wish and faced

Clarkham on his own terms. Nothing visible had changed between them, but Michael's new stance was apparent to Clarkham immediately.

"That's more like it," the ex-Isomage said. "More honest."

"I didn't want to become a mage," Michael said softly.

"I did. I've been working through my apprenticeship, or whatever it should be called, for centuries longer than you've been alive. Your interference is unsettling and unwelcome. You've caused me much grief."

The magnitude of grief caused by the Sidhe-human conflicts was beyond Michael's ability to describe. All of human history . . . He shrugged.

"Your maturity is a sometime thing, weak at best," Clarkham said. "Still, you don't seem unreasonable. And your ambition isn't nearly as strong as mine. Perhaps we can discuss things, and you can realize how hopeless your prospects really are and how much harm you might cause if you try to fight both Tarax and me."

"All right," Michael said.

"We're in one of my test environments," Clarkham explained. "Like an artist's sketch. It's part of my larger world. It's quite accomplished, I think. It has firm roots and mimics most of the complexity of our birth universe. It is not nearly so large, of course."

"Is it complete?" Michael asked.

"No," Clarkham admitted. "Come with me. We'll find a cool place."

They walked over the fields. Michael felt the quality and density of this test-world with the palms of his hands. It was indeed fine, almost indistinguishable from Earth. He could not do something this powerful and real—not yet, perhaps not ever.

Yet he itched to try. The part of himself that aspired to be a mage—the ultimate poet, creator of worlds—was impressed but not overawed.

In a depression within the prairie lay a small town hammered together from gray planks and splintered posts. On one side of the single dirt street was a barber shop, a saloon and a hotel, on the other a gun shop and a feed and general store, all deserted. Michael stretched his mental fingers wide, searching for the facts in this world he might need to know, and he curled those fingers back empty. This world was a test case, finely wrought, but not profound.

Derivative. For the first time since he had swallowed the wine, Michael smiled. Clarkham saw the edge of that smile, and his face became thinner, nose sharper, cheeks paler.

They walked the deserted dirt street, and Clarkham held open the swinging doors to the saloon. Michael passed through into welcome, cool shadow. Clarkham pulled out a seat at a rickety round table and Michael sat.

"This is all I have," Clarkham said, indicating with his arms the room and the world beyond, and not just one world, but the others Michael could still feel at the back of his palate. "You helped remove the rest from me. I cannot return to Earth now. Not in person, not physically."

Michael thought of the footprints on the dusty floor. *Whose, then? A Sidhe—perhaps Tarax himself, or Biri—clearing out Clarkham's gate to the Realm, disposing of Lamia and Tristesse—carrying them to the Tippett Hotel . . . Leaving them there as a warning to the Ban, perhaps, that humans must not cross there . . .*

Would he ever know? Probably not.

"I could not go to the Realm, but now that's dead too, and soon the Earth with it, no? So no regrets. You've taken nothing from me I didn't deserve to lose. Complacency is a mage's worst enemy. Complacency and lack of vigilance."

"The Earth is dying?" Michael asked, feeling like a child again, asking questions of a teacher. *The role he wishes upon me. Power lies in placing others in their weakest postures.*

"Tarax didn't do a very good job of bringing his ship up on the reef, did he? Pushed out the captain and then couldn't navigate. He forgot to toss away the unnecessary, the deadly cargo—the underpinnings of the Realm. Chaos, the mist of creation. Now they pollute the Earth. Soon anything will be possible. When anything is possible, nothing is real. Might as well spill turpentine onto a fresh oil painting." Clarkham sat across the table from Michael and folded his arms, looking strong and young and satisfied, his face dark in the saloon's cool gloom. "His qualifications to be the mage of the new Earth seem weaker to all of us day by day. Perhaps even to himself."

"All of us?"

"The Serpent still dreams. And who can say there aren't others? Less obvious candidates even than you. And you have moments when you don't even want to be a mage." His smile was perfectly candid and friendly. "The contest must be decided soon. We all have loyalties to our people, and without the people, what use is a world? Like Adonna, I once considered populating my own worlds, but . . ." He sighed. "You've seen the results. By the way, how did you escape? Mine was a particularly nasty trap."

Michael saw no reason for lies. "Tarax released me."

"On what condition?"

"I would train his daughter, and he would tell me where you've hidden Kristine."

Clarkham's smile broadened. "Interesting. The Law of Mages. No candidate shall harm a fellow candidate or lessen his chances. But as you see, I don't necessarily follow those rules. Tarax's daughter—a Sidhe? I seem to recall his woman was a pure Sidhe. Adonna made the same mistake." He leaned forward and put his elbows on the table. "Thirsty?"

Michael shook his head. He did not want the taste of the wine diluted or washed away. "Why is it a mistake?"

"It *can* be a great mistake for a mage. If you choose not to be a mage—if you sensibly decline this position you've half unwittingly put yourself in—then there is no threat. But I tell too much. You are still my enemy."

Michael nodded. "Yes," he said. "You killed Tommy."

"He killed himself. All too easy a death. Do you know humans, Michael? You think you are one of them. You are, mostly. But you don't know them. Have you followed your history lessons, read the newspapers? We are not fighting in order to serve an exalted race, Michael. We strive to serve animals . . . unprincipled, cruel, blind and willful. When the Sidhe last left Earth for the Realm, humans were already on their merry path to making it unlivable even for themselves. Now they have the power to destroy everyone.

"Humans are willful and blind. They do not appreciate. They look upon those possessed by genius and chew them over and spit them out. Artists and poets are just so many . . ." Clarkham's face paled again. He brought color back with another broad smile. "Their scientists have the upper hand. Taming a garden gone to seed."

"The Sidhe tried to take magic away from us," Michael said. "Without magic, we could only learn how to use the world. The scientists have made us strong."

"*Us?*" Clarkham mimicked incredulously. "You rank yourself with the scientists?"

"I hope to," Michael said.

"A candidate mage condoning the worship of a corrupt and runaway world. Amazing how far humans have fallen."

Michael suddenly felt a surge of boredom. He pushed it aside lest it dull his apprehension and sense of peril. "You are about to try to strike a deal with me," he said.

"I am?" Clarkham feigned surprise.

"You are," Michael said, the insane self-assurance coming to the fore again. *So much to keep in balance.*

"It might not be the deal you imagine. Your talent is strong but undeveloped. We could help each other. Alone, I can create a suitable world . . . But together, the three of us can control Tarax's ambitions and create a new Earth for all the races, or as many as will accept us."

"Three?"

"You have a certain attraction to Tarax's daughter. Her power can be useful if handled properly. And I can keep the worst from happening between the two of you, once you merge." His eyes seemed to cloud. "Euphemisms. Once she seduces you, or you her."

What he had felt in Shiafa . . . Tonn's wife on the Blasted Plain. Connected. Horribly connected. Those who aspire to become mages . . .

"What about her loyalty to Tarax?"

"I doubt she feels any *loyalty.*"

Michael glanced down at the worn-smooth table top. "What kind of world would you make for all the races?"

"World-building is relatively easy," Clarkham said. "It's control of the world's inhabitants that causes trouble. Humans are especially difficult. They would likely start tinkering with the very foundations, unless they're kept tightly reined in. Sidhe might be more manageable. At least the Sidhe have a sense of their limits."

"How would you control them?"

"Rigidly," Clarkham said, eyes narrowing. "They have opposed me. They must never be that strong or willful again."

"Isn't there any other way?"

Clarkham shook his head slowly. "If you think otherwise, you're being foolish. Human history, Michael. Wars and exterminations and crimes and cruelty. Distorted minds and distorted societies. I doubt you have any idea of the depth of depravity humans are capable of."

"The Sidhe are responsible for many of our problems."

"Probably," Clarkham conceded. "But the roots are still there The Sidhe merely tried to train the branches. And whoever caused the problems—as mage, I still have to solve them. Rigorous weeding and trimming. Could you face up to that?"

Michael pushed his chair away from the table. The wine's finish was losing definition. "If I cooperate and bring Shiafa's power to you, will you free Kristine?"

Clarkham made a magnanimous swing of one hand. "She is of no use to me except as a means to control you. I certainly do not lust after her."

"Nobody implied that you did," Michael said.

Clarkham stood and leaned across the table on his extended arms, fingers splayed against the dark wood. "Do not try to join this conflict, unless you join on my side. You have certain abilities but no sophistication. You do not know the potentials. Whatever you do, you must not oppose me. I've taken your measure, Michael Perrin. I know your weaknesses."

Michael nodded agreeably.

"We cannot afford the virtues of patience and kindness and honor," Clarkham continued, his eyes contemplating the distances beyond Michael. "If we are to be mages, that is."

Michael's palms tingled. He lifted one hand as if to rub his nose and saw a pearly excrescence on his palm. "You've always wanted to be a mage, haven't you?" he asked.

"Yes."

"I didn't," Michael said. "I've never really had a choice." That much had become quite clear to him. He rubbed his tongue against the back of his palate, drawing forth saliva to further dilute the taste of the wine.

"Consider my offer seriously. The alternatives are not pleasant," Clarkham said.

The saloon darkened, and the walls of the basement returned. The bottle lay spilled on the floor, where it had slipped out of his hands. Michael bent to pick up the cork and reinsert it, but there was no liquid left.

When he straightened, he saw a spot of color on the opposite wall. The wall itself seemed intensely grainy, detailed, every speck and shadow of it clear. Michael squinted, and the spot of color resolved itself into a sleeved arm and hand. As his eyes swept up the arm, he seemed to paint with his gaze a flat figure on the wall, dressed in white garments that partook, in their transparency, of some of the wall's concrete gray. Still flat but now complete, the figure's face became animated. Michael backed away; he dimly recognized the Sidhe.

"You must think your house very full," the Sidhe whispered, his voice a mere vibration of the wall.

"Tonn," Michael breathed.

"I had hoped to bring you more, but even a mage cannot survive the forces I've faced. This is a very weak shadow to bring you, a weak bequest . . ." The figure smiled and seemed with that expression to almost lift from the concrete. Michael pressed close to the stair rail.

"You cannot best the Isomage without far greater knowledge than you currently possess. There is only one place for you to gain this knowledge . . . the Serpent. This shadow cannot convey it to you. Adonna favored you for some time; you sensed that? You hold much promise, and the others . . . well, Adonna had reasons for being less fond of them. You must take what the Serpent has; he will not give it to you without his own freight of past evil. But take it you can, if you are careful, without breaking the Law of Mages. You must act soon . . . This is the last shadow the Realm can conjure. There is no forest with wood enough to contain a mage."

The shadow of Tonn faded until nothing but the grainy wall remained.

Michael swallowed. *Will I ever become as insubstantial as that?*

33

On the first floor, Michael knelt before the mage of the Cledar. The bird regarded him straight on, drawing his milky nictitating membrane over white-rimmed eyes.

"You brought me into this," Michael said, half-accusing.

The bird abandoned spoken words, communicating with Michael by *evisa. Better to be a part of change than to simply stand aside and react.*

"How much of Waltiri were you?"

Enough to love Golda. This war has made strange demands on us all.

"Did you know Tonn's shadow was here?"

Yes.

"Were you cooperating with him all along?"

Our goals evolved in the same direction, separately.

"And why are you waiting here?"

For the end, or for you to fulfill your promise.

Michael stood and shook his head slowly. "I'm not the boy you lured into Clarkham's house. I've lost so many selves since then, I hardly know who I am."

That is the curse of a leader.

"I've never been a leader," Michael said softly. His eyes misted over, and he looked around the living room, filled with birds of all kinds, from large white owls and red-tailed hawks to pigeons and sparrows "You're much younger than the Serpent," Michael said. "Are you as old as Tonn?"

Older, now.

"The writing on your wings . . . the terms of your curse?"

The mage of a race must wear its shackles.

Michael nodded, lips drawn together ruefully. "How long will the curse last?"

Until we again have faces. The bird opened its beak and cocked its head to one side. *The Serpent will soon be released. Tonn's death and the end of continuity among the Sidhe mages will break his bonds. Those who were born in their present forms, however, will not be released. None of my people will be released.*

"The cockroaches won't rise up to become Urges, and the Spryggla will not drown at sea . . ." Michael mused, smiling at his vision of the apocalypse avoided.

Be warned about the Serpent.

"I'm warned."

And accept my apologies.

"I'll consider it," Michael said. "One last question. Is Shiafa a danger to me?"

Either mortal danger, fatal diversion, or ultimate boon. Her fate is in your hands.

"I've been led to believe it's the other way around."

You can change. She cannot.

"Tonn's wife . . ."

Adonna was a failure. His cruelties tainted all he did.

Michael could not decide how to say good-bye to the mage of the birds, so he simply turned and walked out the front door. Shiafa sat cross-legged on the lawn, surrounded by grass green-black and jewel-like under the bright nacreous morning sun. She watched him closely as he locked the door.

"How long was I in there?" he asked, blinking in the daylight.

"I am not well-acquainted with time," Shiafa replied.

"You and I are going to have to talk," Michael said. "But first, we're traveling."

"Where?"

"To meet with the Serpent Mage."

Fear and horror crossed her face, but she did not protest.

Michael drew aside a slice of air, revealing darkness and a spot of green, and beckoned Shiafa to pass through. She did, and he followed, closing the rent behind.

Night lay like a cold black ceramic bowl over the grass fields surrounding the loch. The water sat still and silent and practically invisible; without a probe of his surroundings, he would have hardly known where the shore was. Deep in the lake, hundreds of feet below the surface and under a rocky overhang, the Serpent slumbered. Michael could not detect his Breed assistant anywhere.

"Do you feel him?" he asked Shiafa, a patch of dark gray in the obscurity.

"Yes," she said, voice unsteady. "He stole our souls . . ."

"Tit for tat," Michael said, not entirely stifling the upwelling of crass levity again plaguing him. *You do not know the perils . . . you do not feel the true danger.* The voice in his head was his own, a part of himself having assumed the role of Clarkham, the Serpent, and the mage of the Cledar all at once. "He's not going to hurt anybody now, least of all you."

"He makes me harm myself," Shiafa said. "What my people feel . . . anger and horror weaken us. We cannot draw from the center. We become like hunted animals in our minds."

Michael walked down to the shore and held out his hands. The pearly excrescence still covered one palm; he had been at some pains to hide it from Shiafa, even from the bird mage. He did not know precisely what it meant now, and what few clues he did have did not comfort him.

His function, he thought, was similar to that of an organ activated within a body during trauma. That would imply a connection between the worlds and their inhabitants that was completely beyond anything he had learned before, but it was not implausible. Perhaps even Clarkham knew such a "truth," if it could be called that.

At any rate, all questions of his own needs, his own decisions, might soon be swept completely away. In an emergency, his assignment might be predetermined, and if that was so, then very likely what remained of his individuality—all he had left to hold on to—would fall away like some bothersome hangnail.

He hoped to find a way to avoid that.

Kristine.

He held back the anger and impatience. *You must find her . . . soon . . .* But first, he must keep hold of a world to bring her back to.

I know your plans, Michael. The Serpent's words came out of the loch as clearly as if they were side by side. *You are Tonn's final revenge.*

Shiafa groaned softly, hearing the words in her own head. Her disgust was almost palpable.

"I have been told twice that I need what you have," Michael said. "You told me so yourself."

It can be yours.

"I don't think you ever seriously intended me to have it. You would have fashioned me into a weapon. That shows how little you understand, after all."

You could have had my heritage.

"I don't think you would have given me all of it. You didn't tell me your curse is soon done with."

The Serpent began a long, undulating rise to the surface. *You make your way between worlds, and around this one, as if you were a mage. Your candidacy was only in doubt because you spurned what you most need.*

"I'm a flower," Michael said. "I've had the relationship all wrong, all along. We don't make worlds. Worlds make us. Or both. Or neither. There is no priority. I am a rose put forth by a bush grown by a world. So were you, once. But you rotted. Your whole generation . . . all the Sidhe and humans of your time . . . just rotted."

If you want what I have, you should come swim with me.

Michael removed his shoes and shirt. He stepped down to the waterline in the tar-like darkness and hesitated. The water smelled of peat and age. Walking in up to his ankles, he considered the depth of the lake and how easy it would be for a body to be lost here forever—nibbled by the fish the Serpent fed upon, stripped until its tea-colored bones lay scattered on the silty bottom like so many pieces of broken crockery.

Come live the life I've lived. Maybe then you'll deserve to raid my memories.

The Serpent swam several hundred feet below the surface, its watery darkness no more profound than the clouded night over the loch. Michael dived into the water, pulling himself toward the middle with the strokes he had learned in gym class. The icy water tasted sour. He drew more heat from his center and kept on swimming until he dog-paddled directly above the Serpent.

My curse comes to an end soon. Adonna's last power fades, and the words he wrote on my belly fade. I'll stand beside the other candidates. No need for a feeble boy to carry on in my place.

Michael could feel the pressure of the Serpent's ascent beneath him. A harsh metal moon cast a weak gray light through a gap in the clouds and turned the water around him into shimmering mercury, rippling slowly around his stroking arms. "What in *hell* am I doing here?" Michael asked himself, spitting out water. The Serpent swam barely a hundred feet below him now, insinuating its coils through the murk. Sixty feet. Thirty. Twenty.

Michael took a deep breath and sank, letting the water close over his head. His eyes stung, but he forced them open and stared down. Ten feet. Five feet. With the few scattered photons of filtered moonlight, he made out an oblong shape, now stationary beneath him.

My world, the Serpent said. *Have you earned what you wish to take?*

No, Michael responded. *But I'll try anyway.* And if he succeeded, wouldn't he, too, be breaking the law of mages? Adonna's shadow had implied he would not, but that seemed most convenient.

He set aside the confusion. That law, doubtless, had been devised during times of prosperity and calm, when transitions of mages could be leisurely and honorable. Such excuses, at least, came easily to his mind. He was still a thief. And if it all turned out well in the end—would it justify what he was about to try?

Strong motivations. Even bravery.

The Serpent's head gave off its own light now. The small, clouded eyes and underslung scythe of a mouth, with two curves of tiny white teeth, were all too apparent. Michael felt as if his heart would stop. The Serpent could swallow him whole in a couple of bites, an act of topsy-turvy, turned-sidewise cannibalism . . . or simple survival.

Then it's a contest, the Serpent said. *You're worthy of a contest. See if you can take what you need.*

The Serpent broke the surface. Michael did likewise. At the same moment, the moon broke free of clouds and shed a rich, cold platinum light on the smooth loch. The beam drew a line down the Serpent's wake, and Michael saw its skin glittering with jewels and the fresh strong arms it used along with its tail and thickened fins to propel itself through the water.

"You really are part of the original sin, aren't you?" Michael accused, his voice echoing from the hills and rocks of the opposite shore. He realized what he was doing. Despite everything, he had come away from his first meeting with the Serpent intensely impressed. He was shedding those last bits of regard; what he had to try now, he could not in all conscience do to something—someone—he respected.

Michael swam to the shore. The Serpent followed, matching his pace, its blunt eel nose never more than three yards behind.

Michael stood in the shallows. The Serpent relaxed in the sand and mud, quiet. It lay a few yards from the shore. Again the moonlight dimmed.

Michael did not try to probe the Serpent's thoughts; what coiled and tensed within him could be given away by that.

My time has come around again, Michael Perrin. My face returns.

The Serpent humped and thrashed itself onto the pebbly beach. The moon glistened on its skin through random breaks in the black clouds. Michael's palms tingled furiously now, making his arms ache. Shiafa—

He touched her mind lightly. He still had not found sufficient strength within himself. Ashamed, he asked for her help—again—and felt a surge of sexual response, magical strength, intertwined. She did not know what to do with her power, but she knew what his "borrowing" meant. He could hardly avoid entanglement now.

She nearly had him.

The sadness that welled up in Michael was as painful as the feeling in his hands. *Kristine.*

Sixty million years of mixed sanity and madness, dreaming and plotting. The Serpent, whatever he had done, deserved this coming moment of freedom from the Sidhe curse—

Michael recognized the subtle wash of the Serpent's persuasion and blocked it. His emotions were being played with on more levels than he could watch. The Serpent's probes were incredibly subtle, undetected until now . . .

It knew the danger Michael presented.

Michael asked himself, *What in God's name are you*

The loch shore exploded, bushes and grass flaring for an instant into daylight brilliance, burning with a horrifying gasp of air that shook the waters and made them shrink back toward the center

Who did that

And the Serpent writhed on the shore, arms pulled from their grasp on the rocks, a face emerging from its carp-eyes and underslung, moon-shaped mouth, it is changing, now it has a face again, who is

The horror of my people carried in this (Shiafa)

mixing the fires, going out after such fury, the moon gone and the sky like a helmet

Uncoil. Lunge. Who is

Michael, not the Serpent, which seems stunned. Michael stands over it, the Serpent's thickness rising to above his waist, the face coming out and a handsome face, not very unlike that of a Sidhe, the first face of ur-human seen on Earth for sixty million years, brother to Sidhe one would think.

And within its mind Michael works his way rapidly, putting to work tools he did not know he had, tossing out the Serpent's personality and thieving from those reserves of knowledge he knew he would need. Unable to avoid some aspects of becoming the Serpent, for knowledge is the man (and becoming more entwined with Shiafa with every instant of his use of her powers) and breathless above the Serpent watching

Who flamed the bushes—diversion but by whom?

How many minds have I

The sixteen-year-old boy has shrunk to nothingness, leaving only a trail of memory

Shiafa is in his place

Lord, lord of my youth, wherever you have gone, whatever you may be unless you are just another stronger of us who aspire to make worlds I cannot ask your help this is not right but I need your help

The Serpent fought back suddenly, and Michael's head seemed to explode in fire as had the brush along the shore.

The flames crisped the letters of the Serpent's curse onto Michael's soul.

You have not earned any right to do this to me.

"Then give me what I need!" Michael cried out into the night. Shiafa shouted some of the words with him, a poorly slaved extension.

You would have us live with them, after what they did to us . . .

"An end to the war! And no revenge!"

Never.

But Michael learned from the Serpent, took what he needed. He saw the meaning of the excrescences on his palms and knew what he was. There had been many like him, sixty million years ago; with their passing, the world's unruliness had been practically guaranteed.

They had not been mages. They had served the mages that had created this world and many others (!) like it. They had been called makers. In the absence of the intricate organization that the Serpent remembered, Michael would have to be both maker and mage, craftsman and creator.

The Serpent struggled against him, kicking up the rocks. Several large stones struck Michael and Shiafa, drawing blood from his outstretched hand and forehead and doubling her over with a gasp, but he did not flinch.

Even as the transformation continued, the symbols on the Serpent's belly glowed with a new malevolence and with new life. Its sounds, as it rolled and flopped on the beach, knocking free some of its jeweled scales, were agonized beyond any pain caused by Michael.

More and more, the Serpent was returning to the form of Manus—the mage's name, sixty million years ago, before humans had lost their final battle with the Sidhe, and he had been made to carry the eternal burden of defeat.

Michael consumed its—his—memories as rapidly as he could, but they were fading and contorting horribly under his anchored probe. Manus writhed on the shore, steam rising from the letters on his dark, golden-colored skin. The jeweled scales all fell away, littering the beach like a spilled chest of treasure.

The mage now had two arms and two legs. His tail had diminished to a black nubbin at the base of his spine. With a moan, he turned over on his back. His face was once again completely human—but blank.

Michael's probe searched through a vast, empty cavern.

"Nothing," Michael gasped, rising to his knees. He felt a wave of nausea, his exhaustion little short of insensibility. "Where did he go?"

Shiafa backed away from the water and the combatants on her hands and knees, crab-wise. "He's there." She pointed with one long finger at the body barely visible near the quivering water.

"There's nothing in his memory."

The one-time Serpent Mage stared up at the sky, face as blank as a corpse's, chest heaving and hands clenching and relaxing. He made small mewling sounds and writhed feebly on the pebbles. The moon reflected from the mage's eyes, as flat and dull as the eyes of an old dead fish, as empty of thought as a snake's. The letters marked by the Sidhe millions of years past lay like gold-encrusted welts on his stomach.

Using the knowledge he had stolen, Michael could read them now and could see how they had changed as the Serpent's form had changed.

For as long as the Sidhe know darkness, what is within, without. That had been the curse marked by the Sidhe mage, sixty million years past. But a new line had appeared.

What is without, within.

Michael crawled close to the mage, reaching out to touch him. The flesh was warm. He appeared to be in healthy middle age, though the subtle differences in his features precluded accurate judgment.

Michael felt the presence of an opening gateway and saw the mage's assistant run toward them. Dawn was a blue patch to the east. The Breed woman stood in vague silhouette against that blueness, between her master and the loch's still waters, and knelt on the pebbles. She touched him, her hand just inches from Michael's.

Then she turned her eyes to Michael, squinting to see him more sharply in the half-darkness of the moon and infant day. "You are not him," she said flatly. "You've come back, but you are not him."

Michael was too sick and tired to answer. He pulled back from the naked man and lay beside Shiafa, with whom he felt an intense connectedness, not love or lust or even need, but something *a priori*. They lay pressed against each other on the rocks, waiting for the sun to warm them.

The mage's assistant could have done anything to them then; they were as helpless as beached jellyfish. But she simply crouched with her hand resting on the mage's stomach, near the letters that glittered with a light of their own. Slowly, she drew back her fingers into a fist, raised the fist as if to strike something, anything, and then stood. "So long," she said. Michael wondered vaguely if she were leaving.

"I've been with him, off and on, for a thousand years," she continued. "He waited for this day, when Tonn's death and the confusion would free him."

"What's wrong with him?" Michael croaked. "I did nothing that would have . . . left him like this."

" 'What is without, within,' " she quoted. "For sixty million years, he had a man's mind confined in the body of a serpent. *Blessed* Adonna," she croaked, her words thick with sarcasm. "Blessed, forgiving mage of the Sidhe. One curse was not enough. Now that the first has ended, he's made a second by twisting the words. The mage has a man's body—"

Manus rolled over and stared blankly at Michael and then at his assistant, eyes as shallow as road scum after a light rain. He opened his mouth and made a noise like air escaping a balloon.

"—and the mind of a serpent," she finished, nudging him lightly with a toe. Manus recoiled. "Adonna has finished with him. What do you have?"

"I'm sorry," Michael said, feeling a wash of distant horror, as if an inner crowd screamed through a thick stone wall. "I don't know what you mean."

"Did he lose it all, then?" the Breed asked. "All his knowledge, all his thoughts?"

Michael closed his eyes and followed a trail of light through the darkness behind his eyes. Once, he had been a boy and had lived in a boy's body, with a boy's mind, like a very small but well-made cottage.

The boy was gone, and the man who replaced him lived in a palace, crumbling and crooked but magnificent beyond description and filled with mysteries. It would take him years to explore that palace and learn all its passageways and perils.

"No," the Breed said, standing over him. "You did the mage a favor. He didn't even know. You've taken from him and preserved. Now what will you do with what you've stolen?" She turned to Shiafa. "So the whole sad chronicle starts again." She shook her head vigorously, hair flying out against the gray sky, and marched back to the rent in the air. She lifted her leg and hopped through, drawing the ripped edges together after her.

Manus rotated his head to stare at the gray, stone-like sky above them, his human jaw opening and closing rhythmically, his human legs twitching.

Michael managed to pull some strength from his *hyloka* and got to his feet, then helped Shiafa to stand beside him.

"You have his knowledge?" she asked, eyes feverishly bright.

Michael nodded. "Some of it." He felt a sob coming and could not stop it; the sound shook him once, violently, and he hiccoughed it back, covering his lower face with one hand. Some seconds later, in control again, he removed his hand from his mouth and said, "I don't even know how I took it."

His head filled with voices, all unfamiliar. He stumbled over an image of the mage's youth, when the child Manus had wandered through a grove on old Earth, surrounded by huge trees beside which sequoias were puny—trees of no shape Michael had ever seen, with trunks like rubbed ivory and leaves as translucent as glass.

Tumbling after this came memories of the meeting with the last serious human candidate. Manus had used all his remaining powers to cast a shadow, appearing to the Nazarene on a rocky hill in Judea, almost two thousand years before.

Michael saw the face of Christ, strong and fine-boned, eyes black but hair brown almost to red, his eyes drawing almost all attention away from the body, which was broad-shouldered and of medium height.

Michael held his hand over his face, squeezing his temples and nose, and saw Elme and Aske and the garden where their children had played—and the infant Crane Women, grandchildren of Adonna, dancing around the bejeweled Serpent, while Adonna himself played the larger game of godhood among the mountains of Ararat and across the river plains of the Tigris and Euphrates.

And then Michael saw the position above all worlds, where those who would seriously make worlds must stand. The place called Null.

The tears returned to Michael's eyes. Now that he had part of the mage within him, he could assess the truth of Manus's long, tortured life . . .

And he could feel the emotions that had stayed alive within the mage for sixty million years—the horror and rage at what had happened to his people, the dismay at how what had once been paradise had decayed into factional fighting and self-destruction.

None had deserved what had been visited upon them.

The giants of those past ages had been as powerless as children against circumstance.

The depth of Michael's pretense could not be judged. Still, it was far too late to take another course. Adonna had removed a potential rival from the contest; Michael had not broken the law of mages, for Manus had never truly been a candidate; the curse would obviously have prevented that.

Now there remained only Tarax, Clarkham and Michael. And at last Michael had most of the expertise he needed to begin applying his talents with some small hope of success.

"I know where we should go next," he said. Already, he thought of Shiafa as a part of him, practically inseparable.

"To battle my father," Shiafa said.

The vacant Manus tried to rock back and forth. Michael pressed his hand to the mage's forehead. Applying Manus's own knowledge, he brought to an end the life of the world's oldest living creature, the last of the first race of humans. The mage's eyes clouded; the last faint gleam of awareness went out of them. Michael lowered the corpse's eyelids with two fingers.

"No," Michael said, "not to fight Tarax."

Shiafa seemed almost disappointed. "To find Kristine?" she asked hesitantly. *Kristine.*

He shook his head. A far voice said, *One step at a time,* and he hardly recognized it.

Michael held out his hand and she grasped it. Something not entirely pleasant passed between them. Manus's memories now told him specifically what would happen if he stayed with Shiafa much longer, but for the moment, he still needed her power.

34

No need to return to Los Angeles. To Michael, all places on Earth were pretty much alike now; all places offered equal opportunities for entry to Null, and that was the next step he must take.

A mage or maker could, not create mature worlds within worlds already established. He wondered that this had not been obvious to him sooner; young worlds contradicted old in fundamental ways and could not thrive when bound by the *a priori* rules. The nacreous globes that had extruded from his hands had been suppressed by his location, not stillborn because of his inexperience. He wondered, then, that Clarkham had made as much progress as he had—for he was certain the Isomage had never been to Null.

Had the possibility been made clear to him, Michael realized through Manus's knowledge, at age two or three he could have functioned as a maker and spun tiny infant worlds, toy worlds as it were. What potentials lay buried in humankind; what potentials might be released now that the altered Earth suggested so much?

They buried the mage Manus in the hills beyond the lake, under a crisp copper-green sky shot with ribbons of cloud. Shiafa helped him move the body without a sign of her previous fear and disgust.

When that was done, Michael stood on a hill overlooking the loch. Shiafa stood beside him, glancing at him now and then uncertainly, hopefully.

"You are no longer Tarax's," Michael said finally.

"No," she admitted.

"You cannot serve him now."

She shook her head.

"Do you know why he sent you to me?"

"To be a trap," she replied, eyes narrowing as if in anticipation of a blow to the face.

"How many curses were exchanged during the War?" Michael mused. "Overt curses, hidden curses, curses doubling back on each other. How clever in their cruelties our ancestors were. But this curse . . . That Sidhe men and women can be the destruction of each other. Did you know this?"

"No."

"If I become a mage after taking a Sidhe mate," Michael said, "the Sidhe part of me, however small, will assert itself. I will become obsessed with my mate, bury myself in her, adore her until all my powers are drained. We will eat each other alive. And yet to have the power necessary to make the highest sorceries, I need to draw power from a woman. Sidhe women carry the magic. And because I have Sidhe in me, I cannot become a mage of humans alone . . .

"I must love, and steal, and then . . . I must escape. And I will not escape unless my mate is transformed, otherwise I will continue to be held by her. The second part of the initiation. First, you kill your favorite horse . . . then, kill or transform your mate." Michael shuddered. "Females don't know this?"

"I did not."

"The Ban of Hours knew. This is what it takes to be a mage among the Sidhe. Since I have Sidhe blood, I could be trapped. Tarax took his chances. Your father."

Shiafa was shivering. "You do not have all my power," she said.

"I haven't tried to take it all at once, only to borrow it. The more I borrow, the more I need. But I can't take any more without mating."

"Use the Serpent's power. Leave me here."

"I took no power from the mage. What little he had left, I've already exceeded. His other powers were blunted at the end of the War, when he was cursed."

"But you have to leave me—"

"I can't," Michael said. "If I face Tarax in Null, just as I am, I will lose, and all my people will suffer. I can probably defeat Clarkham, who acquired his magic in other ways. But not Tarax."

Shiafa sat on the grass. Her shivering had progressed almost to the point of convulsions. Michael touched the top of her head. "Do you hate me?"

She shook her head, a motion barely distinguishable from her shivering.

"Draw from the center," Michael suggested.

"There's *nothing* at my center," she countered. "I'm as empty as a gourd. I've never been anything. Not to myself."

"What do you want to be?" he asked.

The question seemed to calm her. "A fine lady of the Sidhe. I don't want powers or importance. I reject the courts and councils. I reject my father's goals. I would take all of that and give it away . . . to you, if you need it . . . But it won't be given away. It sticks with me. I can't give, and it is useless within me, and if you take it, it destroys both of us."

Michael sat beside her. "What does a fine lady of the Sidhe do?" he asked.

"I imagine my mother was a fine lady. She worked hand in hand with her mate and—she was gone. I never knew what happened to her. Ideally, a Sidhe woman should aspire to the simple joys of living within a well-tended world, among Sidhe—"

"And humans?"

Shiafa seemed unable to absorb the suggestion. Michael sighed. "Still your father's daughter."

"Then reject me!" she spat, edging away from where he sat. "Find what you need somewhere else!"

"If only I could," he said. *How close to Tarax's trap have I come? The easy way, the obvious way—borrow what you need, rather than face the uncertainty.* He tried to find a solution in all of Manus's memories, but there was none. Just as Manus had not understood souls, only stripped them from the Sidhe, so had he taken away love from Sidhe mages.

Nobody's solutions worked perfectly for Michael.

If you would do everything you can to avoid losing and waste all your energies before the battle truly begins—seeking ultimate assurances and security—then you only destroy yourself.

And where did that wisdom come from? Not from Manus. Not from Adonna. Not even from the Crane Women or the mage of the Cledar.

It came from young, unpolished, uncertain Michael Perrin.

"All right. I won't use your powers any more," Michael said.

"Who will, then?" Shiafa asked, not believing him.

"I don't know. Perhaps you."

"To do what? Work for my father's cause?"

"I don't know." He was still attracted to her. He would have to fight that; right now, compared to Shiafa, Kristine seemed a pale and feeble object of passion.

What could Kristine offer a mage? She was mortal, human, not even especially beautiful compared to some of the beauties he had seen—the Ban of Hours, for example. What good would she do a young mage, what could she teach him or give to him?

Nothing. She was a totally impractical love. He didn't even know that what they had was truly love. It might be evanescent. He might rescue her and find her drifting away from him within weeks or months. If he bonded with Shiafa, they would never be able to leave each other . . .

He might—he would find some way to hold back the mutual destruction. *You are what you dare . . .*

But that was not something he would dare. He would not defy the warning image of Adonna's wife, nameless, turned into a monster and condemned to slide across the Blasted Plain.

No wonder the Sidhe mage had hidden his final revenge.

No wonder all of history was cruel, revenge stacked upon revenge, punishment upon punishment.

Break the cycle.

"I'm returning you to Tarax," Michael said.

"I don't even know where he is," Shiafa said.

"I think I do. He's where I should be now. So we'll go to him together."

35

Stolen memories:

Of a time when the Earth occupied the center of all space-time, and the sky was full not of stars but of jeweled lights, other worlds not far away to which one could travel on *epon* in a few days' time . . .

And when days were determined not by the orbit of a sun but by the duration of a haze of light that suffused all creation.

Manus, initiate and candidate for the position of mage of humans—one among tens of thousands of candidates—undergoing his discipline in the forests and mountains, among immortal trees and clean, sweet snow-smelling peaks that never rebelled to kill but sometimes managed a little defiance simply to *challenge* . . .

Consorts and wives Manus shared with other candidates . . . some of the consorts themselves candidates to be the supreme creator, maintainer, master of the craftsmen, makers, tenders and designers bearing the honorific of *Gardener* or *Weaver of Lace*, keepers of the paradise where a thousand different varieties of beings lived, dominant (in numbers only) being Sidhe, humans, Spryggla, Cledar—and Urges, from whom most but not all of the makers were chosen, hence the legend of the demiurges, workmen of the gods.

Memories of a sky as pure and entrancing as sapphire or lapis, filled with the airborne Sidhe Amorphals and the Cledar, master singers and the inventors of non-vocal music; and of oceans so pellucid that swimmers and sailors could see a thousand feet below the surface and witness the deep sports of the Pelagal Sidhe.

Manus had been young in those times. By his maturity, the golden age had tarnished and the sweetness between races soured. By his accession to magehood, his inherited realm had become a welter of skirmishes and infighting, threatening to erupt into outright warfare.

Accustomed to the purity of sweet reason and orderly debate, very few in his time were prepared to face the upwellings of hatred and suspicion. Almost none were immune to the sickness that passed among all the races. Sides were chosen, and those who supported the humans—virtually all races but the Sidhe—quartered creation and gave the Sidhe the least desired section.

That was when the war truly began . . .

And Manus had been powerless to prevent it. He had, in fact, been swept up in the sickness, as had the then-mage of the Sidhe and the mages of the other races.

The outcome Michael had known already, but Manus's memories added horrifying detail. The true Fall . . .

What many thought of as humanity's fall, distorted in the myth of Adam and Eve and the serpent, had been in fact the beginning of a climb to a new maturity in a creation left to go completely out of control.

Space had spread almost without limit. The creation had merged with wild and discarded continua, and in the necessary coming together of laws for existence, the fine-tuning of the mages and makers had been abrogated. Unfamiliar and alien intelligences had appeared at these distant borders. The triumphant Sidhe, alarmed that in their victory they were declining into easeful ways, had set out across the Great Distance, as these newly accessible regions were called. Followed the war called Quandary, lasting millions of years, of which Manus knew very little, imprisoned as he was on Earth.

Then the Sidhe had returned, neither victorious nor defeated, but somehow lessened by their journeys . . . And only one of them had aspired to be maker and mage: Tonn. Tonn had been the last to go to Null, where creations were arranged, and to work true magic to shape the Realm.

For the ten thousand years since, Null had gone unoccupied.

Michael knew the combinations of discipline necessary to open a mage's gate. From the hill overlooking the loch, he used Manus's memories and spread wide a black gash in the rock and dirt, unlike the gates in the air he had made before.

This gash opened into a near-total lack of qualities, with the most minimal of enforced patterns.

Michael and Shiafa stepped into Null.

"Beneath" Null roiled the mist Michael had seen beneath the Realm, but even more unstructured and painful to witness. "Above" Null stretched a negative plane of dissolution, where badly contrived creations could be recycled, falling back to the mist. Null could be used as an eraser, should a maker or mage decide a new creation must be eliminated.

These two, mist and negative plane, spread across all manner of distances and dimensions; and "between" them, where no untrained human eye could track or decipher, lay Null itself, a simple structure of black cubes resembling an enormous mineral specimen. But Null was not made of rock or of anything else.

It was a place marker, a beginning point.

It had never been "made" by anybody. Existing before all creations, or all peoples, Null had a timeless and *a priori* reality that Michael found difficult to comprehend, even with Manus's memories.

Tarax already stood on the uppermost cube, lost in concentration. In his hands he held a pair of calipers, the two points of the calipers spanning a featureless ivory-colored sphere floating before him.

Michael entered Null on the next cube down. Shiafa closed her eyes and moaned as she appeared on the surface of a third cube a short distance away, if distance meant much here—and it did not.

Tarax glanced away from his measurements and smiled at Michael as an equal. *Welcome, candidate,* he said. There was no sound in Null and hence no voices but those conveyed by mind. Even these communications seemed tinny and weak. It was obvious to Michael that nobody could remain in Null for long without losing all material form, and perhaps all mental order as well. It was not meant for habitation; it was meant only for the highest kinds of creation.

Thank you. Michael's chivalric politeness did not seem out of place here. The sheer, oppressive lack of order had to be compensated for.

My daughter should not be here. She is not equipped for these reaches.

I have given part of myself to her that she might come and witness.

Witness what, our struggle?

If we struggle.

Tarax indicated the sphere between the calipers. *This is nearly finished. It can support all those now alive on Earth. Would you condemn both our peoples to destruction to assume your own petty prominence?*

Michael was fascinated by the difference between Tarax's nascent creation and the tiny pearls he had grown. *You would abandon the old world completely?*

What use is it? It is harsh and uncontrolled. My people live there with difficulty. As flawed as the Realm was, it supported us in comfort.

Do you have room for all the races?

Tarax spread his arms wide. *I welcome all.*

I don't think my people would know how to live in a creation so isolated from Earth.

They would learn.

Michael now knew the full extent of the law of mages. Candidates could not simply "have it out" in Null; they were here by sufferance. What that meant precisely—who was suffering their presence?—Michael could not find in Manus's memories. But at any rate, while they were here, they could not settle the issue by any form of combat—

Except one. Michael felt the pearly excrescences spread across both of his palms.

He had an advantage over Tarax. His creation would not begin from scratch. The example of an unruly, unpredictable garden gone to seed, hothouse growths subsumed, wild and self-sustaining growths dominant—the example of Earth and all space-time around it lay buried within Michael, innate, felt if not understood. And the maker part of him could use that as a beginning.

Tarax would try for a pure creation, outside and beyond the despised Earth. He would attempt what Adonna had ultimately failed at—creation *ex nihilo.* That was a very Sidhe thing, style and bravado. Michael admired that.

But even with Manus's memories, he could not compete on that level. (If you merge with Shiafa . . .)

He tossed that murmur aside and glanced at Tarax's daughter. She stood bravely on the black surface. *I've brought your daughter back to you.*

Is her training finished?

She knows as much as I knew when you brought her to me. I trained her as the Crane Women might have.

Tarax's creation increased in apparent diameter. He expanded his calipers and measured it again, nodding. *Then you will learn where your human woman is.*

Did you send Shiafa to me as a trap? Michael inquired.

You have evaded the trap, if I did.

There are people on Earth who would consider such a trap villainous, the tactic of a desperate coward.

Tarax seemed unperturbed. *Why do you think I care for the opinions of humans?*

Where is Kristine?

I can tell you where she is, but not how to get there. Clarkham has her in one of his endless sketches for a creation.

I already know that much. I've fulfilled my bargain. Tell me what you promised you would tell me.

In number, it is Clarkham's fortieth creation, and you may find it among one of the bottles of wine he made in the Realm . . . or in the wine he stole from Adonna, the celebrational nectar of the Sidhe mages.

Wine for the Sidhe? *Where does he keep these wines?*

You've tasted some already. He hid them in various places.

Michael subdued his growing anger. *This is not our bargain,* he said, the nacre spreading between his hands as he brought them together. Shiafa looked on, squinting against the unaccustomed nonquality of Null's space-time extension.

Never trust a Sidhe. You've heard that adage, no doubt.

Michael grinned and turned to Shiafa. *You are free to choose. I do not need your help or power now.* His confidence had taken a perverse leap with Tarax's statement. Whatever etiquette existed in Null, whatever rules implicit in the law of mages, simply masked a jungle law—

Survival of the fittest. Or more succinctly, the finest.

And Michael had been born and raised in a jungle creation, not in the hothouse Realm Tarax carried in his deepest instincts.

Michael withdrew all his balancing judgments and restraints. He pulled back all the controls, those he had known and those he had never even been aware of.

A maker has no conscience, he said to Tarax. *Where is your maker, Priest?*

I am my own maker.

Michael's grin became positively feral. *Did you discover this talent within you, or learn it?*

Tarax did not reply. His ivory globe was now nearly as broad as he was. The calipers vanished from his hands. *We cannot compete here, Man-child.*

This is the only competition that matters, Michael responded.

He spun the nacre between his palms into a pearl the size of a baseball. Rose-colored lines washed around the little sphere. Manus's memories approved—this was a vigorous creation. It carried its own inner light and confidence. Tarax's large bone-colored globe was a patchwork, virtually stillborn effort. It would grow, perhaps even become a coherent creation, but it would be no better than Adonna's Realm, and probably worse. Tarax was aware of this, Michael suspected.

Within his own pearl, Michael felt all the contradictions and difficulties of the unruly Earth. Spice in the mixture. Give the creation a little autonomy; allow it to surprise the maker. Leave the sting in the bee, the thorn on the rose, and the spider in the garden. These incongruities will remind the inhabitants of the thorns within themselves, the evils that spring not from worlds but from individuals, and perhaps they will not soon forget, and not soon succumb to the disaster that befell all races sixty million years before.

Michael's little pearl-creation pulsed with its own confidence and eagerness. *This world already lives,* he thought. *I simply have to give it freedom. It requires very little power from me, merely encouragement. This world is like a child.*

Michael felt a burst of joy within him that transcended any emotion he had ever known before. He was once again a child rolling mud into a ball. The greatest art of all time—creation of a world—was really no more profound and exalted than a child's play.

And into the pearl went this aspect of innocent enthusiasm, to counter the wisdom of the bee's sting and the rose's thorns. The pearl threatened to burst into light.

Tarax kept his bloated bone-sphere close to him, apparently worried lest it be released too early.

Michael laid his fingers on the surface of his pearl and, lifting it above the black surface of Null, pushed it away from him across the "distance" to the mist. Shiafa's thoughts as she watched were like a song.

You do not need me, she said. *I am free.*

Michael turned with tears in his eyes, his face glowing red. *I don't know what it is I've done. You helped me come here. But you are right. I do not need you.*

With his thoughts, there poured forth a residue of the energy he had put into the pearl. Shiafa added part of her own self, her own thoughts. And in those thoughts lived a small, self-contained world that impressed itself on both of them for the merest instant.

And in this tiny world—

Michael and Shiafa lay down under the spreading boughs of an ivory-trunked tree in the lost creation of their ancestors. They removed their simple hand-spun and hand-sewn clothes and reveled in their beauties and flaws, taking as much pleasure in the flaws as the beauties. They cataloged their differences, Sidhe and mostly-human. They replaced the tensions that had once plagued them and savored such flavors like bitter herbs in a rich stew.

They held each other in the suffused light of the old world, moving against each other, their friction bringing on a delicious passion free of all guilt and necessity.

They *loved,* Michael no longer a teacher, Shiafa no longer a student. For a dangerous instant, they were totally connected; but that instant existed only in a shared fantasy, the connection robbed of all its dire consequences.

They parted.

The little world dissolved.

Shiafa wavered in the uncertain reality of Null, her face as bright as the moon, eyes closed, still savoring the dreamworld they had made for each other. Then she did something she had never done for Michael or for anybody else in her life; she opened her eyes and smiled at him, directly and without reservations.

Michael nodded to her—respect, relief, all his best wishes.

Shiafa turned to her father, then, and nodded.

Go, daughter, Tarax said.

I will give you my power, she said. *You are my father.*

Tarax shook his head. *There has been more than enough betrayal. Go.*

Shiafa lowered her gaze, reached out, and pulled aside a curtain, revealing sunlight and rugged desert hills—perhaps Israel. She stepped through the curtain and departed from Null. She had been released from both Michael and her father.

Michael's pearl had orbited Null several times. It dropped abruptly to the mist, where it waited like seed in a womb for the proper moment to lay itself over the desperately ill Earth. Tarax still held his bone-egg, now nearly as broad as Null itself, if Null had any breadth.

There is no battle between us, Michael said. *I wish you luck.*

The desperation in Tarax's face then was beyond what Michael had expected or desired. The Sidhe was failing as a maker, but no others were available.

The Maln had destroyed the last of the Urges ages ago.

Michael moved forward to help. The bone-egg bubbled, wildly overextended, developing far too many qualities for a single creation. To Michael, it was obvious Tarax had been too deliberate, too cautious.

It's dangerous, he told the Chief of the Maln. *Send it out to dissolve. Start again.*

No, Tarax said. *It is the best I can do . . .*

It's flawed.

Leave!

Michael watched the bone-egg swell between the mist and the hideous solvent "sky," Tarax laboring beside it like an ant under a boulder. For a moment, Michael wondered if Tarax's world-sized abortion would harm the Earth and his own nascent creation.

But Manus's memories told him, this is what Null is for. Nothing that goes wrong here can affect the worlds beyond. Only if Tarax tried to apply his abortion beyond Null—something he did not have the strength to do, in Michael's judgment—was there danger. At any rate, there was nothing Michael could do to stop him.

Before Michael departed from Null, he allowed himself one last comment to Adonna's self-proclaimed successor.

There's no substitute for talent, he said.

Tarax did not respond. White hair sticking out from his head with the effort of controlling the bone-egg, he looked after Michael with a pitiful yearning totally uncharacteristic of the Sidhe priest.

The past makes victims of us all, Michael realized even more sharply. The last of his animosity simply evaporated.

He pulled the gap shut after him and stood on the sidewalk before his parents' house, in the glow of a sizzling streetlight, the night a frightening dark sheet of warm metal laid over the city and half the Earth.

The pearl's convergence with Earth had not begun yet. Whatever would happen, would happen in its own time.

He opened the door to the house. In the living room, his father was presiding over a meeting of neighbors. The electricity was out, and candles had been placed around the room, on the fireplace mantle and on top of the entertainment center and hall credenza. As Michael entered, a plump middle-aged man wearing a golf sweater and baggy slacks was engaged in a vehement diatribe on the lack of city services. Michael glanced around the room. He recognized most of the people there: Mr. Boggin, the plump speaker, and his wife Muriel; the Wilberforce family, six- and seven-year-old daughters sitting before the blank television; grandmotherly Mrs. Miller, widowed before Michael's return from the Realm; the Dopsos; and Warren Verde, a bookseller friend of John's.

"Any news?" John asked quietly.

"Your son is involved in all this, that's what Ruth and Mrs. Dopso have been saying, isn't it?" Mr. Boggin asked. John didn't answer. "Well?" Boggin persisted, facing Michael. "What do you know? What can we expect?"

Michael frowned. The man's thoughts smelled of sweat and fear of his own inadequacy. Mr. Boggin knew he was not the sort of man to survive a major crisis on stamina or wits.

"There's been a kind of battle," he said.

"These invaders," Warren Verde interjected. "Have you been talking with them?"

Michael nodded. "More than that."

Mrs. Miller moaned and twisted her hands in her lap.

"I've been working to see what can be done to put things right again." That, he knew, was about as much as they could take right now. "Where are the guests?" he asked his father.

"Moffat and Crooke and several other people took them away. They arranged for rooms at some downtown hotels."

One thing at a time. And the time had come.

"Dad, did Mr. Waltiri ever give you a bottle of wine?"

John smiled. "Two bottles," he said. "We never drank them. Waiting for a special occasion."

"Are they in the wine closet?" John kept a fair collection of wines in a cool first-floor hall closet.

"I think so. Ruth?"

"I haven't touched them," Ruth said. Her eyes had not left Michael since his entry.

"Then they should still be there. Do you need them?"

"Who's Waltiri?" Mr. Boggin asked.

"The composer," Verde said. "John used to know him, didn't you?"

John had told the guests very little, perhaps for the same reasons Michael had chosen to cut his explanation short. People who rigorously lived their normal lives could not stretch their imaginations to encompass what he now knew.

"I'll get them for you," John said.

"I'll come with you." Michael followed his father into the hall. John took out his key chain and unlocked the closet door, then shook his head. "Can't see anything in there. I'll get a flashlight or a candle." He came back with a candle, but Michael had already located the two bottles on the bottom of the right-hand rack, using his sense of smell more than anything else. One bottle carried the double sundial of Clarkham's winery. The second carried no label whatsoever; this dark, almost black container was oddly shaped, slightly pinched in the middle. The glass had a glazed, metallic sheen.

"Arno had no idea what was in that one," John said. "He said I might save it for a very special occasion. I take it this is that occasion?"

"Perhaps not yet," Michael answered. "May I take them?"

"They're yours. Arno . . . wasn't human, was he?"

"Part of him was human," Michael said.

"The part that died."

"Yes."

"You sound distant," John commented. "Something big happened, didn't it?"

"Yes."

"Your mother is worried sick, more about you than the way the world's going, I think. Can you reassure us?"

Michael hugged his father tightly. "I'm still my father's son and my mother's son," he said. "It'll take me some time to tell you what's been happening. Right now, I have one more thing I have to do."

"Involving the Sidhe?" John asked. Ruth came into the hallway and leaned against a wall, her arms crossed. Michael went to her and hugged her, as well.

"Not involving the Sidhe," Michael said.

"Where's Shiafa?" Ruth asked.

Michael laughed and shook his head. "I'm not sure where she is. But she's fine."

"It's not that I'm prejudiced," Ruth said.

"I'm going to look for Kristine," Michael explained.

"In a bottle of wine?" John asked.

Michael lifted the unlabeled bottle. "It's probably just as well you didn't try this," he said. "It's very old."

"How old?"

"Maybe sixty million years."

"That's impossible," John said, and then laughed dryly. "I suppose it isn't. Let me know what it tastes like?"

"I'm going out the back way," Michael said. "Try to keep the people calm. I think everything's going to work out."

"But you're not sure?" Ruth asked.

"No. I'm not sure."

She gave him a sad and intense look, her face pale and tight in the vibrating light of the candle. "I can't believe you're still my son," she said. "Have you met your great-great-grandmother yet?" Her eyes narrowed to slits.

"No," Michael said, smiling now, knowing what she was getting at. "Great-great-grandpa's Hill wife hasn't come my way."

"If she does," Ruth said, "be sure to tell her something for me."

"What's that?"

"Tell her, 'Boo!' " Ruth said. John took her outstretched hand, and she extended her other hand to Michael. He grasped it firmly.

36

Michael was certain there was more to Clarkham than had met his eye. Clarkham's concealment of his creations' gateways in bottles of wine was a master stroke. That all of Clarkham's worlds were derivative might or might not be relevant; he certainly did not wish to underestimate the Isomage.

Clarkham had, after all, escaped the combined plots of the Sidhe Councils—with Michael as the barb on the end of a spear-shaft centuries long. And Clarkham was much older than Michael.

That was balanced now by the millions of years of memories from Manus. But Michael had hardly had time to catalog the broad features of those memories, much less take full advantage of them. (What would he become when he had absorbed the entire treasure?)

He carried the bottles down the dark street, vaguely making his way by the candlelit windows of the houses. He avoided the few people he saw—some drunk, some young and rowdy, some furtive and frightened. They carried Coleman lanterns and flashlights and made a great deal of noise. Their world was crumbling. He did not want to think about them now, or about the responsibilities of a maker and mage.

He concentrated on Kristine. How long had it been since her kidnapping? Weeks? Months? What had happened to her in that time?

What did she remember? Had Clarkham locked her in some dismal dreamworld, as he had Michael? Did she think Michael was dead?

He was going back to where his first journey had begun, Clarkham's always-empty, always-full house. Once inside, he would drink a toast.

But from which bottle?

The stolen bottle of mage's nectar, however old it was, did not seem the most promising. Clarkham had not considered it important enough to take with him. Or perhaps Waltiri had hidden it from him. And Clarkham had simply given away or abandoned the other wines, perhaps thinking it next to impossible that anyone would learn the secret of his worlds' gateways.

But by now, Clarkham knew the secret was out. Michael had intruded once already. No doubt the Isomage, or whatever was left of him, would be on the alert.

Michael stood on the front porch of Clarkham's house. Despite all that had happened, the house still seemed nothing more than a slightly rundown dwelling in a moderately ritzy neighborhood.

In the upstairs dusty-floored guest bedroom, Michael took his Swiss Army knife from his pocket and cut the lead foil on Clarkham's bottle. With a pop, the cork came out cleanly and in one piece. Michael smelled the varnish-like stain on the cork's end and smelled the bottle.

It had not soured.

The gate was clearly inviting him.

He took a sip and washed it across the back of his tongue, as his father had taught him. He closed his eyes.

The flavors paraded, and he tasted again the distinct divisions. He counted carefully, using all of his heightened senses to mark the borders on each range of tastes.

Thirty-five, thirty-six different flavors—one dusty and grassy, the world where Clarkham had last conversed with him—and then thirty-seven, richer by far, thirty-eight, thirty-nine—

Like counting the iron gates in the alley between worlds.

And forty. He bore down with all his discipline on that flavor: harsh, metallic and stony, and yet behind it lurked the most complex subtleties of all the succession. He thought for a moment, as he crossed, that this fortieth flavor might have once been the finest but had somehow begun to turn, separately from all the others.

Michael was nearly hit by a car as his feet touched hot asphalt pavement. The car screeched to a halt, and the driver cursed at him, then swerved into another lane.

Stunned, Michael left the intersection and stood on the sidewalk. There, he looked up at the street sign. The placards for streets in both directions were blank.

A hot, mellow sun shone down on the pastel stucco-walled buildings with awnings stretched out halfway across the sidewalks. Old streamlined cars—Buicks, Fords, Chevrolets and a single white Packard—with bright paint jobs and glittering chrome rolled down the streets on wide white-sidewall tires. Men and women in summer attire passed by—Bermuda shorts, sunglasses, Hawaiian shirts, spaghetti-strap print dresses with short-sleeved jackets.

Michael stood to one side under a black-and-white striped awning. So many people . . . Where had they come from? For that matter, where was he? He had never suspected Clarkham was capable of creating a world this complex, with such a distinct feel of reality.

Michael entered a men's clothing store to gather his wits. The sunlight through the windows filled his eyes with gold and momentary blindness. Silhouetted in the store window, legless and headless mannequins modeled wide-lapel sports coats and Arrow shirts, surrounded by a small mockup split-rail fence. A smiling cast-iron black jockey in red and white livery offered a silver ring beside a chair. Michael sat and rubbed his eyes. The taste on his tongue was fading, yet the world was still here, detailed and undeniable. It felt real.

All but the blank street signs.

"May I help you, sir?" asked an unctuous salesman in a pinstriped suit. Michael looked up. The salesman's face was round, black hair greased slick, a thin pencil mustache beneath his sharp nose. The salesman smiled, revealing brilliant white teeth.

Michael quickly probed his aura. The salesman had no aura. He was as alive as the mannequins in the window, and as thoughtful.

Michael got up from the chair without replying. The salesman looked over his shoulder at two other salesmen toward the rear of the store. "Sir?"

"I'm fine," Michael said.

"I should hope so, sir. May I help you find suitable apparel?"

"No, thank you."

"Very well."

"What's the date?" Michael asked abruptly.

"We're having a summer's end sale. You know that summer apparel is never really out of date in Los Angeles. Some fine buys."

"The year, I mean."

The salesman smiled broadly. "The gentleman has been reading too much John Collier, perhaps?"

"I'm serious."

"Nineteen and thirty-seven, give or take a few minutes."

"Thank you."

"Think nothing of it."

Michael left the shop and strolled down the street, probing the people he passed. None were more than animated figures—brilliantly animated, but no more real for all that.

He passed the alcove entrance to a stone-walled office building. A shoeshine stand squatted in one corner, attended by an elderly white-haired black (*Negro*, he almost wanted to say) in a denim wraparound apron. The black smiled at several men as they passed. "Shine? Finest shine." He focused on Michael, starting from Michael's shoes and glancing upward. Michael's suede Hush Puppies did not invite an inquiry.

The shoeshine man was empty, also.

Clarkham had populated his world with vacuous ghosts. In a way, these inhabitants were worse than the dark figures Michael had avoided in Clarkham's dream-prison. Without the discipline, one would probably accept these as people.

He turned back abruptly and entered the alcove, passing through the revolving glass door. In the lobby, he glanced at a magazine stand replete with issues of *Life* magazine and stacks of newspapers and pulps. The vendor, a young, skinny woman with hair netted in a tight bun, smoked a Camel cigarette, lost in some blank reverie. *Truly blank*, Michael thought. *Emptiness mimicking emptiness.*

His respect for Clarkham grew, tinged with horror. Why did Clarkham wish to populate worlds with simulacra? That seemed a perversion of what being a maker or a mage was all about—providing a habitat for real people.

But perhaps he was missing the big picture, Michael thought. Perhaps these were simply test subjects, architect's toy figurines. He stepped into a wood-paneled elevator with three other simulacra, one of whom—a gray-haired woman in a black silk suit—smiled at him with matronly good-humor.

He returned the smile. The operator, a Latino with deep-set black eyes, asked what floor he wished. Michael said, "Fourth, please."

Anyplace where he could get off and be quiet, away from the simulacra. Where he could spread a large-scale probe across this world and measure its extent . . . Feel for Kristine.

The door opened at the fourth floor, and Michael stepped out into a cool, shadowy hallway. Near the end of the deserted hall, adjacent to an etched glass-front door marked "Pellegrini and Shaefer, Novelties and Party Favors" in gold letters, he paused by a white ceramic water fountain. Michael spread his probe.

And screamed, withdrawing it immediately.

Head crawling with fire, he slumped to the floor. His mouth seemed to instantly fill with the taste of decayed meat. *Trap,* he thought, pulling in all his senses and calling up a pulse of *hyloka.*

But after a few minutes of silent recuperation, he realized this world was not a trap. What he had felt had not been intended for him. The boundaries of this world—no more than five or six miles on a side—were truly corrupted.

He pulled in the range of his probe and braced himself, taking a deep breath. *Kristine.*

Point by point, he swept the streets and buildings, touching briefly on the hundreds of empty caricatures populating the mockup city. *It's a film set,* he thought. It wasn't as hollow as the sets he had seen in the Western lot at Moffat's studio, but it was nearly so.

A sham.

It couldn't be intended as a serious rival for the worlds the other candidates had constructed. And it obviously wasn't the last of Clarkham's tests. How many mock-worlds had Clarkham created? And how accomplished had he finally been?
Kristine.

As he probed, he felt the foundation of the little world, riddling its secrets, automatically comparing its rules and qualities with the overlay he had recently set loose on Earth. The underpinnings here were smoothly textured, almost slick, difficult to analyze, even more difficult to get a grip on. *The words of Tonn's wife.*

For a moment, he felt a trace of Clarkham, but that passed, and he could not recover it. And almost immediately after, he forgot about that brief touch, for he found *her.*

Michael's release of breath was clearly audible up and down the length of the still hallway. She was alive, she was reasonably well—and she did not remember who she was.

Kristine was wrapped up in Clarkham's world and thought herself a part of it—just as Michael had.

He punched the button for the elevator and anxiously watched the brass arrow point to the raised floor numbers. The arrow passed the 4, and the doors did not open. At the end of the hall, he heard heavy footsteps shuffling. But he could feel nothing.

The chair. The turning chair.

In the house next door to Clarkham's, on his first passage through to the Realm, Michael had paused to look into the living room and had seen an over-stuffed swivel rocking chair with its back turned toward him. The chair had been rocking, and as Michael had watched, it had started turning . . .

The guardians of Clarkham's gateway could have numbered more than two. Tristesse had been stationed by the Sidhe; Lamia had acted as a watcher for both Clarkham and the Sidhe. But the third—

Whatever had been in the rocking chair—

Might have been controlled solely by Clarkham.

Michael had little doubt that the shuffling footsteps he heard at the end of the hall and the occupant of the chair were one and the same.

He swore under his breath and tried to open a gate. But he could find no purchase; the seamless glass-smooth creation allowed for no exits. He swallowed, hoping to wipe the taste of the wine from his tongue, but it lingered. Thinking of the water fountain, he walked quickly to the ceramic basin and turned the handle. The cool water did not erase the taste.

For a moment, Michael felt very foolish. He had just spun loose a thing of incredible complexity and power, an improving overlay for the sick and injured Earth; he had absorbed the knowledge of the world's oldest living being—

And yet he still was afraid. He damped the fear quickly and stood in the middle of the hall, wrapped in a grim calm. Being merely human could get him killed. He explored Manus's knowledge of guardians and other artificial and altered beings. The brief tastes of memory—changelings, conjured devils, witch-waifs, abortions like Ishmael and transformed monsters like the vampiric Tristesse—did not match what he heard approaching.

A door opened and closed around the corner at the end of the hall. Something sniffed delicately. "Hello," a muffled voice said. "I see you've gotten this far."

The voice was barely recognizable.

"Clarkham?" Michael asked.

Again the delicate sniff. "Have you found her yet?"

"I've found Kristine."

"That's good. You'll pardon me if I don't show myself. I still have some pride. We've never met, you know."

Michael raised his eyebrows. "I beg your pardon?"

"No, we never have. Puzzle it out. Reports from distant shores. Corruption and bad decisions. Vicarious thrills."

"I don't understand."

"I won't get in your way. My ambitions, at least, are few now. And don't confuse the other with me, though we are both failures. The other brought your woman here. You'll contend with him, not me. I regret many things, not least of all . . . him. You can go now."

"Who are you?" Michael asked, confused.

"To tell all would be most painful. Find out for yourself. Earn the facts."

Michael thought of the rocking chair. "You were in the house next door to Clarkham's."

"Yes."

"Who were you waiting for?"

"Arno. To apologize. I told him I'd be waiting when I left him the key."

"Did you expect me?"

The sniff was less delicate this time, and much less pleasant. "You can go."

The elevator door opened with a chime. Michael hesitated, then entered. The simulacrum operator smiled toothily at him. "Lobby?" he asked.

Michael nodded.

"Nothing on the fourth floor," the operator said, smirking.

The door closed with a squeak, but behind that squeak, Michael heard a distant wail of anguish. Even through his controlling discipline, his neck and scalp prickled.

The daylight brightness had diminished slightly. He passed the shoeshine stand and turned left down the street in Kristine's direction. When he had first located Kristine, he had seen a distinctively narrow three-story white wood-frame building wedged between two other brick and stone structures. Considering the limited size of Clarkham's creation, Michael didn't think it would take him long to find the site.

The street changed character within a few hundred yards. The buildings aged and darkened; brick and stone replaced stucco, styles reverted to those of the teens and twenties. The air cooled and tasted gritty.

The people changed, too. Less care was spent on their details. Their faces became blander, more standardized; the worst of them were mere blank-eyed mannequins.

Michael became aware, after walking a mile and a half, that he was much closer to the edge of corruption. He took care to limit the extent of his probe in that direction.

Despite his discipline, he couldn't help becoming more excited—and anxious—the closer he came to Kristine. The undercurrent of his anxiety was excruciating. So much had happened since they last met; even if he could bring her out of this creation and back to Earth—even if Earth was recovering through the influence of his overlay—would they still feel for each other with as much intensity and depth?

So little time together, and the time so strange . . .

Memories of Manus's ancient loves came to Michael unbidden, colored by rich emotions and contexts he couldn't begin to interpret. There were hardly words in English to describe what the memories conveyed.

Now the figures around him were little more than place markers in barely-sketched clothes. Michael could see and feel the shifting qualities of their presence, holding them together only marginally here on the edge of a corruption that burned.

He saw the narrow white building, sandwiched between two five-story brick apartment complexes. A fire escape crisscrossed its front and ended a few feet above arm's reach over the sidewalk. Beneath the folded ladder, a simple square cloth awning shadowed the building's double glass and wood doors.

Michael felt for Clarkham's presence, gingerly skirting the painful borders of the creation. There was nothing definite; his probe kept being drawn back to the office building where the unseen figure had addressed him, and Michael kept pulling away from that sensation of lostness and resignation.

He pressed the latch on the brass handle of the right-hand door and opened it slowly, stepping inside. A wall of tarnished mailboxes waited with timeless patience on the left, beside a janitorial door shut and padlocked. To his right, an ancient map of Los Angeles hung behind dusty and cracked glass.

So much detail . . .

Stairs covered with frayed oriental-style carpet rose beyond the wall of mailboxes. He began climbing, not needing to refer to the building's directory, knowing which floor. *She is here.*

Kristine, Michael knew, at this moment sat in a worn leather armchair behind a beat-up wooden desk in a small office on the top floor, the third.

He climbed the next flight of stairs, past the second floor landing and doorway, the door hand-lettered in black: "Pascal Novelties amd Party Supplies." Not and—amd. The detail was repeating, and inaccurately. Clarkham had made much of his creation out of rubber-stamped combinations, prefab units, as it were. Michael thought of the large teeth on both the salesman and the elevator operator: identical.

On the third floor doorway, in gold letters on the clear glass, he read:

TOPFLIGHT DETECTIVES
Ernest Brawley Rachel Taylor
Divorces Investigations Confidential

Behind the door, at the end of the very narrow hallway that ran the length of the building against the right-hand wall, Michael heard Kristine speaking to someone in an undertone.

He walked at a measured pace down the hall, restraining an urge to run and find her immediately, simply to see her and know by the evidence of his eyes that she was alive and well.

The corruption was so close, barely a few hundred yards away, practically singing against the fabric of the streets and buildings, vibrating in the wood like a threatened quake or tremor. How had she withstood it for so long?

The door to the last office was half-open. Michael pushed it all the way. Kristine sat facing the door, black Bakelite desk phone sitting on the desk in front of her. She held the receiver pressed against her ear and slightly lowered from her heavily lipsticked mouth.

Kristine's hair been arranged in an upswept, split bun above her forehead and pulled tightly back behind into a more full bun. The style was not particularly attractive. She looked hard, weary. Her eyes barely reacted when she saw him.

"Yeah," she said into the phone. "Bring me the timecards, and I'll believe

Jimmy was there, like you say. Look, I've got company. I gotta go." She dropped the receiver with a clatter into its cradle. "There's a buzzer downstairs. We come down to meet you. We like it that way." She appraised him coldly. "What can I do for you?"

He smiled. "It's time to leave," he said.

She stiffened and dropped one hand below desk level. "Yeah? Where are you going?"

What came next was pure inspiration. He remembered Bogart and Stanwyck playing through their timeless roles on the television screen the night his father had first introduced him to Waltiri.

"You mean, where are we going," Michael said casually.

"The persuasive type, huh?" Kristine asked, eyes sweeping him again with faint amusement. She popped a stick of gum into her mouth and sized him up again, eyes languid. "You aren't dressed for the part. Ernie has a good tailor—"

"It's not what I'm wearing that counts," Michael said. "It's what I'm thinking."

"Is a penny payment enough?" She kept her hand below desk level. Michael sensed that it was just an inch or two away from a gun. She knew how to use it, too.

"More than enough. For you, it's free." He began to feel gloriously giddy. "You look and act tough, but I know better. I'm thinking you don't belong here."

"We never met before, Mister."

"Think back to before you came here. Remember a kiss?"

She smiled wryly. "Sing me the tune on the radio. Maybe that'll refresh my memory."

Just the words Stanwyck had used.

Michael wet his lips and sat on the corner of her desk, watching her hidden arm closely. He began to whistle, hoping he could reproduce at least the basics.

She stopped appraising. Her large green eyes opened wide. The face behind the thick makeup softened.

"I know that . . ." she said.

"You should. It's our song."

"What's it called?" she asked. She placed both hands on the desk, empty. She seemed ready to stand, perhaps run.

"Opus 45," Michael said. "Concerto for piano and orchestra, the *Infinity*."

Kristine pushed the chair back. "There's no music like that here," she said.

"It's a case of kidnapping. Simple."

"Who's simple, and who's been kidnapped?"

"You," Michael said, pointing. "Now you know. We have to get out of here."

Her confusion put an end to the enjoyment. Michael held out his hand. Kristine reached for it, hesitated, then grasped it firmly. The warm touch of her skin was ecstasy.

"Your name is Kristine," he said.

"I'm not that simple. Kristine Taylor. I mean . . . Kristine Pendeers."

"Who am I?"

She smiled. A tear traveled down one cheek, dragging a streak of mascara after it. "You're *Michael*," she said, taking a deep, tremulous breath. "Oh, God. Michael! Where in hell are we?"

"Not far from hell at all," he said. "Come with me."

But first, she ran from behind the desk and wrapped her arms around him. Not so much had happened after all, he decided—not enough to matter. He cried, too.

37

The difficult part now began: getting home. Michael led Kristine through the double doors onto the street. "Something hurts my head," she said. "I haven't really been able to think about it until now, but it's hurt for a long time."

"This whole place is rotting away," Michael said.

Kristine made a face. "That's what it feels like. Can we leave?"

"I'm trying."

"What happened to you? How long has it been?"

Michael shook his head and held his finger to his lips. "I have to think." He pulled her close and nuzzled her cheek, then let her go and drew his palms together to feel for a way out.

"God, all this *gunk*," she said, touching the caked makeup on her lips and cheeks. "What ever made me do it?"

Michael tried again to locate a seam in the apparently seamless matrix of Clarkham's world. The substratum beneath the detail and solidity was masterfully smooth, smoother than it needed to be—as if Michael's father were to spend weeks polishing the underside of a table. Again, there was more craftsmanship than practicality or actual achievement in this world.

"It's going to be hard," Michael admitted, letting his hands drop.

"We can't leave?"

"There has to be a way." He was calling up facts from the Serpent Mage's memories, but in all that Manus knew about makers and creating worlds, there was little about one-way entries. *Detail,* he thought. *How do I use Clarkham's craftsmanship to get out?*

"We're going to walk toward the center. That's where the reality is most complete," he said.

"I'm ready. I have some questions. I think I have, anyway. How long have I been here—months, years?"

"Months, maybe."

"Am I older? I feel older."

"You don't look any older." In truth she looked like a little girl hiding behind the mask of a stage hooker, but he wasn't about to tell her that.

"Is this place like the Realm?"

"In a way," Michael said. "It's much smaller, and it's not made the same." They looked at each other intently. "I love you," Michael said. "It was awful, losing you."

Kristine's face became comically serious. She stared at him so intently her eyes seemed to cross. "I haven't felt the time, however long it's been. He made me into somebody else. And the funny part is—nothing happened, and I didn't *really notice.* I wasn't bored, but most of the time I just sat behind that desk or walked around the city, thinking I was on a case . . . Taking phone calls. God, I don't remember what people said. It's all jumbled now, like a bad dream. Not a nightmare, I mean, but badly thought out, artistically bad."

They brushed past figures that became more and more convincing and detailed as they approached the center of Clarkham's creation. "I have a thought," Michael said. "It's crazy, but no crazier than anything else . . . Do you know a liquor store or a good restaurant around here?"

"There's a fancy French place called La Bretonne. Lots of mobsters go there."

"Take me there," Michael said.

"Why?"

"We need to order a good bottle of wine."

La Bretonne was on the ground floor of a stately stone building at the very heart of Clarkham's creation. At four or five in the afternoon—the apparent time of day—it was just beginning to open for its supper "crowd." Neither Michael nor Kristine was dressed for the occasion, and a haughty maitre d' with slicked-down black hair and prominent teeth adamantly refused them service.

This did not stop Michael. Leaving Kristine at the front, he walked to the prominent oak rack of wine bottles set into one wall and paced before it, finger to his lips. The maitre d' followed and berated him for his crudeness and bad manners.

"I will call the police, *m'sieur,*" he threatened with a terrible French accent.

Michael chose a sauterne—Chateau d'Yquem 1929—and skirted around the man, uncorking the bottle as he rejoined Kristine.

The maitre d', red-faced and huffing like a pigeon in heat, stalked off with loud threats to call the police. Other employees—penguin-like waiters and busboys—stood well clear of the scene, watching with mixed empty amusement and empty irritation.

Michael offered the bottle to Kristine, more out of politeness than any expectation she would be able to use the taste as he intended to. She took a swallow and nodded. "Good wine," she said, returning the bottle.

"Clarkham's a connoisseur of wine. I'd expect him to stock his world with a good cellar." He brought the bottle to his own lips and took a hearty swig. It was indeed a good sauterne, bloody gold in color, and it carried a distinct sweet message of warm sunny fields and evening mists, of a definite *place* on Earth. Michael gripped Kristine's hand as the maitre d' returned, still livid and voluble.

A shadow fell over the restaurant's interior. Kristine paled and held Michael's hand with painful pressure. "I know who that . . ." she began, not needing to finish. Michael recognized it, also.

In front of La Bretonne, hidden behind a stone pillar, was the presence he had met on the fourth floor. The simulacra in the restaurant froze and lost definition.

Michael tried to place himself in the middle of the wine's flavors and to take Kristine with him, but the wine soured on his tongue. The livid gold liquid in the bottle foamed black, and he hastily set it on a table top.

"It came around the agency sometimes," Kristine said quietly, her face drawn with fascination and fear. "I didn't know what it was—it didn't fit in. I never saw it, but I always knew when it was there."

"Mr. Perrin," a voice called behind them. They turned. Between the dark, gritty black outlines of the maitre d' and a waiter stood David Clarkham. He appeared much older than when Michael had last seen him, pallid of face and long of arm, gaunt as a scarecrow. "You're disrupting everything. That's not unusual for you, is it?"

Michael smiled confidently, though he did not feel confident. He had once thought himself a match for Clarkham . . . Had once believed that the Isomage did not present much of a danger.

Now, he was not so sure. The presence outside the restaurant was stranger and more frightening than Tristesse or Lamia.

"How clever that you head for my wine collection. I never would have thought of that. It's brilliant, but it won't work. You think the battle—the competition—is over, don't you? I trust you believe you've won, too."

"I don't know that," Michael said. Kristine stared at Clarkham with rising color, her face grim.

"I know you, too," she said. "You're the one who threatened me on the phone and brought me to this foul place."

Clarkham sighed deeply. "I would be quite proud of this world, but for some major difficulties, not entirely my fault," he said. "One of the difficulties is that creatures of genuine, original flesh and blood cannot escape. As you've no doubt discovered, this world has a smooth and flawless foundation. For any would-be mage, it's the equivalent of a pit with sheer ice walls. That was not my original intention, believe me. You cannot leave."

"And you?" Michael asked.

"Whatever advantage it is, I can come and go as I please. How did your entry in the competition fare?"

Michael shook his head. "I haven't been back yet to see."

"Eager to rescue your woman. Laudable—if your ambitions are purely human. A mage has to be more deliberate and disciplined. What will you do if things go wrong on Earth? You're not there to protect your people."

That was true enough. Michael felt a surge of guilt—and anger that Clarkham, of all people, could chide him. He probed Clarkham quickly, shielding his reactions against the expected suffusion of evil. But the Isomage seemed almost—not quite—free of corruption.

"I've shed my latest accumulation of dross," Clarkham said. Outside, the unseen presence made a deep, unpleasant noise like coughing. Clarkham appeared momentarily irritated. "This world accepts my difficulties . . . sanitation facilities are abundant, you might say." He put his arm around one of the low-resolution simulacra. "Better than using humans, no?"

Kristine looked as if she might be sick. Her hand tightened on Michael's, and his anger compounded. He brought it under control immediately. *Null,* Manus's memories recommended. *A world ill-conceived can be aborted . . . in Null.*

And if the world envelops the maker?

No creation is completely seamless. That came to Michael almost as a truism, compounded of Manus's knowledge and his own experiences in Null.

The presence approached the door of the restaurant slowly. Michael caught a glimpse of it through the front window before it passed behind a wall again: large, dark and of no definite color.

"If you can leave," Michael said, drawing conclusions rapidly, "then you must not be flesh and blood."

"That should have been obvious to you long before now," Clarkham said. He walked to a table and pulled out four chairs. "Let's have a light supper and talk. The food here is exceptional. You can even have another bottle of that magnificent sauterne. This time, drink it from a glass, which would be more appropriate, don't you think?"

Michael gently urged Kristine forward. She glanced at him resentfully, and he read her combined weariness, fear and hatred of Clarkham without a probe. She was on the edge. She did not know what Michael had become; all she knew was that he had been delayed for a long time before rescuing her, which implied he was not necessarily more adept or powerful than Clarkham.

"We have another guest," Clarkham said. "Michael has met him already. My dear," he addressed Kristine softly, "do not be frightened. He is in some ways my better half, though sorely afflicted. He made this world. He made me."

Clarkham gestured toward the doorway. Silhouetted against the late afternoon light, a small, corpulent man entered La Bretonne, darkness sloughing off him like dust. His skin was pocked and riddled with lesions, giving it a quality of distressed and decaying wood. He wore a wool suit as well-tailored as could be expected, considering his shape and condition.

"Excuse me," he said.

His voice was the same as Clarkham's.

"My original," Clarkham said. "More than a father to me."

"And you are something less than a son," the presence said, waddling slowly toward the table.

Judging from Kristine's expression, there was no question of sitting at table with the two. She was not in the least interested in their relationship; all she saw was a walking horror and a spectral, smiling captor. Michael, though suddenly and almost coldly curious, deferred to her.

"We won't eat with you," he said.

The corpulent presence stopped a few yards from the table, shuffled its feet in indecision, and then said, "I understand."

"How disappointing," said the other.

"Michael," Kristine moaned.

"It's all right," Michael said.

She obviously didn't believe him. "It can't be. This is horrible. I'd rather be back in the office, talking on the phone, not knowing . . . What are you going to do?"

He took her hand and felt for how much strength she had left. Very little. Facing her, he put his hands on her shoulders and stared at her. "I'll never do this to you again," he said.

"Do what?"

He held the palm of his hand before her eyes and spun a brief, soothing dream of UCLA's grassy quadrangles and mock-Renaissance buildings. Then he pulled out a chair at a nearby table and sat her there. Face blank, she relaxed.

"Gentlemen," Michael said, indicating the table where the more presentable Clarkham stood, hands gripping the back of a chair, "let's talk."

"I thought you'd be interested."

"I apologize to her," the presence said. A small, sooty layer pooled around his feet.

"You're both David Clarkham," Michael said cheerfully, sitting. The others sat, the presentable one next to Michael, laying his napkin in his lap, and the dark, corrupted one opposite.

"Yes," said the dark one. The presentable figure smiled and raised a hand in deferment.

"And you are the only Clarkham I've met until now," Michael addressed the presentable one.

"He is the only one," said the other.

"You made him."

A nod.

"He's a shadow? Or a simulacrum?"

"He is me. Like you, I had some of the talents of a maker. Curious that two such rarities as you and I should occur within a millennium, both springing from Sidhe and humans—you more human than I, and more rare for that."

"Makers spin worlds, not people."

"Worlds are extensions of one's self. They are solid dreams. Since I . . ." The dark Clarkham made a half-swallowing, half-choking sound and called for water. A poorly resolved waiter, white smudging into black, brought a glass goblet. He drained it quickly. "You know the mistakes I made, long ago."

Michael raised an eyebrow. "Not in detail."

"The details are not important. Suffice it to say I chose a less tortuous path to express my talents, to gather discipline about me. I did not have the boon of the Crane Women's teaching . . . That was reserved for those favored by the Councils, and I have never been their favorite. The 'down side' of this path, as one of your businessmen might put it, was a wasting spiritual disease. I found I had not prepared myself properly. I gained power but could not avoid corruption. It is a cruel malady, for I could only shed its effects by passing them off on others. For a time, I managed to control the worst effects . . ."

"Shahpur, for example."

"Yes. Shahpur. The Sidhe compounded the effects of my malady when I was defeated in the Realm and the Blasted Plain was scorched around the Pact Lands. I could not remain on Earth or in the Realm. My disease became so hideous then that I would have quickly polluted thousands, perhaps millions. I could not kill myself; I would have, had there been a way. I would have done that simply to atone for what happened to my . . . women. Lovers. But death is not an option and never will be."

"Had you created this world then?"

"I was working on it even as they defeated me. You are aware that in its latter days, time in the Realm, compared with time on the Earth, was most unreliable? Occasionally it would speed up, occasionally slow down. But that's of little relevance here. I had a luxuriously long and peaceful time to 'spin' this world, as you say. I put everything I was capable of into it. And after . . . I retreated here."

"We always end up in civilized discussions, don't we?" the presentable Clarkham commented. Michael ignored him.

"I had to come here. I corrupted everything around me. At least here, I could shed my evil on the periphery."

"A serious problem," the other said. "When one's production of nastiness exceeds the capacity of whole populations of sacrificial victims. When only a world can hold it all."

"Yes," his original agreed. "I had had enough of making worlds. I became convinced I was not good at it, and my handicaps were hideously distracting. So I spun something other than a world. I remade myself. Something of a shadow, something of me . . . finely tuned, finely wrought. This is what the Sidhe Councils set you against." He indicated the dapper Clarkham, who nodded and smiled.

"This has been my adversary . . . and you control him?"

"Not at all. He is too like my younger self, centuries ago. Willful. He made plans on his own. He discovered he also had some ability to spin worlds. He tried a few—of little quality, quite derivative, worse than my own. You have encountered at least one, I believe.

"In the Realm, when you confronted him, you removed most of the reality I had given him. You almost destroyed him."

The facsimile's smile went away. "You made a ghost of me. That's why I lured you here. What little I can do outside, I will not have you there to interfere with. And what little I can do is more than what Tarax can do, now that *he* has failed."

"Like you, I had real talent," the original declared to Michael. "This much must be obvious." A soot-dripping arm waved at the surroundings. "Not even Adonna could spin a creation so solidly detailed and appointed."

"I still don't think you have a real grasp of the problems involved in being a mage," the facsimile said, leaning forward on one elbow. "Especially a mage of humans. I cannot imagine a more fractious and divided audience. Split by religions and philosophies so distorted by the Sidhe that some are beyond redemption . . . But we cannot blame the Sidhe for all our sins. Have you considered what sort of policing a mage would have to do? What sort of punishments he would have to mete out? A mage is more than a creator; he must also control, and guide."

Michael said nothing, concentrating instead on finding a seam in the foundations around them. *Let them talk.*

"My life has been full of bitterness," the original said. "It is only fair that my other self should be given an opportunity, free of interference."

"He hasn't escaped your malady," Michael said.

There—something too small to squeeze travelers through, but large enough for a ribbon of chaos—

"No," the facsimile said. "It eats at me, too. And I have to divest myself of the results now and then. But I cannot do otherwise. Like my original, I do not have the option of suicide."

"What sort of mage would you be, dropping your corruption on innocents?" Michael asked. "You've done enough damage already."

"What about the damage done to us?" the original wailed, standing abruptly. The chair legs caught in the plush carpet, and the chair fell over backward, knocking a hazy simulacrum as it delivered a fresh bottle of wine. The wine spilled to the floor, part of it landing on the dark Clarkham. The liquid hissed and blackened. "I can't even enjoy wine now! It sours before it ever touches my lips."

"I enjoy it for him," the other said. He looked at Michael intently. "What are you doing?"

Michael did not answer.

"He's *doing* something." Lips curled in effete distaste.

"What are you up to?" the original asked, backing around the fallen chair, away from the table and Michael.

"There's nothing you can do," the facsimile said doubtfully. "Still . . ."

"Hold his woman," the original commanded.

Michael pushed his chair back and stood between the facsimile and Kristine.

"There's something wrong," the original said, raising his dark, woody palms and feeling the space around them.

"You cannot escape," said the other, brushing a hand through his hair. He had aged visibly in the past few minutes and was now roughly as old in appearance as he'd been when Michael first confronted him in the Realm.

"You must flee!" the original instructed his second.

"You're staying," Michael said. With remarkable ease, he bound the facsimile to the floor with a clinging, tenuous skein of shadow-cords, the arms of a dozen ghosts of himself.

"You are a monster," the facsimile said, struggling only for a moment. "A sport! You're still a weapon of the Sidhe. Still aimed and fired by Tarax!"

Michael ignored him; his charges weren't worthy of comment. There was nothing in particular he had to say to either of them. He pitied both, a little— but his thoughts were on Shahpur, bound in white sheets and filled with Clarkham's corruption; on Tommy, disintegrating on the sidewalk before the Waltiri house; on Emma Livry, lying burned, in agony, until rescued by the Ban of Hours; on Coleridge and Mozart and all the dozens of human geniuses ultimately tormented by Clarkham's struggle to find someone capable of expressing his desires strongly enough to make them real.

Michael circled the original Clarkham and picked up the bottle. The bottle had landed on its side and still contained some wine. Michael had thought he recognized the label—*Doppelsonnenuhr*, the double sundial. It had seemed only reasonable that Clarkham would have brought some of this vintage with him. It would probably not give them a way out; it had been grown in the Realm, after all, and its flavor led either into Clarkham's worlds or back into the Realm, which was no more. Besides, it seemed likely that both Clarkhams were telling the truth—once in this world, there was no way out . . .

But the wine provided the seam in the smooth foundation. It was neither flesh and blood nor of this world; its reality was subtly *other*, and through it, Michael could feel the qualities of the chaos "above" Null, eager to come in and erase, devour.

Michael partly corked the bottle with his thumb and began sprinkling its contents around the tables. A large spot of wine already seethed around the original's feet. Orange light glowed beneath the dark stain.

"I don't know what you're doing," the original Clarkham said, dabbing at himself. Larger flakes of soot fell away beneath the glistening wine. "Are you going to destroy us, after all?"

Michael didn't respond. Grimly, he shook the bottle and continued sprinkling.

"You were wrong, then," the original said to the facsimile.

"He's making a bloody mess, I'll give him that."

Michael was aware that the second Clarkham, without moving, was working against the bonds. Soon he would be free.

"I think he knows what he's doing. He's more capable than even you imagined."

The shadow-bonds broke and disappeared. The facsimile shrugged his coat back up on his shoulders. Michael gave him a sharp glance: *stay away from her.* The facsimile did not challenge him.

"It's best," said the original, folding his hands over his ample belly. "I can almost feel relief."

The second Clarkham was fading, escaping. Michael glanced at the bottle; still a half-inch or so of the wine remained, the dregs. Turning quickly, he splashed the dregs over him.

The surprise on both their faces was at once funny and horrifying. Where the wine stained his suit and dripped from his face, the second Clarkham began to glow orange. He tried to wipe away the wine, but couldn't. He was held by advancing chaos.

"You do things even I would not have guessed possible," the original said, with an air of peculiar enthusiasm. "Incomprehensible things. My wine. You use me against myself." His eyes were full of wonder.

The wine stain expanded and shot fingers under the wall, into the street. The daylight outside suddenly clouded over.

I've done this before—something like it—to Lin Piao Tai.

"You're going to destroy my world, aren't you?" the original said.

"Yes," Michael answered.

"You know, if I had known a way, I might have helped you and the woman escape. It was really his idea to bring you here. I have nothing against you. Truly. I've grown tired—"

The waiters, maitre d', and all the other simulacra vanished. The original Clarkham's sooty evil sloughed more rapidly. A thick blanket of black, formless dust surrounded him.

Michael stood before Kristine and passed his hand over her eyes again. She looked around quickly. Before she could speak, Michael lifted her to her feet and wrapped his arms around her. "Just a little world," he said. "For us. For now."

Between his palms spread the purest and whitest nacreous sheet. "Are we leaving?" she asked.

"We're going home," Michael said. "But first, there're going to be some special effects." He gripped her tightly as the nacre spread around them both. "Take a deep breath," he said.

"I hold you no ill will," the original Clarkham said. "This is truly best. I can see that."

Michael turned to look at him. In the middle of a prodigious fall of soot from his head, in the span of his now-featureless face, where his eyes would have been, two molten drops of silver flowed.

"My regrets," Clarkham said, and the silver fell to the carpet. The La Bretonne shook, and the walls bloated and spun outward like released balloons. "Dear God above us all, I wish I had it to do over again—"

The nacre closed, and that was as Michael preferred it.

38

As Michael held Kristine tightly within the whiteness, eyes half-closed, weary and resigned to whatever might come, he knew he had done his best. No one could have asked more of him, not even the Crane Women.

"Where are we?" Kristine asked.

"I've made a little world to protect us," Michael said.

"Oh." Then, "What does that mean?"

"It means I'm holding you," he said. "And I'm happy."

"Don't talk down to me," she said, not at all in anger. "Where are we, and where are *they?*"

"We're somewhere near Earth. They are dying or dead by now, and their world with them. Erased."

She considered this for a moment, conflicting emotions crossing her face in rapid succession. "You're positive?"

"As positive as I'll ever be about David Clarkham." He nuzzled her. "I'm very tired, and I'm very happy to have you. Let's wait until later for explanations."

She stroked his cheek. "What in hell are you?" she asked tenderly.

"Later. Please."

Kristine suddenly relaxed. "I don't know what it is about you. I feel very safe. I don't know what's going on, but I still feel safe."

The thought of what he had just done to the two Clarkhams and of all he had been through—all he had lost, most of it never to be regained—and the long path he had taken to come here, wherever *here* was, and that Kristine should tell him this, putting her seal of approval on him . . .

"You're crying again," she said. His back began to knot up and his shoulders to curl inward. "No," she crooned. "Relax."

But it had to come. He felt the Serpent Mage's memories within him, filled with tales of all his ancestors culled from a million years of "listening," and he thought of Manus in defeat.

He thought of Eleuth.

"Shh," Kristine said, holding him as tightly as she could, as if he might fly away.

And of Shiafa, sad Shiafa finally free—she at least was not lost—and even sadder Tarax, power and desire without, finally, the necessary talent.

Within the tiny lifeboat world, settling slowly down to Earth, Michael wept and shivered and came to terms with what he was and what he would have to be.

"I'm not going away," Kristine said. "Whatever you are. You make me safe."

The whiteness took on color and dissolved around them.

They stood in Clarkham's house, on the second floor, the ancient bottle of wine standing upright and undisturbed a few feet away.

The Earth still existed . . .

And accepted them.

39

Fall gave way to winter, and winter to a dry, clear spring.

40

A different dawn.

To the eyes of most, the pale rose horizon and dusty gray zenith would not have seemed different. But to Michael, who did not look with his eyes, the changes were obvious.

For one thing, there had been less violence around the Earth during the night. Strife between humans and Sidhe had decreased markedly in the past few months; now, he could see a decline in strife between humans and humans. He was pleased; there was good reason to believe he was responsible.

For weeks he had worked to lift a mental haze that had lain over the Earth for thousands of centuries. The accumulation of discarded dreams, lost memories, cast-off fragments of personalities from the migrating human dead—the general miasma of a mental environment gone ages without cleansing—had created a mind-muffling "smog." The smog was now largely gone.

His people could think more clearly. Their passions did not magnify and distort, and they were less quick to destructive anger.

If he did nothing for the rest of his life—however long that was—then his creation of the overlay and cleansing of the mental environment would be sufficient, he thought.

But he did not intend to stop. He had other responsibilities.

Kristine slept beside him, a large, very pregnant pale shape in the bedroom's dawn-lit obscurity. They had moved into the Waltiri house just after their return; John had made new furniture for them to replace what had been ruined by the birds.

Michael seldom slept. Night was the time he surfed outward on a spreading wave of perception and kept track of his Earth. On such nights, there seemed to be ineffable rustlings in the world, sounds of growth and change, flowers thrusting from buds.

When Kristine had become round-bellied and big-breasted, she had told him, "I don't know who's more pregnant, you or I. At least on you, it doesn't show."

The Earth turned beneath him, a remarkable pearl covered with rock and soil and oceans, people and clouds and sky. Much had changed since the Sidhe migrations and the death of the Realm, and much had remained the same. Sidhe, for the most part, avoided human cities and human machines and usually chose desolate parts of the land and sea to rebuild their own communities. So it was that Sidhe now lived among the hills and cinder cones of Death Valley, and in the sandy wastes of the Sahara and the Gobi and scattered across the outback of Australia, where they could work their magic and adjust their ways in relative peace.

There were exceptions. A large Sidhe community now existed in Ireland, mostly Faer and Amorphals; a thousand Sidhe had settled in the heart of London, a thousand more in Jerusalem and several hundred in Peking.

Life went on. In Los Angeles, cars still crowded the freeways and power still pulsed through wires across the country. The Sidhe would have to adapt to these things.

Pelagals prevented all killing of cetaceans and other marine mammals and regulated fishing. Humans would have to adapt to this.

Riverines harried rafters on the Colorado River. Apparently, both humans and Sidhe took this as a kind of sport. Firm friendships had been made.

Airline pilots sometimes found their craft inhabited by Amorphals. There had been no air disasters since.

Sidhe horses and riders, under tough restrictions, were grudgingly accepted in equine competitions.

And on the negative side—

Sidhe tribal sorcerers in the Middle East had been called upon by radical Moslems to raise the dead of past wars, that they might fight the Jews again. Human dead could not be literally resurrected, but the Sidhe had obliged by raising shadows and dreams of ancestors, breathing a kind of life back into the ghostly residues. These "dead" promptly occupied Arab villages, driving out the living and refusing to fight or do much of anything else. The Moslems had sworn vengeance. There was little Michael could do about such travesties.

The five thousand human captives of the Sidhe had been repatriated. Their presence so far had not made much difference in the arts, but less than a year had passed . . .

The mage of the Cledar and his retinue moved to jungles in Mexico for the time being, to establish an enclave where they would wait until a way could be found to return them to their ancestral forms. Michael spoke with him frequently, traveling sometimes to Mexico or sometimes just conversing by thought.

Michael spent much of his time consulting with Sidhe and with the deep cetacean minds of the Spryggla and the scattered, tragically fractured cockroach minds of the Urges.

Their time was coming again. Much had been lost, but there was grudging cooperation between the races now. The sundering was done with. Years, perhaps centuries, would pass before most things could be set right, but that was a short time indeed.

Michael pressed his thigh against Kristine's and she sighed, adjusting her bulky abdomen without waking. He smiled and felt a love for her beyond expression, and with that love came not fear but apprehension.

What stability the Earth had now, as always, was very fragile. At any moment, his magehood could topple into singing shards. There was no final security, no certainty. He could not see the future. Yet he was not afraid. Fear would only paralyze him.

Michael laid his head gently on her stomach and listened, smiling. She stirred again but did not awaken.

MICHAEL AND KRISTINE arrived just before opening time at the front door of the trendy little Nicaraguan restaurant on Pico. Bert Cantor came down the street with Olive's arm in the crook of his own and saw the pair. Olive responded to his elbow-nudge, focused on them and smiled broadly.

"I know you," Bert said brusquely, shaking Michael's hand. "Didn't you used to work here or something? But who's this?" Bert eyed Kristine's obvious condition.

"This is Kristine Pendeers. Kristine, Bert and Olive Cantor."

"Very pleased to meet you," Olive said, smiling with delight. "When are you due?"

"Three weeks, roughly," Kristine replied, resting her arms on her abdomen and smiling with anticipation of relief.

"Men. They just don't *know*, do they?" Olive sympathized, clucking and urging Bert to open the door.

Kristine agreed to be polite, but her glance at Michael was sufficient. He knew what her pregnancy felt like. Sometimes he even read the child's burgeoning, liquid-dreaming thoughts and conveyed them to her.

"You know, you have a lot of explaining to do," Bert said, slipping his key into the lock. "I read things in the newspaper that are nothing like what we used to read in the newspaper." He sighed and held the door open for them. "Not *good* newspapers."

"Not everything's perfect," Michael conceded.

Jesus shouted "*¡Hola!*" from the kitchen, and Michael waved back with a big grin.

"The beautiful lady, she's your girlfriend?" Jesus asked, twirling a plastic bag full of dried black beans.

"She's my wife," Michael said proudly.

"Eh! Wait until Juanita hears. Juanita, the *brujo* has a *bruja.*"

"Such talk," Olive said, waving both hands at the kitchen. "Your folks, how are they? And why didn't you invite us to the wedding?"

"They're fine," Michael said.

"It was a small ceremony," Kristine explained.

"You've told her all about . . . ?" Bert asked, raising his brows and corrugating his forehead.

"I have," Michael says.

"And she married you anyway!" Bert marveled.

"*I* would have, too," Olive said, casting a defiant look at her bemused husband. "Bert and I, we think . . . we *know* you had something to do with what's been happening."

"Yeah, a *hypothesis,* call it," Bert said. "How things got so much worse, then better, though all confused. You were the only one who knew anything . . . I admit, though, you sounded quite . . ." He twirled one finger around his ear, then glanced at the front windows and door and said, "Business hasn't been worth much lately. Oh, what the hell, let's close today and celebrate. And talk. You have to fill us in."

And Michael did, Kristine helping him with certain parts he left out. Jesus fixed black-bean tortillas, Juanita served, and everybody ate as Michael spoke in a quiet voice of what had happened. He told very few people these things; there was no pride in him now, only practicality, and he knew not many would believe, and most of those he did not want to deal with.

Juanita crossed herself several times.

"No more meat? Not beef or chicken?" Ben asked at one point.

Michael shook his head. "Plants are growing that will replace meat," he said. The changeover, like everything else, would take time, but at least the groundwork was laid.

"What about the people?" Olive asked. "How will we get along with all these others here now—the faeries and such?"

"Not eating meat's part of the way we'll get along better," Kristine said. "They can't stand it."

"Oh, don't we know!" Bert said, shaking his head vigorously. "Had a few of them walking up the street a month ago, out of place, dressed like they dress, acting like tourists, and they came in here . . . Such looks! Made me feel ashamed, somehow, and mad, too. No worse than going around in black coats and wide-brim hats, I suppose, and frowning at the gentiles—but still . . ."

"So many peoples were transformed into animals," Michael reminded them.

Bert's face paled. "I think we're going to have to come up with new definitions for *traef.*"

"And what about us?" Olive persisted. "What's going to happen to us, all the people here? Can we just accept them, accept all the changes?"

"This is the way things are," Michael said. A finality in his tone made Olive draw her head back and purse her lips, on the edge of disapproval.

"And you're responsible for all this?" Bert asked, preparing to be astonished again.

"Oh, no," Michael said. "Not at all." He laughed, and Kristine laughed with him, thinking it very likely that some of Michael's advisors were even now hiding out in the garbage behind the restaurant. "Not at all!"

"I KNEW THERE would be something different tonight," Kristine said, weary of attendant marvels. She sat awkwardly on the Morris chair John had dragged onto the patio behind the Perrin house.

"What's that?" Michael asked.

"The mage hasn't guessed?" She mocked surprise. She was getting testier as her time narrowed to days. "Your mother. She's keeping mum, but she's a nervous wreck. John looks absolutely terrified."

"So what is it?" Michael persisted.

"Somebody's joining us for dinner. Somebody *not* human, I'd say. You're usually the one responsible for nonhuman guests, but not this time, I take it?"

Michael shook his head, all innocence.

"Who does your mother know that isn't human?"

Michael's eyes widened. "She's never met her in person, but—my great-great-grandmother," he said.

Salafrance Underhill arrived at seven in the evening, her long red hair tied back in a prim bun, dressed in a cloak the color of autumn leaves. Ruth answered the door herself, saying, "She's my problem, I mean my guest, really. When she called, I invited her here. I'll greet her at my own front door."

For a moment, the two women faced each other over the threshold, and Michael saw his great-great-grandmother for the first time. Side by side, Ruth and Salafrance Underhill looked remarkably alike, but there was no denying Salafrance was a pure Sidhe and Ruth was largely human.

"Great-granddaughter," Salafrance said, her voice even more beautiful than Ulath's, almost as entrancing as the voice of the Ban of Hours. "You have dreamed of me. I've felt your dreams across the world and beyond."

"Hello," Ruth said, struggling to control her shivering.

"Is it customary I should wait out here?"

"No," Ruth said. "Come in."

Salafrance drifted through the door, seeming as tall and slender as a tree, her long face and cold eyes difficult to read as she looked from person to person, lingering on Kristine and her improbably wide belly and then turning her full attention to Michael, who stood by the couch in the living room, feeling awkward and young all over again.

"I did not know my love for men would lead to this," she said. "I followed the way of Elme for five hundred years, but out of an inner perversity, not by plan. Granddaughter, this is your husband?" She indicated John with a nod of her long chin.

"His name is—" Ruth began.

"Yes. I have been watching you all for some time. I hope that does not upset you."

Ruth swallowed hard but shook her head.

"I have much to apologize for. I did not prepare my children adequately. I am afraid they issued foolish edicts and did not understand who or what they were, and how they must choose mates wisely. You suffered for this, Great-granddaughter."

Michael could read his mother's emotions, barely held in check—half an urge to order Salafrance from her house, and half simply to weep. She did neither. Salafrance sat in the living room at Ruth's invitation and gestured for Kristine to sit beside her.

"Does he read your child for you?" she asked.

"Michael?" Kristine asked, embarrassed. "Yes. He does."

"And is it a maker, as well?"

"We don't know," Michael said.

"Male or female?"

"Female," Kristine said. "The doctors confirmed it."

Salafrance smiled ironically. Her almond eyes could have been regarding anybody in the room at any given moment, without the slightest impression of darting about. "Power is carried by the female . . . Great-granddaughter," she said, focusing her full attention now on Ruth.

"Yes?"

"I am proud of you, most proud."

Ruth smiled. Michael knew that his mother would never come to love or even be comfortable around Salafrance Underhill, but she could now be comfortable within herself.

She had not failed her heritage.

At dinner, as Salafrance picked at rice and vegetables, she asked, "Where is the nectar of mages?"

"I gave it back to my father," Michael said.

"It's in the wine-cellar. The closet, actually," John said.

"It has waited long enough, don't you think?"

"Sidhe don't drink, Grandmother," Michael said quietly.

"Do you know the rule—always forbidden, on occasion mandatory?"

Michael nodded.

"This is such an occasion," Salafrance decreed.

"I'll bring it," John said, pushing his chair back from the table.

"I am told, and I have felt, that you are in control of this world now, of its making and its song," she said to Michael. "This is so?"

"It is so," Michael said.

"What sort of mage are you?"

Michael smiled. "That's a broad question."

"Are you obvious, dancing with the song at all times, watching the steps of all who dance with you?"

"He doesn't meddle," Kristine said defensively. "Hardly anybody knows what he does or who he is." Michael patted her hand.

"I . . . don't want to control everybody or act like a policeman," he said. "I don't think I should have any real authority over how people behave or make moral judgments. I won't impose my will on others. I'm a poet, not a master. I may tune the instruments, but I don't lay down every note of the song."

"And if it comes about that the races try to destroy the balance again?"

"I'll write that bridge when I come to it," he said, irritated that she should see so quickly what worried him most about the future.

"You are a very young mage," Salafrance said. John returned with the opaque, time-darkened bottle of wine.

"What is its provenance?" Salafrance asked.

John was puzzled, uncertain how to answer. "Arno Waltiri gave it to us."

"The human who shared his body with the Cledar mage . . . ?"

"The same," Michael said. "He had it from David Clarkham. I've heard Clarkham stole it from Adonna."

"We should all drink . . ." Salafrance said. "Except for Kristine, who bears perhaps another maker, one who will drink this wine in her own due course."

"I don't think I could stomach it anyway," Kristine said.

The bottle was sealed with a thick slug of wax impressed with a tiny sharp design, two triangles nested like a Star of David. When John cleared the wax plug from the bottle's neck, working carefully to avoid breaking the ancient glass, an almost palpable aroma filled the room, richer by far than Clarkham's wines, beyond bouquet, more like a visit to a summer-heated fruit garden.

"Who took this bottle, and when, I do not know, but I know whence it comes," Salafrance said. "The sigil tells me. It was once in the collection of Aske and Elme themselves. It may be the last bottle of its kind, and it carries special virtue. It is fitting that the first human maker and mage in untold ages should drink of it and be confirmed. That is what Elme would have wished, and Aske would have been proud beyond his time."

"You knew them?" Ruth asked, awe-struck.

"I am not *that* old, Great-granddaughter," Salafrance said, and Michael sensed the depths of her humor. "I have met those who knew them. So has Michael." Her look was potent with meaning. Michael almost shivered.

"Now that both Councils have dissolved, and new orders are found, and new songs to which we dance, let us toast the new mage in humble surroundings, toast a humble creator who vows not to enslave for order's sake but to do what he must, and that alone: tend a garden fit for all God's creatures and weave a lace pleasing to most."

Not once, in all his time with Sidhe, had Michael ever heard them refer to a god beyond Adonna or Adonna's Yahweh.

"Which god is this, Grandmother?" Michael asked.

"You feel this God in your blood, do you not?" she asked. She held up her glass, and the others followed suit. "The God that requires only our remembrance *in extremis*. The gentle, the mature, the ever-young, that demands nothing but our participation and growth. The composer of the Song of Earth and all worlds. Invoke this God, Michael, and be a maker and mage."

Michael examined the color of the wine in his glass: both golden and brown, all wines become one wine, and said, "To all of us, of all races, and the matter we are made of, and the ground beneath our feet, and the worlds over our head. To strife and passage and death and life." He held his glass higher. "To horror, and awe, and all strong emotions, and most of all, to love."

Salafrance drank, and the others drank as well.

When they were finished, John put down his glass and said, "I think it must be an acquired taste."

"It's wonderful," Ruth said.

Michael frowned, drawing the flavors back and forth. He honestly did not have an opinion. In a few decades, perhaps he would appreciate what he tasted now.

"What's it like?" Kristine asked, curious and envious.

He shook his head. "I don't know," he said.

"All that suspense, and you don't know?" she chided.

The rest of the evening went well, with Salafrance telling her own story and Ruth listening closely. There was much about life in the hills and alleged witchcraft and conflict between the early farmers and the clannish Sidhe. Salafrance told of a lonely and rebellious young Sidhe female—herself—coming down out of the hills into the towns of humans, enchanting and being enchanted in turn by a strong young human male and being taken to his cabin to bear children. In time, Salafrance could not stay apart from her kind; the love was strained by forces neither could control, and they parted, Salafrance leaving their children with the man, who found his house filled with witches and warlocks: his own offspring.

Kristine slept in the crook of Michael's arm as the hour passed midnight. Salafrance said near dawn that she must leave, and Ruth escorted her to the door, where they had a few words alone.

Then Salafrance extended her arms and took her great-granddaughter into them, hugging her close. "Humans have always taught us how to love," she said.

She departed into the dawn, and Ruth returned to the kitchen, her face wet with tears. John sealed the bottle again and placed it in the wine closet. Michael took Kristine home in the Waltiris' old Saab.

THE BIRTH WAS late. Three days later, on a bright spring morning after a long-awaited night's rain, the sidewalks dappled with moisture and the grass still beaded, Michael opened the front door to retrieve the newspaper. Something feather-touched his aura, and he paused, listening.

"Man-child," came a voice above his head. He looked up and saw Coom staring down at him from the roof, her long fingers tightly gripping the tile.

"You still have much to learn."

He turned. Nare stood on one leg on the lawn to his left, wriggling her long fingers before her flat chest.

"Even a Lace-Maker and Gardener needs a few tens of years to mature and reach his potential," said Spart, sitting cross-legged on the lawn to his right, smiling at him with her head cocked to one side. "May we teach?"

Michael's chest swelled with gladness, and he laughed. "Only if you'll teach our child, too."

"Man-childs," Coom said. "Our specialty!"

SO IT WAS that Michael Perrin came into his time, and the Earth found its youth once more.

Afterword

I have led a dull life, disliking chaos and favoring calm and work and family. Pardon my airs for even thinking of such, but any biography of me will likely be a boring read. Still, there have been a few moments of high interest. One involved the first version of the book you have just read. (Unless, like me, you are in the habit of reading all extraneous matter before sitting down to the main bulk.)

This experience haunted me for years. It happened at a critical period, late adolescence, in the winter and spring of 1970–1971; I was a late bloomer socially and a hider of deep emotions, what I have since characterized as a "warm-hearted iceberg," and so it was inevitable that I should fall hard for the first young woman who consented to go out on a date with me.

Actually, I fell for Kristine even before the date. She was tall and slender and coltish, wide-hipped and long-legged, hair close-cut in a shag, a style worn by Jane Fonda at the time, unaffectedly bohemian; quite my opposite. We were both students at San Diego State College and had happened into the same beginning drama class. I asked her to accompany me to the showing of a documentary on Fellini's *Satyricon* (or more properly, *Fellini Satyricon*) at the late, lamented Unicorn Theater in La Jolla. Kristine consented.

I got lost and arrived late at her rented house on Ingraham Avenue, near the beach, and we got even more lost making our way to La Jolla, but we made it in time to listen to a pretentious question-and-answer session with the documentary's director. After, we went out for a late-night coffee and talk.

I was smitten. Not once did I say any such thing to Kristine; but indications must have been plentiful. I asked her to pose for a painting I was planning, a surrealist, adolescent bit of memento mori called *The Madonna of Probability*. I had sketched a rough of this picture a short while before our date, always with her in mind . . .

She consented, with the proviso that she must pose with her clothes on. I didn't have the presumption to imagine it would be otherwise.

At the time, I was painting and writing in tandem, working on my first novel, which I called *The Infinity Concerto*. The central idea of the novel had interested me since I first gave that same title to a short story in my first years in college; some key elements I had conceived in high school, particularly the episode of the Chinese sorcerer whose power was limited to things golden or yellow.

After that date, I expressed my buried emotions by making Kristine a character in the book. I worked on *The Madonna of Probability*, actually quite a hideous picture, a young woman standing against a dull leaden sky carrying the swaddled skeleton of a child. (Not all of my paintings were quite so morbid!)

Our only other "date" was a few hours in San Diego's Balboa Park, where I sketched her as we sat on a grassy stretch before the Globe Theater. The sketch was so inadequate that today I cannot remind myself of the full details of her face by looking at it; nor can I recall what she looked like enough to bring a picture to mind. I was idealizing her, not seeing her clearly; also, I was never an expert at human features. (To this day I have not sketched portraits of my beautiful children; perhaps for this reason, that I would be inadequate to the task.)

During this outing, I told her I had made her a character in the book I was writing. She seemed flattered. I promised that when the book was published, I would send her a copy.

When I dropped her off at her apartment, she stepped from my car, turned, leaned into the doorway, and asked why I was doing all this. I did not admit my infatuation; I was trying to play it cool, yet my feelings must have been more than obvious, even overbearing. I must have seemed a little odd.

We met in class, and at rehearsals for a silly student play (not written by me, thank God) in which she was to be an artist's model, and I some other role. I was not the artist in the play, but I painted a few deliberately awful pictures for background.

We did not go out again.

Writing the book, it soon became clear to me that the character of Kristine had to be removed from the narrative at some point, for reasons of plot; my character could not finish his arc of development encumbered by a partner. I remember writing these scenes in a kind of trance; she did not die, but was involved in a hideous accident that took her away from the protagonist's life, dropping her into the "mist of creation," a place where anything was possible.

I had not spoken with Kristine for more than a month. She had turned down another date at one point, and I did not have the courage to ask again; it was obvious she sensed my infatuation and was not at ease around me, and who could blame her? One-sided infatuation is not a comfortable responsibility. In many respects, she was more mature than I, although we were the same age.

After a time, I did not even see her on campus.

I experienced odd moments. One evening, listening to the adagio of Mahler's unfinished Tenth Symphony, I had an epiphany of life and death as intense as anything I have felt before or since. It was not directly connected with Kristine. But hearing of a car accident at Sunset Cliffs, days later, I thought of her.

I had already ended her part in the novel. The protagonist was suffering intense grief over his loss. The book was far from finished, but *The Madonna of Probability* was nearing completion. Adding the final touches one evening, I decided to call Kristine to let her know the painting was finished, and she could see it if she wished. I did not phone immediately; the thought of calling bothered me. I blamed my reticence on lack of courage. Perhaps I did not want to impose on her any more. Still, something compelled me.

The next day, in my last class of the day, a comparative lit. course, I again fell into an unpleasant mood and wrote a poem, part of which is now in *The Serpent Mage*. The poem strongly hinted of a loved woman's death. I dreaded making the call. At home, late in the afternoon, I stood in a dark hallway and dialed the number of Kristine's apartment.

A roommate answered. *Hadn't I heard?* she asked. Kristine had left school about two months ago and returned to Marin County. She had been killed there in an automobile accident. (Not in the Sunset Cliffs accident.)

I ran outside and stood in an empty lot nearby, in shock. When I returned to my room, I simply sat, stunned. For weeks I went through the motions of being alive, but inside, I was shattered. I had faced the death of loved ones before—grandmother, uncle, acquaintances. But none seemed quite so immediate, so strange and final. And what haunted me—frightened me—was that I had seemed to know what would happen to her from the very beginning, from the time I first imagined her holding a symbol of death.

I went through various rituals, trying to escape this not wholly appropriate grief. There had been little enough between us. She had been friendly and kind and little more. And now I was going through the fire. I was facing not just the ultimate end to all possibilities of love, but a puzzle straight out of *The Twilight Zone*.

I had modeled a character in the novel after a living woman, and then had removed her; and the living woman had died. I didn't take the more bizarre aspects of this too seriously; that way lay true madness, and I have never fancied madness. But it seemed obvious that I had sensed Kristine's impermanence; in the plot of my life, at least, I had known she would be removed.

In bed one night a few weeks after, I gathered all my mental forces and tried to break through the barrier of death, to communicate with Kristine. (I really *was* a little odd, no?) I had done this once, five years before, to communicate with a recently dead uncle: nothing had happened then. But what I now experienced burned and horrified me; I imagined a kind of shell of Kristine, memories present but soul gone, having a relation to the living woman like that of a flake of dead skin to live flesh. She or it seemed to occupy a sphere of newly dead around the Earth, protecting us from harsh outer realities much as dead skin protects the pink growing flesh beneath. I doubt this was any genuine revelation, but it hurt me so much that I recorded it in a diary, then ripped that page out and threw it away. Here were truly things I did not want to know.

I worked on my novel in a kind of heat. I had to see how it all turned out. The protagonist wandered through the last chapters, bereaved, experiencing more and more revelations, until at the end, he was restored to a more solid world, and regained Kristine.

With such wish-fulfillments, I began to purge myself. I finished the novel, took out a student loan for one hundred and twenty-five dollars to have it retyped, submitted it once—receiving a kind rejection slip from Betty Ballantine—and shelved it.

The work was neither complete nor mature. Its core was true, but its form was awkward; the emotions and ideas were fine, perhaps more intense than anything I would write later, but it was not publishable.

Too amorphous, too tied in with half-understood emotions, the book languished for years. Occasionally I would give thought to revising it, but I was working on other books and stories that would eventually sell and be published.

Then, in 1979, the book reshaped itself in one evening of inspiration. In a heat, I wrote the details down in a small blue notebook. The plot was completely different, but much of the core remained. Arno Waltiri, Opus 45, Kristine, the quotation from a nonexistent book by Charles Fort, and the ensorceled Chinese were still there. My early protagonist—originally the son of Arno Waltiri—had evolved into Michael Perrin. Intricate plot and carefully worked-out fantasy elements—an entire historical scheme, incorporating much of the myth I so fondly studied—replaced the amorphous surrealism.

Here at last was a book that could be written and sold. Still, I waited a few years before I broached the idea to then Ace editor Terri Windling over lunch in a Chinese restaurant in San Francisco. She asked to see the proposal.

Eventually, *The Infinity Concerto* became part of a package contract with very different novel called *Blood Music*. (Yet a third proposed novel, *Eon*, was rejected by the publishers because they did not want to risk a three-book contract with a fledgling writer.)

I knew that *The Infinity Concerto* was really only the first half of a longer novel, but the second half would have to wait, to be written separately and published as a second book. In due time, the second half was written and published.

I dedicated the first part to a beloved teacher, Elizabeth Chater, who had read the first version in 1971 and given me much needed praise and support. The second part, the part with Kristine, I dedicated to her. It was my way of sending her a copy.

Adolescence is far behind me now. I'm a full-time writer. I do very little artwork. I've been married twice, and now I'm a father of two; I've been through a few traumatic times, and many more joyous ones. Yet in that winter and spring, life laid down the bricks on which I now stand. I gathered themes I'm still working with.

As for the obvious mystical elements of those months . . . I've had weaker but similar instances of what might be called clairvoyance or second sight. They have not come so frequently as to convince me that they are irrefutable evidence for psychic phenomena; but I cannot deny the multiple documentation of painting, manuscript and poem, of my disturbing "foreknowledge" of Kristine's death. I remain, oddly enough, a skeptic in psychic matters, perhaps because I wish to believe so strongly. I resist easy and comforting answers.

How does this final work compare with the first version? I suspect the first was better in some respects, more true and immediate. But the ideas and emotions are better worked out in this final product. I think the balance favors the newer version; I did not so much distill and reshape the ideas as guide them with a steadier hand.

Since those years, I have gained a reputation as a writer of science fiction. It may surprise some that my first novel was fantasy, and that it was grounded in such experiences. Almost needless to say, I am very fond of this book, and pleased to see it bound in one volume, revised and polished: one novel in two parts, as originally intended.

Notes and Acknowledgments

My special thanks to those who helped with this novel: to Terri Windling, who revived it; to Poul and Karen Anderson, exacting readers; to Jim Turner, Ray Feist and David Brin for critiques and encouragements; and of course to Astrid, who read it endlessly in its various printouts. My debts of inspiration are many—portions of this book go back thirteen years—but Jorge Luis Borges is at the top of the list, and once again, Poul.

The language spoken by the Sidhe is not completely artificial. Many readers may recognize Indo-European roots and borrowings from various extant languages; most will likely not recognize that other words are derived from some very obscure Irish cants. If you're curious to find out more, please refer to a marvelous book by Robert A. Stewart Macalister, *The Secret Languages of Ireland,* first published in 1937 by the Cambridge University Press. A good university or public library may have it. Lovers of languages—or dabblers, such as myself—will find it fascinating.

Appendix

The Film Scores of Arno Waltiri (Highlights)

1935 *Ashenden*
1939 *Queen of the Yellow River*
1940 *Dead Sun*
1941 *Sea Scorpion*
1942 *Warbirds of Mindanao*
1942 *Ace Squadron*
1943 *Yellowtail*
1946 *Northanger Abbey*
1948 *Descartes*, a.k.a. *The King's Genius*
1950 *Let Us Now Praise Famous Men*
1951 *Some Kind of Love*
1958 *The Man Who Would Be King*
1963 *Call It Sleep*